Praise for
This Kingdom Will Not Kill Me

'Ilona Andrews casts the kind of spell every fantasy lover craves – an irresistible plunge into another world. I was captivated from the very first line'
Danielle L. Jensen, *New York Times* bestselling author

'If you thought Ilona Andrews was at the top of her career, you haven't read *This Kingdom Will Not Kill Me*. Exciting, complex, with indelible characters and a heroine who cannot die: loved it'
Charlaine Harris, No. 1 *New York Times* bestselling author

'Fantasy, romance, danger – this book has it all. Addictive. I need the sequel stat'
Felicia Day, *New York Times* bestselling author

'*This Kingdom Will Not Kill Me* will delight long-time readers and new readers alike! A fantastic cast of characters, a world you want to spend endless hours in and a perfect blend of humor and high stakes. You don't want to miss this one!'
Katee Robert, *New York Times* bestselling author

'Brilliant! Absolutely brilliant! I loved every page and could not look away! This is the kind of book that will make you forget the world exists – it's gripping and fun and fabulous!'
Sarah Beth Durst, *New York Times* bestselling author of *The Spellshop*

'An Ilona Andrews book is always a treat, and *This Kingdom Will Not Kill Me* is their best book yet! Perfect for anyone who's ever wanted to step inside their favourite fandom – for better or worse. Filled with Andrews' signature heart-stopping action, rich world-building and emotional depth, *This Kingdom Will Not Kill Me* kept me up well past my bedtime, but it was so, so worth it'
Jessie Mihalik, author of *Silver & Blood* and *Polaris Rising*

'With a fun premise and wonderfully deep world-building, *This Kingdom Will Not Kill Me* gives us an ordinary heroine who takes charge and refuses to let the world dictate her fate. Great for fans of Sarah Rees Brennan's *Long Live Evil*'
Django Wexler, author of *How to Become the Dark Lord and Die Trying*

'Another glorious entry in the Ilona Andrews legendarium. Both a send-up of, and a love letter to, your favourite fantasy tropes, by a master of the genre. Self-aware, tongue firmly in cheek, but also full of heart. The perfect balance of humour, romance and thrills in one brilliant book'

Brigitte Knightley, *New York Times* bestselling author of *The Irresistible Urge to Fall for Your Enemy*

'All the brilliance I've come to expect from Ilona Andrews and more: humour, high-stakes adventure, smouldering romance and a good sprinkle of thought-provoking questions. Perfect for anyone who has ever wanted to jump into a book and rescue your favourite characters'

Elisabeth Wheatley, author of *Tears of the Wolf*

'With intricate plotting, brisk pacing and snappy dialogue, this self-aware take on the portal fantasy is a delight'

Caitlin Rozakis, *New York Times* bestselling author of *Dreadful*

'As addictive as chocolate and more exciting than a rollercoaster, *This Kingdom Will Not Kill Me* is fantasy at its best. I devoured this story and then immediately read it again. Ilona Andrews has knocked it out of the park with this one!'

Jeaniene Frost, *New York Times* bestselling author

This Kingdom Will Not Kill Me

Maggie the Undying
❖ I ❖

Ilona Andrews

TOR

First published 2026 by Tom Doherty Associates / Tor Publishing Group

First published in the UK 2026 by Tor
an imprint of Pan Macmillan
The Smithson, 6 Briset Street, London EC1M 5NR
EU representative: Macmillan Publishers Ireland Ltd, 1st Floor,
The Liffey Trust Centre, 117–126 Sheriff Street Upper,
Dublin 1 D01 YC43
Associated companies throughout the world

ISBN 978-1-0350-8937-6 HB
ISBN 978-1-0350-8938-3 TPB

Copyright © Ilona Andrews Inc., 2026

The right of Ilona Andrews Inc. to be identified as the
author of this work has been asserted in accordance with
the Copyright, Designs and Patents Act 1988.

All rights reserved. No part of this publication may be reproduced,
stored in a retrieval system, or transmitted, in any form, or by any means
(including, without limitation, electronic, mechanical, photocopying, recording
or otherwise) without the prior written permission of the publisher.

Pan Macmillan does not have any control over, or any responsibility for,
any author or third-party websites (including, without limitation, URLs,
emails and QR codes) referred to in or on this book.

1 3 5 7 9 8 6 4 2

A CIP catalogue record for this book is available from the British Library.

Map by Jennifer Hanover
Interior art by Shutterstock

Printed and bound in the UK using 100% Renewable Electricity by CPI Group (UK) Ltd

This book is sold subject to the condition that it shall not, by way of
trade or otherwise, be lent, hired out, or otherwise circulated without
the publisher's prior consent in any form of binding or cover other than
that in which it is published and without a similar condition including this
condition being imposed on the subsequent purchaser. The publisher does not
authorize the use or reproduction of any part of this book in any manner
for the purpose of training artificial intelligence technologies or systems.
The publisher expressly reserves this book from the Text and Data Mining
exception in accordance with Article 4(3) of the European Union
Digital Single Market Directive 2019/790.

Visit **www.panmacmillan.com** to read more about
all our books and to buy them.

To the Book Devouring Horde and all other readers who have dreamed about getting lost in a book.

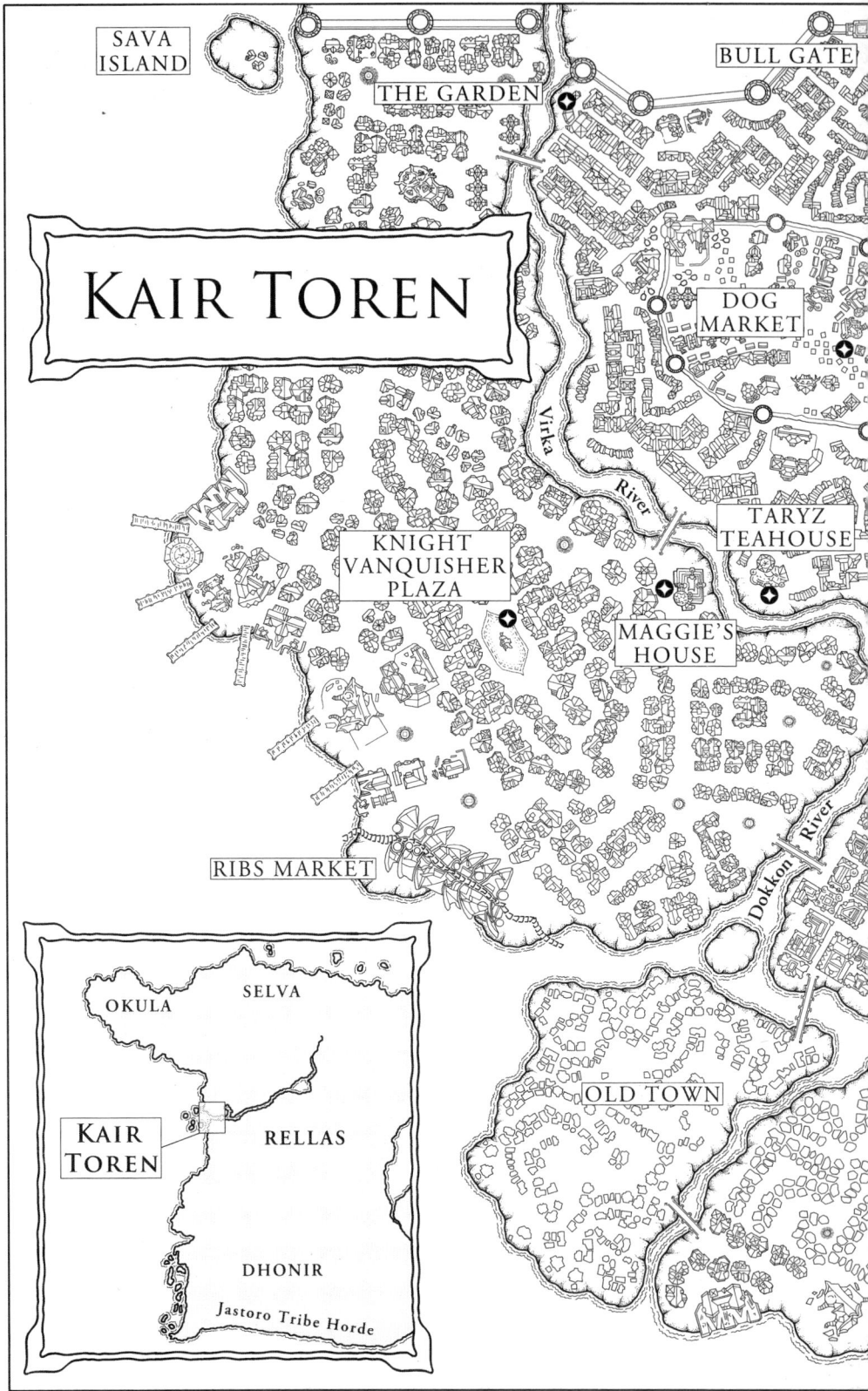

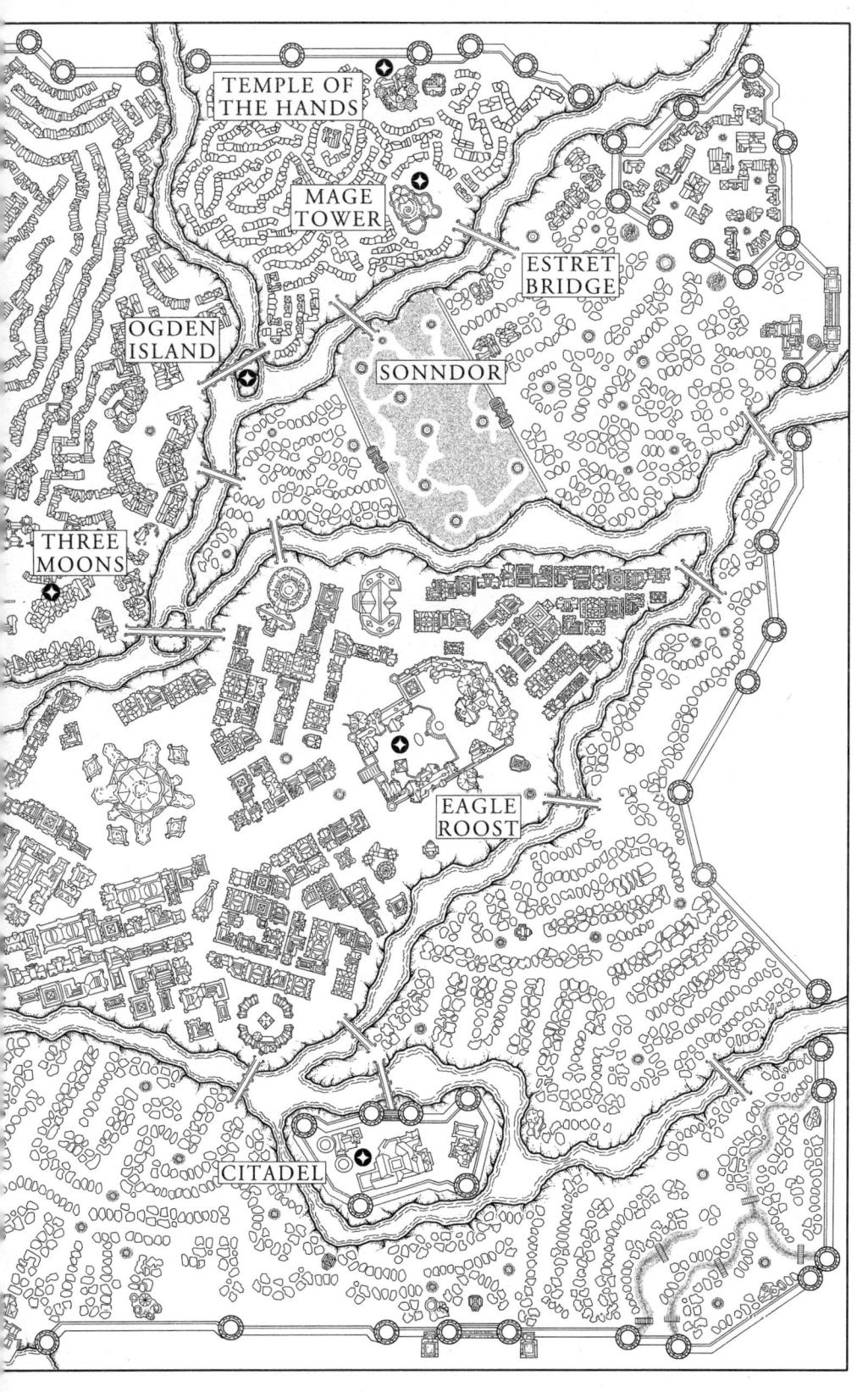

PART I

BAG OF MONEY

Chapter 1

Month of Planter, Day 6

Rain drenched the city, cold and relentless. It leached all color from the medieval-looking buildings, turning the world gray and soaking through the filthy rag in which I had swaddled myself. The sour stench rising from the grimy folds was truly epic. I couldn't feel my toes, and my fingers were going numb.

The three-story buildings towered over the alley like the walls of a stone canyon, boxing me in. Sometime between yesterday evening and this morning, my stomach had turned into a painful bottomless pit. I hadn't eaten in three days. I wasn't even shivering anymore. My body didn't have the energy.

I checked on my rock again. It lay in a puddle by my feet, a cream-colored chunk of building stone about the size of a large grapefruit. Any bigger, and it would be too hard to grip with one hand. I had found it this morning and carried it through the rain for two hours until I found the right bridge.

The rock was still there. I touched it with my foot to make sure. It felt solid and real.

I peeled myself from the wall and leaned a little to glance out of the alley. In front of me a narrow stone bridge spanned the width of a rain-swollen river. Another wall of medieval buildings loomed on the other side. Behind them, a tower soared, a spire rising at least six hundred feet, silhouetted against the storm-choked sky and topped by a huge flower of translucent, milky glass. The flower's petals were shut into a bud, guarding the observation deck in its center from the storm. Every few seconds, bright gold sparks dashed through the enchanted glass.

A dozen dark shapes circled the flower, surfing the wild air currents. My brain expected them to be birds, but birds had only one pair of wings, not two. The feeling of wrongness was overwhelming.

Yep, the Mage Tower and the strange bird-things were still there, too.

I huddled against the wall.

I couldn't touch the Mage Tower, but I knew it was real. For one, I had pictured it differently. In my head it was a flawless pale needle, elegant and almost dainty. If this had been a hallucination, what I saw would've matched the vision in my head, but the reality was nothing like that. This tower jutted up, defiant, its walls worn but strong, as if it had grown from bedrock. And it felt *old*. Like it had stood there for thousands of years and would stand just like that for another millennium, timeless and indifferent, while the city around it crumbled into dust, rebuilt, and crumbled again.

No, it was real, like this endless rain, like the pain in my freezing bare feet, and like the gnawing ache in my stomach.

In the distance, a bell tolled four times. Four PM.

It wouldn't be too long now.

To say that this was not the way I envisioned spending my Sunday would be a criminal understatement. Today would've been my one day off. I should've spent it watching Netflix, nibbling on a pizza, and reading while lounging on my couch in my tiny apartment, in my soft sweatpants, warm and dry. Not wrapped in a dirty rag, shivering in a grimy alley, while the sky dumped gallons of cold rain on my head.

I wasn't a big reader through most of my childhood, but when I was sixteen, my first serious boyfriend broke up with me, and it was hell. My brain kept rehashing every moment of the relationship in excruciating detail. One afternoon, as I lay on my bed, wallowing in self-pity, my mom handed me a thick fantasy book, and when I turned my nose up at it, she told me, "Maggie, you need to live in someone else's head for a bit."

I'd thought I would read a few pages. When I came up for air, five hours later, my breakup was an afterthought. Some seriously messed-up stuff happened on the first page, and I had to find out how it turned out. Somehow by the end of those five hours, the book had wrung me dry. I could deal with life again.

I'd tried every genre under the sun since, but fantasy was my vice of choice. There was something about blades and magic that did it for me. Deadly swordmasters, thieves prowling through moonlit streets, dark magicians, warrior princesses, ruthless nobles, majestic dragons, hideous monsters, I loved it all. Put a hot dude in armor with a sword on the cover, and my eyes glazed over while my hand crept to the BUY button, budget be damned.

I had read enough fantasy books to fill a library, but that very first series was my special treasure. Set in the city of Kair Toren, capital of the kingdom of Rellas, the story revolved around the power struggles of eight noble families, and it was so full of fantasy tropes, it would be clichéd except that the superb writing moved it right past stereotypical into classic. The characters felt so real, they practically jumped off the page.

The series had two books, *The Thieves of the North* and *The Lords of the East*. The third one had never come out.

I had been rereading those two books for the last ten years. Whenever life got to be too harsh, I would grab them off my bookshelf, and they never failed to pull me out of whatever funk I had going on at the time. I could quote passages from memory. I had stalked the author's abandoned website religiously for any hint of a release date. I haunted the fan groups looking for rumors and stewing in collective frustration. Adrian Latour, the author of the series, was always an enigma. He didn't do social media or appearances, and his bio, with a blank square where the author photo should have been, consisted of a single sentence: Adrian Latour, man of dreams and chronicler of stories. After the second book came out, he seemed to vanish. He never wrote anything else, and nobody offered an explanation as to why he stopped working. The story just cut off. One of my favorite characters was left standing on a box with a noose around his neck for a decade.

Three nights ago, after a long day of delivering groceries, I went to sleep in my apartment south of Austin and woke up in Kair Toren.

A hint of movement on my left made me turn. Something small padded through the rain toward me. I brushed the water off my face.

A red furry creature padded out from the rain-soaked alley and stared at me with unblinking dark eyes. Its head was round, with curved marten ears that stood straight up, a button nose, and very long whiskers. It didn't walk, it slunk, its longish body sitting low on four short legs that ended in webbed hand-paws armed with sharp retractable claws. It was as if an otter and a Ragdoll cat had a baby and dyed it red.

A stelka. A female one. Males had tufts on their ears.

Stelkas infested Kair Toren and its five rivers, catching fish and rats, eating garbage, raiding cellars, stealing everything that wasn't nailed down, and generally being a nuisance. Like overly smart foxes, except that normal foxes at least hesitated before they scurried over to take a bite out of someone five times their size. Last night, exhausted and desperate, I'd fallen asleep under some busted crates, and this morning I woke up because one of these red assholes decided to chew on my leg.

The stelka opened her mouth and showed me sharp white teeth.

It couldn't be.

I crouched and tilted my head, trying to get a better look.

There it was, a white patch on the stelka's chest that looked like a lopsided half-moon. I had seen a dozen stelkas in my three days of stumbling around the city, and only one of them had a white patch like that. I must've been really delicious.

"You followed me." My voice creaked like I had crawled out of the grave.

The stelka eyed me.

"Nope. Not happening."

The little creature took a step forward.

I showed her my rock.

Another step.

I gripped the rock and hit the cobblestones with it.

The beast shied back and hissed.

A piercing screech tore through the air above us. I glanced up. One of the weird birds swooped at the tower in a suicidal dive and rammed the petals.

For a moment, the entire flower went dark, barely visible in the rain.

Oh crap.

The bud pulsed with pale light. Tongues of golden lightning erupted from the petals, snaking toward the birds. They tried to flee in a panic, but the lightning chased them, stabbing at their wings.

One of the bird-things cried out, plunged from the sky, and smashed onto the paver stones between me and the stelka with a wet thud. It was about the size of an eagle, with a long whip-like tail tipped with a fan of dark feathers. Its wings were wide, its long hind legs were sheathed in contour feathers, and all four of its appendages ended in paws armed with sharp talons.

A lorsse. Those long dinosaur-looking jaws were a dead giveaway. So that's what they looked like. In the books, they came out during storms and were attracted to magic.

The bird-thing clicked its needle teeth and tried to rise.

The stelka lunged forward. Her mouth closed on the creature's neck and bit down. Blood drenched the feathers. The lorsse went limp. The stelka growled at me, clamping the neck in her teeth, slung the dead lorsse over her back—it was bigger than she was—and took off deeper into the alley, back the way she had come.

That's right. And don't come back.

I slumped against the wall. Kair Toren in a nutshell. One moment you are flying high and screaming at the world, the next someone bites your throat and drags you off into a dark alley. It was unhinged, but I was almost sorry to see the stelka go. In the past three days, that little beast was the only living creature that had acknowledged my existence.

I'd read this type of story before. It was a portal fantasy, a subgenre that had grown really popular in fantasy romance lately. It seemed in every other book some poor office worker woman about my age got hit by a bus or collapsed from overworking and ended up in a fictional world.

I knew exactly how things were supposed to go. I was meant to appear in this new world as a woman of prophecy with magic holy powers so I could assist the kingdom with their blight or curse problem. I would be met by a prince or some high-ranking and stunning noble, and upon heroically demonstrating my abilities, I would become the center of attention, while a gaggle of ridiculously handsome men followed me around, pledged their swords to me, and pleaded with me not to overexert myself.

Failing that, I could wake up in the body of the female lead, usually a daughter of a prominent noble house, after she flung herself into a lake in despair over being shunned by a villainous prince and died, conveniently vacating her body for my soul to take it over. I would pretend to suffer from amnesia, while an army of maids waited on me hand and foot, and plot my revenge, during which I would be fawned on by a dangerous and ice-cold male lead, who would turn into a devoted puppy in my vicinity.

Alternatively, I could come to in the body of the villainess, usually another daughter of a prominent noble house, after she flung herself into a lake, etc., etc., despair, death, maids, hand and foot, and then I would convince everyone that I was just misunderstood and win over the dangerous and ice-cold male lead, who would abandon the heroine for me.

If not the heroine or the villainess, I could be their best friend. Their younger sister. A lesser noble. A chamber maid. I would've happily taken the fucking chamber maid.

That's not what I got.

I woke up choking on rainwater in a muddy ditch. Naked. Without any magic powers.

When I'd finally coughed all the sludge out of my mouth, crawled out, and saw the Mage Tower rising above the city with its magical glass petals, I thought I had lost my mind.

The Rise of Kair Toren was not a pretty-princess-rides-a-unicorn kind of fantasy. I'd stumbled on a ragged blanket someone had forgotten in the rain, dug it out of the mud, and wrapped it around me, stench of urine and all. Because if I didn't, I would be assaulted, murdered, sold, or forced to suffer any of the other tragic things that happened to women running around alone and naked in this city. I needed to look like a beggar, and the less attention I drew to myself, the better.

In our world, there were homeless shelters, police stations, and emergency rooms. I could've walked into any one of those and said, "I have amnesia, help me." And I would have been helped.

Kair Toren had none of that. If I were to stumble into a Guard station as I was, wrapped in my nasty rag, they would throw me back out on the street and tell me to thank my lucky stars they hadn't done anything worse.

The city was huge, filled with tall stone buildings that had sturdy doors and barred windows. The pouring rain had chased everyone indoors, and the stores were shuttered. Theft wasn't an option. I couldn't even panhandle, and if I tried, I'd be beaten up. The beggars of Kair Toren were brutal and notoriously territorial. My first evening here, I'd had the bright idea to try one of the temples for charity and ran into a pack of them fighting in front of the entrance. I had never in my life seen people ripping into each other out in the open like that. The last time I'd watched someone fight was in high school and that was mostly two guys rolling around on the ground. These people were literally beating each other to death with rocks and stomping on prone bodies, and nobody was doing anything about it. I got out of there as fast as I could.

I drank rainwater when I was thirsty and prayed I wouldn't get dysentery. I squatted in alleys when I had to pee. I'd torn two armholes in my blanket and tied it around myself so I could run away fast if I had to. I hid wherever I could to sleep and had only managed a few hours in the last three nights. I had to fight off ravenous magic otter-foxes. The first day I was in denial and expecting the nightmare to end, the second, I was desperate and scared, and now only a grim determination remained. I'd invested weeks of my life into those cursed books. I knew them cover to cover. I would survive. Kair Toren wouldn't kill me. I wouldn't give it the satisfaction.

Last night, I stumbled onto a large plaza with a blue obelisk in the center. In the books it was called Bluestone Square, and there was a signboard by the obelisk where the government posted announcements. When I found it, I learned two things: I could read Rellasian and yesterday was the fifth of Planter, the last month of spring, of the year 3044.

I was at the end of chapter one of the first book. Today after four PM a man called Lecke would cross the Estret Bridge. He was a scummy, sniveling prick, the kind of character that makes you wait an entire book for a rock to fall on his head and crush his skull.

When Lecke was eighteen years old, his parents died in a mill fire. He didn't set it, but it had served his purposes beautifully. He had wanted to get out of the countryside for a while, and now he could sell everything they owned and take off for greener pastures. Unfortunately for him, his two younger brothers, one ten and the other seven, didn't perish with his parents; so Lecke strangled them in their sleep, threw their bodies into the nearest ravine, and told the village that they had gone to live with his nonexistent aunt and uncle. That was only the beginning of his career, and it had gone from bad to worse. Now he made his money as a fence, buying and selling bloodstained jewelry and other valuables brought to his door late at night by people with vicious eyes.

Today, Lecke would be carrying a bag of money from a particularly good haul. I had to get that bag.

I studied my rock. Normally, a man in Lecke's profession would have a bodyguard, but he didn't trust anyone. Instead, he carried a knife and was very good with it. Trying to attack him, with my head swimming from hunger and only a rock as my weapon, was suicide. But I was out of options.

As if on cue, someone walked out from the mouth of the street at the other side of the river and stepped onto the bridge. The Estret was one of the city's narrower bridges, about a hundred feet long but only fifteen feet wide, guarded by a hip-high stone rail. Surprise was my best bet. I had to snatch the bag and run, because if he caught me, it would all be over.

I scooped up a handful of mud that had accumulated by the wall of the building next to me and smeared it on my face. If I did manage to get away, no need to be recognized later.

The figure kept walking, unhurried despite the rain.

I grabbed my rock, tugged the ragged blanket into place, and ventured out into the open. My bare toes had turned into icicles long ago. I didn't walk, I lurched like some zombie.

Get the bag. Get the bag. Get the bag . . .

The distance between us shrank, the curtain of rain thinning as we came closer to each other. I could see his cloak now, a deep hunter green. Yes, this was my man.

If worse came to worst, I could grab the bag and jump into the river. I swam in the ocean every summer vacation since I was little.

I glanced over the rail. The waters of the Koreg River churned below, dark brown from silt.

I would probably survive it. Probably.

I stumbled to the other side of the bridge, as if avoiding Lecke. He showed no sign of noticing me.

Twenty feet. Ten. Five.

The world snapped into terrifying clarity.

We passed each other on the opposite sides of the bridge like two ships in the night.

I spun around and charged at him, swinging my rock.

He must've sensed me coming because he turned, but not fast enough. My rock connected with his skull. Lecke stumbled. I leaped at him and thrust my hands under his cloak. My fingers clutched thick canvas, and something inside it made a metallic *clink*.

I yanked the bag away from him with all my strength, throwing the weight of my body into it. It came free.

I did it!

Lecke lunged at me. Something sharp and cold bit into my side, and I saw him up close, deep-set piggish eyes staring at me from a face twisted with rage.

He'd stabbed me.

The cold blade bit into me again and again, slicing through my insides. I tried to back away, but the stone rail of the bridge dug into my butt, and he was so fast.

Lecke grabbed the bag and jerked back. I clung to it.

"Let go!" he snarled.

I had a death grip on that damn bag. No force in the universe could make me let go.

The bloody knife slashed in front of me, drawing an icy line across my neck. Heat wet my skin. Bright, shocking red sprayed Lecke's face and cloak.

He'd cut my throat. He'd killed me. No more curling up in my apartment with a book. No more Netflix. I would never see my parents and my brother again. All my dreams and hopes, all the things I didn't get to do, it was all over. My small comfortable life ended right here.

He wouldn't take this bag even if keeping it was the final thing I did in my short life. I gripped the canvas sack and, with the last of my strength, hurled myself backward over the rail into the river. The gray stormy sky yawned at me, tilted, and then cold dark water fell on my face and swallowed me whole.

Chapter 2

I choked on muddy water. Before my brain could process the situation, my body took over. I flipped onto my stomach and retched.

I was still alive and drowning again.

How was I alive?

Every spasm hurt like hell. I felt the pain all the way in my toes.

The last of the water spilled out of me. I coughed, my throat raw, and opened my eyes, half expecting to be back in the same ditch somehow.

No, not a ditch. Above me, high up, was some sort of dark roof or ceiling. I was on my hands and knees in about six inches of water. My left hand was squishing slimy mud. My right was still clutching the money bag, its cord wrapped in a tangle around my wrist.

How . . . ?

I untied the cord and pulled the bag open with shaking fingers. Coins. Handfuls of them.

I hugged the bag to my naked chest and sobbed. For a few moments nothing existed except the bag and overwhelming relief.

Gradually it dawned on me that I was naked again and that what I could see of myself looked unwounded. Lecke had stabbed me. I was sure of it. I closed my eyes, and my memory served up the knife slicing into me in a flash of pain. Yes, he'd definitely stabbed me. And then cut my throat. I checked my neck. No blood. No wound. No scar that I could feel. Nothing on my stomach either.

Even if he hadn't stabbed me, the river should've killed me. I should've drowned.

Where the hell was I?

I looked around. The rain still sifted from the sky, but it was no longer a drenching shower. I had attacked Lecke about thirty minutes after four PM. Now dusk was creeping in. Dark water stretched in front of me and to the sides, flowing around a narrow strip of muddy ground choked with weeds and low bushes wrapped in a thorny vine. A stone column rose behind me, supporting the roof above my head. Far in the distance, the top of the Mage Tower fluoresced weakly against the encroaching darkness. When I'd waited by the bridge, it had jutted almost directly across from me, and now it was much farther away, which meant the river had carried me downstream.

I had washed up on Ogden Island, a small, marshy chunk of solid ground at the junction of the Koreg and another small river. Ogden was the only island downstream of the Estret Bridge that would still let me view almost all of the Mage Tower. I knew this because one of the characters chose this spot for an ambush and had a whole page of inner monologue about the beauty of the Mage Tower and how this was the only island where so much of it could be seen. On other islands the trees or buildings blocked the view.

I was sitting under Ogden Bridge right by a busy neighborhood. I needed to get the hell out of here before someone noticed me or Lecke came looking for his blood money.

Getting up proved to be a heroic challenge. My stomach didn't have a gash, but my whole body hurt as if someone had pummeled me with a baseball bat. After three tries, I stood and leaned against the column, which was likely a bridge pier, took a short breather, and stumbled forward, keeping my left hand on the stones and my right cradling the money. Every step hurt, but I was losing light and fast.

I rounded the pier and squinted at the narrow stretch of shrub-covered ground. Something rested on the muddy shore, halfway in the water. The air reeked of an unmistakable, slightly sweet stench.

A dead body. I waded through the ankle-deep water toward it.

It was blue-black and bloated. I couldn't even tell if it was a woman or a man. It looked like it would fall apart at any moment.

I retched, but there was nothing in my stomach, so I just dry heaved until I peed myself. I would've cried, but I didn't have the energy for it.

The body wore a cloak and some sort of tunic and pants, ripped and stained. A rope with torn ends wrapped around the corpse's waist. There must've been a weight attached to it. This was a planned drowning, never meant to be discovered. The floodwaters had dislodged the corpse from the riverbed and carried it to the island.

I waited until my eyes stopped watering from the stink, walked over to the body, crouched, and unhooked its cloak. Getting it off the corpse proved a lot easier than expected. I pulled, and it came free.

I had to wash it. The river was cold, muddy, and dark. I gritted my teeth, dragged the cloak into the water, and sloshed it around.

A small shape slunk out of the twilight to the right of me. I turned my head.

You've got to be kidding me.

The little stelka hugged the ground and showed me her teeth.

My voice came out ragged, like a growl. "I will end you. I mean it."

The stelka hesitated, unsure.

If I ever went back to my world, I would burn every copy of *The Thieves of the North* I could find. I would build a Viking funeral pyre out of them on a raft, push it into Lake Travis, and howl like a wolf while flames consumed it.

The cloak stank, but not as bad as I expected, so I put it on and staggered around the shore of the small island. The fabric was wool but soaking wet and cold. I could really use some shoes . . . No. Stuffing my feet into boots filled with human sludge was beyond me. Barefoot it was.

The stelka watched me, wary.

The assassin who hid on this island, waiting for his victim to cross the bridge, mentioned that one of the piers had metal handholds for maintenance. I scanned the three piers. The middle pier offered a row of rusty metal brackets. My way out. I tied the bag of money around my neck and took one last look around.

Something was wrong with the river's current ahead. Something odd . . .

There it was, about fifty yards away, a section of the river that seemed unnaturally free of ripples. It was the same color as the rest of the water, a muddy brown, but it was moving at a different speed, slower, as if it were fighting the rushing current.

I had no idea what the hell it was. It wasn't in the books. I was absolutely sure it wasn't. I would've remembered that. Every instinct in me screamed that it was bad and I had to avoid it at all costs.

The translucent mass cut across the current to the left, heading straight for the island.

Fear shot through me like an electric shock. I spun around and sprinted to the pier with the handholds, stumbling over fallen branches and weeds. The shrubs caught my cloak. I ripped it free and kept going, jerking my feet out of the mud.

Behind me something let out a desperate shriek. I looked over my shoulder. The little stelka was flailing in a clump of thorny shrubs, stuck up to her chest in mud.

The dark thing sped toward us. An eerie feeling squirmed along my back, like a clammy, wet hand brushing my skin. The stelka screamed, a pitiful frantic cry.

Damn it.

I reversed, tore back through the shrubs, yanked the little beast free, and heaved her onto my shoulder. She sank her claws into the cloak and my skin, clinging to me for dear life.

I crashed through the bushes, heading for the pier. Mud squelched under my feet. I slid on the sludge, caught myself, slid again, and skidded into stone. My fingers caught the first metal handhold, and I scrambled up. Three breaths, and I had climbed onto the bridge and whipped around.

Below me, a translucent body slid out of the river. It was formless and stretchy, like a ten-foot-wide amoeba swirling with terrifying darkness. It licked the shore of the tiny island, slid over the corpse, and slipped back into the water.

The corpse was gone as if it had never been there.

What the actual fuck . . .

The terrible creature lingered by the edge of the island, waiting, its surface rippling like some horrible oil slick. It couldn't climb up the pier, could it? Surely it couldn't.

I held my breath. On my shoulder the stelka froze, completely still.

The monstrous thing sank below the surface.

A moment . . .

Another . . .

The dark thing floated back up, pushed away from the shore, and the river took it, pulling it under the bridge.

I exhaled.

And realized I had a wild animal clawing into my shoulder. At that exact moment, the stelka realized she was clinging to a weird human. I jerked, she squeaked, I stumbled back, and she leaped off my shoulder and raced off into the night, vanishing between the houses at the other end of the bridge.

Okay then. So that happened.

I slumped against the bridge's rail. The dark water rushed below me. I was definitely in Kair Toren. The Mage Tower was where it was supposed to be, the Bluestone Square was as described, Ogden Island, the bridge I was on, Lecke walking across Estret right on schedule—all of that matched. But there was also the body on the shore and then there was that thing, whatever the hell it was. That thing shouldn't have been here. It shouldn't have even existed. It wasn't in the books.

Maybe this wasn't just a book.

I should've realized this sooner, but I had been too caught up in trying to survive. Dying must've given me some clarity. Wherever I had ended up, this world wasn't limited by the pages of the books I knew. This place was something else, something much bigger. Something alive and very dangerous.

I swallowed, hid my money under the cloak, pulled the hood over my head, and forced myself to turn away from the river toward the city.

The rain had eased but the streets were still deserted. Night had pounced, drowning Kair Toren, the outlines of tall buildings charcoal sketches against a deeper gloom. Darkness pooled in the mouths of alleys and stretched onto the roads. Here and there a few windows were lit from within, taunting me with warmth.

I had to get off the streets.

Kair Toren had several licensed inns but to stay in one of those, I wouldn't just need money, I would need identification papers or the crest of a prominent family. Licensed inns were required to keep records of their guests and they screened their patrons. I wouldn't even get through the door in my corpse cloak and bare feet.

There were unlicensed, illegal inns. I knew of a couple, but I would have to find them in the dark, and walking into those and flashing my ill-gotten gains would get my throat slit again. The people who ran those places had no problem killing their patrons for a few coins and dumping them into the nearest river. Been there, done that, no thanks.

My toes started their transformation into icicles again. The adrenaline rush was wearing off. A gnawing ache spread through my body. I was sore everywhere.

I had to find shelter, clean up, and get a change of clothes. Food. I needed food. My stomach actually hurt, as if the hunger had become an open wound.

There was one place where I could get all those things. They wouldn't care about my cloak, they wouldn't ask any questions, and they wouldn't murder me as long as I paid my way. It would be expensive as hell, but I had no choice. Yes, that could work.

I looked up, trying to get my bearings. I was on Ogden Bridge, and the Mage Tower was in front of me and to my left, which meant north was to my left as well. Kair Toren was a huge city, and I'd have to get almost all the way to the Bull Gate. At least an hour of fast walking, maybe longer. The rain had finally stopped, which meant the human predators would soon emerge. I had to hurry.

I turned, crossed the bridge, and started down the cobblestone street, hugging myself against the cold.

The city crawled by, the dark alleys and side streets yawning at me as I passed. I kept moving, listening for every noise, alert to every flicker on the edge of my vision.

My feet ached. My shoulder burned where the stelka had clawed me. My stomach hurt, begging for food. The wet cloak refused to dry. I was freezing. A sob broke free, and I bit down on it. Survive first, cry later. I just had to make it to my destination and not get jumped along the way.

There had to be shorter routes, but I only knew how to get there from the Bull Gate, because one of the characters took that path in the books.

It felt like I had been walking forever. I couldn't even think anymore. I just focused on putting one foot in front of the other.

The street narrowed, its houses three or four stories high and built without any spaces between them. Lanterns lit the way, attached to the buildings every thirty yards. I was almost to the outer wall. The roads here were meant to channel the flood of invaders into a narrow kill space if the gates were breached. The city paid to have them well lit in case the city watch had to chase a criminal trying to enter or exit.

The street ended, as if cut off with a knife, and the Bull Gate rose ahead, the empty space in front of it lit by torches and braziers, their light playing on the massive bronze doors shut tight. High above, the city guards prowled the wall.

I stopped. I needed to take the third street from the gate on my left. There should have been a house with a blue door on the corner . . .

The huge city gates opened with a loud *clang*.

It was after sunset. Only someone in a very high position could force the guards to let them in.

Three riders entered the city, followed by a cart. All three rode Andikan warhorses, big, quick-footed, and mean, with grullo coats that looked like gray smoke. The leading rider's horse had a bald face—a white marking that covered the entire front of his head. It looked like he had killed another horse and wore its skull as a helmet.

Everard. The Sleepless Duke, riding Villain, his war stallion. Crap.

They called him the Sleepless Duke because he ruled over a vast stretch of territory on the northern border and that territory was continuously raided by the aggressive nations from the northwest and the Crimson Empire from the east. The Selva Dukedom was always at war. Ramond vi Everard had no time to sleep. He had picked up a sword at the age of three and never put it down, just like his father and mother before him. He was a violent isolationist, who responded to threats with overwhelming force and shocking brutality.

And he was not supposed to be here. Something monumental must've happened because Everard wasn't allowed in the city without a royal invitation. Sauven Savaric, the current king of Rellas, feared him so much, it was almost a phobia. This wasn't in the book either. Why? This seemed like a pretty major development.

If he was sneaking into the city, he wouldn't want witnesses. Of all the people to run into . . .

There was no place to hide. I flattened myself against the nearest house and looked down.

The riders bore down the street, their dark cloaks swallowing the light as if they had cut out pieces of midnight sky and wrapped them around their bodies.

Don't notice me. Don't see me.

Villain reached me. The size of this horse was truly shocking. I raised my head a fraction of an inch. The stallion glared at me with a bright blue eye, and I caught a glimpse of the rider, broad shoulders stretching his cloak, his hood hiding everything except for his clean-shaven square jaw.

I held my breath.

The stallion stopped.

Crap. Crap, crap, crap.

I was right by a lantern. He could see me in excruciating detail, everything from my bare feet to the hood of my wet cloak. I didn't even want to imagine what I smelled like.

"Hold out your hand."

That voice raised every hair on the back of my neck. He sounded like he ordered people to their death in battle.

Not holding out my hand wasn't an option. If he cut it off, would it regenerate, or would I have to kill myself to regrow it? Would it regrow at all? If I died again, would I come back to life or was it a limited-number-of-times kind of thing . . .

"Your hand."

Damn it.

A hard clump blocked my throat. I swallowed and raised my right hand.

I don't want to die again. Please no.

A cold weight fell into my fingers. He'd dropped a handful of coins into my palm.

"Get off the street and buy some shoes."

What?

Villain started forward. The riders passed me. The cart rolled by into the night. The hoofbeats scattered down the street, receding.

I stared at the money in my hand. A large silver coin, about the size of a silver dollar—a noma—and two copper coins that had to be dens. My memory informed me in a detached mechanical way that each noma equaled one hundred copper dens, and each den equaled four quarters. A quarter would buy me a pint of cheap ale, a den would buy me a young chicken, and a noma would buy me a weaned calf. Thank you, numerous rereads.

The fear slowly melted away. The last echoes of it drained out of me into the night.

The Sleepless Duke had given me money. The actual, in the flesh, Ramond vi Everard had handed me coins.

Oh my god.

Okay, that was cool beyond all reason. Entirely too much excitement, very scary, but so freaking cool. I shivered. Wow. Okay, I needed to get where I was going now before anything else happened.

I backtracked, counting the side streets. One. Two.

Here it was, a house with a blue door on the corner of a side street, marked by twin lanterns with a small red flower painted on the glass. Squire Way. Found it.

I ducked into the side street. It wound, twisting left, then right, then left again. I followed it. As long as I didn't take any turns, it would get me to my destination.

I would need to pay an entrance fee. The question was, how much? The door charge wasn't a means of making money, it was proof of one's ability to pay. The real fees would be spent inside. For prominent people, the door charge would be nothing. For me, it would be a serious amount of money, and the prices in Rellas didn't always make sense by modern standards. In this world, cows and fish were relatively cheap, and books and soap were hellishly expensive. Offering too little would be insulting, offering too much would brand me a sucker. I had to find the middle ground.

I didn't even know how much money I had.

I crossed a street.

Another.

Average daily wages for an unskilled laborer were about two dens. An experienced mercenary made five or six. Would ten dens be enough?

I squeezed Everard's coins in my hand. He'd given me a whole noma. It wasn't much money for him, but for a woman without shoes or underwear, it was a huge amount. It would have been better to put it into my bag, but then I wouldn't know which money was his. I wanted to wait until I could look at it. Kair Toren had beaten me down, but the coins in my hand were proof that kindness existed. Someone in this awful city had been nice to me, and good things did happen here. It was hope in my fingers.

That was so random. If you had asked me which of the characters in the novel were the most likely to hand a coin to a beggar, Everard would be near the bottom of that list. In the books he was a rare presence, an ominous power that both fueled Sauven's mental illness and held it in check from afar. Whenever he appeared, someone was going to die.

Something rounded the corner behind me. I turned my head just enough to catch it in my peripheral vision. A man, wearing a dark half cloak, heading in the same direction as me.

He crossed the street to my side.

It could've been a coincidence, but it probably wasn't.

I picked up the pace.

He did, too.

Anxiety splashed me in an ice-cold rush.

Ahead, the alley bent to the left. I turned the corner, clenched Everard's money in my fist, and sprinted, squeezing every drop of speed out of my body. The money bag slapped against my chest as I ran. Houses flew by.

Behind me heavy boots pounded the cobblestones.

The street spat me out into a large plaza. In the back of it, a big stone building stood, four floors high and lit up like a Christmas tree against the dark backdrop of the city. There was no time to take it in. I saw rows of windows with ornate bars glowing with a welcoming yellow light, two solid rectangular towers in front connected by a third-floor loggia, and between them arched doors standing wide open, leading inside. Two men guarded the doors. They carried maces on their hips, and they looked like they would brain you with them if you glanced at them the wrong way.

I ran to the doors.

Behind me the man burst out of the alley.

I braked in front of the guard on my left. He held out his hand. I dropped Everard's silver noma into his palm.

The guard bowed and indicated the open door with his hand. The entrance waited in front of me, a long narrow hallway lit up by lanterns.

My lungs burned. I sucked in a breath and glanced over my shoulder. The asshole who'd chased me had turned around and was walking away, back toward the alley.

A swarm of glowing golden butterflies flowed out of the entrance, as if the building had exhaled light and beauty into the night. The butterflies bounced on the draft, trailing tiny gold sparks, swirled toward me, and melted into the night air. Like magic.

No, not like. It was magic, not distant like the Mage Tower zapping the lorsses, but right there in front of me. A wonder. It was impossible back home, but here it was real. It existed and it was beautiful.

I caught my breath, swallowed, and walked unsteadily into the Garden of Soft Blossoms.

Chapter 3

Three steps into the hallway, my legs decided they'd had just about enough of my nonsense and tried to fold under me. I stumbled and caught myself on the stone wall. My head swam.

The hallway had to be about forty feet long and only about twelve feet wide, just enough for two swordsmen to defend it standing side by side. Right now, it might as well have been a mile long. Getting through it felt impossibly hard.

The doors at the other end stood wide open, and I could see a hint of the main floor. It was all light and bright colors. The sound of laughter and the scents of cooked meat and spices floated in with the draft. My mouth watered. I had never been so hungry in my entire life.

Standing here and drooling, as fun as it was, wouldn't get me any closer to food and rest. I wasn't out of the woods yet.

I pushed from the wall, took a test step forward, and didn't faceplant on the floor. So far, so good. Small slow steps. No rush. I started toward the light.

A beautiful melody echoed through the building, fast and compelling, with a rapid beat.

The hallway ended. I stepped onto the main floor.

I stood on the edge of a huge square room, with tiled floors and cream-colored stone walls that rose two stories high. A colonnade wrapped around the perimeter of the square, supporting a second-floor balcony guarded by a wooden rail. Most of the floor and the balcony was taken up by wooden tables and chairs. Here and there patrons dined, laughing, talking, and getting drunk. Waiters, dressed in white tunics with dark red trousers and matching sash belts, flitted between the tables delivering food and drinks.

In the center of the room, under a chandelier of glowing orbs, a round stage stood, encircled by a shallow moat about three feet wide. The water in the moat was the color of rubies, and it shone, reflecting the light. The line in the book said, *The red dye in the water stained fabric and skin, keeping drunk patrons from storming the stage*, which had made me think of watered-down red Kool-Aid when I read it. The liquid in the moat didn't look like Kool-Aid. It looked like red wine, rich and almost purple.

On stage, ridiculously beautiful women danced, clad in dresses of bright green veils. They twisted and turned in time with the music, the diaphanous fabric flaring just enough to hint at the bodies beneath, but never offering more than a glimpse. The light of the chandelier played on their dresses, and when they raised their arms and bent their bodies, the veils shone with metallic gold.

So pretty...

The music sped up and so did the dancers, all but flying around the stage. They were so graceful, their movements mesmerizing, almost hypnotic. I had never seen anything like it. After days of rain, mud, and hunger, it didn't seem real. Maybe I was really dying on the street, and my brain was hallucinating, trying to offer me something beautiful before I finally kicked the bucket.

The music stopped on a high note. The women held their poses for a moment, like living statues, then withdrew along a narrow, raised path to the back of the room and vanished behind green curtains.

A man strode to the stage and halted by the red moat. He wore a light gray doublet and dark gray trousers tucked into tall boots. A teal cloak hung off his left shoulder, more of a fashion statement than a protective garment. His back was to me, so I couldn't see his face, only his curly dark hair, cut short, and the color of his skin, a russet brown.

He pondered the empty stage as if puzzled and waved his hand. A globe of red water shot up from the moat fifteen feet into the air and snapped into a monstrous fish.

Oh!

The creature swam above the stage, circling it. Its long eel-like body kept going and going, long and slightly translucent, the sharp ridged fin along its back bristling with red spikes. It was big enough to swallow a human in one gulp.

Goosebumps crawled up my arms.

The fish's grotesque jaws snapped, catching its tail. It exploded into a dozen stelkas. They rained onto the center of the stage and dashed into the dining room, darting between the tables. To the side a waiter gripped his tray and jerked it up over his head as a beast shot by his legs. People chuckled.

The stelkas burst into geysers of crimson flower petals. They swirled, flashed with light, and turned into golden butterflies.

Oh wow.

The glowing swarms floated over the dining floor, bouncing on the draft, spreading in all directions.

It was too much. Too bright, too colorful, too everything...

The nearest group of butterflies changed its course, drifting close to each other instead of fanning out. They were heading right for me.

No time to react. A second, and they swirled around my body, clinging to my cloak. One landed on my shoulder, one tried to wedge itself in my hood, and the third rammed my right cheek...

People were looking at me.

I didn't belong here. I was wearing a cloak that smelled like a corpse. There was river muck in my hair. My bare feet had probably left muddy footprints in the hallway. I couldn't have been more out of place if I had set myself on fire.

The butterflies exploded in a puff of soft sparks. Something zinged my skin, like a weak rubber band slapping against my face.

A woman blocked my view, hiding me from the other patrons. She wore a red gown cut too low, and her brown hair was braided into an elaborate lattice and secured with silver ornaments. She looked like a fairy princess in search of someone to seduce.

"Welcome, my lady. How may the Garden serve you today?"

I opened my mouth.

A paralyzing fear gripped me. I tried to make words, but nothing happened. I hadn't spoken to a human being since I got here. I'd understood Lecke, but it's not like we'd exchanged pleasantries while I robbed him and he stabbed me to death. What if I said something, and English came out instead of Rellasian. What if she asked me questions?

I'd run away. The door was right there. She wouldn't chase me.

The princess woman waited.

I had to say something. I strained, and miraculously my memory served up the right phrase.

"A private respite and a light dinner." My voice sounded hoarse.

"Do you seek serenity or luxury?"

It worked. Holy shit, it worked.

"Serenity." I couldn't afford luxury. I probably couldn't afford serenity either, but those were my only choices.

"It is our privilege to serve you today. Klemena will guide you to your room."

A woman in a simpler red gown stepped forward and bowed to me. She looked to be in her late teens. "Please follow me, my lady."

I didn't qualify as a lady by any metric, but there were no commoners in the Garden. Here everyone was *my lord* and *my lady*. One of the perks of paying an arm and a leg to get through the door.

I trailed Klemena to the right, into the passageway defined by the colonnade and the low wooden rail connecting the stone columns. She held a side door open for me. We passed into a hallway lit by ornate lanterns. Klemena shut the door behind us, cutting off the loud noise of the main floor, and I could breathe again.

Six doors led to other rooms, three on each side. Klemena led me to the third door on the left, the farthest from the main floor, and held it open.

I walked into a square room about the size of a large main bedroom. Bright lanterns glowed on bare stone walls, one of them highlighting a small door in the far wall. On the left, a square stone bath waited, sunken in the floor, filled with steaming water, and big enough to sit four to six people comfortably. Pink and white petals floated on the surface. A tray on the rim of the bath offered a bar of soap the size of a small matchbox, a bottle of what was likely scented oil, a sponge, a comb, and a folded towel. On the right, a small table and two chairs provided a place to sit down.

"May I attend to you, my lady?"

"No. I'm fine." I dropped one of the two dens Everard had given me into her hand. Only one of his coins left. "I need a change of clothes."

"What style?"

"The kind of dress that the wife of a successful craftsman might wear. Something that wouldn't make me stand out on the street."

"Shoes?"

"Yes, please."

"Will you require a companion, my lady?"

"No." Sex was the absolute last thing I needed right this second.

Klemena bowed. "I will return with your dinner."

"Thank you. Could you please bring me water instead of wine?"

"Yes, my lady."

She exited and shut the door behind her.

I dropped my cloak. It fell in a soggy mess at my feet. Something moved on my right, and I almost jumped.

An old metal mirror, pitted from the moisture, spanned the height of the wall.

My heart hammered so hard and fast, it hurt.

I took a long breath, trying to calm down, and looked.

A woman in her mid-twenties looked back at me. About five feet four inches, pale, average build, long brown hair, face pretty in a normal-person way, and terrified eyes. No jewel-toned irises, no raven locks, stunning features, or perfect proportions. I hadn't taken over anyone's body. I was still me. My hair was a gunky mess, my legs and face were splattered with mud, and a leather bag hung around my neck on a cord. I had hit a man with a rock and then died for it. But I was still me.

I should've been more freaked out. I should've cried or broken down but running for my life straight into the sensory overload had wrung the last of my emotions out of me. I was numb and running on fumes.

I slipped into the bath and sat on the stone bench, submerged to my collarbones. The water was luxuriously hot and smelled faintly of lavender.

Suddenly nothing mattered more than getting clean.

I opened my hand over the rim of the bath. The last of Everard's copper dens slipped from my fingers and landed on the smooth stone with a soft clink. I took the bag off my neck, put it next to the coin, reached for the soap, and began to lather my hair.

Getting Kair Toren off of me took a minute.

Midway through it, Klemena returned with a stack of clothes and my dinner: a slender glass bottle filled with water, soup, fresh bread, and roasted fish with some vegetables on a wooden tray. The light dinner. The regular dinner had five courses. I hadn't eaten for three days. I couldn't be trusted not to gorge myself on it and then throw it up.

I gave Klemena one of the nomas from the bag. It would cover the bath, the clothes, and the dinner. If I had been renting a room at one of the cheaper legitimate inns, it would've paid for a week-long stay with meals. Klemena asked me if I wanted to keep my old clothes. I told her no. She bowed, collected my discarded cloak, and left. As bad as it smelled, they would likely burn it.

I devoured half of the soup and most of the bread before I almost got sick and had to stop. Now I sat in the bath, leaning my head on the wall behind it, with my hair brushed out and my stomach gurgling. The rest of my meal waited on the platter. I would finish it as soon as my digestion settled. I'd eaten so fast, I had barely tasted the food.

The water in the bath was still warm. *They must heat it somehow.*

Everyone in the capital knew about the Garden of Soft Blossoms. It sat outside proper society, and yet it was accepted the way upscale strip clubs were accepted in our world. Calling it a brothel would be like referring to the Met as "a little art gallery."

The Garden had two cornerstones: discretion and safety. It was a place of expensive courtesans, male and female, but it offered much more. People came here for entertainment, for gourmet cuisine and rare ales and wine, to get pampered and to escape from their lives. For younger nobles and the heirs of richer merchants, this was a place to flex in front of their friends and throw their family's money around. They could get roaring drunk, pass out at their table, and when they woke up, all their valuables would be right where they left them.

The staff of the Garden would take care of me, not because they were sex workers with hearts of gold or because they felt sorry for me, but because I gave them money. If that man had caught me before I had paid my fee, he would've dragged me off in plain view, and neither of the guards would have lifted a finger to help me. The noma in my hand bought my safety. Had I fumbled with my bag instead of throwing that coin at the guard, I wouldn't be here right now.

I squinted at Everard's copper den next to my bag of money.

Saved by the Sleepless Duke. If this was a fanfic, people would've trashed it for sheer implausibility.

There was a relief on the wall across from me, a marine monster winding around a column, carved in great detail down to the scales and wide fins. It looked like a weird hybrid of a dragon and one of those giant extinct reptiles that ate dinosaurs in the prehistoric oceans. I was in the Idrid Room, the place where Orsana Kallira, an aide to the Underchancellor of Ceremonies, was murdered.

Would be murdered. It wouldn't happen for another eight months or so.

She would be sitting right here, probably in the exact same spot I sat, waiting to sell the kingdom's secrets to an agent of the Crimson Empire, when the Shears caught up with her. In the book, they stabbed her so fast and deep, she didn't even have a chance to scream. The entire bath turned red with her blood.

Orsana and I had that in common. We both died. Violently.

The canvas bag next to the coin assured me that I hadn't hallucinated my own murder. It had happened. And yet, here I was, alive and soaking in the tub.

There was only one possible explanation. Whatever force had brought me to Rellas wanted me to live.

Why was I here?

Was I supposed to do something? Why dump me naked into a ditch and then have me wander around, starving and cold, for days?

And how did I get here? There was absolutely nothing in the books about visitors from another world. No mention of portals, gates, nothing like that.

In most portal fantasies, some terrible, traumatic event occurred for a person to cross into another world. Usually, they died. They were stabbed, they fell off bridges, their ovens exploded. They were hit by a truck. It was such a common trope, there was a name for it. Death was a requirement, because without dying one couldn't reincarnate in a different world.

Nothing like that had happened to me. I had a routine day, took a shower, crawled into my bed, read some online comics, and fell asleep. My oven couldn't explode because it was electric. Nobody had stabbed me in my sleep because my alarm system hadn't gone off. There was no truck-kun.

Was I dead in my world? Was I missing?

If I was missing and the time back home flowed at the same pace as here, by now my parents would be frantic. We texted each other every day. They were probably searching for me. My brother was probably getting emergency leave from the army to help them.

Suddenly I missed my family so intensely that I pulled my knees to my chest, trying to curl into a fetal ball in the water.

I missed my parents. I missed my brother. I missed their voices, their texts, their hugs. I missed their jokes and their laughter.

I missed my home. Things didn't exactly go the way I had hoped after I finished college, but I had managed to build a cozy life for myself. My apartment was small, but it was comfy, full of books, and mine. I didn't love my job and my grocery-delivering side gig, but I tolerated them well enough. They were the price I had to pay to sleep in a soft bed under a solid roof, drink coffee in the morning in my cute kitchen, and play games on my Steam Deck at night. I lived in a nest of safety.

There was no safety in Kair Toren. It was the kind of place you wanted to visit only from the comfort of your home, while wrapped in a blanket and sipping on some hot cocoa for courage. You dove into it, let it thrill you and crush your emotions, and then surfaced, grateful to be back in your own little corner of existence.

I wanted to go home. I closed my eyes and pictured myself on my tiny balcony, sitting in the rocking chair my brother had bought for me and hauled all the way to my third-floor apartment. There would be a view of the picnic area and two large oaks in front of me and a round table on my right with a steaming cup of my favorite green tea in a mug that said *Good morning. I see the assassins have failed.*

I imagined myself in that chair and wished for it with all of my being.

Nothing happened. I was still in the bath. I had already tried dying. That didn't work either.

Maybe there was some purpose to my being here, something that only I could accomplish and then I would get to go home. Or maybe this was it. This was my life now.

A hard lump blocked my throat.

Okay, no. I was safe for the moment, true, but falling apart in the Garden wasn't the wisest thing to do. I needed to stay sharp.

Worrying about what really happened wouldn't get me anywhere. It didn't matter what took place in the "real" world because right now this world was real enough to harm me. It had injured me, starved me, killed me, and resurrected me, and I had felt all of it. Lecke's knife hurt. Drowning hurt. My feet still ached from running on the streets, and my whole body hummed like every cell in it had simultaneously developed a toothache.

This was my reality right now. If five years later I woke up in my bed like none of it had ever happened, it wouldn't matter because I still had to survive today. And tomorrow.

I needed a plan. First, I had to avoid dying at all costs. I had no idea how my resurrection worked. Would I revive every time someone killed me, or did I have a limited number of lives? I didn't want to find out. Not only that, but the pain had been excruciating, and the echo of that hurt still rattled around deep inside my bones. Thinking about it made me shiver, which was a mistake because all of me was terribly sore.

Survival was crucial, but so was safety. Even if I could revive every time I died, I could still suffer while I was alive. Broken bones, cuts, bruises, hunger, all of that would hurt just as much. The difference was, after it killed me, I would resurrect and endure it all over again. Now that was a cheery thought. Yay.

I had to find a secure place to stay. Somewhere safe where I could hole up while I figured out what to do next.

The Garden didn't rent rooms. All patrons were kicked out by two AM with very rare exceptions.

I had been here for at least a couple of hours. It was probably close to ten or eleven PM. The majority of the inns were in the Inn Quarter to the east, all the way across town and walled off in their own section. Kair Toren liked to keep track of their visitors. If they got unruly, the city could simply lock them up within the Inn Quarter and call it a day. The current arrangement had come about because a century ago, a rebel princess had snuck her army into the city by having them pose as merchants and random travelers and then tried to take the capital. The municipal regulations had relaxed a little since then, but not much.

The asshole who'd chased me was probably still out there. The area around the Garden wasn't the safest part of the city and that was partially by design. The element of danger added to the thrill. If someone got uppity and tried to rob some of the wealthier patrons, the Garden would stomp on their neck fast, but I was a nobody. An anonymous woman alone on the street in the middle of the night was fair game.

I really didn't like the look on that man's face.

At least I had clothes and money now. I would have to chance it. I had no choice. I needed to get dressed, ask Klemena where the closest inn was, and then wait by the exit until a larger group of patrons left, so I could tag along. If I found an inn, I would have to try to bribe the staff. Maybe if I parted with enough money, they would let me in . . .

A knock echoed through the door.

I sank deeper into the water. "Enter."

A tall woman walked into my room. Klemena followed three steps behind her, a deferential look on her face.

The woman examined me. She wore a stunning gown of deep Prussian blue accented with gold embroidery, with a slim bodice and a voluminous skirt. Her long dark blond hair was gathered into a single braid that began on her right temple, curved over the top of her head, then twisted to the back on the left, forming an almost Fibonacci spiral at her nape. It framed her face like a crown, secured in place with gold flowering-vine ornaments topped with blue gemstone flowers. I had no idea how to even start this hairdo.

Her features were striking rather than beautiful: dark blue eyes under strong eyebrows, narrow nose, and firm, full lips, and her expression frosted them over, adding just the right touch of authority and self-assurance. She was so composed, she looked almost regal. Everything about her, the way she walked in, the way she stood, the way she wore that amazing gown communicated that not only did she *not* suffer fools gladly, she suffered them not at all.

Galiene of Sosna. The most desired woman in Kair Toren. She couldn't have been anyone else. She was everything I had imagined. Wow.

The Garden was run by two women. The first, Hade, was the senior proprietor. She would be in her seventies by now, and she'd been gripping the reins of the Garden for forty years. Hade was well connected and still formidable despite her age. She knew where the literal bodies were buried, and a lot of powerful people across the entire realm would breathe easier once she died.

Galiene was Hade's chosen successor. She had taken over the daily management of the Garden, with Hade remaining in the background. She was one of my favorite supporting characters in the books. Galiene wasn't just striking, she was smart.

Not everyone in the Garden sold their bodies. Galiene didn't take clients, and it was a deliberate strategic choice, one which she and Hade had settled on years ago. She didn't shmooze or try to ingratiate herself. She didn't make small talk, and she never revealed anything about her life. Galiene appeared when a problem presented itself, resolved it with her usual poise, and moved on. The staff both feared and revered her, and she was truly the queen of her domain.

All of that made her irresistible to the rich and powerful, especially men. She was off-limits and therefore captivating. The authority she wielded just added to her allure. They lined up for a chance to conquer her, both to have her and to own the bragging rights. She listened to their advances with a small smile, while they emptied their purses trying to impress her, and she privately laughed all the way to the Garden's underground vault.

It would all end in blood and fire. That subplot was the first time in my life I had screamed at a book. She was this cool, powerful woman who wanted nothing to do with the swamp that was the political underbelly of Kair Toren, and the narrative had crushed her in the worst, most painful way possible. Galiene was one of the reasons I needed the third book to come out. I wanted my vengeance, damn it.

Galiene studied me for a long moment.

"You don't have anywhere to go, do you?" She had a rich, resonant voice.

There was no point in lying. "No."

"You can stay within the Garden tonight. One night only. No charge."

What?

"There is always a charge." I should have phrased that better.

"Not this time. It's not for your sake. I don't know you."

"Then why?"

"You thanked the servant."

Damn it. Servants weren't usually thanked, especially not in places like the Garden. It must've seemed so odd to Klemena she had reported it. The twenty-first-century social norms had tripped me up. I always thanked my waiter. If I had my hair done, my nails, or my eyebrows, I thanked whichever professional had done it. It was an automatic, ingrained response. I did it without thinking. I couldn't do anything without thinking from now on because it would get me killed again.

But thanking Klemena didn't seem significant enough to prompt this sudden charity. Where was Galiene going with this?

"I don't understand," I said.

Galiene sighed. "Years ago, I also came to the Garden late at night, without shoes and with only a handful of coins to my name. I, too, asked for a bath and a meal. And I thanked the servant who brought my dinner to me and helped me wash my hair."

Oh. I knew some highlights of her backstory, but not this part. Her parents had run a prosperous inn in another city. The family was well-off and respected, and Galiene had grown up in pretty dresses and dainty shoes, learning how to keep the books and manage a thriving inn. The future looked bright until her father had witnessed something he shouldn't have, and the entire family was slaughtered to keep them silent. Only fifteen-year-old Galiene survived. She bought a tattered cloak from a beggar and walked all the way to the capital with what little money she'd managed to grab, sleeping in the woods and eating whatever she could buy or scrounge. It took her almost three weeks. I had no idea she'd ended up at the Garden barefoot. Her pretty shoes must've fallen apart.

Galiene fixed me with her cold stare. "That night changed my life. Today the Divine tapped me on the shoulder to remind me of the kindness I had been shown."

That's right. Galiene was devout.

The dominant religion in Rellas and on most of the continent revolved around the Divine, a genderless, benevolent supreme being. If you were virtuous and good, the Divine would reward you with another life. If you were a horrible person, your soul would fall into the Void and be torn apart.

Their theological doctrine held that worshiping the Divine directly was impossible, since no human could comprehend the eternity of the Divine in its entirety. Instead, the faithful worshiped Aspects of the Divine, defined by their function: the Artisan, the Warrior, the Scholar, and so on. Galiene worshiped the Host, the Aspect of Hospitality, just like her parents and siblings had, and she was deeply committed to honoring her chosen Aspect. It was her last link to her murdered family.

"I will show you the same kindness," Galiene said. "You may stay here for one night. In the morning, you will have your breakfast and then you will be on your way. The Host will know that I haven't forgotten her blessing, and I'm still grateful. You will do well to remember that my gratitude has limits. Do not abuse my hospitality. Klemena will show you to your room once you dress."

She turned and left the room. Klemena moved out of her way, bowed to me, and followed Galiene out.

I wouldn't have to go out on the streets in the dark. I wouldn't have to deal with human predators. I would sleep in a real bed and leave in the morning, in daylight.

The relief was so overwhelming, I would've collapsed if I wasn't already sitting.

I would survive tonight.

Chapter 4

It took me another fifteen minutes to crawl out of the bath.

I had tensed up when Galiene entered the room, and once she left and the tension drained out, fatigue mugged me. I was so tired. Getting out of the bath became a matter of life or death because if I stayed in any longer, I would've fallen asleep and probably drowned. I would likely come back to life, but I didn't want to tempt fate.

Despite my earlier pledge to empty chamber pots, Kair Toren enjoyed advanced indoor plumbing, complete with ceramic toilets, sinks, terra-cotta pipes, and classic labyrinth-like sewers under the city. I discovered a toilet with a wooden seat behind the small door. And toilet paper. I had never been so grateful to find a little basket of toilet paper sheets folded like napkins in my whole life.

Butt napkins. The essence of luxury.

I remembered reading a giant discussion about toilet paper on the fan boards. For some reason, certain people had been very attached to the idea of chamber pots and corncobs. They claimed that anything more advanced would be unrealistic. Personally, it never bothered me. In our world, the Han had used toilet paper since the sixth century, and China mass-produced it by the 1300s. Rellas had advanced architecture, metallurgy, and magic, and it manufactured massive amounts of paper to power its bureaucracy. Toilet paper seemed like a surmountable challenge.

I got out of the bathroom, washed my hands at a sink in a small alcove, and looked through the stack of clothes Klemena had left. When a thin pair of panties slipped through my fingers, I almost cried in happiness.

In Rellas, like in many feudal societies, forms of address communicated how dangerous you were. *Lord* and *lady* meant landed nobility, many trained and well-armed fighters, and a solid chance of getting killed if things went badly. *Sir* and *dame* meant a knight, a highly skilled, professional soldier, also a high probability of injury and death. *Terr* and *tress*, on the other hand, were reserved for ordinary people, merchants, tradesmen, artisans, anyone without formal military rank or a noble title.

The clothes Klemena had brought me placed me firmly into the tress category. The outfit started with a dark green chemise, a thin, loosely fitted underdress.

The sleeves looked like something that had popped right out of a medieval movie: trumpet shaped, with a drawstring casing running along the forearms. Pulling the string shortened the sleeves to above the elbow, leaving the arms bare, which was probably handy for cooking and cleaning. I left the sleeves down.

Over the chemise, I wore a simple sage-green gown, which I had promptly put on backward on my first try. The dress had a deeper neckline, so about an inch of the chemise showed above it. Its bodice laced on the sides to adjust fit, and its loose ungathered skirt came down to my ankles. The fabric felt like a sturdy version of linen.

The dress came with a built-in bra, which seemed to have an underwire of some sort. Its short sleeves ended right about where a T-shirt sleeve would hit. The left sleeve had a small inner pocket on the inside of the arm, just big enough to hide a few coins. I slid Everard's den into it.

The simple cloth shoes with thin soles were a little loose on my feet, but I would make do. A gray cloak completed the outfit. It featured a deep hood and a large inside pocket with a grommet in it to which you could chain your purse. I hid the rest of my money there.

I had asked for an outfit that wouldn't make me stand out, and neither the clothes nor the shoes looked new. The color of the dress had faded, the hem of the cloak had frayed, and the shoes had grime stains, the kind that form on fabric after frequent use. I didn't care. Shoes were amazing. Clothes were pretty up there, too. And the boost of confidence I got from no longer running around literally butt naked was truly priceless.

I braided my hair into a simple plait—I hadn't seen a single woman with a ponytail or a plain bun—tied it with a bit of string I pulled from the cloak's fraying hem, and looked in the mirror.

Good enough.

"Klemena?"

No answer.

Hmm. I opened the door. The short hallway was empty. My attendant had vanished.

I eyed the door at the other end of the hallway. Behind it lay the main floor of the Garden and all the wonders and dangers it held.

Hiding in the room and waiting for Klemena would be safer, but there was magic beyond that door. I had no idea how long I would be in Rellas. For all I knew, whatever force had brought me here could yank me out of this world and hurl me back into my own bed at any moment. Even if I was stuck in Rellas, once I walked out of the Garden tomorrow I would probably never return. I simply didn't have the money. This was my only chance to take it all in. If I missed it, I would kick myself for the rest of my life.

I walked down the hallway, edged the door open, and slipped out.

In front of me, the main floor gleamed, like a swirl of bright paint with an occasional burst of glitter. The mage who had conjured the butterflies was gone. The dancers were back, wearing golden dresses that would've been skimpy back home and were scandalous here. They danced more slowly this time, framing a man in the middle of the stage like flowers.

The man was shockingly beautiful, tall, lean, dressed in black, his skin the color of deep ochre, his black hair worn in a long braid over his shoulder. He sat in a chair, leaning a strange stringed instrument against himself like a cello player and drawing a bow across the strings, seemingly lost to the music. The melody that spilled out sounded almost like a person singing, beautiful and haunting.

The main floor was about half full. Most of the patrons were men in expensive clothes, although I counted four women in beautiful gowns. Three of them watched the musician, while the fourth flirted with a handsome man at her table. The man wore red and white—one of the Garden's attendants.

Three men emerged from the entrance tunnel. The first, dark haired, tan, and muscular, had to be a bodyguard of some kind. He wore dark pants, mid-calf boots, and a black doublet with silver embroidery. He walked in, scanned the floor as if he were looking for threats, and stepped to the side.

Another man followed, with a second bodyguard close behind. He was about six foot two or six foot three and solid, with broad shoulders and a wide pale face, made wider by a chin strap beard. His light brown hair, probably naturally wavy, fell on the left side of his face in a fringe cut. He wore black as well, but his outfit must've cost about ten times more than his bodyguard's.

His boots were made of some leather-like material I had never seen before, with large scales forming gold and burgundy patterns. It looked like he'd skinned a couple of small fantasy dragons and wrapped their hides over his feet. His black trousers flared above his boots, and a small decorative belt crossed each of his thighs, with large buckles that were probably gold. He wore a red undertunic with golden embroidery and an elaborate black doublet with more gold embroidery. His black belt was wide and studded with gold. A scarlet cloak edged with black dripped from his shoulders but left his chest exposed, presumably so everyone would note the gold chain around his neck.

His clothes were too loud. I'd read that phrase before, but I'd never seen it so clearly illustrated. Nothing he wore was garish or gaudy, quite the opposite. Everything was exquisitely made and tasteful, but every individual part of his outfit, from boots to cloak, was a statement piece with its own voice. Put together, they screamed in unison.

The woman in the fairy queen dress who had waylaid me earlier approached him, giving him a deep bow probably reserved for Big Spenders.

Lord Fancypants ignored her.

She murmured something and waited. A moment passed. Another. He turned toward her, giving me a view of his back and his family crest embroidered on his cloak—a golden shield edged by a black chain with the black head of a monster in the center. The head was depicted in profile: a huge reptilian mouth gaping to display a forest of sharp teeth, a long thick neck, and needle spikes protruding from the back of the neck. Bright red blood dripped from the monster's mouth . . .

A kroast.

Ice drenched me.

A black kroast on a field of gold and scarlet. *Ulmar Hreban.*

I gripped the wooden rail so tight, my fingers hurt.

Before the end of the year, this man would claw his way to unchecked power. He would set Kair Toren on fire. The capital would burn for three days, while the soldiers under his command rampaged through the streets, maiming, raping, and killing as they wanted with nobody to stop them. People would call it the Night of a Thousand Fires. After he was done with the capital, Hreban would lead the King's Army to suppress a rebellion and settle personal scores. He would demolish villages and murder thousands with inhuman cruelty.

But before he did all that, he would kill Galiene of Sosna.

Very few people knew that Galiene had a daughter. She had given birth to her quietly five years ago. Her father wasn't in the picture. Galiene chose to raise her child away from the Garden.

Hreban wanted Galiene. Not because he loved her, he wasn't capable of that, but because other men wanted her and couldn't have her. He had more money than anyone else in the kingdom except for the royal family, and he liked the symmetry of the richest man and the most desirable woman. I was in the first chapter, which meant he hadn't approached Galiene yet, but I knew what happened in the books. When Galiene refused to become a trophy, he bribed her daughter's caretakers and stole the child.

Galiene became his slave. She did everything he asked, while he tortured her with glimpses of her daughter. If she was good, she would get half an hour. If she failed to please him, he would punish the child instead of her. He broke that woman so completely, Hade, who had raised her since Galiene was fifteen, didn't recognize her when she saw her on the street.

This went on for almost eight months. Even Hade, with all of her connections, could do nothing about it. The Hreban Family was one of the Eight Great Families. He had too much influence, too much money, and too many hired soldiers, while in the eyes of Kair Toren, Galiene was a commoner who worked in the sex trade. They wouldn't call her a "sex worker." They called her a whore.

And when Hreban finally got the status he wanted, he decided that Galiene was beneath his new station in life. His bodyguards killed her daughter, stabbed

Galiene, and set the house on fire. She died choking on smoke and cradling her child's corpse.

Hreban turned away from the attendant, his expression flat, his mouth downturned in an adult man–pout. Something had displeased him. The woman in the fairy dress hovered nearby, waiting for something.

I scrutinized his face. A slab of a jawline, wide mouth, hooded dark eyes. He was forty-two years old and looked his age.

I graduated with a degree in political science, and before I switched to that major, I studied criminal justice. Both of my majors taught me that monsters in human skin didn't look like monsters. They looked bland and ordinary. I knew this, but some part of me, raised on Disney and anime villains, expected to see the inner brutality of Ulmar Hreban's soul reflected in his face. I subconsciously wanted him to look like a villain, because evil that violent and cold should have to come with some sort of warning label.

But no. Despite his finery, Hreban himself looked perfectly unremarkable, even mildly attractive in that particular way that resulted from a lifetime of wealth, good food, and expert grooming. If you put him in a suit and trimmed his hair, he would pass for an aging tech bro about to give a TED talk on the power of AI and the miracles of angel investing. By the end of the second book, he had spilled so much blood, it could fill a lake, but if I had run into him in a grocery store, I wouldn't have given him a second glance.

"A gilded toad," a male voice said next to me.

I almost jumped.

A man leaned on the column on the other side of the rail, barely a foot away. His pale gray cloak hid him from top to bottom, but he had left his hood down. Tall, around thirty, light skin with a hint of a tan, longish brown hair, defined jaw, strong eyebrows, a regal nose . . .

Handsome. Like should-be-on-a-poster-somewhere handsome. His tired old cloak and his face seemed mismatched. Like bumping into a stranger on a crowded street and catching a glimpse of an elven prince under the hood of a worn-out sweatshirt. His eyes were striking, a rich golden hazel. I had no idea who he was, but he had just called Hreban a toad in public and didn't seem concerned about it.

The man leaned forward slightly, shortening the distance between us. Suddenly I was uneasy. The ornate wooden rail barely came up to my waist. It didn't feel like enough of a barrier.

"Do you think the toad knows he is a toad?" he asked.

He was referencing a folktale from the second book. The story said that three centuries ago Mad King Eble lost his mind and thought that a toad he found in the garden was talking to him and giving him sage advice. He'd commissioned golden vestments for the toad and forced his counselors to give their reports to it. One of the counselors was renowned for his honesty, and when the king asked him directly if the toad would want even grander clothes, the minister replied, "Your Majesty, no matter how you gild it, a toad knows it's just a toad." The king crushed the toad with his fist and then chopped the minister's head off.

The man was looking at me. I had to say something.

Don't say the wrong thing, don't say the wrong thing . . .

I kept my voice quiet. "It isn't wise to disparage the head of a Great Family."

"For you, perhaps."

He wasn't afraid of Hreban. Who the hell was he? Brown hair, hazel eyes, beautiful face . . . Beauty was subjective. No crest, no scars, no unique facial features. Without something specific, I could think of a dozen characters that would loosely fit the bill.

"If you recall, that story didn't end well for the counselor," I said.

"Ah, but I wouldn't be the counselor."

"Who would you be?"

"The king, of course."

"Then let's hope you're less mad than Eble."

His lips curved.

An attendant ran up to the fairy queen hostess. The hostess bowed to Hreban and said something. He nodded, and he and his bodyguard followed her to the side. There would be a staircase there, just out of sight, leading to the second floor.

"There he goes, hopping off. Good riddance." The man looked back at me. "You and I have something in common."

We had nothing in common. "And what would that be?"

"We're both in a place we shouldn't be, pretending to be someone we are not."

What did that mean?

His eyes narrowed. His mouth was still smiling, but the way he looked at me made me want to take off like a rocket.

"Who are you? I mean, who are you really?"

Panic squirmed through me. "Nobody worth noticing."

"Too late for that."

He put one hand on the rail about to hop over it to my side.

"My lord," Galiene called out.

The man let go of the rail.

Galiene approached us, a female attendant behind her. Klemena chose this moment to pop out of some side door on the left and almost ran into Galiene. The queen of the Garden arched an eyebrow, and Klemena bowed her head and fell in step with the other attendant.

The three of them reached us. Galiene looked at the man, her expression flawlessly polite. "You seem to have mistaken one of our guests for an attendant, my lord."

The man smiled back at her, looking unrepentant, like a cat who'd been caught seconds before he was about to steal steak off the counter.

"My apologies." He didn't sound particularly apologetic either.

"Your room is ready, and your companion is eager to meet you."

The man gave me a mock sigh. "Alas, one shouldn't keep such a rare beauty waiting."

"Very considerate of you, my lord." Galiene's tone had just a touch of dryness to it.

He glanced at me. "We'll meet again."

"I doubt it." Why did I just say that? Talk about tempting fate.

"This way, my lady," Klemena said.

They parted us like tugboats pulling two ships in the night. Klemena led me to the right, while Galiene walked him to the left. I followed my guide up a different staircase to the third floor.

Asking about the identity of the man in the cloak was pointless. They would never tell me. Whoever he was, he could pay premium rates. The rare beauties of the Garden didn't come cheap.

Klemena led me to a door and pushed it open. A small bedroom greeted me, lit by two lanterns. Their light fell on a large bed with a blue blanket and plush blue pillows. There was a brown and white rug on the floor, another door that probably led to the bathroom, and a window on the right, but all I saw was the bed. I was suddenly so tired.

"Sleep well, my lady."

Klemena bowed, exited the room, and shut the door. I heard a bolt slide into place. She had locked me in.

The door had a sturdy bar on my side. I lowered it, dropped my cloak, untied the strings cinching my dress, pulled it over my head, kicked off my shoes, fell onto the bed, and passed out.

Planter 7

A knock echoed through the room. "My lady?"

I opened my eyes. Morning light filtered through the window on my left. We were on the third floor, and the window had no bars. I could see a chunk of a beautiful morning sky and ghosts of three moons slowly fading into it.

I was still in Rellas. I had half expected that a night of decent sleep would send me home. After all, that was how I got here, going to sleep in my own bed. But no luck.

"My lady?"

They wouldn't let me sleep in. Right. Galiene had fulfilled her hospitality obligations, and now it was time to prod me on.

"Yes?"

"Your breakfast is served. I will take you to it when you are ready."

Wood slid, followed by the quiet creaking of the old floorboards. Klemena must've unbarred the door and walked away. The footsteps retreated but not far. She was waiting for me to get up. *You don't have to go home, but you can't stay here.*

I sat up. The soreness was still there, but it was muted now. Amazing what food, drink, and a full night of sleep could do. I got up and dragged myself to the bathroom. It was the same setup as downstairs: a toilet with a wooden seat and a small sink.

No toothbrush. Bummer. No faucet either, but there was a ewer of water and soap. I made do.

Klemena took me down to the second-floor balcony. I sat at a solid wooden table right by the balcony rail. Below, the Garden's attendants cleaned the first floor, wiping the tables, heaving chairs up onto them, and then sweeping the tile.

Across from me, on the other side of the second-floor balcony, Galiene and an older woman who had to be Hade sat at a table, sipping tea from green cups as they did every morning. Two sides of the same coin, separated by four decades. Both in elegant, formal gowns, Galiene in Prussian blue and Hade in dark royal purple. Both wearing the same hairstyle, that elaborate braided spiral, except that Galiene's hair was dark blond while Hade's mass of curls was completely silver. Both poised and maintaining the same expression, calm, pleasant, but stern. The only difference was age. Galiene's pale face was unlined, while Hade's dark brown skin showed the wear and tear of surviving to her seventies.

The two of them ignored me.

Klemena brought a tray with a teapot, a little dish of honey, a solitary cup, and two plates, one with two square pastries and the other with two eggs, sunny-side up. She placed the plates in front of me, and deposited a perfectly normal fork, a knife, and a cloth napkin on the table. If I squinted at it just right, I could pretend I was back home at the Egg and Fork, a little breakfast place where I sometimes treated myself. So surreal.

The tea was strong and black and tasted a little like chocolate with a hint of fruit and some new-to-me spice, a sweeter, more potent cousin of cinnamon. I put a little honey in it, reached for the pastry, broke a small piece off, and looked at the filling. Some sort of smoked fish. I popped the piece into my mouth. Delicious.

I drank my tea, ate my pastry, and tried to sort things through.

Although the books never mentioned transdimensional portals, there were two places I could check about the possibility of such travel: the Temples of the Aspects and the Mage Tower. Both dealt in magic.

The Temples had to be approached with caution. If I barged into the Red Basilica and started spouting things about other worlds, they might declare me mentally unhinged, they could brand me as a heretic, or they would believe me, which could be the worst of the three outcomes. The clerics of Rellas were savvy political animals; the advantages of having sole access to someone from another world wouldn't be lost on them. They wouldn't help me get home. They would confine me and exploit my existence to increase their influence.

Contacting the Mage Tower would be even more dangerous. Archmage Damaes Serras, the master of the Mage Tower, was the magical equivalent of a nuclear warhead. Damaes was not the best-adjusted person and that was putting it mildly. In the second book, he turned a knight into a pillar of fire—the man deserved it—and then roasted bacon on a little stick while the guy burned to death. He didn't eat the bacon. He just wanted to make a point.

The Archmage had to be avoided at all costs. If he figured out that I couldn't die, he might spend the next couple of decades murdering me in creative ways to see how far he could push my resurrection powers. I had no desire to become an eternal fireball to satisfy Damaes's intellectual curiosity.

Looking for a way home would have to wait. I needed to figure out a safe place to stay first.

Before I left the room, I'd dumped Lecke's bag on the rug and counted my ill-gotten gains. The bag felt heavy, but most of the coins inside were dens. I had nine nomas in silver and another five in change, roughly five to six thousand dollars in terms of purchasing power. I could rent a modest room for a couple of months, buy some clothes, and feed myself, if I didn't make any extravagant purchases. After that, I would have to earn more money.

I finished my tea and refilled my cup.

Robbing some scumbag every couple of months wasn't an option. My inability to die was magical, but not the kind of skill that could result in meaningful employment. I hadn't woken up in the body of a trained blademaster or a skilled mage, so I couldn't take advantage of muscle memory and honed reflexes. I didn't mind that part. Taking over someone's body meant that person stopped existing. I hadn't stolen anyone's life. I wouldn't have to pretend to be someone else and lie to their family and loved ones. Whatever happened now would be my life alone.

I didn't have any professional abilities valued by Rellas. Nobody would be impressed by my expertise in Google Docs integration or my mad driving skills. I was bad at sewing, slightly better at knitting, useless at weaving or embroidery, and too old to be accepted as an apprentice into any guilds or shops. I could make a mean fajita, but that was neither here nor there.

On the other hand, I could probably do more math, despite being appallingly bad at it by modern standards, than most of the educated people here. Fractions, a new superpower. If I busted out basic algebraic equations, I'd blow their minds.

No magic, no fighting, and no trade skills. But what I did have was knowledge. I knew things about this world and about its people, intimate things, secrets that could topple noble houses and upend politics. I could present myself to one of the power players in the city and dazzle them with my secret expertise.

The political landscape of Rellas was dominated by the Eight Great Families. They were wealthy landholders, each with their own personal army and unique brand of magic.

In Rellas, magic was a force shaped by two principles: knowledge and practice. Some people were born with a talent for it, and you either had it or you didn't, the way some people in our world could smell ants and others couldn't. That type of magic wasn't hereditary, and it was rare. Anybody with a predisposition for it could become a gifted cleric or a mage, and if they studied and practiced, they could grow stronger and more powerful. The Temples and the Mage Tower constantly competed for talented recruits.

The magic of the Great Families was something else entirely. You couldn't have it unless you were born into the bloodline. It was hereditary and limited in scope, but devastatingly powerful. When the Eight Families went to war, the world burned.

The Great Families had been playing musical chairs with the throne of Rellas for the last eight hundred years, and how long each dynasty lasted depended on how good they were at pitting the other seven families against each other. The latest royals, the Savarics, had raised political scheming to an art form, but they'd been growing less and less stable with each generation. Sauven Savaric, the current king, had been teetering on the edge of a full psychotic break for a decade, and the tensions among the Great Families were at an all-time high.

Because of this, my knowledge would be in high demand. But becoming a retainer would mean trusting my safety to a lord or lady, and I wouldn't trust any one of these shitheads to pass me the salt at lunch. The crap they did to each other made your hair stand on end. I met Everard last night in passing for two seconds, and as cool as it was, he'd scared the hell out of me. And he wasn't even actively evil, like Hreban, who would drown the country in agony.

I glanced across the balcony. Galiene and Hade were chatting quietly. Galiene smiled at something. She had probably kept me from dying again last night.

No, being an independent information broker was the way to go. I would need to keep a low profile and be very careful. This world responded to me. I tried to take Lecke's bag, and he'd stabbed me. My actions had consequences.

Once I started messing with things, Rellas would react to the changes I made. If I wasn't careful, my information would become obsolete fast. I needed to be very selective about what secrets I sold, and as soon as I was able, I would need to hire people who would feed me new facts to compensate for the alterations to the storyline. Every change I made, even a minute one, endangered me. Especially a change involving the main players. Like Hreban.

Galiene smiled again.

In my head, I could see her in jeans and a sweatshirt, sitting at the next table at the Egg and Fork across from a little girl with the same blond hair. She would drink coffee from a big white mug, while her daughter, in a cute dress, nibbled on a pastry.

The safest, wisest thing to do was to sit on my information and make only the smallest alterations for my own benefit.

My plate was empty. It was time to go.

Several months from now that little girl and her mother would suffer and then die a senseless, horrible death. Because a self-indulgent sociopathic narcissist with delusions of grandeur felt like it.

Galiene had saved me from the streets. She didn't expect anything in return. It had been a random act of kindness.

Fuck it.

I got up and turned left, walking along the balcony toward Hade and Galiene. Klemena followed me, hovering within reach. I stopped before their table. The two women looked at me.

The balcony was deserted, but for all I knew, there could've been people listening to us in the hallway or in the nearest rooms. I really wished I could've had this conversation in private, but the chances of getting Galiene alone were less than zero. In her place, I wouldn't trust me enough for that.

I turned and looked at Klemena, then back at Galiene.

The queen of the Garden nodded, and Klemena backed away a few feet.

"What is it?" Galiene asked.

"You were kind to me," I said.

"Don't tell anyone, and we will be even," she said.

Hade gave her a razor-sharp smile.

I stepped closer and lowered my voice. "Men like Ulmar Hreban don't see other people as human beings. He doesn't want you. He cares only about what you represent—the means to prove to other men that he is superior. He will stop at nothing to obtain that."

Galiene drank her tea. "Thank you for the warning." Her expression told me that my warnings were not needed.

"Elaut sold you out. You will find the money hidden in his pillow."

Her eyes went wide.

"When you reject Hreban, he will take Adelai and use her to torment you. You will do everything he asks, and at the end, he will kill you both. When his knights run her through, you will think of your brother and the blood on his white tunic, the one your mother embroidered. You will not resist as they cut you down. You will die in a fire, bleeding and hugging your daughter's lifeless body. You must bring her into the Garden. Hreban cares about public opinion and won't risk attacking it directly. Don't wait. Go right now. This is the only help I can offer you."

I turned and walked away, down the stairs, across the main floor, through the tunnel, and out the door into the sunshine. Nobody followed me.

Chapter 5

The bells of the Red Basilica rang a melodious din. The higher-pitched, smaller bells struck a quick rhythm, punctuated by the deeper clang of the larger bells, and finally a single deep chime of the great bell rolled through the city and lingered, reverberating in the air. Noon.

I paused and leaned against a wall of the building to rest my tired feet. Past me, the current of the passersby flowed through Bluestone Square.

Kair Toren was a riot of people, sounds, and color. Most buildings in this part of town had simple lines, sturdy towers, and thick walls, built with a beautiful calico stone, a sandy beige with swirls of cinnamon and white curving through it. And there was a surprising amount of glass. Across the square, the sun glinted on the upper floors' windows and a beautiful glass sign in red and teal marked an alchemy shop.

Countless people moved against that backdrop, traders, shoppers, city guards, knights . . . I saw actual knights in armor. I had expected it to be clunky and rigid, but it was sleek and fitted, and they moved in it as if they were wearing sweatpants. People carried swords and maces on their belts, and their long cloaks flared as they walked. Women who weren't in armor wore dresses and gowns in every color, actual gowns, and their hair was braided and styled with hair jewelry. Men out of armor preferred jerkins and tunics, although I saw a couple in robes.

As I watched, a woman in a pretty cloak, accompanied by four guards, passed me, walking some relative of a Tasmanian tiger on a chain leash. A craftsman with two teenage apprentices followed, lecturing them on the right way to pickle cabbage, and behind them an old man carried a wooden frame on his shoulders with brilliantly colored birds perching on each side.

Across the street, a woman in a wheelchair rolled in the opposite direction, surrounded by a gaggle of young girls. One of them held the door of the alchemy shop open, the second pushed her chair, and the other two scurried into the store, as the woman's raised voice carried over in the familiar cadence of a teacher giving a lecture, "Remember the rule. Everything is poisonous, everything is hot. Touch nothing and do not put your hands in your mouth . . ."

I'd read about it over and over, I'd imagined it, and here it was, right there. Right in front of me. All this wonderful magical weirdness. I wanted to just wander about like a toddler at an amusement park, going, "Ooo, look at this." But there was no time.

I had hightailed it out of the Garden like my butt was on fire. For the first fifteen minutes I just walked, paranoid that they would chase after me. By the time I reached the Bull Gate again, I'd decided I was in the clear and concentrated on the most important thing—putting a roof over my head.

I went to the Inn Quarter. It took me an hour and a half of determined walking to get there. I tried the White Stag, the Squire's Rest, and the imaginatively named Softer Beds, the three cheapest inns in the quarter. All three required the Rellasian equivalent of a "credit card for incidentals," meaning they wanted proof of identity.

I offered to prepay. I offered to pay double. That just made them more suspicious. They booted me out the door, and the Softer Beds clerk went a step further, called me a lowlife, and told me to never come back. Apparently, only their beds were softer, not their service. Asshat.

I had to find a private room to rent. The books didn't deal with real estate in detail. There were references to characters purchasing properties or finding lodging, but none of it was specific enough.

I returned to the signboard in Bluestone Square. I vaguely remembered seeing something about rent, when I was stumbling about in the rain, looking for a date on the official announcements pinned to it. I was right. The front of the sideboard was for official use. The back served as the medieval equivalent of Craigslist, announcing everything from lost dogs to rooms for rent.

I'd gotten to that signboard around ten AM. It was two hours later, and I had seen five rentals so far. Three wouldn't rent to a woman unattached to a guild or a workshop, one was a straight-up hovel with one communal bathroom for seven people, and the landlord of the last one gave me the creeps.

I had about seven or eight hours of daylight left, and I was down to my last available rental. If this one didn't work out, I would have to move on, and I had no clue where another signboard might be. Maybe this one would work out. I would get to it as soon as my feet stopped hurting.

A whiff of freshly baked bread floated past me. My mouth watered. I turned.

A peddler was coming up the street toward me. He carried a tray with a strap around his neck, and it was full of pastries. Fresh, flaky, golden pastries, with crispy crust. Oh my god.

How was I so hungry? I had breakfast six hours ago . . . Oh.

The vendor zeroed in on me like a wolf spotting a lame rabbit. "Mushroom handpies, tress?"

Yes, all the handpies. All of them. "How much?"

"A quarter."

I reached into my cloak, dug two quarters out of my bag of money by feel, and dropped them into his palm. He plucked a little envelope folded from some sort of leaf from the stack on his tray, slid two handpies into it, and handed it to me.

"Thank you, terr. Do you know where Prodoe Street is?"

The peddler pointed over his shoulder. "That way, on the other side of the Kar Crescent. I'd go around if I were you, though."

"Why?"

He shook his head and walked away.

Mysterious. Why would I need to go around?

I bit into a pie. The crispy, buttery pastry practically melted on my tongue.

Mmmm. How could mushrooms and bread be so tasty?

I wolfed down half of the pie. My stomach gave it a standing ovation. It was time to get going.

I started walking. The square ended, flowing into a street, and the city blocks crawled by. Every place I had seen so far was within fifteen minutes of the square, so that signboard only advertised nearby rentals. There had to be other signboards out there. Kair Toren had several markets. Maybe I would go to one of those next.

The street curved slightly to the left, widening. Ah, so that's why they called it a crescent. I followed it, rounding the bend.

Yes, I hadn't found a place to rent yet. But the sun was shining, and I had a delicious handpie. Life wasn't so bad . . .

The bite of the handpie turned to cement in my mouth.

A man sat in the street in a puddle of half-dried blood. He was young, maybe eighteen, and so thin he looked like a little kid, slumping against the building, thrown there carelessly, like trash. Gore caked his face. Thin streaks stretched from his pale blue eyes where his tears had made a path through the blood. His lips were swollen and split. His arms ended in bloody stumps, partially charred with black. Someone had hung a signboard around his neck and tied his severed hands to it. Two city guardsmen in teal and black tabards with the white towers on them stood by the body talking in low voices, their expressions flat, their eyes haunted.

The signboard said *I STOLE FROM BARON HREBAN*.

It felt like I had sprinted face-first into a brick wall.

The contemplation. Ulmar Hreban's special brand of atrocity.

Nausea squirmed through me. I'd read about it over and over in the two books, but never in my life did I think I would actually see it. Common sense told me I needed to walk away, but my feet must've sprouted roots, because I couldn't move.

The thief must've broken into Hreban's mansion. Hreban's guards had caught him, beat him, cut off his hands, partially cauterized his wounds, and thrown him on the street.

He looked so desperate now, his eyes dead but still full of pain. When they dumped him here, he would've known that he was about to die and nobody would save him, so he just sat and stared at the sky, bleeding out and waiting for the end. His life must've been hard and brutal for him to risk breaking into Hreban's mansion, and then it ended in agony on this street.

A city of three hundred thousand people, and nobody lifted a finger to help him. How was that even possible? How could anyone ignore this? Did all of them go blind? Why weren't the guards moving the body? They were just standing there.

The younger guard on the left raised his head and looked at me. Our stares connected. His eyes were filled with shame and fear. He looked away.

It hit me like a hammer. Hreban had paid the city guards to watch the body. They were standing there to make sure nobody removed it. He had a pet phrase for it, *sunup to sundown*. He could've ordered his private guards to secure the corpse, but he paid off the City Guard instead. He wanted everyone to see his special punishment and know that nobody could stop him, and moreover, that the city condoned it. A preview of what awaited Rellas when he rose to power, and I was the only one who understood.

There was nothing I could do for the dead man. It was too late. And even if it hadn't been, even if he was still alive and dying, what could I have done? Hreban had everything, the name, the magic, the wealth, the private soldiers, and I couldn't even rent a room at an inn.

If Hreban ever found out that I had helped Galiene, he would do this to me, and nobody would do anything about it either. The thief probably had people who knew him. Family, friends. I had no one.

I felt so helpless. So angry and scared and helpless.

The young guard raised his gloved hand and motioned to me. *Move on.*

This was so wrong.

The guard took a step forward and jerked his hand toward an alley branching off the street. *Go!*

I forced myself to turn and fled into the alley, walking as fast as my feet would carry me.

I walked into the Three Moons just as the East Tower bells struck, announcing five PM. Historically, medieval taverns were supposed to be filthy places, noisy and dark, with floors covered in layers of rushes or straw and soaked in a lovely mixture of mud, vomit, rotten food, and horse manure brought in on boots.

The Three Moons was the opposite of that. Large windows let in plenty of light, the wooden floor had been scrubbed clean, the tables had actual chairs instead of a wooden plank propped up on a couple of barrels, and the clientele skewed, if not affluent, then at least comfortable. The patrons had good clothes, groomed hair and beards, clean faces, and decent shoes. The sign outside, a carved wooden board with a stylized depiction of the planet's three moons, had three circles of colored glass hanging from it on thin chains: green, amber, and red, meaning they served green ale, mead, *and* wine.

This early in the evening the place was only a third full. I walked to an empty table about midway between the bar and the door and sat down.

This was a terrible idea.

A young man with light brown skin and jet-black hair delivered two wooden beer tankards to the neighboring table, stopped by mine, and offered me a smile. "What will it be, tress?"

"Favonian red mead," I told him. "Cold, please."

The smile gained a forced quality. "I'm afraid we're all out."

"Then I'll take the Denavi ale. But I want to try it before I order."

"Yes, tress."

He turned and walked away, making sure to look casual. I watched him make his way to the bartender, a large man in his mid-thirties with blond hair and a deep tan. The bartender glanced at me. I smiled at him. A hurried discussion occurred in hushed voices, and then my waiter slipped through the door to the right of the bar into the back rooms.

They had a dilemma on their hands. I had given them the passphrase, but neither of them recognized me. They would have to run it up their chain of command.

Seeing that dead man had shaken me to the core. By the time I had gotten to the next rental, I was ready to take it no matter what. Anything to find a hole to hide in.

The room belonged to a young family of bakers who had clearly fallen on hard times. The man's name was Ert, the woman's name was Hille. They had two kids, a boy and a girl, in clean, worn clothes, about seven and five years old. Ert and Hille baked handpies and bread in their small kitchen, and then Ert would go out to sell them on the street.

Their house was narrow and shoddy. The communal bathroom on the first floor stank like the sewers, and I'd nearly gagged from the reek when they showed it to me. There wasn't anything to be done about the stench.

The room they wanted to lease was all the way on the third floor, up a rickety old staircase that groaned under my feet. It was cramped, old, and grimy with a coffin-size bed that had no mattress, only a quilt over wooden boards. The flimsy door featured wooden bars on both sides.

Ert and Hille were clearly desperate. They didn't care about my lack of papers, but they wanted a week's rent in advance and informed me that they would lock me in at night. As the man of the house had put it, *It's not that we think you'll murder us while we sleep. It's just safer that way.*

I paid them seven dens for one week. The room wasn't worth half of that, but I didn't have the heart or the will to argue. As soon as the money exchanged hands, the bakers left me to "settle in." I took my shoes off my hurting feet, lay down on my new, awful bed, wrapped in a threadbare blanket and instant buyer's regret, and thought about my options.

Saving Galiene and her daughter was an impulsive decision. It was probably a mistake, but I didn't regret it. The memory of the dead man's battered face haunted me like a ghost, but if I had a chance to do it over, I would save them again. Even if this world turned out to be just a book and she and her daughter were only characters, I didn't want them to suffer and die. That asshole Hreban wouldn't get to kill them. It was in my power to warn her, I did it, and it was done and over with.

But I couldn't afford any more impulsive decisions. Not dying was great, but could I come back if my killer dismembered my body? Could I regenerate a cut-off head? What if they killed me, weighed my body down, and threw it into the river like that poor corpse whose cloak I took? Would I just keep coming back to life and drowning over and over, unable to swim to the surface?

What if I were buried? If I was buried in loose soil, I could probably dig myself out. I would likely die a few times from suffocation, but eventually I would claw my way to the surface. But what if they buried me in a coffin? How would I get out? Also, Kair Toren cremated their dead. What if I was cremated?

What if my body was fed to pigs? I had watched a movie where the villain went into great detail about feeding corpses to pigs and not trusting a man who kept more than three pigs. Or was it four? Would I resurrect as sentient pig crap?

I didn't know, and I did not want to find out. If someone like Hreban got ahold of me and discovered that I was unkillable, he would torture me. That old clichéd saying about a fate worse than death was true in my case.

I wanted to vanish into a secure burrow, like a mouse, and get my bearings, and this tiny room failed to deliver that safety. The door was so old and warped, even I could kick my way through it. My biggest security measure wasn't that door, it was that damn staircase. It would probably collapse if someone in armor tried to climb it.

Being locked in every night wasn't amazing either. If the house caught fire, I'd be trapped.

The only way to truly get some security would be to buy or lease my own house and hire soldiers to guard me at night. Besides, trading in information required discretion and a private base. I had to get my own place, the sooner, the better.

I lay in bed, stared at the ceiling, and finally came up with a plan. It wasn't a good plan. It involved a great deal of risk, and risk was exactly what I was trying to avoid. But if I pulled it off, the payoff would be worth it. I ran through my scheme three times, looking for pitfalls until my brain began to overheat. If I hesitated any longer, I would think myself right out of doing it, so I put my shoes back on and came here to the Three Moons.

Now I had to live through the next twenty minutes and exit in one piece.

The waiter emerged from the back room and walked over to my table. "We have a couple varieties for you to try. Would you like to come with me for samples, tress?"

"Yes."

I got up and followed him through the door into a hallway. He paused to close the door behind me. I turned left, walked to the third door, and waited for him.

The waiter blinked, chased me down, and opened the door for me. A long stone staircase led down to the cellar. The staircase was steep, and more than one person had broken their limbs, and sometimes their neck, after being pushed down those stairs.

"Lead the way," I told him.

He took a lantern off the wall and started down the stairs without hesitation. Apparently murder by stairs wasn't on the agenda today.

We descended the staircase and turned left to a huge, old wooden door. The door opened to a wine cellar. We passed through a dark tunnel formed by beer and wine barrels stacked on their sides almost to the fifteen-foot ceiling, and reached another door, even better reinforced than the last one.

My guide knocked three times, then swung the door open. We went through that doorway and ended up in a well-lit room. A long old table, flanked by two benches, stood in the center, its surface stained and scarred. Today it held a stack of papers at the far end and a map of the city drawn on a four-foot-long, square piece of sturdy parchment. To the left, a small bar, a simple wooden counter with shelves behind it, offered a variety of cups and tankards.

A man looked at me from the table. He was tall and lean, with warm, golden skin the cosmetics companies would call *sand* and tawny light brown hair, cut a bit longish, so it framed his handsome face. He drew the eye in that classically attractive way: a sculpted jaw he kept clean-shaven, strong, angular features with a touch of elegant arrogance, and smart amber eyes. Right now, everything about him was sharp and dangerous, like a well-honed dagger, but when he went about his day job, he was charming, sophisticated, and effortlessly handsome.

In our world he would be in movies and make millions. People would line up to see his films, and they wouldn't be disappointed, because he was an excellent actor.

He must've come directly from a meeting or some formal occasion because his clothes didn't fit his current expression. He wore a high-collared white shirt left open to display a muscular neck and a narrow golden chain around it. A leather vest embroidered with golden thread caught his narrow waist. His dark brown pants were tucked into soft boots. A leather pauldron shielded his left shoulder. His burgundy cloak, designed to fit over his right shoulder, lay on the bar, casually discarded.

He was thirty years old but looked about five years younger. Solentine Dagarra. The head of the Shears and bastard son of Trihorn Border Margrave Izarn Demarr. Ruthless, dangerous, and deeply paranoid. He was one of my favorite characters. So handsome, so smart, so witty, and yet so deeply fucked up.

Solentine met my gaze.

Wow.

The Rise of Kair Toren had more viewpoint characters than you could shake a stick at, but Solentine was definitely near the top when it came to sheer page numbers, because he delivered both drama and shocking violence. Most people had a circuit breaker that tripped and stopped them because some things were simply not done to fellow human beings. In some people, it malfunctioned, but in Solentine it was either permanently broken or didn't get installed in the first place. He was infinitely dangerous, and right now he was looking at me like I was an annoying bug he needed to crush.

It sank in: This wasn't fiction. This was my reality. I was standing in a soundproof room, the servant behind me was likely a trained killer, and I was looking at Solentine Dagarra. In the flesh. I could reach out and boop him on the nose.

Oh god, he would kill me.

Solentine smiled at me. Alarm punched the base of my neck and rolled down my spine in an electric shock. Oh no, that wasn't good. Not at all. Dying at the hands of the Shears would hurt.

Coming here had been a terrible mistake.

Mistake or not, now I had to survive. I needed to establish my credentials and show I wasn't afraid. But I was afraid. Very afraid.

I forced the words out. "The head of the Shears. I'm honored."

"Tell me how you know our password, and I'll decide what to do with you," Solentine said in a cultured baritone. Even his voice was off the charts.

"I don't give away information, I sell it. Right now, I have something you want, so I came here to trade. You're missing one of your men."

There was a barely perceptible shift in the way Solentine held himself. A little less relaxation in the line of his shoulders, a little more rigidity in the spine, a harder edge to his gaze. I had his undivided attention.

"I can make you tell me everything you know," he said. "It won't be difficult."

"True. However, if you do that, the Shears will never again profit from my services. I'd like to establish a mutually beneficial business relationship, so I'm willing to make certain concessions. I'll tell you what happened to Miro, no strings attached. In a week, I'll come back for my payment. If I like the value you put on saving a life, we can make a deal again in the future. If I don't, this will be our first and last transaction."

It was a huge gamble, but Solentine suspected everyone and everything. A week would give him enough time to check out the information I offered him. The delayed payment guaranteed I would stick around, which should make him comfortable enough to let me walk out of here unharmed.

A stupid leg-breaker would torture the information out of me and then kill me. Solentine was a very smart man. He would want to use this week to have me watched and to try to find out everything he could about me. Who sent me? Where did I come from? Did I have a secret agenda? Could I prove to be useful in the future? So many fun questions that would gnaw at his brain.

And if I played my cards right, down the line, he might trust me enough to not only pay me but provide me with a false identity. It would take a lot of work, but it was possible.

He pondered me for a long moment.

My skin felt too tight. I had a powerful urge to scream and run away as fast as I could just to ease the pressure.

Come on. Let the curiosity win.

"Where is he?"

Got him. "He broke into Baron Horost's estate and was caught. They have him in the dungeon, last cell on the right as you enter."

The Shears had started a century ago as a crime syndicate specializing in espionage, sabotage, and rumors. Solentine had taken them over eight years ago and continued the policies of his predecessor, forging the former syndicate into a shadow army of informants, thieves, and assassins. The Shears embedded capable and well-trained people all throughout Rellas. They were the tailors, the chefs, the barbers, the embroidery maids. Some simply gathered information and passed it on. Others ran around the rooftops in black outfits, broke into impregnable fortresses, and stabbed people in the back when the occasion demanded.

The Shears still took lucrative contracts and sold information to the highest bidder just like they did decades ago, but now they were dedicated to Solentine, and their actions stemmed from his agenda. Right now, a large part of that hidden agenda revolved around finding out who was supplying iron to the rebel group picking up steam in the north of the kingdom. Miro, one of Solentine's best black-outfit operatives, followed the trail of breadcrumbs to Horost and got himself nabbed through an epic turn of bad luck.

The day after tomorrow, Solentine, who sat on the crossroads of several currents of information, would attend a dinner at Horost's estate to gauge the Baron's possible involvement in the diverting of the iron ore. During that dinner he would purposefully lose a large sum of money, and a drunk Horost, already flattered by Solentine's presence, would magnanimously give him a tour of the dungeons so he could boast about his general awesomeness. Solentine would see Miro and rescue him a couple of days later.

I wouldn't change the plot in any significant way. The sequence of events would remain the same, except that now Solentine would go to Horost's little rave expecting to find evidence of Miro being held there. If it worked, I would cause a minimal disturbance and net a decent sum of money. Hopefully enough to get me out of the third floor of the bakery.

Solentine leaned forward. His eyes narrowed. "How much do you know?"

Danger, danger. I met his gaze and kept my voice calm. "Any additional information will cost extra."

"Did he break?"

This was a test. Miro wouldn't break, even if he was tortured to death, and Solentine knew it.

"No. He's pretending to be a common thief, and Horost's men are inexperienced. They've beaten him too badly, so they must allow him a couple of days to recuperate before they can torture him again. Do you require a map of the estate?"

"I assume the map will cost me extra?" Solentine asked.

"Yes."

"It won't be necessary." His posture relaxed a fraction. He thought he had my number.

"I will come back here in one week for my payment. Do we have a deal?"

"Yes," Solentine said.

"It's been a pleasure."

I turned. The waiter opened the door for me and then led me all the way to the front room of the tavern. I smiled at him and kept walking, out the door, merging with the foot traffic flowing through the street. I'd walked for almost five minutes when my control finally snapped, and cold sweat drenched my face.

Survived. Somehow. So far so good.

Solentine would have me followed. I didn't bother glancing behind me. I wouldn't spot whoever was tailing me anyway. I walked up the street, made a left, then a right, and came to a large building with a wooden bolt of fabric above the entrance. I swung the heavy door open and went in.

The inside of the shop was spacious. On the left, a counter guarded the front door. Rows of tables on both sides offered bolts of fabric. More fabric hung from wooden racks by the walls. At the wall opposite the entrance, two doors led deeper into the shop.

I lingered by the nearest table, pretending to care about linen.

Two women entered, one after another, the first middle-aged, the second barely fifteen. The older woman wore a dress similar to mine and carried a full shopping basket, while the younger had a nicer outfit, almost a gown. A man followed them, young, with a larger shopping basket on his shoulders.

All three went in different directions and started shopping. One of them was likely Solentine's.

I mulled about a bit more, made my way to the counter, put a den on the wooden surface and slid it to the clerk. "I need to use your other exit."

He nodded and swiped the coin.

I meandered over to the door on the left, opened it, and slipped into a long hallway.

This shop took up the entire block. The exit at the end of this hallway opened to a different street, which branched into two others. The Shears had frequently used this shop as a getaway. The agent tailing me wouldn't follow me through the building into the hallway because that would be too obvious. They would leave the store, go around the block, and then quietly trail after me.

One, two, three . . . five. Long enough for my tail to exit.

I opened the door and stepped back into the main room. Let's see which of the three worked for Solentine.

The younger woman and the man were still in the store. It was the older lady. *Ha!*

I crossed the main floor, went out the front door, made a sharp left into an alley, and took off. Nobody followed me.

One very dangerous meeting down, one to go.

Chapter 6

I walked through the doors of the Taryz Teahouse in one piece.

The teahouses had come to Kair Toren almost three hundred years ago, when Dhonir, a small nation on the southern side of the continent, joined Rellas, becoming the Dhonir Duchy to escape the aggression of a nearby warmongering Crimson Empire. The teahouses were a staple of the city now, and drinking tea had become the dominant way to hydrate. Boiling water was the simplest way to disinfect it, and tea leaves made it taste better.

The Taryz Teahouse occupied a large, coveted plot in Golden Leaf, named so for the beautiful trees that grew along the river and turned bright yellow in the fall. The neighborhood straddled the line between the middle-class district of the Fens to the east and the affluent Anchor Drop estates to the west, just across Virka River. The farther north you went, the more dangerous the streets became, but here the cobblestones were clean, and robberies were rare.

The layout of the Taryz Teahouse echoed the Garden, although it was nowhere near that luxurious. It had the same arrangement of the extra tall main floor and the second-floor balcony running the length of the room, followed by two floors of smaller rooms: quiet, elegant, and very private. Many underhanded deals were hammered out in those rooms and people were occasionally murdered here. With the utmost discretion, of course.

The fourth floor consisted of a small room that opened to a large outdoor terrace. That's where I went, up a very long staircase, following a polite server with a platter supporting a small teapot, a cup, and a little glass dish of honey.

Unlike most of the fandom, I'd never crushed on Solentine. I had spent way too much time in his head and his problem solving would give you nightmares. But I liked him, because I knew what had shaped him and understood why he did what he did. The Bastard of Dagarra knew he was messed up and twisted, and yet his priorities never wavered. It was always about family. He was ruthless and brutal, but to his relatives he was a beloved and loving son, nephew, and cousin.

I admired that loyalty. I grew up as an army brat. We moved so much during my childhood that nothing was permanent. Schools, other kids, sports teams, all of it came and went, "for now" rather than "for always." I never got a chance to form lasting friendships, but my brother was always there for me. No matter what happened, he was a constant the way Solentine was a constant for his family.

I wanted Solentine to survive, despite all the awful shit he had done, but as much as I rooted for him, I had no illusions. Putting myself on the Shears' radar was extremely risky. If Solentine wanted to get rid of me, he could simply snap his fingers, and it would be done. In a week I would have to interact with him again to get my payment. I needed some way to lessen the danger of that encounter. I needed a bodyguard. Someone that even he would have a difficult time killing.

At his core, Solentine was an assassin. An exceptional assassin, true, but he relied a great deal on the element of surprise. I needed a warrior. Someone who could stand up to an assassin. Rellas was a place that valued martial skills. Finding a great swordsman wouldn't be that difficult but convincing them to work with me was a whole other story.

The stairs ended and I followed the server onto a roof terrace.

The Taryz Teahouse had never forgotten its roots, and the echo of its native Dhonir was everywhere—in the ornate stone rail of the terrace with protective symbols carved into the posts; in the metal windchimes shaped like strange animals tinkling gently in the wind; and in the long stretches of beautiful green fabric, draped at an angle over some tables to shield the patrons from the sun. The shading canvas stirred in the wind, as if the teahouse were a ship and these were its emerald sails.

Right now, with the afternoon sky threatening rain again, the terrace was mostly empty, and I saw him right away, a man sitting alone at the table closest to the western rail. He would be drinking Thieves Tea, a strong smoky brew, although he was not a thief.

He wore an old cloak, so faded you could no longer tell its original color. It hid most of his build, but his broad shoulders stretched the fabric, and he leaned in his chair with the kind of effortless, controlled grace particular to very strong men.

He sat under a green sail, half in the shadow and half in the light. The cloak's thick hood was down, and the morning sun warmed his olive skin, while the wind blowing from the river stirred his dark brown hair. His face was striking. His features were powerful and chiseled, a hard jaw, a strong nose, high cheekbones, a firm mouth . . . He was looking away from me across the river, and I couldn't see the color of his eyes, but they should've been gray. The trait ran in his family.

His sword rested on the table. A simple wooden sheath, a downcurved guard, a grip of reddish-brown leather, a blade that was about forty inches long, and most importantly, a small white pebble embedded in the round pommel. Location, outfit, features, sword—everything checked out.

Everything except his age. He'd become a professional soldier at seventeen and served in the King's Army for twenty years, so he was at least thirty-seven. The exact line in the book said, *A harsh life of battles and marches added years to his face. He looked like a man who was a decade older.*

The man in front of me was in his very early thirties at most. He didn't look old enough to have a fifteen-year-old son and he didn't look worn down by life either. He looked tempered by it. Heated to the breaking point by danger, quenched by experience, and hardened like a blade to a sharp, unbreakable edge.

I had about two seconds to decide what to do.

He had the sword. Nobody else would be here, in this teahouse, looking across the river at that house, and carrying that sword. The owner of this weapon wasn't just a soldier, he was a blademaster, knighted at the age of seventeen for exceptional bravery and skill. I didn't know if he was the best swordsman in the kingdom, but he was in the top five. The people capable of separating him from his sword could be counted on the fingers of one hand and none of them would be sitting on this terrace.

Don't screw this up, don't screw this up . . .

I walked over to his table and sat down across from him. He looked at me. His eyes, more green than gray, took my measure from under dark eyebrows. No apprehension, no surprise. Only calm, calculating intelligence and invincible will.

He's real.

He wasn't a character. He felt more real than anything or anyone in Kair Toren so far. I was looking into the eyes of a living, breathing man, who was infinitely dangerous, and I couldn't look away, because that connection, that reality, was magnetic. It was the kind of moment when, after being trapped in a confusing nightmare, you realize that you are dreaming, and you have the power to wake up.

The server placed my teapot and my cup in front of me and departed with a soft smile.

I poured a cup of tea. The waters of the Virka flowed past us, on their way to join the Dokkon, the city's main river, a quarter of a mile to the southeast. Across the river the estates of Anchor Drop hugged the water, some with docks, others without, all wrapped in sturdy walls and sitting on about an acre or so each.

The estate directly across from us abandoned the walls completely. Instead, the entire house was a wall, a large square built with Kair Toren's trademark swirly stone, three floors high and about sixty feet deep, with a courtyard in the center. A single stubby tower rose at the left corner of it. The first floor had no windows. The second and third floors had a few, but all of them were guarded by thick bars or shutters. No points of access. The only obvious door lay on the opposite side of the estate, facing the street.

The place was a fortress. It took safety to the next level, even by Kair Toren's standards.

"If human suffering had color, that house would be churning with black and red," I said.

The man across from me said nothing.

"The estate to its left is owned by a respected physician. The estate to the right belongs to a minor noble family. They think their neighbor is a trader who has done well for himself. A good businessman, a bit reclusive, but pleasant. Nobody knows."

He drank his tea. I sipped my brew. The black tea was aromatic and slightly floral, vanilla, lavender, and a hint of citrus. Any other time, I would have savored it.

He was giving no indication whether any of my words were landing.

"A thriving kingdom must always be at war," I said. "That's how it justifies and trains a professional army. These wars don't have to be large. In fact, it's better if they are not, and it's best if they're fought on foreign soil or at the frontier. The kind of conflict that doesn't affect most of the kingdom and allows the citizens to ignore the fact that every day someone is dying on their behalf, for reasons most of the people involved do not understand or care about."

No reaction.

"Of course, a professional army creates the problem of veterans. Highly skilled at warfare, great at surviving, and not always fit to reenter civilian life after all the blood and horrors they witness. A professional soldier with twenty years of experience is a living weapon that can be used against the state when hired by a rogue noble as a mercenary or incited to violence. The state must then find a way to anchor these veterans. They need an incentive to not become a destructive force."

I poured another cup of tea. He hadn't stabbed me yet. I took it as an encouraging sign.

"When a veteran reaches the eighteenth year of their twenty-year service, they are offered the Last Tour. It is a terrible tour of duty, in a place where the risks are high. If the veteran survives it, they are awarded a parcel of fertile land no less than one gere."

About eight acres. Typically, near a forest with monsters or a border with a hostile nation, where the veterans could act as a buffer. *Praemia militia*, invented by Ancient Rome of our world for its legionnaires, never bested, often imitated, and eventually transformed by our modern government into the GI Bill. Instead of rewarding our veterans with a parcel of land, we sent them to college and hoped they would learn to cope.

"In addition to one gere of land, these veteran soldiers are also given the Green Purse, enough money to hire farmhands, obtain seed, purchase two oxen or a single horse, and work the farm for one year. They can become farmers, or sublet the land, or they can cash out. It's a tempting proposition for a soldier with a family. The promise of a peaceful life."

He refilled his cup. His face looked like it was carved from stone.

"So, a soldier takes that Last Tour. He survives against all odds and receives all that was promised. He returns to the city with his limbs and mind intact and discovers that the wife he left behind was murdered and his son has gone missing."

Nothing. Not a hint of emotion. I was on very thin ice, and I could hear it cracking.

"He searches for his son and finds out that he was taken and sold by a slavemonger who lives in an impenetrable fortress. He keeps looking for a way in but can't find any, so every day he comes to the rooftop terrace of the local teahouse. He drinks the same tea he learned to enjoy during his first campaign, he watches, and he waits for fate to knock on his door."

"And you would be fate?" he asked.

His voice matched him, confident, powerful, controlled. His eyes turned cold. Yep, he would kill me. I wasn't getting off this terrace.

"No. I'm just a woman who made a deal with dangerous people. I get my payment in one week, and I need a bodyguard."

If I got him on my side, no fighter in the kingdom, aside from the members of the Great Families, could touch me.

Don't babble. Babbling makes you appear nervous. Stay calm. Like an icicle. Think icy thoughts.

"Normally I would offer money."

I couldn't afford him. Even if I threw all the money I had at him, it wouldn't be enough.

"But you don't want money. You want Derog Olgren."

He stared at me. "What kind of deal did you make? What is your profession?"

Lying of any sort would get me murdered. I could feel it emanating from him.

"I sell information. I know things. Surprising things, secret things, things I shouldn't be aware of. Things people think are private and hidden."

He tilted his head to the side. "Impress me."

"You were in Gassargand, trying to take the city. You and three others scaled the First Wall and were running across an old aqueduct when the ground gave way. You fell into an underground chamber. It was old, older than the city. The only light came from the hole your bodies made as you tumbled down. There were tunnels leading from the chamber into the darkness."

I was all out of tea, and my mouth was as dry as the Gassargand desert.

"A creature came out of the tunnels. It walked upright like a man, and it wore armor and carried a battle hammer, but it was covered with gray fur, eight feet tall, and its head was the head of a monster. It smashed Mertio's skull with a single blow, and you saw his head crack like a broken egg. The three of you fought it until the mortar bombardment resumed, and the sounds of explosions drove it back into the darkness."

"We used to tell that story at every campfire for years afterward," he said.

"I'm not finished. Of the four of you, Mertio was the youngest. He was barely into his second year, but he was good with a spear and brave. He reminded you of your younger brother, and you used to look out for him. You ended that day on the Second Wall, and when everyone went down for the night, exhausted and nursing their wounds, you snuck back to the aqueduct to get Mertio's crest off his body so his family would have something to bury. You tied a rope around an old stone pillar and dropped into that hole without a torch, carrying only your sword. Mertio's body was gone, so you walked the tunnels in darkness until you found the creature and its siblings eating Mertio's corpse, and you killed the three of them in a room with a statue of a bronze god with a bloated stomach."

He stared at me. As far as I knew, he'd never told anyone about that last bit.

"Is it magic?"

"Not exactly."

"Then what is it?"

"One day, if we become friends, I might explain."

And I had no idea how I would do that. *Hi, in my world, you are a character in a book* wouldn't exactly fly. He would think I was mentally ill.

The intensity in his eyes made his gaze difficult to hold. "Do you know where my son is?"

I frowned. "No. I have a guess."

"Tell me." His voice was almost a growl.

"There is a boy in the Knight Order of the Redeemer with the gift of farseeing. He is the right age, and he has blue-black hair like your wife and your light eyes. He was rescued by a group of knights from slave traders in the wilderness. But the boy lost his memory. They call him Syllind, the Redeemer's chosen. He answers to Lin."

It was the oldest literary device in existence—surprise amnesia. The books never confirmed Lin's parentage, but it would have to be a cosmic coincidence for him not to be Reynald's son. The gift of farseeing was very rare.

I had many favorite characters. Solentine was one, Galiene, Pelegrin . . . But I always felt for Reynald the most. He'd spent his life serving the country. In return, his wife was murdered, and his son was stolen by slavers. Despite all of it, Reynald tried to do the right thing till the very end. He fought with all his strength and skill for it, and no matter how hard it tried, Kair Toren couldn't crush his will, so it killed him instead. It was a horrible death.

The blademaster stood up and leaned on the stone rail, his palms planted on it, his gaze fixed on the house.

"Redeemer's chosen," Reynald said. His voice was suffused with menace. I almost scooted back in my chair.

Rellas had many knightages, groups of knights affiliated for various reasons. If a knightage pledged itself to one of the Aspects and met certain requirements, like number of members and paying all the proper religious dues, it became a knight order.

There were three prominent knight orders in the kingdom. All of them pledged themselves to the Aspect of the Warrior, but in different forms. The Defenders worshiped the protective Warrior, concerned with guarding and securing their domain, while the Conquerors favored a more aggressive approach.

Of the three orders, the Order of the Redeemer was the newest and the smallest. They were big on renouncing your old, wretched existence and seeking redemption through a life of service, specifically martial service. The best comparison would be the Foreign Legion, but wrapped in religion, with a big chip on their shoulder, and actual magic powers.

"Getting into the Redeemer Tower will be very difficult," I warned. "They guard their squires, especially the ones with magic, with extreme prejudice. It will take someone with a great deal of influence to get you in."

The Redeemers overreacted to any perceived slight, and trying to take away one of their squires wouldn't go over well. Even Reynald, with all his skill, would not make it out of the Tower alive.

"As of now, I don't see any opportunity to reach your son. Instead, I can give you Derog Olgren. I can't guarantee a reunion, but I can help you with your revenge."

He turned to me. "What's your name?"

"Maggie."

He didn't look impressed. I felt the need to add something more. The pressure of his stare was overwhelming.

"Maggie what?"

Maggie Haley would mean nothing to him. Despite everything I had told him, he was ready to get up and leave. I could see it in his eyes. I was about to lose my only chance at keeping myself safe. I had to say something to make him stay. Something, anything . . .

"Maggie the Undying."

Reynald gave me a look. He was clearly skeptical. "Really now? Undying in what way exactly?"

Showing how desperate I was would only make him leave faster. I shrugged. "Stick with me and you'll find out."

"Fine, Maggie the Undying. Get me into that house, and I will protect you."

I'd got him. Oh wow. "It's a deal."

Reynald looked back at Derog's fortress. "There are at least eight guards in the house at all times. One door leading from the street to the courtyard, one door leading from the courtyard inside. Both are reinforced and guarded."

"Three," I said.

His eyebrows crept up.

"There is a basement-level escape passage with a hidden door that comes out near the dock. Derog uses it to ship the slaves by river when his usual route is compromised. The passage branches off into two hallways. One corridor leads to the basement, where the kids are held. It's protected by a door that's barred from the passageway side. The other corridor leads up the stairs to the kitchen and serves as Derog's escape route. The slaves never enter that part of the house, and he doesn't want to be hindered by dealing with additional doors in an emergency, so it's a straight shot."

Reynald studied the opposite shore.

"The door is reinforced," I told him. "You would need a battering ram, so breaking it isn't an option."

"Do you have a plan?" His voice told me that he clearly didn't think I had a plan, and if I did have one, it was probably stupid.

"Yes. You're going to sell me to Derog, and I'll take it from there."

A hint of steel flashed in his eyes. "And you were doing so well up until this point. The answer is no. Out of the question. First, you're too old. Derog deals in children and adolescents. Second, you will be raped, beaten, and worse."

"Trust me. He'll buy me, and I'll stay safe. I have an asset that Derog is looking for."

He was looking at me like I had lost my whole bag of marbles. "What asset is that?"

I gave him a big, bright smile.

Chapter 7

"This is reckless and foolish," Reynald muttered under his breath.

"It will be fine," I told him. "I have it in hand."

He nodded at the statue of the Knight Vanquisher in the plaza in front of us. "That's what Ralinbor of the Wilds said before his final battle."

"I thought he said, 'This kingdom isn't big enough for two sons of Aymar.'"

"That, too."

We were waiting two streets north of Derog's personal fortress, in the shadows of some building in the Knight Vanquisher Plaza. The night had fallen, and the enormous knight thrust his halberd to the sky as if trying to impale the three moons glowing against the darkness. The statue had been erected twenty years ago to commemorate King Sauven's victory over Ralinbor of the Wilds.

Ralinbor Savaric possessed a rare brand of magic, which allowed him to control a particularly nasty species of monster. He was also Sauven's half brother and best friend. They were raised together, separated in adolescence due to political circumstances, and then reunited in their early twenties. Ralinbor was Sauven's ride or die.

Sauven had promised Ralinbor great rewards for supporting his claim to the crown, but when it came time to deliver the goods, he dragged his feet and made excuses. Ralinbor saw the writing on the wall—now that his brother sat on the throne, Ralinbor, with his army, vast lands, and powerful magic, had become a threat to his rule.

Two years into his reign, Sauven accused Ralinbor's maternal uncle of treason and had him beheaded. Ralinbor took his army and marched on Kair Toren. The story had an ugly ending with Ralinbor dying in battle, his wife being brought to the capital, tried for treason, and executed, and their orphan son burning to death. Although that last one was in doubt.

Sauven won, but his victory was bittersweet. He'd killed his brother, the one man in the whole kingdom he'd genuinely cared about. Perhaps because of that, instead of a triumphant smile, the knight's stone face bore a perpetual disapproving frown. I didn't need any more disapproval in my life right now. I was getting plenty as it was.

"There must be a better way," Reynald said.

He'd had almost four months to figure out a better way and he hadn't. Pointing that out would be counterproductive.

A woman in her fifties walked into the square, carrying a lantern and moving like she had a destination in mind and needed to get there. She wore a dark dress with a knitted shawl wrapped around her shoulders.

Here we go.

The woman stopped and raised the lantern, the light catching her face. She had harsh features and skin like old parchment. Her hair, which might have been blond at some point, had grayed to a kind of beige. She wore it pulled back into a braid and coiled on the back of her head.

Darotha. When you needed some questionable crap done in the west part of the city, she was the person to see. She had three great qualities: She stayed bought, she kept her mouth shut, and she hated Derog. His men raided the beggar slums once and took away some kids. Darotha took offense to that. Those were her beggar children. He sent his people into her backyard, took her kids, and did not return them, apologize, or make amends, and she couldn't do anything about it because he was sitting in his fortress surrounded by guards.

Darotha didn't make a stink. She didn't confront Derog. She simply waited and held on to her grudge. Derog had no idea, but she'd stab him in the back with a rusty knife in a heartbeat. When I offered her that knife two hours ago, she'd grabbed it with both hands.

"I still don't understand why we need her," Reynald muttered.

"We need her because I can't sell myself, and you can't sell me either. Derog's people might have seen you before, when you were asking questions about your son, and even if they hadn't, you're too scary."

There was no way to tone him down. The slavers would never open the door to him.

"I'm not going to buy my vengeance with your life."

"I'm Maggie the Undying. It's not a figure of speech."

Darotha saw us and headed right over.

"We're not doing this."

That sounded very final.

"I'm going into that house one way or another," I told him softly. "There are children in there who will be sold and brutalized unless someone stops it. I need to know if you have my back. If you don't help me, I'll have to stab Derog myself, and I've never stabbed anybody in my whole life."

I only hit people with rocks. That was more my speed.

Darotha was halfway across the plaza.

"Are you going to abandon me?" I asked. "In or out?"

"In, damn it," he growled.

Darotha reached us and looked at me. "You sure you want to do this?"

"I am."

"Follow me. Keep your head down, look at your feet, and don't talk."

I looked down and trailed her across the square. At the mouth of the street, I glanced over my shoulder. Reynald was still under the arch, deep in the night shadows. I gave him a little wave. He didn't wave back.

We walked through the dark streets until we reached Derog's estate, one solid wall facing the street, a single door like black satin in the center of it. The woman knocked on the door. A small window opened, revealing a slice of a man's face.

"I have merchandise," Darotha said.

The window shut. Metal clanged. Win. Darotha had cost me three nomas, and she was worth it.

The door swung open, revealing a hard-faced man in his thirties. A thin scar carved through his cheek, drawing a pale line on his skin that ran all the way into his dark hair. I caught a glimpse of a long stone tunnel behind him.

Darotha reached over and slapped the back of my head. "What did I tell you about staring?"

I bowed my head.

The guard's gaze slid over me, long and sticky, almost viscous. A cold draft swirled from the tunnel, throwing damp air into my face. A nauseating shiver squirmed through me. I didn't want to go into that house. I wanted to turn around and run away as fast as my legs would carry me.

"Come with me."

Darotha started moving, and I followed her into the tunnel. It punched through the entire width of the building, exactly sixty feet, and at the other end, another archway led to the courtyard, brightly lit by a row of lanterns. The courtyard was large, at least thirty-five, maybe forty yards across and paved with cobblestones. A well rose to the right, and in the center of the courtyard, an old wine tree stretched its branches from a flower bed. I concentrated on the tree. If I looked nervous in any way, it was game over.

Reynald was right about Derog's business preferences. He liked to buy young. Slavery had been illegal in Kair Toren for over three hundred years. The very first Savaric king had outlawed it, and their entire dynasty rested on that law. Buying and selling slaves fell under Crimes Against the Kingdom, federal treason with an automatic death sentence. Even a noble of a prominent family caught with slaves would be purged. Most of the slaves Derog acquired would be smuggled outside of the country to be sold at foreign markets.

Despite the law, a few Rellasians still risked buying human beings, and they wanted them young, so they would be easier to control. Cute kids and attractive teenagers were in high demand. At twenty-six, I was way out of Derog's favorite age bracket, which was why I had chosen to pretend to be a vulnerable adult. Explaining that term to Reynald had taken some time.

The guard who let us in was staring daggers at me. I raised my chin a little and looked at the tree. It really was a pretty tree. Stout, with a thick trunk that spiraled up in that corkscrew way particular to wine trees. During the day, it would bloom with pale pink flowers that looked a lot like oversized roses. If you cut it, its sap would run ruby red, like cabernet sauvignon . . . And the door in the far wall opened.

Crap, crap, crap. I looked down at my feet.

A pair of brown boots came into my view.

"Where did you get her?" The man had a quiet voice.

"My sister sent her to me from the countryside," Darotha said. "Her late husband's daughter from a previous wife. My sister's got a house full of her own kids and a husband in the ground. They are bad off, and they need the money."

"How old is she?"

"Twenty."

"Too old."

"She has the mind of a child," the woman said. "She's sweet, obedient, good with kids. She keeps herself clean."

Thick calloused fingers grasped my chin and lifted my face. The man in front of me was large, with broad shoulders and the kind of seasoned strength you sometimes saw among the older MMA trainers, the guys who stood in the fighter's corner and screamed incomprehensible advice and curses during the matches. He was in his fifties, with skin the color of sand and longish dark hair brushed back from his forehead. His face, with a sharp nose and dark hooded eyes, showed no emotion. Derog Olgren. The slavemonger.

His eyes studied me.

Like being caught in the claws of an old eagle.

Behind him, another man stood, holding a coin purse and a book with a quill in it. He was in his late thirties, pale, with short, dark blond hair. Lasa, the bookkeeper.

I tried to look oblivious and trusting.

Derog turned my head left, then right.

"She's untouched," Darotha told him. "Healthy. Not diseased."

That first one was not strictly true. I wasn't a virgin, but I doubted they would check. My value wasn't between my legs, it was in my mouth.

Derog grimaced and let me go. "It's supply and demand, Darotha. Customers who risk buying a fucktoy want something extraordinary."

"She's docile. She won't run off, and she will do whatever you tell her to. Smile, Maggie."

I produced a bright plastic smile.

Derog's gaze sharpened. He reached over, pressed his thumb against my upper lip, and pulled it up, exposing my teeth. Ugh.

"Open your mouth."

I opened and held still.

"Close it."

I did.

"I'll take her."

Lasa stepped forward. "Two nomas."

Darotha drew back in outrage. "Five!"

"Two nomas, ten dens."

"Four nomas, forty dens."

Telling Darotha that she could pocket whatever money she sold me for might have been a mistake.

"Three nomas," Lasa declared. "Take it or leave it."

"Fine."

He dropped three silver coins into Darotha's palm. The woman squirreled them away. "This man is in charge of you, Maggie. You be a good girl and obey him. I'm leaving now."

I raised my hand and gave her a small wave.

"Follow me," Derog told me.

I followed him and Lasa through the door into a large, well-lit hallway.

"Ciskan?" Lasa asked.

"Mhm," Derog said.

"I'll make the arrangements. Talpot is waiting for you in the pen, as you ordered."

We kept walking.

Ciskan was an auldor, a minor aristocrat, the lowest rank of Kair Toren's civilian nobility. It went king, duke, margrave or earl, baron, and everything below was an auldor. Some auldors had riches and land, others barely scraped by. Ciskan owned a thriving winery. He was wealthy, reclusive, and odd, and he had a crippling phobia of bad teeth. His fear was so severe that even something minor, like a gap or slightly crooked tooth, sparked an anxiety attack. One time he was forced to carry on a conversation with a man whose teeth had turned black from decay. After five minutes Ciskan fainted, fell down the stairs, and had to be treated for a concussion and a broken arm.

Derog had been supplying Ciskan with dentally sound slaves for the last seven years. Unfortunately for the two of them, Derog obtained slaves in two ways: by kidnapping them or buying them from desperate families. Both methods targeted the poor, and finding an award-winning smile among malnourished children was very rare. But I had enjoyed the benefits of twenty-first-century dentistry. All those years of high school braces had given me an

Instagram smile, and my mouth was a poem in enamel to Crest 3D White. To Derog, I was a sure way to make a significant profit.

We turned the corner and stopped before a heavy wooden double door in the wall on our right. Lasa removed the inch-thick metal bar securing it and held it open. A stone staircase led down, and I could see a small section of brightly lit stone floor.

A long bloody smear stretched across the left wall as if a heavily bleeding person had leaned onto it, tried to climb the stairs, and then slid down. The blood was old and brown. There was so much blood. Someone had died here.

I want out. Let me out.

Derog started down. I had to follow.

It would be fine. I would just count the steps and not look at the blood. *One, two . . .*

Behind us, Lasa shut the door and caught up. I was so on edge, I could feel him behind me. I knew exactly where he was without looking.

Twenty-two. We had run out of stairs.

Derog turned to the left and I made myself mirror his movement. A large room stretched in front of us, illuminated by wall lanterns shielded with metal cages. Wooden double bunks lined the walls. Directly opposite us, a doorway allowed a glimpse of a latrine, sectioned off from the rest of the room by an interior wall. To the right of it, a big wooden door, reinforced with iron strips, loomed in the wall. The entrance to the escape tunnel.

Five children huddled together in the middle of the floor, standing as close to each other as they could. A dark-haired boy of eleven or twelve, and four girls, three under seven and one teenager, probably sixteen or seventeen, wrapping her arms around the younger kids. All clean, all dressed in identical plain, undyed linen outfits like prisoners, and all, except for the boy, wearing identical frozen expressions on their faces.

Another boy, blond and sturdy, slumped against the bunks on the right side. His eyes were shut. Blood drenched his shirt and spread in a puddle on the stone floor. A big puddle. Oh no.

Two men flanked the kids, one older, with a sparse, dark beard and a shaved head. The other was younger, in his early twenties, pale, tall, and beefy, built like a defensive lineman. There was a faint echo of Derog in his face, in his hooded eyes and the shape of his brow, but his features were softer, less defined. That had to be Talpot, Derog's nephew.

Derog looked at the injured boy, then looked at Talpot. The slow-moving hamster wheel that powered Talpot's brain turned a couple of times. He held himself straighter.

"The first goal of a business is profit," Derog said. "There are other goals. Growth, client retention. But all of them are driven by profit."

Talpot relaxed slightly, probably thinking it was a lecture. A mistake.

"To sustain profit, one must have quality merchandise. What did you do with my merchandise, you shit smear?"

Talpot opened his mouth.

"You broke it." Derog's voice snapped like a whip.

Everyone in the room flinched, except me. I was too petrified, so I just stood there, staring straight ahead like a mannequin.

Derog stepped forward, grabbed the boy by his neck, and jerked him up with one hand. The boy's head lolled.

"I can get a healer . . ." Lasa murmured.

"It wouldn't do any good," Derog said. "He's cold. He's been dead for at least three hours."

Oh fuck, oh god, oh god, oh god, oh god. . . .

Derog pulled the boy's shirt up. "You stabbed him in the heart. A clean, quick kill. Congratulations, nephew. What a feat."

He let go and the body crumpled to the floor, splashing into the blood.

The kids stood frozen. Not a single gasp. Nobody cried. They just went immobile like statues, their faces blank, except for the other boy, who glared at Derog with blatant hatred.

Derog pulled a rag off the bunk bed's rail and wiped his hands. "You killed him, and you didn't tell anyone for three hours. Do you think I am stupid, Talpot? Do I strike you as a man of limited intelligence?"

"No, terr." Talpot bowed his head.

"I promised your mother that I would take care of you. That's the only reason you're not bleeding out on the floor next to him."

Talpot stayed immobile, like a statue.

"You owe me a boy," Derog said. "And by *boy*, I don't mean one you snatch in front of his parents and the entire street, so I'll have a city-wide panic with the guards breathing down my neck and have to suspend all deliveries for weeks. I mean a boy quietly obtained; a boy of good quality. Do you understand me?"

Talpot unhinged his jaw. "Yes, terr."

Lasa was staring at me with single-minded intensity. I must've broken character somehow and now he was watching me like a hawk, waiting for me to stumble. My life was hanging by a thread. There were five children in this room. If I died now, nobody would get out.

I walked forward, picked up the rag Derog had dropped, knelt in front of the boy's body, and put the rag onto the blood, gathering it like it was spilled water.

"What are you doing, Maggie?" Derog asked.

I looked up at him. "Mess."

"That's right," Derog said. "It is a mess, isn't it? A slow-wit understands,

Talpot, yet my only nephew doesn't. Bring the girl a bucket of water and get the body out of here."

Talpot stomped away. Out of the corner of my eye I saw Lasa. The suspicion had melted from his face, and he was making notations in his book.

I went back to mopping up the blood. It was cold. Cold and sticky on my fingers.

Chapter 8

The blood refused to come out. I scrubbed and scrubbed, but the stain had settled into the grout between the stones. I would need bleach. Did they even have bleach in Rellas?

The horror of what had happened loomed in my mind, like a terrifying dark ghost that bent over me, watching me scrub the grout. Falling apart to deal with it wasn't an option, so I ignored it and kept scrubbing with a blank look on my face.

The younger kids had started crying the minute the door leading upstairs closed behind Derog. The older teenage girl tried to calm them down, then another man came down the stairs, told them to shut up, dropped into a large chair in the corner, and propped his feet in beat-up boots on an old wooden trunk. He was about Talpot's age, but where Talpot was thick, this guy was leaner, with a face that reminded you of a weasel, and skin so pale it was slightly green. His longish brown hair was pulled away into a sparse ponytail, and the jerkin he wore over his bare chest had burned patches on it.

I hadn't counted on the kids being watched. That altered things.

The oldest girl led the three younger children to the latrine, then brought them back. The boy crawled onto his bunk and sat there, watching the weasel-face. He was eleven or twelve, thin, small, with dark tan skin, short brown hair, and very dark eyes. From where I knelt on the floor, his irises looked almost black.

I kept scrubbing.

Derog and his revolting crew showed up in the second book, in one of the later chapters. A talented young thief who went by River Fog traveled to Kair Toren at the request of a prominent noble family. They hired him to steal a child from Derog. It was a particular child, and Derog had referred to her as a "custom order for a special customer." The family had tried to purchase her, but the slavemonger refused to sell her even at a sky-high price, which meant whoever had hired him to obtain the child in the first place had to be powerful enough to scare him.

A lot of that chapter revolved around River Fog scouting the house and remembering all the terrible shit that happened there, because years ago, he, too, was one of the children sold through it. At some point he encountered Talpot on the street, and it took all of River Fog's will not to murder him. He stopped only because it would jeopardize his job, and he took pride in being a thief who never failed. He could pick any lock, steal the object he wanted, and vanish without a trace.

In his reminiscing, River Fog also shared that he had once run into another of Derog's child victims. The man, by then an adult, told him that he had loosened a board in the latrine and dug a hole through the wall into Derog's escape tunnel. He worked on it for weeks, removing the board to work on his tunnel, then sliding it back in place until one night he realized that only a single stone stood between him and the escape. A good push would have knocked the stone free and opened the way to freedom, but he was exhausted, and it was almost morning. He decided to make his escape the next night. But during the day one of Derog's roughnecks noticed the loose board and nailed it in place, never realizing there was a tunnel behind it.

Every night for the next week the boy would go to the latrine and stare at the board. He was too weak to pry it free, so he would have to break it. It was old and would splinter from a kick, but the sound of the snapping board would bring Derog's guards. He never got the courage to kick the board and several days later he was shipped out to a country estate, where his life became a living hell.

That should have been a big obvious clue that the children were watched, but I had read right over it. I thought he just had an irrational fear. In my defense, I usually skipped that chapter during my rereads because in the end, once River Fog delivered the child to the prearranged place, an assassin murdered him and the girl. The whole thing was one giant setup by River Fog's employer, who had wanted the child dead.

I hated reading about child abuse and murder. I could read about horrible crap as long as it happened to adults, but crimes against children skeeved me out, so I had only read that chapter two or three times. As far as I could remember, Derog, his nephew Talpot, and the bookkeeper, Lasa, were the only people mentioned by name. I had no idea who the guy guarding us was.

I was reasonably sure the escape hole was already dug, because the man who'd made it mentioned it was during the cholera outbreak. The city had been under quarantine, which was why he had been stuck with Derog for so long. The outbreak had happened four years ago.

I had to find the tunnel and figure out how to break the board without alerting the asshole in the chair.

I wrung the rag out, straightened, and lifted the bucket.

The oldest girl jumped off her bunk. "I'll help you."

Perfect.

She grabbed the other side of the bucket's handle. Together we carried it to the latrine, passing the boy on his bunk. He glanced at us and went back to mad dogging at the guard.

The latrine had a sink and a simple shower on the left and a wooden box on the right with three holes cut out, one for an adult butt and two others smaller. We set the bucket down. I turned, trying to bring the guard into my view without looking obvious. He was conducting a fascinating study of his own nails.

I turned to the girl and held my finger to my lips.

Her eyes widened.

She was a pretty girl with round eyes somewhere between blue and green and braided hair on the darker end of blond. Swirls of old bruises covered her face, no longer purple, but a sickly greenish yellow. She was maybe five foot six or five foot seven, and strong, not fragile. I had gone to high school with girls just like her. They played volleyball and ran track.

I kept my gaze on her, moved to the first latrine, and gently knocked on the board next to the hole. Solid.

She watched me.

Second hole. Solid.

Third. Hollow.

The girl blinked.

I motioned her over with my hand. She dragged the bucket over and began slowly pouring the bloody water into the hole, blocking me from the guard's view. I bent, trying to find the edges of the board. It wasn't hard since I had a helpful cluster of nails to guide me.

Neither she nor I would fit. The rest of the girls were too young. It would have to be the boy.

"What's behind there?" she whispered.

"A hole that leads to Derog's back door."

The board was nailed well. I'd need a pry bar, which I didn't have. No, breaking it was our only chance. It looked thin enough.

"Does the guard ever come into the bathroom?"

"Only when he has to go," she whispered.

We needed to do it now. The longer we waited, the higher the risk that Derog would ship one of the kids out during the night.

"What's your name?"

"Clover."

"Are you good at kicking?"

She glanced at the board and nodded.

"Get the boy," I told her.

She walked over to the sink. I followed her. We stood side by side.

"Kaiden, bring me the girls' laundry."

He didn't respond.

"Kaiden!"

"Do what she says," the guard growled.

Kaiden slid off his bunk, went over to the wicker basket in the corner, picked it up, and carried it to us, looking like he wanted to punch somebody.

"Bring it over here," she told him, pointing at a spot between us.

He set the basket down with a sour look on his face.

"Don't react," I whispered.

He glanced at me.

"Show me your left hand."

He glanced at Clover. She made big eyes at him. He showed me his left palm. Good. He knew right from left.

"The last latrine by the wall has a hole behind the board," I murmured. "I'm going to make some noise. When I scream, Clover will kick the board. You'll crawl into the hole. There is a loose stone at the end. Push it open and crawl out into a tunnel. Turn left and run until you find a door. Open it. Nod if you understand."

He nodded.

"Remember, turn left. If you see the stairs, you're going the wrong way, straight to Derog. Open the door and come right back. If they notice you are gone, they might kill the lot of us. You'll have to be very fast. Do you understand?"

He nodded again.

I washed my hands under the water. There was a child's blood under my fingernails. I shook my hands, wiped them on my dress, turned, and walked into the room. My heart was beating so fast, it actually hurt a little.

I needed to draw attention, and then I would need to hold it for at least three to four minutes.

I crossed the room and stood in front of the guard. This was a stupid plan. I would regret this.

I stared.

The guard looked at me.

I stared some more. Most people didn't like to be stared at.

"What the fuck are you looking at?"

I stared.

"Are you fucking deaf?"

I stared.

He kicked the trunk out of the way, jumped to his feet, and started toward me. Well, that was easier than I thought.

"So, you're gonna eyeball me now? Is that it?"

I opened my mouth.

"What?" he demanded.

"Shit smear," I told him.

"What?"

I sucked in a deep breath and screamed at the top of my lungs. I was loud and scared beyond all reason, and my body delivered all the decibels I had in me.

The guard backhanded me across the face. The hit burned like he'd scalded me. I rocked back and stumbled. Something hot and salty wet my lips. Blood, this time my own.

"Shut the fuck up."

The small kids burst into tears. I hadn't heard the board breaking. There was no telling if they'd managed it, but it was too late to stop now.

"Shit smear!" I told him.

He grabbed me by the neck and squeezed all of the air out. Panic hit me. I wanted to claw at his hands, but I had to hang there, limp, instead.

The world was turning dark.

The upstairs door swung open, and Derog marched into the room, followed by a thickset guy who looked like he crushed bricks with his forehead for a living.

The guard let go of me and backed away with his hands in the air.

"What the fuck are you doing?" Derog snarled. "What in the honest fuck do you think you're doing?"

"She provoked me, terr."

I sucked in air and coughed. I was still alive somehow.

"How?"

"She was looking at me." As soon as the words came out, the weasel-face realized that he'd made a crucial mistake.

"So you hit her because she was looking at you?" Derog asked, suddenly calm.

"She called me a shit smear."

"She has the mind of a child, you moron." Derog grasped my chin. "She doesn't know what the words mean. She probably heard them for the first time today. Smile, Maggie."

I blinked away tears and gave him a smile.

"She said it like she knew what it meant. And then she screamed."

Derog studied my mouth. "You scared her. Of course she screamed. Your face isn't scratched. She made no effort to fight you."

The weasel-face stared at me.

Derog put his finger in my mouth and tested my teeth. I almost threw up in his face.

"She has teeth like a noblewoman, and she's worth more than I pay you in a year. And you hit her in the face. What would we do if you knocked any of her teeth out? Would I pull yours out and put them into her mouth?"

The bruiser next to Derog stirred. "Apologies, terr, but his teeth aren't pretty enough."

The slavemonger turned his head and looked at the big guy for a long moment.

"Close your mouth, Maggie."

I did.

"You're not wrong, Murt," Derog said to the big man, "but you are missing the point. The point is, if one of you touches her again, I'll hang you by your balls off the tree in the courtyard."

The two guards held still.

"You," Derog pointed at the weasel-face, "come with me. You!" He pointed at Murt. "Guard. I don't want to come down here again tonight. No more trouble, no more screams."

Murt nodded.

The weasel-face tossed a ring with two keys to the big guard and gave me a this-isn't-fucking-over look. He was right. It wasn't over until all of them were dead.

Derog headed toward the stairs, weasel-face in tow, stopped, and turned. "Where is Kaiden?"

Shit.

"He has the runs, terr," Clover said from the latrine's doorway. She was standing with her feet together, her head slightly bowed, still keeping Derog in her view but not looking straight at him. Her arms were bent slightly at the elbows and her hands were together, right over left.

It looked like a pose a maid from a noble household might assume. Her face was serene, her expression perfectly neutral. I got the feeling that if Derog threw a bucket of blood at her right now, she'd stay just like that.

Derog's gaze sharpened. "Does he?"

He started toward the latrine.

We were busted. It was over. I could sprint to the upstairs door, but I wouldn't, because the kids would be left behind. And weasel-face would catch me.

Kaiden stumbled out of the latrine.

Had he gone through the hole or not? I couldn't tell. He didn't look like a child who had crawled through dirt.

I had failed. The escape had failed.

But the kids were alive. It would be fine. I would think of something else.

"Come here," Derog ordered.

The boy walked over, defiance all over his face. My heart was in my throat, and it had squeezed itself into a painful rock that kept me from breathing.

Derog frowned. "Have you been drinking from the faucet?"

Kaiden looked at him. If he'd had a weapon, any weapon, he would've tried to stab Derog.

"I asked you a question," Derog said.

"No."

Derog shook his head. "If he doesn't improve by morning, tell the guard to get a healer."

"Yes, terr," Clover said.

Derog turned and he and the weasel-face went up the stairs. The door clanged shut.

Murt glared at all of us and put his meaty hand on the short club hanging from his belt. "Bed. Now." He stabbed his finger in my direction and then pointed at the nearest cot. "Maggie, sleep here."

I walked to the bed, took off my boots, and lay down.

At the other side of the room Kaiden crawled into his bunk. Clover settled to the left of him, by the little girls. Their faces told me absolutely nothing.

Murt walked over to the lantern in the wall by my bed, stuck the key into the lock of the cage, and opened it. "Everyone goes the fuck to sleep."

He blew the flame out and moved on to the next lantern.

"Nobody cries."

The door at the far end of the room swung open, and Reynald slipped in. I blinked to make sure I wasn't hallucinating. He'd lost the cloak. He wore a dark gray shirt and dark pants, loose enough to move in but without much slack. His sword rested in his fingers, pointing down, almost an afterthought.

"Everyone sleeps," Murt intoned.

Reynald moved across the room, silent as a ghost.

"And then everyone gets to keep their pretty teeth in their mou—"

It was so fast, I didn't actually see it. Reynald had moved, the big guard fell mid-word, and Reynald wiped his sword on his sleeve.

I bolted out of the bed and shoved my feet back into my boots. Kaiden was looking at Reynald like he had seen a god in the flesh. Clover sat up in her bed, her face shocked. The little girls froze, not sure whether to cry.

I had to get the kids out of here. Clover was still sitting on her bunk.

"Get the kids." I cleared the distance to the nearest child, the smallest girl, scooped her out of her bed, turned, and saw Talpot at the bottom of the stairs with a lantern, his eyes wide.

We hadn't heard the door open. He wasn't supposed to be here. He had snuck in, the slimy bastard.

Reynald sprinted toward him.

"Guard!" Talpot screamed, fumbling for the knife on his belt. "Gahh!"

Reynald's blade slid into Talpot's chest, once, twice, so fast, like a scorpion stinging. Reynald turned his back to him and walked away.

Talpot dropped his knife. His mouth gaped open. He struggled to say something, but no sound came. Pink foam bubbled up on his lips. A faint hissing noise came from his chest. A collapsed lung. The air was rushing into Talpot's chest through his wounds with every breath, compressing his lungs and his heart. He would die slowly, in pain.

Talpot sagged to the floor. His neck veins bulged out, the skin gaining a slight blue tint. Fear squirmed in his eyes, raw and sharp, the terror of a man who knew he was dying and could do nothing to stop it. The dead boy's face flashed before me. *Good. Die, you scumbag. Be afraid and die.*

Footsteps thudded, and two men charged into the room from the other door, cutting off our escape. They must've been in the kitchen and heard Talpot scream.

Reynald stepped toward them, his broad back to us. I backed away from him into a corner. Clover lunged for the stairs, holding two children by their hands, but I grabbed her and yanked her back, next to me and the boy.

"No! The safest place in this house is right here. Don't distract him."

She pulled the girls closer to her and wrapped her arms around them.

Reynald waited, his blade down.

The two guards advanced. Derog liked to hire beefy intimidating goons, the bigger the better. Reynald was about six feet tall, and these two towered over him. They were both larger and heavier than him by at least thirty pounds. The guy on the left was the scarred guard who had let me and Darotha in, and his coworker on the right looked like a seasoned brawler. No fat, just muscle, big arms, thick legs, and a mean look in his eyes.

The brawler hefted a wooden club, swung it, and roared, "He's in the pen!"

The girl in my arms flinched. I hugged her to me and said, "Don't be scared. This is already over."

And once it was done, Reynald would walk us right out of here and go back in to paint the walls red.

The brawler charged, swinging the club. Reynald sidestepped as if he were floating and slashed across the brawler's stomach. The other guard stabbed at the blademaster from the side, aiming for his neck. His blade pierced only air. Reynald slashed at the man's extended arm, opening a gash above his wrist. The guard dropped his sword and howled, red drenching his hand.

The brawler fell, clutching at his gut.

It was insanely fast. They'd clashed in a blink, and now one of them moaned on the floor and the other stumbled away, clenching his arm. Clap your hands once, and the clash was over.

Another guard ran down the stairs, a giant of a man, brandishing a huge sword. He had to be close to seven feet tall, broad, with long troll arms thicker than my legs and huge shovel hands. Where the hell did Derog even find this guy? What was he feeding him?

I held my right arm out and backed a little deeper into the corner, herding the kids behind me.

The injured swordsman grabbed his sword off the floor with his left hand. His right arm hung useless, dripping blood. The giant glanced at him.

Reynald took two steps toward the stairs, his back still to us. He wasn't maneuvering to get into a better position.

It was because of us, I realized. Reynald had a choice: to kill the slavers for his vengeance or to protect us, and he'd made protecting us his priority.

The giant roared.

The two men charged at the same time, the giant from the right and the injured swordsman from the left. Reynald dodged the giant's swing. His blade kissed the man's throat. The giant stumbled back, and Reynald continued the swing, letting the sword drop as he turned left and bringing it back up in a beautiful arc to slice the swordsman's left arm. The blade barely seemed to touch skin. A red drop swelled at the swordsman's wrist. His arm gaped open, split in half from hand to biceps.

The swordsman dropped his blade, both of his arms awash in blood. He screamed, half from pain, half from frustration. Reynald's first cut had damaged something in his right hand, and he couldn't even use it to stanch the flow of blood along his left arm.

The big man was still on his feet, bleeding but mobile, stalking Reynald across the floor.

On the stairs, Talpot had turned blue. His legs drummed the ground.

On the other side, the brawler moaned on the floor in a puddle of blood. His wound gaped open and the intestines inside looked like a mess of bloody rope.

Reynald was torturing them. He could've finished each of them with a single strike. Instead, he forced them to experience pain and despair. This was a punishment for every child who had ever come through the doors of this house.

The big man was breathing harder. Reynald had barely nicked him, but the wound steadily bled. He was getting weaker, and he knew it. He had circled Reynald and was now between us and the door, cutting off our escape.

Reynald didn't look worried.

The huge swordsman raised his sword over his head, lunged forward, but stopped just short of committing to a strike.

The blademaster watched him calmly.

The giant stomped forward again and pulled back.

Reynald sighed. "You don't have much time before you bleed out. Do what you're going to do."

Three men came running from the kitchen.

Kaiden darted forward, right past me.

"Kaiden!"

The boy grabbed Talpot's knife and dashed up the stairs.

He'd spent so much time being afraid of these men, and here was Reynald shredding them like they were cabbage. They bled, they cried, and Kaiden had endured so much abuse. He was only twelve years old at most. He thought this was his chance. He was going after Derog.

I thrust the girl in my arms at Clover. "Stay with Reynald!"

She bobbed her head up and down.

I grabbed the club from Murt's corpse and sprinted up the stairs. The door stood ajar. I dashed through it and into an empty hallway. Left or right?

A loud thud from the left. I turned and ran down the hallway, chasing the source of the noise. Rooms flashed by. I turned the corner. More rooms. It didn't sound that far. I should've found it.

Another thud and a short scream. I'd passed it. I doubled back, looking into each room as I ran.

A doorway gaped on the right, revealing a large room, with bookshelves and a desk. To the right, Kaiden had pressed himself against the wall. His right arm was bleeding, the knife gone. Lasa was standing five feet away, a sword in his hand.

Something in me broke. All the energy and will I had exerted to keep from losing it and screaming my head off since landing in that rain-filled ditch turned to anger in a flash of heat. I charged like a bull, swinging my club.

Lasa tried to parry, but I was so mad. The world turned red. I batted the sword aside, growling like some deranged monster, and hit him. My club grazed his shoulder. He stumbled back, and I was on him, screaming, snarling, beating him in a frenzy, again and again. He shrieked and tried to back away, but he was between me and the desk and there was no place to go. One of the blows caught his head. Blood sprayed my face. Lasa dropped down, trying to lift his arms to shield himself, and I hammered him like he was a flying cockroach trapped with me in a shower. I couldn't swing my club fast enough.

Lasa collapsed. I pointed my club down, grabbed it with both hands, and drove it straight at his face. It hit with a wet squishing sound. I did it again, then again, and straightened.

Lasa's face was human hamburger meat. His chest didn't rise. He wasn't breathing.

I had killed someone.

Kaiden gaped at me from his spot by the wall.

"You little jerk," I snarled.

Something cold touched my neck. Kaiden shot out of the room like a bullet from a gun.

"When something seems too good to be true, it usually is," Derog said.

His sword pressed against my skin, forcing me to stand straight.

"Come with me," Derog ordered.

He walked me out of the room, and we started in the direction of the courtyard door.

We turned the corner. Reynald blocked our way, all of the kids behind him. "Go back downstairs or she dies," Derog said.

If this was a movie, Reynald would pull out a gun and shoot Derog between the eyes. It wasn't a movie. The metal of the sword was cold against my throat, pressing right where I could feel blood pulsing through my neck.

It was probably the adrenaline, but Reynald seemed to grow darker, while his eyes turned brighter, a piercing green. "Give me the girl."

"Don't make me cut her to prove a point," Derog said.

I saw it in Reynald's eyes. He would let Derog go to keep me alive. He would let him walk out with me.

Once Derog stepped out that door, he would vanish into the shadows and set about tracking us down one by one. We had made a fool out of him, and he couldn't afford for it to get out. He would find the children and murder them. Killing him was the only way to ensure they survived. It had to end today, right here and now.

I met Reynald's gaze. "Remember my name. Wait for me."

I raised my right foot and stomped on Derog's boot as hard as I could.

Ice sliced across my neck. The world went black.

Chapter 9

I woke up to pain and the wailing of children.

The world was soft and fuzzy, out of focus. I blinked a couple of times and saw Reynald's face. He was sitting by me, dark and scary, lost in thought.

It would be a great time to quip something witty, but everything hurt too much.

"Ow."

Reynald's gaze snapped to me. Relief shone in his eyes.

"Well," he said. "'Undying' is a bit of a misnomer, isn't it?"

"Yes, but 'dying horribly and then waking up in a lot of pain' is a bit of a mouthful."

I raised my hand. He grasped it and pulled me into a sitting position. The little girl I had carried threw herself at me, sobbing. Double ow. I winced, hugged her, and petted her back.

Clover made a strangled noise. Her eyes were red, and tears stained her face. Her voice shook. "I thought you died, my lady."

Aww.

Behind her, Kaiden stared at me, a desperate, vulnerable look in his eyes. He looked like a little kid who'd been pummeled by life so many times, he didn't expect anything good to ever happen again, and my heart squeezed itself into a painful little ball.

"Hey," I told him.

He spun around, hiding his face.

"I'm fine," I told them. "It's all good. Everything is good."

Everything wasn't good. Everything hurt like hell. The little girl hugging me felt like someone was stabbing needles into my body.

I looked at Reynald. "Is he dead?"

He nodded.

"Good." The relief that flooded through me was indescribable. I had never been so happy in my entire life. "How long was I out?"

"About half an hour," Reynald said.

Less than last time. Or at least I was guessing it was less, but then last time I had been stabbed several times, my throat was slit, and I'd drowned. There was a lot more damage to heal.

I suddenly realized that I was still in the hallway. They must've been afraid to move me.

"Do we need to go? I can try to get up."

"Why would we need to go?" Reynald asked.

"To escape."

"Everyone is dead," he told me.

"But we need to leave. What if the guards come here and discover all the dead people?"

"Why would they come here? In all these years they've never bothered with this house."

"What if Derog's clients show up?"

"I hope they do." Reynald smiled.

I shivered and instantly regretted it. Shivering hurt.

He was on my side. At least for now.

I met Reynald's gaze. "My brain is a little slow right now."

He nodded. "I can tell. We have five children in our custody. We must provide them with a safe place to stay until we can return them to their families or determine what to do next. We're in a fortress of a house. We can hold it against a small army. In a little while, I will get a boat and dispose of the bodies in the bay, as is the time-honored Kair Toren tradition. We will clean the blood. We will sleep safely and eat well, and after you recover, we will go through Derog's ledgers."

And there would be a lot of ledgers. Years of them. Lasa kept meticulous records.

Reynald was right. Derog was a slaver. If he had paid off any guardsmen, they wouldn't stick their necks out to get revenge for him. His only living relative was his sister who lived in another province, and we would be able to handle her if she showed up. The Kair Toren underworld would note that we had killed Derog and his crew and leave us alone because they were creatures who ate their weak and avoided their strong. By their logic, Derog was strong, and because we took the house away from him, we were stronger. Nobody knew anything about us, and nobody would want to test us. Why would we go anywhere when we could just stay here?

"Are things a little clearer?" the blademaster asked.

"Yes."

"Good. Come on, little one." He reached for the little girl holding on to me like a baby lemur. "Let Maggie get a breath."

Planter 8

I stretched my legs and leaned back in my new office chair. It used to be Derog's chair and office, but he didn't need them anymore. In fact, I now had an entire suite to myself: a luxurious bedroom, a palatial bathroom with running water, and this personal office with a desk and a lovely window.

I had offered the suite to Reynald. He gave me a short laugh and settled into a slightly less luxurious set of rooms previously occupied by Lasa. We put Clover into one of the other suites, the little girls in the room next to her, and Kaiden on the other side.

Twenty-four hours had passed since the massacre. It had been justice, but it was still a massacre. Shortly after I resurrected, we bathed the small kids in the huge bathroom downstairs and put them to bed. Then the four of us wrapped the bodies of Derog, Lasa, and some other guy Reynald had killed upstairs in canvas we found in storage and carried them down to the basement. It was backbreaking work, and I was deeply grateful most of Derog's employees had helpfully run to confront Reynald in the pen. Now we had a row of anonymous bodies swathed in cloth and trussed up with rope. Reynald had been scarily efficient at wrapping them up and I was too chicken to ask where he had acquired that particular skill.

Once the corpses were handled, we took long baths, scrubbed ourselves clean, and fell asleep, or in my case passed out into a black dreamless hole.

In the morning, we fed everyone and cleaned up most of the blood. Some traces of it were still there, too faint to see. Removing the blood completely was almost impossible, but Clover had found some kind of powder that was probably a quicklime variant, so we made do with that. She also insisted on stripping all the linens off the beds and boiling them with detergent in this massive pot we found in the laundry area in the courtyard. Apparently, this was a common thing, because the pot came with three-foot-long wooden tongs for stirring the boiling laundry.

While she boiled linens, Reynald and I took stock of Derog's blood money. Most of Derog's cash was with a banker and out of our reach. The small safe in his room yielded us two hundred nomas, the equivalent of two gold grests, probably the purchasing capital, household budget, and payroll. Reynald had used some of it to buy a lovely boat, which was now parked at our dock. Tonight, he would make the corpse run.

I had settled in the office to look through Lasa's ledgers. I'd cried after the first one, then I went numb, and now I was angry. It was a cold, crystallized kind of anger and it grew out of me like an iceberg. At some point Clover asked me if I wanted dinner. I thanked her and told her no. I couldn't stomach any.

The bells of the North Tower tolled, distant. It was ten PM. Outside the window, night had fallen.

The ledgers lay in neat stacks on the desk. The worst of Kair Toren documented with annotations in Lasa's fluid, perfectly legible handwriting.

In my senior year of high school, we had to write a book report on a favorite novel or series. I did mine on The Rise of Kair Toren. After I submitted my outline, my teacher asked me why I picked that book series and not some other, so I told her all about the characters, their conversations, their funny moments, the plots they brewed, and the tragedies they lived through. The magic, the beauty, the horror. Everything. I told her I had reread them three times, because everything was falling apart in Rellas, and wading into that darkness again and again kept my anticipation of justice fresh. The reckoning was coming, and I would relish it. I couldn't wait to see the bad guys fall and my favorite characters—the few who had survived—get their happy ending.

I remember she smiled and asked what would happen if the third book never came out. And I, high on my teenage horse, told her that it had to come out. Things had to be fair. Karma was a bitch, she was sharpening her scythe, and there would be a harvest.

I graduated, went to college, grew up, and learned that life wasn't always fair. Sometimes there was no third book. No resolution no matter how many times you reread or how hard you wished for it. It gnawed at me. I just couldn't let it go.

In fact, thinking back on it, those books had shaped my path through life. Somewhere between those rereads, I must've subconsciously decided that I would make sure the nightmare unfolding in Rellas wouldn't repeat itself in our world. That's why I'd started out in criminal justice. Except that I overdosed on reality in my first year by reading too much about the terrible things human beings did to each other. I realized that it was smothering me, so I chickened out and switched to political science. Teenage me thought Rellas was as dark as things could get. Post-criminal-justice me knew better.

Lasa's ledgers were as bad as the worst of my real-world crime reading. They were made of human suffering. Pages and pages filled with matter-of-fact stories about children abused, sold, and butchered in secret.

But if Derog was still alive and I had somehow stolen those ledgers, I could have taken them to the Justice Chamber, and the royal prosecutors would have ripped the slavers apart. Derog knew this. He paid his bribes and hid his dirty dealings by writing in code, pretending to be a legitimate businessman, and paying his taxes on time. He didn't do flashy spending. He didn't draw attention to himself. He didn't parade around in black, red, and gold with a sour pout on his face because people didn't jump to do his bidding fast enough.

No, for all the heinous shit Derog had done, when compared to Ulmar Hreban, he was definitely small-time.

Someone rapped their knuckles on the doorframe. I turned in my chair. Reynald stood in the open doorway.

"Come in."

He came in and sat in a chair, throwing one leg over the other. He looked fresher somehow. Like a man who, after enduring restless nights for weeks, had finally slept till morning.

"Rough reading." He nodded at Lasa's ledgers stacked on my desk.

"Like swimming through a sewer."

"Is there anything in there about Matheo?"

I passed him a ledger with a knife in it. I'd needed a bookmark and that was the only thing handy.

He took the knife out, looked at it for a moment, set it on my desk, and read the entry. It was very short. *One puppy, fourteen weeks, mother didn't survive. Shipped to a southern buyer.* Code for "We stole a fourteen-year-old boy. We killed his mother. We shipped him south."

Reynald raised his gaze. "Puppy?"

"Derog paid taxes. He pretended to be a livestock trader. Dogs and cattle."

"What does this mean?" He pointed to a small star by the entry.

"Special request. He didn't grab your son at random. Someone paid him to do it. There is another thing. If you look at the other entries, the buyers are identified by initials or code names. 'Southern buyer' doesn't appear again anywhere. Why southern buyer? Why so generic?"

"Someone targeted Matheo," Reynald said.

"Do you have any enemies I don't know about? Can you think of anyone?"

He shook his head. "All of my enemies are dead. No, it has to be Silveren."

Silveren was the Lord Commander of the Redeemer Knights. The books didn't spend much time on him. He was fanatically devoted to the Order of the Redeemer and would do just about anything to help it thrive. When Hreban rose to power, Silveren put the military might of the Redeemer Knights behind him, hitching his wagon to the only horse willing to help him draw ahead.

The entire Order of the Redeemer consisted of people who had done something so screwed up that they were willing to risk their lives to atone for it. They were capable of terrible things, and for some of them it didn't take much to cross that threshold a second time. Their leader was a ruthless, stone-cold killer. Hreban waved the banner, but Silveren carried the sword.

"You think Silveren was Derog's southern buyer?"

Reynald nodded. "My son has the gift of farseeing. Any knightage would want him."

He wasn't wrong. In the 1970s, both the CIA and the USSR became obsessed with psychics and actively recruited people who claimed to be capable of remote viewing—perceiving distant objects and locations in real time with their minds. Matheo was the real thing. He didn't see the past or the future, he saw the present, and his visions were brief but clear. It made him the perfect scout. He could catch glimpses of the enemy commander's map in their tent from miles away or spy on a conversation that happened in a secure room in another end of the city. The Redeemers would hold on to him with every tooth and claw.

"The Redeemers are desperate for talented recruits," Reynald continued. "I think Silveren approached Derog and paid him to steal Matheo. Then Derog sent my son, escorted by a couple of his less valuable lowlifes, to a prearranged spot, where the Redeemer Knights ambushed them, killed the witnesses, and 'rescued' Matheo. If any questions arise, the only thing the Redeemer Knights are guilty of is saving a child from some slavers."

"If you're right, Silveren must view Matheo as a double-edged sword. Matheo claims that he lost his memory, but there is no way to verify that. For all Silveren knows, Matheo remembers everything. If he is allowed to escape the Redeemer Tower and this matter is investigated, he might link Derog and Silveren, and Silveren wouldn't want that."

Reynald's face was grim. "Yes. We must be certain that we can pry him free. If we show our hand too soon, Silveren might kill Matheo rather than let him go. I don't want my son to suddenly suffer a fatal fall from a horse or have a 'regrettable training accident.'"

He fell silent. We sat quietly for a while.

The books didn't do Reynald justice. He wasn't a stunningly handsome man like Solentine or the guy in the Garden, but there was something about him, something compelling and forceful that dragged your attention to him. If you put him in a room full of men, I'd instantly zero in on him, and I wouldn't be the only one.

Right now, he sat completely relaxed. He was in a house he had taken away from a gang of slavers, with eleven corpses in the basement, in the middle of a very dangerous city, in the company of a woman who had mysteriously come back from the dead, and absolutely none of it bothered him.

He hadn't looked like this back in the basement. He'd looked like a demon, and he had kept cutting grown men down like it was their first day with a sword.

Reynald could turn on me at any second, and the demon would return and cut me down. But right now, it didn't feel like he would, so instead of being scared, I felt . . . safe. Probably for the first time since I crawled out of that muddy ditch. It was almost addicting.

Reynald stirred. "I owe you protection for your meeting."

And had I known we would get a fortress of a house at the end of this adventure, I wouldn't have gone to the Shears in the first place. But then I wouldn't have contacted Reynald or saved the kids either.

"Thank you. I will need it."

"What are you planning to do with the children?" he asked.

I picked up Lasa's latest ledger and tossed it to him.

"The three younger girls were 'quietly obtained,' meaning kidnapped from the neighboring villages and towns. The locations of the 'breeders' are listed. We can take them home and their parents will be overjoyed to get them back."

Reynald would be overjoyed to get his son back. I wished so badly there was something I could do to spring Matheo out of the Tower.

"I will help you with this," he said.

"Thank you."

"What about the other two?"

"Kaiden has nowhere to go." I flipped through the right ledger and passed it to him.

"One puppy, twelve weeks, local breeder, breeders no longer available, sold by the trainer, requires a course in obedience." Reynald frowned.

"A twelve-year-old orphan from Kair Toren sold by whoever he was apprenticed to."

Reynald's gaze darkened.

"My plan is to keep him with me until I figure out something better," I said.

He would be a handful, but he was my handful now. I was responsible for him. I wouldn't toss him out in the street or pawn him off on someone else.

"What about Clover?"

I sighed. "It's on the next page."

Clover's entry was short. It said, "Puppy, seventeen weeks, trained as LM by KR, not intact, damaged, extremely poor condition, recommend disposal."

Reynald looked at me.

"Someone dumped Clover on Derog's doorstep half dead. Her condition was so bad that Lasa actually argued for letting her die. For some reason Derog kept her alive."

Only Derog could overrule Lasa.

"She's been here for almost two months. You can still see the bruises on her face."

"What about LM and KR?"

I shook my head. "I don't know. She doesn't seem like a noble or a merchant's daughter. I think she might have been employed by a wealthy family."

The way she'd been standing when Derog asked her about Kaiden was practiced and demure.

I could tell by Reynald's expression that he understood what was left unsaid. Whoever had employed Clover had punished her and then sold her to Derog. This went beyond simple theft, incompetence, or household politics. This was rage.

"I will help her in any way I can," I said.

These two children had gone through more suffering in their short lives than some people endured during their entire lifetime. And the worst part of it was, I knew it was real.

I'd read those books cover to cover, and there was no mention of Clover or Kaiden, yet here they were. They existed just like the other random people I had met: the bakers, the inn clerks, the landlords, the Garden attendants . . . Each of them had a life, a past, and hopes for the future. They weren't abbreviated characters; they were actual human beings. The amount of detail in the city itself, the people I met, the lives they led, it seemed impossible to have come from one person's mind. It was too much.

Technically, yes, I could've just fallen through some dimensional hole into a pocket world imagined by the author in greater detail than he was able to record. Maybe he was a supergenius and knew the location of every rock and the story of every one of the three hundred thousand residents of Kair Toren.

Except that it didn't feel like a fictional world. It *felt* real. I had been sure of it ever since I looked into Reynald's eyes on the roof terrace. The books might have described and recorded the events that happened here, but this was its own separate reality. It existed independently of the fictional series, and it was headed for a cliff at breakneck speed.

Several months from now, Hreban would manufacture suffering on a mass scale. He would do it out in the open, without fear of retribution. There would be no Justice Chamber to stop him because he would be running it. Nobody would escape unscathed.

Thinking about it made my stomach churn. What would happen to Reynald and the kids? True, I'd helped them for now, but it wouldn't last. Their lives would turn into nightmares, and I was the only one who knew about it. I hadn't saved them. I'd just postponed the torment. I'd given them hope, and then Hreban would set their world on fire.

What was the point of being thrown into this world and watching it all burn?

"Will you try to get Matheo out of the Tower?" I asked.

Reynald stirred. "Yes. He is my son. I promised my wife . . ."

"At her grave. I know."

He looked at me and shook his head. "What will you do after we return the children?"

"I'm going to destroy Ulmar Hreban."

The moment my mouth shaped the words, something changed. It felt right, as if I had blundered out of the woods onto a path. Almost like a bell tolled somewhere.

Reynald raised his dark eyebrows. "You're going to destroy the richest man in Rellas? The head of a Great Family?"

"Yes."

"Why?"

"Because I will not let Rellas burn."

Reynald and Matheo, Clover and Kaiden, Galiene and her daughter, Solentine, the bakers, the nameless handpie seller, I would give them all a different future.

Just wait, Ulmar. You thought you could murder people left and right as if they didn't matter. I will fix you right up. Fucking watch me.

Reynald pondered me. "How are you planning to go about it?"

"I don't know yet. I have six months to figure it out."

"Not a lot of time."

"You're right. Unfortunately, your timeline to rescue your son is even shorter . . ."

Reynald was a careful man. Cautious, even. But he was also a grief-stricken father desperate to find his son. He'd been trying for months and gotten nowhere, and he was at the end of his patience. I saw a hint of that when he was on that roof, thinking about storming the Redeemer Tower.

There was an excellent chance that if I told him exactly what would happen, he would lose his shit and go on a killing spree, which would likely end with his head separated from his body. The fictional Rellas had killed him, and I didn't want to take a chance that the real Rellas would want to do the same. I had to keep things vague.

"You have about five months at most. Less than that actually. More like four and a half, before the end of the High Court Session. You have to pry Matheo out of the Tower before the first assassination, because after that it will be very difficult."

Impossible. It would be impossible.

"And Reynald, if you fail, you must leave the city before the Winter Hunt. I don't care how angry you are. If you value your life at all, you must leave. Once the second murder happens, that entire mess of Hreban and the Redeemers spins out of control and sets Kair Toren on fire . . ."

Reynald rose from his chair and stared at me.

"What?"

"Maggie," he said, his voice quiet. "Can you see the future?"

Chapter 10

Crap. Crap, crap, crap.

I'd said too much. I'd concentrated so hard on not saying anything that would immediately set him off, that I had put way too much out there. Damn it.

Too late to back out now. Even if I did make something up, he wouldn't believe me. He was focused on me like a wolf who had spotted a lame bunny.

"Not exactly. I know a version of it."

"Tell me."

I didn't want to go there.

"Tell me what's coming. Please."

"A civil war and everything that brings. Slaughter, atrocities, famine. A complete breakdown of society, aided by the invasion of the Crimson Empire and a plague. It begins with three powerful people being murdered one after another, and things really fall apart after the second murder, the assassination of the crown prince. King Sauven isn't in his right mind already. After losing his eldest son, he becomes unhinged."

And that was just the start of it.

"During the investigation into that assassination, the capital burns for three days. They will call it the Night of a Thousand Fires. Rellas fractures as the Eight Families revolt and start clawing at each other, trying to get to the throne and pull the Savarics off it. Then it's tragedy after tragedy. Nobody is spared. Even the countryside endures atrocities. The king's forces march to meet the rebels and come across a small town called Applegrove. The town refuses to open its gates. The commander in charge takes Applegrove and decimates the male population. Every tenth male, no matter their age, is put to the sword. They spare no one, not even babies. The river by the town runs red with blood . . ."

The look in Reynald's eyes made me stop.

"Too much?" I asked.

"Do I die before I rescue my son?"

Danger, danger . . .

"Look, it's probably better not to know."

"Tell me," he growled.

"Yes." Technically not true, but true in spirit.

Reynald closed his eyes for a long moment, then opened them. "How do I die?"

"During the Night of a Thousand Fires, a woman you don't know tries to run away from a group of pikemen chasing her. You interfere, and they impale you. You lose the use of your legs but survive for another three months as a beggar on the streets, until a random scrounger slits your throat for the few coins you had managed to gather that day."

He stared at me.

"I'm sorry," I said and meant it.

"Clover?"

"I don't know. Some people have big parts to play, some small. I don't know what happens to her and Kaiden."

The blademaster sank into his chair.

The silence lay like a brick between us.

"How does it end?" he asked.

"It's a mystery."

The second book stopped with the civil war still raging and the invasion by the Crimson Empire going full force.

"How does Hreban fit into this?"

"I suspect he is the architect of this mess." I had suspected it since finishing the first book. "I don't know exactly how he brought this about, but while other Great Families are shocked and reeling, he jumps on a chance to seize authority."

"As if he were expecting the opportunity to present itself," Reynald said.

I nodded. "Hreban craves power. He thinks he is entitled to it. Yesterday morning I was walking through the city . . ."

I told him about the thief. Every gory detail was branded in my mind, and it spilled out of me like a geyser.

"He calls it *the contemplation*. He doesn't see people as people, he sees them as tools he can use. In his view, a faulty human tool should be discarded, but not before they fully understand the depth of their failure. That's why he partially cauterizes their wounds—to prolong the suffering. He wants them to realize the errors that led to their end and have time *to contemplate* . . ."

The expression on Reynald's face cut me off. It was hard, cold, and merciless, as if a different man suddenly sat in his place. A dangerous man who'd made up his mind and wouldn't be deterred. I almost scooted back in my chair.

"Is this something he does often?"

I sighed. "Not yet, but he will. After the second assassination, Sauven grants him unchecked power."

"To Ulmar Hreban?" Reynald's eyebrows rose slightly.

"Yes. Hreban is the one who burns the capital, he is the one who butchers

Applegrove, and after he does all that, he starts mass executions. He lines the King's Way with prisoners in *contemplation*. Fifty people per batch. They die slowly, while the city watches, and when they pass on, he brings more out. Around-the-clock executions for a week."

There was a demon sitting in the chair in my office, and he was contemplating murder.

"It's not that simple," I told him. "Right now, the only thing Hreban is guilty of is killing the thief."

"That's enough for me," Reynald said.

"You and I are on the same page. Hreban perpetrated torture and murder. He should be brought to justice. But killing him now would just postpone the inevitable. People like him rise to power not because they are incredibly capable but because the situation is ripe for it. Hreban murdered that boy and dumped his body to test Kair Toren. If eliminating Hreban could solve this problem, the city would've roared in outrage. Instead they let him get away with it."

Reynald's expression turned calculating. "Rellas has become accustomed to the Great Families wielding unchecked power."

"Yes. And the higher he rises, the less accountable he becomes. Power attracts supporters. After Hreban receives the royal mandate, he reaches out to the Order of the Redeemer. Silveren has misgivings but in the end he sees a way to elevate his order above the Defenders and the Conquerors. The Redeemers become Hreban's enforcers."

"You're telling me that a holy order willingly chooses to support Ulmar Hreban? The man despised by the entire knighthood?"

"Yes. By that point enough things happen to throw the other two knight orders off-balance. They leave Kair Toren, and Silveren jumps on that opportunity. With knights at his back, Hreban is unstoppable. Competing merchant guilds who wouldn't do business with him enter losing deals to curry favor. Councilors who denounced him crawl to his house bearing gifts to save themselves. In the end, nobody can keep him in check."

"All the more reason to remove him now."

"But even now, before any of this happens, Hreban is likely not alone. He must've made alliances and bargains. If you kill him, whoever is working with him will simply take his place and continue."

And Reynald and the kids would still be in danger. The nightmare would still come to life.

I shook my head. "No, this will be complicated. I can't just eliminate Hreban. I have to dismantle him while the entire kingdom watches. He thinks he is untouchable. I will reach out and touch him. I know his secrets. I'll drag all his dirty laundry out into the light for everyone to see. It will take time, money, people . . ." And I didn't have any of that.

He leaned forward over my desk. "I will do this with you."

"No."

He gave me that Reynald look, the same one he had treated me to when I announced I would sell myself to Derog.

"I'm capable—"

"Three hours after we met, you sold yourself into slavery and then died."

Well, yes, it sounded bad when he put it that way.

"You need help. You need me to keep you alive."

"You have done enough for Rellas," I told him. "You served the country for twenty years. You fought and bled for the kingdom. You deserve to rescue your son and go far away from here, to live a calm, safe life. Matheo needs a living father."

"I'm a knight," Reynald said. Steel vibrated in his voice. "I swore an oath to defend my country. A kingdom isn't land or cities, it is people. If what you say is true, we are on the threshold of great suffering. I will do whatever it takes to shut that door."

"No. There will be consequences."

"We will deal with the consequences."

I wasn't explaining it very well, and the danger he radiated made it harder to think.

"I've already meddled to save someone, and then you and I came here and killed Derog and his crew. Now an entire sequence of events won't happen, and I don't know what will happen in its place. I only know what was supposed to happen. I may have made things worse."

"I doubt it," Reynald said.

"Our actions will alter the future in unpredictable ways. What if we stop the assassination of the crown prince and King Sauven is assassinated instead? What if your son is blamed for it and dragged through the streets chained to a horse? What if you die? What if Clover dies? You won't come back to life like I do."

Here is a giant sack of what ifs, *deal with it.*

"I have six brothers," Clover said from the doorway.

I turned. She stood on the threshold, her face pale, her body rigid. Oh great. "How long have you been there?"

"Since I asked you if you could see the future," Reynald said.

"And you didn't mention it?"

"She has a right to know."

I raised my hands. *Really?*

"While we are on the subject." Reynald looked past me at the open door to my bedroom. "Come out."

I turned in my chair.

Kaiden crawled out from under my bed on all fours.

You've got to be kidding me. "Kaiden! What are you doing hiding under the bed?"

"I heard you crying. I thought something bad happened." He stared at Reynald. "How did you know I was there?"

"I heard you," Reynald said.

"I was very quiet!"

"Quiet enough for them. Not quiet enough for me."

Kaiden sat on the floor, his face stunned.

"You said every tenth man in Applegrove will be put to the sword," Clover said. "I was born in Applegrove. My parents are there. My grandparents and my brothers, our whole family is there. I don't want any of them to die."

"You may want to convince them to move," I told her.

"Where would they go? My father is a blacksmith, like his father and his father's father. Our family has lived in Applegrove for generations. You can't just pick up a forge and carry it off in your pocket. My father isn't going to uproot the family and abandon everything we've built just because I tell him that my new lady knows the future."

I would have to address this *my lady* thing, but right now I had bigger problems.

"If you die—"

"If I have to die so my family is safe, I'll do that," Clover said. "I'm not a knight, but I'm not afraid. I used to be. I used to think that as long as you didn't get involved and kept to yourself, you'd be safe. But that isn't true. I also thought that death was the worst thing that could happen to you. That isn't true either."

"You are a child. I don't think you understand the full gravity of this decision."

"She's seventeen years old," Reynald said.

Right. He was knighted at seventeen after a bloody battle, where he'd cut his way through enemy forces. Different world, different expectations.

"I'm in, too!" Kaiden announced.

Great.

"You—shush." I took a deep breath. "The three of you are asking me to gamble with your lives. Think about the people involved. These are the Eight Families. All of them are horrible bastards. I saw Ramond vi Everard once. I didn't even get a good look at his face, and he scared me half to death."

Reynald blinked. Everard's name always made an impression. He was the scary bastard all other scary bastards were afraid of. I had to strike while the iron was hot.

"The Sleepless Duke divides the world into friends and foes. You either obey him, or you are against him, and if you oppose him, he will kill you, your family, your neighbors, your pets, and just to be thorough he will burn your house and salt your fields. He solves every problem with violence, and if that doesn't work, he applies more violence. He is just one of the people who will be drawn into this mess up to their eyeballs."

Clover looked worried. Kaiden looked undeterred, but he was barely twelve.

I met Reynald's gaze. "You may have to cross blades with Everard. Think about it."

In a fight between Everard and Reynald, Reynald would lose, and he knew it. It would be an amazing fight, but Everard had the Fatefire.

Reynald's light eyes turned resolute. "Thank you for your care for me and my son. However, I'm not the kind of man who runs and hides from his responsibility. I will not teach my son to take the coward's way out."

His face told me that we were done arguing and I had lost. I looked at Clover.

Clover raised her chin. A determined spark lit up her blue eyes. "Do either of you know how to run a household? Where to purchase supplies and at what prices, which traders are reputable, how to balance a budget?"

"No," I said.

Reynald shook his head. His lips curved in a small smile.

"I know the prices, so we won't get swindled. I know the right traders, I know medicine, I know etiquette, I know how to file the right forms with the government."

She had a point.

"If we do this, Maggie will need to look like a lady. I'm proficient in hair, cosmetics, and attire. I can dress you in the latest fashion, so you will present the impression you want to the world. You have a huge house and no idea how to take care of it. You can't even do your hair properly. You need help."

I opened my mouth. She didn't let me get the words out.

"Maggie will be the head of the household, Reynald will be head of the household guard, and I will be the steward maid. I'll be staying here. I won't let my brothers die. The Hreban Family will not take anything else from me. And I owe Reynald and you a debt for saving us. I pay my debts. I will help save Matheo and destroy Ulmar Hreban. This is settled. Come, Kaiden."

For once Kaiden didn't argue. He jumped to his feet and followed her out.

Okay then. I looked at Reynald.

"You heard her. It's settled," he said.

The hell it was.

"I will do this with or without you, Maggie," Reynald said. "I need to know if you have my back. If you don't help me, I'll have to change the future myself, and I have no idea what happens next. In or out?"

He'd remembered what I told him in the Knight Vanquisher Plaza almost word for word. Wow.

His lips curved.

"What about Matheo?"

"My son is safe for now. He will wait for me."

"Are you sure?"

"I can bear to be separated from him for a few more months if it means he will grow up in a peaceful kingdom. Let me join you. Help me save my son from a future of suffering."

I gave up. "Then I am in."

"Good." He stood up. "I'm going to drop off the bodies. I'll be back in a couple of hours."

I stood up, too. "I'll help you."

"It will be grisly work."

"I said I was in. I'll manage."

I took a deep breath and followed him down the stairs, to a basement full of corpses we needed to load onto the boat.

<hr />

Dead bodies were heavy as hell.

I knew this. It was one of those academic facts you learned from reading, never expecting to encounter it in real life, until you had to drag eleven corpses about a hundred feet through a stone passageway and then carry them over a grassy bank to a boat in the middle of the night.

In the fantasy books filling my shelves, heroes slung limp humans over their shoulders with a manly growl and then hauled them like they weighed nothing. The level of bullshit involved was criminal. Reynald was a lot stronger than me, and he grunted, strained, and took frequent breaks.

Finally, all the corpses were in. Reynald paused on the dock and held his hand out. I took it—it was rock steady—and he carefully helped me into the boat. He put his hand on the mooring line and stomped twice on the dock boards.

I glanced at him.

"For luck," he said. "It's tradition."

This world or ours, sailors were superstitious everywhere.

Reynald freed the mooring line, climbed into the boat, and started tying and untying various ropes. The sail caught the wind, unfurled, and the boat slipped into the current, still slightly rough from the recent rain. Reynald secured the lines and moved to the big wooden rudder at the stern, about a foot from where I sat on my bench. The corpses, trussed up in canvas, lay on the bottom of the boat like cordwood.

We sat silently, watching the estates of Anchor Drop slide by, darker shadows in the night, marked by an occasional lantern. The sky above us was smudged with clouds.

When Reynald told me he'd bought a boat, I defaulted to one of those small fishing boats people towed behind their trucks all over Texas highways as soon as the summer heat started. Which was ridiculous, but that was where my brain went. What Reynald had purchased was nowhere near that.

The boat looked like something ancient Vikings might have taken upriver to raid the English monasteries. Except it was less of a dragon boat and more of a swan. It sat low in the water, a graceful, sleek wooden vessel about thirty feet long and seven feet wide with a single mast supporting a complex moss-green sail. Its sides curved from the raised stern, swooping low in the middle, then rising again at the bow, crowned with a small figurehead of a horned sea serpent. The serpent sported a mouth of scary teeth, and they weren't wood. Someone had ripped those fangs out of the mouth of an actual marine monster and glued them in. You had to admire the dedication.

The boat sped down the river. We rounded a bend, and the current dumped us into the much wider, calmer Dokkon, the main river of Kair Toren. The cold breeze flung moisture and a hint of salt in my face.

We skirted a wooded island with roofs peeking through the trees, passed a big trader ship with a bloated hull, and then two people in a small fishing boat. They didn't pay us any mind, and I didn't look too closely at what they were doing either.

The river widened. Docks crowded the banks, with wooden ships of all sizes moored for the night. A sea of dark masts and stowed sails rose on both sides. A few more minutes, and the Dokkon carried us out to sea.

The ocean spread before our boat, endless and calm. The clouds melted away, and an enormous sky reigned above, studded with glittering stars. Three moons spilled their light on the water: Prata, a giant silver crescent with gold tiger stripes; Drao, a much smaller ruby-red waning gibbous; and Broe, the smallest of the three, a grass-green, last-quarter moon. The view took my breath away. I smelled the briny salt water, I felt the wind and the steady movement of the boat under my feet, so it had to be real and actually happening. But it was so . . . magical.

We turned left and kept going, farther from the mouth of the river, within the view of the coastline.

Ahead something shimmered in the water like a spill of faint fluorescent paint. Reynald steered for it. The swirls of faint blue and pink drew closer and closer, rippling through the water. The boat slid through them, and I saw the outlines of glowing algae suspended like a floating island over the ink-black depths. Tiny fish with luminescent fins darted through the frilly leaves.

The boat slowed to a leisurely drift.

Reynald let go of the rudder, fiddled with the lines, and sat on the other bench across from me.

"It's lovely," I told him.

He nodded. He seemed lighter, almost carefree. "I've always liked the ocean."

"When did you learn how to sail?" He had been born in the northern highlands, a rough region bordering Selva's mountain range. Once upon a time his people had been sea raiders who invaded Rellas and settled deeper inland, but they'd given up their sea legs a couple of centuries ago.

"During the Corios campaign." His voice was quiet and light. "They had us raiding the coastal forts in small boats, trying to keep the defenders guessing when and where we'd show up."

Corios, meaning the "middle sea," was a landlocked sea about twice the size of Lake Superior. It cleaved the continent in two, separating Rellas in the west from the Crimson Empire in the east, and it was a bad-tempered sea. Its storms sank a lot of ships, to the delight of the marine monsters swimming in its depths.

"The second week in, our captain took an arrow to the chest and went overboard. The wind blew us farther from the coast. We drifted for hours before we figured out how to work the sails. I decided that sailing was something I should know how to do."

"You're a very good sailor," I told him.

He smiled. "Thank you."

It felt like we had stopped moving completely. We just hung there, between the ocean and the sky, watching the trails of three moons shine on the water.

"What are we waiting for?"

"The wind," Reynald said. "We'll need it to pick up before we start."

I didn't mind if the wind didn't pick up for a while. It was so beautiful here, almost romantic. Floating on a starry night across a magical ocean, just me and Reynald . . . And eleven corpses we needed to dispose of. So Kair Toren.

Reynald stirred. "About Hreban . . ."

"Yes?"

"I know a bit about him. He was born rich, like his father, and his grandfather. Generations of wealth."

"*The gift of Mirror Heart is wrapped in gold*," I murmured. It was a line in the first book.

"And misery."

True.

Each of the Eight Families had their own special brand of magic. The Everards had the Fatefire, the Arvels had the Enduring Flame, and the Hrebans had the power of Mirror Heart, meaning they knew exactly what someone was feeling. They could tell when people lied. They knew when their opponent was unsure, desperate, or terrified. It made them excellent judges of character and brought them unimaginable wealth.

From a very young age, Ulmar sensed people's hidden motives. They approached him and his family with smiles on their faces, pretending to be solicitous and loyal, while he soaked in their greed, jealousy, hatred, and derision. It convinced him that he was inherently superior, and that people were fundamentally selfish and needed discipline and punishment to be useful.

"Ulmar is a reflection of what he feels," I said. "He sees people as sheep, a stupid, panicky commodity to be bought and sold. He isn't the sheep dog that protects the flock. He is the shepherd with a big heavy stick."

Taking a tour through Hreban's head killed your will to live. He had forever ruined empath and telepath characters for me.

"The other seven Great Families hold him in contempt," Reynald said.

I had caught some of that in the books, but it was nice to get a first-person account. "Why?"

"Rellas is a kingdom of knights and merchants. There is a reason why knights are listed first. We are surrounded by enemies on all sides. Without the protection of the knights, the merchants would not exist."

"But the Hrebans are not the only non-martial Great Family."

Reynald nodded. "True. However, the other three contribute in their own way. The Yolentas provide steel for weapons, the Jals produce grain for provisions, and the Graives build roads and castles. The Hrebans buy and sell a great many things but produce little. They made their money trading in luxuries and precious metals, and they are proud of it, which is why their crest is awash in gold. Gold is soft and heavy, Maggie. You cannot make a sword out of it."

Also, true. Not that Ulmar hadn't tried. Once he'd decided that he wanted power, Hreban realized that he needed martial achievements. Ten years ago, he got his chance. An impregnable castle had rebelled, and Sauven needed someone to go and sit on it until the rebels saw the error of their ways.

The campaign promised to be long and boring, with minimal casualties and few opportunities to show off, and nobody except Hreban wanted to deal with it. For some bizarre reason, Sauven decided to let him.

Hreban was given two battalions of the King's Army, all seasoned troops to compensate for his inexperience. He marched them to Lerem Castle, and then he hurled them against the walls again and again, in defiance of every military strategy and against the advice of his knights, until the defenders literally ran out of soldiers and arrows. He took the castle in a month, but he lost more than sixty-five percent of his army.

After, when Sauven screamed and threw things at him, Hreban countered that he had saved the kingdom money because none of those casualties would need to be paid and new soldiers could be recruited for less. To Hreban, the loss of experienced, battle-seasoned veterans meant nothing, because in his view, people were expendable and infinitely replaceable. There were always more of them. He would've made an excellent modern CEO.

That campaign made Hreban into a laughingstock among the knighthood. He had never gotten over it.

"If what you told me is true, then the Fool of Lerem Siege suddenly became a master strategist," Reynald said.

"As I said, it's likely he has allies. Someone with a greater vision who is behind him steering his boat."

"Do you know who that is?"

"No." I knew who it wasn't, but that still left plenty of suspects.

He gave me a long, probing look. "There is something you're not telling me."

There was a whole lot I wasn't telling him. "Yes."

"You mentioned there would be three murders. The second is Kiel, the crown prince. Who are the others?"

I really didn't want to have this conversation. *Let me out of this boat.*

"I don't want to tell you."

I should've thought of some clever answer, but instead the truth came out.

Reynald studied my face. "You don't trust me."

"I do trust you. I told you about my magic. I'm alone in this boat with you."

I'd been in his head. Reynald would kill me if I became a threat, but he would never backstab me.

"Then what is it?"

Reynald was a knight kardar, from *kar*, an old word for banner. In battle, he led his own detachment of knights and fighters with junior officers under him. He was used to being in command. He also had serious doubts about my ability to get things done. Oh, he believed I could see the future, but like he said, my first plan had ended with me dying. If I wasn't careful, he would bulldoze right over me, wreck the flow of events beyond repair, and then get himself killed. He knew just enough about the future now to royally screw things up.

I had to earn his trust. I had to demonstrate that my schemes worked, and that I was capable. I had to come up with a brilliant plan . . . and I had nothing.

Making grand pronouncements about bringing Hreban to justice was good and all, but now I had to actually do it, and when I tried to come up with a plan, all I got was a dark emptiness with a faint buzzing sound. The enormity of the stakes paralyzed my poor traumatized brain. If I made a mistake, Reynald and the kids would die and Rellas would collapse. No pressure.

I had to buy some time.

"You're half right," I said slowly. "It is a matter of trust. You don't know me, Reynald. If I told you to do something right now, would you do it?"

"If I understood the reasons behind it and agreed with them."

"Exactly." I nodded. "You wouldn't act just because I told you to."

His eyes narrowed. "So, you're expecting blind obedience?"

This conversation was going off the rails in a hurry.

"Not at all. But I know you. Once you decide on a course of action, you follow through even if it is unwise, like the time you decided to climb into an underground catacomb in Gassargand alone, without telling anyone. You knew there would be a monster waiting for you there, a monster you and three other experienced soldiers had failed to kill the first time around, and you climbed in there anyway."

"It had to be done."

"That's exactly what I'm afraid of. That I will tell you what I know and then you'll decide to do something about it and get yourself killed."

"I'm resilient."

"I know. But in my version of the future, you still died. And unlike me, you didn't come back from it." I sighed.

He pondered me.

The best defense was an effective offense.

"I'm not completely dense, Reynald. I know why you didn't tell me that Clover was standing there or that Kaiden was hiding under the bed. You realized that I cared for the kids, and having both of them there would convince me to lean on you. It's one thing to talk about the kingdom ending and people dying, but it's completely different when two children are standing in front of you, and you know you are their only hope to survive. You have no resources, except for the deadly blademaster in the room willing to lend a hand."

His face shut down.

"I understand why you did it."

He waited, his expression blank.

"You think that I'm your best chance at saving Matheo."

If I was missing back home and not in a coma or just dreaming in my bed while the events here passed before me at a thousand minutes per second, my parents would be frantic. My dad would do anything and everything to find me and bring me home. He would sell his soul to the devil if it would help. I was Reynald's devil, and I was sitting right here.

"I give you my word that I will do everything I can to keep your son alive. You asked to join me, not the other way around. So trust me and be patient. Let me prove to you that my way is the best way."

I tried not to hold my breath. He'd notice.

"Fair enough," he said. "Since we've decided to be straightforward with each other, you're right. You do have a blademaster on your side. I will protect you. No more heroics. No more dramatic dying."

"I'll do my best."

"Good. Then we're on the same page." He nodded. "I like that turn of phrase. It's clever."

I had brought a new idiom to Kair Toren. Heh.

A breeze fanned me. I tasted salt on my lips.

Salt! That was it! That was the thread I could tug on. So many things hinged on it.

But how the hell would I pull that off? Not only it would be dangerous and complicated but if we managed to . . . The mercenaries. Holy crap, what would I do about the mercenaries?

This wouldn't be just altering the flow of events. This would be like hitting it with a hammer. Here I was worrying about Reynald crashing through the timeline like a battering ram, and I was contemplating dropping a meteorite on it.

"I understand your point," Reynald said. "But I do not like being kept in the dark. Do you at least have a direction?"

"Yes." I had a direction, all right. I just wasn't sure we could pay the price.

"Then I will trust you for now. Let's see it through."

The unspoken *but* was loud and clear. If I failed, that would be the end of our alliance. He would strike out on his own, and who knew what sorts of havoc he would wreak.

I had to get my shit together and fast. If we went after the salt, I would have to deliver at all costs.

A breeze stirred my hair.

Reynald rose and grabbed the first corpse by its shoulders wrapped in canvas. "The wind is up."

I picked up the legs, and we heaved the body overboard. It hit the water with a heavy splash. Ten corpses followed, sinking below the surface.

"Won't the bodies float back up when they start to decompose?" I asked. The last thing we needed was for Derog's dead crew to wash ashore with the tide.

"Hold that thought."

He pulled a small barrel from a spot at the front of the boat, unsheathed a knife, and pried the snug lid open. A stench hit me, reeking of rotting fish and something else, something sickening and gross.

I gagged.

Reynald emptied the barrel into the water and tossed it into the ocean. He moved through the boat, fast like he was on solid ground, and pulled a line. The sail unfurled, and our vessel slid across the sea. We turned left, drawing a wide U around the spot where we had dropped the bodies.

Something moved beneath the luminescent ocean as we sped by.

I looked over my shoulder.

A huge triangular fin pierced the surface, trailing a long yellow spike.

Another. A third . . . A massive body broke the surface, half as big as our boat. I caught a glimpse of broad armored jaws, and then it dove under. The ocean behind us churned as if boiling.

"What bodies?" Reynald asked and gave me a wide smile.

Planter 9

It was well after midnight. I sat in my office again and watched the three moons in the night sky in the open window. I had unlocked the shutters and slid the glass aside. Reynald warned me that it was a safety issue, but we were on the third floor. Coming back to the house after that boat ride felt almost stifling. My brain kept tripping and thinking I smelled blood. The brisk night air was so refreshing.

Tomorrow I would clean this house until the last traces of the slavers disappeared. That was my mother's trick. When we moved during my childhood, as my father got transferred from one duty station to the next, my mother would always clean the new apartment or house before we moved in. She claimed that once you cleaned a place, you made it your own.

I missed my family so much.

The house was quiet, the room filled with soft comfortable light from a couple of lanterns. Clover had stayed up until we came back, brewed "restful" tea, and served it to me without being asked, as if I were some sort of princess.

I picked up the cup and drank from it.

The moons looked back at me from a foreign sky.

I had never thought of myself as a violent person, and yet I had beaten a man to death with a club. I'd killed someone with my own hands and then helped to feed the evidence to a monster fish. And I hadn't done any of those things normal people were supposed to do after they resorted to violence. I hadn't cried. I hadn't gotten sick. I didn't feel a lot of guilt.

And I didn't regret it. I would do it again. Because tonight five children slept safely in their beds without fear of being abused. This house would never again be used to steal kids from their parents and then sell them to the highest bidder. Maybe I just thought I was a nonviolent person because in my old life nobody had ever backed me into a corner with a knife to my throat.

This was a different world, and it played by different rules. I didn't have the safety net of social services and law and order to back me up. There was no 911 to dial. Funny how you take things for granted until they are gone.

If I went through with my plan to stop Hreban, I would likely die again, no matter how determined Reynald was to keep me alive. Worse, I would have to kill again. And I would have to somehow keep Reynald, Clover, and Kaiden safe.

It scared me so much, I shivered. If I was one of those isekai heroines I'd read about, by now I would be well on my way to building an empire by inventing popcorn or nail polish, or purging the blight with my holy powers, or taking control of a village of goblins and earning their undying loyalty. Instead, I was here, trying to cobble together a half-assed plan. I felt stupid and scared. I was in so over my head, it wasn't even funny. Keeping it together through today was my limit.

I would have to be very careful not to get too arrogant. When I woke up in the Garden, I thought I could just nudge a few things but keep the flow of the events mostly the same. That was hubris. I was too far in now and the changes I brought were irreversible. Just because I knew one version of Kair Toren's future didn't mean I could accurately predict what any one of the people involved would do in the next moment. We would need informants, which meant we would need money . . .

Solentine slipped through the window and landed soundlessly on the floor. He was dressed in gray and black from head to toe. A soft doublet hugged his body, leaving the sleeves of a black shirt bare. Black gloves, black boots, black sash, black belt with an assortment of knives, and a gray hood.

"Hello there, Ezio," I said. "Imagine meeting you here. Killed any Templars lately?"

"I understood none of that." He leaned against the windowsill.

Of course not. References to twenty-first-century video games were solely for my own amusement.

He tilted his head and studied the room. This whole thing with him framed in the window in that sinister getup with the moons above him was unbelievably cool. If I didn't know he was a horrible bastard who could murder me in less than a second, I would have fainted in my chair from the sheer badassery of it.

"Love what you're doing with the place."

"Thanks." If I screamed, Reynald would come running, but it would be too late.

"What have you done with the corpses?"

Had the Shears seen us dump the bodies? I needed to say just the right thing . . . "I could tell you, but I have to charge."

Ha! Oh wait, he wouldn't get that either.

Solentine looked at me. "You're a mystery, Maggie."

And he already knew my name.

"You speak like a native of Kair Toren, but nobody remembers you. You have no friends, no lovers, no parents, or employers. Nobody recalls you entering the city. You simply appeared as if by magic."

You have no idea how right you are.

I smiled. It seemed better than some half-baked witty comeback.

"I gather you've decided to stay?" he said.

"For a while."

"Good. I enjoy mysteries."

He tossed me a small purse. I caught it. It was light. Cheapskate.

"Your payment. We're even."

"Then our business is concluded."

Solentine smiled. The hair on the back of my neck stood right up.

"Oh no. I have a feeling we will be seeing a lot of each other in the future. Close the window after I leave, Maggie. There's no end of unsavory characters out there."

He leaped out into the darkness.

Okay. That was the second-coolest thing I had ever seen in real life. Everard riding in was the first. And as soon as my hands stopped shaking, I would shut that damn window.

I pulled the strings of the purse open. Judging by the size and weight, he'd paid me less than ten nomas. You'd think the life of his agent would be worth more. Oh well. Every little bit helped.

I emptied the purse onto the desk. Six gold coins clinked and shone in the lantern's light. A small fortune. Solentine, you beautiful bastard.

Things were looking up.

PART II

BARREL OF SALT

Chapter 11

Clover's brunch was a religious experience. She'd made eggs and folded crepes that had some sort of cottage-like cheese in them and served them with smoked fish, green jam, fragrant tea, and slices of salted meat that looked but didn't taste like ham. The jam was sweet, tart, and refreshing, and I could've eaten my weight in that smoked fish.

I dipped a slice of freshly baked bread into my perfect over-easy egg, took a bite, and savored it.

Mmmm.

We sat in the kitchen around one end of a huge wooden table. Clover and I had scrubbed this space to within an inch of its life. In fact, we'd scrubbed so hard, we had probably made the room bigger by rubbing a layer off the walls and the floor, but we both wanted to eradicate any trace of the slavers. We didn't discuss it, we just did it in silent agreement.

The kitchen looked like an entirely different room now. We had washed the grime off the walls, revealing the pale stone underneath, and exorcised the small piles of sticky debris accumulated in every nook and cranny of the floor. The massive table, smoothed from years of use, was free of food stains and old spills. The morning sun flooded through the open window, giving us a beautiful view of the courtyard and the wine tree.

This morning, I woke up, looked outside my window, and saw Reynald practicing swordsmanship in the yard. He wore a simple loose tunic, pants, and boots, and he spun and moved like a whirlwind, slicing, stabbing, slashing, and thrusting, shifting flawlessly from attack to defense. He held his sword as if he were fused with it. It was just a sword, but in his hand, it became a dozen different weapons. Sometimes it thrust like a rigid spear; at others it seemed to flow, flexible like a whip, slicing though unseen opponents; and then it became an axe, cracking invisible skulls with a single blow.

There was a line in *The Thieves of the North* I loved. It said, *"And the fighters clashed, writing poetry with motion and blade."* That's what it was. Poetry. The way he moved was oddly beautiful and almost superhuman. Like watching an Olympic gymnast launch into an impossibly high jump, spin through the air, and perfectly stick his landing. It was mesmerizing.

And hot. The books had neglected to mention that part. Ninety-nine percent of the time, Reynald was a study in control—calm, collected, even cold. But you knew there was heat and violence inside, and there it was, burning everything in its path. I'd stood there, just outside of his view, and watched the demon from the basement until he finished.

Now he was sitting across the table, chewing his crêpe, looking perfectly ordinary and relaxed. The scary, menacing Reynald from last night was gone. The graceful, powerful Reynald from this morning was gone, too. You wouldn't even suspect that he could kill all of us in a blink.

Next to him, Kaiden was on his third helping. We'd fed the younger girls earlier. They were playing in the courtyard now. It would take time to get over Derog's basement, but right now, their bellies were full, their hair was brushed, and they were having fun chasing each other around the wine tree.

"The food is delicious," I told Clover. "Thank you."

She gave me a shy smile. "You're welcome."

"Clover, you're the best." Kaiden stuffed another chunk of crêpe into his mouth.

That reminded me. "You don't have to keep using that name," I said to her gently. "You can go back to what your parents called you, if you would like."

Clover's mouth turned into a hard, firm line. I'd guessed right. Clover used to be a maid.

"Clover isn't your name?" Reynald asked.

"Some noble households in Kair Toren have a custom of renaming their maids," I told him. "Usually there is a theme. Months of the year, constellations, colors . . ."

"Flowers," Clover said.

Reynald stopped chewing.

"It's a way of dehumanizing," I said. "They erase your past identity by giving you a new name. Whatever you were before doesn't matter. Now you are Jade, maid of the Hreban Household."

"It would be Sapphire, not Jade," Clover corrected. "Lady Hreban names her maids after gems and semiprecious stones, but she doesn't like the color green."

"You're right," I told her. I had almost forgotten that part.

"Why?" Kaiden asked.

"Green is the primary color of Duke Everard's crest," I told him. "When the Sleepless Duke fights on the battlefield, he summons bright green Fatefire that coats his blade. He strides through the battle in his black armor, and his Fatefire burns so hot that it kills everyone around him."

Reynald rolled his eyes. "It just means he isn't man enough to trust in his blade."

Unlike Everard, Reynald had no magic. I sniffed the air. "Is that jealousy I smell?"

He gave me a dark look.

"Why doesn't she like Everard?" Kaiden asked.

I turned back to Kaiden. "When Lady Hreban was twelve, her father took her to the Duke and Duchess of Selva, the current Sleepless Duke's parents. He wanted to form an alliance through betrothal. The Duchess talked to the future Lady Hreban for half an hour and announced that she didn't have the right temperament to be her daughter-in-law."

"Is she bad tempered?" Kaiden asked.

"She's mean and arrogant," I told him. "Her parents are even meaner and more arrogant, so they berated her for weeks over it. She has never gotten over that humiliation. Everard is out of favor because the king is scared of him, but he is still very powerful. She can't openly hate him, so she chooses to hate the color of his magic instead."

I went back to eating my food.

"Why is the king scared of Everard?" Kaiden asked.

A loaded question.

"Decades ago, when Sauven was a little shit of seventeen, he thought he could do anything he liked," Reynald said. "He rampaged through Kair Toren every night, plowing his way through the brothels and drowning in wine. If a man looked at him wrong, he killed him. If he wanted a woman, he took her. He was the treasured crown prince, the favorite child, and nobody dared to call him on it."

It helped that Sauven had traveled around with a pack of hangers-on eager to do his bidding, and his squad would attack anyone who even coughed in his direction.

"Every year, the royal family hosts the Winter Hunt," Reynald continued. "The Eight Families always attend. That year, Lorest and Katorna vi Everard came down from the Selva Dukedom with their mother."

"Lorest was the current Sleepless Duke's father," I explained. "And Katorna is his aunt. Back then they were fifteen and fourteen."

"Sauven saw Katorna and decided he wanted her, so he put his hands on her," Reynald said. "There was a struggle. She punched Sauven hard enough to blacken his eye."

"She also kicked his legs out from under him," I added. "He was embarrassed."

I hadn't expected Reynald to know that story. It wasn't something people talked about.

"Sauven demanded that she be given to him to be punished as he saw fit," Reynald said. "Lorest told him that Katorna belonged to the Selva Dukedom. In the absence of his father, Lorest was the voice of Selva, and it was his duty to protect its people, so Sauven would need to go through him to get to her."

He wasn't explaining the context well. I turned to Kaiden. "Do you know why people call the Selva Dukedom the shield of Rellas?"

"Um . . ." Kaiden blinked.

"Because it shields us from the nations of the northwest and the Crimson Empire," Clover said.

"Exactly." I nodded. "Selva lies in the north, bordered by mountain ranges on both sides. It protects the kingdom from foreign invasions, and it's a big territory, one-fifth of Rellas's lands. The Everards have ruled it for centuries. Their armies are powerful and skilled, and their magic is devastating on the battlefield. The Savaric royal family can't afford to openly offend them. When Sauven assaulted Katorna, it wasn't just him violating her personal boundaries. It became Savaric versus Everard and Rellas versus Selva."

Reynald speared another small slice of salted not-ham and cut it with surgical precision on his plate. "If Sauven had just apologized, the whole matter could've been dismissed as a child's squabble. But Sauven was used to doing whatever he wanted. Lorest had put his hand on his sword. He was fifteen years old, and at the time he was short and thin. Sauven was seventeen, almost a head taller, and much bigger. He decided he liked those odds. Sauven's father, the king, saw where it was headed and ordered Sauven to sit down."

"Did he?" Kaiden asked.

"No. He drew his sword." Reynald's smile was devoid of humor. "Which turned the whole mess into a formal challenge."

Formal challenges were the bedrock of Rellas's martial culture. No matter how secure the Savarics were on their throne, going against that tradition would knock them right off it.

Kaiden leaned forward. "What happened?"

Reynald took a swallow of his drink. "The challenge was accepted. Lorest hit Sauven in the jaw and knocked him to the ground. While Sauven was trying to find his feet, Lorest ignited his Fatefire and drew a circle around them with his sword. When Sauven staggered up, he found himself in a ring of green flames nobody could cross. And then Lorest beat the shit out of him, while everyone watched."

"Sauven was bedridden for over a month," I added. "A part of his soul died in that circle. Until that point, he'd thought he was untouchable. He was a prince, and everyone was his father's subject. That day he learned that he was mortal and that some people do not bend to the throne of Rellas. He was never the same after that."

"His hatred of the Everards is like a pet viper he keeps in his heart," Reynald said. "Once in a while it bites him, and he does witless things to dull the pain."

Sauven had spent the better part of his life trying to murder Lorest in various schemes. He got his wish in a roundabout way. The Crimson Empire had poisoned

Lorest vi Everard about fourteen years ago and Ramond vi Everard became the new duke at sixteen. When Sauven learned about Lorest dying, he was beside himself with happiness. He had ascended the throne by that point, and he summoned the new duke to Kair Toren, expecting a sixteen-year-old boy he could suppress.

Unfortunately for him, Ramond vi Everard was a carbon copy of his father. He'd ridden into Kair Toren in his black armor, on his vicious Andikan stallion, dismounted before the great staircase leading to Eagle Roost, and shot Fatefire in eight different directions, like the rays of a star, to prove his identity. As the green flames burned and colored Ramond's face, Sauven saw the ghost of his fallen enemy returned to life. He fled into the depths of Eagle Roost, abandoning his court atop that staircase.

"Don't repeat that to anyone," I told Kaiden. "Sauven is unhinged, and Everard is a monster. You don't need to be involved with either."

"I'm not a baby," Kaiden told me.

"I know you're not," I told him. "That's why I trusted you with this conversation."

We ate in silence for a few breaths.

"So, what's your real name?" Kaiden asked Clover.

Clover raised her chin. "It doesn't matter."

"Why?" he asked.

She cut her pancake. "When I was twelve years old, a Maid Mother came to our town and scouted me."

"Clover, are you a lady's maid?"

She nodded.

That's what LM stood for. I knew she had to be a part of a noble household, but I hadn't expected a lady's maid.

Maids had all sorts of jobs. There were laundry maids, kitchen maids, chamber maids, etc., and most of them came from the villages of a noble's estate. They were the closest to the family, and it was essential that they were trustworthy.

A lady's maid was often her closest confidant. She made sure that the lady was properly dressed and put together for every occasion and kept track of social functions and her lady's budget. Ladies' maids required specialized training, and a woman ascended to that position in one of two ways: by apprenticing to a lady's maid and eventually inheriting her job or by going through training with a Maid Mother. Either way, it took years.

Formally educated lady's maids were in high demand and their services weren't cheap. In the hierarchy of the household, they stood near the top, right behind the stewards.

That was why Derog had kept her alive.

"It was a great opportunity," Clover said. "I left my family and came to Kair Toren. For three years, I lived with other girls and studied. I had top marks in everything. My Maid Mother told me that I had a bright future. When my training was finished, I was placed in a household related to a Great Family. There are girls who would kill for that position."

I had a really bad feeling about this.

"For two years I served as the lady's maid to the household's young lady. We were the same age. I was never reprimanded. I was praised, and the lady I served called me her friend. She named me Clover because I had a 'soft and gentle beauty.' I was paid well and sent money home to my family. I didn't make any mistakes. My service was flawless."

Yep, this would not end well.

"Two months ago, she was engaged to the son of an earl. There was a celebration. She celebrated with pastries. He celebrated by raping me."

The three of us froze. Clover kept working on her pancake.

"The servants found me and dragged me before the lady, and then she slapped me until her hand hurt."

Oh god.

"Then she kicked me, and after she got tired, she ordered the servants to kick me. I woke up in the basement of this house."

Clover speared a piece of a pancake with her fork and dabbed it into a small puddle of jam on her plate.

"So it doesn't matter what my name was. The girl who had that name is no longer here. Things that happened to me would've broken her. But I survived. I'm Clover, exactly what they made me. I'll keep the name. It's mine now, and I'll make them regret giving it to me."

She bit into her pancake.

"Which household?" Reynald asked. His voice was terrible.

"Earl Sunner," Clover said. "Ulmar Hreban is my former lady's brother-in-law."

Shit. So that's what she'd meant when she said the Hreban Family wouldn't take anything else from her.

"Why did you stop eating?" Clover asked. "Is the food not delicious?"

The three of us grabbed our forks.

"It's excellent," Reynald said.

"Very delicious," I told her.

"Mhm!" Kaiden said around a mouthful of pancake.

"I'm so glad." Clover gave us a sweet smile.

⊐⊂

Brunch was finished. We lingered around the table, drinking tea.

"We need to hire guards," Reynald said.

Hiring guards seemed like a perfectly reasonable idea, but the mood had gotten heavy, and he was so deadly serious.

"What was it you said? Something about being able to hold this place against a small army?"

The blademaster gave me a look. "I have to sleep, and there will be times I might have to leave the house."

I sipped my tea. "If only we knew someone who was an expert in martial arts and also aware of a lot of veterans in need of a steady paycheck."

Reynald raised his eyebrows at me. "You're bold this morning."

"Clover's delicious brunch restored me to my natural state. Who are you thinking of hiring?" I asked.

"A man named Gort Magnar."

One of my college professors was a retired homicide detective. He used to say that cops did not believe in coincidence. Yesterday I decided to go after the salt. Today, Reynald wanted to hire Gort, who was in the salt subplot up to his eyeballs.

I hadn't even done anything yet. I had only decided to do it, and here was Rellas, shoving the mercenary dilemma at me front and center.

Reynald paused with his cup halfway to his mouth, watching me.

"What?" I asked.

"Waiting for you to tell me some earth-shattering secret about Gort."

The most earth-shattering thing about Gort was that he was devoted to Reynald. He would follow him through fire and death. When Reynald was an officer in the King's Army, Gort was his sergeant-at-arms, his right-hand man. If we brought him and his sons into the house, and I did something Reynald didn't like, one word from the blademaster, and Gort would chop my head off with his axe. And he wouldn't lose a wink of sleep over it. But it didn't even matter. Of the two of them, Reynald was the better killer, and if he really wanted to do away with me, he wouldn't need Gort to do it for him.

And Gort had a grudge against Hreban. The kind of grudge that would put either Gort or Hreban into their grave.

"Anything?" Reynald prompted.

I could tell him what I knew, but it wouldn't hurt to find out how he would present Gort. It could tell me more about where Reynald and I stood.

I shrugged. "I told you. Some people have big parts to play and others small. I don't know everyone's story. What's Gort like?"

"He's a solid soldier. Good with an axe."

I waited.

"He has a leg that never healed right, a souvenir from a hard campaign. It doesn't slow him down unless there is a forced march coming. If you needed a man to defend a bridge, you could put Gort there and tell him 'Nobody crosses this,' and he would die on that bridge with about a hundred bastards that tried to get past him."

That checked out.

"He's a survivor," Reynald continued. "He also badly needs the work. He has a wife and two grown sons, both mercenaries like him. He trained them himself and they have experience, but their last job went sideways."

"What happened?" Clover asked.

"They didn't get paid, and they didn't take it well. Now people are afraid to hire them."

"They didn't take it well" was code for "They almost started a revolt in the lands of the noble who'd hired them, drove a flaming cart through the fortress gates, and nearly kicked him out of his own tower." Because that's how the Magnars rolled.

"Should we be afraid?" I asked.

"No. Gort and his sons follow orders."

At his core, Gort was a professional soldier. The son of a blacksmith in a small village, he had enlisted in the King's Army when he was nineteen. He met Shana, his wife, while he was in that service, and he'd fully intended to do his twenty years, get the Green Purse, and settle down. It was a good, simple plan, but it was shattered on the rock of Ulmar Hreban's ambitions.

Reynald had been transferred by that time, but Gort had been part of Lerem Siege. He'd made it almost all the way, until he took an arrow to the side during one of the final battles, fell off a siege ladder, and broke his leg. His side was fine, but his leg didn't heal right. He was discharged with eighteen years in. No Green Purse, no chance at his own farmstead, nothing. Hreban was the reason why Gort's sons had become mercenaries instead of tradesmen or farmers.

Between his hatred of Hreban and his loyalty to Reynald, Gort was almost tailor-made to be our guard.

Reynald was waiting for my answer.

"Do you trust Gort?" I asked.

"Yes."

"Then hire them. We can afford it. We got paid last night."

Reynald narrowed his eyes. "How?"

"The head of the Shears scaled the wall and dropped the payment off."

"And you're just telling me this now?"

I hid a smile. "Why are you mad? This helps your case. Clearly, we need Gort and his sons to guard us at night."

Kaiden snickered.

"Maggie, if anybody from the Shears comes here again, I need to know about it. Not after it happens but immediately, while it's happening."

"It was the middle of the night. What was I supposed to do, scream?"

"Yes."

He stared at me. I stared back. It was really difficult to hold his gaze.

"Next time I will scream," I promised.

"Thank you." He didn't sound grateful.

"Will you come to my rescue?"

"Yes."

He said it with absolute certainty. If I screamed, he would come running. It felt so . . . reassuring.

"How long will it take you to find Gort?"

"I know where he is. He can be here today. We will likely need a few more people, but Gort and the boys are a solid start. His wife is a good cook, too. She'd be an asset."

He went back to his tea. I let him drink a mouthful.

"If Shana came to work for us as a cook, do you think she would make her famous rudberry pastries?"

"She better," Reynald said. "As much as Gort's been boasting about them for years . . ." He stopped and swore.

I laughed, and the kids laughed with me.

Chapter 12

Reynald hadn't lied. It didn't take Gort long to show up. Reynald had found a small table and a chair in one of the storage rooms and carried them out to the wine tree. Apparently, this was my Magnar family–meeting chair. I sat in it now, with a small box of money in front of me.

Clover was to my left, standing, her hands folded before her, and Reynald was to my right. It was early afternoon and Kaiden had run to the door to let Gort and his sons in.

Gort's name meant *shield* in the Old Tongue. The man looked exactly as you would imagine a human shield would look. He was tall and broad and built like a football defensive end who'd given up cardio to be the strength-training coach: six foot three inches tall, just under three hundred pounds, burly shoulders, huge biceps, thick neck, and a scowl on his face. Naturally pale, he'd acquired a permanent tan over the years. His hair was gray and cut short. He looked to be in his late forties or early fifties.

Two younger versions of him followed. Gort 2.0 was twenty-one years old, while Gort 2.1 was nineteen. They were a couple of inches taller than their father and looked similar enough that people mistook them for twins at first glance.

All three men wore brown pants tucked into sturdy boots, dark short-sleeved tunics over thinner shirts, and thick belts. All three were armed. Gort and Gort 2.0, on his father's right, carried battle-axes on their belts. Gort 2.1, on the left, bucked the trend and went with a sword.

"A human wall is walking toward us," I murmured.

"That's why we're hiring them," Reynald said next to me.

Gort stopped in front of me. "Right then. I'm Gort. This is Willem." He pointed to the son on the right. "That's Lutren." He pointed to the son on his left.

Will and Lute. Up close, telling the brothers apart wasn't that difficult. Will, the oldest, was a little taller and had slightly paler, ash-blond hair. Lute had more gold in his hair, and while Will was calmly menacing, Lute seemed like the type to start some shit just to see what would happen.

According to the books, Gort started in the King's Army at nineteen, did eighteen years, and then he worked for another ten years as a mercenary.

Nineteen plus eighteen, plus ten . . . forty . . . forty-seven.

Gort made sense. He looked around fifty. According to the books, he'd served with Reynald for nine years, before the blademaster was transferred to a different post.

Gort was exactly as described but Reynald wasn't. Their lives weren't dissimilar. Even if I took into account the author's possible biases and assumed Reynald had great genes, he still looked younger and less worn out than he should've been. And when he spoke to me, and the way he smiled that one time in the boat and this morning, he acted younger than a harshly lived thirty-eight. It bugged me. If this was wrong, then I could be wrong about the salt as well.

"This is Lady Maggie," Clover told Gort.

Gort glanced at me but then looked at Reynald. It was exactly as I'd expected. *We* weren't hiring the Magnar family. Reynald was hiring them, and they would listen only to him.

I opened the small box in front of me and placed a stack of silver nomas on the table. "We offer a sign-on bonus of one noma each, room and board, and daily pay of seven dens for you, five dens for each of your sons, and five dens for your wife, if she chooses to work as our cook."

Gort's eyebrows crept up. He glanced at Reynald. "Those are war rates. Generous war rates."

"There is a reason for that," Reynald said.

"If you're injured on the job, we will cover the cost of healing your injuries," I said. "If you are permanently maimed and lose a limb on the job, you will get a one-time payout of two gold grests to compensate you. If you die on the job, your heirs will receive a one-time payout of three gold grests."

And he better not die, because we couldn't really afford it.

Gort's eyebrows rose again. "Death bonus?"

"That's the way she does things," Reynald said.

He and I had bickered over the work-compensation clause for over an hour. Reynald maintained that this was foolish, and no army ever paid soldiers money for dying. According to him, the surviving spouse was entitled to the full pay a soldier would've received by the end of the campaign and that was that. I finally asked him if he thought Gort might kill himself for three grests or if he was worried the kids would do their father in to get their inheritance, at which point he gave up.

"That's the first time someone's offered me money for dying," Gort said.

I looked at Reynald. "Did you talk to him?"

"No," he said. "It's common sense."

"Taking care of the people who work for you is common sense." I looked Gort in the eye and gave him my best serious stare. "Did Reynald explain the nature of the job?"

"He said we will be going after Hreban."

Gort's face said everything that needed to be said. The hatred in his eyes was burning hot.

"We are," I told him. "But it's more complicated than that. We are going to shift the currents of power in the kingdom. We will do dangerous things that will piss off a lot of people. The Eight Families, the three knight orders, the Justice Chamber . . . There may come a time when all of them will be looking for our heads."

"I want to see Hreban fall," Gort said.

Same. "Hreban sees himself on the throne in Eagle Roost. Before we are done, all of Rellas will see him for what he is. I promise you, he will never sit on the throne."

Making promises like that would get me into all sorts of hot water with fate.

"Then I'm in," Gort said.

I looked at his sons.

"We're in," the two of them said in one voice.

"What about Shana?"

"She is in," Gort said.

"Then it's settled. You start now." I looked at Will and Lute. "We have three small children who were kidnapped. I need them taken back to their parents. One is from Stilla Britin, and two are from Lagie."

"Less than a day's trip," Will said. "We'll be back before morning."

Of the twenty-two hundred combined pages of the two books, Will and Lute had exactly seventeen and a half devoted to them. I only knew one secret about their past and one secret about their future. I had to make it count.

"Treat this as a mission into enemy territory," I told them. "Drop the children off and come right back. No milk runs."

Will froze. Lute went bright red.

Gort narrowed his eyes. "What does she mean by that?"

"They know what I mean. Clover will show you where the kids are."

"This way," Clover said and walked off.

Lute followed her, clearly grateful to escape.

Will lingered. "How . . . ?"

"She does that," Reynald told him. "You'll get used to it."

Will gave me a long look, then followed his brother. We watched the three of them enter the house.

"Milk runs?" Reynald asked.

"That's what they call their little detours. It's less about the milk and more about the milk maids," I told him. "They are handsome, and pretty farm girls like them."

Gort squinted at me.

His mouth said, "So, you're the real deal." His face said *Prove it*.

"You should've listened to Eges," I told him.

Nothing changed in Gort's expression. "Fair enough."

Eges had served with Gort in the Hreban campaign. The morning before the charge that left Gort with an injured leg, he'd had a bad feeling and tried to convince Gort to hang back. Gort hadn't.

"Now I have a question for you. How old were your sons when Reynald was transferred to the west?"

Gort looked at Reynald.

"Don't look at him," I said. "It's a simple question."

"Will was ten and Lute was eight."

Will was twenty-one, which meant Reynald was transferred eleven years ago. That lined up with the books.

A lot of the details matched exactly, like the way Derog and Gort looked. And then there was Hreban, who was described as having a powerful presence, but who had looked very ordinary aside from his daring fashion sense, and Reynald, who seemed younger and more forceful than he should've been. The age and looks were a minor discrepancy, but we couldn't afford too many of those. Every inconsistency was a potential pit with sharpened stakes at the bottom. I had no idea how or why these minor deviations had occurred, but they bothered me.

Gort was looking at me.

"We are all settled," I said.

Gort offered me his shovel hand. "Shake on it."

Some things were universal. I stood up, took his hand, and shook it.

"Do you need help settling Shana in?" Reynald said.

"She is waiting with our cart around the block. Just point us to the rooms, and we are good to go."

I waved at the west wing. "Take anything you like in there."

"Will do."

Gort turned and headed for the outside door.

Reynald circled the table and leaned on it with both hands, so our eyes were level. His eyes were very green today, like spring grass in sunlight. They seemed to change color depending on lighting, on what he wore, on if a bird flew overhead . . . And I was thinking entirely too much about his eyes.

"Is there something you would like to ask me?"

Why not? "How old are you?"

"Thirty-eight."

"What year were you born?"

"3006. Became a squire at twelve, in 3018, knighted at seventeen in 3023, served for twenty years, received the Green Purse last year in winter."

"You don't look thirty-eight."

His dark eyebrows came together. "How is thirty-eight supposed to look?"

Put like that, it did sound ridiculous, but I had marched into this conversation, and I had to keep going until I got myself out of it.

"Like Gort."

"Gort is forty-seven. Nine years older than me."

"I meant that Gort is forty-seven and he looks fifty. You are thirty-eight and you look thirty." In-great-shape thirty. Not the-war-life-ground-me-into-dust thirty.

"Gort was a battle sergeant. He marched on foot with the bladesmen and spearmen. I am a knight. I rode a horse."

He had a point.

"Come to think of it, where is Striver?" Reynald and his stallion were inseparable.

"He died."

"I'm sorry to hear that."

Was Striver supposed to be dead during this time? I didn't know. The book started with Reynald riding on Striver into Kair Toren expecting a happy reunion and instead finding out that his wife had died and his son had been kidnapped. Striver was in numerous flashbacks but there was no mention of him in the main plot after that opening.

We stared at each other some more.

"Would it help if I grew a beard?" he asked. "It might make me look older."

Now who was being ridiculous. "No."

"We must resolve this now, because I need you to trust me, Maggie. There might be times when I tell you to do something for your safety and you must do it without hesitation."

Another good point.

"I asked you to stop the civil war and save my son. You asked me to wait for your plan and to help you acquire manpower. I'm doing both."

Also a good point.

"Would you like to see my papers?"

A better person would've said no. I wasn't that person. "Yes."

He turned around and walked into the house.

I sat at my table. The sun was shining. Fat happy bees bumped into the wine tree flowers and crawled around the plump red petals.

The door swung open and Reynald emerged. He walked up to the table and placed a folded piece of paper in front of me. I opened it.

The Grant of Green Purse to Reynald Etir Karis . . .

"Does this help?"

It still nagged at me, but it was here, written in beautiful calligraphy and sealed with the stamp of the Scribe Chamber.

"Yes," I said.

He picked up the paper, folded it, and slid it into his tunic. "We know who I am. Who are you, Maggie? Where do you come from?"

"Somewhere else."

"Where would that be?"

I didn't answer.

He leaned closer. It was an annoying habit that made him very difficult to ignore. I braced myself.

His voice was quiet, almost intimate.

"Do you have any papers to show me, Maggie?"

"No."

"Then we must remedy that. The sooner the better because no one in the kingdom can escape the Seventh Chamber."

He said *the Seventh Chamber* in a way most people would say *the Spanish Inquisition*—when they weren't being funny about it. Rellas had seven chambers of government. The Justice Chamber oversaw the criminal justice system, the War Chamber dealt with the military, and so on. "The Seventh Chamber" was the common people's code for the Treasury. It collected taxes. No force in Rellas was more feared.

"At the end of the summer, after Derog fails to report his yields, the Treasury will come knocking," Reynald said. "We have three months to procure an identity for you, forge a deed of sale for this house, and account for every noma in your purse."

I blinked at him.

"I leave you to contemplate how we can accomplish that," he said. "I'm sure you will come up with something."

He turned around and walked away.

Had I hurt his feelings?

He had trusted me, he had put himself in harm's way for my sake, and I had demanded to see his papers. When we were in Derog's horrible basement, instead of looking for the best position, he'd blocked the way to me and the kids, making sure nothing would get past him and hurt us. That told me everything I needed to know about who he was. If I screamed right now, he would come running and he would kill all threats he found. Because he had decided to protect me, and he kept his word.

You don't look thirty-eight . . . Ugh.

The Book-Reynald was a man of few words and lots of thinking, and all of that thinking was laid out in detail on the page. I'd spent so much time in his head, our interactions should've been easy. It should've been like hanging out with an old friend.

Interacting with the real Reynald was anything but easy. It was tense. So much was riding on him having faith in me and I kept blundering about.

There had to have been a more diplomatic way to go about that conversation. I felt so uneasy about it.

Too late now. Besides, what would I have said? *In my world, you're a character in a book and you were described as older and more beat down, so I'm trying to suss out the reason for the discrepancy before something I can't predict bites us in the butt?* Yeah. That would go over well.

I sighed. I needed to strike the first blow against Hreban and make it count. If I pulled it off, Reynald would trust me. The problem was, my plan was risky, expensive, and came with a massive moral dilemma attached.

Setting that aside, Reynald was right—I needed an identity. My original plan would have been to establish greater ties with the Shears and ask them to make me some fake papers. That could still work, but it required Solentine to trust me, and that twisted bastard rationed trust like it was water in the Sahara.

Trust, the bane of my existence.

We required more money as well. We'd just doubled our forces. We would need to feed, clothe, and arm everyone. Buying the boat had taken a big chunk out of our budget. Solentine's money would float us for a while; however, that money would run out.

Trading in secrets was lucrative but doing it too often would alter the chain of events beyond recognition. I had to be picky. I knew what I wanted to offer to Solentine next, but the timing wasn't right for it.

Money, money, money . . . Where could I get some?

I had to find a source of legitimate income that could cover our collective butts when I presented it to the government. It was time to invent popcorn or something. A farm, a shop . . . If only I had some kind of marketable skill that would apply to this world.

A bee landed on my sleeve, its fuzzy fur red from the wine tree's flower pollen. I sat very still. Bees were delicate and precious, as our world had found out.

The bee crawled across the fabric, leaving a little trail of vermillion, buzzed, and took off slowly. I brushed at the smudge of red.

I wonder if this pollen will wash out.

Oh.

Right. Why hadn't I thought of this sooner?

Chapter 13

Planter 10

I opened my eyes. Above me, the ceiling of my new bedroom glowed slightly, its thick beams, sealed with resin, bright in the light of the morning sun.

Today was the day we went to the Dog Market.

I'd spent yesterday figuring out two plans: one for the salt and one for our legitimate business enterprise. I'd made a single shopping list, handed it to Clover, and informed her that this morning we had to go to the Dog Market. It was the closest and largest market nearby, named so not because puppies were sold there, although they were, but because of a massive stone statue of a demonic dog that perched at the top of the market's main gate.

The Dog Market was a wondrous place. All sorts of goods were sold there: weapons, armor, clothes, groceries, potions, magical creatures . . . So many interesting things happened at the Dog Market in the books. I had to see it.

Get up, make myself presentable, and go to the Dog Market. Yes. Yes-yes-yes . . .

There was an odd wetness on my chest.

I touched it. Slimy . . .

I flung the slimy thing off me and leaped out of the bed like there was a surprise cobra in it.

A fish lay on the floor. It was about a foot long, with a narrow body and shiny iridescent scales with a gold cast and purple stripes. Plum-colored fins, edged with crimson, thrust from its spine and belly. The mouth under its bright red eyes bristled with a forest of thin, sharp fangs.

What the hell?

The room was empty except for me and the fish. Was this some sort of weird message from the Shears? Was Solentine telling me to sleep with the fishes?

I had locked my window last night because Reynald insisted on it. I glanced at the window. Still locked and bolted in place from the inside. My door wasn't locked though. Reynald's suite was only a few feet away across the hall, and I felt better knowing that if I screamed, he would come running. Putting a locked door in the way of my possible rescue didn't feel prudent. Theoretically, anybody could've come in and put a fish on my chest.

Was this some weird prank?

If it was a prank, my money was on Kaiden, because of his age, and yet it didn't seem like something he would do. But who would break in to our house just to slap a fish on me?

I peeled off my nightshirt, washed up in the bathroom, and got dressed. The offending fish waited on the floor. I got a piece of paper from my desk, picked the fish up by the tail, slid it on the paper, and wrapped it up. Then I put my shoes on, took my fish, and went downstairs.

The house was quiet. Nobody in the hallways, nobody in the courtyard . . . A faint noise came from the kitchen. Ah!

I walked into the kitchen. Shana was sweeping the floor. Behind her the oven was going, and the warm air, seasoned with the scent of freshly baked bread, washed over me. The kitchen window stood wide open. A large shallow bucket rested on the windowsill, and a sandy-gold horse head was halfway into it, munching.

"Morning," Shana told me. "Greet the lady of the house, Honey."

Honey raised her head, looked at me with big amber eyes, and went back to eating.

Shana had arrived yesterday in an old cart pulled by Honey, a woodland mare. Honey was large and broadly built, with a golden dun coat dappled with dark chestnut spots and narrow brown stripes on her legs. Her coat pattern made me think of a spotted antelope mixed with an okapi. Her profile was convex, her muzzle broad, and her ears were oddly shaped.

"What is she eating?" I asked.

"Vegetable peels. No sense letting them go to waste."

At home, horses were powerful but delicate creatures. Any sudden change in diet could result in colic, which, if severe enough, would kill the horse. Rellasian woodland horses didn't have that problem. They'd evolved from a different equine ancestor than the warhorses, which was why mercenaries and caravan guards loved them. They weren't fast or particularly obedient, but they didn't scare easily, they stayed near the camp even when not tethered, and they foraged for their own feed, eating just about everything like goats did.

Looking at Honey was confusing. When I'd met Villain, Everard's huge stallion, he felt like a horse. Honey felt like a horse's distant cousin. Probably a couple of times removed. There was nothing like that back home.

Shana was confusing, too. She was a couple of inches shorter than me, stocky, broad, and obviously very strong. Yesterday her graying blond hair had been put away into a braid. She'd worn chainmail and carried a mace, and the way she handled herself made you think that real-life whack-a-mole was her favorite game.

The chainmail was gone, traded for a simple dress. The mace had vanished, too. Her hair was pulled into a low croissant-shaped bun secured with a simple wooden hair brooch. I had seen several women with this style. It seemed to go hand in hand with being a little older and running errands.

Yesterday she'd looked like a human tank. Today she was a plump, nice middle-aged lady who had never held a weapon in her life. Just cleaning up the kitchen with a broom. Perfectly harmless. Sweep-sweep.

"What do you have there?" Shana asked me.

I put the paper bundle on the table and unwrapped it. "What kind of a fish is this?"

Shana squinted at my catch-of-the-bed. "That's a young purple pike. They're delicious. Hard to catch, too. Where did you get this?"

"I found it."

"Where?"

"Around."

She looked at me. I fought the urge to fidget.

"Did you go fishing?" Shana asked.

"Not exactly."

She squinted at me.

"Where is everybody?" I asked.

"The boys got back from delivering the kids a couple of hours ago. I sent them to bed. They're no good as guards if they are tired."

Made sense.

"Our cart won't fit through your entrance," Shana said. "There's no point in keeping it. Leaving it outside the wall is asking for it to be stolen, so Gort and Reynald left to sell it."

Our house did have a small stable with two enclosures, but the front tunnel was too narrow for any kind of horse-drawn cart. It was too low for a rider as well. Anyone trying to come through would have to dismount. Derog had been paranoid about being raided.

"Where is Clover?"

"She went with Reynald and Gort. After they sell the cart, they'll go to the Dog Market. We need arrows and bolts, and a few bows . . ."

"They went to the market without me?"

"Clover has your list. Don't worry, she'll buy everything on it."

That wasn't the point. I wanted to go. "Did they take Kaiden with them?"

"Yes."

"Why didn't they come to get me?"

"You were resting."

I could follow them, but Reynald would have a cow if I went out without an escort.

They'd left me behind. Ouch.

This proved exactly what I had feared. Gort and the Magnars only listened to me because Reynald was willing to follow my lead for the time being. Clover was grateful to me for saving her and Kaiden, and she clearly believed me when I said I knew the future, but I was failing in some basic Rellasian life skills, and she had decided that she knew better than me. I was in real danger of being treated like one of those bumbling genius mage characters, who knew the mysteries of the universe but had trouble putting on socks and couldn't be trusted to do anything.

So far I'd told them some secrets about their past, but the past had already happened. I had to prove that I could predict things. I had to deliver results and when I did, it had to hit like a ton of bricks, so when I told them I could see the future, they would believe me completely and without reservations.

Shana sniffed the fish on the table. "What are you going to do with it?"

"Um, throw it away?"

Shana gave me a hard look.

"It's a mystery fish. I don't know where it came from."

"It came from Virka River." Shana jabbed her wooden stirring spoon at the wall, in the direction of the river.

"How do you know that?" Although it was probably a safe bet since that river was literally just outside the house.

Shana set the spoon down, grabbed a narrow knife from the knife block, and pried the gills of the fish open. "Look, see how pink they are? The gills darken when the fish is out of the water for a while, and with this kind of fish they go purple very fast. This pike was swimming less than an hour ago."

"If you say so."

"It's a perfectly good fish. I'm taking it," Shana announced.

"What for?" I asked.

"Soup!"

She took the fish and tossed it into the sink.

Okay then. I picked up the fish paper, threw it into the trash bucket, grabbed a rag from the sink, and started wiping down the table.

Shana stared at me.

"Yes?"

"What are you doing?"

"I scrubbed this table way too hard to let the fish slime stink it up."

"I'll take care of it."

"No need."

I rinsed the rag under the faucet and hung it back on the sink. "Can I help you with anything?"

"No, my *lady*." She'd put a bit of force into that *lady*.

"I'm not a lady. Can I peel something? I'm fast."

"If I need something peeled, I will let you know."

"I can—"

Shana pulled out a teapot and a cup and set both in front of me on the table. "You can sit in this chair right here and have your morning cup of tea. The pastries will be ready soon."

I opened my mouth.

Shana pointed at the chair. I had seen this exact look on my mom's face when my fifteen-year-old supergenius self told her that I didn't need to study for drivers' ed because I already knew everything there was to know about cars and I was an excellent driver.

I clicked my mouth shut, sat in the chair, and poured some tea.

"I'll get you some honey," Shana said.

"Thank you."

She put a jar of honey in front of me. I spooned some into my cup and tried the tea. Like being kicked in the teeth by a caffeine horse. Wooo!

"Is this firepit tea?"

"Yes. Too strong for you?"

"No, I like it."

It reminded me of an assam tea blended with some sort of sweet spice or fruit. Mercenaries and soldiers all across Rellas drank this tea by the campfire in the early mornings before long marches and in the evening before the night watch. One famous knight had even declared that there were three essential ingredients to winning a war: a commander who was admired by their troops, weapons of Rellasian gray iron, and firepit tea.

Shana sat in a chair across from me, poured herself a cup, and loaded it with honey with a slight frown on her face.

"Am I confusing?" I asked.

She nodded. "A bit. I'll figure you out. Gort says you know people's secrets."

"Something like that."

"He's hiding something from me. He won't tell me what it is, and the kids don't know either. Do you know?"

Gort wasn't half as slick as he thought. "I have a good guess."

"Is he sick?"

"No. It's not another woman either, if you're worried."

She barked a short laugh. "Oh, I know it's not another woman."

"It's not important now, because both of you are here," I told her.

"How do I know you're telling the truth?"

I had to impress her. I would need to ask the Magnars to do some strange things in the near future, and having Shana's support would go a long way. I had to choose carefully.

"You could've picked Kurem of Las. He came to you the night before your wedding and begged you not to marry Gort."

She paused with her tea halfway to her lips. I gave her a few moments to recover.

"Do you ever regret it?"

"Picking Gort?"

"Yes."

She sighed. "No. I love him."

"It must've been a hard life with him being gone so much."

"If Gort was a blacksmith or a farmer, I would still love him. But he is a soldier. That's what he knows how to do."

In Rellas, being a mercenary was a job like any other. Most people didn't choose it because they loved war. They picked it because they were out of options, and it was a way to make a living. The nobles frequently squabbled with each other and their conflicts sometimes flared into small-scale wars, with the official blessing of the Throne complete with papers and royal seals. The nobles hired mercenaries to get the upper hand, and when they didn't, the Throne often did, to supplement the King's Army.

"You're right, it wasn't an easy life," Shana said. "It was tough, and yet we made it through. Hreban stole my husband's Green Purse from him. But you pay well. We're going to get our justice, and once this job is over, if we live through it, we'll get a farm of our own. We've earned it."

That was their dream. They talked about it when the going got tough. One day they would get a farm with fruit trees and a little house. They would have a calm and peaceful life, free of marching through the mud to almost certain death. Will and Lute wouldn't have to risk their lives to put food on the table.

All Gort and Shana wanted was something a little bit better for themselves and their kids. Just like my parents.

I sipped my tea.

There were hundreds of Gorts and Shanas out there, working to get their own little farms and a little slice of peace. Two weeks from now, eighty of them would die.

I had a hard decision to make.

"Maggie," Reynald said on my left.

"Yes?"

"We've run out of land."

I stopped.

We faced the harbor. Ahead the stone wharf stretched, and beyond it the ocean shimmered, the water a flawless turquoise darkening to a heartbreaking blue.

To the left lay the fishing docks. About a hundred yards away, a team of fishermen was pulling a huge fish onto a ramp leading from the water. It was trapped in a net, hooked by enormous ropes to a big wheel-and-pulley contraption, and one of the fishermen led a pair of horses connected to the wheel, winching the net ashore. The fish glistened with purple and blue, its spiny fins bristling in the thick net. Its head and chest were as big as one of those oversized Ford Transit vans, and I couldn't even see its tail. Four stelkas bickered by the pulley, fighting over the fish guts someone had dumped on the stone. None of them had a crescent-shaped white patch on their chest.

Normally I would've gaped at the scene, but right now I just wanted to get to our destination. We needed to go north along the coast, away from the fishing dock and toward the commercial wharf.

"Which way?" Reynald asked.

"To the right."

We made a right and headed down a wide street, parallel to the wharf, with massive warehouses rising on both sides.

Reynald, Gort, and Clover had come back from the market an hour and a half ago, followed by three delivery people pushing carts loaded with their purchases. I told them I needed to go to the docks, and Reynald immediately volunteered to escort me.

I had included "outfit that would make me look like I'm from a minor noble house" in the shopping list, and Clover had come through with flying colors. I wore a green gown the exact shade of lawns from the weed killer commercials, a cloak of slightly darker green, and my hairdo was a work of art secured with a pricey silver ornament shaped like a flower. My shoes were much better, too. I looked like I had just enough money and status to be annoying.

Next to me, Reynald broadcast kickass bodyguard. He wore his outfit from the teahouse, and he'd added a lancer's coif to it. The coif fit over his face and hid everything except a narrow part around his eyes. Originally the coif had served to protect the faces of Rellasian lancers from their heavy helmets, but now it functioned like a local version of a sheisty. Masons wore it to keep from breathing in stone dust, butchers put it on it to keep the gore from their face, and private guards and mercenaries used it to look more scary.

Together with the hood of his cloak, the coif took Reynald from menacing into downright sinister territory. A good thing, too. The more threatening he looked, the more credibility it would give me.

I'd been turning the problem of the mercenaries in my head over and over, trying to account for all possible consequences, and gotten nowhere. It gnawed at me. I knew what I wanted to do. Unfortunately, it was completely opposite of what I should do, and I had trouble justifying my choice.

There it was, on the left. A warehouse with a painted wooden shield above the door. A copper warhammer on a field of dark cobalt blue striking a gray anvil. The Keepers of Iron. The Yolenta Great Family.

"Do I look like a noble?" I asked under my breath.

"Yes," Reynald told me. "Green suits you, Maggie."

Great.

I made a beeline for the open door. Reynald got there before me, stepped inside, pulled his coif down off his face, and glowered.

The interior was filled with goods, some in barrels, others in chests, grouped by type, with samples on display: chunks of ore in different colors, some sort of powdered stone, big hunks of crystal . . . Quartz, maybe?

A seller hurried out from behind a short counter, keeping an eye on Reynald, and bowed to me. "How may I help you, my lady?"

"Do you sell pink salt?"

"We do, my lady. Right this way."

Clover's outfit did its job. Excellent.

He led me down the aisle to a group of barrels. One of them stood open, filled to the brim with small, coarse pebbles of pink rock salt.

"We also offer raw rock and fine grinds," the seller said.

I needed to aim for just the right mix of clueless and put-upon. The kind of woman who normally couldn't be bothered to step foot into a shop like this.

I looked at Reynald. "Is this what they call a trader rock barrel?"

"Yes, my lady," Reynald said.

The barrels stood about twenty-five inches high. My grandpa used to have an old bourbon barrel about that size. He used it as a side table on the porch, by his rocking chair.

An overly obsessive reader once calculated the volume of one of these barrels based on Rellas's units of measurement to settle an argument on a fan forum. It came in right at sixteen gallons. According to that post, a gallon-sized chunk of Himalayan pink salt weighed about eighteen pounds, based on halite's density. The actual weight per gallon varied, depending on the size of the particles and type of salt. Either way, a sixteen-gallon barrel was very heavy.

And I had no idea why I remembered that so precisely. The numbers just popped right into my head.

"They seem small," I said to Reynald. "Much smaller than grain barrels."

"They are very heavy, my lady," he said, his expression completely neutral. "They are sized for ease of transport. Grain barrels are larger because grain weighs less."

The seller grabbed one of the rock pebbles and held it up to the sunshine coming through the door. The small chunk glowed softly with diffused light.

"Our pink salt is of the finest quality. Directly from Gassargand."

"Directly?" *Tell me more. I need to know when your ships arrive.*

The seller hit me with his best buy-my-stuff smile. "Yes, my lady."

"But is it fresh?"

The trader blinked.

"Salt is always fresh, my lady," Reynald said with a completely straight face.

"Absolutely!" The seller nodded. "It was mined just a few weeks ago across the sea and shipped here. Our ships arrive every three weeks, my lady!"

"When is the next one due?"

"Next Fifday, my lady."

We had four days. Very little time. I needed to hurry. I looked at Reynald. "Should I wait for the fresher salt?"

"I assure you, there is no difference in quality between this barrel and the next shipment," the clerk promised.

"It wouldn't be significantly fresher, my lady," Reynald told me.

I wrinkled my nose at the barrel. "And the whole barrel is pink salt? It is for my mother-in-law. It must be perfect."

"Of course, my lady. The entire barrel is the best grade of pink salt. The calla resin seal proves it."

He swept his fingers along the rim of the barrel, indicating a wax-like seal stamped with the Yolenta crest.

"You see, the seal is intact. Unlike wax seals that melt and flow when exposed to warmth, this resin seal will crumble if cut or heated. The full might of the Yolenta Family stands behind this barrel. The Keepers of Iron do not lie. When your mother-in-law's chef opens it, the salt will be just as beautiful and fresh as the moment it was mined."

I pondered the barrel. "Very well. How much is it?"

"The whole barrel?"

"Yes."

"One grest, my lady."

Ouch.

I nodded to Reynald. He reached into his clothes, pulled a single gold coin out, and handed it over to the seller. Our budget had just taken a big hit. Reynald gave the seller our address and we exited the warehouse and went back the way we came.

"Where to now?" Reynald asked.

"I need to see the pier in front of this warehouse, but I don't want to be obvious about it."

He considered it for a moment. "Follow me."

At the next intersection, he started weaving his way through the streets, edging east. We walked for a couple of blocks, made a left, and came to a stone stairway leading up, its steps worn smooth by the salty wind, rain, and countless feet.

We took the stairs. Reynald kept pace with me.

The stairs kept going, climbing higher and higher, until finally we stepped onto a tall bridge guarded by a stone rail. It soared over the roofs of the harbor warehouses, mirroring the coastline.

Below and on our left, the ocean glittered, a placid expanse of blue, rolling to the hazy horizon. The wide ribbon of the stone wharf bordered the water, and long stone piers stretched from it, out into the ocean, flanked by large ocean-worthy trading ships. Between the piers, shorter wooden docks offered the smaller vessels a place to moor. The Combs, the city's infamous main wharf.

A sparse current of people moved past us: fishermen with carrying yokes across their shoulders, balancing pails of water filled with fish; dockworkers hauling cargo in sacks; teenagers with shopping baskets running errands and carrying messages; a couple of young priests in robes with bladed staffs on their backs... Everyone had a place to be and was on their way there, minding their own business.

I knew where we were now. This was the Spotter's Rampart, a chunk of the wall left over from the ancient fortifications. Most of them were long gone, swallowed by Kair Toren as it grew over the centuries. But this stretch of the old rampart proved useful, so the city kept it, and the Chamber of Works maintained it for the kingdom's sake.

Reynald and I walked side by side, keeping close to the left rail, out of the way of other passersby. I scanned the ships and the flags flying from the tall masts. Copper, cobalt, and gray. Shouldn't be that hard to find.

"Aren't you going to ask me about the pink salt?"

"I'll wait," he said. "I'm demonstrating trust."

Smartass.

I scanned the harbor as we walked. It was hard to tell the warehouses apart from this height, but the Yolentas would have one of the larger stone piers. They did a lot of trade.

We kept walking.

"What's bothering you?" he asked.

"Why do you think something is bothering me?"

"You didn't speak on the way to the docks, and then you almost walked into the ocean."

I sighed.

"Two weeks from now, eighty mercenaries are going to die. I can stop their deaths."

"What's the downside?"

"Every change we make alters the flow of events. Remember how I said that our actions are like pebbles we cast into a placid pond? They cause waves and ripples. This wouldn't be a pebble. This would be a huge rock."

"Do they die for a good cause?"

"No. They are sacrificed for nothing. It is a senseless slaughter."

I caught a glimpse of his face under the hood of his cloak. His jaw was set. He didn't like what I was telling him.

Ahead a scattering of rubble lay in our path. A chunk of the stone wall had broken off and fallen on the bridge, breaking into gravel. We reached it.

Reynald offered me his arm.

For a second, I stared at it.

Oh. He was helping me cross it. I rested my fingers on his forearm, picked up my skirt with my left hand, and stepped over the gravel.

He made no move to step away from me. He kept walking with my hand on his arm.

To keep holding on or to let go? What was the etiquette here?

Back in the warehouse, I was pretending to be a lady. A lady wouldn't hold on to her guard because he had to have both arms free to do his job. But we weren't pretending to be anyone right now.

His arm was steady as a rock. I could feel the hard muscle underneath through the fabric of his shirt.

This felt so oddly intimate. I had walked side by side with men before, I had held hands with men before, and it never gave me warm fuzzy butterflies like this. We had connected, and there was power in that connection. It drew me in. I wanted to keep my hand right where it was and keep walking just like this.

I glanced at his face.

He hadn't pulled his coif up. His expression was relaxed, softening the harsh contours of his features within his hood. His eyes were a light gray-green. He was still broadcasting menace and dangerous edge, but it was directed outward, at other people. Walking with him like this felt like the safest thing in the world.

He looked at me. There was a hint of warmth in his eyes.

Oh wow. All those people crushing on Arvel and Solentine had no idea what they were missing.

The rules of conduct for unmarried men and women were strict. Touching was generally discouraged unless there was romantic interest, deep friendship, or a family connection. Walking together like this was sending all sorts of signals I shouldn't be sending. First, we had only known each other for three days. Second, neither of us was emotionally stable at the moment. Third . . . I liked touching him entirely too much. I had to let go.

I gently raised my hand. He smoothly let his arm drop, and we once again walked side by side.

"Tell me about the mercenaries," he said.

"These people have families. Children, spouses. Instead of ending, their lives will go on and the paths of their families will diverge from the future I know."

"That is a significant change," he said.

"Yes. I promised myself that I would only do what was absolutely necessary. There is no logical reason to save the mercenaries. More, saving them is risky. First, it will be dangerous and second, it has a chance to send the future in a new direction that could endanger us. You, Clover, Kaiden, and the Magnars."

He didn't say anything, leaving me space to talk.

"When Shana found out she was pregnant with Will, she cried," I told him. "Her father had abandoned her when she was a child, her mother had died, and the day after that funeral, she had enlisted in the King's Army. She liked being a soldier. She didn't know anything about having babies, and there was nobody to teach her and no home to go back to."

Reading about it had broken my heart.

"But she loved Will before he was even born, and she loved Gort, and so she left the army and went to live with her in-laws in a tiny village that was barely large enough to support a single forge. The house was already crowded with Gort's parents, his brother and sister-in-law, and their kids. The family lived hand-to-mouth, and Shana and Will were more mouths to feed. She didn't fit in. Meanwhile Gort volunteered for every mission that would earn a bonus. It took him three years, but he got her out of that house and into a shack of their own."

Reynald probably knew most of this, but I had to get it all out.

"When Gort lost his shot at the Green Purse, he became a mercenary, because that was all he could do. Two years later, Shana joined him as part of the supply convoy. They took their kids with them. A lot of mercenary companies do this. On a long campaign, there will be a supply train following them with wives and husbands and sometimes kids."

Reynald's face told me nothing. He just listened.

"The mercenaries who are going to die are not the youngest or the healthiest. It's an old-dog campaign."

Old-dog in mercenary speak meant a slow-paced campaign, the kind that didn't pay that well, but didn't call for any long marches or heroics either. Old-dog campaigns were fought by veterans, experienced, steady, but past their prime.

"These people are the second tier, looking for a simple, short campaign and willing to work for less, because few jobs come their way these days and they have to take what they can get."

They were like Gort and Shana. Trying to keep afloat.

"You want to save them," he said. There was no judgment in his voice. No emotion at all.

"Yes. Eighty people. Eighty families. That's so many lives. But if we do save them, there's no telling what the consequences will be. Preventing this event from happening doesn't mean that the powers behind it will just abandon their schemes. It could cost more lives than it will save in the long run."

"But you don't know it will?"

"I don't. I wish I was wiser. I'm afraid of making a mistake that other people will have to pay for."

I realized we were standing still. "Why did we stop?"

He nodded at the ocean. "The Yolentas' pier."

To the right and just up ahead, a long stone pier cut into the ocean. Three large ships waited by it, their complex segmented sails stowed and secured. Long flags with copper, cobalt, and gray streamed from their masts.

I needed to stop venting and concentrate on the reason we had come here.

The Yolentas' pier ended in front of the three warehouses. On each side, a narrow street ran deeper into the city, perpendicular to our bridge and passing under it. The street that we had taken to get to the storefront was directly under us, running along below the bridge.

I crossed the bridge to the other side and looked at the two side streets. The street on my left curved and veered north. The one on my right ended in a small plaza with two other streets, one going southeast and the other eastward. Narrow alleys branched off from both like capillaries from larger veins.

I needed a plan. Luckily for me, I had an experienced tactician next to me. Reynald had planned hundreds of battles and skirmishes.

I kept my voice low. "In four days, the next shipment of the overpriced pink salt will arrive at this pier. I want to steal one of the barrels and replace it with the one we bought."

"Stealing a barrel from the Keepers of Iron." Reynald raised his eyebrows. "Why not?"

He looked slightly wicked, like a villain planning something dangerous yet fun.

"Can we do this?"

The blademaster surveyed the tangle of streets below. "Yes."

"Safely?"

"No plan is foolproof, Maggie. But probably."

"I promise I will explain everything once we have that barrel."

He shook his head.

"What?"

"Wondering what sins the Yolentas have committed."

"Maybe I just want to steal their salt."

"No. That's not you. The Yolentas have done something special. Something that's more than their usual schemes and backstabbing."

"You're right."

I turned and leaned my back against the rail. The ocean on the other side of the bridge was so beautiful.

Reynald leaned on the rail next to me, his profile a grim suggestion in the hood of his cloak, the humor gone. And just like that we were back to the deadly warrior vibes.

"Once when I was younger, the force I led was pinned down by the opposing army," Reynald said. "They outnumbered us, and things looked bleak. I'd made some enemies among my peers. I didn't expect reinforcements."

His voice was calm and measured. Reynald wasn't a bootlicker. With him, it was always mission first. Achieve the objective with the fewest casualties possible. He didn't care to stroke people's egos, and he wasn't always liked by his commanders.

"Just when I thought we were done, another knight came to our aid with his troops."

This wasn't in the books. Reynald Karis was telling me something about himself that he probably kept private. He was trusting me with it.

"Nobody would've blamed this knight for not showing up. It was heavily suggested to him that he shouldn't try so hard on my behalf. Yet he rendered aid anyway, because he had judged it right and that was the kind of man he was. He knew there would be consequences. People would make things difficult for him. When I brought it up, he looked me in the eye and said, 'Fuck 'em.'"

I blinked. "That's really what he said?"

Reynald nodded.

"I had expected something more . . . profound."

"So did I. But he was a soldier, Maggie. Not a sage. His superiors wanted him to let other soldiers die to settle a grudge. He held them in contempt. He didn't worry. He didn't waver. He felt nothing but disdain and a distinct lack of fear."

His expression turned harsh.

"Fuck the kind of people who would sacrifice eighty souls to further their ambitions. You can't bear responsibility for their actions. I've lost people before. Trust me when I say this: The weight of knowing you could've saved eighty lives and didn't is too heavy to live with. If you want to save the mercenaries, do it. I will stand with you. The powers behind it will do what they will do, and we'll deal with that, too."

"You will back me up?"

"I will."

I could've hugged him. Instead, I nodded, pushed away from the rail, and we walked side by side back the way we came.

"We can steal the barrel," Reynald said, his expression thoughtful. "Just one question."

Anxiety nipped at me. "What kind of question?"

He looked at me, his expression deadly serious. "Will it be fresh enough, Maggie?"

Damn it. "I know that salt is a mineral. I wanted to find out when the next shipment was coming in."

Reynald laughed. It was such an unexpected sound. When he smiled, his whole face lit up, his eyes turned bright and green, and I wanted to smile back at him, but when he laughed, it was on a whole other level.

"It's not funny," I told him.

"You're wrong. It's hilarious. You're hilarious."

We reached the staircase.

"Hold my arm, Maggie. I don't want you tumbling down the stairs."

"I can walk on my own, thank you very much."

He laughed again.

I picked up the hem of my gown and concentrated on not falling.

Chapter 14

Planter 11

I surveyed the purchases arranged on the laundry table. It was barely morning. A faint breeze swirled through the courtyard, bringing with it a hint of the ocean. The sky glowed with gentle blue, veiled here and there with pink-tinted clouds. Kair Toren had pulled out all the stops for this sunrise.

Yesterday when we came back from the docks, Reynald talked to Gort for a while. Our precious salt was delivered by cart and installed in a secure spot with a strict warning to not touch the seal. Reynald spoke to Kaiden at length about it. When Clover found out how much we had paid for it, she turned slightly green and went to recalculate the budget.

In the evening Gort had left. He came back late, completely plastered, and announced that Will had a job on the Yolentas' dock crew. Apparently, the Yolentas often hired veterans for their loading and unloading, reasoning that people who knew how to handle themselves would be good at protecting cargo. Gort had served with one of the supervisors and whatever sob story he told the man over the ale mugs and a plate of greasy tavern food had worked. This morning Will had departed before dawn.

We wouldn't know anything until he came back, and I needed to use this time to get our legitimate business up and running. I had no illusions—this was the calm before the storm, but I could either wait and marinate in my anxiety or work. I chose work.

I claimed the section of the courtyard with an open firepit, where Clover had previously boiled laundry in the huge pot. I'd made a small fire, hung one of our spare cauldrons over it, and dragged a scale and a set of weights I found in Derog's office to the utility table sitting there. Then I got paper and one of the reed pens from my office and arranged our purchases, while Clover anxiously hovered nearby.

"I bought everything on your list," Clover said.

I glanced at the gathering of barrels, jars, and vials. "I see that."

"A short barrel of pan oil at fifteen dens," Clover recited. "He wanted twenty for it, which would have been highway robbery."

Pan oil came from Rellasian olives and served as the main oil in local cooking. It was also pricey. The short barrel contained about five gallons or so, and it had cost us a pretty penny even with Clover's haggling skills.

"A short barrel of bulko oil at three dens."

Bulko oil came from fat, green berries. It was inedible because of its off-putting taste, so it was produced for industrial uses—grease for wheels and axles, quench medium for armor and weapons, and first aid burn ointment. It was nontoxic, possessed decent antibacterial properties, and best of all, it was solid at room temperature and had the consistency and texture of coconut oil.

Clover eyed the cauldron. "You can't cook with bulko oil, my lady."

Again with the *my lady*. "Maggie."

"Maggie. It tastes awful."

"We won't be cooking with it."

Clover glanced at the cauldron and waited to see if I would say anything else. I didn't, so she forged ahead.

"A large vial of maidenflower oil at three dens and two quarters. It was on sale, and I got her down another half den."

The clear glass vial held about two cups of dense, bright purple liquid. I opened the cork and waved my hand above the rim, fanning the scent to me. It smelled of vanilla with a hint of rose and just a pinch of something else. Lilac, maybe? Maidenflower oil was used to add fragrance and color in baking. I knew this because in the books Shana made a dessert with it.

"Two large loaf pans at two dens and ten small pans at two quarters each."

She would go through the whole list. There was no stopping her.

"One bucket with a wooden stirring spoon at one den."

Right.

"A large crock of yogurt at one den . . ."

Yogurt would come in very handy.

"One sack of lye at two dens and a quarter."

A decent-sized sack, too. Kair Toren had an abundance of salt-tolerant plants and lye was cheap.

"Two pairs of heavy work mittens, and two pairs of stonecutter spectacles at two dens each."

Safety first.

Clover frowned at our collection of supplies. "What is it all for?"

"Do you want me to tell you, or do you want to be surprised?"

She thought about it. "I want to be surprised."

"In that case, let's mix the lye."

I put on the stonecutter spectacles, which were large, ridiculously heavy, and attached to a leather band that went around my head, put on the work mittens, and set about mixing the lye. Five drems ought to do it for the test batch. I measured the powder and mixed it into water.

The simplest recipe I knew called for olive oil, coconut oil, and lye at thirty-three percent each by weight.

"I need five drems of bulko oil and pan oil, each."

Clover reached for the scales. "See, I didn't forget anything when we went to the market."

"Me."

"I'm sorry?"

"You forgot me. I wanted to go to the Dog Market. You knew I wanted to go but you left without me."

"You were tired and resting," Clover said carefully. "Are you unhappy with how much money I spent?"

"No, and that's not the point."

I took the cauldron off the heat and set it on the stone block. Should be hot enough to melt the oils. I added the bulko oil to it and watched it liquefy.

"I had a friend who worked for a merchant."

Me. I was the friend. In college I'd switched to political science aiming at law school. In my senior year, I interned at four different law firms and found out that I hated law with the passion of a thousand suns.

A series of random jobs followed. I got hired by an insurance agent, and six months into it the agency went bankrupt. I tried to be a journalist and couldn't keep myself fed. I tried civil service and watched my supervisor stress-cry in a closet on my first day while my coworker assured me that I would get used to it.

I ended up at a storage place run by an elderly couple. It gave me plenty of time to read and figure out what I wanted to do with my life, while putting a roof over my head. Sort of. The job market was lousy across the board. Last year my roommate finally threw in the towel and moved back with her parents, so now I spent my days off delivering food to make up for her portion of the rent.

I realized that Clover was waiting on me.

"As I said, I had a friend who worked for a merchant. The merchant was elderly, and she would get confused when managing the accounts. The previous servant warned my friend not to correct her because she would get flustered and upset. He told her to smile, nod, and say, 'Yes, tress,' and then do things the way they were supposed to be done once she left."

My elderly employers knew just enough about QuickBooks to complicate both their life and mine.

The oils were melted, and the mix had sufficiently cooled. I carefully poured the premeasured lye into the cauldron and set about stirring it.

What I wouldn't give for a stick blender right now.

I met Clover's eyes. "The point is, I don't want to be that merchant. I don't want to be placated. If you find fault with something I want to do, I would rather know about it."

The yellow mass in the cauldron got a little lighter. Maybe this could work after all.

Stir-stir-stir.
Stir.

Clover raised her chin. "I didn't wake you up because you didn't have an appropriate dress. The Dog Market is the best one in this part of the city and the one we will frequent. If you are to pose as a lady, you must look like one when you are going out, otherwise someone might remember seeing you in a shoddy dress and old shoes and wonder why a lady of noble birth would dress like that."

"Why didn't you tell me?"

"Because you would want to go anyway."

"Fair point. Anything else?"

The pale mass in the cauldron reached the consistency of soupy mashed potatoes. The technical term was "come to trace." I tried to draw a little heart with the tracings dripping from the mixing spoon. It didn't hold. No, not quite there.

"Also, please stop cleaning."

I stopped stirring for a second. "What?"

"Please stop cleaning. Especially the toilets. It makes me uneasy. I am more than capable of handling basic household maintenance. You don't need to insult my skills."

"I cleaned because it had to be done. We have a giant house. We all pitched in."

Clover sighed. "I know. But that's over now. There are things that only you can do. Please do those things and leave other things to me."

I resumed stirring. "It really bothers you that I scrubbed the toilets?"

"What kind of maid lets her lady clean the bathrooms?"

The light finally dawned. Clover had left her home and studied for years to become a lady's maid. When she was thrown out of the earl's household, her entire identity had been ripped away from her. She desperately wanted to get back to the place where she was competent, efficient, and admired for her skills. She required a lady, especially now, because she had something to prove, and for better or worse, I was it.

"Very well. I will leave the cleaning to you."

"Thank you, Maggie. I swear I won't go to the market again without you."

The contents of the cauldron turned into thick banana pudding. I drew a heart on the surface. It stayed. No yellow streaks, and the shine was just right.

"It's ready." I took a ladle and scooped the mass into the first small pan.

"But what is it?"

"Soap."

The soap in Kair Toren was both expensive and not that great. It was hot-processed using rendered animal fat, which was pricey. Even the soap in the Garden, which served only the best to its customers, had no scent and had felt kind of rough. When I was looking for a place to stay, one of the prospective landlords took his time moaning about the price of soap and then patting himself on the back for including a grape-sized chunk of it with the weekly rent.

"But you didn't use tallow," she murmured. "Can you make soap with bulko oil?"

"We're about to find out." The basic principle was the same: Add lye to fat and let it saponify. I had no doubt that this soap would lather. But nailing down the details would take a lot longer.

"If this works . . ." Clover's face took on a faraway look, and then her eyes shone. "Half a den."

"I'm sorry?"

"That's how much it cost us to make a small pan. If we make a large pan, we can cut it into finger-thick bars, ten bars per mold. If we charge five dens per bar, we can make half a noma per batch. We bought two short barrels . . ."

"We won't know if it worked until it cools enough to handle. Help me keep track. This is test batch number one at five drems, even. Now we need to make batch number two."

We had a long day ahead of us.

Kair Toren didn't just have beautiful sunrises. Its sunsets rocked, too.

The western half of the sky shone with gold and amber, as if someone had built a hot fire and scattered the still-glowing coal over the soft azure expanse. Plump clouds floated in it, soaking in the color and turning yellow and lavender.

At the laundry table, Shana dipped her hands into a bucket of water, lathered them with the latest bar of soap, and contemplated the bubbles. Sample bars filled the table, each carefully labeled with a number, twenty-four in total. On the bench, Clover made the latest annotations on our list of ingredients.

I stretched my chest and shoulders, trying to work the kinks out. We'd been at this for over twelve hours.

The first batch worked but had too much lye. It wouldn't go to waste, since we could use it for laundry. The second batch didn't have enough lye and came out slimy. It took me four more tries to nail down the precise ratio of the three ingredients. Then we added yogurt to create a creamier lather and a softer, more fluid soap. That took several batches, and then we added the maidenflower extract. The challenge wasn't to just make cheap soap, but to produce a superior soap bar at a low cost.

I was so tired.

At some point Reynald parked himself near us, working on sharpening some arrowheads. He and Gort had discussed our arsenal and decided it was sorely lacking. They had bought some bows and crossbows and a heap of arrows and bolts, which now needed tending to.

Then Shana came out to see what we were doing, and Gort followed shortly after. He and Lute sat on a bench nearby now, working on patching some chainmail and helmets. Gort and Shana were never too far from each other. If she was in the kitchen, and he had nothing to do, he would end up there. If he was working on something in the courtyard, she would come out and knit, keeping him in her view.

"It's between batch number twenty-two and number seventeen." Shana passed the bar to Kaiden. "How did you even think of adding maidenflower to it? Where did you learn to do this?"

"I had a friend who was interested in soap when I was Clover's age."

Cheyenne was my best friend through the last two years of high school. The soap-making craze was in full swing back then, and one day she announced that we should corner the high school market. I learned to make soap, got slightly obsessed with it, and kept making it long after Cheyenne moved on to other things.

We had grown apart after high school. Cheyenne was a banking underwriter now. She worked for a local credit union, had bought a house ten minutes from her parents, and got engaged. I found out about it when I delivered a grocery order to her new house.

For some reason seeing me drag a pack of bottled water to her front door had deeply disturbed Cheyenne. She tried to give me a ridiculously large tip in cash on top of what she had already put in through the app. I declined. She texted me the next day saying that there was a teller opening at her bank. I thanked her and told her I already had a job. She didn't text again.

She thought I needed help and was trying to rescue me. I appreciated that but I wished she had invited me to catch up over lunch instead. I didn't need another job, but I could've used a friend.

Kaiden lathered his hands, rinsed them, lathered them with the other bar, sniffed the soap, and held the one with the deeper purple up. "This one."

"It's number seventeen for me, too," Shana agreed.

My back still hurt. I glanced at Clover.

"Number seventeen," she confirmed. "It softens the skin, and the scent is refined. I would've bought it for any noble household without hesitation. There is no soap like this anywhere in the city. If we brought this bar into the soap guild, all the soap makers would bow to it."

"I've finally found my true calling," I announced. "I shall be Maggie the Soap Queen of Kair Toren. I will rule this city with my clean, soft hands . . ."

Reynald laughed.

"You should take a rest," Shana told me. "The fumes are getting to you."

I used to feel alone sometimes. Not lonely, just alone. I texted with my parents and my brother every day or two and hung out online, but my in person interactions with other humans were limited to accepting payment and handing out keys at my storage job. I was never a social butterfly and the few friendships I built in college just kind of faded out. I'd dated but never found someone I wanted to stay with. That was fine. I wasn't pulling my hair out in despair, but occasionally I became aware that it was just me and four walls.

Now I had a whole house of people to talk to. When Will came back, we would go inside and have a well-earned dinner and all the chairs around the table would be full.

I hadn't thought of home or my parents for over twenty-four hours. It made me feel guilty, as if I had somehow betrayed them. Logically I understood that this guilt was absurd. Staying in Rellas wasn't a choice. It's not like I had a magic wand I could wave to teleport me home. I wasn't deliberately choosing to stay here at the cost of panicking my parents and my brother.

The problem was that if someone had handed me that wand right now, I wasn't sure I would use it. Leaving meant everyone in this courtyard would have to fend for themselves. Some of them wouldn't survive.

I had to see the Hreban thing through. Stop Hreban, then search for a way to go home.

Maybe that was where the guilt was coming from.

Someone pounded on the front door. Gort nodded at Kaiden. The boy ran into the tunnel. A moment later Will staggered into the courtyard, looking haggard. He landed on a bench across from me, propped his feet up on an empty pan-oil barrel, and closed his eyes.

"How did it go?" Shana asked.

"I will never complain about a forced march again," he said, his eyes still closed. "This was worse than Egendarr."

Lute grinned. "Hey, Will? Let's spar."

Will didn't bother looking at him. "Are you tired of living?"

Lute chuckled.

"A day of honest work is good for you once in a while," Gort said.

"Thanks, Dad. I've had enough honesty till next year. I'm full up."

"The salt ship?" Reynald asked.

Will opened his eyes. "Coming on Fifday, like you said."

We had two days to prepare.

"We'll be unloading early," Will continued.

"How early?" Gort asked.

"They warned us to be there by four bells."

Four AM. They didn't want anyone to pay too much attention to that salt, so they would unload it before the wharf filled with workers.

"This might be harder than we thought," Will said. "They watch us closely."

"How many guards?" Reynald asked.

"Two, and three clerks on the warehouse crew."

Gort grunted. "We'll need a diversion."

"It will have to be something flashy," Will said. "Their guards are dedicated."

Silence fell.

"How is the pier lit?" Reynald asked.

"Reinforced barrels with logs," Will said. "One on each side of the pier where it joins the wharf and two along the pier's length. Lanterns inside the warehouse."

Reynald's face turned thoughtful. He walked over, picked up bar #17, and smelled it. "In the north, they make soap out of gorefish blubber instead of tallow."

"Tallow is better," Shana said. "If gorefish blubber catches fire, it flares up. They make oil out of it and use it for Kair Toren's lighthouses."

Reynald looked at Clover, then at Kaiden.

"How fast are you?"

"Very fast," Kaiden said.

Reynald took our mixing bucket, walked over to the wine tree, and set the bucket on the stone wall wrapping around the tree. Then he went back to the bench and picked up a round helmet.

What was he up to?

Reynald waved Kaiden over. Kaiden trotted to him. Reynald gave the helmet to him and drew an invisible line on the stone with his foot.

"Stand here."

Kaiden stood.

"Toss the helmet into the bucket."

Kaiden threw the helmet. It bounced off the rim and clattered to the ground. Bucketball, not Kaiden's best talent.

"Again," Reynald said.

Kaiden chased the helmet down and tossed it into the bucket again. This time it landed.

Bucket, gorefish blubber, diversion . . .

Oh. I got it.

"Safely," I said. "If anyone gets hurt, it's not worth it."

"I remember," Reynald told me. "Trust me."

"Question." Lute raised his hand. "Why are we going through all this trouble for some overpriced salt?"

Because the fate of the kingdom depended on it. "Get me that barrel and I will explain everything," I said.

Chapter 15

Planter 14

I leaned on the wall of Spotter's Rampart. Behind me lay the city, shrouded in darkness. In front of me most of the harbor was dark, too, except for this stretch of the Combs. Large barrels dotted the wharf and the Yolentas' pier, blazing with orange flames. Each barrel came with a polished metal circle affixed to the rim. It jutted straight up, like a wheel on a cart, reflecting the light from the fires and illuminating a chunk of the pier like a streetlamp.

A huge ship floated at the end of the pier, its carved hull wide, almost bloated compared to the graceful, leaner waverunner moored at the next dock. The waverunners were built for speed, while the Yolentas' trade vessels were meant to carry as much cargo as safely possible.

At the end of the pier, a small harbor crane swung back and forth. On board the ship, dim shapes loaded barrels onto the crane platform. Once full, the crane swung to the pier, and a couple of burly workers heaved the barrels onto handcarts.

A line of dockworkers moved along the pier, carting barrels to the warehouse and returning to the ship with the empty carts, like worker ants marching from the anthill to a picnic and back again. One of these workers was Will, but from this distance I couldn't tell where he was. They were all large men, pushing identical handcarts, and the orange glow reduced them to dark silhouettes.

Next to me, Shana peered at the line of dockworkers. We waited side by side, wrapped in our cloaks.

A gust of wind swirled around me, flinging cold marine air in my face. I shivered.

"I need to make you a shawl," Shana murmured.

"It's almost summer."

"Yes, and if I start now, it will be done by the fall."

"We'll have to live that long."

"That's your job. Keep us breathing."

The human conveyor belt below kept moving. The person behind this scheme was very careful. The first and last batches of barrels, twenty-five each, would contain only pink salt. We needed to target the barrels in the middle batch, roughly a hundred of them, marked with a small triangle burned into the lid.

The burn mark was so small, only someone looking for it would notice it. There wasn't a lot of light on that pier. The easiest way to find it was by feel.

Nothing would happen until Will put one of those barrels into his cart.

I pulled Everard's den out of my sleeve pocket, rubbed it between my fingers for luck, and put it back. Please let it go well . . .

"It will be fine," Shana murmured next to me. "My boys have done far worse. The stories I could tell."

"I'm worried about the kids."

"Clover and Kaiden can handle themselves. They know their parts. They've practiced."

Reynald was a big believer in "practice makes better." Kaiden had spent the last two days sprinting through our courtyard and chucking various objects into empty baskets and barrels, while Reynald and Gort took turns supervising. Those two would have made excellent high school football coaches. Gort especially.

I had spent the last two days stressing out and making a large batch of soap. Yesterday we had strapped a tray to Lute and sent him, some sample bars, and his winning smile toward the market. He came back in half an hour without the soap but a noma and a half richer. I didn't dare to sell more until we registered our shop, but it was a good sign, and Clover stopped sweating bullets over our production costs.

The kids were down on the wharf, waiting. Reynald was down there somewhere, too, hiding in the alley to our right, ready to step in if things went badly. Gort was farther east, waiting in one of the plazas with Honey and a leased horse cart. If everything went well in the next few minutes, we'd be loading one of the marked barrels into it.

I needed things to go well. So much was riding on it. I needed a win in the worst way. If this went to plan, I would have Reynald's confidence, and eighty people wouldn't have to die.

A dockworker passed by the farthest barrel, right by the ship's gangplank, and stumbled.

"That's my boy," Shana murmured.

The signal. Will had found a mark on his barrel.

I picked up the lantern resting by my feet. Shana grabbed a long pole, and we hung the lantern on its end. We waited. We had to time it just right.

Below Will disappeared into the warehouse.

Breathe. Breathe, breathe, breathe . . .

Will emerged from the warehouse with an empty cart and pushed it back to the ship, keeping his place in line.

"There he is," Shana whispered.

We watched him as he reached the trade vessel. The two powerlifters deposited another marked barrel into his cart. Will made a careful U-turn and headed back to the warehouse.

Three...

Will reached the second fire barrel. Thirty yards to the warehouse.

Two...

We had to time it just right, so he would be between the barrels, in the dark.

One. Now!

I raised the lantern pole and bobbed it up and down.

A loud scream came from the right, a woman yelling at the top of her lungs. "Stop! Stop! Thief!"

A beggar boy in rags sprinted along the wharf toward the line of dockworkers, cradling a large clay jug to his chest. Clover chased him, screaming, a stick in her hand.

"Thief! Help!"

The dockworkers, overwhelmingly male and young, saw a pretty girl yelling for help and did exactly what Reynald expected them to do. They stopped and moved to the right, trying to block the thief from escaping. Will let go of his cart and stepped in front of it, almost as if he were protecting the cargo.

A lone dockworker pushing a cart covered by a tarp came out of the street to our left. Lute with his replacement barrel.

Kaiden saw a wall of bodies closing together in front of him, whirled toward Clover, saw her stick, spun back around, and hurled the jug he was carrying into the nearest fire barrel.

Flames exploded, sending chunks of burning logs all over the wharf.

The dockworkers shielded their eyes against the flash.

Kaiden darted past them into the alley to the right.

Lute pulled up next to Will's cart, picked up the tarp, tossed it over Will's barrel, grabbed Will's cart, and smoothly wheeled it away back the way he came.

Clover shrieked in outrage and alarm. "That's a noma's worth of gorefish oil, you little shit!"

The burning logs sputtered on the wharf. There were few things more alarming than a fire at the harbor. The sailors on the Yolenta ship collectively lost their shit. Someone roared, "Don't just stand there, you assholes! Put that fucking fire out!"

The crowd by the pier fractured. Half of the workers ran for the water barrels to put out the fire, three went to check on Clover, and a few who still had cargo in their carts wheeled them into the warehouse. Will was one of them.

One of the warehouse workers sprinted after Kaiden into the alley and stumbled back out, hands up. If I had run into Reynald on a dark street, I would have done exactly the same.

Nobody noticed Lute and his cart.

We'd pulled it off.

I let out a breath and slumped onto the stone rail.

"I'm going to make my rudberry sambocade," Shana said. "I think they deserve it, don't you?"

✦

". . . and like I told you, fire always works," Gort pontificated. "You could steal the whole pier if you had a big enough fire."

I sat at the head of the table and tried not to fidget.

The entire day was a blur. We got home and went to bed. Except I couldn't sleep. I kept turning over and over until I finally gave up. Nothing could happen until Will returned, safe and sound, from the wharf. All I could do was wait.

Just after lunch I sent Kaiden, in his clean clothes and with his hair brushed, to check on Will, and he came back and reported that everything seemed to be normal. The barrel swap had gone unnoticed.

It was almost dinnertime now. Will would be back any minute. One by one, everybody trickled into the kitchen, until all of us were packed in there, eyeing the stolen barrel sitting on a tarp on the floor.

Come on. How long . . .

As if on cue, Reynald loomed in the doorway and stepped into the kitchen. Behind him Will staggered in and tossed some coins on the table.

"What took you so long?" Lute demanded.

"I had to settle up," Will growled. "I told them I'd had enough excitement and dawn-to-dusk days. Honest work takes a lot out of a person. You should try it."

Lute looked at the coins. "Doesn't pay that much though, does it? I'll stick with soldiering, thanks."

"Oh, when do you plan to start?" Will dropped into a chair and turned to Gort. "Next time, it's his turn."

I looked at Gort, too. "We'll need something to bust the barrel open."

Gort stood up. "I have just the thing."

Shana slid a big plate of food and a tankard of ale in front of Will and put a platter of triangular pastries on the table, perfectly golden brown and smelling of delicious fruit and freshly baked bread. Clover distributed cups and tea.

"Don't we get ale?" Lute asked.

Shana stopped and looked at him.

Lute raised his hands. "Fine, fine."

Gort returned to the kitchen carrying a large war maul. It looked like an oversized hammer.

"Now?" he asked.

"Not yet."

Gort leaned the maul against the wall next to the barrel and sat down. Everyone was here, finally.

I was so nervous, my hands trembled. This was it. Either I was Maggie the Undying who could predict the future, or I was a delusional woman who had no idea what she was doing. Everything was riding on this, and I'd run across enough inconsistencies to realize that nothing the books talked about was guaranteed. I could've hedged my bets and opened the barrel privately, but I needed the full power of that reveal. I needed to shock them. Go big or go home.

If only.

I took a deep breath. "I asked you to do all of this and didn't explain why. You trusted me. I appreciate that trust more than I can express."

Reynald's face was like a stone wall. No emotion at all. I had a vision of the empty barrel and him getting up from the table and walking away.

"Reynald told you that I know other people's secrets. I do. I also know some of the future."

Will raised his eyebrows. Lute gave me a skeptical look. Shana glanced at Gort. Her face said *What did you get me into?*

So far this was going awesome.

"So is that like visions?" Will asked.

"Not exactly. I know a version of the future. In that version Hreban rises to power and the kingdom burns. I'm trying to stop it. If anyone finds out about me, I will be in danger. This knowledge is valuable, and someone like Sauven, Everard, or Hreban would kill to possess it."

The skepticism was so thick, you could cut it with a knife.

I took a swallow of my tea for courage. "Gort, you are not supposed to be here."

He glanced at me. "Where am I supposed to be?"

"Getting ready to march on Falcon Point."

Gort's mouth dropped. He caught himself, but it was too late. I had finally managed to shock Gort Magnar.

Shana pivoted to her husband. "Falcon Point?"

Her voice was soft and mild. Across the table, the two brothers went perfectly still.

Gort reached out and patted Shana's fingers with his huge hand. "A small fort in the north Middle Fields. Quick job, easy money."

Shana turned to her sons. "Did you know about this?"

They shook their heads.

"I didn't tell them," Gort said gently. "I didn't tell anyone. I hadn't even signed yet. We were just talking."

Shana took a long, slow breath. "Who is the recruiter?"

"Filderon," Gort said. "You remember him. We worked with him before."

"You promised me that you were done."

Gort cleared his throat. "We needed the coin."

Shana didn't say anything.

"It was going to be the last one," Gort said.

"That's what you said the last time. And the time before that."

"This time, it would be," I said.

The table went quiet.

Shana met my eyes, and suddenly I had the urge to back up with my hands in the air.

"What will happen at Falcon Point?" she asked.

I drank a bit more of my tea. My throat had gone dry. "Filderon is recruiting people for a short campaign to settle a land dispute between two nobles. He is offering generous rates with a third of the money up front on signing."

"Strange," Will said. "Last time getting money out of him was like pulling teeth."

"What's with this sudden generosity?" Lute said.

"It was last-minute, and the client who hired him was desperate," Gort said.

"Filderon is lying," I told them. "The client who hired him doesn't want any of this to come back to them, which is why Filderon is requiring everyone to bring their own gear. The company can't look like an organized fighting force. They must resemble bandits."

The more I talked, the scarier Shana looked.

"The company will leave for Falcon Point in two days. Gort will suspect that something is off when Filderon refuses to fly any banners. By that point it will be too late. On paper, Falcon Point is owned by a minor noble. In reality, that minor noble is Dreantia Yolenta."

Gort stopped patting his wife's hand. Lute swallowed. Will's face turned grim.

Dreantia was the head of the Yolenta Family. It was her barrel sitting on the tarp.

Attacking a fort owned by the head of a Great Family was writing your own death warrant. Especially attacking a fort that belonged to the Keepers of Iron. Their cavalry was the heaviest in Rellas. Their crest bore a hammer, both the symbol of their craft and a promise of their retribution.

"What happens next?" Shana asked, her voice flat.

"A day into the march, Filderon will send a scout to warn Falcon Point's defenders that bandits are about to attack. The garrison will ask Dreantia for reinforcements. She will pull a company of knights from Kryss Britin, a town half a day's ride from Falcon Point."

The Magnars listened, food forgotten. To my right, Reynald's expression had grown dark. A mercenary company, no matter how well trained and supplied, was no match for the Yolentas' knights. Even if Dreantia didn't dispatch her best, even if she sent her second, third, or fourth best, they would mow through the mercenaries like wild horses trampling a field of weeds.

"Filderon will throw the company against Falcon Point and clear off during the charge. Dreantia's knights will arrive, crushing the mercenaries between themselves and the fort. Most of the company will die in the battle. Gort will survive, but he will be captured with a few others, convicted of banditry, and executed."

Clover sucked in a sharp breath.

"His body will be thrown into a mass grave at the foot of the fort. I'm so sorry."

The kitchen went as silent as a tomb.

"Well," Shana said slowly. "We can't have that."

The brothers jumped to their feet at the same time.

"Sit down!" she snapped.

They sat.

"Why?" Shana asked me.

Now that was an excellent question.

I drank more tea. "Kryss Britin is a trade hub for Yolenta goods going north. The goods come off the ships and caravans, are given a quick inspection, and then are shipped to Kryss Britin, where they are inspected again and sent to their final destinations. That is where this barrel was headed."

I nodded to Gort. "Time for your maul to shine."

He looked at Will. "Do you want to do the honors? You've earned it."

My hands shook. I hid them under the table.

Will got up, walked over to the barrel, grabbed the maul, and swung. The big war hammer smashed into the wood, right in the middle. The barrel creaked but held.

You've got to be kidding me.

"Hit it, don't tap it," Lute said. "It's not an ale keg."

Will made a face and swung again. Wood cracked like a gun shot. The barrel burst, spilling salt on the tarp amid shards and splinters. In the middle of the salt heap, five smooth gray ingots reflected the light.

Relief washed over me, so overwhelming I almost passed out. I was right. I was right, I was right, I was right. I hadn't screwed up. I would do a victory dance, except if I tried to stand right now, I'd probably fall over.

Reynald rose and picked up an ingot. He hefted it in his hand, examined it, and placed it on the table. "Gray iron."

There were many kinds of iron in Rellas. Hard iron was for tools because it was strong and durable. White iron was for the mages because it was soft and pliant and took enchantment well. Blue iron was for armor because it was light, resilient, and didn't rust. Gray iron was for weapons. It was tough and flexible, and it held a sharp edge the longest.

Everyone stared at the ingot. Gort picked up a smooth brick and let it fall on the table with a heavy thud.

Reynald turned to me. The expression on his face was indescribable. There was admiration in his eyes, surprise, and something more I couldn't quite place. He was looking at me like I was a magician who'd made an elephant disappear in the middle of a crowded street. I would remember that look in his eyes for the rest of my life.

I allowed myself a small knowing smile. *That's right, Sir Reynald. Drink it in.*

"I don't understand," Gort said. "The Yolentas own the iron mines. Why are they smuggling ingots in barrels of salt?"

"Dreantia Yolenta has an older brother," I said. "Normally the oldest sibling heads the family, but Diodor doesn't care about wealth or profit. He cares only about working with metal. I'm not even sure he understands the full value of money, but Dreantia does."

"He makes the blades, and she makes the coin," Shana said.

"Yes." I nodded. "Diodor's daughter, Indora, is ambitious and impatient. Dreantia has her on a short leash, and Indora wants her father to take over the family, so she can run it instead of her aunt. But she lacks support, so she needs to borrow someone else's hands to shove Dreantia aside."

"What about the iron?" Clover asked.

"I'm getting to that. There is a reason why the Yolentas are the Keepers of the Iron, but not the Lords of it. All iron in Rellas belongs to the Throne. The Yolentas are allowed to work the mines, but the king determines how much of the ore they keep, how much they sell, and to whom. Especially when it comes to gray iron."

To Rellas, gray iron had the same strategic value that plutonium did in our world. Sauven wanted to know exactly what happened to it.

"Dreantia is skimming off the top," I said.

They looked at me with blank expressions.

"She underreports the mine yields and secretly sells the excess outside of the kingdom. She is choosy about the price, not the buyers."

"That's treason," Reynald said. "Sauven will rip her heart out."

"Dreantia knows that. She's been bribing the right people for years. Even counting all those bribes, she makes a nice profit, and all of it goes directly into her secret vault."

I drank the last of my tea. This would be a longish explanation.

"Indora discovered that her aunt was embezzling and sensed an opportunity. If this theft is exposed, Sauven will lose his shit and Dreantia will lose her life. Indora's father would be the natural successor. Reporting the theft would do no good. Dreantia pays her bribes on time, so if Indora tried to turn her in, nothing would happen and Dreantia would be informed. Indora must draw attention to the embezzlement without leaving herself vulnerable."

"There is a nice little rebellion brewing on the border with the Selva Dukedom," Reynald said, his eyes iced over. "And the rebels require iron for weapons and armor. When the word of them arming themselves reaches Sauven, he will send the royal inspectors to the nearest iron producer, the Yolentas. They are the most obvious suspects. Bribing the inspectors won't work. They fear Sauven much more than they love money. They will open Dreantia's books, discover the theft, and her life will be forfeit."

He had put it all together.

"Exactly," I said. "The iron for the rebels has to come from somewhere. Indora can't steal it from the Yolentas' mines—they are watched too closely by her aunt's people. Nor can she buy it abroad, because Dreantia pays attention to her spending."

"Hreban." Reynald spat the word like it was poison.

"Yes. Hreban is quietly training a private army. He will need weapons and armor. He and Indora struck a deal. He supplies her with iron he buys elsewhere, and she smuggles it in with pink salt and distributes it to the rebels. In return, when she takes over the family, she will funnel weapons and armor to his troops."

The partnership between the monarchs of Rellas and the Keepers of Iron was centuries old. As a ruler, you would want your most trusted ally to run the mines. When dynasties changed, so did the identity of the Keepers, although the Yolentas had kept the iron the longest. They had the gift of Copper Glean. Their magic allowed them to find mineral wealth beneath their feet and granted them enhanced understanding of metallurgy.

When the Savarics took the throne centuries ago, the Yolentas were their greatest allies. But time and greed had eroded that bond. Indora Yolenta had no qualms about throwing her lot in with Ulmar Hreban.

"But why Falcon Point?" Will asked. "How does it connect?"

"Dreantia isn't stupid. She also wants to know where the rebel iron is coming from, and she suspects that there is a traitor in the family. Last month Dreantia replaced the head commander of the knights guarding Kryss Britin with Sir Drogen, her loyal dog. Indora paid off the inspectors, but with Drogen looking over their shoulder, her barrels won't pass. She needs the knights to disappear for the day so she can push her salt caravan through."

"It's a distraction," Lute said. "But why would the knights drop everything and ride to rescue a small fort?"

"That's the best part." I smiled at him. "Falcon Point is where Dreantia hides her stolen gold. She will do anything to protect it."

"That is clever," Clover murmured.

I faced the Magnars. "Filderon is due to ship out in two days. If we do nothing, all of those mercenaries will die a pointless death. If we do something, we will draw attention to ourselves."

And hit the timeline with a hammer the size of Gort's maul.

Silence claimed the table.

"The company can't ship out without the broker," Will said. "Filderon is the linchpin."

"Take him out and it all falls down," Lute said.

"How is our friend Filderon?" Shana said. "I haven't seen him in ages. We should have dinner."

"If the four of you take action against Filderon and it's discovered, you will never work as mercenaries again," I warned. "You know what happens to mercenaries who kill a broker."

"We will be blacklisted," Will said. He didn't sound the least bit upset about it.

"Oh no," Lute said, his voice bland. "Whatever shall we do?"

Gort faced me. "What happens to Filderon after Falcon Point?"

"He gets his payout and buys an estate near Praul Britin. He grows grapes and makes wine."

"Is it any good?" Gort asked.

"He thinks so. Calls it Falcon's Tears."

Gort looked at Reynald.

"Don't be seen," the blademaster said.

Gort smiled.

The two Magnar brothers grinned at me in unison. Next to Gort, Shana bared her teeth. They looked like a family of werewolves about to sprout fangs and claws. If their eyes started glowing, I wouldn't be at all surprised.

Gort rose. "I'll go set up a meet. We'll want to discuss this job somewhere quiet."

"What if he rejects that invite?" I asked.

"Oh, he'll see us." Gort's eyes turned cold and angry. "When he was trying to lure me in, he kept mentioning the boys, and I couldn't understand why. It's an old-dog job."

"He didn't want two grown men coming around asking how their father died," Reynald said.

And if Gort and both his sons died at Falcon Point, the only one asking questions would be Shana, and Filderon must've decided he could handle her. That fucking slime.

"Go get him, love," Shana said.

Gort motioned to Lute. "Think you can play the part?"

"I have this." Lute nodded. "I'll tell him all about how times are tough, and my brother is breaking his back at the docks."

The two of them left the kitchen.

"Well, it's about time for dinner." Shana nodded to Kaiden. "Come with me. I'll need things from the cellar."

"I'm going to wash the wharf off." Will headed into the hallway.

In a moment it was just Reynald, Clover, and me.

"I'll see Gort and Lute out," Clover said. She got up and turned to me. "You were amazing, my lady."

Aw.

Clover left the kitchen.

Reynald stood up. I looked at him.

"Regrets?" he asked.

I shook my head. "Filderon is a man who sacrifices other people to put coin in his pocket. He deserves everything that's coming to him."

Reynald leaned slightly toward me. A little light played in his green eyes. He was strikingly handsome right now for some reason. Suddenly I was acutely aware of the space between us. I knew exactly where his hands rested on the table and how close his face was to mine.

"For the record," he said, his voice quiet, almost intimate, "I also think you're amazing."

The world stopped. *Say something, don't just stare at him . . .* "Thank you, Sir Reynald."

He gave me a scorching smile and left the room.

All of the air went out of me, and I slumped into my chair. That was too much.

Entirely too much.

Chapter 16

Writing with a reed pen wasn't my favorite.

I had found all sorts of paper in my office: the rougher sheets; the smoother ones; thin, brownish everyday paper; the pale formal paper; even the thick fancy paper, embossed with an ornate border and accented by a thin magenta thread. I probably would've found a bullet journal if I looked long enough. All of that was great. The reed pens were something else entirely.

Rellasian reed pens were carved out of hollow reeds, which were then tipped with a metal nib and filled with ink. Lasa, the horrible shit smear that he was, had used them to produce a feathery, beautiful script. How he'd managed that escaped me. I kept scratching the paper and leaving holes everywhere.

Outside the last of the sunset had burned down to twilight, the sky like purple velvet. Fortunately, I had two oil lanterns—the larger floor lamp and the smaller one for my desk. They weren't as good as electric lamps, but they weren't bad either, and their soft yellow glow turned my study into a cozy den.

My handwriting was never great and had gotten worse. I typed at the speed of light and texted like a pro, but neither of those options were available here. Besides, I was taught to write fast and clearly. No frills, just legible letters. Writing in Rellasian was an exercise in pretty whorls. I still couldn't get over the fact that I knew how to do it. I set the pen to paper, and Rellasian script came out. I'd tried the Shears cypher for laughs and that worked, too. If I ever got into the Shears' HQ, all their secrets would be mine.

I had been at this for the better part of two hours. Now that we'd found the contraband iron, we had to decide what to do about it. I had a lot of things to write down.

A knock made me raise my head. Reynald stood in the doorway.

During the day, when he was doing things around the house, you forgot who he was and what he was capable of. But right now, half wrapped in the gloom, he looked frightening. His broad shoulders stretched his charcoal shirt. He seemed to have congealed from twilight, complete with an impassive expression on his face. Deadly swordsmen in my fantasy books loomed a lot, but I'd never seen anyone "loom" in real life. Reynald could give a master class in looming. If he wasn't on our side, I'd be climbing out the window to get away.

"Come in," I invited.

He stalked into the room and sat in the chair across the desk. The golden glow of the lanterns played over the hard jaw and the defined contours of his cheekbones. His gray-green eyes were cold and thoughtful, communicating just enough danger to catch your attention and hold it right there, on him. You could put him on a cover just like that, with a sword by his chair, and I would buy it so fast, my phone would catch fire.

I also think you're amazing . . .

Perspective. He wasn't trying to impress me. He was just sitting in a chair.

"What are we going to do about the iron?" he asked.

Right. Back to business.

"It's a valuable secret. We could sell it to the Shears," I told him. "The rebellion in the highlands is just south of Selva's border. If it flares up, Sauven will demand that Everard put it down and then find some fault with how he does. The Sleepless Duke will lose soldiers, time, and money, and in the end, he'll be accused of slaughtering helpless peasants or some other nonsense Sauven's pack of counselors cooks up. Don't get me wrong, Everard is ruthless, but he doesn't go out of his way to be cruel unless he is trying to make a point. There is no point to be made in the hinterlands."

"We are ornery people," Reynald said. "If we don't rebel every decade or so, we get bored."

Spoken like a highland man. Long ago that area was settled by geriben, who raided Rellas in their blade boats. They were an independent and proud people, who kept the memories of their raiding glory alive, and they had no love for Rellasian bureaucracy. It didn't take much to set them off. If they weren't rebelling, they were communicating their intention to rebel.

"Everard needs this rebellion like a hole in his head. Since the Shears are allied with him, they've been turning the kingdom inside out trying to figure out the iron supplier. They will pay top rate."

He thought about it, his fingers tapping the right armrest. "What's binding the Shears to Everard?"

"The Shears are led by Solentine Dagarra."

"Ah."

Nothing more needed to be said.

This portion of the continent was split between Rellas in the West and the Crimson Empire in the East. The two countries shared a long border, interrupted by the Corios Sea. When they warred, their invasions happened either in the south, across a vast plain, or in the north, where three mountain ranges formed the Trihorn.

Solentine's father, Margrave Izarn Demarr, held the southern edge of the Trihorn, while the Sleepless Duke shielded the northern side. The Demarrs and the Everards had to cooperate. They were both vassals of Rellas, but Izarn was much more vulnerable to Sauven's whims and paranoia. More, he had to maintain a large standing army that was beyond his means. The Throne sent him an annual grant, and without that money the defense of the border would collapse. Izarn couldn't afford to piss Sauven off.

To keep everyone safe, a secret agreement was reached between the Everards and the Demarrs.

"Publicly, the Demarrs are cool toward Selva and hold themselves as if the Sleepless Duke is the necessary evil they must endure to guard the border," I said. "Privately, Solentine aids Everard in his ambitions using the Shears, at least for now. In return, if the Demarrs need help, Everard will come to their aid."

"Good to know," Reynald said.

While we're on the subject . . . I handed him a small envelope.

"What is it?"

"Leverage against Solentine. If something happens to me, and you suspect the Shears are involved, you can use this to pressure him."

Reynald studied the envelope. "Can I look at it?"

I nodded.

He opened the envelope, freed the single piece of paper inside, and read it. His eyebrows crept up.

Yeah. Solentine regretted a few things he had done in his life, but he was only ashamed of one. That one.

Reynald slid the paper back into the envelope.

"Solentine is very dangerous," I said. "You're the superior swordsman, but he has magic, and he won't meet you head-on. He's more likely to shoot you in the back and call it a day."

"He wouldn't be the first to try." Reynald shrugged, then frowned. "You said Solentine supports Everard for now. Does he switch his allegiance?"

"Yes."

"To Hreban?"

"No. Not at all. The Demarrs go at it alone." And it would become their undoing.

"What causes the rift?"

Now that I'd met Solentine, I could picture it in my head, him standing in the middle of a terrible battle, splattered with blood and screaming. It would be a wordless, horrible howl, the sound of grief and rage so awful that it had to be vented or it would've torn him apart.

"Solentine is loyal to his family, while Everard is loyal only to Selva. The Sleepless Duke makes a choice that Solentine can't live with."

Reynald nodded, his expression thoughtful. "Makes sense. Only a fool expects loyalty from a man who salts fields and burns villages to the ground."

Loyalty among the Great Families was a touchy subject. Some, like Bors, inspired it. Others, like Hreban, ruled through intimidation and money.

"There is also this." I passed another folded piece of paper to him.

Reynald looked at it. "What language is this?"

"It's the Shears' cypher."

"What does it say?"

"'Don't get into the carriage. Krasta has magic, and he's fast with a knife.'"

"Is that a warning for Solentine?"

I nodded. "He's getting desperate to find the source of iron. He took a shortcut and crossed a kir from the of Tangle."

Kir meant a gang boss, and as criminals went, Krasta was one of the more vicious. Curiously, kir also meant "sergeant" and there was probably some deep meaning in that.

"What happens if he gets into the carriage?"

"He'll win, but it will cost him the use of his left arm for about a month."

"Everything I've heard about the Bastard of Dagarra says he can take care of himself," Reynald said.

"Yes, but I don't want to take a chance on Solentine being stabbed in the throat instead of his shoulder. I was thinking of asking Will to sneak the message into the Three Moons."

"You feel something for Solentine," he said.

"I know what drives him. He is a horrible bastard, but if you earn his loyalty, he will fight for you till his dying breath. I don't want that breath to happen any time soon. He is useful."

And that sounded a lot better than *I spent too much time watching him struggle and now I'm emotionally invested despite my common sense.*

"I'll take care of it," Reynald offered.

"Thank you. As you can see, Solentine is at his wits' end. We can sell the secret of iron to the Shears. It would earn us some coin and let us keep the element of surprise. Hreban would continue his present course for a while, unaware that he was being targeted."

"I sense a *but* coming."

"We could also leak the existence of the iron to the Throne. We would lose the surprise, but we'd rattle Hreban's cage. He's been too comfortable for too long. Planning to kidnap Galiene's daughter, killing a man and paying the city guards to watch the body . . . He thinks he is untouchable."

It rankled me.

"I think I know why that is," Reynald said. "Silveren."

"You think Hreban and the Redeemers are already allied?"

He nodded.

"Why? When Hreban approaches Silveren after coming to power, Silveren seems to be conflicted about it. He hesitates."

"Because Hreban is not a strategist, but Silveren is. I fought with Silveren once, years ago. The man is sly, subtle, and guarded. He doesn't seek personal recognition, he avoids it. I watched him formulate the plan of assault and then nudge the commanders in the room toward it until they saw it, and when they claimed it, he congratulated them on their superb strategy. He observes, he waits, and he strikes only when he is sure. I doubt he's changed in the last few years. I cannot see him throwing his lot in with Hreban on a whim."

In the books, after Hreban claimed his top-dog spot, he made a grand show of traveling to the Redeemer Tower and asking Silveren in front of the entire order to be his sword for justice and protection of the kingdom. But that could've been staged. In fact, it probably was. Hreban wouldn't have risked public humiliation of being turned down. He had to know in advance that Silveren would agree to aid him.

An existing alliance with Silveren would explain why Hreban was feeling bold. He had an entire knight order at his disposal. If things went badly, Silveren's people had many ways of solving inconvenient problems.

Reynald leaned back, his expression thoughtful. "I understand Hreban. Gaining the support of a knight order would go a long way to helping him climb up. The Defenders and the Conquerors each have a Great Family behind them. Allying with them is more complicated, while the Redeemers have no backing. I know what he gets out of it. But what's in it for Silveren?"

"The Redeemers rise in status above other holy orders."

Reynald grimaced. "Status they would lose immediately if either Arvel or Bors decide they care. Too much risk for too little gain. No, it's bigger than that."

"So Silveren is using Hreban? To what end?"

"I was hoping you could tell me."

Estol Silveren wasn't a POV character. He didn't have a lot of page time either. He was the son of a baron from the southwest. His family was well-off. He came from a long line of knights, and like his father, he had distinguished himself on the battlefield. In war, he was clever and demonstrated flashes of brilliance.

When he was twenty-three, he was sent overseas on one of Rellas's foreign campaigns. The detachment of the army under his command had taken a small town and burned it to the ground. It was unclear how the fire had started, but many people died, and Silveren was deeply affected by it. He resigned and joined the Order of Redeemers, seeking forgiveness and absolution. His rise through their ranks was meteoric. Within five years, the aging Preceptor passed him the reins. Silveren was thirty-one now, and so far, he'd stayed completely neutral, surfing the sea of political intrigue without getting his hair wet.

"I don't know," I told him. "Hreban holds him in high regard, which for him means refraining from openly sneering in Silveren's direction. When chaos starts, publicly the Redeemers act mostly as one would expect. Once Hreban's private troops are done rampaging, they put out the fires, keep the peace, and obey Sauven's commands."

"And privately?"

"They do things that would turn your hair white. Especially Silveren. You're right, he must have some kind of plan, but what is it?"

"I don't know, and that troubles me."

It troubled me as well.

There was something I was missing here, which wasn't surprising. Latour was infamous for inserting seemingly random scenes into the narrative. They would sit there without any obvious reason for their existence, until three hundred pages later some shocking revelation would make them crucial and relevant. One of them could've related to Silveren and without the final book, I would never make the connection, no matter how many times I'd reread.

The lack of the third book was so fucking frustrating.

"What do you want to do?" Reynald asked.

"I want to rattle Hreban's cage."

"You want to leak word of the iron." His eyes lit up.

"Yes."

"So do I."

"Rattled people make mistakes. I want to see what he does."

"Then we're in accord. I want to stab Hreban and see if Silveren moves to counter."

We shared a look across the table.

"It is far riskier than selling it to the Shears," I said.

"I'm willing to take the risk," he said. "Let me handle this as well."

"What will you do?"

"I have a friend who works for the Justice Chamber."

I waited but he didn't volunteer anything else. Whoever this friend was, the books didn't mention them.

"It's my turn to demonstrate trust then."

His grin had a slightly evil edge to it. "Don't worry, Maggie. Your trust is not misplaced."

Chapter 17

Planter 15

Outside my window the sun was setting. Somewhere in the distance bells rang eight times. The Magnars had been gone for two hours.

I heard footsteps and looked up. Clover appeared in the open doorway and knocked on the doorframe. "Are you sure you don't want any dinner?"

Shana had cooked the whole dinner before she left, complete with dessert, but I couldn't stomach a single bite. "I'm not hungry."

"Snacks? You didn't even have any sambocades."

"I'm good. But thank you for thinking of me."

She frowned and left.

Last night, after Reynald and I talked, he had gone out. In the morning he informed me that the errand was taken care of. Reynald's friend moved fast. I'd sent Kaiden out to the wharf just after noon for general reconnaissance, and according to him, men in armor in black and purple tabards had swarmed the Yolenta warehouse. He couldn't even get close. Hreban had people in the wharf. By now he would know that the warehouse had been raided by the Justice Chamber, and he would deduce why.

We'd made enemies of two Great Families today and if they ever found out about it, there would be hell to pay. And yet it didn't bother me. All of my anxiety was going toward the Magnars. Filderon was overjoyed that Gort had changed his mind and had invited the Magnar family to join him for dinner at the house he leased. They had put on their mercenary garb. I wished them to "Survive, get paid," which was an old mercenary saying for good luck. Lute and Will laughed at me and then they left.

I'd set this in motion. I had known exactly how it would go if I told the Magnars about Falcon Point. It was too late for regrets. I'd sent four people to either kill someone or get killed, and I desperately hoped it wouldn't be the latter.

I had to get out of the office. Sitting here was just making me stir-crazy. I took my desk lantern and went outside.

Instead of a typical roof, our square of a house was topped by a battlement like a castle, a flat stone walkway bordered by a waist-high parapet on both the outer and inner sides. The floor was slightly slanted, allowing the rain to run toward the drain holes in the outer rampart.

In the northeastern corner of the battlement, someone had set up a table, two benches, and a triangle of canvas that you could stretch over the table and attach via a hook to a ring embedded in the rampart. To get to the battlement, you had to take a flight of stairs from the courtyard, which was exactly what I did.

I sat at the table. The evening sky glowed a beautiful lavender washed with gold. Beyond the wall, the Virka flowed, its waters olive-green from the silt. The dying sunlight reflected from the calm surface, and in places the river shone like a jewel.

Across the water, an attendant lit colorful glass lanterns on the roof terrace of the Taryz Teahouse. The evening breeze stirred the bright green triangles of canvas that shielded the patrons from the sun and rain.

A flock of small draga birds flew above the river. Bright white, they looked like a cross between a heron and a hawk that somehow had stolen a white pheasant's tail and dip-dyed it in sunset clouds. Beneath the birds, a boat loaded with barrels floated by, guided by a single helmsman with a large oar at the rear of it.

The world looked like a magical painting.

"Enjoying the scenery?" Reynald said.

I almost jumped. Damn it.

He smiled at me and set a platter with a teapot, two cups, and a dish of triangular pastries on the table.

"What are you doing here?"

"I came to check on you." He sat in the other chair and nudged the platter toward me. "And I brought Shana's sambocades."

The sambocade was a medieval elderflower cheesecake. I'd never tasted one, but a dedicated group of fans had once made all the recipes from the books, and I remembered the pictures. Sambocade looked kind of like a pumpkin pie with some berries on top. This looked more like a pocket of dough.

I took one of the triangles and bit into it.

Oh. Oh wow.

The pastry was buttery and flaky, and the filling was light and creamy, with a subtle berry taste that reminded me of a ripe, sweet blackberry without any seeds. It was light, fluffy, sweet, and it melted on my tongue. I should have never tried one of these because now I was ruined for life.

Reynald poured the tea. I drank from my cup. It was a different flavor this time, a light aromatic brew that tasted faintly of honey, jasmine, and something fruity with a hint of whipped cream.

"What is this?"

"Night blossom. It's a tea rich people drink before bed."

"Did this come out of Clover's 'for the guests' stash?"

The need for a superior tea option to be served to future clients had been explained to me a couple of days ago at great length.

"Possibly. Better drink it before she catches us. I tried to find wine, but we have none. I would've thought we had inherited some from Derog."

"He was adamantly against spirits or wine of any sort. If one of his employees showed up smelling of ale, he would kick them out."

"Ah," Reynald said. "Explains things."

I sipped from my cup. The tea was delicious.

He watched me. "It will be fine, Maggie."

"Filderon is a shrewd, suspicious bastard," I said. "He will be protected."

"The Magnars knew that going in."

I looked at my tea. There was a tiny white flower floating in it.

"You're a worrier," Reynald said. It didn't sound like criticism, just a statement of fact, but I felt the need to defend myself anyway.

"If it wasn't for me, they wouldn't be doing what they're doing right now."

"If it wasn't for you, Gort would be marching to his death in a few days."

I ran my finger along the rim of my teacup. "He wouldn't. You convinced him to abandon Filderon and come work for us."

"Which would never have happened if you hadn't sat at my table at Taryz Teahouse."

Technically true.

"Breaking Ulmar and Indora's budding alliance will leave Hreban without his source of arms," Reynald said. "But the mercenaries didn't have to be a part of it. You could've kept quiet, and nobody would've ever known. Instead, you stuck your neck out for people you've never met."

He was right. I could think of half a dozen ways to quietly shatter that link, the most obvious of which would be writing a letter to Dreantia about what her niece was doing. Now Dreantia would find out when Filderon's mercenaries failed to show up, leaving her inspector to discover the contraband.

I sighed. "Yes, preventing the slaughter at Falcon Point didn't have to be a part of it. It might've been better if it wasn't. There is a risk that the Magnars will be found out, and that may draw attention to us. Indora will survive this mess—she's too shrewd—and she will be looking to get even. Especially since we had the warehouse raided. Right now, she doesn't know we exist. After Filderon dies, who knows?"

He gave me a long glance. "Why did you do it?"

"My father was a soldier. When I was a child, he would leave to fight in wars. I was young, so I didn't always understand where he went, but I remember being scared that he might not come back. His death would've crushed my little world."

Trying to put childhood anxiety into words was surprisingly hard.

"I'm not sure if we can stop Hreban and prevent the civil war. I will do everything I can, I just don't know if it will be enough. But I can save these people today. I'm still worried about the consequences, but was it even a choice?"

"No," he said. "Not for you. Although some people would've let them die and never lost sleep over it."

"I've barely gotten any sleep in the last few days. I can't afford to lose any more."

Reynald studied me for a long moment. "Let me tell you a secret that everyone knows. Mercenary brokers like to talk about rules and traditions, but they are soldiers for hire. They serve the coin and pray to the Hireling. The very Aspect they worship sells his services for money. If they were truly fond of rules and traditions, they would choose a lord or a city and swear their allegiance. Instead, they work for the highest bidder."

True.

"When I convinced Gort to aid us, he told Filderon he wasn't interested. His name isn't on any roster. Nobody will suspect the Magnars, and even if they do, nothing will come of it. No matter how connected Filderon is, no one will risk their neck to avenge him. He will be dead. Do you know what a dead mercenary is worth?"

"Two boots and a sword?" Gort said this once in the books.

"Their boots are garbage, but yes. You can take his sword so you will have a spare. That's it. And if someone chooses to make an issue of Filderon's death, I will take care of it."

He said it in a very final way. *Don't worry about it, I will handle it.* And he would. Reynald didn't make empty promises.

"You have me, Maggie," he said. "I don't know the future, but I know the present, and I've decided to walk this path with you. As long as you will have me by your side, I won't allow anyone to harm you."

The most precious commodity in Kair Toren—the trust of Reynald Karis. I finally had it. Not for now, not conditionally, but for however long it took.

I'd thought I had to deliver the contraband iron to earn it. Instead, it was saving the eighty mercenaries that did it. The deadliest blademaster in the city would lend me his sword. Now I just had to decide what to do with it.

I had worked so hard for this moment. We'd scored a hit against Hreban, we stopped the rebellion and the needless loss of life, and we'd prevented the death of the mercenaries. The Magnars should be able to handle Filderon. The next pivotal event in the storyline wouldn't happen for months. Plenty of time to prepare.

I should've been relieved. Instead the unease wrapped around me like a heavy, smothering blanket.

Reynald squinted at the roof terrace of the Taryz. "The Conquerors are out in force."

On the terrace several people in armor and red tabards sat around a table. One of them waved their arms. The sound didn't reach this far, but it looked like they were laughing.

"I had no idea they drank tea," Reynald said.

"Well, blood of their enemies does get old after a while."

He cracked a razor-sharp smile. He was really handsome today, all edge and green eyes.

On the terrace, one of the Conquerors jumped up. The others pulled her down back into her seat.

"Have you seen the Borses' Rageglow?" I asked.

"I have."

"And Arvel's Enduring Flame?"

"Yes. I've seen the magic of all four warrior families."

"What is it like?"

He sighed. "The Enduring Flame shines like a curtain of golden light. It's showy. When Arvel stands in the middle of it, he looks like a saint, one of the Aspects' reincarnations. His skin and hair glow, and his eyes light up. When the flame is burning, he is untouchable. He can expand it to cover himself and his allies. If you're in his inner circle, you are invulnerable. The competition to be one of Arvel's chosen is cutthroat."

That's why they called Arvel the Golden Knight. It had to be beautiful.

"Everard's Fatefire is terrifying," Reynald continued. "It coats his sword, blazing with green and black. When he strikes, the Fatefire flies off the blade and burns everything in its path. It can cut through a man in armor and the horse he's on from a hundred paces away. Every strike leaves a line of green flames in its wake, and he can keep it blazing for a single breath or a quarter of an hour. When Everard is on the field, the air reeks of smoldering flesh and the battlefield burns with scars of fire. The screams of the dying assail your ears. The black smoke that rises from the bodies stings your eyes and scrapes your throat."

I mentally scratched Fatefire off my "To See While in Rellas" list.

"The Rageglow is bright red, like arterial blood," Reynald said. "It sheathes Wynand Bors and his Conquerors in glowing armor. They grow stronger, faster, and impervious to pain. Their weapons cut through solid steel like butter. The magic severs their grip on reality, and as they lose themselves, they scream. It's a sight you never forget. If only the Rageglow gave Wynand some wisdom, he would be sitting on the throne in the Eagle Roost."

On second thought, I didn't need to see the Rageglow either.

"The Exultant Call of the Savarics has no color," Reynald said. "You don't see it, you feel it. It reaches into you and envelops your heart. You feel stronger, faster, more powerful, and you know you're not alone. Your friends are standing with you, and no enemy is great enough to bring you down. Your courage grows like a tree within you, unbreakable, and you run into battle. And even as you die, you still feel victorious."

Wow.

"It's that power that has kept the Savarics on their throne for three centuries," Reynald said. "One cannot discount it."

He fell silent. I was sitting on a wall in a magical city, and a hot, deadly swordsman had brought me tea and pastries and was entertaining me with his war stories. Dreams fanfics were made of.

So why couldn't I relax?

I needed the Magnars to come back in one piece. That would take a huge load of anxiety off my shoulders. I checked the streets. Still empty.

"Do you know what they call Wynand Bors behind his back?" Reynald asked.

I blinked at him. "So it's true?"

He smiled.

"They really call him the 'Lord of Assholes'?"

"Never to his face," he said.

I laughed softly. "What did he do to earn that title?"

The books never explained it.

"It was his uncle, actually. He was the Lord Commander of the Conquerors before Wynand."

"One-Armed Verold?"

"That's the one. Losing the arm in battle didn't slow him down any. About twenty years ago, each of the three knight orders had ceremonial guard duty for one day and night during the Midsummer Aspects festival. On the first day, the Defenders stood guard, and the Conquerors behaved themselves. On the second day, the Conquerors were on duty, so again everything went well. On the third day it was the Redeemers' turn to guard, and the Conquerors went wild. They got drunk, they chased the festival cows, they picked fights . . . One of them climbed the statue of the Nurturer and attempted to *conquer* her."

I laughed.

Reynald's eyes sparked with humor. "Neither the king nor the clerics found it funny. So Wynand's uncle is on one knee in the throne room, while Sauven is raging and throwing things at him from his desk. This went on for some time. Finally, Sauven shakes the long scroll with all the charges on it at Wynand's uncle and yells, 'These are not the actions of knights! These are the actions of deranged assholes! And what are you? Who do you think you are?!' And Wynand's uncle says, 'I am the Lord of Assholes, Your Majesty.'"

I laughed so hard I snorted.

"So Wynand inherited the title," Reynald said.

"But is he worthy of it?"

"Oh yes. Many times over." Reynald turned his head. "There they are."

I looked in the direction of his gaze and saw four people coming down the street, through the twilight. Three were tall and one short.

"You can stop worrying now, Maggie," Reynald said, his eyes warm. "The future won't get the better of us. I promise you, we will win this war."

PART III

HEART OF A KNIGHT

Chapter 18

Planter 17

"These aren't even the right color. They look like they're sick. What if they poison our food instead of preserving it?" Clover sniffed at the big bright green fungus growing from the clay trays.

"Grums don't get sick. They're mushrooms," the vendor countered. "If you can't afford them, stop wasting my time!"

"Forty dens for six and no more."

"Sixty!"

"Forty-five!"

"I have children to feed."

"Feed them these mushrooms then!"

"They're not edible!"

Next to me, Reynald in his work clothes and lancer's coif quietly heaved a sigh.

I had finally made it to the Dog Market.

The Magnars had returned victorious but banged up. Gort had a black eye, Shana had taken a shallow gash to the side, and both Will and Lute came back with cuts and bruises. Filderon had had bodyguards who were in on his scheme, and when the Magnars confronted him, all hell broke loose. Apparently, he was also meticulous about following client instructions, because he'd written the whole Falcon Point plan down. Will found it when they searched the house and pinned it to Filderon's corpse with the broker's own knife.

Shana had taken yesterday to rest, but this morning she was back in the kitchen, cheerfully doing scary things like chopping the head off a big fish with one swing of her cleaver. She needed groceries, I needed more soap supplies, and so to the market Clover, Reynald, and I went. Reynald's menace meter was all the way up, and people gave us plenty of room.

The Dog Market was everything I'd hoped and more. It occupied several city blocks bordered by a wall, and despite the morning hour, it was already crowded. We had gone to get Shana's groceries first, then to order my soap stuff, and were on our way down the Center Row, toward the gate, when Clover spied the grums. Big, fat, and green, they resembled foot-tall, weird mushrooms growing in pots, and they were highly prized because they somehow kept food from spoiling. According to Clover, we didn't have any and it was vital that we get some, so she'd launched her haggling barrage.

I didn't mind the delay. I was having an awesome time.

Most merchants self-segregated by the type of their merchandise, selling their wares in clearly labeled rows. There was a Grocery Row, a Forge Row, and a Fabric Row, and so on. Between the defined rows lay the no-man's land, where merchants whose goods didn't fit a specific category hawked their wares.

The Center Row, where we were now, was exactly that kind of place, and I was doing my best not to gawk. It was weirdness. So much wonderful weirdness. Magic amulets, odd trinkets, a stall that sold colorful powders that might have been dyes or spices, jewelry, glass sun catchers, bizarre-looking knives . . . It was like a dozen books from an epic fantasy list had gotten together with some dungeon master manuals, had a drunken party, and thrown up on a flea market.

Across from us, a vendor was selling little beasts that looked like tiny Pomeranians crossed with miniature foxes. To the left, another stall offered hair ornaments, delicate like lace, each beautiful blossom woven from silver wire and studded with tiny gems. So pretty . . . I looked at them for a while, until I finally saw the prices. Ouch.

Past the jewelry cart, a toy-peddler was putting on a show at his stall. He held up two wooden knights with very realistic looking swords and pretended to have them clash as a gaggle of kids watched. The knight in royal purple with a black cloak and a steel crown on his helm was definitely King Sauven, and his counterpart wore lavender and green, which made him Ralinbor of the Wilds.

When it came to the Savarics, good and bad were rather arbitrary. Both half brothers had been terrible people, but one of them sat on the throne and the other was dead. History was written by the winners.

I drifted closer to watch.

This year marked the twenty-fifth anniversary of that battle. Sauven hated any reminder of it, but twenty-five was a number of significance in Rellas. Despite all the "mad king" vibes Sauven was putting out, he wasn't irrational all the time. He had episodes of paranoia and violent outbursts, but between them, he was calculating and shrewd. As a seasoned political animal, Sauven would make the most of this anniversary. There would be celebrations and festivals . . .

The vendor swung Ralinbor's wooden sword at Sauven's chest. Sauven parried. The vendor's helper, a lanky teenager who was probably his son, hopped out from behind the stall holding a stuffed toy monster with wide wings.

The monster swooped above the two knights. A dursan, one of Ralinbor's pet abominations, the ones he used to command in battle.

The kids gasped.

Sauven ducked and swung his sword at Ralinbor's neck, and the knight's head went flying. The children squeed. Yay joyful beheading.

"Horrid little things, aren't they?" a male voice said by my side.

I turned. The man from the Garden stood next to me. He wore a plain brown cloak and a lancer's coif that hid his face, but the eyes were unmistakable. A rich, golden hazel, slightly wild.

All my alarms screeched.

I kept my voice calm. "Do you mean the toys?"

"Those, too."

I stood facing the side of the toy stall. The jewelry stall was behind me and slightly to my right and the grum stall was even farther. The man from the Garden had come up between the toy and jewelry stalls, from the other side of the row, and positioned himself to my right, so the jewelry stall blocked him from Reynald's view. Everything about this was deliberate.

He tilted his head, looking me over. "We meet again, my lady. You're moving up in the world. From a barefoot beggar to someone who can afford embroidery. Quite a leap."

He'd seen me in my corpse cloak. He'd probably watched me come into the Garden and then deliberately waited for me to emerge from the baths, so he could talk to me. Why?

"You haven't changed a bit," I told him.

"Oh?"

"You were a lord in disguise then and you are a lord in disguise now."

He chuckled softly. That voice was off the charts. I didn't even know what to compare it to. Melted chocolate, warm velvet, amused wolf . . . All of the above?

A sound of a commotion made me look over my shoulder. At the grum stall, two men crowded Clover. The older one waved his arms around, irate. Reynald glanced at me. Our eyes met, and he moved into the space between Clover and the two men.

"Your nursemaid is otherwise occupied," the man from the Garden said.

"Is that your doing?"

"Yes. I cherish privacy, and we have many interesting topics to cover. Why don't we take a stroll, my lady? You didn't answer any of my questions in the Garden. I'm still so curious. Come with me."

Yeah, no. "Does that usually work for you? Do you just slide up to a woman and tell her 'Come with me,' and she allows herself to be meekly led away from her bodyguards?"

"Sometimes."

"I'm going to stay right here. If you would like to say something to me, now is your chance."

"You're getting more interesting by the moment," he muttered. "Why are you here?"

"Why are any of us here?" He wasn't giving me much to work with. Maybe if I frustrated him enough, he'd slip up. "To pursue happiness and discover the meaning of our lives."

He laughed softly.

"Or are you asking why I am at the market? To buy supplies and look at interesting things. Why are you at the market?"

Tell me something.

He moved to the side so fast, he almost glided.

Reynald bore down on him from behind the jewelry stall. He'd circled from the other side. Somehow the man from the Garden had sensed him and moved out of the way.

The two men stared at each other, both with their faces covered and their hands not too far from their swords. I had landed in the middle of a medieval spy thriller.

The man from the Garden narrowed his eyes. "Do I know you?"

Reynald's voice was casual and even. "Draw your sword and let's find out."

"Tempting, but I have places to be. Another time, perhaps." He leaned to the side, meeting my eyes. "Have no fear. I'll find you again."

"Not if you value your life," Reynald said.

"If you want to see something interesting, my lady, you should head north, to the pavilions. Trust me, it will be worth a look."

The man backed away and took off, vanishing into the market.

Reynald and I turned left at the same time and started north.

Clover caught up with us. "I bought six grums . . ." She saw my face and fell silent.

We headed deeper into the market along the Center Row.

"Who is he?" Reynald asked quietly.

"No idea. We met in the Garden."

Reynald's eyebrows came together.

"Not that kind of meeting," I told him. "I was watching Hreban make an entrance, and he stopped by and said a few words."

"What did you talk about?"

"He called Hreban a gilded toad. The attendants treated him with deference. He is a lord of some sort."

"I know him from somewhere," Reynald said. "I know the eyes and the voice. I just can't place them."

A faint yell came from ahead. It sounded like a woman who'd choked off a scream.

The crowd was growing thicker.

A woman about my age hurried past us, going in the opposite direction, wide-eyed, her face pale. Terrified.

Yep, that's exactly the kind of "interesting" I was expecting him to point out.

Another woman, an older one this time, in a good quality dress, with a maid and two bodyguards, barreled up the street. Reynald not so subtly put himself between us and them. The small group rushed past us.

Ahead, the Center Row widened, flowing around three large pavilions, set in a column. A crowd had gathered in front of the first one, squeezing into a knot of tightly packed bodies.

I had to see what it was.

Three guards in chainmail with teal and black surcoats marched up from behind us, toward the crowd. The leading guard bellowed, "Part!" and the crowd opened in front of them. They strode into the gap, and I ducked in after them. Clover and Reynald barely had time to squeeze in behind me. I turned sideways and pushed my way to the front.

The press of bodies eased, the crowd ended, and I halted on the edge of it. In front of me, across twenty yards of clear ground, stood a simple open-air pavilion with a clay tile roof resting on ancient wooden beams. A row of timber columns held up the roof. Every column had two bracers, one on each side, that stretched from it at an angle to support the rafters.

The corpse hung from the central column.

The sight of it was so shocking, it didn't seem real. There were other people around it—guards, a knight in chainmail and teal tabard—but I saw only the body.

The dead person was a man, middle-aged, naked, his arms tied to the bracers of the pillar. His head drooped, his salt-and-pepper hair falling forward over his face. His torso was split from his collarbones to his groin, the skin and muscle pierced by hooks attached to twine and pulled back, the twine disappearing behind the column. He was laid open like a book, all of his insides on display.

The horror of it was so heavy, it bounced from my brain. My mind needed a moment to come to terms with the visual input. I stared, numb, while my eyes catalogued everything in excruciating detail: bare muscle, bloodied bone, a mangled liver, the gory sack of the left lung that seemed almost chewed on, the cut to the right thigh that had drenched the leg in blood . . .

"Dame Gler," one of the older guardsmen was saying, "we need a ladder . . ."

The officer of the City Guard, a knight of about my age, didn't seem to hear him. She was standing there frozen, trying to process the body. The cluster of people around us was quiet, almost afraid to speak. The crowd had formed a crescent around the grisly scene, held back by some animal instinct, as if coming too close would somehow infect them.

This wasn't a true crime show with carefully blurred bodycam footage. This was real life. The stench of blood was so thick, I could taste it on my tongue. Flies crawled on the exposed lungs and intestines . . .

A hand landed on my shoulder. I jerked, turned, and saw Reynald looking back at me. Next to him, Clover gaped at the body, her face pale, her eyes shocked.

My brain restarted all at once. The meaning of what I was seeing penetrated though the shock and punched me with an icy fist.

He was early. It was too soon.

Why now? Was it because of something I had done?

Oh god. I should've seen this coming. Everything was going wrong.

Reynald leaned toward me. "Talk to me."

I would have to tell him. Fuck.

"Maggie?" he prompted.

"We're in trouble," I whispered.

Around me the crowd pressed tighter as more people came in.

We had to get out of there. I spun around.

Reynald caught me by the arm. "Slowly."

He was right. The killer was probably nearby, watching the spectacle right now. We didn't need to draw attention to ourselves.

I took Clover's hand and nodded. Reynald glowered at the crowd blocking our way. Somehow, despite the tight press of the bodies, people parted before him, and we followed. A moment and we were in the clear.

I took off toward the exit, forcing myself to maintain a stable pace, with Reynald hovering over Clover and me like a hawk. We walked in complete silence, weaving through the current of shoppers, until we cleared the gates and the stone demon dog on top of them bared his fangs at our backs.

Outside of the market, I sped up as fast as I could without running. Clover chased after me. Reynald broke into what my dad used to call double time.

"What's going on?" Clover asked.

"We have a problem," I told her.

"How bad?"

"Very bad. We have to get home right now."

We turned around the corner. Reynald put his arm in front of me as if he'd braked suddenly while driving and wanted to keep me from flying through the windshield. A group of riders on gray horses with white tails stomped their way down the street, two per row. They wore polished gray breastplates and cloaks the color of fresh blood. The single rider in front carried a banner on a tall spear: black, scarlet, and gold.

A carriage followed them, drawn by a single massive gray horse. Ornate but not delicate, blocky, with thick walls, it was the medieval equivalent of an armored limousine. Nothing like what you would imagine Cinderella might ride in. The curtain on the window was pulled aside, and I could see the passenger. Ulmar Hreban.

The carriage passed us. Hreban looked at us, obvious boredom stamped on his face. His gaze slid over me, and for a moment I looked straight into his eyes. They were mean, menacing, and empty.

The carriage rolled on, another pair of knights following it.

Hreban, here, at this moment, of all people. It was as if Kair Toren were taunting me. Every time I dared to get even the slightest bit comfortable, the city reminded me where we stood.

I wouldn't take this punch lying down. I would stop this from happening no matter what it took.

We gathered in the kitchen at the big table once again.

I looked at the stack of papers in front of me. When we were cleaning, Clover and I had found a board made of soft wood. Derog used to pin the guard shift schedules to it. I put it up on the wall behind me. I would need visual aids to keep it all straight.

Reynald had explained the dead body. The faces looking at me were grim. Our world had come to terms with serial killers, but Rellas had no frame of reference. That kind of horror was raw and shocking.

Reynald sat at his usual place on my right. He had promised me that he would stand by me. He'd given me his word. I was about to kick that promise off a cliff.

I took a deep breath.

"People tend to kill for a specific reason. The most common are greed, passion, or revenge. The perpetrators seek to benefit from the murder, and they often know their target. The man who left the body in the Dog Market isn't like that. His victims never met him. Their deaths do not benefit him. He kills because he likes it."

I had learned way too much about serial killers during my brief stint in criminal justice. This one hit all the marks for the organized category: He planned his crimes in advance, he went about killing in a methodical fashion, he abducted his victims to torture them in a safe location, and he improved with each crime. He was a monster.

"This killer derives pleasure from his murders, first when he fights his victims, then when he dissects their bodies, and finally when he watches the effect his handiwork has on other people. He doesn't feel remorse, and he can't be cured of his urges."

"So he needs to be put out of his misery," Shana said.

"Yes. He will kill a new victim every week. Every Firsday, he will display them in the same way he has done in the market."

I took a nail and pinned the piece of paper with dates on the board. My fingers shook a little. This was not the way I wanted to deliver this explanation. I'd wanted to have a plan in place, so when I explained what was about to happen, I could immediately shift to "and this is how we stop it." I had expected to have time to formulate that plan, Divine fucking damn it.

"The murderer will choose different public locations, but he will display each body exactly the same way he displayed the first. Splayed open. There will be a total of six victims." I held up six fingers. "So this one and five more. I don't know his name or where he comes from, but people will call him the Dog Market Butcher."

I wrote "Dog Market Butcher" on the piece of paper I had attached to the board. This would've been much easier with dry-erase markers.

"How does it involve us?" Will asked.

"I've told you before that Hreban has great ambitions. He seeks the throne. By midwinter, King Sauven will give Hreban nearly unlimited power. The Order of the Redeemer will back Hreban, and he will drown the kingdom in fire and blood."

"Sauven was always a few arrows short of a full quiver," Gort said. "But that is too far even for him. I could see him raising Arvel like that, but Hreban?"

"Sauven Savaric isn't in his right mind," I said. "He has fits of paranoia and they are getting worse."

"It runs in the family," Shana said.

I nodded. "It does. Sauven isn't oblivious. He is aware of what is happening, which is why he's trying to hammer out a solid foundation to support his son, Crown Prince Kiel. To Sauven, dynasty is everything."

And every time Sauven would cobble together some kind of rickety scaffolding to hold his firstborn up, Kiel would wreck it with his arrogance and narcissism, but that was a topic for another day.

"Sauven trusts very few people these days, the most important of whom is Colart Jenicor."

I picked up a picture of a heraldic shield I had cut out from one of the scrolls in my study and pinned it to the board. A golden sun with stylized rays rising on a field of black.

"The Sun Margrave," Reynald said.

"Who is the Sun Margrave?" Kaiden asked.

"He's the man who leads the Justice Chamber," Clover told him. "When people commit crimes against the kingdom, he is the one who brings the cases before the High Court."

"Margrave is a military title," Reynald explained. "It means *lord who defends a border*. The Sun Margrave also guards a boundary, the one between lawlessness and order."

"Colart Jenicor is an exemplary Sun Margrave," I said. "Although he wields great power, he doesn't use it for personal gain. He cannot be bribed, coerced, or intimidated. None of the Eight Families can sway him. He serves Rellas itself and he has never wavered in that service."

As far as attorneys general went, Colart Jenicor was above reproach.

"King Sauven knows he is losing his grip, and he also knows that if he pushes things too far, Colart will be there to pull him back from the cliff. The Sun Margrave has been there from the very beginning of Sauven's reign. Sauven relies on his counsel. It is of great comfort to him."

I leaned on the table.

"You asked why Sauven puts Hreban in charge. Because after the entire city becomes paralyzed with fear from the constant killings, the Dog Market Butcher will murder the Sun Margrave in front of the whole court and then vanish into thin air. Colart Jenicor will be the sixth victim."

Reynald's face iced over.

"The next day Hreban and his guards will stumble on the killer's hideout and cut off his head. Ulmar Hreban will become known as the savior of Kair Toren."

"Aspects preserve us," Shana swore.

"With the Sun Margrave dead, there is nobody to steady Sauven. Before he can fully come to terms with that murder, Crown Prince Kiel is assassinated during the Winter Hunt."

I might as well have thrown a grenade on the table. They stared at me, shell-shocked.

"When his son is also murdered, Sauven spins out of control. His paranoia blinds him. He sees plots and conspiracies everywhere. He makes Hreban the next Sun Margrave, because he sees him as an outsider and therefore free of corruption. He gives him the power to kill or detain anyone who gets in the way."

The room had gone completely silent.

"There is more." I had saved the worst for last.

"What more can there be?" Clover demanded.

"The Sun Margrave is supposed to die at the conclusion of the High Court's session, on the eve of the twenty-fifth anniversary of Sauven's victory over Ralinbor of the Wilds. He will be escorted to that ceremony by three squires of note, one from each of the knight orders. The Defenders, the Conquerors, and the Redeemers will each contribute a squire."

The knight orders constantly competed for power and prestige. Escorting the Sun Margrave delivered a lot of prestige. It was a public chance to flex.

Reynald was looking at me, and I couldn't tell what he was thinking.

I had to keep going. "When the killer attacks, the Sun Margrave will order the squires to save themselves and get help. Only the Defender squire obeys. He abandons the margrave and runs, forever shaming the Order of the Defender."

"What about the other two squires?" Shana asked.

"The Conqueror squire is hit on the head and collapses. He is later ridiculed for not landing a single blow on the killer, is sent away from the capital, and is killed in a border skirmish."

I looked at Reynald. He was sitting very still.

"The third squire, the one from the Order of the Redeemer, fights to his last breath to defend the margrave and dies trying to save him."

The words didn't want to come out of me. I had to squeeze them out.

"It's Matheo, Reynald. The third squire is Matheo. The Dog Market Butcher will kill your son."

The silence in the kitchen was so deafening, it hurt.

Reynald opened his mouth. His voice was calm and cold. "Why didn't you tell me?"

"Because I was afraid that you would storm off and try to break in to the Redeemer Tower. You had no reason to trust me. I didn't want you to fail and die. And I wouldn't have wanted you to succeed either. Everything is connected, Reynald. If you managed to kill Silveren somehow, there is no telling what it would do."

He was looking directly at me, and his gaze was difficult to hold. It took all my willpower to stare back.

"You should've told me."

"I was going to. I thought I had time." I pointed at the board. "This isn't supposed to be happening yet. The Butcher's first victim isn't supposed to show up until the first of Harvest Month. That's more than four months from now."

"What could've caused him to start now?" Reynald asked.

"Us. We caused this."

"How?"

"The Butcher kills prominent knights from all three holy orders. They flood the city with their people trying to find him. At the height of his rampage, the City Guard triples the patrols. Everyone is looking for him, and yet he comes and goes like a ghost, and then Hreban just coincidentally finds him in some remote warehouse, where Hreban has no business being."

Reynald's gaze darkened. He saw where I was going.

"Hreban has eight guards with him. Way too many for a daytime trip to the docks and more than enough people to arrest the Butcher, and yet the Butcher ends up conveniently dead. And then Hreban profits from his death, first by being hailed as the savior, and then by becoming the Sun Margrave."

Reynald leaned forward. "The Butcher belongs to Hreban."

"I have no proof, but it is the only deduction that makes sense. It is too convenient otherwise." I shook my hands. "This is what I mean when I say everything is connected. We sicced the Justice Chamber on the Yolentas' warehouse where they found the smuggled iron. Hreban could've reacted in a dozen different ways. The most logical one would be to leave Kair Toren. Then if Indora Yolenta implicated him in the iron scheme, the Justice Department would have to go to his domain and question him there on his terms."

"It would take a direct order from Sauven to pry him free and drag him back to the capital," Reynald said. "And Sauven wouldn't issue an order against the head of a Great Family without indisputable proof."

"Exactly. Instead of taking that safe and smart route, Hreban must have told the Butcher to start ahead of schedule. If Kair Toren is gripped by panic over the horrible murders, the Justice Chamber will shift their focus to finding the killer. It takes the attention off Hreban. He can remain in the capital, and once he kills the Butcher, nobody will care about the iron."

I couldn't tell if I was making sense to him or not.

"The killer started early," Kaiden said.

I almost jumped. He was so quiet, I had forgotten he was there. "Yes."

"So the Sun Margrave won't get killed at the end of the Court thing," Kaiden said.

"Matheo might not be there," Will finished.

"That means the kid won't die, doesn't it?" Lute asked.

I shook my head. "I looked at the calendar. Do you know what happens in five weeks?"

"The opening of the High Court Session," Reynald said.

I had no idea how he had pulled that out of his brain on demand. I'd had to look it up.

"Yes. The annual ceremony when the Sun Margrave walks up the King's Way to the Eagle Roost castle and hand-delivers the docket to Sauven in front of the entire capital. Colart will be escorted by three squires. The same three squires that will escort him at the end of the session . . ."

Reynald swore.

"Do you remember how I said that messing with the future is like throwing rocks into a pond?" I asked. "That is still accurate but not in the way I thought. When you throw a rock into a pond, it makes ripples and then these ripples smooth out and it's like the rock was never there. The future is resisting us. It's trying to stick to the existing pattern. Instead of being murdered at the closing of the High Court, the Sun Margrave will die at the opening. Nothing changes, Matheo still dies, and Hreban still rises to his reign of terror."

I dropped into the chair.

On my left, Clover turned paler. A hint of fear shivered in her eyes. Gort looked troubled. Shana wrinkled her brows, her mouth a thin line. Will frowned, thinking. Lute looked like he'd been sucker punched, and even Kaiden at the end of the table seemed lost, as if he had suddenly fallen into a deep hole and didn't know how to climb out.

I felt so hollow. All this time I'd been so worried about doing too much and ending up with a future I couldn't predict. I should've been worried about not doing enough. The timeline was fighting me, and it was winning.

I had given these people hope. They'd worked so hard, and in the end, it had been for nothing. The future continued to steamroll forward.

"I just can't stop this train," I murmured.

Will gave me a puzzled look. I must've said the English word for train. There was no Rellasian equivalent.

Would anything we did matter? Would the mercenaries we saved die somehow in other ways? Should I just send the kids out of the city? But where? Where could I put them that the war wouldn't touch . . .

"It doesn't matter," Reynald said.

"What?"

His voice was calm and measured. "The timeline has moved up, but it doesn't matter. You've given us a five-week lead. I've taken castles in five weeks."

A change had come over Reynald. The way he sat with his back straight, the set of his jaw, the look in his green eyes, everything communicated assurance and power. The man from the basement was back, and he wasn't just confident, he was unassailable, like a rock in the middle of a raging sea. This must've been why people followed him into the slaughter.

"As of now, nothing has happened," Reynald said. "Yes, we've just lost several months, but Matheo still lives. The Sun Margrave still lives. All we have to do is find the Butcher and remove him from the picture, and we have a five-week head start."

"We'll find that fucker in five weeks," Gort said.

"Someone knows him," Will said.

"Yes, the city isn't that big," Lute added.

The demon from the basement leaned toward me slightly. "The future can resist all it wants. In the end, it will surrender. I have no intentions of losing this war."

He was right. We hadn't lost the war. Both the Sun Margrave and Matheo were still breathing. We still had a chance.

"You don't know the Butcher's name," Reynald said. "But you do know something about him."

True. Even if I couldn't account for all of the consequences, even if we did change things, I still had the core knowledge from the books. I knew things about the major players. Facts, quirks, habits, secrets. More, I knew how they thought.

If the future did resist change, it would make things more predictable, not less. The Butcher would stick to his once-a-week pattern. He would target the same victims.

Reynald's eyes said, *It will be fine. We have this. It's under control.*

He'd pulled me out of the sea onto his rock. All I had to do was stay on it.

I took a deep breath and let the angst go. Whatever happened, had happened. Now we had to deal with it.

"Could it be that man from the Garden?" Reynald asked.

"No. The Butcher is older, and dark haired. The man from the Garden has blond eyebrows."

The serial killer was a subplot. He was mostly mentioned in passing, except for three scenes: one where a character was targeted by the Dog Market Butcher, brought to his lair, tortured, and murdered; the Sun Margrave's death; and Hreban's discovery of the Butcher; they were presented in gory second-by-second detail.

"The killer is a man." I began writing a list under the Butcher's name. "Dark brown hair, neither too tall, nor too short. Strong, muscular. Between thirty-five and sixty years old."

The description in the book mentioned shoulders that showed the strength of a mature man. Latour specifically stated through one of the characters that the onset of maturity happened after thirty-five and before the old age of sixty.

"That describes half of the men in Lower Berem," Shana murmured.

Lower Berem was Hreban's domain.

"Anything specific?" Reynald asked. "A friend, a spouse, where he's from, if he's a soldier or a mercenary?"

I shook my head.

"He duels his victims until they can no longer fight, then transports them to his place, where he tortures them. Ritual is very important to him. Dissecting and displaying the body is as vital as the killing. Usually, repeat killers like him have a type. Their victims look similar. He doesn't. He doesn't care what his targets look like or what their age or gender is, as long as they are famous knights."

That's why his reign of terror was so scary. He was killing people who not only knew how to defend themselves but excelled at it. If he could kill them, an ordinary person wouldn't stand a chance.

"He's very good with his sword," I said.

"How good?" Gort asked.

"Good enough to be a problem," Reynald said. "I recognized the man he hung in the Dog Market. It was Shuhoven."

I had no idea who Shuhoven was. The series spent very little time on the victims aside from stating that they were all famous knights. Half of the time, the books just said things like "another body was found in the morning. The Butcher had struck again" and moved on to the intrigue and Great Families' machinations.

Gort whistled. "Are you sure?"

Reynald nodded. "I saw the scar."

There'd been a scar? All I could remember was the mangled organs, the blood, and flies breeding on his insides.

"Shuhoven the Spear?" Will asked.

"Yes," Reynald answered.

"I heard he retired," Will said.

"And he has a bad arm," Lute said. "Had. Had a bad arm."

Gort grunted at them. "He had two bad arms, and I still wouldn't have fought him unless I was buying time for you and your mother to get away."

"Who is Shuhoven?" Kaiden asked.

"A renowned knight," Reynald said. "He was famous for driving his spear through multiple fighters in one thrust."

"It's hard to do," Will explained. "It takes a lot of strength."

"Then you have to pull the spear out," Lute said. "And the bodies don't want to let it go."

"Now you're stuck with your weapon inside another person," Will said.

"Any asshole can come up and stab you," Lute said.

They sounded exactly the same. It was like listening to one person whose voice bounced from one speaker to another. Will and Lute, spear experts, coming through in stereo.

"Shuhoven would do it in a single pull," Gort said. "Unbelievable upper body strength."

Reynald grimaced. "He was a show-off. He used to do this thing before battles—once the troops lined up, he would stand on his horse. He claimed he needed the height to survey the field."

"Why did he really do it?" Kaiden asked.

"So the enemy would see him standing there on a horse with his spear," Reynald said. "I once told him that he made an excellent tar—"

Gort coughed.

"A story for another time," Reynald said. "The angle of the wounds suggests Shuhoven was upright and moving when they were made, so Maggie is right. The Dog Market Butcher duels with his victims, then he cuts them open and displays the bodies for everyone to see. It's a message."

"This is what I did and how I did it," Will said. "It's pride."

"It's hubris," Reynald corrected and turned to me. "What about the other victims?"

"I know of two, besides the Sun Margrave: Eliarde of the Silver Eagles and Jeor Baes. But both of them die later. Eliarde is number three and Jeor is number five."

"He kills Eliarde?" Gort frowned.

Dame Eliarde was Arvel's second cousin. She hadn't inherited the Enduring Flame of the main family, but she got the lesser version of the talent called the Amber Coal, which made her both stronger and more durable than an ordinary knight. She was deadly.

"Did he ambush her?" Lute asked.

"No. He fought her," I told him. "She lost."

The table went silent. Even if the Magnars all banded together, Eliarde would go through them like Shana's cleaver through a fish.

"How does Hreban find him?" Reynald asked into the silence.

"The killer has a lair on the coast. That's where he tortures and slices up his targets. When he takes Eliarde there, she can hear the surf. Hreban was buying a warehouse, didn't like the condition of it, and wanted to see what else was available. Supposedly he ended up walking into the wrong building with his guards as the killer was cleaning up the gore."

Except that if he and the Butcher were in on it together, he would know exactly where to find his pet serial killer.

"Do we know what area of the coast?" Gort asked.

I shook my head. "Somewhere remote where nobody could hear the screams."

Kair Toren was founded because of its safe harbor and access to the West Ocean. It had literally miles of docks and warehouses. We could search for months and not find anything.

"How does he transport his victims?" Will asked. "He can't just walk around dragging people and bodies back and forth."

"In a cart," Clover told him. "That's how I would do it. I'd load them into a delivery cart, stack some goods on top, and wear some cheap clothes and beat-up shoes. I could make circles through Kair Toren all day, and nobody would pay me any mind."

The brothers gave her an odd look.

"And you said he vanished into thin air after killing the Sun Margrave," Reynald said.

"Yes."

"Morr beads?" Gort wondered.

"Most likely," Reynald said.

"What are more beads?" Kaiden asked.

"M-O-R-R. Battlemages carry them," Will told him. "It's illegal to use them but they do anyway. They break one, and magic shoves them to a safe spot half a mile away."

"You'll be in camp, sharpening your sword, and they pop up out of nowhere, and then you cut yourself," Lute said.

A very specific example there.

Morr beads came up a couple of times in the books. They were small black beads with red cracks strung onto a bracelet or a necklace. When the user crushed a bead, they would be teleported to a predetermined location, but the beads weren't exactly foolproof. One of the mages using them exploded upon arrival at the Mage Tower, and then Archmage Damaes got pissed off because the potion laboratory stank like rotting human fluids for days.

"Morr beads cost a lot of money," Gort mused.

"Not if Hreban is paying your way," Shana told him.

"So how do we find him, if we don't know who the next victim is?" Clover asked. "Or do we have to wait for Eliarde?"

"Eliarde is a member of the Silver Eagles," I told her. "They are an elite knight unit. There are only fifty of them and they are very proud of making that cut. She is . . . difficult."

Sometimes overtly arrogant people hid severe insecurities, but in Eliarde's case, her arrogance hid more arrogance. Her entire family thought their relation to the Arvels placed them above the rest. She was born into a life of privilege, with everyone constantly reassuring her that she was special and entitled to everything she ever wanted. She was beautiful, talented, celebrated, and cherished, and she was very aware that everyone else was less-than.

"She has an inflated sense of her self-worth," Reynald said. "She won't listen to a warning from us and attempting to follow her around until the Butcher strikes will be impossible."

How could we find him . . . If he had been targeting regular fighters, it would be one thing, but he was targeting knights. They spent half of their time in their HQs and when they did go into the city, it was usually on horseback.

Knights . . . on horses . . .

Ah!

"I don't know who he kills next, but I do know where he will leave the body," I said. "He'll tie it to the statue of the Knight Vanquisher."

Gort's eyes narrowed. "That's six blocks from here."

Reynald pivoted to me. "Is there a chance he'll change the location?"

"I don't think so. He spent months planning the order of his victims and the dump sites. He made drawings. He won't want to deviate from his plan. It's a compulsion. He must carry it out exactly as he envisioned it."

Reynald bared his teeth in a sharp smile, like a wolf who has sighted his prey. "Gort and Kaiden, with me. Will, Lute, stay here. Nobody comes through the front door until we're back."

Chapter 19

I climbed the stairs to my rooms. I needed to write down everything I could remember about the Butcher. Any detail could make a difference.

Why had Reynald taken Kaiden with him? I'd have to ask him when he got back.

Twenty minutes later I stared at six sheets of paper. I had reproduced the Eliarde torture scene exactly. Word for word. Every gruesome detail.

How? I didn't have a photographic memory. If I had, my college days would've been much easier.

What about something else from the books? Something random.

"I trusted you. I've known you since you were twelve years old. You've stayed at our house." Solentine's voice rose, raw with anguish. *"You've eaten our food. My father taught you how to handle a dagger. You stood right here, in this hall, and swore to aid my family in every battle!"* Solentine swept the bottle off his desk and hurled it against the wall. It bounced and rolled across the floor, coming to rest at Everard's feet.

"You were the closest thing I had to a brother."

Word for word.

This was not normal. Why was this happening?

A faint slapping sound pulsed through the room.

This had to have some sort of significance. In most portal fantasies, heroines who popped into books wrote down everything they remembered in some secret diary so they wouldn't forget it. Apparently, that was not going to be an issue for me.

Slap.

Maybe I just *thought* this was perfect recall. I didn't have the book in front of me, so I couldn't compare. But it seemed right, it felt right . . .

Slap-slap.

What the hell was that noise?

I stood up, leaning over the desk.

An eighteen-inch fish lay on the floor between the open door and my desk.

It was white striped with orange and speckled with red and turquoise, and it resembled a bug-eyed red snapper with long fins.

Was I seeing things?

I held still and listened. The study was empty.

I looked over my shoulder. I could see my bedroom through the doorway, and it was empty, too.

I looked back. The fish was still there.

No strange sounds. No intruders lurking in the corners.

The fish flopped, slapping its tail against the floor.

I jerked back.

Slap. Slap-slap.

The sound of someone's steps as they ran up the stairs came from the hall, and Will appeared in the doorway. He saw the fish and halted.

"Fish," I told him.

"I see it."

Oh good. I wasn't imagining it.

"Where did it come from?" Will asked.

"I have no idea. It wasn't there when I came in."

"How did it get here?"

"I don't know."

"Is it magic?"

"I don't know."

The two of us stared at the fish.

Slap.

"Is this some sort of Kair Toren custom I don't know about?"

Will shook his head. "Nothing I ever heard of."

"Could you please put it out of its misery?"

Will walked over, pulled out his knife, and sliced through the back of the fish's head. The fish went limp. I handed Will a rag and he wiped his knife on it.

"This is the second fish that's showed up in my rooms. The first time I thought it was Kaiden, but he's out with Reynald now."

"Why would Kaiden leave fish in your rooms?" Will asked.

"Why does a twelve-year-old boy do anything?"

"Good point."

We looked at the fish some more.

"Did you want something?" I asked.

Will pulled a small, sealed envelope from his tunic and passed it to me. "Someone rang the bell and left this by the door."

While we were waiting on the salt ship to come in, Gort had rigged a rope and a bell to our front door. Unlike Derog, we didn't have the manpower to have somebody sit by it. If one of us went out, we'd pull the rope when we came back, which rang the literal bell in our courtyard.

"I might have seen a priest walking away," Will said. "It was hard to tell with the cloak, but I think they had a blade staff."

Blade staffs were polearms, like spears and halberds, but while spears thrust and halberds chopped, the long, sharp blades at the end of the blade staffs were used to slice. Rellas was a martial kingdom, and a lot of priests practiced martial arts. The blade staffs served as preferred weapons for a number of denominations, so much so that when people saw one, they usually assumed a priest wielded it.

I tore the envelope open and pulled out the paper inside.

Drugh knows. He's coming.

Shit.

Drugh was Filderon's sort of son-in-law. He was trained as a knight, although never knighted, and he ran his own mercenary company, acting as both a commander and a broker. He was also bad news.

I showed the note to Will.

"Hireling damn it. I swear, we weren't seen."

"I believe you. We don't know what happened. Maybe he told Drugh he would be meeting you."

I had a little bit of ammunition against Drugh but nothing that would knock him off-balance if he was truly determined to avenge Filderon. The relationship between the two men was strained, and they barely talked, but according to the note, Drugh had decided to do something about it.

Who had left the note? Who would know that the Magnars had done away with Filderon, that Drugh was looking for them, and that they were here, in this house? I spun the roster of characters in my head. Maybe, possibly, the Shears, but delivering an anonymous note wasn't Solentine's style.

"What do you want to do?" Will asked.

"We sit tight until Reynald and your father come home. If Drugh shows up, don't open the door."

He nodded and turned to walk away.

"Will?"

"Yes?"

"Please take the fish with you."

⌑

Reynald studied the note.

They'd been gone for two hours; so long that I was beginning to worry Drugh had jumped them somewhere. When they'd finally returned, we had gathered in the kitchen. Gort was sketching something on a large piece of paper spread on the kitchen table, while Kaiden tinkered with some small object in the corner, perched on a chair cross-legged.

"Are we paid up with Taryz?" Reynald asked.

"Yes."

A few days ago I went up to Taryz Teahouse, passed a noma to the proprietor, and told her I wanted the "favorite customer" service. If anyone left a note for us, they would pass it to us, and if we wanted a private room, we could have one at a moment's notice. Should something unpleasant happen in that room, Taryz wouldn't ask questions and might even get rid of the evidence if the tip was large enough.

"Gort, you and the family need to go to Taryz tonight and drink some tea," Reynald said. "Be seen. Let the waiters know that if someone were to come asking, you drink tea there just about every evening at seven bells."

Gort nodded.

"Do you have anything on Drugh?" Reynald asked me.

"Yes, but he's stubborn and it might not be enough."

"No matter," he said. "I'll make sure it will suffice."

"If you say so." He had promised me he would handle the complications. Drugh and his two hundred mercenaries were definitely a complication.

"This concerns me more." Reynald frowned at the note.

Same. "Could be someone among the Shears."

It sounded thin even as I said it.

"Whoever wrote this knows too much about us," Reynald said.

We needed to solve this mystery. And I had no clue how to go about it.

"Done." Gort straightened.

I went to look. He'd drawn a map of the Knight Vanquisher Plaza in black ink.

The plaza was roughly egg-shaped and depicted from above, with two streets that ran north stretching from its wider end, and a single street at its narrow end going south. In the center the statue of the Knight Vanquisher reared. It wasn't just a drawing, it was a piece of art, beautifully inked in delicate detail, down to traces of the cobblestones on the street. I'd had no idea a brush that tiny could even fit into Gort's steel pincer fingers.

"The lay of the land," Gort said.

"It's beautiful."

"Thank you."

"You should've been an artist."

"To make a living, I'd have to do portraits, and I can't paint people to save my life. When it comes to living creatures, I paint what I feel, not what I see. Maps are easier. Straightforward."

"Do you see the problem?" Reynald asked.

I studied the map. "No."

"Look at the buildings." Reynald traced the border of the plaza with his fingers, sliding them over the roofs.

The buildings were close together. They formed two continuous walls that bordered the edges of the plaza without any gaps. What was it he wanted me to see . . .

"No places to hide?"

Reynald nodded.

"Let's say I'm the killer," Gort said. "I like to plan. I select the places for my corpses carefully. Before I ever bring a body here, I'm going to walk through this plaza on different days and at different times. I'll memorize the entrances and exits. I will take note of the people and their patterns. When do people come in, when do they leave, who locks the doors at night. I might memorize the faces of the regulars, those who visit every day."

"Makes sense."

Gort tapped the buildings one by one. "Pan oil merchant, a harness maker, a shoemaker, and two accounting houses. This is a trade plaza. It's deserted at night. The two accounting houses have guards they lock inside, and they don't come out until morning."

"If a killer shows up with a body and sees people loitering about in the plaza after dark, he'll run," Reynald said.

"So, what's the plan?"

"The plaza has no places to hide, but the side streets do," Reynald told me.

"We'll put Will here and Lute here." Gort touched the two streets leading north.

"I will take this street here." He tapped the third street, which led south. "But there's a lot of distance between those streets and the center of the plaza. We don't know which direction he'll be coming from, and if he's as good as we think, none of us should take him on alone."

I stared at the plaza.

"It would be good if we could hide in one of those buildings."

Reynald smiled at me and touched the roof to the west of the statue. "I'll take the oil merchant."

"How? Did you bribe them?"

He shook his head. "No. Didn't bother asking. They would never let me into their warehouse overnight."

"Then how are you going to get into the building?"

Something heavy landed on the table in the middle of the map. A thick padlock with its arm out.

"Done!" Kaiden said.

"How?"

He grinned at me. "My dad was a lockmaker." The smile faltered, then slid off his face. "I'm good with locks."

I'd had no idea. It struck me—I knew almost nothing about Kaiden. According to Lasa's notes, his parents had died, and he must've been apprenticed to someone, because the entry mentioned his "trainer" had sold him.

"The lock on the oil merchant's door is the weakest," Gort said. "And there is no guard inside."

It made sense. Pan oil wasn't dirt cheap, but you would have to steal barrels of it to make it worth the risk, and then you would have to sell it somewhere. There were better thieving targets in that plaza. The oil merchant didn't bother with a guard.

"It's not a bad lock," Kaiden said. "It's not a good lock either. Thirty breaths. Maybe fifty."

"Once the killer shows up, I will engage him," Reynald said. "If he tries to retreat, one of the others will block his exit long enough for me to press the advantage."

Anxiety squirmed through me. I didn't like this plan.

"In addition, we'll put Shana on this roof here." Gort tapped one of the western roofs. "If things get out of hand, she'll shoot him."

"Where am I going to hide?"

"At home," Reynald said. "You'll stay here and wait for us to come back."

No, I didn't like this plan. Not one little bit.

Reynald nodded to Kaiden. He swiped the lock off the table and scurried out of the room.

"What do you know about your friend from the Garden?" Reynald asked.

"He is not my friend, and next to nothing."

"Do you have any guesses as to who he might be?"

"No. You're obsessing about him."

"I know him from somewhere," Reynald said. "I can't place it, but my memory tells me to be wary. Why was he at the market, where the body was displayed, with his face covered?"

"You also had your face covered."

"I was escorting you, and I didn't want to attract attention. Your clothes and hair don't communicate the right level of wealth. You can't afford me, Maggie, and that discrepancy would draw the eye. People would come to the wrong conclusions."

By Rellas's standards, my usual dress put me somewhere in the lower nobility. Reynald didn't read as a lower-nobility bodyguard. Gort fit the bill—an aging mercenary who had decided to take a cushier job. Will and Lute would pass as well, skilled and dangerous, but too young to have developed a reputation.

But Reynald was well known. If people saw one of the top swordsmen in the kingdom guarding a woman who clearly couldn't afford to hire him, they would conclude that I was paying him in other ways.

"Thank you for protecting my honor." And I'd just said that with a straight face.

"Don't mention it. The man from the Garden. Tell me about him."

I recounted the meeting in the Garden.

"A lord," Gort said when I finished.

Reynald nodded, his face grim. "What does he look like without the coif?"

"Very handsome," I said.

Gort and Reynald shared a look.

"What kind of handsome?" Gort asked.

"Beautiful. Like the kind of face that makes you stop and stare. He has these captivating eyes, light hazel, like golden amber. They almost glow. Long eyelashes, too."

Reynald rubbed his face.

"I'm not helping, am I?"

"No."

"Sorry."

"No matter," he said. "He will appear again and when he does, he will tell me everything I want to know."

"He didn't seem scared of you," I reminded him.

The demon from the basement gave me a narrow smile. There was no humor in it. "And that will be his undoing."

Chapter 20

Planter 18

The morning sun spilled into the courtyard, warming up the laundry benches. I squinted at the sunshine.

Gort sat on the other side of the bench, twisting a thick wire into some sort of object. Occasionally he squished it with a pair of tongs, then twisted again. Across from us, Kaiden sat cross-legged on the wall around the wine tree, messing with another lock.

In the center of the courtyard, Reynald and the Magnar brothers clashed. All three wore padded gambesons, formfitting quilted jackets shielding their torsos and arms. Will's gambeson was blue, Lute's pale green, and Reynald was in dark, charcoal gray.

Both Will and Lute towered over the blademaster by about four inches and the quilted gambesons made them seem even larger. Both were remarkably strong and fast. Both were younger and had the training and experience of professional mercenaries. At twenty-one and nineteen, they were seasoned veterans, who identified weaknesses and zeroed in on them like hungry wolves.

They should've dominated Reynald, yet he moved through them like water. I'd been watching them for twenty minutes. Both brothers were out of breath and their necks and hands were covered with red welts, while Reynald hadn't even broken a sweat.

The books said he was one of the best swordsmen in Rellas. But reading about it and watching it were two different things. I was used to movie fights. The clashing of the blades, the dramatic scene with two guys crossing their swords and pushing against each other, the long sequence of spectacular moves . . . This was nothing like that.

The Magnars circled Reynald. At first, they attacked at the same time, but he kept using them against each other, so now they were taking turns.

He waited for them, his sword held in both hands, the blade pointing up over his left shoulder.

Will struck from the right, swinging his axe in a short, vicious arc. Lute hung back. Reynald turned, gliding past the axe, and rammed the pommel of his sword into Will's solar plexus.

"Ooh," Gort grunted.

Will's mouth fell open, and he landed on his ass and stayed there.

Lute thrust, fast as a snake. Reynald knocked his blade aside, turned, grabbed Lute by his neck with his left hand, and kicked his leading leg from under him. Lute crashed on his back, the point of Reynald's sword half an inch from his throat.

It was all so fast. I barely followed this one. Most of the time I couldn't. They would clash, and then one of the brothers would be either on the ground or walking away, cursing.

Will clambered to his feet, trudged over to us, grabbed a pitcher of water from the table, and drank from it.

Gort kept working on his wire.

Will wiped his mouth with his arm and growled. "The man isn't human."

"There are people in the kingdom who would trade years of their life for one lesson from him," Gort said. "Learn while you can. You'll live a little longer."

Reynald offered Lute his hand and pulled him to his feet. He raised his arm slowly and thrust the blade, turning his arm. "Look at the angle."

Lute mirrored his stance and thrust. The point of his blade quivered.

"Imagine the muscles in your arm," Reynald said. "Feel them work."

Lute thrust again.

"Slower," Reynald said.

Another thrust.

"Slower."

Lute thrust very slowly. The point of his sword danced.

"Don't worry about keeping it steady for now. Concentrate on learning the motion."

Lute squared his shoulders and tried again.

"Better," Reynald said.

"Feels awkward."

"Do it just like that thirty times every morning until it starts to feel natural. Break it into three sets of ten."

"Why thirty? Why not a hundred?"

"Too many and you'll overwork your shoulder. You won't get there any faster, and we have a fight in seven days."

Will took a deep breath and headed back to the center of the courtyard.

I wasn't great at sports, but I played volleyball and swam in high school. I could tell when someone was phoning it in during practice. The brothers were giving it their all, and tonight they would be sore as hell.

Will landed on his butt again. I sucked in a breath in sympathy.

"It's good for them," Gort said, still examining the weird-looking tool in his fingers. "Knowing that even though you're big and strong, a smaller, older opponent can still kill you."

I nodded at the tool in his hands. "What is that?"

"A lockpick for Kaiden. I need to make six more. He gave me drawings." Gort smiled.

I glanced at Kaiden. He slouched on the wall, the lock forgotten, watching Reynald. His face looked grim. Almost haunted.

"How did you find out he was a locksmith's son?"

"Reynald told me," Gort said.

Kaiden followed Reynald around like a devoted puppy. He should've been excited watching this fight. Instead, he looked like he was at a funeral.

I had two younger cousins on my mom's side. I remembered visiting them a few years back, when they were twelve and eleven. They were borderline feral and bouncing off the walls. Kaiden was usually so quiet, half of the time I forgot he was even there and right now he might as well have been a ghost.

Our stares connected. Kaiden looked down at his lock and started fiddling with it.

"What about from the Southerner's Guard?" Lute asked.

Reynald moved into a stance, sword in both hands, the blade resting over his left shoulder. Lute mirrored him.

"Got it?" Reynald asked.

Lute nodded.

"Come on," Reynald said.

The younger man charged, his sword raised for a strike. Reynald parried and turned around Lute, somehow grabbing his opponent's arm and locking it in the bend of his elbow. His sword slipped around Lute's blade, as if it were liquid. Lute's sword went flying and clattered onto the stone. Half a second, and Lute was on one foot, off-balance, bent forward, with Reynald controlling his arm and the blade of Reynald's sword touching his neck.

Gort raised his thick eyebrows.

How did he do that? Did he catch Lute's sword with his cross guard and pry it free? It was so damn fast.

Reynald let go. Lute fell and cursed.

It was beautiful and so controlled. Reynald never stumbled, he never missed. He owned his battlespace. Everyone else was just a guest in it.

Watching Reynald was dangerous for me. When he took a blade into his hand, he transformed into a different man and that man pulled me like a magnet. It wasn't just his muscular body and the way he moved; it was the eyes. Cold, calculating eyes. Merciless. Powerful.

I needed to have my head examined.

Seven days until the Butcher displayed his next kill. Thinking about that was like pouring cold water over my head.

"What's bothering you?" Gort asked. "Is it Drugh?"

"No."

A messenger from Taryz had come first thing in the morning. One of Drugh's mercenaries had stopped by asking about the Magnars. Tonight Reynald and I would go to the teahouse and try to settle things.

"Then what is it?" Gort asked.

"The Butcher is good enough to kill Eliarde."

In the courtyard, Reynald thrust past Will's swing and stopped the tip of his sword an inch from Will's throat.

"Reynald knows his limits," Gort said. "He won't throw his life away or ours. If he says he can do it, it's because he's calculated the odds."

"I understand that. And I know Reynald is amazing. I can see him being amazing right now. But nobody knows how good the Butcher is."

Gort shrugged. "True."

"There's a part of Reynald that wants to find that out," I said.

"Also true," Gort said.

"That's what I'm afraid of."

Gort cut a new length of wire. "You can't afford doubt in a swordfight. You come to it to win, or you don't fight at all."

Lute staggered to us and sat on the ground by the benches. "I'm done. Just done."

"Weak," Gort told him.

"You try him, old man. All you do now is tinker and complain."

"Don't make me get up off this bench, boy."

"Maybe you should. Watch out for those knees breaking."

The doorbell rang. Lute groaned and dragged himself to the front door.

Will parried Reynald's cut with the haft of his axe.

"Good," Reynald said.

"About Drugh," Gort said. "This is a mess of our making. Our family should fix it."

I didn't have much in the way of secrets to hit Drugh with, so I had come up with a backup plan. They didn't need to know about it.

"It will be fine. I'll take care of it." Hopefully. "Reynald said he'd help me."

"We could . . ."

I pitched my voice low and intoned, "'Reynald knows his limits. If he says he can do it, it's because he's calculated the odds.'"

"Aspects preserve us," Gort muttered. "The boys are bad enough. Don't you start."

Lute trotted to us, all fatigue forgotten. "A noble is here to see you."

What?

"He won't tell us who he is. He brought a bodyguard with him."

"Did he ask for me by name?"

"Yes."

Strange. Did Solentine send someone my way? "Did he say what he wants or who sent him?"

"He wants to ask you a question. He didn't say anything else."

If this was coming from the Shears, it was in our best interest to let him in. However, that was highly unlikely. I was still an unknown to Solentine. He wouldn't recommend me to any clients. And if he wanted information, he would come himself.

No, this visit was a bad idea.

"Please inform him that I'm not receiving visitors. Let's see what he does."

Lute nodded and went to the door.

In the courtyard, Reynald paused, looking at me. Will decided it would be a great chance for a surprise attack and struck. Reynald stepped out of the way without looking. Will's axe whistled past the blademaster. Reynald kicked the back of Will's right knee and shoved him forward, his gaze still on me. Will went down. His knee slammed on the ground. He grunted.

"Hey!" Gort growled. "That was a cheap shot, boy!"

Lute jogged back to me from the front door. "He says his name is Earl Berengur."

Oh.

I jumped to my feet. "Please ask him to wait. Clover!"

She stuck her head out of the kitchen window. "Yes?"

"We have a visitor. Could you please fix my hair?"

She beamed. "Of course, my lady!"

I sat at the table by the wine tree, wearing my green gown, with my hair hastily braided and pinned into something Clover deemed decent. She waited on my left. Reynald assumed the bodyguard position behind me and to my right. He had changed into a dark jerkin, put on a cloak with the hood up, and pulled the lancer's coif over his face. The menace meter had gone all the way up.

"Do you know Earl Berengur?" he asked quietly.

"Not personally."

"Do you know why he is here?"

"He's looking for his brother."

"How did he find you?" Reynald asked.

"That's what I want to find out."

He nodded and waved at Lute, who waited by the tunnel. Lute went to the front door. A moment later two men emerged from the tunnel into the courtyard.

The first was about six feet tall, with dark hair and broad shoulders. He wore Southern scalemail, a kind of knee-length tunic of overlapping metal scales, and a plain metal pauldron on his left shoulder. Solentine's pauldron had been a fashion statement. This one was functional, with a rerebrace, almost a full metal sleeve. The man didn't carry a shield, and he would use that arm to block in a fight. A simple sword hung from his belt. His skin was an even, warm beige, his features were sharply cut, and his hooded eyes were alert and watchful.

His bodyguard was larger. He loomed three or four inches over Berengur and wore the same armor, except for a full-face helmet, which hid his features. He also carried a simple sword.

They could have been private guards, mercenaries, men-at-arms, or sergeants of some knightage. If you met this pair on the streets, you wouldn't give them a second glance. This was not their real armor. They didn't want to be recognized.

The dark-haired man approached the table and put a crest on it. Regular crests, the kind trusted servants and guards carried to show their affiliation with a noble household, were painted over wooden pucks, lacquered, and then wrapped with a cord, so they could be suspended off belts or wrists. Sometimes they were embroidered on clothes. This thing was solid metal. A miniature shield, a green background with a white tower, wrapped in rising rose vines bearing blue flowers. The crest of Berengur.

Who *had* sent him my way? It had to be the Shears. I couldn't think of anyone else, but I had to find out for sure.

"Please sit, my lord."

I invited him to a chair with a sweep of my hand. Clover and Reynald had been teaching me etiquette, and I was getting better at imitating a noble.

Berengur sat. The huge man parked himself behind him, directly across from Reynald. I couldn't see his face because of the helmet, or Reynald's because he stood behind me, but I would've bet money that the two of them were staring impassively at each other.

"What can I do for you, Lord Berengur?"

"I'm told that you sell information. I'm looking for a man, and I will pay generously."

That's what I thought. To tell him or not to tell him? That was the question. If I told him, would it make things worse? I wasn't worried about the impact on the timeline. I was worried about Pelegrin. If I made a mistake, he would lose his life.

Berengur waited for my response.

Silence stretched.

"Do you sell information?" he prompted.

"Under the right circumstances. I'm trying to decide if helping you would do more harm than good."

"What is the meaning of that?" His voice held a hint of warning.

"Let me ask you a question. A horse that carried you into battle has gone lame. There is no cure. He will never bear a rider again and the injury prevents him from being a stud. What would you do with this horse?"

Berengur frowned. "I would put him out to pasture. He would've given me years of faithful service and deserves a peaceful life. I don't see how this is relevant."

Maybe this would work out after all.

"Clover, please bring our guests some tea."

"Yes, my lady."

She turned and smoothly glided toward the house.

I faced Berengur.

"Your brother is alive."

Berengur didn't seem surprised that I'd guessed who he was looking for. If I truly was a competent information broker, I would've heard about it. He'd been looking for his baby brother for over a year.

"He isn't a captive. He is within the borders of this kingdom in a place of his choosing. He remains there of his own free will."

Berengur's face told me he didn't believe me. I couldn't blame him. He'd been scammed more than once.

"And how much will his location cost me?"

"Nothing."

He studied me.

"I won't be charging you today. I know you love Pelegrin. I know you and your mother are both worried about him. You lost track of him after the Halaros campaign. That was by his design. He doesn't wish to be found."

"And why is that?" His tone told me he was clearly skeptical.

"Pelegrin wanted to be a knight from a very young age. He admired your late father. Part of it is your fault. You used to tell Pelegrin stories of your father's bravery, stories you'd embellished. You made him into a heroic figure, a man of flawless character, who embodied the knightly virtues."

"How do you know that?"

"That's not important."

Clover brought out a platter with a teapot and poured the tea into two cups. She set the cups in front of us, placed a dish of honey between them, and withdrew a polite distance away.

"Like you and your father, Pelegrin joined the Defenders. The knight orders spend a great deal of time discussing the knightly virtues, while training their squires in violence. And yet, they never address what happens when those two halves of knighthood come into conflict."

He furrowed his eyebrows. "I do not follow."

"Pelegrin was knighted at seventeen and given his first command at eighteen. He was very young. His view of the world was simple, but I don't need to tell you that war is complicated and messy. It demands brutality and sacrifice. Pelegrin was put in an impossible situation, and he had to make a decision that conflicted with everything he had been taught to believe. It haunts him. He dreams of it over and over. He thinks he failed the legacy of your father and failed himself as a knight."

Berengur stared at me, his face shocked.

"He's deeply damaged by what he endured. He let the war touch his soul, and he felt too much. When he looks at his hands, they're still covered in blood, and he's searching for a way to wash it off."

"Where is he?" He didn't say it like a demand. It was almost a plea.

"He has chosen to recuperate at a monastery. He hasn't taken vows and has no plans to do so, but he conducts himself as a monk. He does manual labor. Growing things in a garden soothes him. He is accepted by the other monks, and the abbot, who is very experienced in these matters, is helping him to come to terms with his past. It's a simple life and that is all he can handle right now. He is healing, slowly, gradually, but he is healing. If you go there and force him to return to your castle, you will take the little bit of peace he's found from him. He will obey you, but one day you will walk into the great hall and find him hanging off a beam."

Berengur drew back.

"I urge you with everything in my power to let him recover. When he is ready, he will return to you on his own."

Silence fell. I drank my tea.

"You truly believe he will take his own life?"

"Yes. He's already thought about it. He hasn't done it because it would be selfish, and he doesn't want to hurt you or your mother."

In the book, Berengur found his brother, and his mother begged Pelegrin to return to their castle. He did. He ate, he bathed, he seemed to be functioning, but he rarely spoke, and then there was a scene where he stared at the beam of the great hall for way too long. Then, in the chaos after the crown prince's assassination, Arvel, the head of the Defender Order, wished that he had Berengur by his side, but the earl was gone to "tend to his family in mourning."

Pelegrin had hanged himself. I was absolutely sure.

My father hadn't come unscathed out of his service. I knew a lot about PTSD and the damage it brought, but convincing Berengur that I was right without modern psychology and veteran suicide statistics on my side was tricky. I had to put it in a framework he would understand.

"We place such a crushing burden on knights," I said. "We tell them they're supposed to be heroes, defenders of the realm, people of superior character. Then we send them into a slaughter and force them to butcher. They experience fear. They exist in constant vigilance, always ready to fight for their lives. It exhausts their body and soul. They watch their friends bleed out and die, and they have no time to grieve. Nobody warns them about this. Nobody sings songs about a young man trying to push his guts back into his stomach, or being so scared that the world turns dark, or being knocked off your horse and drowning in a muddy field in heavy armor while riders stomp on your back."

The two men in front of me were very still.

"We do this to them and then we expect them to return to a peaceful life as if nothing happened. Some of them get a taste for the killing and can't let it go. Some of them learn to distance themselves from their war selves. Others, like Pelegrin, need help and time."

"What did he do?" Berengur asked.

"He was put in charge of a border village that was a vital point in the supply chain for the front line of the Halaros conflict. The village sympathized with the Crimson Empire. The Emperor's agents promised them ten years free of taxation if the region raised the Crimson Banner."

Come to our side, everything will be great, we have cookies. Of course we won't tax you. What are you even talking about? By the way, we'd love to sell you an ocean property in Nebraska . . .

"The village didn't resist openly, but the first night there, Pelegrin lost two of his soldiers. He found them in the morning with their throats slit. The next night he lost another to poison, then two more to hunting arrows. The Empire's forces were nowhere near the village. This was a homegrown rebellion. Pelegrin gathered everyone in the town square and told them that the next time one of his soldiers was killed or harmed, he would take the life of a villager. A life for a life. He hoped it would stop."

"It didn't," Berengur guessed.

"They didn't believe him," I said. "They thought he was young and soft. Another soldier died in his sleep, and Pelegrin picked an old man, the village head, marched him to the center of the village square, and ran him through. The man's daughter, a young woman about my maid's age, drew a knife, and stabbed the battle chaplain in the back. He was the only unarmored member of Pelegrin's command, and he died on the spot. Pelegrin dragged her to the body of her father and cut her throat. The killings stopped.

"The villagers thought that not being soldiers would protect them," Berengur said. "Once he executed an old man and a young woman, he communicated his willingness to retaliate, and they realized they were not immune. His actions prevented further deaths, both soldier and civilian. He has nothing to be ashamed of. Nothing he has done would damage his standing as a knight. Those are the realities of war."

"And that is precisely the problem. In his eyes, he is a monster, and yet he was hailed as a hero when the conflict ended. To Pelegrin, either nobody understood that he was a monster and when they found out, the whole world would turn on him, or everyone knew what he had done and they cheered him for his evil deeds, which was even worse. How could he ever measure up to his father's legacy, the man who in his place would have brought the villagers to his side by his authority and the sheer force of his will alone?"

Berengur choked on air. "Our father did things far, far worse . . ."

"You didn't tell Pelegrin any of that."

"Of course not. Pelegrin was only seven years old when Father died. He was a child!"

I drank my tea. "You were trying to protect him then and I'm trying to protect him now."

"Why?" Berengur asked.

"Because I understand his burden, and his story moves me. My father has also seen war, and his soul took years to heal. My heart goes out to your brother, and I feel the weight of everything he has endured."

He stared at me.

"I can tell you the name of the monastery."

I'd given him enough to find it anyway.

"In return, I want two things."

"Name them."

"First, swear to me that you will go alone, without your mother, that you will not speak to your brother or let him see you, but meet with the abbot privately instead, and that you will do your best to heed his counsel."

"I swear," Berengur declared.

"Second, I need to know who referred you to me."

"His name is Shod. He works in the Three Moons and sells information on the side."

No hesitation. Dropped his contact's name just like that. This visit was connected to the Shears after all. Good. One worry off my shoulders.

"You will find Pelegrin in the monastery of the Pious Planters, north of Praul Britin."

If he hurried, he could make the ride in two days.

"You have done me a great favor." Berengur jumped up. "I will not forget this, my lady. The crest is yours to keep. Should you need me for anything, show this crest to the guards at the Citadel and they will take you to me."

He turned to leave. His bodyguard bowed to me. It was a deep slow bow. He straightened and followed his liege to the tunnel.

I took the crest off the table and studied it. I hadn't factored it in, but a favor from one of the Defender officers could come in handy.

"You said some things that are thought but not spoken," Reynald told me. His voice was quiet and solemn.

"Perhaps if they were spoken, fewer soldiers would hang from beams."

Reynald pulled his lancer's coif down. "Do you think he will follow your advice?"

"I don't know. I've done my best to convince him. It's up to him now."

"Whatever he chooses, the earl owes us a favor," Reynald said, his voice calm and measured. "Berengur isn't the wealthiest of nobles or the most renowned of knights, but that tower on his crest is well earned. He remembers his debts and he doesn't flinch."

To have a tower on your crest meant your family was stalwart. Reliable and loyal. The kind of family that honored its commitments and knew the meaning of duty.

"Good to know." I tapped my fingertips on the table, thinking.

"What is it?" Reynald asked.

"Berengur is allied with Arvel."

Doran Arvel, the head of the Arvel household and current Lord Commander of the Defender Order. Of all the Eight Families, the Arvels had the best reputation. Doran, in particular, was viewed as the kind of knight all others should aspire to be. Brave, honorable, a gifted general dedicated to his duty and devastating in battle. The main character to put all main characters to shame. The Golden Knight.

"And?"

"Shod, Berengur's informant, works at the Three Moons. That tavern serves as the Shears' headquarters."

Reynald's eyebrows rose. "Solentine supports Everard, but a Shears agent is feeding information to Arvel's faction?"

I nodded. "Probably not exclusively to them, or Berengur wouldn't have given him up so easily. Shod is moonlighting, and he isn't choosy about who pays him."

Solentine would lose his shit. Now I just had to figure out the right time and price to sell this juicy tidbit to him.

This wasn't in the books. I had just gotten my first piece of real intel all on my own. Ha!

"What happens to Arvel in the future?" Reynald asked.

"I told you that the crown prince is assassinated. It happens during the Winter Hunt. The security for the Hunt will be provided by the Defender Knights. After the assassination, suspicion falls on Arvel, and he shuts himself and his knights within the Defender Citadel. Hreban decides against trying to take it."

"A wise choice," Reynald said.

The name of the order was a clue. Defender Knights specialized in defense. Once fortified in their stronghold, they were immovable. Especially while wrapped in the magic of Arvel's Enduring Flame.

"Meanwhile, the city burns. Eventually Arvel and the entire Order ride out of Kair Toren, intending to rally and return. A tragedy happens, and someone close to Arvel is killed. When Arvel learns of it, he changes his mind and retreats to his territory instead. Sauven sends for him again and again, but Arvel never comes back to the capital."

Reynald frowned. "He abandons the Savarics?"

"He does."

"And Everard?"

"He leaves the city in the very beginning of the Kiel mess, before Hreban shuts the gates, and goes straight to Selva."

They were always in opposition to each other, Everard and Arvel. Even their branding seemed to identify them as rivals: Everard's crest of green, black, and silver, while Arvel's colors were white, azure, and gold.

"Arvel always maintained that his loyalty was to the Throne and nothing could shake it," I said. "As long as the Savarics held the Eagle Roost, he would heed their orders. Everard can't even bother to pretend to care about anything except the Selva Dukedom. One is the renowned and honorable Golden Knight, the pillar of the realm, and the other is the heartless and cruel Sleepless Duke, a violent isolationist."

Sauven had spent a good deal of his reign reinforcing that status quo. Which was why Arvel was celebrated in Kair Toren, and Everard was greeted with suspicion.

"I sense a *but* coming," Reynald said.

"But when the Crimson Empire invades, they both react the same. The Empire crosses the eastern border in the north and the south."

"A two-pronged assault."

"Yes. Their northern offensive targets the lower Trihorn, bypassing Selva, so Everard could've just sat back and let them invade Rellas. Instead, the Sleepless Duke moves his forces and hits the invading army. He suffers great losses but halts the northern invasion. Meanwhile, Arvel disobeys a direct command from Sauven, breaks his oath of loyalty, marches across half of Rellas, and crashes into the legions from the south. It costs him a third of his army, but he fights the Empire to a stalemate."

Reynald sighed. "It is as expected."

"How so?"

"Everard was born to protect the Dukedom. It's the purpose of his life. He carries responsibility for the lives of the people in his domain. If Rellas crumbled, the Dukedom would be next. He's acting out of pure self-interest."

"And Arvel?"

"Arvel has never failed. He's admired and celebrated everywhere he goes. If all the adoration and praise were replaced with suspicion and accusations, he wouldn't be able to deal with it. He would turn his back and retreat to a place where he would be beloved no matter what. But he is still a knight and a gifted commander. Arvel's lands are in the Western Middle Fields. The advance of the Empire would pin him between the sea and the Copper Mountains to the south. He calculated the odds and decided fighting the battle in someone's else backyard was better."

I took a deep breath and blew the air out. We had to stop what was coming.

The private rooms on the third floor of Taryz were really nice.

A large solid table occupied the middle of the room. Its top resembled gold oak with a darker wood inlay sealed in several coats of resin. Reynald and I sat on one side of it in carved wooden chairs, facing a large window. Outside, the Virka flowed to the Dokkon under the evening sky. If I leaned all the way to the right, I could see our house on the other side.

The door was on our left. I thought Reynald would do that thing badasses usually did in movies and books when they either choose a chair facing the exit or dramatically move one to face it, but no. He sat with his back to the door and didn't seem the least bit concerned about it.

The bells had struck seven about fifteen minutes ago.

I slipped Everard's den between my fingers.

"What is that?" Reynald asked.

"A man once gave me three coins. They saved my life. I kept the last one for luck."

I put the coin away, picked up the small teapot from the ornate metal platter, and refilled our cups. The tea in Taryz was top-notch. This one tasted a little like chocolate and something else, something slightly tart. Rose hips?

The wooden door opened, and three men entered. All three were large, in their late twenties or early thirties, wearing dark gray tabards and dark cloaks secured with a metal clasp in the shape of a dargan's head. Dargans resembled wolves, and these three did as well.

Same clothes. Same hair: very short on the back and the sides of the head, but long enough to pull back into a short ponytail on top. Drugh understood the power of branding. Anyone familiar with the mercenaries of Rellas would see one of these guys and instantly recognize which company they belonged to.

The leader took our measure. He was slightly shorter than Reynald, with light brown hair and a harsh face. He'd asked for the Magnars and found us instead, but he didn't seem at all surprised. Drugh Harra in the flesh.

Drugh headed for the table and sat across from me. One of his guys, the blond one, leaned against the wall by the door. The other man, with darker brown hair, moved to the window and stood behind Drugh.

Drugh fixed me with a heavy stare. "You are not Gort."

"I am his employer."

"I'm not here for you."

Too bad. He wasn't getting his hands on the Magnars. Drugh wasn't a bad man, but he was dangerous, and no matter how much bad blood there was between him and Filderon, the broker had been his mentor. I needed this to go well, because if it didn't someone would end up dead.

"Filderon was a greedy man in the truest sense of the word. Some people are greedy until they get comfortable and then they decide they have enough. For Filderon, enough didn't exist. He was always looking for a way to grab more."

No reaction.

"That's why he lied to you that day in the cemetery, when you were holding your mother as she wept. Your father never asked him to take care of you. Your father knew what kind of man Filderon was, and he didn't expect to die in that campaign. Filderon recognized talent when he saw it. He understood your worth and reasoned you would make him a lot of coin. That's why he convinced you to abandon knighthood. What was it he said? 'Knighthood is for people born into money. It keeps them from being bored. You have a mother to take care of.'"

Still no reaction.

"That's why he took your wife under his wing. He'd ignored his cousin for most of his life. The only reason he showed up at his funeral was because he realized there was an inheritance. He didn't even know your wife's name, he just knew there was a sixteen-year-old orphaned daughter, and she would be an easy target. That's why he didn't want the two of you to marry. Once you did, he'd lose the money. She came to the wedding with only a quarter of her dowry."

The commander of the Dargans was a tough nut to crack.

"When Indora Yolenta sent a sack of gold to him to lead eighty people to the slaughter, Filderon wavered. Not because it was wrong, or because he felt guilty about it. It was because he knew that there was no coming back from that. It would finish him as a broker so there would be no more money to be had. But the offer was just too tempting. So much money. He already had the estate picked out where he would retire. That's why he tried to get all of the Magnars in. He didn't want Gort's sons looking for him after their father died at Falcon Point and disrupting his sweet new life. You've read the instructions pinned to his chest. Things like trust and loyalty didn't matter to him at all."

That was the Dargans' credo: trust and loyalty.

I had run out of things to say. The silence lay heavy.

Drugh opened his mouth. "Do you think you've told me something I didn't know? There is a reason I stopped speaking to him."

"Then why are you here?"

"Because right or wrong, Filderon was there. He robbed me blind, but he gave me a way to support my mother. He taught me. He was shrewd and patient and he didn't hold back. I am where I am because he showed me the ropes. Hedena knew her uncle was after her dowry, but he gave her a safe place to stay. When she was scared and grieving, he put a roof over her head and food on her table. She was not alone. She belonged somewhere, and when she was ready, he pulled in all his favors to apprentice her to the weaver of her choice. He treated us as his own. He sat at our wedding for both of our fathers, and he left everything he owned to us. He was family. That's what the Magnars took away."

And I had just crashed and burned. Damn it.

"My wife is sad. She wants someone to be held accountable." Drugh stared at me. "I'll make it simple. Tell me where the Magnars are, and I will let you walk out of here."

It was time for plan B. "No."

Drugh stared at me.

"Filderon was your family. The Magnars are mine."

Drugh sighed. "Not smart. You think being a noblewoman will protect you."

No, I was sure it wouldn't. "I accept responsibility for their actions. The person you're looking for is right here."

The mercenary commander raised his eyebrows.

"You have a choice, Drugh. Either you kill me here and now, or we come to some kind of arrangement. But I will not let you hunt down Gort and Shana and their sons. Filderon was going to send them to their deaths. He got what was coming to him. If you persist, I will expose every dirty secret he had. By the time I'm done, his name will be mud and everything you and your wife have built will be splattered with it. Decide what you're going to do."

Drugh looked at Reynald. "And what about you? Are you fine with dying here, too?"

"Hadn't planned on it," Reynald said.

"Too bad, because that's what—"

Reynald pulled down his lancer's coif.

Drugh went white. The man behind him froze, too. The guy by the door wasn't quite sure what was going on, but he caught the change in body posture and snapped to alert readiness.

Nobody spoke.

Drugh opened his mouth. "You . . ."

"Go home and console your wife," Reynald said. "And I will forget you were ever here."

Drugh stood up, nodded, and marched out of the room. His backup fell in behind him without a word. The door swung shut.

Wow. I knew Reynald had a reputation. I just hadn't realized the full meaning of it.

I leaned forward and peered at Reynald's face. His expression was calm and relaxed. He looked like himself.

"I'm so impressed," I said. "How?"

"The Dargans did some business with the King's Army," Reynald said. "We've met before."

"Wow."

Reynald refilled our cups. "This is tea is expensive. Might as well finish it."

I drank my tea and exhaled. At least my fingers hadn't shaken this time. Maybe I was getting better at handling the life-and-death pressure.

"This was your plan?" Reynald asked.

"Drugh was raised to be a Conqueror Knight. They're all about loyalty to their own. He respects that. Killing me would bring too much scrutiny, and he isn't the kind of man who would murder a woman he just met in cold blood. It would be different if I came at him with a sword, but I was armed with a teacup."

I took another sip.

"Also, Drugh knows Filderon would sell his own mother for a noma. They've been estranged, so he isn't sure what his mentor has been up to, but he's sure it wasn't good. I told Drugh a lot of personal things I wasn't supposed to know. He must wonder what other secrets I keep. Dargan Company and Hedena's weaver shop are thriving. Like you said, Drugh knows what a dead mercenary is worth."

"Two boots and a sword," Reynald said, his face thoughtful.

"And Filderon's boots were shit."

I drank my tea and looked outside the window. We'd handled Drugh.

If only the Butcher would be as easy to deal with.

Chapter 21

Planter 19

There was a fish on my desk. It was a foot long with a blunt snout, small eyes, jet-black body, an asymmetric tail, and bony plates on its head. It looked prehistoric. I had known something wasn't right when I came up the stairs after breakfast and saw a trail of wet spots leading across the hallway to my rooms.

I picked up my reed pen and poked the fish with it, trying to get a look at the gills. Yep, pink.

The trail of wet spots stopped on my desk, right on the stack of cheap paper. I had started hiding the paper after the second fish, but we had had a late dinner last night because of the whole Drugh thing, and I'd forgotten to put it up. The stack was soaked through.

I picked it up, wrapping it around the fish, and took it downstairs, to the kitchen.

"Blackfin," Shana declared.

"Is it delicious?"

"Yes. Where do you keep getting them?" Shana asked.

"I don't know. I thought they were pranks at first. But now I think they're gifts."

Shana frowned at me. "From whom?"

"Someone who loves fish. Do we have any meat?"

I came back to my study carrying a small plate with a chunk of not-ham on it. I put the plate on the desk.

I should probably hide.

The study didn't offer many hiding opportunities. It was mostly shelves and small chests. There was a larger chest in my bedroom for spare linens and blankets. I went into my bedroom, pulled the linens out, and climbed into the chest. From there I could see a chunk of the study with my desk and the plate of meat on top of it. I closed the lid. Claustrophobic, but tolerable.

I climbed out, got the knife I used as a bookmark, and wedged it between the lid and the rim. The lid closed, leaving a half-inch gap. I checked it from my desk. It didn't look suspicious. You would have to really pay attention to notice the lid.

I got into the chest, stuffed some linens into it to make a cushion, and closed the lid. Good enough. Comfortable even.

I settled in to wait. Sunshine flooded the study. The sounds of Reynald and the Magnar brothers sparring floated through the open window.

When we were in high school, Cheyenne had planned on being a high-powered business executive with cutting-edge fashion sense and an office in a skyscraper. She'd listen to this business guru motivational speaker who talked about "ideating" and thirty-thousand-foot views. One of his favorite mantras was *"Stop. Look around. Take a deep dive and understand that your choices brought you where you are."*

I was sitting in a wooden chest in a house once owned by slavers in the middle of a magical city watching a plate with a chunk of meat because someone kept leaving fish on my desk. Which of my choices had landed me here, exactly?

I hadn't thought about home once since I saw the body in the Dog Market. Guilt landed on me like a brick.

So much had happened.

Back home, having a stressful day had meant a customer got annoyed or one of the food delivery apps sneezed, so I had to hustle to make up the money. Here a stressful day meant trying to stop a serial killer and bargaining with a mercenary for the lives of your friends.

Were the Magnars my friends? I didn't even know.

Sitting in the chest wasn't good for my mental health. I dealt with anxiety by doing something: making soap, writing down scenes from the books, plotting, sneakily cleaning my room, reading the books in my study. Derog had a remarkably varied library.

There was nothing to do in the chest but contemplate the confrontation with the Butcher. I just sat here and marinated in apprehension.

A faint creak announced my door swinging open.

Here we go.

Kaiden walked into the study. He moved completely silently, walking on his toes. He hadn't knocked and he didn't seem to be in a hurry, so he wasn't looking for me. He was sneaking in. Why? Everybody else was in the courtyard.

The boy glanced at the bedroom. He seemed to be looking straight at me.

I held my breath.

Kaiden turned away and went to my desk. He looked at the plate, tilted his head, looked at the not-ham from the side, frowned, and moved on. His hand glided over the desktop. He picked up something, looked at it, and walked out the same way he came, silent like a ghost.

Well then.

I gave it five seconds, climbed out of the chest, and checked my desk. My favorite reed pen, the one that didn't scratch the paper, was gone.

I slipped my shoes off and padded down the hallway toward Kaiden's room barefoot. His door was cracked open. He must've thought he was completely alone up here, so he hadn't bothered locking it. I pushed it with my fingertips, revealing a simply furnished room: a bed sitting against the wall, a desk with a chair, and some shelves Will had installed. They were mostly bare except for a single book and a weird rock. Several locks waited on the desk with the lockpicking tools Gort had made neatly arranged in the lower right corner.

Kaiden sat on his bed with my reed pen in his fingers. A large chest stood open by his feet.

He looked up. Panic shivered in his eyes. He stared at me like a frightened rabbit.

I kept my voice soft. "Want to tell me about it?"

He sighed and pushed the chest toward me. I came over and looked. An assortment of items lay inside: a worn knife sheath, a random lock I'd found in the study, a whetstone, a shaving brush, an arrowhead, one of Shana's wooden spoons, a wooden hairpin I'd seen Clover use . . .

I pointed at the sheath. "Is that Reynald's?"

He nodded.

"And the shaving brush? Will's?"

He nodded again.

Shana had a small basket in the kitchen where Clover put the week's grocery budget. The coins were in plain view, but he hadn't taken any. None of this stuff was valuable. They were just small mundane objects we had handled.

We looked at the collection some more.

"Kaiden, how did your parents die?"

He looked down at his feet. "Mom got sick. She came home and her skin was burning up. She went to bed. In the morning there were circles of welts on her face and her breath whistled."

Ring fever. Highly infectious and hard to cure. Sometimes it came into the city on ships, usually from the south, and burned entire city blocks before they caught it.

"I wanted to take care of her, but Dad took me to Sart's house."

"Who was he?"

"A tailor." His tone dripped hate. "He borrowed money from Dad. Dad told him he had to take me as an apprentice. Sart didn't want to, but Dad said the debt was registered so if Sart didn't take me, he would take his shop. I didn't want to stay there. I didn't want to be a tailor, but Dad said he had to take care of Mom and he would come back for me in five days. He said not to worry. It would be fine."

"He didn't come back," I guessed.

Kaiden shook his head. "I waited five days, then I waited three more. Sart would get drunk every night. One night he forgot to lock the room, so I snuck out and went home. The door was boarded up, so I had to get in through a window. It was gone."

"What was gone?"

He met my eyes. "Everything. Mom, Dad, all of our things. Everything was gone. And then our neighbor came out and said Mom and Dad died. The city had burned our things to stop the plague. She told me to go back to Sart because that's what Dad wanted for me. He signed a contract, and he wouldn't want me to be a runaway apprentice. She said I had to honor my father's dying wish."

Oh god. His father had realized what was coming and he had gotten his son out before Kaiden either got sick or the city quarantined him in some cell while all of their belongings were destroyed. Kaiden would've come out an orphan with nothing to his name. Awful things happened to beggar children on Kair Toren's streets.

"If you had stayed, you would've died, too," I said gently.

Kaiden stared straight ahead at the wall.

"How long were you with Sart?"

"A year and a half. He was a shit tailor. He would drink and then he would beat me. I tried. I really tried because that's what Dad wanted, but I got tired of him hitting me."

"You fought back?"

He nodded. "He sold me to Derog in the morning."

And we had rescued him. We were his new family. He wasn't just stealing. He was collecting pieces of us.

I was looking at the chest of Kaiden's fears. He probably opened it and looked at his little treasures when he felt unsafe. If we disappeared from his life, at least he would have something.

He knew we were about to do something very dangerous. We had included him in the Butcher talks. Excluding him wouldn't have worked—he would've just eavesdropped until he figured it out and it would've made him worry even more. But he was only twelve years old.

How to handle this . . .

"Your father didn't want you to be a tailor. He didn't want you to get beaten either. He just wanted to keep you safe, and he was out of time."

"I know," Kaiden said.

"Reynald is very skilled. Yesterday we went to confront Drugh. He brought two huge men with him. And then Reynald showed his face, and they fled."

Kaiden glanced at me. "Fled?"

I nodded. "They were very manly about it, but yes, they escaped as fast as their dignity let them."

My brother, who thought military slang was funny, would've called it a "rapid advance to the rear."

"And he will have the Magnars with him. And me. I will be there and even if I die, I will come back, Kaiden."

He looked down at his feet again.

Stealing was a coping mechanism. Taking it away cold turkey could do more harm than good.

"I will need my pen back. It's the only one I have that won't make holes in the paper."

He handed the pen over.

"Stealing is wrong. It makes the people you stole from feel unsafe and vulnerable."

He still wasn't looking at me. "Will you tell Reynald?"

"No. I won't tell anyone."

Some of the tension went out of his shoulders.

"A good thief steals without getting caught, but a better thief can return what he stole without being discovered. It takes more skill because the target is looking for their belongings, so they will be more alert."

Kaiden didn't say anything.

"When you steal things from us in the future, you must return them after two days."

His gaze snapped to me.

"If you get caught, I won't help you. If you are going to be a thief, Kaiden, be the best thief you can be. Do you understand?"

"Yes."

"Good. Just for the record, you aren't leaving fish in my study?"

"What fish?"

"That's what I thought."

I got off the bed. "Would you like a hug?"

He shook his head.

"Well, if you ever need one, you know where to find me. Two days, Kaiden. Don't get caught."

Half an hour later Reynald found me on the floor of my study. I'd heard a noise in my bedroom when I returned, so I had moved the plate with the meat to the floor and leaned against the wall.

Reynald took it all in and sat on the floor next to me.

"What are we doing?"

"Waiting for the fish fairy."

"I didn't quite catch that."

I must've said *fairy* in English. Tiny, winged humanoids weren't a part of Rellasian mythology.

I passed him my notes. I'd finished them while watching the plate.

"What is this?" he asked.

"This is what the Butcher does." Two scenes from the first book in nightmare-inducing detail.

He read the pages. I watched the plate.

Reynald finished and set the pages aside.

"I need to visit the Scribe Chamber," I said.

"Why?"

I told him.

"I'll take you," he said.

We fell silent. Minutes stretched by.

Something rustled under the bed. I kept still.

Another rustle.

A fluffy round head poked out from under the blanket dripping to the floor. The little red stelka looked at me, flicked her ears, and slunk over to the plate. She sniffed the not-ham, looked at me and Reynald, showing off the white crescent-shaped patch on her chest, bit the meat, and carried it off. As she ducked back under the bed, I caught a glimpse of my old gown. She'd made a nest out of it.

Reynald watched my new pet vanish under the bed with a stoic expression.

"That's one thing about you, Maggie. Being with you is never boring."

Chapter 22

Planter 24

The Rabeh Bridge spanned the Koreg River at a narrow point, stretching one hundred yards across the water. Its gray stone was worn down by countless feet, its rail smudged by time and the touch of many hands. It felt ancient, its lines simple but timeless.

As Reynald, Kaiden, and I walked across it now, it felt like passing from one world into another. The sounds of the bustling city behind us receded with each step. Ahead, at the other end of the bridge, a beautiful garden bloomed. Slender willow-like trees dripped long thin branches to the river, washing their scarlet leaves in the water. Behind the red willows, taller trees rose, bright green and bearing big white blossoms.

It was Planter 24, Resday, the final day of Rellas's eight-day week. Tonight the Butcher would leave a mangled body at the Knight Vanquisher Plaza. All the preparations had been made. All the plans had been gone over. There was nothing left to do. We were out of time.

"Where are we going?" Kaiden asked for the third time.

"You will see," Reynald said.

We crossed the bridge. A wide, paved path unrolled in front of us, stretching into the distance, flanked by greenery and flowers. Other paths branched from it, each marked with a signpost.

I pulled the scrap of paper from the pocket in my sleeve and checked it. "Row 202."

We started down the path.

Above us, ragged clouds slid across the sky, dappling the garden in light and shadow. Little winged lizards, colored like gemstones, scuttled up the trees and occasionally leaped off and glided to other trunks. Birds chirped in the canopy.

As we passed the paths branching off, I caught glimpses of wooden signs that hung from the tree branches. Most were sealed with several coats of resin, but a few were worn and weathered. Some had small pieces of colorful glass embedded in them, and when the sun caught them, they glowed like jewels.

"Where are we?" Kaiden asked.

"Sonndor," I said.

Kaiden eyed me. "And that is?"

"The cemetery," Reynald told him.

Kaiden fell silent.

Finally, we reached the right row and made our turn onto a narrow path paved with stone blocks. Lines of trees greeted us on both sides, each identified by a stone marker with a number on it. The wooden signs on their branches swayed gently in the breeze.

We passed more red willows, some goldenberries that reminded me of dwarf oaks, and a handful of twisted marse trees, their split trunks braiding over each other.

Let's see, 202–18, 202–20, 202–22. There.

I stopped before a twisted marse, its leaves a beautiful green streaked with purple veins. Over a dozen wooden signs hung suspended from its branches. This plot had been recently tended to—the weeds had been removed, and new flowers had been planted in a ring around the tree's roots, their blossoms small and white like little stars. The clerics of the Dridag had done a good job. Well worth the fee.

Two wooden signs, brand new and sealed with resin, hung off the branches. One had a glass flower with pale blue petals and the other had a small lock attached to it with a tiny chain.

Kaiden stared at the signs.

"Your father was born outside of Kair Toren," I told him. "But your mother's family is from the city. I didn't think he would mind joining them. I'm sure that if we could ask him, he would want to be with your mother."

Kaiden stared at the tree.

"She found your parents' ashes," Reynald told him. "They were stored in the Temple of Dridag because nobody paid the burial fee. Maggie paid the fee and had them buried here."

"This is your family tree, Kaiden," I said gently. "All rites have been performed. Your parents' ashes are nourishing the roots. Your grandparents are buried here as well, and their parents. Five generations. You can come and visit them whenever you want."

He blinked and turned away from me, hiding his face.

Reynald opened the bag he had brought and took out a small wooden canteen filled with water. He held it out to Kaiden. "Make your offering."

Kaiden took the bottle. His voice was hoarse. "What do I do?"

"Pour the water on the roots and talk to your parents," Reynald said. "Tell them how you've been. Ask for guidance if you need it. Request their blessing. Maggie and I will be over there. Take all the time you need and then find us when you're ready."

The boy stepped toward the tree. Reynald and I strolled farther down the path.

Finding his parents hadn't proved difficult, only time consuming. The Scribe

Chamber kept meticulous records. Now Kaiden knew where they were, and nobody could take them away from him again.

The people of Rellas had several ways to bury their dead. They were a mix of many waves of settlers and invaders, and each had brought their own traditions and rites. People from the north, like Reynald, sometimes built cairns or erected stone pillars over the graves. Coastal southerners did water burials, sinking their corpses off the islands in the ocean. But the majority of Rellas burned their dead and buried their ashes under the roots of their ancestral trees. A family tree took on a whole new meaning.

The unbroken line of trees on our left ended abruptly, and we came to a massive statue. A huge beast, carved out of wood and sealed with resin, gripped a slab of stone with four enormous, clawed paws. Its body bulged with muscle, promising sudden explosive power. It was sheathed in razor-edged scales as large as my hand. They blended into a mane of blades on its thick neck and turned feather-like on its colossal wings, which were tipped with bone spikes. Its tail split into three long, flexible whips, studded with spur-like protrusions, and they curved around the beast as if aiming to strike.

I stopped. Reynald halted next to me.

The creature's head, lowered slightly toward us, was a meld of lion and dragon, with terrible square jaws and a mouth bristling with fangs. Its eyes seemed to stare straight at me, alive with malevolent intelligence and rage.

Someone had thrown paint on the statue's paws. There were cuts and gouges on its legs. People had tried to destroy it, but all that their efforts resulted in was mere scratches. The great beast stood undaunted.

"A dursan," Reynald said next to me.

One of Ralinbor's creatures? "This can't possibly be to scale, can it?"

"I've seen bigger."

Bigger? It was larger than the huge steppe mammoth I once saw at the Smithsonian. This thing was movie-dragon size, and it looked like it existed to kill and rip its prey apart.

"How could it fly?"

"Magic," Reynald said. "Its power isn't limited to humans. Beasts use it as well. The dursans infest mountain ridges all across the continent. Do you know the story of Ralinbor's Rebellion?"

"Sauven and Ralinbor were half brothers and the best of friends. Then Sauven took the throne and realized some people thought the wrong Savaric had entered the Eagle Roost. Ralinbor's maternal uncle was one of them, so Sauven accused him of treason and had him beheaded. Ralinbor turned on him and marched into Kair Toren with his army. He was killed, his rebellion was put down, his wife was brought to the capital in chains, tried and executed, and his only son died in the fire set by the king's knights."

"That about sums it up," Reynald said. "Ralinbor of the Wilds inherited the power of Exultant Call from his father and the affinity for the dursans from his mother. He tamed them, and he called on them in battle, which was how he got the name 'of the Wilds.'"

The idea was horrifying. "How did he lose with those things on his side?"

"They have magic and they're powerful, but they are still creatures of bone and blood. They can be killed. Fatefire can cut one. So can a weapon coated with Rageglow."

Wow.

Reynald shrugged. "Ralinbor didn't lose his war on the battlefield. He lost it weeks before, when he failed to adequately equip his troops, neglected to put together a functioning supply chain, and chose the wrong place and time to engage his enemy. He counted too much on the dursans, but they are just animals. No matter how powerful a magical beast is, it's no substitute for proper planning and strategy."

A stone bench waited across from the statue, on the other side of the path. I sat on it. Reynald joined me.

"Why is it here?"

"This statue was commissioned by Wynand Bors's father, Sagred," Reynald said. "He'd managed to kill a dursan single-handedly during the conflict, and he was very proud of it. He presented this monstrosity to Sauven on the first anniversary of the battle. 'Behold the mighty enemy we vanquished.'"

"But Sauven didn't want a reminder of his dead brother," I guessed.

"So Sagred Bors found out," Reynald said. "Sauven would've loved to set it on fire, but he'd needed the Conquerors' support, so he had it put somewhere in the Tangle."

The Tangle was the collective name for the northern slums. The last place Sauven would ever visit.

"Someone must've realized that it had been defaced. It was still a royal gift, so it was carted off and must've ended up here. I've never seen it before. I've only heard the story. This was before my time."

The dursan glared at us, scarred, stained, and yet defiant. I had the strangest feeling. A kind of vague anxiety, as if I were looking at a sign of things to come.

"It's fitting that it's here," Reynald said quietly. "Ralinbor's mother and his uncle were his only living relatives besides Sauven. Ralinbor died on the battlefield. His wife was tried, convicted, and beheaded. His son perished in the fire when Sauven's personal guard set Kair Tred on fire. Everyone is dead now. It stands here as a monument to the fallen family."

"I'm not so sure," I told him.

He gave me an odd look. Like he was both amused and admiring. If I didn't know better, I'd say Reynald Karis, the ice-cold blademaster of Rellas, found me endearing.

"What?"

"I'm not even surprised anymore," he said. "Tell me more, Maggie."

Somehow, he loaded a lot of meaning into my name. Was I reading too much into this?

"I know of a boy who woke up in a burning house to the shouts of his enemies in the courtyard."

It was one of those random Latour scenes. No hint when or where it took place. No names. No explanation as to why it was in the narrative. It was just there to drive the fandom out of their minds with speculation.

"The house was engulfed in flames. He couldn't get to the window, so he hugged his puppy and ran into the hallway through the fire. The burning boards collapsed under him. He fell three floors, all the way into the stone cellar, landed badly, and passed out from pain and smoke. Two days later, when the knights who'd set his home on fire were long gone, a man rode up to the still-smoking ruin. He searched through the wreckage and found the boy in the cellar. The boy's legs were broken, but he'd kept the puppy safe in the fall. The man took the boy and his dog with him because he was the child of a woman the man once loved, and he raised the boy as his own son."

Reynald pondered the statue. "Do you think the boy was Mirabor Savaric?"

"I don't know. I can't say either way. But he could've been."

That was my personal pet theory. It would so much more interesting if Ralinbor's son survived.

"Who was the man, do you think?" Reynald asked.

"It's hard to say. Aelis Savaric was supposed to be so beautiful, her smile could stop a heart. Many people were in love with her."

The sun broke through the clouds, and I turned my face to the warm sunshine.

"Are your parents alive?" he asked.

"Yes." Somewhere. "Yours?"

"Dead. My father was killed, and my mother died on the battlefield two years later."

"I'm sorry."

"Thank you."

Suddenly I missed my parents so much, it hurt.

"What does your father do?" Reynald asked. "He must be retired from the army by now."

How to explain a civil engineer?

"Yes. He earned our country's version of the Green Purse and then became a kind of architect."

"So you are from a scholar family?"

"I suppose. You could say I was a scholar."

"What did you study?" he asked.

"Power. How to acquire it, how to keep it, how not to abuse it. How to exercise it for the greater good of as many people as possible."

"Fitting," he murmured.

"What about your father? What kind of man was he?"

"Kind." He sighed, looking at the trees across the path. "Many people feared him, but he was a good father. He loved my mother, and he loved me. I wish we'd had more time."

There was a world of pain and regret in those words.

"I need to be there when you take the Butcher down," I said.

"You're not a trained fighter, Maggie," he said gently.

"And yet, of all of us, I'm the most likely to survive that fight. I will come back to life. I'm Maggie the Undying."

"I don't want you to be hurt."

"I won't be."

"'Dying horribly and then waking up in a lot of pain,'" he quoted.

"Do you remember everything?"

"Only the important things."

He wasn't going to derail me. I needed to see this through. "I cried when you died, Reynald."

I could feel the tears building now, a wet frustrated heat just behind my eyes. I'd spent the last week worrying and going over every possibility, every contingency, and the pressure cooker of it finally broke me.

"I . . . witnessed it happen many times, and I cried every time."

I had read about it, not witnessed it directly, but I wasn't ready to tell him that.

"I wanted so much for you to succeed, to save your son, and get far away from Kair Toren. You must survive. I cannot come here to bury you. I can't have you turn into one of those wooden plaques hanging off the branches. I can't do it. It will destroy me."

I'd said too much.

A warm hand closed over mine. The words died in my mouth. Suddenly we were connected. Everything else disappeared. It was me and him, and he was holding my hand in his.

"I won't let him kill me." He swore it like it was an oath.

It felt so reassuring and safe and so achingly right. I wanted him to wrap his arm around me, pull me close, and tell me that it would be fine. I wanted to keep touching, to feel him, to kiss him. I craved it. I required it. It wasn't just a need; it was as if I were in pain and only he could make it better.

I wanted Reynald.

Holding on to him was a colossal breach of etiquette. I had to let go.

I looked at him and forgot to breathe. His eyes were hot and green, and he looked at me like he wanted me. He was all in. There was no way I was misinterpreting that. The densest woman in the world would've known exactly what was going through his head.

This man had already lost so much. His parents were dead, his wife had been murdered, and his son had been kidnapped. And here I was, lying to him.

I had been lied to before by someone I loved. I had moved on, but it still hurt years later. And my lie wasn't the ordinary kind. No, it was huge.

I'm not from Rellas. In my world, you're a character in a book, but here you are, real and alive, and I don't know how that's possible. I don't know what brought me here or why. I don't understand why I can't die. I don't know if there is a magic counter that keeps ticking every time someone kills me and if one day I might run out of lives. I don't know how much time I have in this world. I don't know if I have a future here.

I knew how Reynald thought. He'd witnessed me dying and coming back to life, and it had disturbed him so much, he'd made it his mission to make sure I didn't die again. Right now, we both felt the beginning of something, but if I kissed him, there would be no going back. I wouldn't be able to let go, and his eyes told me he wouldn't want to.

If we got together, and then I died and *didn't* come back to life, it would rip him apart. He would blame himself for failing to keep me safe.

If whatever weird force that had thrown me into Rellas yanked me back out without warning, he would look for me. Finding me would become his life's goal, just like saving Matheo was a goal, except he would never find me no matter how hard he tried. He would never know what had happened.

And even if none of this came to pass, even if I kept resurrecting and stayed in Rellas, I couldn't offer him honesty.

I knew this world was real. I felt it. But if I stopped lying, I would have to tell him how I knew the things I knew. He would have to wonder if his life was just a book. What would it do to a person if they were to find out that they were a figment of someone's imagination? If that was true, the woman Reynald loved and cherished had died for the sake of emotional impact and their son was kidnapped to raise the stakes. His life and death would become just someone's idea of entertainment.

And I'd had a front-row seat to all of it. I'd been in his head. I knew his inner thoughts and doubts, things that were so deeply private he never told anyone about them. Sharing those things should've been his choice, but the book had robbed him of that right. I knew his weaknesses and how to manipulate him. It would never be a relationship on equal terms.

He was a very smart man. He would see all of the pitfalls.

I would give anything to kiss Reynald Karis right now. But he deserved a peaceful, happy life.

I gently freed my hand.

Oh, I was so, so stupid. Letting go hurt.

Reynald drew back ever so slightly, making a minute adjustment to his pose and expression. I wasn't sure how he managed it, but everything about him was suddenly aboveboard. Without saying a single word, he had surrendered control of the space between us to me, and his expression reassured me that I owned it and could do with it whatever I wanted. He wouldn't invade my space again.

"I need to be there when you take down the Butcher," I said. "I will do everything the way you tell me to, but I need to be there. You can't keep me from coming with you."

He sighed and looked at the sky.

Birds sang in the branches. The dursan glared at us with its vicious eyes.

"If I were to foolishly agree to this, you would have to follow my orders exactly."

My pulse sped up. "I promise."

"No noble sacrifices for the greater good."

"None."

"Good. I've watched you die, too." Reynald's eyes turned hard. "I never want to see it again."

"I can't promise that."

"You don't have to promise anything," he said. "As long as I am by your side, I will make sure you don't die again."

We fell silent, sitting side by side, looking at the gardens around us.

I reached into my sleeve, pulled Everard's den out of the pocket, and put it in his hand.

"Your lucky coin?"

"Please carry it with you tonight."

"Thank you," he said. "I'll give it back to you when it's over."

Kaiden came striding down the path. His eyes were red. He handed the empty canteen to Reynald and hugged me. He didn't say anything. He just hugged me, quickly and quietly, and then we set off back to our home.

Chapter 23

Planter 25

I sat on the barrel of pan oil and stared through the crack between the slightly open window shutters. The crack let me see a narrow slice of the night-drenched plaza. Prata, the largest moon, was full, enormous in the night sky, and its pale light encased the statue of the Knight Vanquisher, turning it silver. The night was bright.

On the other side of the window, Reynald waited, dressed in a plain tunic and trousers, his lancer's coif resting on his shoulders. He hadn't even bothered with armor. He'd brought his sword and that was it.

I had traded my gown for some dark pants and a tunic, and Gort had given me a short sword "just in case." I was also presented with a lancer's coif and told to wear it. Generic clothes and covered faces for everyone. Reynald was taking no chances.

The statue was in the center of the plaza, and the pan oil warehouse, in which we were hiding, sat west and slightly north of it. If I leaned all the way to my right, I could see one of the northern streets. Lute was probably hiding somewhere in there. If Reynald leaned all the way to his left, he could probably glimpse the mouth of the southern street where Gort would be waiting. The only roof accessible to Shana was on the most southeastern building, so she was lying in wait somewhere not too far from her husband.

It took Kaiden about five seconds to pick the lock. Reynald sent him home after that, and he obeyed without complaining.

Reynald and I had slipped into this warehouse just before midnight. It had to be two or three in the morning now. The sun rose at six thirty or so, and the first workers would be on the street half an hour before that. The closer dawn crept, the higher his chances were of discovery. Our killer was overdue.

Reynald didn't seem to care. Five minutes after we came in, he had straddled an oil barrel, leaned against the wall, and closed his eyes. He wasn't asleep. If I stirred, he opened his eyes to check on me. He simply waited.

It wouldn't be too long now.

Unless the killer got cold feet and decided to not show up. He should've been here by now.

A faint creaking squeaked through the night. I froze, sure I had misheard.

Creak, creak, creak . . . The axle of an old cart straining under a heavy load.

A lone man crossed the plaza from the north side, pushing a handcart. He wore an old cloak, and his hood was up.

My heart hammered a million beats per minute.

On the other side of the window, Reynald uncoiled soundlessly and moved to the door, pulling up the lancer coif over his face.

The man stopped and pulled back a corner of the tarp covering the top of the cart. He glanced at the statue, rubbed his chin, and took a rope with a pulley out of the cart.

It was him. It had to be him.

"No matter what happens, stay inside," Reynald whispered. "Trust me."

He opened the door and walked out.

The man turned to him.

Reynald kept heading toward him, his steps unhurried.

The man took a few slow steps back, glancing to both sides.

I couldn't see shit. I got up and tiptoed to the doorway, staying in the shadows. I could see the southern street and the hulking shape of Gort blocking it. Will and Lute were probably blocking the other side. We had boxed him in.

Reynald lifted the edge of the tarp with his sword, looked at the contents of the cart, and let the tarp fall.

The killer pulled off his cloak and tossed it aside. He was a hair shorter than Reynald, but wide in the shoulders and across the chest. His dark hair fell to his shoulders, parted in the middle to leave his face open. I couldn't see his features from where I stood.

"It's like this then," he said. His voice was low and harsh.

Reynald stepped away from the cart, his gaze fixed on the killer.

"You think you're a problem," the Dog Market Butcher said. "You're only an inconvenience. A slight one."

Reynald said nothing.

"You think you're good enough. You're not."

Reynald advanced. The killer moved back, maintaining the distance. They were stalking each other across the cobblestones.

The Dog Market Butcher was about the same size as Reynald, but he moved differently. Reynald never planted himself. He was always light on his feet, and even when he stood still, he seemed poised to strike at any moment, in any direction. By contrast, the Butcher's footsteps were heavy and deliberate, and he held himself as if he expected Reynald to ram him head-on.

"I don't know you, and you're not on the list."

The Butcher pulled a blade from the scabbard on his belt. It was a double-edged sword, simple, functional, very similar to what Reynald carried.

"Still, you clearly went to a lot of trouble arranging all of this." The Butcher drew a circle with the tip of his blade. "So I'll show you a thing or two before you die. The rest of you, stick around. I don't want to have to chase you down. I still have real work to do."

Reynald remained silent.

A slight uncertainty touched the Butcher's face, breaking through the bravado. He saw himself as a predator. He was used to taunting his human prey, as they tried to figure out why he'd attacked them. He liked things to be on his terms. Suddenly he was being hunted, and his opponent was refusing to take the bait.

The Butcher struck.

He lunged forward, his sword parallel to the ground, the blade tip slightly angled down, and thrust.

Reynald parried with the flat of his blade, letting the Butcher's sword slide to his right.

The Butcher reversed his swing. His sword cut upward and over and came down on Reynald like a sledgehammer. Somehow Reynald moved out of the way, and the blade carved empty air. Reynald took a step back.

The Butcher recovered and smiled, his mouth a slash across his face. "Somebody taught you something, boy."

He must have read Reynald as a much younger man.

"Let me show you a little more."

The Butcher charged, swinging his sword in a barrage of strikes. Left, right, left, left, right . . . It was very quick, just glints of reflected moonlight. He swung that sword like it weighed nothing, lightning fast, and Reynald was barely parrying. He took a step back, another, then a third. The Butcher drove him across the plaza, the sheer ferocity of his attack unstoppable and unrelenting.

Another blow. Another step.

Reynald kept backing up. Why wasn't anybody helping him? Why weren't Gort and the brothers rushing in there and stabbing the hell out of this bastard?

They were past the statue, and I moved, trying to keep them in view.

The Butcher shifted his stance, gripped his sword with both hands, lifted it above his head, and brought it down with all his strength. Reynald leaped back. The killer reversed his blade, spinning it, and sliced in a horizontal slash across Reynald's chest. The blade caught the front of Reynald's tunic.

He was cut. He had to be cut.

If I sprinted now, I could throw myself at the Butcher and it would give Reynald an opening.

Stay inside. Trust me.

I didn't know if I had that much trust in me.

Gort wasn't moving. There had to be a reason he was staying put. They must've had a plan, but nobody had bothered to tell me. Right now, the plan seemed to be to let Reynald get hacked to pieces while we all stood around like brainless jackasses who filmed their friends' fights with cell phones instead of breaking them up.

Strike, strike, strike.

Reynald turned to his left and took a few steps. The Butcher followed. They were in profile now, with Gort behind them, watching, motionless, like some kind of referee.

The Butcher squared off for another attack.

Reynald waited, both hands on the grip of his sword, its blade resting on his shoulder, point up. The Butcher also clasped his sword with both hands, propping the blade on his right shoulder. For a moment they were mirror images of each other.

The Butcher swung. It looked like another devastating overhead strike, and it started like one, but then he rolled the sword off his shoulder and to the right, stepping forward as the blade sliced through the air.

Reynald stepped to his right and thrust straight at eye level. As the Butcher's blade completed its arc, it should have taken Reynald's head off. Instead, it slid against Reynald's sword all the way to the cross guard. The tip of Reynald's blade sliced the Butcher's left cheek. The killer stumbled back, shocked. With a flick of his wrist, Reynald dropped his sword to the side and down, sliced the Butcher's left thigh, pulled back, and thrust. The blade bit into the Butcher's side, just above the hip bone.

It was so fast, Reynald barely seemed to move. Cheek, thigh, waist, the whole left side of the Butcher was bleeding. He backed away from Reynald, holding his sword in a high guard.

"Who are you?" the Butcher growled.

Reynald started toward him. He said nothing. He just advanced on the Butcher, and it was terrifying. Like watching Death coming.

It wasn't just me. The Butcher saw it, too. His stance shifted from confident to guarded. He bared his teeth like a cornered animal and snarled. A faint purple light sheathed his body.

The Butcher blurred. He actually blurred, swinging out of focus, encased in a shivering purple outline.

Reynald struck, too fast to follow. Metal clanged—the Butcher parried. Whatever that blur was, it made him faster.

They clashed, slicing and blocking. There was no way to parse what was happening. They had devolved into human shapes and swinging swords, colliding to the beat of ringing metal.

Blood wet one of the swords, bright red blood, and I couldn't tell whose blade it was. I only saw it for half a second. Was it Reynald's blood? Was it the Butcher's blood?

My chest hurt from the grip of fear.

I took back everything I'd thought about swords and poetry. This was terrifying. There was no beauty in it. It was brutal and horrible. I didn't want to watch it anymore. I just wanted it to end with Reynald still standing.

Something moved behind Gort. I was so focused on the two fighters, I didn't even know how I saw the flicker on the edge of my vision. It was a man in a gray assassin's outfit running down the street toward Gort.

Oh please no. Please, please, please no. Anybody but him.

Solentine sprinted.

I pulled the door open and jabbed my hand at Gort. *Behind you!*

He spun around, his axe swinging before he even saw anything. Solentine's footsteps ignited with silver. He veered away from Gort to his right and ran up the building, two long daggers in his hands. Gort hurled his axe. It slammed into the wall, missing Solentine by a couple of inches. The head of the Shears twisted his body and dashed across the vertical wall, his body parallel to the ground.

The Butcher saw him. His blur flared with purple, and he slid away from Reynald and Solentine, to the west and toward me, covering twenty-five yards in an instant.

A crossbow bolt clattered on the cobblestones, a quarter of a second behind him. Shana had missed.

The purple light died. The Butcher stumbled, still running but no longer blurring. He was out of juice and running straight for Lute's street. Of the two Magnar brothers, Lute was the weakest. The Butcher would kill him, hurt him, or use his morr beads, and we would never find him again. He had a head start and Reynald was across the plaza.

Morr beads transported whoever broke them, but never more than one person or a heavy load. *They must have a weight limit . . .*

I shot out of the doorway toward the Butcher.

He didn't see me.

For a terrifying second I was flying toward him. The plaza seemed to stretch into the distance. I just had to tackle him and wrap him up. No matter how strong he was, I could buy us at least two or three seconds.

The Butcher's head whipped around, and I saw his face, an angry cold mask.

We collided. I grabbed onto him, clutching at whatever I could, and yanked him toward me.

Pain exploded across my stomach. Something cracked. Breath burst out of me. He must've hit me.

Another hit. It felt like a horse had kicked me. My grip slipped, and I landed on my butt on the ground, a chunk of dark hair in my hand.

The world slowed to a crawl.

The Butcher raised his sword, and I saw his face, furious and filled with rage.

He stared straight through me as if I weren't a person but some obstacle he had to destroy.

The sword thrust toward me.

Green fire streaked across the cobblestones, like a jet of arcane napalm, straight between us. The front end of the Butcher's blade slid off and fell to the ground.

The Butcher's eyes went wide. He stared at the half sword in his hand and pawed at his wrist. Something popped like popcorn in my head. The Butcher vanished.

Twenty yards away, Reynald was holding a sword dripping green magic. Black smoke coiled from him, streaming downward to hug the cobblestones.

Green fire.

The line of flames died, snuffed out like the flame of a candle. A scar gouged the plaza.

When he strikes, the Fatefire flies off the blade and burns everything in its path. Every strike leaves a line of flames in its wake. The air reeks of smoldering flesh. The black smoke that rises from the bodies stings your eyes . . .

He was looking at me. His eyes glowed. I could see them all the way from where I sat. They were a bright, paralyzing green.

Behind him, Gort swung into view, walking over. He didn't seem surprised.

I scrambled to my feet and ran for the house.

✧

I pounded on the door of the house. "It's me. Open up!"

The door swung open, revealing Kaiden and Clover. I yanked my coif off my head.

Clover's face blanched. "What happened?"

"Leave the door unlocked." He would cut through it if he had to. "Go to Clover's room and bar the door from the inside. Do not come out. Don't make noise. If Reynald knocks, don't open the door to him."

"Why?" Kaiden demanded.

"Do as I tell you!"

Kaiden opened his mouth, but something in my face must've told him now was the wrong time to argue. I slammed the door closed behind me and we took off across the courtyard to the inner door.

Ramond vi Everard, the Sleepless Duke, the Lord of Selva, wielder of the Fatefire, twenty-nine years old, six foot one, dark hair, pale green eyes that turned an intense, true green when he used his magic.

True green, my ass. It was a bright electric green that burned into your brain.

Of course he didn't look thirty-eight. He wasn't thirty-eight.

I rode a horse.

He sure did. The one with a skull face on its head.

I will take care of it.

And he did. The Dargans did a lot of business in the north. When Reynald took off his mask, Drugh saw the Sleepless Duke and he got out of there like his ass was on fire. That should've been a clue. Reynald was respected but not feared and that had been fear.

Trust me.

I was so oblivious and stupid. Everard's whole life revolved around Selva, and I had told him the civil war was coming and Rellas would go to shit. He would do anything and everything to control me because I was the key to his survival. A woman who knew his rivals' secrets. A priceless gift. He must've been overjoyed when I sat on that bench in the cemetery and stared at him like a lovesick fool.

We cleared the stairs and burst into the upper hallway. The kids ran to the right, past me. I lingered until I saw them disappear into Clover's room, and then I ducked into my suite. I would lock the door and—

Solentine leaped onto my windowsill. I had left the fucking window open again. Damn it.

"Don't move," Solentine ordered.

A low growl came from my bedroom. The stelka emerged from under my bed, her little fangs bared.

"Guard vermin. Charming," Solentine said.

Quiet steps came from the hallway.

He was coming. There was no escape.

Everard walked through the open door.

Nothing of Reynald remained. This was the demon from the basement. Before, even during the fights, he had dampened himself somehow. He wasn't hiding anymore.

He walked in, and the room was his. He owned it. His presence filled it, unignorable, a sharp, immediate threat that demanded you focus on it to the exclusion of everything else. There was no predator to compare him to. He was in a class of his own.

He leaned against the wall and crossed his arms, and when I looked into his eyes, I saw a cold, calculating intelligence looking back. If I'd had any emotional capacity left, it would have scared me more than Solentine and his daggers, more than the Fatefire or the Butcher, but I was too shocked and numb. The enormity of the betrayal had knocked all the fear out of me.

The stelka dashed under the bed and stayed there.

"Are you hurt?" the Sleepless Duke asked me.

Somehow, I made my mouth work. "No."

"A pity," Solentine murmured.

Everard ignored him. His voice was slow and measured. "What happened to staying inside the building? Did you misunderstand? Were my instructions vague or confusing?"

How had he hidden this? How in the world did he manage to tone himself down to pretend to be Reynald?

He was waiting for me to answer.

"He was about to disappear or hurt Lute," I said.

Everard fixed me with his stare. "Morr beads are calibrated to a specific weight. Do you know what happens when you add another human to that weight?"

"No."

"Neither do I. The magic could've cut you to pieces and strewn them between that plaza and his destination."

"Lute—"

"Is a trained killer. You're not."

"Can we get back to what's important?" The head of the Shears slid his daggers back into their sheaths and sat on the windowsill.

"Nineteen days ago you left the safehouse in the morning 'to think' and disappeared. The two human-shaped statues you brought with you refused to tell me where you had gone."

Solentine's tone was even and deliberate.

"We have a partnership. I've committed resources and people to our shared cause. And for reasons that right now escape me, I'm personally invested in your survival and continued well-being."

Oh he was pissed. Solentine didn't run hot when he was mad. He got chillingly cold.

"Nineteen days. Not a word. No sign of life. Nothing. I was sure that you had been recognized and Sauven had you stashed in some dark hole. I considered what I would do if you turned up floating face down in the Dokkon. Instead, I find you here, in the company of a woman without an identity. A woman who showed up out of nowhere, who has access to information she shouldn't have, and who likely has been planted here by one of the Eight Families to get close to me or you."

"The world doesn't revolve around the two of you," I told him.

"Be silent," Solentine told me.

"Or what? You're going to kill me? Ha." I just didn't care anymore.

Solentine turned to Everard. "What are you doing here?"

"Saving the kingdom."

Solentine looked at him for a moment. "Divine, I think you might be serious."

"I am," Everard told him.

There was something in my hand. I looked down at it. I was still clutching a clump of the Butcher's hair. Somehow, I had held on to it the whole time. I stepped to my desk and dropped the clump onto a piece of paper. Some hair had stuck to my sweaty hand, and I brushed it off on autopilot.

Solentine shook his head. "Fine. What's done is done. Fatefire leaves recognizable scars. There is nothing I can do to erase the gash in the Vanquisher's plaza. Tomorrow the capital will know that you are here."

He was right. That green crap had carved right through the stone.

"Sauven will be told. He will panic and lean on the knight orders. They will scour the city looking for you. If you're recognized, and Sauven can prove you broke the Accords, we're done."

Again, he was right.

"Here's how we fix this. You leave Kair Toren tonight and go straight to Selva. I will tie up loose ends here."

He didn't tie up loose ends. He severed them. That's what Shears did.

"The loose ends work for me," Everard said.

"Just her then." Solentine looked at me. "She is a threat, Ramond."

"No."

"Why?"

"She belongs to me."

Solentine blinked.

I laughed. It sounded exactly how I felt, bitter and apathetic.

"Now isn't the time to be distracted by a woman," Solentine said.

"I'm not distracted," Everard said.

Solentine examined me like I was a poisonous bug. "What do you really know about her? What's her family name? Where is she from? Why did she approach you?"

"I know enough."

"Let me confine her until we get some answers."

"No," Everard said.

"She will be perfectly safe, and once we resolve our current problems, we can revisit this like rational people. Let me close this breach in our walls before the enemy streams through it."

I would not survive that confinement. Solentine had decided I needed to die.

Black smoke slid off Everard, spilling onto the floor. His eyes blazed with green.

Cold sweat slicked my back. I couldn't help it. It was an instinctual, knee-jerk reaction.

"Sol," he said, pronouncing each word slowly, "*she is mine.*"

Solentine stared at the nightmare in the flesh.

A moment passed.

Solentine sighed.

It was over. He wouldn't lay a hand on me. Everard had claimed me as his.

He had known Solentine since they were teenagers. He understood how Solentine's mind worked, so he left him with zero ambiguity. I was now a possession of the Sleepless Duke.

The two of them could fuck right off.

"Why were you in the plaza?" Solentine asked.

Everard leaned against the wall. "Ulmar Hreban hired a man to kill some prominent knights and display their bodies. He aims to assassinate the Sun Margrave and disguise the murder as the latest in the string of random killings."

"To what end?"

"He wishes to become the next Sun Margrave."

"And you know this how?"

"Maggie told me," Everard said.

Solentine looked at me, then back at Everard.

Neither of us said anything.

"Splendid." Solentine raised his hands. "One small question: How does Maggie know this?"

"Magic," Everard said.

Solentine's eyebrows crept up. "Magic! Of course. Why didn't I see that before? For a moment I suspected that you'd taken leave of your senses, but now I am sure of it."

He was jumping on my last nerve. He couldn't touch me, so he had decided to discredit me. It wouldn't work, but my shock was starting to wear off. I was no longer numb. I was angry. I couldn't vent my anger on Everard, but Solentine was right there.

"Let me see if I can guess how we got here." Solentine crossed his arms on his chest. "A young woman approached you with an offer. Some vital information to bait the hook. Perhaps she needed a protector. She presented herself as a victim or she might have tried to seduce you."

"Yes, that's it exactly," I said. "All of the seducing."

"Then in a relaxing moment of peace, she fed you this inane Hreban plot. Ramond, I'm begging you, use your common sense. Does that turn of events seem likely to you?"

"Yes," Everard said.

"Hreban couldn't attain that position in his wildest dreams. He is the Fool of Lerem. Would it help to clarify things if I told you she approached me first? I didn't take the bait, so she switched her target. The only question here is who is behind her."

"Bless your heart," I said.

"And that means?" Solentine raised his eyebrows.

"'Eat dirt and die.' I should've let Krasta slice up your arm. You're an insufferable ass."

"Ah, so you were the one who sent the note. Congratulations, you warned me not to get into the carriage with a man infamous for gutting his rivals with a hunting knife. The cypher was a nice touch, though. If only there weren't several hundred people proficient in it. Is this the part where I am supposed to be impressed? Please let me know. I don't want to miss my cue."

I would strangle him.

"What makes more sense, an agent planted by a Great Family or a woman with mysterious powers who wants to help you for no apparent reason? If her magic was real, she would know things nobody else would . . ."

Everard looked at me. "As of now nothing has changed. Colart still loses his life. Matheo dies. The city burns. The kids still fall victim to the war."

I knew where he was heading. He was reminding me that the Butcher had gotten away, and Solentine had an entire network that could look for him. He was jerking my emotional leash.

"The sooner we climb over this wall, the better," Everard said. He sounded so much like his Reynald self right now. But that man was a lie.

In this moment I hated him.

Solentine opened his mouth. "As I said—"

"Three Drops of Blood."

Solentine stopped mid-rant. "What?"

"When you were twelve years old, you were required to spend one month during the summer at your paternal grandfather's estate. He was a mean old man, and you hated his guts. Your grandfather treasured his grape vines and the wine produced from them. They were the only things he loved in this world. His most prized wine, Three Drops of Blood, came from a one-hundred-twenty-year-old vine, the apple of his eye. That horrible old bastard babied it like it was made of gold."

Solentine held very still.

"One day he punished you. He whipped you with a cane. The next morning, while everyone was asleep, you slipped out of your room, got an axe, made your way down to the vineyard, and chopped down the vine. You left the axe by it, so there would be no question that it was done deliberately. Then you snuck back into your room and pretended to be asleep. Unfortunately, your ten-year-old cousin found the axe and was discovered holding it. Your grandfather beat him to within an inch of his life. Nearly killed him. From your room, you could hear him screaming and the blows landing. Rumian worshiped you. And you did nothing. You sat in your room with a pillow over your head and you let him endure the worst beating of his life."

Solentine stared at me, his face stunned. "You can't know that. Nobody knows that."

Everard smiled.

"Rumian still worships you. That man will do literally anything for you, and you've never told him. You're a coward."

Solentine's hand moved to his knife.

"I was going to warn you soon, but I might as well do it now. After that beating, your aunt Griele arrived and asked your grandfather if he wanted to pick on someone his own size. She put him into sick bed for two weeks. Her swords were always precise. He disowned her, and you and your cousin never had to visit him again. When he died, he left everything to your father, Izarn, who promptly granted the villa and the vineyard to his sister. Griele and your uncle Brune moved in and turned that oppressive house into a warm and happy home."

The look on his face was priceless. I was telling him family secrets only the closest to the Demarrs could know.

"Brune has been approached by a noble who is trying to get him to invest in a silver mine. In twelve days, he will sign documents putting that stupid vineyard up as collateral for the loan. His thirtieth wedding anniversary is coming up and when he heard the proposal, he thought the mine would be a nice present for his wife because the first gift he had ever given Griele was a silver necklace that she still treasures to this day. Brune married into the family and brought very little wealth with him. He always wanted to contribute."

That bug-eyed expression he was making was so satisfying.

"The silver mine does not exist. Your family will lose the vineyard that has been its pride and joy for centuries, and you will have to do heinous things to get it back. It will break your uncle. He will never recover from it."

Solentine opened his mouth and closed it without a word.

That vine incident had made Solentine who he was. It taught him that what he valued most was his family. He felt deep unrelenting shame, and he had sworn that he would never again do anything to harm his loved ones. I had hit him where it hurt.

"You should take a few days and see to it," Everard said.

Solentine clenched his teeth.

"She is never wrong," Everard said. "She may be off on dates, but if she says it will come to pass, it will."

Technically, I'd been wrong quite a bit.

"Go take care of your family, Sol. I'll stay here."

"Your word?"

Everard nodded.

"Don't leave," Solentine said. "I'm begging you. Stay inside these four walls until I return. Don't do anything. I will be back before the week's end."

I took a stack of pages from the shelf and handed it to him. "Light reading for the road. Burn it after you're done."

I had written out the brief timeline of events in case something happened to me and Reynald had to continue alone. This would save me a lot of explanations.

Solentine gave me a wild look and dropped through the window.

"Nicely done," Everard said.

I didn't answer.

The silence stood between us like a wall.

"What happened to the real Reynald?" I asked.

"He died."

My heart squeezed itself into a tiny ball. "Did you kill him?"

"No. It was an accident. His horse fell. He died of internal bleeding three days later."

"When?"

"He passed in the early morning on the sixth of Planter."

I felt sad, worn out, and desperate. My heart hurt.

"Maggie," he said quietly.

"Please leave."

He turned, walked out the door into the hallway, and stopped just outside my room, wrapped in shadow. "You don't have to be afraid of me. I will never hurt you."

My voice sounded hollow. "I liked you better when you were Reynald."

"So did I."

He walked away.

I took a piece of paper with Butcher's hair from the desk and held it up to the lantern. A tiny drop of blood swelled on some of the hair ends. I must've really ripped a chunk out of his scalp.

There was blood on my sleeve, too, and it wasn't mine.

Blood was good.

I folded the paper in half, slipped it into an envelope, and placed the envelope into the top drawer of the desk. I walked down the hallway, knocked on Clover's door, and told the children it was safe to come out. Everard wouldn't hurt them. He considered them his people. Then I went back to my suite, closed the door, locked it, and leaned against it. The triple moons shone their light through the open window.

I'd trusted him. I'd told him things.

He'd sat with me on the wall and tried to distract me from worrying by telling funny stories about the Conquerors, he'd held my hand on the bench in Sonndor, and when he'd smiled, he'd looked so . . .

He'd lied to me and used me. Just like he used other people to get what he wanted.

Everard was a strategist. Stepping between the kids and the slavers, swearing to put himself in front of the disaster that would grip Kair Toren, winning me over step by step; all of it was part of a carefully calculated approach. Everything had been precisely measured and flawlessly executed. Holding my hand had been part of the plan.

Was anything he'd said real?

Probably not.

It hurt so much.

Chapter 24

I had woken up with a dead fish on my stomach. It was freshly caught, wet and slightly bloody, and the mix of water and fish blood had soaked through my nightshirt. My pet stelka must've decided that an emergency snack would make everything better.

I took the fish off, set it on a plate I had stolen from the kitchen yesterday, and left it by the bed. Then I used the bathroom and washed my face and my chest. My left side was black and blue where the Butcher had rammed the pommel of his sword into my ribs. I was pretty sure one of them was either cracked or broken because it hurt like hell if I bent the wrong way.

I brushed my teeth, braided my hair, got dressed, and went downstairs to the kitchen. Hiding in my room wasn't an option. Sooner or later he would find me. Last night, as I lay in bed, I had thought of a plan. It was time to get it started.

Everyone was already there. I took my usual seat. Everard was sitting across from me. He'd tried to look like Reynald today. He was back to emanating that quiet strength, his terrifying magic hidden, his dark smoke put away, but it was too late. I *knew*.

Breakfast was served in silence. Gort was quiet, seemingly absorbed in the food on his plate. He wouldn't look me in the eye. Shana sat next to her husband, her face unreadable. Will and Lute watched me and Everard, waiting to see how things would shake out. Clover had scooted her chair slightly closer to mine than usual and seemed ready to jump up and hover over me at the slightest excuse. Only Kaiden was blissfully unaffected by it all, stuffing his face with handpies.

From my spot at the table, I could see our courtyard and a chunk of the sky through the window on the left side. Thick gray clouds had piled up overnight, like clumps of dirty cotton strewn across the clear blue. It would likely rain later in the day.

The Dukedom of Selva shared its eastern border with the Crimson Empire in the south and the Goryni Kingdom in the north. Goryni, a small nation, occupied a mountainous area and was renowned for its mineral wealth and unbeatable military. They imported a lot of their food. Its treacherous, rocky coastline made commercial fishing and trade difficult, and in a few months, an underwater earthquake would take out their largest functional harbor. When the Crimson Empire invaded Rellas, which would be bleeding from Hreban's rampage, the Gorynians would be on the edge of starvation.

The future Goryni required a port. The future Everard needed allies and reinforcements to hold off the tide of Crimson Legions. They united through a marriage alliance. Selva opened its eastern ports to the kingdom's ships, and Everard married Omelyana of Gor, who brought as her dowry three thousand elite strikers of the Gorynian Guard.

Omelyana was two years older than Everard. She was a talented commander, a superior warrior, and a shrewd politician, seasoned both on the battlefield and at court. She'd had multiple lovers prior to her engagement and was experienced and calculating, and she'd arrived in Selva with no illusions as to the nature of her arranged marriage. Within six months, she would be eating out of Everard's hand.

How that came to be was open to interpretation. Some people chalked it up to magic-dick syndrome, where a character was so good in bed, his partners lost all of their common sense. But it wasn't as crude and simple as just sex, although by all indications Everard was scorchingly hot in the bedroom and sex was a part of it. No, it was far more insidious and subtle.

He paid attention to her. When Omelyana did something that helped him, Everard would spend time with her. He opened his schedule for dinner, a hunt, a hike in the mountains where she would have him all to herself and during those times, he would be all in, listening, interested, and attentive. When she failed him in some way, he never chided her. He never criticized. He simply withdrew from her life, and she would turn herself inside out trying to regain his attention.

It was very clear that Omelyana was obsessed with him, and some people liked to fantasize that he was in love with her. The narrative was vague at this point since there were no scenes from Everard's point of view in the whole series. He was a mystery to the end.

I didn't think he loved her. He tamed her like a pet because Selva needed her strikers to survive, and he couldn't afford to have dissension in his backyard. I had never understood how exactly he managed it or why a sophisticated, smart woman like Omelyana would fall for it.

Now I knew. I almost fell for it, too.

To Everard I was the golden key to avoiding a horrible war. He saved me last night, because the Butcher was about to run me through and he didn't want to take a chance on me permanently dying. The way he had managed me up to that point was nothing short of brilliant. He had recognized that things would be infinitely easier if I wanted to work with him of my own free will and so he became my friend and protector. He would've become my lover if I had worried a little less about honesty. The more devoted I was, the better.

Except now it had all come crashing down around his ears.

He would try to regain control, and he would make it seem like sliding back into the warm embrace of his power was my idea. Right now, with our relationship on the verge of breaking, he would be most agreeable to making concessions. I had to make the most of it, because as much as I wanted to throw my plate at his face, I needed him. He was right. We had failed to stop the Butcher. Hreban was still on his way to his reign of terror and Reynald's son would still die.

"Who did the Butcher kill this time?" I asked.

Everyone stopped chewing.

"Velpor," Everard said. "Highly decorated, recently retired. He was one of Wynand Bors's Conquerors."

"What happened to the body?" I asked.

"The Shears took it," Everard said.

Knowing Solentine's people, they had either destroyed the corpse or stashed it in one of their caverns. They had some sort of preservation chamber in there. A wise choice. Otherwise, we'd have the entire Order of the Conqueror running amok in the capital, exhaling rage and looking for blood. Speaking of that . . .

"I saw blood on one of the swords last night." I kept my voice neutral. "Was it yours or his?"

"His," Everard said.

That meant the blood on my clothes was the Butcher's as well. Score.

I kept my voice even. "How badly is he hurt?"

"Nothing that would incapacitate him. The cut will bleed for a few days, but meanwhile he can go about his business."

"In that case, I have to go out," I said.

"Where to?" Everard asked.

It was like we were the only two people in the room. Nobody else was talking.

"The Defender Citadel."

"Eliarde?" he asked.

I nodded. "We failed. She's the next target on the list. He will come after her, and there is no way for us to approach her."

"Are you planning on using Berengur?"

He'd already plotted my strategy, which was just the way I wanted it. The smarter he felt, the more freedom I would get.

"Yes. Berengur has a good relationship with Arvel, and Arvel is Eliarde's second cousin. She worships the soles of his boots. She would listen to a warning if it came from him."

Everard leaned back, thinking out loud. "Praul Britin is at least two days of hard riding from Kair Toren. Assuming Berengur left the same day you two spoke, that gives him seven days. He may not be back yet."

"It's worth a try."

"I'll come with you," he said.

Oh no, he wouldn't. Not in his wildest dreams.

"That's not a good idea. First, you promised Solentine you would stay here. Second, Sauven is likely aware you are in the city. By now at least one of the holy orders will be looking for you. You are well known to the Defenders. You will be recognized even if you wear every lancer's coif in the city."

He didn't like that. Too bad.

"Your Grace," I started.

A spark of green flashed in his eyes.

"I'm sorry, would you prefer Lord Commander?"

"Formality isn't necessary," he said.

"What should I call you?"

"Ramond is fine."

No. Absolutely not.

"Your Grace, if any of the Defender Knights spied a man of your height and build covering his face and loitering near the Citadel, how fast do you think they would corner him and demand he remove his hood?"

"You're not going out alone."

"I don't plan to. The Butcher's magic is distinct. Someone will remember him, so I'm guessing the Magnars will be going tavern to tavern today."

Gort jerked a little.

"They will," Everard confirmed. "We'll have his name by midweek at most."

"You don't need Gort and Shana and both Magnar brothers. Will is older; more people know him, so he will be more useful to you. Let me take Lute as my escort."

He didn't like that either.

Too bad. I had to win this fight, or we would never find the Butcher again.

"Take a carriage," he said.

"I can't. We don't own a carriage and even if we did, I would have to cross Ashen Bridge, and no carriage is allowed on it without a permit. Not to mention that no matter what carriage we hire, the driver will be working for the Shears."

It didn't matter where we got the carriage. The driver would answer to Solentine. If we insisted on putting our driver in it, they would sabotage it in some way.

"The Shears have the necessary permits," he countered.

"Solentine hates unknowns, and right now I'm a frightening unknown. His people will disappear me, and when you call him on it, he will be terribly remorseful. He'll offer his regrets and tell you that what's done is done and the two of you should move past it."

Everard focused on me. I had never been sighted through the scope of a sniper rifle, but I'd bet it would feel exactly like that. I clenched my hands into fists under the table. Holding his gaze was really difficult.

"What are you scheming, Maggie?"

The man had some sort of sixth sense. I had given him absolutely no indication that I would do anything except go to the Citadel, but somehow, he had sensed that there was more to it.

I looked right into those green eyes and said quietly, but with as much force as I could scrape together, "I'm trying to stop the Butcher, and I want to save a woman's life. You may not have meant your oath to save Matheo and to stop what's coming, but I did. I meant every word. I do not want to see this city burn."

I needed to put him on the defensive.

"When I give my promise, it is cast in stone," he said, carving each word out. "I swore I would see this through."

And yesterday morning I would've believed him with all my heart. But not today.

"It's in my best interests, Maggie. I need Rellas to correct its course to keep Selva safe."

Have you thought of allying with Goryni? I hear Omelyana is a rare talent . . .

"Then let me try to save Eliarde. The brothers are loyal to their father and Gort is loyal to you. I have no plans of walking up to the nearest guard and telling him the Sleepless Duke is hiding out in a deceased slaver's house by the river. But if I tried, either Will or Lute are perfectly capable of stopping me."

Everard frowned. He looked so much like the old Reynald.

Damn it.

"Even if the Butcher is prowling the streets instead of licking his wounds, he has no idea what either Lute or I look like," I said. "You can't go. Neither the Magnars nor Clover can get into the Citadel, but I can. I still have Berengur's crest. He will remember me. This is our best option."

Everard looked at Lute. "Escort her and bring her back here unharmed."

Lute nodded and jumped to his feet.

"You can finish breakfast," I told him.

He sat back down.

Across the table, Everard leaned back in his chair, thinking. He looked cold and regal right now, like some dark monarch contemplating an invasion.

"Be careful in the Citadel. Take care of yourself."

There was genuine care in his voice. *Fool me once, shame on you; fool me twice . . .*

"I'm always careful."

He slid something across the table. A small copper den.

"Your lucky coin."

"I don't want it anymore." I looked at Clover. "Once we finish breakfast, please help me get dressed. I must look like a noble today. The more highborn, the better."

Clover bowed her head. "With pleasure, my lady."

※

It took me over an hour to get out of the house. Clover sprang into action as soon as I got up from the table, as if she had been waiting for a chance to make me over and assured me that I would "look right" when she was done.

Looking right entailed having my hair properly arranged, which took forever. Right now, two wide braids ran along the sides of my head to the back, where they became a single elaborate plait with silver cord braided into it. Six narrow braids crossed in a lattice on top of my head, in the space between the two larger braids. Somehow Clover made me have three times as much hair.

I could never replicate it, which was probably the entire point. It was like wearing a sign above my head that said, "Look, I'm wealthy enough to have someone else to do my hair, and I can waste a whole hour sitting in a chair while it's being done."

While Clover worked on that, Kaiden brought news from the Knight Vanquisher Plaza. It was crawling with people from the Justice Chamber. Everard's strike had left a twenty-five-yard cut in the cobbles. It was only half an inch deep—he must've aimed for minimal damage, but it was there.

After my hair was finished, Clover produced a dress. She had sewn it from the fabric she'd purchased that first time at the market. I'd had no idea she was even working on it. I asked her when she'd found the time, and she just smiled. The gown was a rich forest green, and it fit me like a glove. I couldn't wrap my head around it. She'd never measured me. She'd just eyeballed it and somehow delivered a perfect fit.

Most dresses, like the ones we had bought at the market, came with lacing on the sides. It was the medieval equivalent of one-size-fits-all. You slipped the dress on and tightened the lacing to the right fit.

This gown opened from the back, so I could step into it, and the back slit was secured by two silver-colored snaps. It was clearly custom-made specifically for me. My shoes, dainty boots, also identified me as someone with money. They were pretty and uncomfortable, the kind of shoes worn by women accustomed to carriage rides.

We finished the look with some makeup. I'd planned to steer clear of it, since some medieval cosmetics had fun ingredients like lead and mercury. But Clover assured me that the rouge and eyeshadow were made of only root powder pigments and mica dust and insisted that some makeup had to be applied. Not wearing any would look odd. She offered to help me. I'd commandeered a mirror instead and left her in awe of my YouTube-taught application skills.

The end result was somewhat surprising. I did look like a highborn lady. So much so that when I passed Will in the courtyard on my way out, he did a double take. Lute was more restrained. He just blinked a few times.

Lute was wearing a complementary hunter green and brown, the colors of our shade-down. The clothes were brand new, his hair was brushed, his sword was in its scabbard on his hip. He looked every inch like a guard of a noble family.

In Kair Toren, clothes weren't just a fashion statement. They indicated rank and affiliation. Families prominent enough to have a crest wore their crest colors at formal functions. The middle class—merchants, wealthier craftsmen, and minor nobles—didn't qualify for their own crests, but they still wanted to display their status and wealth, so they color-coded their households, too.

The immediate family wore clothes incorporating the family's chosen color with complementary shades. The household servants wore the same color but either two shades darker or less saturated—the shade-down. Our main color was a warm forest green, and our shade-down was more of a hunter green. Clover had bought green and more green for our family colors. At the time, I was all for it, because the *fuck you* to the Hreban Family couldn't have been louder. But now, I wished it was any other color. Anything but that.

Green suits you, Maggie.

Fucking bastard.

Everard had shown no reaction at all to my new self. He had walked us to the door and opened it. I put my cloak's hood up; Lute positioned himself by my side; and we were off. As we turned the corner, I glanced back and saw Everard standing there, in the doorway, watching us walk away with a flat expression on his face.

As soon as we rounded the corner, Lute said, "I didn't know."

"Even if you did, I wouldn't blame you," I told him. "Your father clearly knew, but I don't blame him either. He is an out-of-work mercenary, and we both know who 'Reynald' is."

Considering all the people scouring Kair Toren right now trying to find Everard, even saying his name in public could land us in hot water.

Lute nodded. "The whole thing was twisted from the start. Will and I are used to doing shit work. We are weapons for hire. We don't ask a lot, except for one thing: Be straight with us and we'll be straight with you. The old man didn't tell us."

"Your old man risked his life for years to take care of you and Will. He saw an opportunity, and he was right. 'Reynald' has been personally training you. I heard your father tell your mother that both you and your brother have improved more in the past week than you have in the last two years. You've already benefited from this arrangement."

"We didn't ask for that."

"I know. If you stick with 'Reynald,' there is a good chance you will become a knight instead of spending your life as a mercenary-for-hire with high risk and low reward. Your father couldn't pass up this chance. He had your best interests at heart."

"That's not his call to make."

"That's the thing about parents—they will do what they think is best and they don't always care how you feel about it. You have to endure it."

We walked in silence for a couple of minutes.

Lute leaned a little toward me. "There's a woman following us."

As expected. "Probably a Shears agent."

Solentine would have left someone watching the house. Most likely at least three someones. One to follow me if I left, one to follow Everard, and one to stay and watch the house. They wouldn't murder us in broad daylight, though.

"Do you want me to do something about that?" Lute put a hand on his sword.

"No need. She probably won't interfere. Her job will be to observe and report back."

"Are we really going to the Citadel?"

"Yes. It's our first stop."

"So, there's a second stop?"

"Yes." Warning Eliarde was important, but the second stop was even more so.

Lute's eyebrows crept up. "Where?"

"Old Town."

"Does 'Reynald' know?"

I smiled. "No. And I don't want him to."

If I explained my plan to Everard, he would lose his shit and lock me in the house.

We crossed the street and turned west, walking along the river on the street that would eventually bring us to the Ashen Bridge.

"You asked me to be straight with you. If Everard finds out where we are going, a little bit of that iron control might slip. If you want to go back to get his permission, now is your chance."

Lute shook his head. "I don't believe I will."

"Oh good. Because we have another forty-five minutes of walking, and my feet already hurt."

Chapter 25

At its southern border, Kair Toren ran into a ridge of hills that stretched southwest to the ocean. The city streets climbed up onto the rises, and below them the Dokkon's numerous tributaries carved their way toward the center of Kair Toren to join the wider river. One of those lesser rivers formed a tight horseshoe loop around a stone crag. A man-made channel, equipped with floodgates, bridged the loop, turning the bend of the river into a ring of water that hugged an oblong island.

The Defender Citadel sprouted from that island like a king trumpet mushroom, taking up all available space. Built with the trademark Kair Toren stone, the castle walls soared fifteen stories high, unified at the bottom, then widening into a collection of fortifications that would allow archers to rain arrows on any approaching attackers.

The Citadel was connected to the rest of the city by a sloping bridge, wide enough to allow six knights to ride abreast. The bridge spanned the open air between the castle and the nearest hill, and at the foot of the bridge, where it touched the street, a fortified gatehouse blocked the way, flanked by two towers and equipped with a heavy gate and portcullis. Right now, the portcullis was up, and the gate stood open, revealing a passageway that led through the barbican and up to the bridge.

Two knights in the beautiful pale armor and white-and-gold tabards of the Defenders kept watch by the gate.

I took my hood down, revealing my spectacular hair arrangement, and approached the knight on the left.

"Greetings, my lady," the knight said.

"Greetings."

I pulled Berengur's crest out of my sleeve and showed it to the knight.

He examined it carefully, brushed his finger over it, checking for something, and nodded to me. "A moment."

He flicked his fingers. A young teenage girl in a plain blue tunic ran out of the passageway and set a small stool in front of me. A boy of about the same age in an identical outfit ran to the bridge.

"Please wait here, my lady," the knight said. "Would you like some refreshments?"

"No, thank you."

I sat on the stool. Lute loomed behind me, projecting his willingness to do bodily harm to anyone who approached.

Minutes crawled by.

Finally, a young knight in armor emerged from the tunnel, stopped a few feet before us, and bowed his head. "Please follow me."

Berengur was back. Yes! I might have a shot.

I stood up and started toward the passageway. Lute took a step to follow. The sentry knight moved, and Lute stared at the blade of a sword blocking his path.

"Just the lady."

Lute glanced at the three knights. The odds were bad, but his eyes told me he was game.

"Please wait here," I said.

Lute's eyes widened. Crap. I shouldn't have said *please*.

He dropped into a bow. "As you wish, my lady."

I looked at the young knight. He indicated the passage with a sweep of his hand, and we began walking.

The long bridge rose slightly, probably to make it easier for the molten pitch and burning oil to roll down at potential invaders. In the second book, a mob tried to storm the Citadel, egged on by a former squire that had been cast out. He'd told them that only ten knights remained inside after Arvel and most of the Defenders had left the city. The knights had let the mob get three-quarters of the way up, and then they dropped a ball of flames onto the bridge. The narrative never explained what it was made of, but it was heavy and the fire coating it was white-hot. Those who weren't crushed or burned fell to the Defenders' arrows. All of the military orders acknowledged that Arvel's knights knew no equal in archery. Nobody made it off the bridge.

My feet really hurt.

Finally, the bridge ended. The heavy metal gates swung open at our approach, their motion silent and smooth. A long chamber stretched before us, narrow and high, its ceiling supported by colonnades running on both sides. A walkway traced the walls above us, accessible only by interior doors I couldn't see. No stairs. If attackers did manage to make it through that door, this chamber would become a deathtrap.

We passed through the chamber into a wide hallway with doors branching off. Men and women walked past us, moving with purpose. Everyone wore light brown, close-fitted pants with brown boots, white tunics, and white tabards with a golden Defender shield embroidered on the chest. They came in all sizes and shapes; tall, short, bulky, slender, some young, some older, but all of them ridiculously fit. They looked healthy, strong, athletic, and ready to spring into action. It was like walking into a medieval version of one of those firemen pet-charity calendars, except that everyone kept their clothes on and there was a distressing lack of kittens.

The hallway ended in double doors propped wide open. Outside, a beautiful courtyard waited. Paved with beige stone and bordered by tall walls on the right and left sides, it was about twice as big as a football field. At the other end of it, across from us, a majestic keep propped up the sky, accessible by a wide staircase.

"This way, my lady."

My guide turned right, and I followed him across the stone tiles toward the keep. The center of the courtyard was clear, probably so the knights could assemble there. To the far left, a long structure running along the wall was likely the stables. On our right, we were passing what could've been a spectator gallery, complete with benches and a white-and-gold overhang.

We reached the keep and kept going around it.

My feet felt like painful pancakes. The next time Everard suggested a carriage, I would take it, Shears or no.

As we passed the keep's staircase, a blond man in ornate white armor stepped out of the doors at the top and began walking down the stairs as if he owned the entire place. A beautiful blue cloak draped his shoulders. Another knight followed him, keeping a respectful distance. Arvel. Had to be.

"Is that Lord Arvel?" I asked.

"Yes," the knight said, his voice clipped. "Lord Arvel does not receive visitors unless there are special circumstances."

Perhaps he thought I would charge up those stairs to fangirl-rush Arvel.

"No worries, sir. I have no plans to ambush the Lord Commander."

Drawing unnecessary attention from the members of the Eight Families wasn't on the agenda today. I already had Everard at home. One terrifying magical knight was enough, thank you. Putting myself on Arvel's radar in any way would only bring disaster. It was much better to let Berengur play the middleman.

I wouldn't have minded a glimpse of his face, though. Oh well.

The damn fortress kept going and going. How did they heat this place in the winter?

Finally, we rounded the keep, and the back courtyard came into view. Long rectangular flower beds spanned its length, filled with white flowers. Their blooms, with five petals and bright yellow centers, reminded me of jasmine flowers except they were the size of large tulips. A strong scent filled the air, bringing up memories of honeysuckle.

In the center of the courtyard, between the two rows of flower beds, a lone knight raised a big bow. His broad back was to us and as he aimed at a straw target near the far wall, the muscles on his shoulders stood out under the sleeves of his white tunic.

At least eighty yards. The red circles drawn on the straw were barely visible, and the bright red bullseye was the size of a small apple.

The bow string twanged. The arrow sliced through the air, biting deep into the bullseye, above the other two arrows already in it. He'd made a perfect triangle.

"Please wait here," my guide murmured and headed toward the knight.

The knight nocked another arrow. His muscles stood out again and he let it loose. The arrow thudded into the center of the triangle. Impressive.

My escort approached him, bowed his head, and spoke in a low voice.

The knight lowered his bow and turned toward me.

He was in his early thirties. His blond hair, a shade darker than his golden tan, was cropped short. His jaw, with a hint of stubble, was square and flared, but not too heavy, balanced by his high cheekbones and a chiseled nose. His lips were narrow, his eyebrows thick and slightly darker than his hair, and his eyes, small and piercing blue, seemed to be caught in a permanent half-squint.

The flowers around him were delicate and fragile, and the white fabric of his tabard was so thin and light, it moved when he turned. If this had been a painting, I would've expected a different man, someone lean and graceful with beautiful, maybe even delicate features. Instead, he was all harsh strength and refined power. The contrast was stunning.

The sun chose that moment to break through the clouds, drenching the entire courtyard in golden light. It spilled onto him and he almost glowed.

Oh wow. The Defenders didn't need to advertise, but if they had to, they could just slap him on a recruitment poster and call it a day.

The man listened to my escort, waved him off, and started toward me.

Here we go. I'd read the books over and over. I knew how the nobles spoke to each other. My manners were refined because, apparently, I'd been learning etiquette from the Lord of Selva. I could do this.

The closer he came, the larger he got. He was at least as tall as Gort. Maybe even taller. Six foot four? Six foot six? All the broad shoulders you would ever need. Not only was he large, but he moved so well, he reminded me of Reynald. *Everard.* I had to stop calling him Reynald in my head. This man walked with the same light gait of a warrior trained to respond to sudden threats.

I'm looking for a man in armor. Six five, blue eyes. I almost laughed. After everything that happened, I must've finally lost it.

He reached me and bowed. It was a shallow bow, polite and perfunctory, a simple courtesy afforded to an unfamiliar woman of noble birth. Well, he probably did have a trust fund judging by the manners.

"Welcome, my lady. What can the Order do for you on this beautiful morning?"

His voice matched him, a smooth baritone. You could tell that he was used to roaring commands in the heat of a battle, and now he was deliberately controlling the volume, taking care to speak softer because it was just the two of us here.

"I'm afraid there has been a mistake, my lord. I'm here to see Lord Berengur."

"Lord Berengur has left us for the time being to take care of a personal matter. However, I have known him for many years. We trust each other to handle problems in each other's stead. Perhaps I could be of service?"

"When will he be back?"

"Not for another week, I'm afraid."

Another week would be too late.

"In that case, I regretfully ask for permission to impose on your hospitality. May I ask your name, sir?"

At least tell me who I'm speaking with.

"Forgive me. I should have introduced myself. It has been a complicated day, and clearly, I have misplaced my manners. I am Earl Bellen. But here, within these walls, the honorifics are unnecessary. Inside the Citadel, I'm just a knight, one of many. May I ask your name?"

Earl Bellen. Bellen . . . Didn't ring any bells. How was he not some kind of major character in the books? Of course, he could be lying to me, but I had no idea why he would. We'd never met.

"Maggie," I told him.

He quirked an eyebrow. "Lady Maggie . . . ?"

"Just Lady Maggie, my lord." Every time someone said Lady Maggie, it sounded ridiculous, and now I was saying it, too, and feeling stupid every time I did.

"My issue is complicated. I came to appeal to Lord Berengur for help."

"Perhaps we better sit down then." He indicated a table and two chairs set at the crossing of paths between the flower beds.

We strolled toward it.

"Does the scent of hafia bother you? Some people find their aroma too heady."

"Not at all," I said. "The scent is pleasant, and the flowers are very beautiful."

"They're medicinal in nature. They help to stem the blood flow from open wounds."

"Beauty and utility in a single form."

"Indeed."

We reached the table, and he held a chair out for me. I perched in it. My feet quietly celebrated.

Bellen sat. The chair seemed slightly too small for him. In our world, physically gifted people played sports. If you were strong and fast, you became a football player, or a basketball star, or an Olympic athlete. In Rellas, you became a knight. I was probably looking at a descendant of several generations of martial tradition. Knighthood was in his blood.

He was something that was lost in our world because it was no longer needed. We had moved past people in armor charging at each other on a battlefield. Romantic history told us they would wash off the blood and gore and turn into gallant poets at the next formal dinner. If that gallantry had ever truly existed, it would've been a disguise, window dressing designed to lull you into forgetting you were sitting across from a trained, experienced killer who would take your life without hesitation. If I left Rellas and returned to my world, I would never be able to see knights in the same way. Not after watching Everard kill. Not after the Butcher. If a Renaissance faire jouster tried to talk to me, I would run away screaming.

"My lady?" Bellen prompted.

"Pardon the hesitation, my lord. Are you aware of the body found in the Dog Market?"

Bellen's face turned hard. "An ugly affair. Not the way a knight like Shuhoven should have gone."

"The man responsible for his murder fancies himself a hunter of people. Specifically, knights."

Bellen frowned. "How do you know this?"

"I cannot tell you that. I can tell you that there was a second victim."

"Who?"

"Velpor. His body was found in the plaza of the Knight Vanquisher. It was removed and hidden to avoid agitating the Order of the Conqueror."

Bellen leaned back. "I didn't hear anything."

"You weren't supposed to, my lord."

I hesitated. One wrong word here and he could detain me. He clearly was high enough in the ranks. But knights were bound by a code of conduct. Defender Knights, in particular, made a big deal out of the knightly virtues. If he did something unbecoming of a knight, it would make his political life within the Order more complicated, and his rivals would use it against him. It was less about his explicit authority and more about how he would be seen by others. I had to leverage that against uncomfortable questions.

"I find myself in an awkward position, my lord. Lord Berengur would have reason to believe the things I'm telling you, and he would understand why I cannot reveal the source of my information. I have no choice but to rely on your discretion."

"You have it." He leaned closer. He was already taking up too much space, and now he blocked half of my view.

"Do I have your word?"

"Yes."

"The hunter of knights will strike again, and he has selected a new victim. He will track her until the opportunity presents itself, ambush her, abduct her, torture her, and then display her mutilated corpse to terrify the city. I want to spare her that fate."

"Who is she?"

"Dame Eliarde."

No reaction. I had expected surprise, outrage, something.

"If I were to warn Dame Eliarde, she would not heed my warning. She has no reason to trust me. She might take it as a threat or a slight against her skill. Depending on her mood, I might not be able to walk away from that meeting. I came here to beg Lord Berengur to deliver that warning on my behalf."

He studied me. "This is a grave matter."

"It is. I do not want her to die, my lord."

He fell silent, considering it.

I waited. I had no arguments left.

Bellen nodded to me. "Although I'm not as renowned as some, my words do carry a little weight. Do not fret, my lady. I will deliver your warning in Berengur's stead."

I exhaled, and I didn't even care if he saw it.

"What can you tell me about this killer?" he asked.

"He is a man who uses magic to enhance his speed. When he strikes, he shimmers with purple and blurs, and his attacks become almost impossible to parry."

Unless you're Everard.

"I don't know his name or where he's hiding. I know he's wounded, but I'm afraid it will only spur him on. He will strike again."

"Who wounded him?"

"A swordsman who interrupted him as he was about to display Velpor's corpse." The best lies were mostly true. "A chance meeting that ended badly. I only heard about it and cannot tell you more."

"Of course."

Sooner or later, the Defenders would find out about the scar Everard left in the plaza, and Lord Bellen would likely decide that the Sleepless Duke might have been involved. It was good to distance myself from it.

"Thank you. I will not forget this favor." I rose.

He stood up. "On the contrary, we owe you a debt. Dame Eliarde is dear to our Lord Commander. Any threat to her safety must be taken seriously by all of us."

"Then I leave assured. Goodbye, my lord."

I turned. He caught up with me.

"Please allow me to escort you."

We started down the path. I would have to walk all the way to the barbican, and then I would have to walk some more to Old Town, and Kair Toren didn't have Band-Aids.

"Would you like to borrow a carriage, my lady?" he asked.

"Is it that obvious?"

He smiled. It softened his harsh face, turning him unexpectedly handsome. It didn't seem fair—like finding out that a gorgeous actor, who already seemed to have everything in life, could also sing like a rock star.

"As a knight with others under my command, it is my job to recognize when someone is hiding pain. You have done so much for us. Please allow me this one small courtesy."

Climbing into a Defender's carriage was ill-advised and dangerous, but my feet hurt like hell.

"Thank you. A carriage would be most welcome."

We walked across the courtyard. He was keeping close to me, almost at the distance Everard was when he hovered over me at the market. Except Everard did it because we were in a crowded place with a lot of potential danger. Bellen and I pretty much had this courtyard to ourselves.

"Thank you for the escort, my lord."

"My pleasure. Escorting beautiful women is the rarest of our duties but it is one of grave importance. You never know where dangers may lurk."

I laughed softly. He smiled at me again.

It was probably force of habit. He was maintaining the "bodyguard" distance.

"What place in all the city is safer than the Citadel of the Defenders? Surely, I'm in no danger here."

He assumed a serious expression, but the smile was still there, in his eyes. "You could trip, my lady. Should that happen, have no fear. I will not let you fall."

Flirting with Lord Bellen in the Defender Citadel. Heh.

Everard's betrayal had hit me like a semi. I felt raw, as if someone had taken a brick to my emotions and viciously smashed them until they turned into one continuous bruise. I didn't want to think about it. I had a big hurdle to overcome today and if I managed it, I would have to go home, and home had turned from my shelter to a dragon's lair.

But here and now I was "a beautiful woman," if only out of politeness, who wore a lovely dress and had amazing hair, and I was being escorted through the Citadel by a handsome knight of remarkable hotness ready to catch me if I stumbled. I let go and enjoyed the moment.

We reached the gates, where a young knight ran up to us. Bellen issued a short order, and a carriage appeared as if by magic, pulled by a large roan horse and driven by a young male squire. The carriage was a rectangular box on four wheels, with a single door at the front and square windows. It was less a leisure vehicle and more a fortified transport like what Hreban had ridden in, although not nearly as ornate.

Bellen helped me into the carriage. Leaning on his hand was like resting your weight on an iron rail. He almost lifted me up into it.

Inside the carriage was a simple bench running along the interior walls. It could fit four people comfortably, maybe six if someone sat on the floor. No frills but so much better than walking.

I settled in and drew the blue curtain back on the window. Bellen was looking at me. His eyes were warm and still filled with humor.

"Thank you again, my lord."

"Think nothing of it." He looked at the driver. "Take the lady where she wants to go. Let no harm come to her. Then return here."

"Yes sir."

"My guard is waiting on the street," I called out to the driver.

"I shall stop for him, my lady."

"Until we meet again, Lady Maggie."

"Until then, Lord Bellen."

The carriage rolled forward. Now we just had to pick up Lute, and we would be on our way.

One visit down, one to go, and that one would be harder than getting in and out of the Citadel in one piece. I had to play this very carefully. It was our only chance to get at the Butcher before he killed again.

Centuries and centuries ago, before the capital became the sprawling beast it was now, a small fishing village had perched in the hills that touched the sea. Sliced off from the rest of the coast by a forked river, the village presented a difficult target and promised very little plunder. When raiders struck out of desperation, the fishermen retreated into ancient caverns dug in the hills by a long-forgotten people, waited them out, and then resumed their simple lives.

Years passed, kingdoms formed and fell, and eventually the potential of the sheltered harbor was recognized. A castle rose on a nearby hill to protect the fertile lands and the budding port. The fortress became a marker for the traders. Travel until you see *kair toren*—the castle towers.

People settled around the castle, seeking protection and the jobs the port promised. The city grew, spreading outward, taking over more and more of the delta, until it swallowed the little fishing village, which became known as Old Town. It lay in the southwest of the capital now, away from the busier docks. Its smaller port catered to specific commercial ships, military vessels, and couriers.

Ironically, no fishing boats docked there anymore. The fishermen had moved out, their huts had been leveled, and large estate-size dwellings sprouted in their stead, home mostly to mid-level merchants, who required quick access to the port.

Our next stop lay at the heart of Old Town, on the slopes of Fifth Hill. I had allowed the Defender carriage to bring us over the bridge and let it go two blocks after that. It rolled back the way it came, and Lute and I wistfully stared after it. Like all soldiers, Lute prized getting off his feet.

"We should buy a carriage," he said.

"Where would we put it?"

"We could build a cart shed."

"Where?" There really wasn't any space.

"By the river. Me and Will could build it."

"Lute, have you ever built a cart shed before?"

"It's a box. Four walls and a roof. How hard could it be?"

I looked around, trying to orient myself. The main road, paved with darker gray stone, climbed up in front of us, winding around the hill upward. The houses were invisible, set back from the street and hidden from view by solid walls, sheathed in flowering vines. The people who lived here liked their privacy and didn't react well when it was invaded.

Let's see . . . the ocean was behind us, the green dome of the Trader's Temple peaked through the houses in front of us. We were in the right general area.

"What now?" Lute asked.

"Now we wander around until we find the correct house."

Lute nodded and leaned to look down the street.

"What are you checking for?"

"The Shears woman. She followed the carriage. I saw her."

It made sense. The carriage wasn't traveling fast. The main advantage of it wasn't speed, it was comfort, and the city streets were crowded. A person in good shape could easily follow us, especially if she was one of the Shears' agents.

"If she followed us, she won't let herself be seen. That would be too obvious. Come on. Let's look for the house. The sooner we find it, the sooner we can get this over with."

Ten minutes later, I stopped before a wall with a gate crowned by a heavy wooden sign that hung on a massive chain just above it. The sign bore sharp, spiky script.

"Okulan," Lute said with all the joy of a man spotting a hungry tiger.

"Can you read the sign?"

"No, but I recognize the writing. The old man has a dagger with that writing on it. He got stabbed during the battle of Sanderan and pulled it out of his gut. It nearly killed him."

Sounded about right.

"What does it say?" Lute asked.

"The House of Morning Sky. The Clan of Harzi." Apparently, reading Okulan was no problem either.

"Shit." Lute stared at the sign. "I can see why you didn't want *him* to know."

The nation of Okula lay in the northwest and shared a border with Selva. If you put Rellas where the US lay on a map, Selva would be Canada, and Okula would be Alaska, except that its weather was a lot warmer. It was a big chunk of land surrounded on three sides by water, and it was populated by a conglomeration of clans. Each clan was a state unto itself, and they competed and fought with each other.

The Okula were excellent sailors and good horsemen. They raided and traded with both nations, and no one knew which of those two options they would pick in any given year. Every three decades or so, the clans got antsy, elected a war chief, and invaded in force, usually Selva by land or southern Rellas by sea. Twelve years ago, Everard had to repel a massive invasion. His mother lost her life on the battlefield. Clan Harzi had been on the forefront of that war.

After the invasion, Okula and Rellas resumed trade relations, which was how Clan Harzi ended up with this house in Old Town. Rellas might have moved on, but Everard hadn't. He would never have let me walk into a Harzi clanhouse. And if I had any sort of common sense, I wouldn't enter one either. Unfortunately, it was our only option.

"Do we have to go in?" Lute asked.

"Yes."

He stretched his neck and squared his shoulders. "Should I knock?"

"You should."

Lute knocked on the gate.

The door swung open, revealing a girl in her late teens. She was four inches taller than me, with a sturdy frame and a wide face. Her skin was a deeper shade of beige with a cool undertone. Her long auburn hair was plaited into an intricate braid, the tip of which had been bleached in the Harzi fashion and dyed to announce her clan color—a muted Carolina blue.

Her clothes also identified her clan: high-waisted blue and white pants, a pale cream tunic tucked into those pants, and a thicker, blue overtunic secured by a wide cloth belt. A slender sword in a soft sheath on her hip completed the outfit.

"Calm winds and tranquil sky."

She stared at me. No response to the traditional greeting. Rude, but fine.

"I seek an audience with the *orsi*," I said. "I bring a secret to trade."

"The *orsi* is busy," she said.

"Then I will wait."

She pressed her lips together, turning her mouth into a hard, thin line. The Harzi were foreigners in Kair Toren. The city welcomed their merchant ships, the goods they brought, and the money they spent, but their presence in the capital was limited and Kair Toren never let them forget that they were perennial enemies who were closely watched.

Clan Harzi was one of the more powerful Okulan clans. If we had been in Harzi Ar, the seat of their power, the sentry woman would've informed me that I wasn't fit to kiss the footprints of the *orsi*, let alone ask for an audience, and slammed the door in my face. But we were in Rellas, and I looked like a noblewoman. They couldn't simply ignore me. It wouldn't be prudent.

"Follow," she said.

Again, rude. At the very least, she should have observed the basic courtesy. They were on edge, which meant that I had guessed right. All was not well, and that would be to my advantage.

I followed her into the courtyard.

The house was two stories tall, built with dark gray stone and crowned with a steep blue roof that looked a little like a witch's hat. Smaller structures flanked it on both sides, with their own steep roofs, forming a U-shaped courtyard, which we had just entered.

"You wait here," the sentry said and turned to leave.

Three strikes. That was my limit.

"It seems Clan Harzi is so poor that they no longer offer resting stools to their visitors."

She glared at me, and I glared right back.

"Should I have brought my own?"

The woman stomped into the house and returned with a small, embroidered quilted pad, which she placed on the stone tiles in front of the door. Just the rug. No stool to go with it.

Fine.

I knelt on the pad, resting my weight on my bent legs. Lute tried to catch me, but I waved him off.

The woman stared at me.

"Please let the *orsi* know that I'm here."

The sentry disappeared into the house and shut the door behind her.

"What are you doing?" Lute murmured.

"Showing them courtesy," I said. "Just because they are rude to me doesn't mean I will be rude to them."

"You shouldn't be kneeling in front of them," Lute said under his breath.

"This is their custom."

Sometimes stools weren't available, and the Okula sat straight on the pads, but this usually happened when they were traveling. They should've brought a stool. Not offering one was rude.

"I'm not kneeling," he told me.

"Nor should you. Your job is to look menacing and glower at everyone who approaches. Maybe do that thing where you put your hand on your sword."

Lute widened his stance and put his arms behind him in a textbook parade rest.

"Perfect," I told him.

"How long are we going to wait?" he murmured.

"Until they see me." I put some volume into my voice. "I'm not Harzi, but I've done everything the right way. They do prize ceremony and hospitality, so they won't throw me out. They will delay, hoping I leave."

"Should you lower your voice?" he asked.

"No. They are listening to us right now. Now they know that I know and also that I know that they know."

Lute blinked a couple of times, shook his head, and fell silent.

After ten minutes, kneeling was not comfortable in the slightest.

After half an hour it started to get painful.

We were about an hour in, and my legs hurt like hell.

The doors swung open, and an older man in an ornate Harzi tunic stepped out.

Lute put his hand on his sword.

"We welcome you to the House of Morning Sky. The *orsi* will see you now."

I looked at Lute. My legs had gone numb. He bent down, grabbed me by the elbow, and lifted me to my feet. Ow.

Blood rushed back into my feet. Every step sent needles through my soles all the way through my calves. Ow, ow, ow.

Lute half helped, half carried me up the three steps and inside the house. We walked into a large room with glossy wooden floors stained dark blue and ornate wooden columns. People in Okulan attire waited on the sides: a few retainers in embroidered overtunics and a handful of guards, their swords in plain view. Most of them were tall and long-limbed, with beige skin warmed by a peach undertone and dark brown, auburn, or red hair, worn in half-ponytails or braided away. Rellasian hairstyles emphasized elaborate lattices and flattering curves, while the Okulan hairdos seemed to mostly revolve around getting the hair out of your face and securing it, so it didn't fly around.

In front of us, on a raised platform, the *orsi* sat in a carved wooden chair. Each Okulan clan was led by a *tair*, the clan lord, a gender-neutral term. The *orsi* were their deputies. The word literally meant "hand." They looked after the clan's interests at their assigned posts and spoke with the voice of the *tair*.

This *orsi* was young, only twenty-two years old. Unlike most of the Harzi around her, she was on the shorter side, a couple of inches taller than five feet and slender. Her outfit, the same style as worn by the sentry that had met us, was decorated with exquisite embroidery depicting a white bird with long feathers amid red flowers. She had a heart-shaped face with delicate features and chestnut-brown hair that rested on top of her head in an elaborate crown of braids, secured with golden cords and clips carved out of bone. A thin band in matching Harzi blue crossed her forehead, identifying her status. It looked tattooed, but it wasn't. It was drawn on with a plant-based dye similar to henna, and they had to redraw it every couple of weeks.

Digi Dareel. The first daughter of the Harzi. Smart, gifted, diligent, and shrewd. Everything the heir to the clan should be.

A simple stool waited for me in the center of the floor. No mat to pad it. Assholes.

I gave everyone a shallow nod and sat. Lute parked himself next to me.

The *orsi* regarded us with large brown eyes, traced with dark eyeliner and accented with gold powder. Four people stood next to her chair: on the right, a tall woman in her thirties and an elderly man whose hair had gone completely gray, and on the left, a middle-aged man in warrior garb next to a tall younger man with sharp features and a mane of auburn hair. The young man wore an expensive outfit. A cascade of gold loops dripped from his left ear.

Ha. All the right people. Time to get this party started.

The tall woman spoke. "What do you want from Clan Harzi?"

"I need a mordok."

The tall woman shook her head. "We do not sell mordoks to outsiders."

"I don't wish to buy one," I said. "I have come to offer the *orsi* a secret that will put her in my debt. Should she wish to be free of it, allowing me to borrow a mordok will suffice."

"You know nothing of us," the middle-aged warrior man said. "We do not need your secrets."

"I think you do, Mrest Eser."

His eyes narrowed. The name was a gamble, but he couldn't have been anyone else.

"Let her speak," the man with golden hoops said. "What's the harm? If we don't like what we hear, we can throw her out."

Oh, yes, my gentle lamb. Come to the slaughter, Tarak. You deserve it.

The tall woman opened her mouth. Digi moved her hand, and the retainer stopped and stepped back.

"I will hear you out," Digi said.

Yessss. "My secret will draw blood. Please be sure that only those you trust with your life remain in the room."

"There are no traitors here," Digi said. "You may speak."

I looked at Mrest Eser. "You should draw your sword. Once I speak, the *orsi* may be in danger."

His eyebrows came together.

"Humor her," Digi ordered.

He unsheathed his blade, a slender, wicked sword.

"Lute," I said, "draw your sword. I might be attacked in a minute."

The sword was in Lute's hand so fast, it might have jumped into it.

"Young woman," the elderly man next to the *orsi* said, "did you come here to die?"

"No, Karet Or, I came here to help your grandniece."

I faced the *orsi*.

"The *tair* sent you here to oversee the trade deal with the Jal Family. You were supposed to be recalled upon its conclusion. You expected to stay here for three months. A year has passed, and you are wondering why your father hasn't sent for you."

The room went quiet like a proverbial tomb. Hopefully, it wouldn't be ours.

"Go on," Digi said.

"Your father knows you are not his daughter. He has no intention of recalling you. He's buying time for your second brother to consolidate his support by taking over your deals with the Northern Clans. Once he's ready, he will accuse you of betraying the clan and will send his sword brothers to bring you back. In chains."

"You lie!" the tall woman snarled, ripping the spear from her back.

Lute raised his sword.

"Stop," Digi ordered.

The tall woman halted, but she really didn't want to. The young man with the golden hoops took a step back. Next to him, Mrest Eser's face sank into grim determination. He was like a man preparing for a death charge. Digi's granduncle stood still like a statue.

"Have you any proof?" Digi asked.

"You must have wondered why your cousin joined you here instead of enjoying the company of his many lovers and indulging in those hunts he loves so much. After all, Tarak has always avoided work whenever possible."

Everyone looked at the young man with the golden loops in his ear.

"Tarak reports your every move to the *tair*. All visitors, all conversations, where you go, what you do, which goods you purchase and from whom. He has done a thorough job. It is the first time in his life he has ever worked so hard. Search him. Your cousin carries the black claw, which gives him the authority to take any life belonging to the clan. He can kill you at will."

Tarak ripped a dagger from his waist and lunged at Digi. Mrest Eser smashed the pummel of his sword into the young man's solar plexus. I had seen Everard do it to the Magnar brothers repeatedly during their practice sessions. Tarak folded in half. Mrest Eser gripped his arm and twisted it. The dagger clattered to the floor.

The older warrior thrust his hand into Tarak's robe and pulled a metal object out. It was solid black and shaped like a miniature dragon claw.

Silence claimed the room. Nobody made a sound except for Tarak trying to suck the air back into his lungs.

Digi regarded me. Her expression was perfectly calm. That was some amazing self-control.

"If I am not my father's daughter, whose daughter am I?"

"Ask the man next to you."

Mrest Eser jerked as if bitten by a snake.

Digi turned her head slowly and looked at him.

Sometimes we don't notice glaringly obvious things because we are conditioned to ignore them. She was probably seeing him for the first time. The same dark eyes. The same shape of the mouth. The same cut of the nose. The pain in his face that could only come from a parent expecting to be separated from his child.

The retainers of Clan Harzi stood frozen, afraid to move. Mrest Eser was a retired general of the Harzi clan. He had been ordered to accompany Digi by the *tair*, and, as the *orsi*, she now held his fate in her hand. She could banish him. She could imprison him. She could order his death to hide her secret.

Digi turned her head, looking at no one and everyone at the same time.

"My father is the best warrior in the clan. He is our savior and the most honored of the generals. I am blessed."

Mrest Eser put his hand over his face.

"Prepare a feast and bring out the best wine. Today is a day of celebration and reunion. I shall honor my father, and we shall sing of his achievements. Tomorrow, we go to war."

And it would be a brutal and quiet war, fought through trade, spices, and assassins.

"What is your name?" Digi asked.

"You may call me Maggie."

"Give Maggie anything she asks for. Let it be known that she is our ally and should be treated as such."

I rose. "The wisdom of the *orsi* knows no bounds."

One of the guards stepped forward and bowed to me. "This way, honored guest."

I limped after him, outside, with Lute holding my elbow just in case. The doors closed behind us.

The guard took us to a smaller door on the left side. We passed through it, cleared a hallway, and exited into a smaller courtyard. An older man sat under a tree, drinking green wine from a wooden cup. His coarse dark hair, salted with gray, was pulled back from his face in a half-ponytail, falling to his shoulders.

Short for an Okulan, with a broad build and powerful arms, he seemed grizzled like an old bear. Scars marked his face, one across the left cheek, and the other on the right temple, where something must've tried to bite off his ear. He looked like he could lift a small car all by his lonesome.

Two large dogs lay by his feet, panting. They looked like an oversized, prehistoric version of a German Shepherd with long legs and thick lupine fur. Two pairs of golden eyes stared at me. The fabled Harzi hounds.

"*The orsi wishes to gift a mordok to this ally of the clan,*" the guard told him.

I understood spoken Harzi. I wasn't even surprised anymore.

The man sipped his wine. "*The orsi should have told me in advance.*"

"*She didn't know, nura,*" I said. Nura was an all-purpose honorific used to address older Harzi men. Beastmasters enjoyed a lot of prestige among the Harzi. Being polite usually helped.

The two men spun to me.

The guard cleared his throat.

The beastmaster sighed and continued in Harzi. "And now they speak our language. What is the world coming to? You come at a bad time, foreigner. I have only one mordok available, and she is a terrible creature. She screams. She bites other mordoks. She bites the dogs. She bites the hand that feeds her."

"But can she track?" I asked.

"What do you have of your prey?"

"A bloody chunk of hair and a blood-smeared shirt."

"Does your prey use magic?"

"He does."

The gamekeeper shrugged. "Good enough. She will track him. Do you know how to handle a mordok?"

"I do, but I would beg you to honor me with a lesson."

"This one has some sense at least," he muttered. "Follow me."

He rose and went to a door on the left. The dogs stood up and trailed him, trotting at his heels. I was next, then Lute, walking side by side with the guard. We passed through the door into a large courtyard. Deep spacious stalls lined the walls on both sides, segregated by bars, wire mesh, or wooden partitions. Creatures moved within, hidden in the shadows. Some were eating, others slept on the straw. A dozen animal smells floated in the air, mixing with a trace of manure.

A howl echoed through the stables, a ululating call that was like nothing I've ever heard before. I almost cringed on pure instinct.

The Harzi guard made a face.

"Nothing to worry about," the beastmaster said. "Just a cub missing her mother."

"What happened to the mother?"

"Who knows? The hunters who sold her to us did not say. A goruk might have gotten her. Or a peibasa flock. Perhaps one of her own kin wanted her territory. It matters not. Now the cub is here, and she is fed and safe."

I had no idea what was making that disturbing noise, but I knew what a goruk was. That beast was about twelve feet long and weighed close to twenty-five hundred pounds, with a body that resembled a giant sloth and overly long limbs armed with steak-knife-sized claws. The goruks were excellent climbers. They scaled near-vertical surfaces. Unlike a sloth, they were fast and carnivorous, and their mouths would give anyone nightmares.

The peibasas weren't much cuter either. They were about eight feet long and looked like velociraptors sheathed in owl feathers. They stood on four legs equipped with talons, had long necks and vicious teeth, and they flew around on oversized wings. The peibasas hunted in packs. Whatever the mother of the cub was, she had to have been large, because they usually went for sizable prey.

"Do you think the hunters might have killed the mother?" I asked.

"It would take many great hunters. The men who sold her to us were few and not that great."

We passed by a cage. The man inside it grinned at me. I took another step.

Wait, what?

I stopped and leaned back to look.

The man from the Garden. What the actual fuck?

He sat on the floor of the cage, one knee bent, foot planted on the floor, his arm resting on his knee. No cloak this time, just a jerkin, pants, and boots, all in charcoal gray. He was lean and long legged. His light brown hair looked a bit disheveled, and a short brown beard traced his jaw. He'd been clean-shaven in the Garden, and I was pretty sure a man couldn't go from smooth jaw to a beard that full in two weeks. And it did not match his eyebrows.

He was smiling at me like a happy wolf panting in the forest.

I pointed at him.

"That one is not merchandise," the beastmaster said.

"He is an intruder," the guard told me. "We found him in the courtyard in the middle of the night."

Aha. "But he didn't steal anything."

"He didn't. We found him before he could try," the guard confirmed.

Crap. I'd worked too hard on making friends with Clan Harzi. I would need them later. I had to fix this right now.

I turned to the beastmaster. "This man is dangerous."

"Him?" The beastmaster eyed the man in the cage.

"He is more than he seems. You caught him because he wanted to be caught. I don't know what his purpose is, but it's not good. He's a lord. Killing or detaining him will bring trouble to the clan."

The beastmaster sighed.

"Why should we believe you?" the guard asked.

"No one allies with a clan just for a mordok," the beastmaster said. "She will want more from us. If we are harmed, she cannot benefit."

"You are wise, nura." I bowed my head.

The beastmaster sighed again. Harzi culture dictated that thieves were to be made example of. More, he had broken into their clanhouse, which insulted them and damaged their reputation. They couldn't just let him go. They couldn't keep him either.

"You said he wasn't merchandise, but may I buy him?"

The beastmaster raised his thick eyebrows. This was the best solution to the problem. The clan would profit from his presence, which would wipe away the black eye on their honor.

"The price will have to be fair," the beastmaster warned. We both knew it was another favor to the clan, but proprieties had to be observed.

"Of course, nura."

We pondered the man in the cage.

"I have never sold a human before," the beastmaster said.

"I have never bought one before."

"What would be a fair price . . ."

"How long have you kept him?"

"Since last night."

"He looks to be about the size of the oruke bull in that stall over there. Should we say the cost of the bull and enough money to pay for a dinner and green wine for the guards who captured him and for his keeper?"

The beastmaster tilted his head side to side, thinking. "Seems fair. That will come to thirty dens."

I switched to Rellasian. "Lute, please hand the man thirty dens."

Lute extracted his purse and counted off the money. Best thirty dens we would ever spend.

"Prepare him," the beastmaster told the guard. The younger man bowed his head and jogged off.

"Come with me, small foreigner," the beastmaster said. "The mordoks are kept just beyond here, in the gardens. Let me introduce you to your new best friend."

Chapter 26

I walked out of Clan Harzi's gates with a mordok on my shoulder and a chain in my hands. The chain was attached to a collar around the man's neck. They'd also tied his feet so he could walk but not run, and his wrists, and they'd gagged him with a strip of cloth. For people who didn't trade in humans, they were remarkably thorough.

We walked down the street without saying a word, as fast as we could without the man tripping. I was leading a human being on a chain. I wanted to end this ASAP.

The street was deserted. *Please stay deserted. Please don't let anyone see me.*

The streets of Fifth Hill didn't have corners or intersections. It was all a single road, and it wound around the hill in a spiral. As soon as we made it around the first curve, I stopped. The mordok riding on the leather pauldron on my shoulder decided that would be an appropriate time for shrieking into my ear.

"Cut his ropes, please," I told Lute.

Lute gave me a cautious look, crouched slowly, and sliced through the tether on the man's legs. His arm restraints were next. I stepped closer and unlocked his collar.

The man from the Garden pulled the gag out of his mouth, stretched, and kicked the restraints to the side of the road. The metal collar made a screeching sound as it slid over the cobbles.

"Much better. We meet again, my lady. As I said we would."

That voice was like the auditory equivalent of chocolate. I should've mentioned that to Everard and Gort.

He gave me a wolfish smile.

Lute was right next to me, with his hand on his sword, and this guy didn't have any weapons, but I didn't feel safe. Something about him communicated danger. I needed to move this conversation to a place where we were not alone on a deserted street. It would take at least ten minutes to get off the hill.

I started down the sloping road. He joined in, walking next to me. Lute's face behind him was sending all sorts of danger signals.

The mordok on my shoulder growled. At first glance, she looked a little like a slender white cat that had somehow sprouted large feathery wings. The wings reminded me of a seagull, her feet with their long non-retractable claws could have belonged to a racoon, and her face looked just like a mongoose. She was tiny and very light, barely two pounds, and only eighteen inches from the tip of her little black nose to the end of her long fluffy tail.

She looked cute, but her claws were wicked, and she was using them to try to shred the reinforced pauldron to which she was attached by a long, thin chain.

"You still haven't told me your name," he said.

"You haven't told me yours, my lord."

"I'm not your lord, but I could be."

He said it like a come-on, but there was a threat wrapped in that smoldering voice. The faster we got down to the city, the safer Lute and I would be.

"What were you doing at the Harzi house?" I kept my voice light.

"They have something that doesn't belong to them. I came to retrieve it."

"In the middle of the night?"

"It seemed like the best option at the time."

"You're clearly a man of some means, although the quality of your wig and beard says otherwise. Why not simply bargain with them for it?"

He smiled. "I see my disguise has failed to impress."

And he had ducked the question.

"It would be better if the beard matched your eyebrows."

He chuckled softly. "Do you prefer me clean-shaven, my lady?"

I had to string him along until we reached the main street. "I do."

He peeled the beard off and tossed it aside. "Better?"

He was a dangerous, scary bastard, but damn, that face. "Yes."

"What were you doing at the Harzi house?"

"Buying a mordok."

I pointed at the beast perching on the pauldron on my shoulder. The mordok promptly bit my finger.

"Ow!" I jerked my hand back. Blood swelled on my skin. That was the second time she'd bitten me today.

The man from the Garden laughed. "Adorable. What's her name?"

"Tzeri."

"How in the world did you convince the Harzi to sell you an animal? They do not trade with the likes of us."

"They do if the price is right. The beastmaster was overjoyed to be rid of her. He told me not to bring her back."

"I can't imagine why."

We were almost to the main road. I could see it below us. People walked across it, heading to the bridge connecting Old Town with the rest of Kair Toren.

"Every time we meet, you've risen in station," the man said.

"How so?"

"In the Garden you looked like a beggar, then a servant; in the market like a merchant's wife; and now you look like a noblewoman. I can't wait to see what will come next. The colors of a Great Family, perhaps?"

"Perhaps." Keeping it cool and noncommittal, that's me.

"And then there is the other thing," he mused.

"What is it?"

"Every time I see you, things take an unexpected turn."

"In what way?"

Just a little farther.

"We meet at the Garden, and the next day the world discovers Galiene has a daughter. More, she breaks a five-year dry streak and takes a lover—and not just anyone. Inhan. The second prince."

"I can't imagine what that has to do with me."

A brilliant move, Galiene. Of all people, Inhan had exactly the right combination of means, clout, and a lack of ambition that would keep her safe. Inhan Savaric had figured out long ago that his best chance at enjoying a long life hinged on convincing his older brother that he was not a threat. Kiel was rabid and aggressive, while Inhan was passive and avoided conflict. He indulged in wine and women, built elaborate moving models, and patronized the arts. When it came to his princely duties, he did the bare minimum, just enough to keep from enraging his father.

Both Sauven and Kiel had written Inhan off long ago, but he was still a Savaric. Not only did he possess considerable resources, but Kiel was directly invested in keeping his brother distracted. If Hreban threatened Galiene in any way, the crown prince would come down on him like a ton of bricks.

We stepped onto the main road and joined the foot traffic. Finally. The bridge curved just ahead. Yes! Made it.

"We meet at the Market, and then things that should've happened do not," the man continued.

What did he mean by that?

"I come to the Harzi house, and you frustrate my plans. You should stop."

"I was more surprised to see you in the cage than you were to see me outside of it, my lord. I had my own plans, which had nothing to do with you, but I couldn't leave you in there. As you've said, we've met three times. We are practically friends."

"Is that what we are?"

I realized Lute wasn't behind me. I turned. He'd stopped in the middle of the street with an odd look on his face.

The man from the Garden stalked between me and Lute, blocking him from my view with his body. He was too close, way closer than was appropriate, and there was a spark of magic in his golden eyes.

"A friend is someone who knows you," he said. "And you don't know me at all, my gentle mel."

I went cold.

Mel meant a year-old lamb-like creature. It sounded like a term of endearment, but it wasn't. When a lamb became mel, it was marked for slaughter. There was a man who said this exact phrase in the books, word for word. He said it to Inhan Savaric just before he slit his throat.

Silveren. The man from the Garden was Estol Silveren. The Lord Commander of the Redeemer Knights. The man who had allied with Hreban and kidnapped Matheo.

Fuck.

"Lute!" My voice sounded too sharp, but I didn't care.

Silveren smiled.

A metal blade slid over his shoulder along his neck.

The smile died. His eyebrows rose slightly. He hadn't expected that.

"Step aside," Lute said, his voice a quiet snarl.

Silveren took a step to the right, then another. Lute pulled the sword back and put himself between me and Silveren. On the other side of the bridge two men stopped to watch. A woman halted on the right. People were looking at us.

"Be on your way," Lute said.

Silveren took two steps back, turned, and strode across the bridge into Kair Toren.

I slumped back. Lute caught me and helped me lean against the stone rail of the bridge.

"What happened?" I asked him. "Why did you stop?"

"I don't know," he said. "I blinked and he was between us. Are you all right? You've lost color."

"I just need a minute."

The first time I ran into him in the Garden, he had called Hreban a toad and mocked him. And then he'd said, *Alas, one shouldn't keep such a rare beauty waiting.* I'd assumed he was talking about a celebrity attendant. He had been talking about Hreban. Hreban was the beauty. They could meet at the Garden in complete privacy without raising suspicion. Galiene's people would simply lead them to the same secluded room one at a time, and nobody would be the wiser.

Hreban must've shared his intentions for Galiene with him. Silveren knew, so he paid attention when that scheme collapsed.

It explained why he'd been at the Dog Market. He knew about the Butcher, so he went to check out the killer's handiwork for himself. But what about the

Harzi? How did they fit into this? Why was he there, what did he want? They weren't a part of Hreban's plan in the book. I was missing something.

Damn it.

I needed to speak to Everard. The sooner, the better.

I pushed from the rail.

"Are you good?" Lute asked, his eyes concerned.

"Yes. We have to get home."

"Agreed."

We started across the bridge.

He said the Harzi had something that didn't belong to them. What could it be? A weapon of some sort?

"Maggie?" Lute asked.

"Yes?"

"What was all of that for?"

"What?"

"Going to see the Harzi. What was it for?"

"For Tzeri."

I nodded toward the mordok on my shoulder. She hissed.

"Mordoks prey on small magical creatures and when they can't get those, bats, mice, and small birds, and they need magic to survive, so the more magical the prey, the better. When a mordok bites something or someone, they imprint on the taste, and they can find them by magic across distance."

"No, I got all that. We let her lick some blood or bite someone's dirty laundry, and then we make those weird noises, and she finds the person."

He'd gathered that from just watching the beastmaster and me. Huh.

"Why do we want her?" Lute asked.

"Because last night I ripped out a chunk of the Butcher's hair. And a bit of scalp. It's in my study. My clothes from last night also have his blood on them. 'Reynald' had cut him, and when the Butcher shoved me away, some of the blood got on my tunic. I hid it in my linen chest before we left, so Clover wouldn't wash it."

Lute's eyes lit up. "We'll be going hunting."

"I hope so. It's worth a try."

Tzeri screeched into my ear. I raised my hand to scoot her, and she clamped onto my finger.

"Ow! Third time today."

"Let me take her," Lute said. "She'll behave for me."

"I don't think she knows how."

"Trust me. Animals like me. Seriously, let me take her."

I unbuckled the pauldron and carefully lifted it off me. He bent his knees a little and I set it on his shoulder and buckled it in place.

Tzeri hissed and snapped her teeth an inch from his ear.

"You'll come to regret this," I warned.

"No worries. We'll come to an understanding . . ."

A figure lunged out of a side street. I caught a flash of steel as it sank into Lute's side. His mouth gaped.

A hand gripped my wrist, and the world swirled into gray nothing.

⬧

Stab.

The pain burned into my side, hot and cold at the same time. It sliced into me, into my organs, and my whole body screamed.

I gasped.

Someone scooped my legs from under me and dropped me onto something hard. The pain in my side exploded into blinding agony. I tried to get up, but a hand clamped my throat and slammed me back down. My head bounced off the hard surface. My vision swam.

Something caught my neck, constricting it.

I blinked away tears. The Butcher's face came into focus. I tried to punch him. My right arm didn't move, but my left did. He caught my fist and forced my arm down.

"Flailing won't help," he said.

Some kind of restraint clamped my wrist. I kicked with my left leg. My heel drummed something hard. I was on a table. I was on *the Butcher's table*.

He stepped to the side. Out of the corner of my eye, I saw a workbench with something metal on it. The Butcher turned back to me, a mace in his hand. He walked to the end of the table. Steel fingers gripped my ankle. The mace swung up and came down. Agony crushed my left knee. I screamed like I'd never screamed before in my life.

Through the haze of pain, I saw him move. He clasped my right ankle. I knew what was coming and that half a second of anticipation nearly broke me. When the blow came, I almost blacked out. I wanted to black out.

He slapped my face lightly. "Not yet. Stay with me awhile."

Tears streamed from my eyes. I couldn't stop. Everything hurt.

He pulled a knife out and began cutting off my dress.

I would die here, on this table. I knew it with absolute certainty. There was no escape.

The Butcher leaned over me, his dark hair dripping over his shoulders. "Are you with me? Do you understand what's happening?"

I stared at him, wishing I could claw his eyes out.

"Good," he said. "You're bleeding from a lacerated liver. I nicked a major blood vessel. That is a mercy. The last one you will ever know. You will be dead in half an hour."

If only I could get a hand free.

"You're not getting the full treatment. You haven't earned it, and you don't deserve it. You are not one of us." He tapped my chest. "You don't have the heart of a knight."

Fuck off, you sick asshole.

"I will make it simple for you. There are things I want to know. Tell me and I will end it fast. Refuse, and I will fill the last moments of your life with agony."

I clenched my teeth as hard as I could.

"You think it hurts now. The next thirty minutes will feel like thirty days. It will hurt in ways you can't even imagine."

Nobody would come for me. Nobody knew where I was. It was just me and him, the light of the lanterns hanging above me, and this table. That would be my world until I died.

And then, I realized with cold horror, I'd come back to life, and he would do it again. And again and again; even if I broke and told him everything he wanted to know, if he found out that I could die and resurrect, I would be a reusable torture toy. If I was lucky, I would lose my grip on reality. If not, I would die in agony and wake up perfectly aware I was in hell, over and over.

"Here's what I know. The first time I saw you was in the Dog Market. You were in the crowd. Everyone was scared and shocked. You were angry. I noticed you. Then someone of your height and build attacked me in the plaza. Today I saw you again, entering the Citadel."

He had been watching the Citadel. I should have thought of that.

"Every Firsday, Eliarde Docell visits her second cousin at the Citadel at exactly eleven o'clock. She rides through the barbican at the first strike of the bell. Today I watched you go in. Then a rider was dispatched. You left in a Defender carriage. I waited. The bell tolled, but Eliarde never came."

He loomed over me, his eyes unhinged and filled with menace. "You knew. You warned them."

I said nothing. My heart was pumping my blood out of my body with every beat. I could feel it draining out of me, taking my life with it.

He swung out of view, and I heard him walking. He circled the table like a shark. His voice vibrated with barely contained rage.

"That was Everard in the plaza. He was probably with you in the Dog Market before that. Didn't see him today. They must be looking for him. Scars from Fatefire are hard to miss."

The sooner I died, the sooner the pain would end. And once it did, I would have one shot at ending this. Only one.

"How did you know I would bring Velpor to the plaza? It's a good question, but I have an even better one."

I didn't say anything.

"Only two people know who has earned the right to the full treatment. You belong to Everard. He trusts you. He has you run his errands. I only want to know one thing." He leaned over me again, his teeth bared. He didn't seem human, and his voice was a snarl. "Did that fuck Hreban betray me and conspire with Everard to stop me?"

There it was, confirmation of everything I suspected. Hreban had hired him.

"Answer me," the Butcher growled.

I stared at him.

His expression relaxed. His voice was normal again. "I guess it's true what they say about the Sleepless Duke. He does know how to pick his people."

He stepped away, then turned back to me. He was holding big sharp shears in his hand. The kind you used to shear sheep or cut through branches.

"He stole Eliarde from me. I'm taking you from him. You're a piss poor replacement but needs must."

He fiddled with the restraints on my right hand and wrenched it upright, so I could see it. I tried to fight him, but my arm wouldn't obey. I had no strength left.

He caught my index finger between the blades.

"Just one question."

The blades came together with a metallic scrape. I screamed. He showed the bloody stump of my finger to me.

"It's not complicated."

The sheers sliced again. My middle finger was gone, and the pain drowned me. I hung in its depths, unable to move, unable to scream, just existing and hurting.

"Did Hreban betray me?"

Screech.

"Tell me and it will be over."

Screech.

I just had to endure it. I was dying already. I was so close. Eventually the agony would end. There was no choice and no escape until it did.

He leaned close to me, and I felt his breath in my ear. "If you want, you can whisper it to me. Nobody will ever know."

My lips were so dry. They had stuck together, but despite the agony, I made them move.

"I will kill you," I said into his ear. "I will make you pay for everything you've done."

He straightened. "No. You never will. And now I need to get on with it. We don't have much time left."

He was right. He made thirty minutes into thirty days. I cried, and I screamed, and I called for my mom, but I never told him anything he wanted to know. I was blind by the time I drew my last breath, but I heard him cursing as I died.

※

Everything hurt. The pain was like air, in my body, in my blood, in every cell.

I opened my eyes.

The wooden ceiling above me was grimy. Familiar clusters of lanterns hung from it, no longer lit. I was still on the table. He'd left my corpse there.

Slowly, oh so slowly, I turned my head and saw him. He sat at a table, with his back to me. A roasted chicken with a drumstick missing rested on a big plate next to him. He'd tired himself out and gotten hungry.

Just one shot. There would be no do-overs.

I tried to move my right hand. I had fingers again. I squeezed them into a fist and raised my arm, half expecting him to whip around and stab me.

He kept eating.

My hand was whole, and he hadn't resecured it. Why would he? I was dead.

I reached for the thing binding my neck. A leather strap.

He reached for the pitcher on his left and I froze.

The Butcher refilled his cup and set the pitcher down.

I traced the strap with my new fingers. It was secured by a metal nail threaded through it. I clamped my fingers around the nail and pulled up. It came free with shocking ease, and I froze again, holding my breath.

He kept chewing.

I pulled the belt to the side and sat up. The same setup held my left wrist. I pried the nail free and slipped off the table.

The pain nearly took me to the floor. My clothes hung on me in tattered bloody shreds. I wasn't me. I was a furious wounded animal, and I moved like one, silent, sure, and careful.

The workbench with his tools was between me and the Butcher. Gingerly, I reached out and picked up the mace he'd used to shatter my kneecaps. It felt solid and real in my hand, and its head was heavy.

I took a step toward the Butcher.

He picked up a knife.

Another step.

He sank the knife into the chicken and carved a thigh off.

Another step.

He put the meat on his plate.

Another step.

He set the knife down.

The final step.

I was right behind him. Inches away and he had no idea. I watched him bite into the chicken. I heard him chew. I saw him pick up his cup and drink from it.

I raised the mace. My whole body hurt, but I bent back, against the pain, lifting the mace as high as I could.

The Butcher reached for his bread.

I brought the mace down on his skull. His head cracked like a walnut being hit by a hammer. Blood spurted out. He spun in his seat. His eyes opened wide, the gray irises stark against the whites, horrified.

I smashed the mace into his face, crushing his nose into a bloody mush. I felt the impact all the way in my bones. He tried to scream and scramble away from me, but I hit him again and again. I heard a voice and realized it was me screaming. No words, just sounds.

He blurred, but I gripped the mace and kept hitting him, again and again, flinging blood into the air. And then he was on the ground, and I was hammering him with the mace, and the sounds became words.

"Die. Die!"

There was blood everywhere, and the mace made a wet squishing sound when it landed and then a sucking sound when I lifted it back up, but I kept hitting him.

Time stopped. It was me, the mace, and him, and if I stopped hitting him, he would get up and torture me again and then I would die and come back and die and come back . . .

I kept swinging the mace over and over. I had to. It was the only way to survive. I was trapped and I couldn't stop.

"Die die die you sick twisted fuck die."

A hand caught the mace and tore it away from me. Strong arms wrapped around me. I flailed, fighting and snarling. Someone lifted me off my feet and carried me backward, away from the body.

"No! No!"

I tried to kick the Butcher's body, but the person carrying me spun around, away from him. I twisted in his arms and saw Everard's face and his green eyes. Long tendrils of darkness spilled out of him, writhing around us. His voice cut through the mix of rage and terror that wailed like an animal in my head.

"He's gone, Maggie! He's dead."

He'd found me.

Everything I'd lived through in the past few hours hit me all at once. A single ragged sob came out of me.

Everard let me go and pulled off his black cloak. The dark smoke boiled around us, raging like a living thing. He wrapped his cloak around me and picked me up off my feet. He wasn't a hallucination. He found me. He came for me.

There were people around us. The familiar screech of a pissed-off mordok sounded outside.

"Pack everything up and bring it to me," Everard ordered. "Secure the body, then burn this place down."

More people rushed into the room.

Everard turned and headed to the doorway. The door lay on the floor in pieces, smoking, sparks of green fire dying on its wood. He walked over it and carried me over the threshold.

Rain slammed into us, a gray curtain of water pouring from above. The sky was pitch-black and churning with storm clouds. A carriage loomed in the downpour, two men in cloaks on the driver's bench. They turned and I saw Will and Lute. Lute's face looked bloodless, his eyes dark and desperate. Tzeri stuck her head out from the inside of his cloak and hissed at me.

Not dead. He wasn't dead. I nearly choked from the relief.

Recognition shone on Lute's face. "You're alive!"

Will jumped off and flung the carriage door open. Everard started to set me inside. Fear strangled me, cold and suffocating. I wrapped my arms around his neck and held on. Some part of me was sure that if I let go, he would disappear, and I would be back on the table again with the Butcher leaning over me, his teeth bared.

Somehow, Everard climbed into the carriage with me clinging to him and then we were on the bench.

I couldn't stop shivering. He hugged me to him, wrapping the cloak over us. His body was so warm, and I was ice-cold.

The carriage took off, rocking as the rain drummed on its roof. It was over. The nightmare was over. Everard was holding me, and I was safe.

The thin wall of fury and will to survive that had held me together tore, and I cried. Angry, violent sobs rocked me. My body spasmed and hurt. The pain was everywhere, in my bones, in my joints, in every cell. I clung to him, and I cried and cried, shuddering.

He shifted, molding his body to mine, shielding me with his arm from the hard wall of the carriage. I pressed my face against his chest and cried harder. I couldn't stop.

He stroked my back and held me.

Finally, the last of the panic and rage leaked out of me. I fell silent.

He was still rubbing my back, gently, lightly, his touch bringing me back to reality. My head rested on his chest.

"Is he dead?" I asked.

"Yes."

"Are you sure?"

"He's as dead as any corpse I've ever seen."

"So we can't question him?"

"Maggie, he doesn't have a face anymore."

"Oh."

The carriage slowed.

"Conqueror checkpoint ahead," Will announced through a small window in the front wall. "Do you want me to turn back?"

"No. Stay the course," Everard said.

If they checked the carriage, they would find Everard. He would have to fight. I tried to push away from him. He shook his head and hugged me to him.

We stopped. Heavy footsteps approached.

Dark smoke coiled about Everard, slipping over the arm I had wrapped around him, curling from him to the floor of the carriage. His eyes turned a bright, murderous green.

A knock resonated through the carriage.

"The Order of the Conqueror, inspecting all carriages by demand of the king!" a deep voice growled.

I froze. I didn't know what to do.

The door swung open. A man in armor peered in at us. His eyes widened.

"Close the door," Everard ordered, his voice like ice.

The knight shut the door and called out, "All clear!"

"Who is in there?" a woman asked.

"No one we want to find. Move along!"

A hand slapped the carriage, and we started forward.

I sagged against Everard.

"Everything will be fine," he promised. "We're almost home."

For once, I believed every word.

Chapter 27

The carriage couldn't make it through our gate. We stopped just outside of it. Everard picked me up again and carried me through the tunnel into the courtyard.

"I can walk," I told him.

"You have no shoes."

"They hurt my feet."

He looked at me for a second.

We reached the house door, and then he brought me down the hallway toward our communal bath. A door swung open. Clover and Shana stood in front of the stone tub of steaming water. Clover saw me and went pale.

Everard tried to bring me in, but Shana blocked his way. "My lord, we've got it from here."

For a moment, he hesitated, still gripping me to him, then he set me on my feet.

"Support her. She is in pain."

I stumbled, but Clover caught me. I looked back to Everard. I didn't want him to go.

"I will be right outside," he promised.

Shana shut the door in his face.

I tried to walk, and the pain punched my knees. I gritted my teeth.

Shana caught me by my waist and steadied me. "This won't take but a moment. Hold on."

Clover stripped the remnants of my bloody shift off me.

"I'm sorry," I told her. "That fucking asshole ruined the beautiful dress you made."

Clover swallowed. "No worries, my lady. I'll make you another one."

"Maggie," I told her.

"Maggie."

I could see myself and I was covered in blood.

"Hold on to me." Shana wrapped her arm around my waist.

I took a step, winced, and took another one. Clover bit her lip.

"It's fine," I told her. "This is just pain from the healing after I died. The fucker shattered my kneecaps."

Whatever magic was keeping me alive had a lot more to heal this time around.

Clover shut her eyes for a moment.

Shana maneuvered me over to the drain in the floor and stood back, holding my hands. "Clover, I need that bucket!"

Clover grabbed a bucket and carried it over. Hot water hit me, smelling like lavender.

"Another," Shana said.

Clover brought another bucket, dumped it on me, and started pulling my braids out and soaping up my hair.

"I can do this," I told them.

"No, you really can't," Clover said.

I didn't have the energy to fight with them. Standing was enough of an effort. They soaped me up, scrubbed me, dumped more water on me, ran the shower, and finally deposited me into the tub. I melted into the hot water. The heat soothed the ache clenching my muscles. I couldn't smell the blood anymore, only lavender.

Shana picked up the bloody rags and walked out of the room. Clover sat on a stool next to the bathtub and held out a cup to me.

"What is it?"

"Hot wine with a bitter powder. It will soothe the pain and let you rest."

I shook my head. "I don't want to sleep."

"It's medicinal. You need it."

"How about tea? I'll drink tea."

"Wine is better." She thrust it into my hands.

I sighed and took a sip. "This soap smells so nice."

"It's from the last batch you made, the one with extra breberry oil."

I sank deeper into the water and took another swallow of wine.

I was home. I was safe. Everard was just outside the door. The nightmare was over.

It was over.

I was scared to close my eyes. If I did, when I opened them, I could be still on the table. This could be a hallucination. A weird vision of safety my brain had conjured up as I died. In a moment I could come to and I would still be . . .

"Clover?"

"Yes."

"Hold my hand."

She gripped my fingers.

Quick, like pulling off a Band-Aid. I shut my eyes.

One . . . Two . . . Three . . .

I was still in the bath. I could feel the hot water and Clover's fingers holding on to mine.

I opened my eyes slowly. It was fine. It was truly over.

"Thank you."

Clover bit her lip. If she started crying, I would come apart.

"What happened after I left?"

"A woman showed up with a carriage. Lute was inside and he was bleeding. I was trying to get him out when Lord Everard came out of the house."

She said "Lord Everard" in the same way one would say, "His Majesty has arrived."

"He saw Lute and his face changed."

I sipped my wine. "Changed how?"

"I can't describe it. It turned very cold. Frightening. He looked like he could kill everyone around him. I have never seen anyone that angry. He was like a storm except it wasn't raging, it was . . ."

"Contained."

"Yes."

That checked out.

"He asked where you were, and Lute told him that the Butcher took you and that he had a beast that could track you down. His tunic was soaked with blood. He kept saying that he lost you and he had to find you, or the Butcher would kill you."

Poor Lute.

"We bandaged him the best we could," Clover said. "Lord Everard ordered him to recount everything that happened since you left the house. Lute did, and then Lord Everard looked at the Shears woman. His eyes glowed green, and she bowed her head and stayed like that until he turned away."

Right. Lute got stabbed, but she was in one piece, uninjured, and in Everard's mind, she had allowed me to be taken.

"We finished working on Lute. A second carriage arrived with more people in it."

The Shears backup.

"Lute and Will got into the driver's seat. Lute gave the little beast a leather pauldron with blood on it, made an odd noise, and the beast flew up, pulling on a chain. Lute said they would have to follow the beast. Lord Everard got into the carriage, and they left."

No horse other than Villain could carry Everard, because something about his magic made horses panic, and the entire city was looking for him. Every second counted, and he'd been reduced to riding in a slow carriage at the mercy of a temperamental magic beast and the man who had failed to protect me and was slowly bleeding out. It was a miracle that the carriage hadn't exploded from his rage.

"How bad is Lute's wound?"

She frowned. "It looked bad to me, but his father said it was a scratch."

If you cut off his hand, Gort would say it was just a flesh wound. "So we have no idea how badly Lute is hurt?"

"Precisely," Clover said.

Right. And now that the emergency was over, Everard would circle back to Lute letting me get snatched by the Butcher while he stood three feet away. Everard didn't tolerate failure. I needed to make sure that Lute was okay.

I gripped the stone wall. "Please help me out of this tub."

"I really think you should stay in."

"I think so, too, but I really want to check on Lute. I don't want him to be in trouble."

A knock sounded through the door.

Clover went to it, cracked it, listened for a moment, and shut it again. Her eyes had gotten very big.

"My lady." Her voice was oddly formal. "His Grace wants you to know that nothing is going to happen to Lute tonight. His injuries are not life threatening, and he did help find you. Lord Everard suggests you stay in the tub and finish your wine. When you have rested, he will escort you to your suite."

When he'd said he would be right outside, I had taken it figuratively. Apparently, he meant it literally. Also, apparently, our doors were made of paper.

"Is he still out there?" I whispered.

Clover nodded, her eyes still as big as saucers.

"I'm going to need more wine," I told her.

It took me half an hour and two more cups of wine to get out of the bath. Clover helped me into a nightdress that was modest enough to cover everything and wrapped a shawl over me for good measure. She also brought my house shoes, so I wouldn't have to be carried everywhere.

I braced myself and opened the door. Everard waited on the other side, as promised.

"Does it hurt to walk?"

"I'll manage."

He offered me his arm. I rested my hand on it, and we walked to the stairs. I was able to move now. The bath and the bitter powder must've helped.

We climbed the stairs in awkward silence. One, two, three . . .

I clenched my teeth. It hurt so much.

Seven . . . Eight . . . I couldn't do it anymore.

"May I?" he asked.

I gave up. "Yes."

He picked me up and started up the stairs. My face was only a few inches from his. His arms were rock steady. His profile was harsh, as if it had been carved from stone, but he carried me as if I were made of glass.

He was so gentle. After everything the Butcher had done to me, I should've been alarmed at being touched, and yet this felt comforting and safe. Not possessive, but protective, as if he were shielding me from a storm with his body. This was completely absurd. I was being carried by the Sleepless Duke. That alone should've sent me into near panic, and instead I had to fight to keep from wrapping my arms around him, desperate for closer contact. Somehow, this was helping more than the bath and the safety of the familiar walls around me.

"Does it hurt worse this time than the last?" he asked.

"Yes."

"Is it more painful every time you die?"

"No. The second time hurt a lot less than the first. I think it's how much damage the body has to heal. He did a lot of damage."

His face had that steel-hard flat expression. He was controlling himself.

"It really wasn't Lute's fault," I said.

"No, it wasn't."

"It happened very fast."

"I know."

"He didn't have a chance to react."

"Maggie, I know whose fault this was. It was mine. I allowed you to go out."

"I insisted."

"And I should've insisted on coming with you. I didn't, because you were angry with me, and I selfishly wanted things to be the way they were before."

"I don't know if that's possible," I told him softly.

"We'll have to find out."

We stopped before the door of my suite. He put me back on my feet.

"Thank you."

"Don't mention it."

He opened the door and walked me to the bed. The lanterns were already on, glowing with soft light, and the bedroom felt familiar and yet not quite safe. I sat on the covers.

Everard walked to my window, checked to make sure it was locked, then went into my office and checked the window there.

"I lock it now," I told him. "After Solentine."

Everard came back. He was dressed in black, and in the gentle light of the lanterns, he looked like a wraith woven from the night shadows.

"May I stay and watch over you?"

I wanted so much to say yes. Now, in the quiet of the bedroom, the ghost of the Butcher stirred, hiding in dark corners, waiting in the gloom under the bed. It would be so nice to fall asleep knowing Everard was right here.

I'd already hugged him and cried on top of him. That part of the carriage ride was a tortured blur. I had crossed every line, and I needed to reassert a boundary. What happened in the carriage had to stay in the carriage.

I needed to thank him for his kind offer and tell him I would be fine.

I wasn't fine.

"Yes." I would regret this moment of weakness later, but right now I needed him to be here, or I would start screaming.

He got a chair from the study, brought it in, and placed it by my bed.

"Lanterns on or off?"

"On."

I wasn't ready for darkness. Not yet.

He nodded and sat in the chair.

"Rest well. You are safe."

I pulled the blanket over myself.

A faint rustling came from under my bed. The little stelka crawled onto the covers, hissed at Everard, and curled up next to me. Her cold nose nudged my side. I petted her soft fur.

For a while I just lay there. I was so tired but sleep just wasn't coming.

"Have you settled on a name for her?" he asked.

"Sushi."

"Odd but pretty."

I petted the stelka. The house was quiet.

"Thank you for finding me."

"This will never happen to you again as long as I live." He swore it like an oath. "I won't let anyone hurt you."

"Did Lute tell you about the man from the Garden?"

"He said you bought him from the Harzi. We'll talk about that tomorrow, after you rest."

"The man from the Garden is Silveren."

"I see." He said it like he was pronouncing a death sentence.

"If he comes here looking for me . . ."

"If anyone enters this house tonight, even if they appear by magic, I will know and I will kill them."

"Silveren is a good fighter."

"I'm better."

"The Tower . . ."

"Even if he empties the Tower and brings every Redeemer knight to this house, I will cut them down and take his head. He will never touch you."

"Because you're the Sleepless Duke."

"That's one reason."

I believed him.

"I'm ready for the lanterns to be off now."

He got up and blew the lamps out. I watched him settle back into the chair in the gloom, closed my eyes, and fell asleep.

Chapter 28

Planter 26

I opened my eyes.

Golden sunshine flooded the room, painting the walls with bright happy light. Someone must've opened the window in the study, because I could hear the birds singing their hearts out in the branches of the wine tree.

I turned my head. Everard met my eyes. He was still in the chair.

"Did you stay here all night?"

"I did."

I didn't know what to say.

"How's the pain?"

I raised my arm, trying to test my body. My joints creaked like an old door.

"Tolerable."

"I'm relieved." He rose. "I will give you some privacy."

He left and shut the door behind him.

My bed was empty except for me. Sushi must've gone out.

I sprawled on my sheets and stared at the ceiling.

I started yesterday with beautiful hair, an amazing dress, horrible shoes, and high hopes. I met a handsome knight and delivered a warning. I won an audience with a merchant princess of scandalous birth and started a trade war of succession. I ruined the plans of the Lord Commander of the Redeemer Knights, who was clearly up to no good, and obtained a magical creature.

And then I was abducted, stabbed, tortured, and killed.

I died, came back to life, and defaced my killer in the most literal sense of the word. I was rescued and bathed, and then I was carried gently by the Sleepless Duke, who sat by my bedside all night and was probably nursing a raging backache.

Zero out of ten stars. Would not recommend.

I'd murdered my second person in three weeks.

The memory of cracking the Butcher's skull was fresh. The visuals were a bit fuzzy, but I remembered the sound of his bones breaking, the wet splats, and the stench of the blood . . .

I'd killed the Butcher. I'd saved myself, but there had been so much pain. The horror of what I'd endured had been too raw. When I thought back to it, I felt trapped. I had probably not been altogether sane in that moment. I should've killed him and escaped, but instead I had stayed, locked into the endless cycle of smashing that mace into his face. I wasn't even sure how long I had stood there, beating a dead man.

When Everard showed up yesterday, he had shattered that weird, agonizing loop. He took me out of that nightmare, brought me home, and promised to guard me while I slept. And then he did.

The books had led me astray.

The Book-Everard was a merciless killer. He didn't believe in degrees of guilt and punishment, and he seemed incapable of empathy. He was portrayed as a force rather than a human being, a personification of his domain. Whenever he appeared in the narrative, someone was about to die.

The real Everard was infinitely more complex. He was deadly and ruthless, true, but also subtle and smart. Smart was the problem here. I couldn't help but admire the deviousness. The problem was, I had no idea where the manipulation ended and actual feelings began, if he even had any.

He had pretended to be Reynald, and he'd been very convincing. His speech had been less refined, he'd grinned, he'd laughed, he'd seemed . . . normal. I had cared for him. I'd liked him. I hadn't ever realized how much until I saw the Fatefire and it had all come crashing down.

The way he looked at me when he carried me up those stairs . . . I shivered and instantly regretted it because all of me was very sore. If I ever met Omelyana of Gor, I would buy her a whole short barrel of the orange cherry wine she loved so much. She had all my sympathy. He was too much.

I needed to get my head on straight, because if things kept going his way, in a couple of months I would be standing by his throne in Selva, gazing at him in adoration with all my Kair Toren plans forgotten. And I would keep standing there for years, until all my knowledge was exhausted, while he planned his wedding to the most politically advantageous candidate.

Yesterday was done. Today was a whole new day.

It sank in finally. We had won. I had taken out the Butcher. He was gone. The Sun Margrave would survive. Matheo was safe.

I took a deep breath. It hurt. My ribs didn't like me breathing.

Now that the immediate threat was gone, Everard would want to know what came next. I had to be smart, sharp, and careful. But first, I had to get out of this bed. Up we go. How hard could it be?

I tried to sit up. No. Not happening. Bending hurt too much.

I groaned at my stiff muscles and rolled off the bed.

I opened the door and found Kaiden leaning against the wall across the hallway. His eyes looked haunted, his expression pinched and tight.

"Did you hurt yourself?" he asked. "I heard a thud and then there was groaning."

After I rolled off the bed, I'd tried to do a push-up and got the biggest *nope* of my life.

"I'm fine now. Where is everybody?"

"Downstairs. Having breakfast."

I didn't like those ghosts in his eyes. We needed to get back to normal and fast.

"Having breakfast without me? I want breakfast, too."

He offered me his arm.

"Are you escorting me downstairs?"

"Yes."

"Thank you, Lord Kaiden."

We headed down the staircase. Moving was a challenge, and my knees still didn't like the stairs, but it was a lot better than last night.

"You're shuffling like an old woman," he said.

What I wouldn't give for a bottle of ibuprofen right now. I wrinkled my face at him.

"We need to work on your manners."

"Did you die again?"

"Yes. But I killed the man who killed me."

"Don't die anymore," he said quietly.

Maybe I could get some of that bitter powder from last night. It seemed to help. "It's not like I tried to die on purpose."

"I know. Just don't."

He looked away. People in Kaiden's life died too much.

"Maybe you should ask Everard to train you, so you can save me next time."

"Maybe you can stay home and not go anywhere, so you don't get kidnapped and murdered."

"That won't work. I'll die of boredom."

He rolled his eyes. A little bit of his former smartass swagger came back to his face. That was better.

My stomach felt a bit queasy. I needed food. Food would make everything better.

I stumbled. My right leg folded, and I careened like a ship in a storm. Kaiden grabbed my hand, steadying me. I straightened.

"That was a close one."

"Like an old lady," he repeated.

"Let's not tell Everard about that."

I looked up and saw Everard standing at the bottom of the stairs. Damn it.

"You were supposed to tell me when she left the room," he said.

Kaiden raised his chin. "She is hungry."

"Then it's good that I have breakfast ready." Everard walked up the few remaining steps. "I'll take it from here."

Kaiden didn't move.

I held out my left hand. Everard stepped to my side, I rested my hand on his arm, and the three of us descended the steps, Everard on my left and Kaiden on my right.

We reached the bottom of the stairs and strolled into the hallway, filled with the delicious aromas of cooked meat and fresh bread; I tried to keep from drooling. Ahead, voices floated from the kitchen.

"You should go," I told Kaiden. "I'm slow right now, and I know you're hungry."

He glanced at Everard, let me go, and started down the hallway. Halfway to the kitchen he turned, walking backward. "No more dying."

"I'll try my best."

He turned the right way around and jogged off.

Voices floated from the kitchen.

". . . I fucked up," Lute said.

"The woman was tortured to death, Lute," Gort growled. "That's not a fuckup. Leaving your weapon outside the latrine in the rain is a fuckup. This is the worst thing that could happen. Where were your eyes? How in the void did he get the drop on you? If it wasn't for my brigandine, he would've shredded your kidney. You would've bled out right there on the street."

"Fine," Lute growled back.

"No, it's not fucking fine."

"What do you want, Dad?"

"I want you to take responsibility—"

I braced myself. I just wanted a quiet meal. Walking into the Magnar storm was a little much right now.

"We're not going in there." Everard steered me toward the door.

"Oh good."

He led me outside to the stairs leading onto the wall. Yes. We were heading to my favorite spot.

"Shall I carry you again?"

"No, thank you. But please catch me if I take a tumble."

He offered me his arm again. I climbed the stairs. It hurt but they finally ended and then we were on the wall. Someone had tilted the sail by the little table so part of it shielded us from the street. We could sit in private and watch the river. I spied a teapot, two cups, a platter of sausage, eggs, and the familiar golden pastries.

I sped up.

"Maggie?" he asked.

"Sambocades," I told him.

He smiled and helped me to my chair.

◆

I was full and happy. Shana's sambocades were the stuff of legends.

Everard reached to refill my teacup. I took the teapot from him.

He raised his eyebrows.

"It's not appropriate, Your Grace."

"I've poured your tea more than once."

"That was when you were Reynald. You're not him any longer." And he would never be Reynald again.

He reached into his jacket, pulled out a folded piece of paper, and offered it to me. I unfolded it. A middle-aged man, brought to life by a talented artist. He had a long face with hollowed cheeks, a full mouth, and a broad nose. A short curly beard, black touched with gray, hugged his jaw. His eyebrows were thick, and his eyes were a startling light gray. He looked intelligent and grim; a worn-out knight tired of fighting for causes he didn't believe in.

The books had tried. There were only so many ways to describe a man and they had hit all of the important points. Both Everard and Reynald had strong features and square jaws. Both had light eyes under dark eyebrows. But they couldn't have looked more different. Reynald was solemn and hardened by the years, while Everard in front of me was magnetic and brimming with power. Also, the books described Reynald as keeping his hair in the style of the men from the Highlands. I had pictured him with a longish mane, but his hair was cut so short, it was barely a dark trace against his brown skin.

Why was he giving me this? A gesture of good faith?

"I had it made for his son."

I touched Reynald's portrait. I never got to meet him.

"I was seventeen years old when the Okula invaded for the third time," Everard said. "I'd been a duke for a year at that point, long enough for Sauven to get over his shock and start plotting to kill me. He issued a royal edict demanding Selva respond to the threat and promised the backing of the royal army. I followed through. He didn't. He fucked around, he delayed, he puttered. He mulled over the rations and the routes. He used any small excuse to be late to the fight. He hoped the Okula would gut me, and he would arrive just in time to mop them up. Heroically, of course."

He smiled. There was no humor in it.

"Midway through the campaign, I found myself pinned down in a mountain pass. It didn't look good for us. The Okulan vanguard kept charging our position, wave after wave, endless. When they came, they looked like a human sea. I was running out of arrows and soldiers. When it looked like the next charge would break us, Reynald's company smashed into them from behind."

Oh! "He was the 'Fuck 'em' knight."

Everard nodded.

"He'd been given written orders to reinforce us and verbal orders to delay. Instead of meandering as he was instructed, Reynald advanced in the middle of the night and marched his knights through a mountain trail that was passable only for goats. His charge threw off the Okula's strategy. We crushed their vanguard between us. Their main force pulled back to regroup. When we met on the field, among the corpses, I told Reynald that if he ever needed a favor, he had only to ask. I considered him my friend."

At seventeen, Everard was probably on his first major campaign as the duke. Reynald would've been a seasoned, war-tempered twenty-five, already in command and expert with a sword. Adolescent Ramond must've looked up to him.

"How did he die?"

Everard's face turned grim. "It was exactly as you said. He came home to find his wife murdered and his son stolen. For months he went to the teahouse, watched Derog, and plotted his revenge. Reynald was always a careful man. He calculated his risks. Had Derog left the house, he might have cornered him on the streets, but the slaver never stepped foot outside of it. Reynald didn't know for certain how many people were inside the estate, if they had children that could've been taken hostage, or if Matheo was still in there."

That did sound like Reynald.

"He dug around and found that Derog had paid bribes to the right people. He was protected. They wouldn't stick their necks out for Derog, but they wouldn't make a move against him either. An official complaint would be useless, and a direct assault by himself was impossible. Reynald needed to borrow someone's power and resources to enter the place."

"And he sought to borrow yours?"

Everard nodded. "He could've have just written, but it was the kind of favor he wanted to ask for in person. He left the city and was on his way to me when Striver collapsed."

How could that have happened? "Did someone shoot at them?"

"No."

"Do horses just die like that?"

"Sometimes."

I hugged myself.

"There was no sign of foul play," he said, his voice suffused with sadness. "The stallion was old, and his heart had simply stopped. Striver was a Jekran warhorse, loyal to a fault. They will run themselves to death for the sake of their riders. Reynald's mind was on Matheo and what he would say to me. He hadn't noticed anything was wrong until Striver went down. He'd fallen badly, hit his head, and the stallion's bulk pinned him to the ground. A random, stupid twist of fate."

So he just lay there, pinned down and hurt? "Did anyone find him?"

"Eventually. He had set out before sunrise, and it wasn't a well-traveled road. They brought Reynald to the nearest village, two hours from Kair Toren. He knew the end was near, so from his deathbed he bundled his possessions into a pack, found a willing courier, and told them he was one of my men and I was expecting the package. His sword would be the proof I needed. The courier happened to work for the Shears, and he took it straight to Solentine."

"How long did Reynald linger?"

"Three days."

Why did it happen? Reynald wasn't supposed to die for another nine months. He hadn't suffered the way he had in the books, but still, it wasn't a good death. He had survived every battle, fought in every war, made it through the plagues, the sieges, and the storming seas, and that's how it had ended. Alone among strangers, not knowing if his final request would ever make it to Everard. Not sure if his son was suffering or even if he was still alive. How could life be so monstrously unfair?

My eyes were watering. I swiped the tears away.

"I made it in time to watch him pass," Everard said.

What? How? Selva was a ten-day hard ride from Kair Toren. Even if Solentine had sent a message by bird or some magical means, Everard would have still had to physically get there. Was there some long-range version of morr beads I didn't know about?

"I sat by his side as he faded, and I swore to him that I would find his son and when I did, Matheo would become my ward. He died in peace, Maggie. Or at least as much peace as was humanly possible to find considering what I had to work with."

Everard leaned back in his chair, his expression mournful and tired.

When he said he'd sworn to rescue Matheo, he'd actually meant it. He'd made a vow to a man he considered a friend so Reynald could let go knowing his son would be looked after.

"Before I got Reynald's message, I'd been considering coming down to Kair Toren. The rebellion was flaring up, and Solentine's messages betrayed a growing frustration with the state of things. Once Reynald passed, I took his body into the city so he could be buried next to his wife."

The cart. Oh my god. When I saw him in the city that night, there were three riders and a cart. Reynald's body must've been in that cart. It had rolled by me, and I'd had no idea. When Everard had given me those coins, he wasn't just feeling charitable. It wasn't mere money; it was funeral alms offered to me in memory of a man who once saved him. He gave it to me because that's what Reynald would've done.

I tried to keep my voice casual. "When did Striver fall? What day?"

"The third of Planter. Early in the morning, sometime shortly after sunrise. The rain was heavy that day."

Goosebumps crawled up my arms.

On the third of Planter, I woke up naked in a muddy ditch, choking on rainwater. I had been pulled into Kair Toren on the morning Striver collapsed. Probably at that exact instant. There was no limit to coincidences in the world, but that one was a stretch.

What did that mean? Did the timeline go wrong at that moment, and was I supposed to put it back on its rightful course? But how? I couldn't resurrect Reynald. I didn't have the power to bring the dead to life. I knew that for a fact because I had tried it when I was looking at the thief. I had stood there and wished with everything I had to undo Hreban's grisly handiwork, and nothing had happened.

If that wasn't it, then that meant the real events had diverged from the books before I had a chance to do anything. This answered absolutely nothing. It just raised more questions.

"I buried him next to his wife and placed his gravestone, as is the custom in the highlands. The next day I went to Taryz Teahouse. I wanted to sit in the spot where he sat and see what he saw. Then a strange woman sat at my table, called me by my dead friend's name, told me his secrets, and offered me a chance at vengeance."

"Why did you trust me? You knew Reynald was dead. That meant everything I said about his death was wrong."

"You were right about enough. Reynald left me his sword and his papers. He'd kept a journal of people and creatures he'd encountered. He'd meant for it to be a military manual, I think. The story of the bronze god was in there. You knew too much. I wanted to know how you had found out so many secret things, so I went along to see where it would lead."

"And then you spent weeks lying to me."

"I did."

"You should've told me who you were."

"You liked Reynald. You admired him. I just watched you cry for him. Would you have traded him for a man who would kill you, your family, and your neighbors? The Sleepless Duke is a monster who solves every problem with violence. He will murder your pets, burn your house, and salt your fields . . ."

I held out my hands, trying to stop the flood of things I'd said about Everard coming back to drown me.

"Being Reynald allowed me to live a different life for a few days. He's who I might have been if I hadn't been born an Everard. But I am the Sleepless Duke."

His face was calm, but his eyes had grown distant. He looked past me, across the river, to the city on the other bank.

"Most of what you've said is accurate and true. Except for the murdering of the pets and salting of the fields. Salting the soil is a massive waste, and the only dogs I've ever killed were the Empire's battle hounds. Calling them pets is a stretch."

I didn't know how to respond to that, so I just stayed quiet.

"I also strive to refrain from killing civilians, but war is war. Homes burn. Fields lie fallow. People suffer. I have razed villages before, and I may have to do it again. The only way to prevent that is to keep the peace in the first place."

It would've been naive and foolish to imagine that a clean war where no civilians died was possible. That was something from fairy tales. Wars were brutal, horrific, and messy. He didn't want to fight one. He was thinking about it now, and his whole body emanated dread.

"I will save Matheo," he said. "And I will do whatever I must to stop Hreban and Silveren from rising to power. I will not let the kingdom burn. Divine knows, I can't stand Sauven any more than he can bear my existence, but we are surrounded by enemies on all sides. If Rellas stumbles, other nations will fall upon it and rip it to shreds. Without Rellas, Selva is doomed. I cannot hold them back alone."

Now was as good a time as any. *What do you really want, Ramond?* "Have you ever wished for more?"

"As in?"

"Rellas. The throne."

"I already have one in Wilkair. It's carved from a solid chunk of malachite and old as the Void itself. It's hard, cold, and uncomfortable no matter what sort of cushion I put on it."

"I think it's supposed to be."

"Yes, I suppose it is a symbolic reminder about the burdens of holding people's fates in your hands. To answer your question, no, I don't want another chair, Maggie. Nor do I want the kingdom that comes with it. If I wanted Rellas, I would've taken it by now. You don't have to worry. Our goals still align. We need each other."

Our goals did align, and I did need him, but right now I was at his mercy. At any moment, he could tie me up, load me into a carriage, and send it up to Selva and nobody could stop him. He wouldn't resort to brute force unless I became a threat. He was too subtle and calculating for that, and his success relied on me volunteering the information. He needed me to like him.

I couldn't stay in this position. The power difference between us was too great, and he was too smart, too shrewd, and too magnetic. He drew me to him.

In the books Omelyana was consumed with seducing Everard. I could recall pages of longing from memory. *She wanted him to touch her, to hold her, to lose himself in her. She wanted Ramond above her, that hard, muscled body slicked with sweat, the green eyes blazing, all control completely gone . . .*

She kept having all sorts of sexual fantasies about him. And now I understood every one of them. He was filled with power and so controlled, he probably calculated his breaths. Imagining him obsessed with me to the point where all his chains snapped was intoxicating.

But I wanted even more. I wanted him to care. That carriage ride, when I was broken, vulnerable, and scared, and he'd held me . . . The way his strong arms felt, wrapped around me. The way he'd looked at me, like he would rip the world apart to keep me safe.

That was a fantasy, too, and it was way too tempting. Ramond vi Everard didn't do love or affection. Better women than me had tried to get them out of him and failed, and yet I couldn't let it go. Being in his presence was a constant test of willpower, and these were just the opening maneuvers as he contemplated the best way to win this war. If he mounted a full assault, I wasn't sure how long I could hold out, and there was a real danger that I would be the one obsessed in the end. I needed to get a grip.

I sipped my tea. "I forgot to ask, where did you find me?"

"On Sava Island. The mordok led us there. It's a small chunk of land off the northern part of the west coast, still within the city limits, but only barely. The island sits close to the shore, connected to the road by a narrow wooden bridge. It held two warehouses and a small dock. Very private. It's a burned ruin now."

"A perfect place to torture people. Nobody would hear them scream. Did the Shears find my fingers?"

Everard gave me an odd look.

"He cut them off," I explained. "Both hands. Did they find them?"

"No," Everard said slowly.

"So my body parts disappear after I die. Good to know."

He looked slightly ill. Ramond vi Everard, a human being. That would be the day.

"You treat Death so lightly, Maggie. As if it were just a thing that happens to you instead of the fiend it is. Every time you die, I wonder if this time it will take."

"Cheer up, Your Grace. The evening is lovely, we're alive, and we still have three delicious pastries left. Matheo is still stuck in the Redeemer Tower, but the Butcher will not end his life." I curled my hand into a fist and made a hammering motion with it. "Because he doesn't have a face anymore."

"Once you recover, I will teach you how to defend yourself with a dagger. You can't keep bashing people to death in a blind panic."

"It's worked well for me so far."

"True, but you might not always have a bludgeon handy."

"I've never used a dagger before."

He smiled. "Then you won't have any bad habits I'll have to correct."

"Do you still have my lucky coin?"

He reached into his jacket and slid a den over the surface of the table. I took it. It felt familiar and comforting in my fingers.

"We won," I said softly. It had cost me so much, but we had won. "I don't care how resistant the future is, the Butcher is dead. Hreban will never be the Sun Margrave. It's over."

Solentine Dagarra swung himself over our parapet and landed on the wall, six feet away. His eyes were slightly sunken in, and the lines of his handsome face were sharper and more prominent. His usually perfectly combed hair stuck out from his head in a disheveled mess. He looked rough, as if he'd spent a couple of weeks fighting with a nasty flu and today was his first day upright.

How the hell did he get here so fast? The Demarr domain was all the way in the Trihorn. It should've taken him weeks to get back and forth.

"I hate to be the bearer of bad news," he said. "But they just found another butterflied body hanging off the Estret Bridge."

PART IV

IN THE NAME OF THE FATHER

Chapter 29

"Fucking shit! Of all the fucked-up, shitty, damn fucking assholes . . . Why?"

I stomped around my study.

"Was that not enough? Was the Butcher not enough?! Fuck you. Fuck you, Latour! I hope you die and rot in some ditch, you filthy motherfucker! Fuck Kair Toren, fuck Rellas, this whole damn world can go and jump in the fire for all I care!"

Solentine blinked and looked at Everard. "Who is Latour?"

"No clue," the Sleepless Duke said.

I finally ran out of steam and collapsed into my chair.

The two men waited.

"Rough journey?" Everard asked.

Solentine nodded. "Thunderstorms over the Glades. Added three hours."

I met Everard's eyes. "He's dead, right? He didn't regrow a face and resurrect?"

"I swear to you, he is dead," Everard said.

"Magic has a limit, and its name is Death," Solentine said. "Last I checked people didn't come back to life. That would be utterly ridiculous."

"Ha!" I put my hand over my face.

"Maggie, the Butcher is no more," Everard said. "I will prove it to you tonight."

"It has to be an impostor," Solentine said. "I got a good look at the body before the guards pulled it off the bridge. It lacked the Butcher's artistry. Cutting humans open to display your handiwork requires a skill set most people do not possess. The cut on Velpor was a single smooth slice. It took the new killer four cuts to open up the body, and his edges are ragged."

"So he imitates without understanding the purpose behind the kill," Everard said.

"In essence, yes," Solentine said. "Also, the Butcher dueled his victims. He was looking for that moment when the tide turned, and his target saw their death approach. The man sought to prove his superiority. The new murderer put an amulor through the target's eye."

"What's an amulor?" I asked.

"A narrow-bladed dagger. About this long." Solentine indicated about fourteen inches with his fingers. "Triple-edged, convex grind. Very stiff. Basically, a sharp, rigid spike designed to crack links in chain armor. The killer stabbed our dead man in the eye with enough force to scramble the brain behind it. Instant kill. The victim didn't even know he died."

"Hreban hired a replacement," Everard said. "It's the simplest explanation."

"Probably Cai of Sunder," I told them. "That's his go-to assassin."

Solentine frowned. "That complicates things."

"Is he good?" Everard asked.

"Yes. Fast, precise, professional. The man doesn't get emotionally involved," Solentine said.

"Can you find him before the opening of the judicial session?" Everard asked.

The head of the Shears shrugged. "Doubtful. I will try, but only saints can work miracles."

Everything I had gone through, all the pain and suffering, and the assassination was still going forward. Not only that—we were worse off than when we started.

The Butcher was an assassin of opportunity. Hreban had hired him for his cruelty and shock value, but before the Butcher became a serial killer, he was a knight. He told me so when he declared that I was not one of them because I didn't have the right heart. Skulking around the city didn't come to him naturally. Cai of Sunder had been trained by one of the best assassins of the age, and assassination was his profession from the start. He wouldn't make the Butcher's mistakes.

I'd managed to escalate things again. Every time I crawled a foot forward, Rellas kicked me two feet back. I'd scream but I had already made enough of a spectacle.

"There is one thing that puzzles me," Solentine said. "We know that Hreban becomes the Sun Margrave."

He'd read the pages I'd given him. "Yes."

"But Hreban himself can't possibly know that," Solentine said.

Everard sat up straighter. "That's true. Sauven is volatile and Hreban is an unlikely man for that post."

"So why does Hreban want to kill the Sun Margrave?" Solentine asked. "Why him of all people?"

I opened my mouth. Nothing came out.

We knew what would happen, because of me. Hreban didn't have me. Trying to assassinate the Sun Margrave was incredibly dangerous. It would infuriate Sauven beyond anything Rellas had seen. Hreban had to have figured out that much. So why risk it?

"Are there any charges in the High Court against Hreban?" Everard asked.

"Before I left, I told my people to look into the High Court docket. There is nothing. There is no bad blood between Colart Jenicor and Ulmar Hreban. They know of each other, but they've never come into conflict."

The two of them looked at me.

I shrugged. "Your guess is as good as mine."

"If Hreban doesn't have an obvious reason to kill the Sun Margrave, it must be Silveren," Everard said.

That made sense.

"We wondered why Silveren decided to back Hreban," I said. "Perhaps they struck a deal. Hreban kills the Sun Margrave for Silveren, and in return, the Redeemers support Hreban's climb."

"But why would Silveren want the Sun Margrave dead?" Solentine asked.

"I don't know. But after the Sun Margrave was buried, Silveren did go to Jenicor's family tree."

Everard leaned forward. "Did he deface the burial plot?"

"No. He just sat there for several hours. Another Redeemer knight came to see him, and Silveren told her that life was a chain that anchored you to the past like a rope that secures you as you scale a wall. One link attached to the other, each coming full circle. If you failed to close the links, the chain would come apart, and you would plummet."

Solentine frowned again. "This new Silveren, the one who is running around the city in disguise, plotting with Hreban, and contemplating the meaning of life, I don't know him. I find it troubling when people act unlike themselves."

"Which Silveren do you know?" Everard asked.

Solentine sighed. "He says little. When he's forced into small talk, he is dull, save for a rare quip. If you attempt to converse with him, he will inevitably turn the topic to the burdens of war or his old injuries. Silveren broke his legs somehow during his service and they bother him when it rains. He tends to Inhan and hangs behind him like a bitter shadow. Considering his face, he should be far more coveted, but he is so unresponsive that he isn't pursued by either women or men. The only time Silveren comes to life is when the discussion touches on matters pertaining to the Redeemers. He is a zealous advocate for his order, and he doesn't back down from either Arvel or Bors, I will give him that."

"That is not the Silveren I met," I said.

"I gathered," Solentine said. "Who did you meet?"

"A dargan in mel's clothing. Sharp, menacing, clever. Hreban walked into the Garden wrapped in loud luxury, and Silveren referred to him as a rare beauty who couldn't be kept waiting."

Solentine raised his eyebrows.

"You said he attached himself to Inhan?" I asked.

"Yes."

"Silveren kills Inhan in the future. Slits his throat and watches him bleed out."

Solentine swore.

"There must be a connection between the Sun Margrave and Silveren," Everard said. "His graveside speech at Sonndor suggests it may not be about him. It may concern his parents or his siblings."

"I'll take a deeper look," Solentine said. "However, that will take time, and the start of High Court is a month away. We could always take a direct approach. Eliminating Silveren would be problematic, but we could remove Ulmar Hreban from the picture."

"No," Everard and I said in one voice.

"Why?"

"It's not about eliminating the man himself, but about removing the opportunity he's taking advantage of," Everard told him. "If we kill him without changing the circumstances that allow his rise, we risk someone else sliding into his place. Better the dursan we know than the one we don't."

"I see," Solentine said. "A pity."

Up to now everything I had done was in response to Hreban's actions. The abduction of Galiene's daughter, smuggling iron, the string of serial murders, all of those had already been in motion. I had stopped them, but that didn't address their source.

No, we had to eliminate Hreban not as a man, but as a force. That's what I had set out to do when Everard was still Reynald and I told him for the first time that I would stop the nightmare that was about to swallow Rellas. But then the salt and the mercenaries became a pressing issue, and I'd defaulted to stopping the disasters as they came.

"We have to take Hreban apart," I said.

"How would we do that?" Solentine asked.

"I don't know yet. Let me think about it."

Hreban had manpower and money on his side. He was truly the richest man in Rellas, and that wealth bought him a lot of protection. Nothing about that had changed since we'd started. But back then, I was a woman lost in a new world, trying to protect two teenagers and relying on a blademaster who didn't trust me. Now I had four seasoned mercenaries, a lady's maid, a locksmith's son, possibly the assistance of the Shears, and best of all, the Sleepless Duke. There had to be a way forward.

"To topple the head of a Great Family, we would need unassailable proof," Solentine said.

"I know," I told him.

We didn't have much time. This was the point where the isekai heroines usually got struck by a brilliant idea in a flash of intellectual lightning. My mental skies were blue and clear. Not a thundercloud in sight.

I had to think of something fast, or both Matheo and the Sun Margrave would lose their lives. I had failed to save Reynald, but I had to save his son. I had to.

"Speaking of families, thank you for averting a disaster about to befall mine," Solentine said.

"Things went well?" Everard asked.

Solentine nodded. "I arrived just as my uncle was doing a final review of the loan. To say he was shocked would be a grave understatement. We had a long and productive chat with the noble in question."

I could only imagine.

"And?" Everard asked.

"He sang like a bird in spring the moment knives came out. At once expedient and yet somewhat unsatisfying. I wouldn't have minded more resistance."

Words to make your hair stand on end.

Solentine reached for the bag by his chair, pulled out a scroll case, stepped over to the table, and offered it to me.

"Demarrs pay their debts. To show my gratitude, I would like to offer you something of great value as well. You have the pesky problem of not having an identity. It makes you vulnerable. As thanks, I've prepared one for you."

I took the case, pried the scroll loose, and unrolled it. A set of papers with a blank first name. The last name: Demarr . . .

Wait, what?

Parents: Brune and Griele Demarr.

Everard stepped closer to the desk and looked at the document over my shoulder. The transformation into the Sleepless Duke was instant. One moment he was reading, and the next he was *there*, an active and immediate threat. His voice could've cut a human being in two.

"This would make her your cousin."

"So it would." Solentine smiled.

※

"No," Everard said.

"That is not up to you," Solentine said.

I did not see this coming. At all.

My face must've said volumes, because Solentine dropped back into a chair, one leg over the other, and braided his fingers on his knee. It was his "hear me out" pose.

I was acutely aware of Everard looming next to me like some deadly storm in human form ready to unleash hell at any second. The head of the Shears ignored him and looked at me.

"Hear me out, Maggie. You are meddling with the affairs of the kingdom. Until now, you've escaped notice, but that won't last. A reckoning is coming. When that happens, you'll need the kind of name that will shield you. You cannot afford to remain a commoner. Truthfully, at the moment, you're not even that. You are no one."

He nodded at Everard.

"Ramond can promise you an identity and a noble title; however, that identity will have a *vi* in it, and the moment people hear it, it will mark you as a woman of Selva. You will be watched and treated with suspicion, rendering you much less effective and painting a target on your back. You don't need that kind of attention."

"Whatever he promises you, I can deliver more and better." Everard's eyes were a lethal, electric green.

"Not in this case," Solentine said. "She needs legitimacy. You cannot give it to her. If you try, you will place her in front of Sauven's archery target."

"It doesn't have to be his family," Everard said to me.

"But it does," Solentine said. "My family is available and willing. Our lineage is sound, our achievements command respect, and we are good at keeping secrets."

"You know him," Everard told me. "You know what he's capable of. Think of what happens if you make a mistake and he decides his family is better off without you."

"I swear on my father's love that I make this offer in good faith. If you make a mistake, I will compensate for it because you will be my dear cousin."

"He can't be trusted," Everard said.

"And yet you trust me with a great many things, your life included," Solentine parried.

Solentine looked like a dog baring his teeth and Everard was a bomb about to go off. I needed to defuse this disaster before the shrapnel started flying.

"It's not about trust. Solentine Dagarra is afraid of very few things, but right now he is afraid of me."

Solentine's amber eyes watched me, unreadable.

He was born of an affair his father had before his marriage. Solentine's biological mother was a knight, and Izarn had no idea his son even existed until almost two years after said knight died in battle. Solentine had been left in the care of a woman who'd neglected him, abused him, and fed him scraps. He was eight years old when his father walked into his life and plucked him out of his misery. Solentine's stepmother had treated him as her own son, to the point of delaying having children so she could devote all her efforts to his well-being. After that, he was raised with all the love and care a child could wish for.

Some children recovered from abuse and went on to live happy lives. Some carried scars. Solentine carried anger. He chose not to inherit the title of the margrave. He didn't see himself as a general. Instead, he decided to look after the Demarrs in a different way, so his father apprenticed him to the previous head of the Shears. When Solentine reached his majority, Izarn gave him his own domain, the Dagarra. Although Solentine had voluntarily stepped away from his birthright, his family was the center of his universe.

"He cares only about one thing: the survival of the Demarrs," I said. "They rescued him from the hell of his old childhood. They love him, they look up to him, and he cannot bear to disappoint them. Everything else is secondary to their safety. I know their hidden thoughts and their secret sins. I know which road they will travel on and where the ambushes lie. I'm either a catastrophic threat or the guardian of their future. Since you will not permit him to eliminate me, his only option is to make me his ally."

Solentine offered me a razor-thin smile. "We understand each other."

He would've never tried this scheme without his aunt, Griele. His father, Izarn, was a brilliant military strategist, but when it came to politics, Griele always saw the bigger picture. This adoption had to be her idea. Brune would go along with whatever his wife decided. He wasn't a stupid man, far from it, but he was neither devious nor introspective. He was dependable, brave, and earnest, which is why Griele loved him with all the fierce love her complicated soul could deliver.

"Did your aunt put you up to it?"

"My aunt and uncle are both committed to this course."

"This won't stand up to scrutiny," I told him.

Solentine pointed at the documents.

"This isn't a forgery. This adoption is legal. We are backdating it, but every other aspect of it is authentic. If you agree, you will become one of us. My aunt and uncle, my cousin, my father and mother, and my siblings will support and defend you, in private and in public. You will be entitled to every privilege the combined power of Demarr and Dagarra can provide. This act cannot be undone."

"And if I betray you?"

Solentine sighed. "If you betray us, I will kill you, Maggie."

He would try.

"But even in death, you would remain a Demarr. You would be buried with every honor and ceremony in our private cemetery." Solentine met my gaze. "I do not make this offer lightly. If you take it, I will truly accept you as my cousin without reservations, conditions, or expectations. You know how I treat my family."

What's scarier than a rabid honey badger in human form? A rabid honey badger in human form who is your loyal cousin.

"Solentine, my powers are not absolute. They are not hereditary either. Often, they're not even accurate. I can't concentrate on an event or a person and get a vision. I know what I know and that's that. There is no way to improve on it, and my usefulness will diminish over time."

He put a metal crest on the table. A shield depicting a rust-colored dagger on a cream background with three moons in different phases above it in a saturated blue. We come at night and stab you. Right.

"No reservations, conditions, or expectations," Solentine repeated. "Except that you commit to being a Demarr. If you say yes, this crest is yours."

"That 'no conditions' part of the offer is what makes this suspect," I told him. "I know you."

"True, but I also know you." Solentine leaned forward. "I made inquiries. Apparently, a woman matching your description had come to see Galiene of Sosna. Galiene rushed off and returned with a daughter nobody knew about and the next day she took the second prince as her lover."

"She was kind to me."

"Kindness deserves thanks. What you have done goes far beyond that. You've warned me expecting nothing in return. You saved the mercenaries from Falcon Point. You put yourself in danger for the sake of others because you do not like to see people suffer, Maggie. Even strangers. I'm offering you a family who will love and shelter you and accept you as their own. I doubt you will repay us with betrayal."

"Don't take this offer," Everard said. "I can give you an identity. I can give you protection, wealth, and status. I can give you the means you require to accomplish your goals."

All at the low, low cost of my freedom.

The papers lay on the table in front of me.

"Everything has a price, Maggie," Everard said. "Yes, you will be gaining a family, but you'll be assuming its burdens. Think about it."

Margrave Izarn Demarr, Solentine's father, was in the upper middle tier of Rellas's nobility, below the Eight Families and their immediate circle. He rarely visited the capital or attended court. However, his influence far outweighed his rank.

In the Trihorn, Izarn commanded both a formidable fighting force and a terrifying reputation, and nobody wanted to get on his bad side. When Izarn besieged a city, he surrounded it and issued his demands. If they were refused, the next morning the defenders would wake up to find their entire command staff slaughtered. Very few people knew how he did it, and that only added to the family's legend.

I was now a part of an elite club that had seen that magic in action. The Demarrs were abnormally fast, had ridiculously good hand-eye coordination, and their magic allowed them to play with gravity. They could run up walls. They could sprint across a wooden beam the thickness of a chopstick like it was solid ground. If you threw them off a building, they would land on their feet like a cat, charge right back up, and stab you in the throat.

It made them excellent assassins. Everyone in that family—Solentine's father, Solentine himself, Solentine's aunt and cousin, and even Solentine's teenage siblings—all of them were gifted killers. If I took this offer, I would become a Demarr, and they would be my relatives.

However, the Demarr family existed on a blade's edge. The Throne's grant didn't cover all of the military upkeep for that oversized army Sauven expected them to maintain. The Demarrs were always strapped for cash, provisions, and equipment. They couldn't afford to piss off either Everard or Sauven. They swam in the ocean between two monsters, scrounging for crumbs and always ready to dodge if one of them decided to strike.

"If Sauven turns on them, he will obliterate them," I told Everard. "If you withdraw your support, the border will fall, and they will fall with it. I understand the situation very well."

If I closed my eyes, I could picture Solentine splattered with blood and howling like a grieving animal over the body of his father.

Everard crouched by me and took my hand into his. His eyes were so warm, his face reassuring and sincere. The feel of his fingers on mine sent little shivers down my spine.

"You don't have to make this decision right now," he said. "Or at all. Use me. Let me be your shield. Let me take care of you."

"Holy shit," Solentine muttered.

"If you reject this, I give you my word Solentine will never bother you again. Tell me what you wish for, and I will grant it."

Solentine leaned forward. "Maggie, not even the Eight Families can take the Demarr name for granted."

I knew exactly what he was saying. If I became a Demarr, I would slip out of Everard's grasp. The Demarrs were Everard's allies, not vassals. He couldn't kidnap their child.

"Trust me, Maggie," Everard said. He was so handsome right now. So irresistible. Saying no seemed absurd. Ridiculous.

"I do trust you," I told him and tugged my hand free. "Where do I sign?"

Solentine exhaled.

Everard's eyes blazed. He straightened and leaned over the table, shortening the distance between us to way closer than was appropriate. His voice was low and calm. "A mistake, my lady."

He didn't say it in a threatening way. He simply expressed his disappointment that someone he treasured had made a regrettably foolish decision. It was problematic but ultimately it would change nothing because he was completely confident in his ability to compensate.

I couldn't sign this paper fast enough.

"I thought we had established trust." Everard looked into my eyes.

"I trust you with my life. Just not with my freedom."

The Sleepless Duke smiled. It was an indescribable smile, knitted from determination, power, and pure heat. "Then I shall have to work harder."

Dear god.

I turned to Solentine. "Hurry up."

Solentine pulled a reed pen and a small jar of ink out of his bag and moved his chair closer to the table. "How old are you?"

Rellas had eight days in one week and four weeks in a month, with three hundred and eighty-four days per year, so I would need to subtract a few months. "Twenty-five."

Close enough.

"Birthday?"

"The first of Snowdeep."

Solentine dipped the quill into the ink pot and wrote on the paper in an ornate script. "You were adopted sixteen years ago, at the age of nine. This coincides with the Blaze of Garr, which flooded the area with refugees."

The Blaze of Garr was the Crimson Empire's attempt at testing Lorest Everard, Ramond's father. They had set fire to the fertile wheat fields on their own side of the border and the resulting wildfire burned the border settlement of Garr to the ground. He retaliated so hard, they sacrificed an entire town for the opportunity to poison him three years later.

"You were a refugee, you lost your memory, and my aunt, who always wanted to have a daughter, saved you from the street. This is not a lie, by the way. My aunt always wanted a girl."

"I know," I said. "She gave up after the fifth miscarriage."

Solentine looked at me, shook his head, and wrote something on the paper.

"Won't the fresh ink give it away?"

"This isn't regular ink," he said. "It will lighten quickly in sunlight, and the scribe in the Demarr regional chamber is a friend of the family. This document will be slipped into the archive, and no one will be the wiser."

"But I have never appeared with your family. Won't people have doubts?"

"They are free to doubt. Their doubts don't matter. Only the proof matters and we have it right here. Should they wish to question my aunt and uncle, they will gladly confirm that you are their beloved daughter. Their household staff will swear on their lives that you are the young lady of that estate. Your status will be unassailable."

He was doing a very good job of selling it.

"All that remains is the name. Maggie is obviously short for something. What is it?"

I sighed.

"Magrane? Magdalinta? Margriete?" Solentine guessed. "Magrefondretta?"

"Now you're just making things up."

"I need a name," Solentine prompted.

"Marigold."

"Marigold?" Solentine raised his eyebrows.

"Yes."

My mother loved flowers and *M* names. She'd wanted to name me Magnolia, but since we lived on the corner of Magnolia Street and Magnolia Blossom Trail, she named me Marigold instead. While there were many Roses, Irises, and Violets, almost nobody was named Marigold.

Especially after *Marigold's Garden*.

When I was a toddler, I used to watch a cute cartoon about a yellow cow and her friends. They grew flowers in their garden and sang songs. The cow's name was Marigold. By the time I reached kindergarten, Marigold was everywhere: on toy shelves, on backpacks, on notebooks . . . The other kids made moo noises at me. I became Maggie in my third week of kindergarten in self-defense and had been Maggie ever since.

"It's a beautiful name," Everard said.

"It is unusual, but lovely." Solentine wrote it on the scroll, matching the existing handwriting with ridiculous precision, and pushed the paper toward me. "Sign here."

I wrote my new name in the empty space.

"Welcome to the family, Marigold Demarr." Solentine smiled at me and met Everard's gaze. "You are standing too close to my cousin. Remove yourself to the appropriate distance."

Everard tilted his head. Somehow the level of danger in the room shot way up. "Move me, Sol."

"Let's not do this," Solentine said.

Yes, absolutely. Let's not.

Everard's voice was almost casual. "When it happens—and it will—remember, you forced my hand."

Solentine blinked and shook his head. "Out of the question. Besides, didn't you want to keep your options open?"

"My options are not your concern."

And he had just told Solentine not to worry about it. Not only was he not moving away from me, his whole body communicated that no force in Rellas could shift him.

"This would never work. You don't even know her," Solentine said.

"What do you mean, Lord Dagarra?" Everard looked genuinely puzzled. "Of course I know her. She is Lady Marigold Demarr, your charming, clever cousin, granddaughter of the Iron Raptor and niece of my closest ally, Margrave Izarn Demarr. I've known her since she was nine years old. We've met every time I've come to visit your uncle's domain. You might say we are childhood acquaintances."

Solentine looked slightly green.

"Thank you for removing the obstacles in my way," Everard said. "So considerate of you."

"Sauven will lose what's left of his mind."

"It is a fine, long-standing tradition in my family to not give a fuck about what the Savarics think. I plan to continue it."

Solentine swore.

"You need me to legitimize this scheme," Everard said. "Have no fear, I will back you up. It's in my best interests."

What the hell were they on about? Somehow Everard had gotten the best of Solentine, but I couldn't quite figure it out.

It didn't matter right now. The adoption was done. I had a family, a lineage, and a crest. I was no longer a person without papers or status.

I had new parents.

Right now my real parents were probably still looking for me. The police search—if there had been one—had likely been called off. Too much time had passed. I was probably presumed dead, and my mom and dad were grieving.

I'd thought of them less and less as time went by. I only remembered them when something terrible happened and I felt sorry for myself. I had no idea how to go home and no clue where to even look for a way to get there, and meanwhile every day here was a fight for survival. People's lives depended on what I did next.

If I explained this adoption to my parents, they would understand. They would even encourage me. Anything to help me endure and survive.

It didn't matter. Signing that paper had felt like a betrayal.

Guilt smothered me like a heavy wet blanket. Everard said something, Solentine said something else, and I didn't hear any of it. I just sat there quietly, struggling to breathe.

Chapter 30

The carriage climbed a winding road veering through the steep hills southeast of the city. I pulled the curtain aside, letting the night air in. Kair Toren lay on my right and below. The night had barely begun, and windows and lanterns still glowed bright, the city shining with sparks of man-made fire like a swarm of fireflies cradled in the gloved hands of the dark, ridged hills. Above it the bottomless night sky soared, with Prata still full, and the other two moons in waxing crescent, Drao, red and angry, and Broe, glowing an eerie, magical green.

Across from me, Everard sat on the carriage bench, a liquid dark shadow. After Solentine had left, Everard helped me down the stairs. Two men came to see him, both wrapped in worn cloaks, probably his retainers. Solentine had referred to them as two human statues and that wasn't far from the truth—both looked stone-faced and stoic. They'd gone into our basement to discuss something. Now one of them was driving this carriage and the other one rode shotgun.

While Everard had his discussion, I went into the kitchen, drank very hot tea with too much honey in it, and nodded as Shana and Clover discussed the menu for the next week. I approved Clover's budget.

I should've gone into my study, but instead I loitered. I sat in the courtyard in the sun for a while, then in the kitchen with Shana, and after Clover came back, I made a fresh batch of soap, half with breberry and half with maidenflower. And every time I zoned out, a little voice in my head asked *What if the Butcher came back to life?*

By the time evening rolled around and Everard came to find me to take me on this trip, I was ready to rip my hair out.

There was no logic to it. Solentine was right. Dead people didn't rise again; unless they were me. This was trauma rearing its ugly head. *Remember how you died? How much it hurt? Remember beating a living person to death with a mace?*

I needed to put a period on this so I could move on. The Sun Margrave's assassination hung over my head like a sword. No matter what I did, Hreban seemed untouchable. If only I had some way to nuke that asshole . . .

"Dark thoughts?" Everard asked.

I glanced at him. Eventually we'd have to discuss my new family name, and I wasn't looking forward to that conversation. "Thinking of Chesterton's fence."

"And that would be?"

"It's a parable. A person comes to a fence erected across the road. It is blocking their way, so the person says, 'I don't see the point. Let's tear it down.' Another traveler comes along and says, 'If you don't know why it's there in the first place, I won't let you break it. Figure out why someone invested time and effort into building it and then we can talk about tearing it down.'"

He considered it. "There are three possible outcomes."

I nodded. "Suppose the fence is blocking the road to a mountain where medicinal herbs grow. The nearby village desires the herbs to prosper."

"They break the fence and profit," he said, "or they break the fence and a dursan hiding on the other side devours them; or they do nothing at all and continue as they were."

"Exactly. Hreban is a fence post."

He raised his eyebrows. "In what way?"

"I've read the code of laws." I'd found it in Derog's study. It was thick and I had mostly skimmed it. "At first glance, Sauven's power comes from military might, but unlike the transient dictatorships, the monarchy of Rellas has deep historical roots. It is steeped in tradition. Sauven isn't claiming the divine mandate to rule; nor is he terrorizing the population to maintain his power. The system endures because it enables most people in Rellas to survive. It works. Yes, there are those who exist in poverty and those who struggle, and there are not enough safeguards to keep the vulnerable from being preyed upon, but most people have shelter, food, and leisure. There is a thriving and numerous..." *middle class* "... group of people who not only survive but do well. Craftsmen, merchants, healers, government officials."

He nodded.

In terms of social order, Rellas was in the beginning stages of a mixed monarchy. It had abolished slavery and serfdom in favor of tenant farming. It had codified the principle that everyone, including the monarch, was subject to the code of laws. Those laws were created and ratified by the Konderar, a council that included representatives of the Eight Families, the knight orders, the Basilica, and most importantly the biggest guilds and merchant companies. Rellas was beginning to flirt with democratic ideas, but right now it was balanced on a sword's edge. It could either right itself and continue evolving or it could tumble backward into a dictatorship.

I would defend this fragile sprout of democracy with my life no matter how many deaths it took to win. It had to be nurtured and allowed to grow. Tyranny had to be avoided at all costs.

"The laws grant Sauven supreme military power. If he were to go mad and become a true terror, killing ordinary people, confiscating their property, and infringing on their freedoms and safety, what would happen?"

"It wouldn't happen, because the other Great Families would hold him in check," Everard said. "*I* would hold him in check."

"Precisely. The Great Families are a fence around Sauven. If he attempts to overstep his bounds, they will contain him, and if one of them steps out of line, Sauven will knock them down and put a new fence post in their place. Except that Sauven is too far gone. His sole focus right now is consolidating his power around Kiel because he must preserve the dynasty. It blinds him and creates an opportunity for someone like Hreban to seize power."

"The answer cannot be removing Sauven," Everard said. "He isn't ready to go and there are no worthy replacements. Kiel isn't fit to rule. It would mean civil war."

"Exactly. So we cannot replace Sauven, even if we somehow were capable of it, nor can we count on Sauven to check Hreban's climb. There is a third force that can exert influence here. They are the ones who constructed this fence in the first place. They bestowed the Great Families with power to keep themselves safe."

"The people of Rellas," he said.

I nodded. "To go back to the earlier story about the village by the mountain: As long as their lives are going well, the villagers will not risk destroying the fence. Like you said, there could be a dursan on the other side. However, if the village is ravaged by a plague, they will break that fence to pieces and use the wood to light their way up the mountain. Probable death is better than certain death. We must convince Rellas that Hreban is a plague. We must show it in a huge, overwhelming way, so his lineage, wealth, and status do not matter and Rellas no longer holds him immune."

"How?"

"I'm trying to figure that out. We must demonstrate to everyone that in spite of Sauven, the balance of power still works."

He studied me from the gloom. "You are very dangerous, Maggie. I don't think you realize the full extent of it."

"If only." I sighed. "Maggie the Useless would be a better fit."

The carriage slowed and came to a stop. A knock sounded through the front wall.

"We're here," the driver called out.

Everard got up, opened the door, stepped out, and offered me his arm. I put my hand on his forearm. He helped me out of the carriage and I stepped away from him.

A cold wind fanned me. I pulled my cloak tighter around myself.

In front of us, the road ran into the sheer rock face, as if a hill had been split in half with a knife like a birthday cake. A fifty-foot gate protruded from the mountain, carved from the living rock—two blocky towers connected by a walkway. Strange animals wound around the towers, depicted in contorted shapes, the carvings so ancient and worn, you could barely make out the edges. Between the towers a dark cave gaped like a hungry mouth.

"Drigildarg. The city of the dead," Everard said. "And here comes our guide."

A faint yellow glow appeared in the darkness. A few moments and a guard emerged carrying a torch. She waited for us to approach and went back into the mountain.

We followed the guard into the gloom.

The tunnel was long and dark, swirling with a draft from deep within the mountain. The torch sputtered, casting chaotic highlights onto the walls. The sound of our steps sent echoes bouncing through the tunnel.

The air grew colder.

A strange feeling gripped me. I was walking through the tunnel next to Everard and I was also back on the table, with the Butcher leaning over me, cutting into my body over and over. The two realities overlapped, both tangible and illusory at the same time.

I killed him. I'd been powerless on that table, but I had taken my power back when I turned his face into mush. I'd reclaimed my sanity and my life. I would not let him haunt me.

Demons were meant to be confronted. I would face mine.

The tunnel ended, opening into a vast cavern steeped in gloom. A stone floor of big square tiles, uneven and worn down by countless feet, stretched in front of us. Here and there, tall stone pillars soared into the darkness above, some crowned by glowing lanterns. The light of the lanterns slid over the pitted stone, playing on the ancient carvings on the cavern walls. In the distance, deeper darkness tinting the twilight offered hints of passageways, framed with stone arches and guarded by fearsome statues.

Kair Toren was only an hour away, but it might as well have been across the ocean. This space felt like its own world, sacred and terrifying. Being in it filled me with a vague dread. I had a distinct feeling that it was better not to look at it too closely, because I might find something I couldn't deal with.

"Do you need to rest?" Everard asked.

"No." My legs still hurt like hell, despite the huge dose of bitter powder I'd taken before I left, but it didn't matter. I needed to get this done.

We came to a fork. In front of us three stone gateways led deeper into the cave, on the left, on the right, and straight ahead. The passageways on the right and straight ahead were lit by lanterns.

Our guide stopped. Everard turned left and I walked with him.

The stone arch defining the left passage was so old, it had been worn nearly smooth. The darkness within it shivered like a living thing. Something was watching us from that deep gloom. I couldn't see it or hear it, but I felt someone there.

We approached the archway. Everard held out a silver noma.

A man congealed from the darkness. He was wrapped in a tattered cloak, dark haired, with dark brown skin, and when the light of the lantern caught his face, his eyes were completely white and opaque, like the silver coin he'd just taken.

The man held out a rope. The other end of it disappeared into his garments. Everard took the rope with his left hand and offered me his right.

None of this was in the books. We were going to the Shears' Larder, the hidden cave within the morgue where Solentine stashed bodies he wanted to keep on ice, but the text never described how to actually reach it.

I put my hand into Everard's. His warm fingers closed around mine. It felt like someone had tied a lifeline to my waist in the middle of a storm.

The man turned without a word and disappeared into the passageway. Everard followed him and I let him lead me into the underground night. It wasn't just dark, it was pitch-black, the gloom so thick, I couldn't see anything in front of my face.

We kept going. There was no sense of progress or direction. It felt like we were walking in circles. The air was freezing now. I shivered within my cloak.

Ahead an eerie greenish glow fought through the darkness. We passed through a narrow doorway into a cavern. It must've been a meeting hall or some sort of formal chamber in its previous life—the walls still bore hints of carved reliefs and here and there columns jutted from the ground, holding up the arched ceiling. But the war between man and nature was long over and nature had clearly won. The human presence was a distant echo. Fungi had claimed the chamber. Huge, shaped like corals, they climbed up the walls and filled the floor, glowing with green. Around them grum mushrooms sprouted, the same type that now grew in our cellar back home, keeping our food from spoiling.

Between the fungi, a dozen stone slabs rose like altars. Most were empty, but the three in the front each held something.

The blind guide led us to the nearest slab and stepped aside, revealing an unmistakably human shape under a shroud of pale cloth. A corpse.

I let go of Everard, marched to the slab, and pulled back the fabric. The Butcher's body rested on the stone, his clothes splattered with blood. He looked exactly as I remembered. Everard was right. He didn't have a face anymore.

The blind guide withdrew, back into the darkness of the passageway.

I stared at the Butcher. Here he was, dead. Dead as a doornail. Permanently unalived.

Everard pulled out a dagger and pressed it into my hand. I almost jumped. He nodded at the corpse. "Stab him."

I gripped the dagger.

"Do you need help, Maggie?"

Hell no. I raised the dagger and drove it into the Butcher's stomach. The corpse didn't move. It didn't even bleed. The knife just went in like I had stabbed a piece of meat.

Everard's voice was almost wistful. "He is dead. I wish he wasn't dead, so I could kill him, but he is a corpse. In this world, Maggie, dead is dead. I know of only one exception. I watched you come back to life. The wound on your neck knitted itself closed and then the blood on your throat evaporated. It was as if it never happened."

The Butcher hadn't regenerated. His wounds were still there, his blood was still there.

Everard reached into his clothes, pulled out a dark cloth, and held it out to me. I yanked the dagger out of the body, took the cloth, and wiped the blade.

"Better?" Everard asked.

I nodded.

"I will bring you here every day if need be. You can hit him, you can spit on him, you can stab him. Whatever you want to do to reassure yourself that he is gone. We will do this however long you want, until you get tired of it. Until the sight of his corpse is just a boring fact."

I cleared my throat. "No need. I've gotten what I came for."

"Good. Let's go home."

Planter 27

"My lady!"

I bolted straight up in bed just in time to see someone rush to me through the dark bedroom. Sushi saw them, too, and snapped her teeth.

The figure jerked back and hissed in Clover's voice. "There is vermin on your bed!"

I hugged my guard vermin to keep her from attacking. Sushi growled but didn't bite me, which was a win.

Behind Clover, Kaiden ran into the room, shut the door, barred it, and whipped around, illuminated by the moonlight streaming through the window. He was gripping a dagger.

"What's going on?" I whispered.

"We're under attack!" Clover whispered back. "His Grace told us to get in here, lock the door, and guard you."

That explained the knife and little else.

I slipped off the bed and quietly opened the window. Prata's moonlight was bright and silver, and every detail of the courtyard was clearly visible. On the right, a rope hung off the outer wall. I pressed against the side of the window. Clover and Kaiden crouched by the windowsill.

A group of dark figures emerged from our entrance tunnel. They had sent someone over the wall and that scout had opened the door for them.

One, two, three . . . Nine.

Who the hell were they?

Had the Conquerors discovered that Everard was here somehow? No, that couldn't be right. Climbing over the wall and sneaking in wasn't their style. They would've brought Wynand Bors, and he would've pounded on the door and bellowed loud enough to wake the entire neighborhood.

Was this Silveren's Redeemers? It seemed like the kind of clandestine crap they would pull.

Was this Hreban retaliating for the Butcher?

Whoever they were, they'd found us.

The door below opened, and Everard walked into the open. He hadn't bothered with a coif or a hood, and he was carrying a huge sword.

This wasn't Reynald's sword or Everard's usual weapon. The books had described Everard's sword in excruciating detail. The Emerald Blaze had a blade like a longsword, with a basket hilt like a rapier, and it was about forty-three inches long. When Everard fought, speed and precision were most important, and protection was his weakness. That hilt guarded his hand, because if he dropped his sword, the battle would be over for everyone.

The monstrosity in his hands right now was at least fifty-five inches long, with a guard that looked like something that should be growing on a longhorn bull's head. He would have to swing it with two hands. That wasn't how Everard fought.

The intruders spotted him and fanned out. Two of them, carrying short, brutal-looking spears, moved to the front.

Everard gripped his sword with both hands, leaned back on his left foot, and raised the weapon to his eye level, holding the massive blade parallel to the floor, pointing at his enemy. His wrists were crossed.

What the hell was going on? Was he going to take them all on by himself?

Behind Everard, the door thudded, and the Magnar brothers tore out, weapons in hand. Lute was half dressed—his tunic loose—and pale, gripping his sword. Will looked like he hadn't even gone to bed.

Everard didn't pay them any mind.

Gort burst out of the door.

The brothers flanked Everard, weapons ready.

"Harst!" Gort snarled.

Will and Lute backed away in unison, falling into a loose stance by the wine tree. Will caught the shaft of his axe with his left hand, while Lute rested his blade on his shoulder.

A battle command. All soldiers in Rellas drilled to instantly obey them, and that one meant hold position. Gort had been a kir, a sergeant, first in the King's Army and then as a mercenary. When he barked an order, disobeying wasn't an option. They wouldn't move until Gort told them to.

One of the intruders stopped just like the brothers.

"Gort?" he asked, his voice uncertain.

Gort turned to him. "Tillmar?"

Tillmar backed away from the group and parked himself by the wall, his sword down.

"What the fuck are you doing?" one of the attackers snarled.

"I'm done," Tillmar told him.

"The fuck you are!"

"Today," Everard snapped.

The eight remaining intruders charged.

They came at Everard in a pack, like wolves trying to encircle a deer, the two spearmen in the lead.

The taller spearman lunged, aiming for Everard's stomach. The Sleepless Duke knocked the spear to the left with his arm and drove the point of his sword into the man's face. The second spearman thrust from the side, and Everard shoved the first intruder at him. The second attacker stumbled, trying to avoid the body. The point of his spear dipped. Everard smashed the flat of his sword against it. The spear touched the ground. Everard stepped on it. The spearman bent his knees, trying to wrench the weapon up, and Everard stabbed at his neck, lightning fast.

It happened so quick, less than two seconds, and then the two spearmen collapsed, while Everard was on his feet in a circle of attackers.

He dropped the point of his sword down, almost touching the ground.

A large man charged at him, swinging a longsword in a devastating overhand strike. Everard stepped to the side, redirecting the descending sword with the flat of his blade. The swordsman realized he was exposed and tried to jerk his arm to the right, but Everard's sword was faster. He struck. The man's head drooped, barely connected to his neck by a sliver of flesh. He took another step then crashed down to the stone floor.

An axeman chopped at Everard from the left. He shied back. The axe whistled by, but another swordsman on the right was waiting, and their blade grazed Everard's back.

Oh god.

Everard thrust at the swordsman, too fast to follow. The swordsman's back was to us, and I didn't see exactly what happened, but Everard's blade slid either into his throat or his upper chest. The swordsman stumbled away, clutching at himself, folded in half, and fell.

The axeman came at Everard swinging. Everard dodged, left, right, floating like his body was made of water. His sword sliced, and the axeman dropped the axe, clenched their arm, and tried to back away. Everard thrust and recovered in a fraction of a second. The axeman went down.

Five bodies in the courtyard.

The three remaining attackers hesitated.

"He's bleeding," one of the shadows growled.

Everard took a step back, toward the southern wall directly opposite our tower. The intruders followed.

Another step.

Another.

If he kept going, eventually his back would hit our stables.

Why wasn't anyone helping him? Why wasn't I helping him? I opened my mouth to tell Kaiden to bring me a bow. I had never shot one before, but I could shoot a gun. I would manage.

Everard stopped.

The intruders closed in on him, weapons ready.

His eyes ignited with a shocking, murderous green. Black smoke shot out of him, licking the pavers of the courtyard. Brilliant green Fatefire ran up the blade.

Tillmar dropped to one knee, head bowed.

Everard lunged, light on his feet. His sword struck, slicing at the nearest attacker. The top half of the intruder slid aside and crashed to the ground. Clover gasped and clamped her hand over her mouth.

The two remaining swordsmen had no time to react. Everard was coming, unstoppable, fast, his sword slicing like the Grim Reaper's scythe. The green blade kissed the second shadow's neck, and the head rolled off its shoulders. The third one turned to run, and the blade severed their spine.

He'd cut them down like they were made of paper.

I realized I had squeezed the windowsill so hard, my fingers hurt.

If anyone enters this house, even if they appear by magic, I will know and I will kill them.

Well, he kept his word.

Everard strode to the kneeling intruder, the glow of the Fatefire throwing green light on his face. The black smoke curled around his feet. He looked like a demon, he killed like one, and now he was moving to take this man's life and nothing in the world could stop him.

"I surrender," Tillmar squeezed out, his voice hoarse.

"My lord!" Gort called. "I know this man. He will talk."

"I haven't decided if I want him to talk," Everard said.

He reached the man. The sword rose.

The man braced himself. His shoulders shuddered.

"Please don't!" I called out.

Everard looked up at me. A long moment passed.

The man stared at the ground.

"Don't move," Everard told him.

The man froze as if petrified.

The Fatefire died.

"I know you are there," Everard said.

A figure stood up on the north side of our house wearing a ninja-like get up. One of Solentine's people. Had to be. He'd left a babysitter for us.

"Get down here," Everard ordered. "I have a job for you."

The figure tossed a rope down and slipped into our courtyard.

Everard looked in Gort's direction. The old mercenary hurried over.

"Take him to the basement."

Gort nodded to his sons. They flanked Tillmar like two hounds and herded him inside.

Everard looked up at me.

"Don't walk down the stairs by yourself. I will come and get you."

※

I chased Kaiden out, Clover helped me throw on one of my two housedresses—it still hurt to raise my arms—and headed for the stairs.

"My lady, your hair!"

"Never mind."

Someone had broken into our home trying to murder us. The condition of my hair was the least of my worries.

I marched out the door and to the stairs. Everard was already there, blocking the way. He saw me. I was on the top of the stairs, and he was one step down. We were almost the same height, and I saw his expression shift. His eyes darkened. A slight smile lifted the corners of his mouth. My brain identified the look and screeched to a halt.

For a moment we just stared at each other.

"Your hair is down," he said. The smile got deeper.

In Rellas, the only time a man would see a woman with her hair down without any sort of decoration would be if they were about to climb into the same bed together.

"For crying out loud, it's not like I ran out here wearing nothing but lace and leather."

His eyes went wide. He opened his mouth. Nothing came out.

And that was exactly the wrong thing to say. Me and my big mouth.

I jerked my hands up, rolling my hair into a bun. "Clover! I need a hairpin!"

She darted out of my bedroom, thrust a hairpin at me, and ran back inside. I pinned my bun in place. "There, it's fine now."

"Leather and lace. I'm still trying to picture it."

"Don't."

"Is it not usually either or? How would one combine the two . . ." He gave me a contemplative glance.

"You need to broaden your horizons. Are you all right?"

"Why wouldn't I be?"

"You were cut."

"I wasn't. I'm wearing chainmail under my clothes."

He moved like that while wearing chainmail? I had lifted some up a few days ago when Gort was working on it. It had weighed about thirty pounds.

"Take my arm, Maggie. I don't want you falling down the stairs."

Grrr. Unfortunately, while I could move okay on flat ground, the stairs were still a problem. I took his arm. We started down slowly, taking the steps one at a time. Each time my foot touched the stone, a spike of pain shot up into my leg.

"I get why going up the stairs is hard, but we're going down the stairs. Why does it hurt more?"

"It's the force of all of your weight landing on your foot. Goes straight into the knee. The first thing the heavy-armor knights learn is to never jump off their horse or they will have no knees left by their middle age. Would you like me to carry you? You can explain more about the leather and lace to me."

"No." I'd had enough bridal carry for a lifetime. "You just fought. Aren't you tired?"

"From *that*?"

Of course, why would anyone be tired from hacking at eight people with an oversized chunk of metal? Silly me.

He stopped on the landing and didn't move.

"Shouldn't we be going downstairs to interrogate that man?"

"Let him sweat. The more he waits, the louder he'll sing. Thank you for playing along. It was just the right touch."

He never meant to kill Tillmar. He had just wanted to intimidate him into talking. He thought I was in on his plan, and I would absolutely take credit for that.

"Any time."

We stood on the landing close enough for Solentine to have kittens if he saw us. My hand was on his arm.

"Are they Redeemers?"

He shook his head. "Not good enough."

"Then who?"

"We'll find out shortly."

We stood together. A minute crawled by.

"Solentine left us a babysitter."

He made a noise halfway between *mhm* and a growl.

"Still upset that I took his offer, I see."

"It was a regrettable decision, my lady."

There was more than one way to say "my lady." Gort said it without any thought behind it, as a common courtesy. Clover said it like a pledge of loyalty. Just now Everard had said it like I belonged to him. Like I was his lover. That "my lady" was a declaration of exclusivity, desire, and intent.

Oh no. The Sleepless Duke had regrouped. I'd frustrated his plans for me by becoming a Demarr, but he had formulated a new strategy. Letting me slip through his fingers wasn't an option. He still needed the knowledge in my head, and I'd opened this door by planting a vision of me in a sexy nightie in his. Brilliant. Simply brilliant.

"That's a bit hypocritical, Your Grace. In my place, you would've done the same."

"In your place, I would have chosen the wiser option. I can protect you better than the Demarrs."

"Yes, but Solentine offers no surprises. I'm familiar with the way he thinks. I don't even know you."

It was true. I had been in Solentine's head, in Hreban's, in Sauven's, but never in Everard's. I knew what he did and how he reacted but never why.

"Then I will have to introduce myself."

He started down the stairs and since my hand was still on his arm, I stepped down with him.

"My name is Ramond vi Everard. Son of Lorest and Elia Everard. Lord of Selva, Cataren, and Audiar."

He took a step.

"Wielder of the Fatefire."

Another step.

"Lord Commander of the Selva Knightage."

Every time we moved, he delivered a new title.

"Lord Commander of the Everard Knightage."

Step.

"Commodore of the Falcon Fleet."

Step.

"Duke of the Realm."

And that told you exactly how little he valued Rellas's title. He had put all the Selva-related honors first.

"Lord Protector of the Northern Coast."

Step.

"Ruin of the Okula."

He got that title when he stopped the Third Invasion. Sauven had to officially bestow it on him because of the historical precedent, and it had nearly killed him to do it.

"Owner of three castles and one hundred fifty thousand kare of land."

Although he ruled the whole of Selva, his personal lands were the size of South Carolina. I knew that one from the forums. What was next, his prized Pokémon card collection?

We'd reached the end of the stairs and continued down the hallway toward the stairway to the basement.

"To summarize, I'm powerful, wealthy, and unattached."

So nice of him to throw that last one in there. Not unmarried. Unattached.

"Interesting choice of words."

He stopped by the door leading to the basement staircase. "Your turn."

"Maggie of no name, poor, titleless, and landless. No fleets or castles."

He flashed a smile, like a hint of a lethal blade in the scabbard. "You have some titles of your own. You forgot Undying."

"Yes, well, there is that."

"Keeper of Secrets."

Funny he should mention that.

"A woman of interesting fashion sense . . ."

"Would you like to know who you will marry?"

"Enlighten me."

"Omelyana of Gor."

He blinked. "Ah. It seems I will require the Gorynian Guard in the future. But why would they seek an alliance with Selva?"

"There will be an earthquake along the White Beard Strait. It will drown their main port."

He rocked his head back and forth, mulling it over. "Makes sense."

"You will manipulate her until she falls in love with you. She'll live for the crumbs of your attention. Your presence will become her reward for anticipating Selva's needs."

"Mhm." He bent toward me slightly. "But will she be happy in my presence?"

I opened my mouth. Shoot. "Yes."

Deliriously happy, in fact. Giddy. Thrilled.

"Well, that's something to keep in mind, then, isn't it?"

You arrogant ass.

He swung the door open and offered me his arm. "Let's see what we can squeeze out of our guest."

Chapter 31

Last week, while recovering from their training sessions, the Magnars had remodeled the basement. They'd trashed the child-sized bunk beds and hung a door for the latrine. Gort had whitewashed the walls, and we'd used some of the lye I'd bought to banish the bloodstains.

The basement looked completely different now, with two plain wooden tables and benches on both sides and hooks and pegs on the walls that supported weapons. When Everard was Reynald, he'd planned to turn it into an armory/last-stand room. It still made me slightly queasy, but I would get used to it.

Gort sat at the left table on a bench. Lute was next to him. He was looking two shades paler than usual and as he turned to glance at us, he winced a little. Will leaned against the other table. The prisoner sat in a chair in the middle of the room.

His hood was down, revealing short brown hair salted with silver and the face of a man in his early forties who'd lived a rough life. A small scar marked the flesh under his right eye. Another crossed his nose and three more cut his left cheek, all old and healed but still clearly visible. A short beard hugged his jaw, dark and touched with gray. His brown eyes were worried, but his expression said this was a man who knew he was screwed, and he wasn't surprised because that was the way his life rolled. He'd accepted it but he was bitter.

Everard helped me to a bench. I sat down. He leaned against the table next to me, arms crossed on his chest.

Tillmar looked at him and swallowed.

"How do you and Gort know each other?" I asked.

"Gort was my kir years ago, my lady," Tillmar said. "Then we fought for the same mercenary company for a while."

"The Strikers," Gort said. "It was a decent outfit, up until the Galador campaign."

"What happened?" I asked.

"Lost half the people and all of the officers in one battle," Tillmar said. "Everyone went their separate ways after that."

"Why didn't you fight tonight?" I asked.

Tillmar sighed. "I've known the kids since Will was twelve. I've got two daughters and a son. I wasn't going to fight Gort's boys. A man has to have a boundary he won't cross."

"And yet, here you are," Everard said. "Breaking into a house of someone you don't know in the middle of the night to kill everyone inside."

The mercenary didn't quite cringe, but he came close to it.

"Who sent you?"

"Otrade."

Gort grimaced. "How in the void did you end up with that piece of shit?"

Tillmar sighed. "I was a kir with Saubra."

"Damn," Gort said.

"Yeah."

I looked at Gort.

"The Saubra Company got hired to settle a family dispute between two brothers," Gort explained. "They did their job, took the castle, and then found out that their broker had been bought off. The lord who hired them didn't get the king's blessing."

In Rellas, two nobles couldn't fight a private war without a dispensation from the Throne. There was an entire process, involving filing the proper papers and then waiting to see if Sauven approved them.

"You never know what King Sauven will do, my lady," Tillmar said. "When shit like that happens, sometimes it's a fine and sometimes it's scorched earth. The Saubra mercenaries went to sleep in the gutted castle and woke up with the King's Army on their doorstep. Everyone kir and above was put to the sword, including the lord. They held the trial right before the castle gates."

"How did you get out?" Gort asked.

"I'd taken off the night before. Just had that feeling." Tillmar shook his head. "Cursed brokers. Did you hear about Filderon? He got paid off to throw away a company. Eighty bodies. Somebody found out before they set out and pinned the evidence to his chest with a knife. Drugh was going to make an issue of it, but that shit stank so much that he backed right off."

"What's the world coming to?" Gort said with a straight face.

"Exactly," Tillmar said.

"How does it work?" I asked Gort. "Is the Throne looking for Tillmar?"

"He left before the trial, so he was never officially convicted," Gort said. "They were mostly after the lord, the broker, and the officers. The kirs got thrown in there to make a louder noise, but they aren't important enough on their own. It happened a year ago, and he isn't hard to find. If they haven't picked him up by now, they won't bother. He's probably safe but nobody will want him on their roster."

"I can't get hired," Tillmar said. "I've been trying for a year. I've got three kids, and this is all I know how to do. My daughter needs redblossom powder every day."

I knew that one from the books. Redblossom root treated diabetes.

The mercenary shook his head. "I haven't earned a den in the last four months, so I was desperate. I ran into Otrade in a tavern. The man is foul, but I was at the end of my rope, and he put fifty dens on the table in front of me. Said he was running a crew for a Great Family."

"Which one?" Everard asked.

"The Hrebans. He just had two spots open up."

And here was our answer. Hreban had finally found us. Now we had to find out why. Would he send more when he found out the first group failed?

"When was this?" Everard asked.

"The ninth of Planter. This was my first job for him," Tillmar said. "Had I known it was this kind of work, I would've never taken the contract. I would've left that money on the table and got out of there."

There was a contract. Very in character for Hreban. He didn't trust people because he could see into their hearts. He trusted signatures, and he was compulsive about it. He'd probably made the Butcher sign a contract . . .

Wait.

"Do you remember what the contract said?" I asked.

"I have it here." Tillmar reached into his jerkin and pulled out a folded piece of paper. "I haven't signed it yet. I was supposed to give it back to Otrade today."

"Where is Otrade now?" Everard asked.

"In the courtyard. He was the one with the southern spear. I sat there and stared at this thing, and something told me not to sign it. So I waited."

I scanned the contract.

> In the Year of 3044, in the Month of Planter, on the 9th Day . . . Blah, blah . . . Let it be known to all who read or hear these words that on this day, a solemn bond of loyalty and obedience is forged between the undersigned:
>
> Lord Ulmar Hreban, Baron of the Realm, Lord of Lower Berem, Vaterna, . . . title-title-title . . . (hereinafter referred to as The Liege)
> and
> Dorr Tillmar, a mercenary of sound mind and unwavering resolve (hereinafter referred to as The Sworn).

What . . . I read out loud. "The Sworn pledges unwavering loyalty to the Liege, agreeing to carry out all commands given, without question or hesitation. This oath includes, but is not limited to:

1. Engaging in acts of violence or subterfuge as directed.
2. Carrying out deeds that may contravene the laws of the kingdom, provided such acts serve the Liege's interests.
3. Protecting the Liege's life, holdings, and secrets at all costs, even to the peril of the Sworn . . ."

I glanced at Tillmar.

He sighed.

I skipped ahead. "Article II: Secrecy and Discretion. The Sworn shall safeguard the existence and terms of this pledge with absolute secrecy. Any revelation of the contract's nature to any third party shall be deemed an act of betrayal. Should such betrayal occur, the Sworn forfeits all rights to life and property . . ."

Gort swore under his breath.

"It gets better." I kept reading. "The Sworn acknowledges that their service absolves the Liege of all culpability for the actions carried out under this agreement. No word, act, or failure of the Sworn may be attributed to the Liege in any formal or informal proceedings, nor used to implicate him in wrongdoing."

"That's not a pledge of loyalty," Will growled. "It's a slave contract."

"It is. This oath is to remain in effect for the entirety of the Sworn's natural life or until the Liege sees fit to release the Sworn from service. The only way out is to die in service of Ulmar Hreban."

"And what does he get for signing his life away?" Everard asked.

"In return for this fealty, the Liege shall grant:

1. A monthly stipend of 128 dens, to be disbursed on the first day of each month.
2. Lodging, arms, and provisions necessary for the Sworn to complete the Liege's tasks."

Tillmar looked down at his feet.

"That's four dens a day," Lute said. "I get five."

"You're not me," Tillmar said. "You still have your good name."

"This is . . . There had to be something else out there," Gort said.

"There wasn't," Tillmar said, his voice tired and bitter.

It wasn't that Hreban was asking for something unexpected. When a person pledged their loyalty to their liege, it was understood that they would do all the liege required even if it cost them their life. It was the way he had gone about it.

Most people wanted something to believe in, and when they found it, they gave it their trust. It was as true in this world as in ours. Back home, people went above and beyond for the company that employed them, hoping they would be treated well and fairly compensated. They gave to charity, directing their money to help someone who needed it most. They voted, expecting those they elected to look after their interests. All of these human transactions hinged on trust.

Pledging your loyalty took that trust and pushed it a step further. When you swore an oath to your liege, that oath was a double-edged sword. The sworn promised to lay down their life should the liege require it, but the liege swore to defend and value the sworn. The oath served as a mutual promise of protection, a matter of honor and integrity. Choosing to pledge yourself was a decision of grave importance, and it required respect and dignity from everyone involved.

This contract reduced that pledge of loyalty to a financial transaction. Tillmar promised absolute obedience and Hreban promised nothing except prompt payment. Will was right. Tillmar had sold himself.

Why even write this at all? It wasn't enforceable or legally binding. Moreover, a pledge of loyalty required witnesses. If the sworn betrayed their vow, those who were there would know of their shame. This contract was completely secret. It forbade Tillmar from even mentioning its existence.

Did Hreban just get off on having it in writing? He clearly valued this oath, judging by the paper. It was thick, with strands of silver thread woven through. The "good stuff" from my study didn't even come close.

A weird feeling pressed on my fingers as I slid them near the signature line.

"Tell me everything about tonight," Everard said. "Be detailed."

Had I imagined it? I slipped my fingers near the signature spot again. Here it was, a weird pressure, like trying to push two magnets of the same polarity together.

"I rent a cheap room in the Tangle's south end," Tillmar said. "I was asleep. A runner came in the middle of the night and told me to go to Bluestone Plaza. I got my gear and went."

It felt like the paper was trying to repel me. I ran my hand all over it. Only the bottom quarter of the contract was affected, directly around the signature line. I couldn't even touch it.

"There were eight of us there: Otrade, Praga, and six others I didn't know. Otrade said we were about to raid a house. We were to secure it and leave as many as we could alive, because he had to ask some questions. He kept asking Praga if she was sure she had the right house, and she kept telling him that she had followed the carriage all the way from the warehouse, and that he needed more people, because the man who'd carried the woman out made her skin crawl."

It made sense now. Hreban had invested too much into the Butcher to leave him unattended. He told Otrade to keep an eye on it, and Otrade had sent Praga. She saw Everard carry me out and the Shears set the warehouse on fire. She must've followed our carriage straight to our house.

The only question now was, had Otrade reported to Hreban right away or did he wait? If I were Otrade, I would've waited until I could question us. The bad news would go over better with some kind of explanation attached. *My lord, your pet serial killer was murdered, but I found the people responsible, and I have them under lock and key. What would you like us to do?*

"Was Praga in the courtyard, too?" I asked.

Tillmar nodded. "She was the one who scaled the wall."

There was no way to tell how much Hreban knew. He could know nothing or everything.

"I had a bad feeling about this," Tillmar said. "I almost didn't show up. That's life, you know. It's . . . short."

Tillmar's bad feelings were right on the money. If I didn't interfere right now, Everard could kill him. Tillmar was a loose end that needed to be tied up.

"Is he any good?" I asked Gort.

"Yes," Gort said. "Good fighter. Smart."

"Is he lying about his family?"

"No."

I looked at Everard. "Can I have him?"

He shrugged. "Do you have a use for him?"

I nodded.

"Very well."

"Will, bring the wooden box, please."

The wooden box was where I kept some of our money.

"Yes, my lady."

Will left.

I rubbed the contract some more. Still a no-go on touching the signature line.

Will returned with the box. I opened it. Otrade had put a half-noma, fifty dens, on the bar. I would need to beat that. I took a noma out.

Tillmar's face went completely flat.

I looked at the silver coin. "Gort?"

"Yes, my lady."

"How much redblossom powder can a noma purchase?"

"Six months' worth," Gort said.

"We better make it two then." I put a second noma on top of the first. "Two nomas a month. Sent to your family."

Gort made 224 dens a month, more than two nomas. I was offering Tillmar a war rate.

Tillmar met my eyes. "What do I have to do?"

"In the morning, go to the Redeemer Tower. Tell them your sad Saubra Company story. Give them lots of details so they have no trouble confirming it. You dream of your friends who were put to death, and when you lie awake at night, they whisper to you from the darkness. You question why you lived, and they didn't. You wonder if you could've saved them. Can you sell that to them?"

Tillmar nodded.

"Good. Look tormented as if the guilt has gnawed at you from the inside until you became a hollow husk of a man."

Lute looked taken aback. Gort did, too. They hadn't seen this side of me.

"Yesterday you thought of ending it all, but you dreamt of a knight in dented armor holding a sage standard on a plain wooden spear. He called to you. You've come to pledge yourself to the Redeemer Order."

"What if they ask about my family? Redeemer pay is shit."

Gort was right. Tillmar was smart.

"Tell the Redeemers that you're no good to your family, since nobody will hire you. You have failed as a soldier, husband, and father. They are better off without you. You cannot live with yourself, and you wish to be reborn. Can you do that?"

Tillmar nodded. "I can."

"Do you think your wife can pretend to be sad and abandoned or do we need to lie to her?"

"Benna is smart. She will play her part," Tillmar promised. "She won't tell a soul."

"Good. You will write two letters. One explaining the true story and the other one so she can show it to people when they come asking."

"What do I need to do at the Redeemers?"

"Be the best Redeemer recruit they ever had. Be humble, pious, and dedicated. Volunteer for unpleasant tasks. Say as little as possible, just show up when they need you."

He nodded.

"They will confine you while they verify your story, so you won't be able to leave the Tower for the first month or so, but that will pass. The first few times you go out, you will be watched. When you feel safe, go to Taryz Teahouse and order Thieves Brew with a sambocade. They will tell you they're out of sambocades. Order something else instead, enjoy your tea and go back to the Tower. The next time you come back to Taryz, ask for the sambocades again and there will be instructions for you."

Tillmar looked past me at Everard. "If I do this, will me and mine be black and green?"

Everything stopped. The three Magnars went still. Tillmar stared at Everard as if he were drowning and the Sleepless Duke was holding a life jacket.

"Do this well, and there will be a place for you and your family in Selva," Everard said.

Tillmar looked at Gort. "I want to do this right."

The older mercenary took Tillmar's sword off the table and passed it to him. Tillmar got up.

Gort moved to the aisle to stand on Everard's right. Lute forced himself to his feet and joined his father. On the other side Will stood up and took a position to Everard's left. Everyone was getting up.

Everard offered me his hand. "My lady."

Clearly, whatever this was required standing. I put my hand in his, stood up, and tried to turn toward Will. There was a space there. Instead, Everard gently but firmly maneuvered me to stand next to him.

"Your Grace . . ."

"This involves both of us."

Tillmar dropped down on one knee, his blade upright, resting with its point on the floor.

I shut up.

The Magnars stood like sentinels, solemn and silent, their faces grave. The way they held themselves transformed the room into a sacred place, as if the walls of our basement had melted away and we stood in the center of the Red Basilica.

Tillmar bowed his head.

"I swear upon my life and the lives of all I hold dear to pledge my blade, body, and soul to the Lord of Selva. His word is my law, his cause is my cause, and there are none above him. So shall it be until the end of my days."

A formal oath. Oh wow.

Dark smoke boiled out of Everard. His eyes turned a piercing, scalding green. He spoke as if etching each word into stone.

"I, Lord of Selva, accept you into my service. From this moment on, you are my sword, and I am your shield. Should you be wronged, I will give you justice. Should you fall in my service, your loved ones will not know hunger. Rise, Tillmar of Selva, and sheathe your blade until I have a need of it."

Tillmar rose and put away his sword.

"In three months, after the Redeemers are satisfied, I will move your family north," Everard said. "They will be protected and well taken care of."

"Thank you, my lord."

The smoke melted into nothing, and Everard's eyes went back to their normal light green. Hreban and Everard. One had tried to buy a man, the other changed the course of Tillmar's life with five sentences. That much power concentrated in the hands of one person. It was at once awe-inspiring and terrifying. There was a reason our society had moved away from that. Mostly.

Everard turned to me. "Are you ready to go, my lady?"

"Yes, Your Grace."

Everard offered me his arm. I rested my hand on it.

Behind us Gort muttered, "You are one lucky sonovabitch, Tillmar. Let's get you some ink and paper."

The Shears agent was waiting for us in the hallway. She was lean, with dark hair, sandy skin, and narrow dark eyes. Her features were pleasant and ordinary, and nothing about her drew the eye at first glance. I'd met literally a dozen women just like her at the Dog Market. And then you looked into her eyes and realized she could kill you three times before you hit the ground.

Avaria, Solentine's second-in-command. He wasn't joking around.

"It is done, my lord," she said.

I could see the courtyard through the window, lit with lanterns. A whole team of people in black and gray swarmed over the bodies. She must've called in reinforcements from the Shears.

"You have all of the measurements?" Everard asked.

"Yes."

"You noted the blood spatter?"

"Yes."

"Take the first five bodies and Velpor's corpse to the edge of Hreban's territory and re-create the scene of their death. Place Velpor's body in the spot I told you to mark. Have someone of the same height drop the sword next to his body. Make sure that the five bodies are deposited first, then Velpor. Arrange the bodies exactly as they fell, complete with blood and their weapons. Wynand Bors isn't wise but he's skilled and his mind is sharp. Do not make a careless mistake like placing a weapon too far out of reach."

She nodded. "Yes, my lord."

This explained so much. In the morning, the Conquerors would find Velpor with five corpses. They would conclude that he was jumped and murdered.

The Order of Conquerors ran on loyalty. When one of their own was injured, they pursued the offender to the end, and they were relentless. Instead of turning the city upside down looking for the Sleepless Duke, they would turn the city upside down trying to shake out the owner of the hit squad.

Everard had thought of all of that before he ever walked out of the house. He fought those five intruders with Velpor's sword in Velpor's two-handed style. In a single move, he had shifted the Conquerors' focus off himself and onto Hreban.

To plan all that in a split second while the house was being invaded and then to execute it flawlessly. He had stopped with five, likely because Velpor could've taken out that many but no more.

The man was frightening.

"Avaria," I said.

She startled. "Yes, my lady?"

"When you searched the warehouse, did you find any papers? Any contracts, anything with the Butcher's name on it?"

"No, my lady."

"What about the people in the courtyard?"

"No papers," Avaria confirmed. "However, we found this by the front door."

She offered us an envelope. Everard opened it, pulled out the paper within, read it, and held it out to me.

H will strike after midnight.

"Another warning," I murmured.

"Too late this time." Everard looked at Avaria. "Who left the letter?"

"We do not know, my lord."

He gave a small sigh. Avaria took a tiny step back.

"You let Maggie be taken," Everard said, "you missed the watcher that followed us from the Butcher's warehouse, and now you failed to note the messenger even though your people were watching the house."

Avaria held perfectly still.

"Get the bodies right," he told her.

"Yes, my lord."

Everard nodded and she took off. I headed for the stairs, and he walked with me. The steps would be a challenge, but there was no way around it.

I was so damn tired. Getting through that conversation in the basement had sapped whatever resources the few hours of sleep had restored. The floor was beginning to look appealing. If I didn't go up these stairs right now, I would curl up against the nearest wall and pass out.

I started climbing.

"That was a stroke of genius with the Redeemers," Everard said.

"Thank you."

If all went well, we would plant a spy in the Tower. We would need one because I'd killed the Butcher. While Hreban had compensated by bringing in a new assassin, the future was irrevocably changed, and having eyes and ears in Silveren's domain would be vital.

"He is tailor-made for them: a verifiable sin to redeem, at the end of his rope, and skilled enough to be an asset," Everard said. "More, he fits the part."

"Yes. He's bitter and jaded, and he looks like he expects life to kick him at any moment."

We reached the landing. I took a little breather and headed for the second flight of stairs. "Do you think Tillmar will stay loyal?"

"Yes. That man is desperate."

Weren't we all.

"The Redeemers can offer him nothing, while I can give him everything," Everard said. "He won't break his oath."

That right there was why I had to keep things in perspective.

I conquered the last step. Yes. Success. Clover had lit a lantern by my door and the hallway was bathed in comfortable light. Just a few more feet and I could fall into my bed face-first and let the world fade away.

"Why did you ask Avaria about contracts?"

I held Tillmar's contract out to him. "There is something wrong with it."

"There is everything wrong with it. The whole thing is an abomination."

"Yes, that, too, but that's not what I mean. Feel it."

Everard ran his hand over the paper and stopped above the signature line. He frowned and raised the contract up, so the light of the lantern shone through it. A complex design curved and wound within the paper, wrapping around the signature spot.

"What is that?"

"I don't know." He held his hand over it. "I can break it, but it would destroy the paper. We need a mage."

Where could we get a mage without attracting attention . . . The Mage Tower was chock-full of them, but I needed a mage that wouldn't report to Archmage Damaes. We had no idea what this contract did. We needed someone with some autonomy.

"Maybe I will make a trip to the Garden," I murmured.

"Not without me, you won't."

"You cannot leave the house."

"You cannot go without protection."

"I have a perfectly good cousin. He can take me."

"I will take you."

"You are a wanted man. Solentine is more than capable of protecting me."

"Maggie, you try my patience."

And here he was, the Sleepless Duke coming out.

He fixed me with his stare. "After everything we have been through, why do you trust Solentine over me?"

"Because he didn't lie to me."

"I didn't lie to you in all things," he said. "When I promised you I would protect you, I meant it. When I told you I could give you everything Solentine offered and more, I meant that, too."

The light of the lantern softened his face. He looked so handsome right now. Strong, trustworthy. Hot. Almost irresistible. I could just wrap my arms around him. He would kiss me and carry me to my bed. It would be scorching hot and dirty, a night I would never forget, and then I could fall asleep wrapped in those strong arms. I didn't even know what I craved more right now, sex, intimacy, or comfort. I wanted all of it.

"This is how Omelyana drowned, isn't it?"

"Drowned?"

"In my future. She looked into your eyes, heard your voice, so sure and sincere, and decided to live just for you. I'm no Omelyana. I have other things to do."

He pondered me. "I've met Omelyana. She is an accomplished woman. In your future, I married her because Selva needed her. By your own account, I worked hard to keep her satisfied."

"Yes, you did."

"If I worked that hard for the sake of someone my domain needed, I wonder how far I would go for the sake of someone I truly want?"

So smooth. His eyes were full of the fire that every woman who had ever wanted a man hoped to see. It was that heady mix of want, need, admiration, and just a hint of a possessive challenge. He didn't make it blatant or obvious. He made no demands. It was just there, and it was intoxicating enough to make you lose all grip on reality.

"You can turn that off now," I told him.

"Turn what off?"

"You said Tillmar was desperate. So am I. I want to save Kair Toren, and you are using that as a lever. But you are down in the desperate ditch with us, Your Grace. No matter what you do or say, you are the Lord of Selva, and you'll go to extreme lengths for the sake of your domain. You need the knowledge locked away in my head, and you know force won't work. Death isn't scary to me, and pain doesn't frighten me either. Not anymore. No matter what the Butcher did to me, I told him nothing. He was cursing when I died."

That wasn't strictly true. I was terrified of pain, but Everard didn't know that.

"You need my secrets, and you will offer whatever I want to get them. Wealth, status, your body. It would be so much more convenient if I was besotted with you. You would use me until I broke, and you wouldn't feel much guilt about it."

The Sleepless Duke studied me. "We're finally putting all of our cards on the table, then?"

Not all of them. I was still keeping back who I was and where I came from, but I no longer felt bad about it. Why should I? He had lied about where he came from and who he was.

"Why not? Let's get it out in the open. You told Solentine that I was yours. I am not. I will never be yours."

He laughed.

Oh you bastard.

"How does that work in your head, exactly?" I asked. "Are you sitting on your throne in Wilkair, while I'm standing demurely to the side, gazing at you in adoration with all my Kair Toren plans forgotten? What a wonderful future that would be, me helping you as you plot alliances and find the most advantageous wedding partner, all the while reassuring me that I'm the one you truly want. Will I be standing just like that for years, until my knowledge is finally exhausted, and you discard me?"

"If you are ever standing by my side, it will be because that's where you are supposed to be. It is where you belong, Maggie. You just don't know it yet."

Argh. "I'm going to the Garden with Solentine tomorrow."

"Sleep well, my lady."

Fuck off.

I shut the door in his face, locked it, and heard him chuckling on the other side.

I pulled my dress strings apart, dropped the gown on the floor, and collapsed into my bed. Sushi immediately curled up by my feet.

"If he comes into the room, bite him," I told her. "I'm counting on you."

I closed my eyes and passed out.

Chapter 32

Breakfast was over but I was still in the kitchen, sipping my second cup of tea, because Shana had served geskirin honey. It had a slight citrus flavor and once I loaded my tea with it, I couldn't stop drinking it. Clover sat at the other end of the table, embroidering a length of green fabric.

I missed orange juice. The fresh-squeezed H-E-B kind. I missed tacos. I missed coffee.

I missed my family . . .

I took another sip of tea.

Kaiden popped into the kitchen and slid an envelope in front of me without a word.

I pried the flap open and pulled a single piece of paper out.

I need your help.
G

There was only one *G* who had interacted with me enough to ask for my help.

"Who brought it?" I asked.

"A girl," Kaiden said.

"Did she say anything else?"

"She said that she hoped you bought some shoes."

That's what I thought. Something had happened at the Garden and now Galiene needed a favor.

Serendipity. For once Kair Toren had come through instead of biting my ankles to trip me. Judging from the way things had gone so far, this was probably some sort of timeline trap that would result in all kinds of problems. That was fine. I would handle them, and I would figure out how the Garden had found me. I had a good guess.

Everard would want to come with me, and I had to avoid that at all costs. Not only were people still looking for him, but after last night, I needed to reassert my independence. I could simply get ready and have the Shears escort me, but that would result in an argument. A better move would be to leave quietly, without giving him a chance to protest, as if he didn't even factor into this equation. I had to pull off sneaking out without looking like I had resorted to sneaking out.

"Clover, I need to go to the Garden."

Her eyes widened. "*The* Garden?"

"Yes. We're going to do the usual lady outfit." I turned to Kaiden. "Are the Shears still hanging out nearby?"

He rolled his eyes. "Yes."

"Please tell them that I'm leaving for the Garden in one hour and if their head doesn't want a certain someone to escort me and run all over the city, he needs to come and pick me up. I will meet him in front of Taryz Teahouse."

"What about His Grace?" Kaiden asked.

"What about him?"

"He won't like it."

"Kaiden, His Grace and King Sauven signed a treaty called the Accords. Because of that, Everard cannot enter Kair Toren unless he is invited. If he is discovered in the city, Sauven will kill him. His Grace doesn't like to be told what he can and can't do, so we need to protect him from himself. That's why in exactly one hour you're going to find a way to distract him and keep him occupied in the basement."

He made a face, shrugged, and took off. I rinsed my cup and headed upstairs. I had to get dressed and do my hair and I needed to get it done quietly, without Everard discovering what I was up to.

I stood on the corner in front of Taryz Teahouse wearing my lower-tier lady outfit, with my hair done up and secured with silver jewelry. I was also holding a basket, which no self-respecting lady of my social standing would be caught dead holding. Etiquette dictated that I should've brought Clover, but this was a clandestine operation.

Considering Hreban's attack last night, going out alone wasn't the best plan, but I had the protection of the Shears. Solentine must've taken a dim view of Hreban's goons attacking our house, because he had beefed up our security. Two Shears agents tailed me from the house all the way to Taryz and a third one was already there, waiting for me.

A carriage rolled up the street and stopped in front of me. The door swung open and I saw Solentine inside.

I abandoned all propriety and climbed in before he had a chance to exit and load me into it. I shut the door, landed on the bench across from him, and the carriage took off.

My newly minted cousin took in my winning ensemble and my basket. His eyebrows crept up.

Solentine was channeling a prince of rogues today. He wore brown pants, boots, and a cream shirt with wide sleeves. Over that he had put a sleeveless tunic of cinnamon-colored leather, decorated with golden designs and featuring a deep V-neck, and then added a formfitting black jacket with short wide sleeves, embroidered with a golden vine bearing two white flowers on his right shoulder. The jacket was open, and a black leather belt crossed his body diagonally from the right shoulder to the left side, buckled in place just above his waist. He'd tossed his cloak on the bench and the leather belt with sheaths bearing his two daggers was on full display.

He'd also shaved and brushed his deep auburn hair. The signs of fatigue from yesterday were gone, as if they had never even been there. The curtain of the carriage window was pulled back slightly, and the golden sunshine slanting across his face set him aglow. He was like a living painting.

Talk about a thirst trap. Luckily for me, I was immune.

"My dear cousin," he said. "Where is your maid?"

"Covering my escape. Would you have preferred picking me up at the house so you could spend the next hour saying things like 'The Conquerors are still looking for you' and 'Please don't be difficult for once'?"

He gave me a narrow smile. "I appreciate your care for my sanity."

"Of course. You are my favorite cousin."

The carriage rolled on. We were headed straight north. It would be a short trip, fifteen minutes or so. The Garden was up by the north wall and the teahouse was an almost straight shot south.

"What is your relationship with Ramond?" Solentine asked.

Straight to the point. "I'm a valuable asset, and he is using everything at his disposal to try to control me."

"Do you have feelings for him?"

"Yes."

"What kind of feelings?"

I sighed. "At the moment, I want to brain him with something heavy."

Solentine nodded. "I know that urge."

"I'm mostly angry with myself. He goaded me, and I took the bait. I don't even know what came over me. When someone says 'let's put all our cards on the table' . . ."

". . . you never put all your cards on that table," we finished in one voice.

I nodded at him. "Yes. That."

"Don't feel bad," he said. "Ramond is very difficult to manage."

"He knows what's at stake. If we don't alter the future, he will have to fight a punishing war. He will halt the advance of the Crimson Empire in the north, but he will take heavy losses. Things will get so dire, he will have to marry Omelyana of Gor to shore up his defenses. I told him all of this because at the time

I thought he was Reynald Karis. Had I known who he was, I would've run away screaming instead."

"Ramond's priorities are set in stone," he said. "If he sees you as the key to halting that future, he will do everything to keep you. And I do mean everything."

"I'm aware."

"I would advise against sleeping with him," Solentine said.

He'd finally come out and said it. "Are you attempting to safeguard my virtue?"

"Far it be from me to dictate what a woman does with her virtue. But you are my cousin now, and I see a disaster looming on the horizon, so I'm trying to shield you from it. Ramond has a way to make you feel . . ."

"Treasured?"

"Yes. Most people spend their lives trying to be noticed, often by the people they are closest to. Ramond doesn't just notice, he sees you. He stands head and shoulders above the rest, and when he takes an interest, you feel important. He'll treat you as a vital ally and acknowledge your talent and effort, and soon you'll find yourself doing ridiculous things for his approval."

"Sounds like you should be careful not to sleep with him."

He laughed softly. "We both prefer female company, but it might've been easier if our relationship was just that. Only my heart would be broken instead of the future of my family."

The carriage came to a stop. I glanced out of the window. In daylight, the Garden didn't look quite as enchanting. Without the lights and music, it reverted back to its previous identity as an ancient fort. I pulled the hood of my cloak over my head. Solentine put his own cloak on and pulled a black coif over his face.

The carriage door swung open, and a tall man wrapped in a faded cloak offered me his hand. His lancer's coif was down, and his eyes were green and unrepentant.

Behind me, Solentine swore.

I put my hand into Everard's, and he helped me down.

I turned to the driver, a young, compact man with a mane of dark hair. "How long has he been with us?"

"He got on at Taryz, my lady."

Solentine descended from the carriage.

"Have you taken leave of your senses?"

"Not that I've noticed." Everard took my basket. For a second, I thought about holding on to it, but playing tug of war with him in front of the Garden wouldn't be a good look. "And for the record, you give me too little credit. I would take great care with your heart, Sol."

Solentine rested his hand over his forehead and shut his eyes, as if he had been hit with a sudden, incapacitating migraine.

"Don't be dramatic." Everard faced me. "It doesn't matter what he tells you. The truth is the Demarr family is formidable but of limited means. The Empire looms large across the border, ready to swallow them, while at home bigger predators hunt each other for power and money. In this ocean of monsters, the Demarrs have to swim in someone's wake. I'm a great monster. They require my support. They cannot survive without it."

"Sauven Savaric is also a monster," I said.

"Yes, but Sauven is far away, and I'm right there in the Demarr backyard." Everard smiled and pulled the coif to cover his face. "Something to keep in mind for the future. Shall we?"

We approached the doors. The two guards at the entrance of the Garden eyed us. It was too early in the morning for the Garden kind of shenanigans, and the plaza was deserted. Galiene and Hade would be taking their morning tea right about now. And here I was, some random woman accompanied by two armed men with their faces covered.

"Tell Galiene of Sosna that a woman without shoes is here," I said.

The left guard went inside.

Moments ticked by.

Two men walked out of the Garden. One was the guard who'd gone to deliver my message, and the other was tall and muscular, with russet skin and short curly hair. A neatly trimmed beard hugged his jaw. He seemed to be somewhere on the crossroads of late twenties and early thirties. The mage from my first night.

The mage studied me for a moment. "She will see you. Just you."

"No," Everard said.

I faced the mage. "I didn't come here for my own sake. Your mistress invited me. If she no longer needs my help, I will simply go home."

The mage studied me.

There was exactly one sentence in the entire series devoted to this man. At some point, Hade got desperate and hired some people to break Galiene and her daughter out of Hreban's mansion. The book said, *Hade's mercenaries failed, and the Garden's only mage met his end with them.* No name, no description, nothing.

Powerful mages were rare. The best analogy in our world would be doctors with an unusual medical specialty, like neurosurgeons. There was something like one neurosurgeon per ninety thousand people in the US. Mages weren't quite that endangered, but the fact that the Garden even had one was odd. For some reason, Damaes chose to tolerate his presence and autonomy. He was literally irreplaceable.

"May I see what's in your basket?"

Everard held the basket out to him. The mage moved the piece of cloth covering the contents aside, looked at them for a long moment, and put the cloth back.

"Follow me."

Galiene's office lay all the way up on the fourth floor in an airy, light tower with tall pale walls and massive arched windows. The window on the left offered a stunning view of the city, the one on the right showed a hillside cushioned in greenery. Beautiful flowers bloomed in ornate pots, artfully grouped on the floor by the windows, their white and vivid red blossoms almost glowing in the morning light.

The wall between the windows was filled with shelves supporting books and treasures: boxes carved from stone and wood, glass vases, and small statues. A large wooden desk stood in front of the shelves. Galiene sat behind the desk looking exactly as I remembered, regal and cold, with her dark blond hair curved at the nape of her neck into a spiral. Today her gown was pewter gray.

On the left, Hade waited in a padded chair, her eyes sharp.

The mage took up a position by the door, just behind us.

I took my hood down.

"You found shoes," Galiene said.

"Among other things. What can I do for the Garden?"

Galiene's face was impassive. Whatever it was had to be bad.

"We are being harassed," she said.

"In what way?"

"Our shipments are going missing, our people are being accosted, and our patrons are being robbed."

It sounded like Ulmar Hreban's petty brand of revenge. He couldn't touch Galiene directly, so he was using his money and hired muscle to complicate her life.

"We've hired additional guards to take care of the last two," Galiene said. "But we can do nothing about the shipments."

"What sort of goods are not coming in?"

"The special sort."

He was going after their aphrodisiacs and drugs. One of the Garden's lures was providing a touch of the rare and forbidden. They stayed away from harder drugs, but they did dabble in lighter stuff that Rellas restricted or heavily taxed. Their shipments were smuggled in.

"I assume that you've tried changing the schedules and routes, and it made no difference?"

Galiene nodded. "It seems Elaut wasn't our only traitor."

"Someone is talking to Hreban, and you want to know who."

"Yes," Galiene said.

"Have you narrowed it down?" I asked.

"Wesla, Orrem, and Arale," Galiene said. "They are the only three who knew of the new shipping changes. We've questioned all of them and all of them deny it. We cannot detain all three of them indefinitely. The Garden would grind to a halt."

"Nor can we afford to lose the next shipment," Hade said.

Wesla was their bookkeeper, Orrem was the head of security, and Arale was the one who took over the Garden after Hreban took Galiene. Right.

"Before we go any further, let's talk compensation," I said. "I need to borrow your mage. I have a magical item, and I need to know what it does."

Galiene glanced at the mage. He nodded.

"Done," she said. "What else?"

I took the basket from Everard and set it on her desk.

Galiene lifted the cloth and stared at the twenty bars in four different colors all stamped with a small shell design. Gort had carved the stamp for us.

"What am I looking at?"

"Soap samples. I'd like you to use them in the Garden to see how they perform and how your clients like them."

"Very well," Galiene said.

"It's Arale."

Galiene and Hade shared a look.

"How do you know?" Galiene asked.

"Orrem was born to a horrible father, who took his frustrations out on Orrem's mother, his sisters, and him until Orrem grew large enough to put a stop to it. He abhors violence against women and sees himself as a protector. He would never ally himself with someone who sought to kidnap a child from her mother."

He also led the raid on Hreban's compound and was blinded in one eye. There were a couple of scenes from his point of view, and I had gotten a good glimpse inside his head. His thought process toward Ulmar was very straightforward: hate and then more hate.

"That leaves us with Wesla and Arale. Wesla is devoted to both of you, but in particular to Galiene. She likely spent the last few days looking ashamed, and that's because she did do something, but it wasn't connected to Hreban."

"What do you mean?" Galiene asked.

"Bring her here, and I will show you."

The mage departed and returned a couple of minutes later with a blond woman. She was slender, around twenty years old, and the guilt on her face was so obvious, it wasn't even funny.

"Wesla!" I loaded steel into my voice, doing my best impersonation of Shana. "Do you know who I am?"

She shook her head.

"I'm the woman with no shoes who saved Galiene's daughter."

Wesla drew a sharp breath.

Just as I thought. By now the rumors about the shoeless beggar woman who had mysteriously warned Galiene had spread through the Garden. I was probably credited with all sorts of mysterious powers.

"I see all," I declared. "I know all. Did you think your theft would go unnoticed?"

She jerked as if struck.

"How dare you take advantage of your lady? She feeds you, she takes care of you, and how do you repay her? Admit your guilt."

Wesla opened her mouth, struggling to say something.

"Speak!" Hade snapped.

"I stole the Queen's Delight," Wesla announced, her voice high-pitched. "I was the one who did it. I meant to only take one, but it was delicious, and I couldn't help myself." She dropped to her knees. "I accept my punishment. Please, don't throw me out."

I turned to Galiene and spread my arms.

". . . I will do anything, please, please, please don't send me away . . ." Wesla dissolved into sobs.

Galiene heaved a sigh.

". . . I have no place to go . . ."

"Nobody is going to throw you out," Galiene said. "Return to your room. I will speak to you later."

Wesla got to her feet and fled.

"All of that over sweets." Hade rolled her eyes. "That child has no sense."

"Yet she can calculate a month's expenses without paper," Galiene said.

"If it's not Orrem or Wesla, it has to be Arale. Search her room," I said. "There might be a small purple pouch hidden somewhere in it. If you find it, do not open it."

Ten minutes later two guards led Arale in. The fairy princess from the first floor, the first person in the Garden to speak to me. She had traded her gown for a red robe and her hair was undone.

"Is this about the shipments?" Arale sighed. "I had nothing to do . . ."

The mage approached Galiene's desk and placed a small purple pouch on it.

"What is it?" Galiene asked me.

"Poison. The plan was for you to be taken away by Hreban and for her to take your place. Since that failed . . ."

In the original storyline, Arale took over Galiene's job, but she kept making mistakes. Shortly after the failed raid, Hade died suddenly. A purple pouch containing traces of poison was found in her room. I'd always thought Arale was the one who'd done it. Without Hade she had free rein, and within a year she had run the Garden into the ground.

"You just couldn't help yourself, could you?" Galiene said.

Arale looked at Hade. She must've seen something terrifying in the old woman's eyes because she flinched. She caught herself in an instant, but we all saw it.

"Everything I have done was for the sake of the Garden," Arale said.

Boom, there she is.

Hade stared at her, and the old woman's eyes were dark and cold.

Arale raised her chin. "Why her? She is neither beautiful nor skilled."

She must've decided that arguing her innocence was a lost cause. Her only chance was to convince Hade that she'd betrayed Galiene for the benefit of the Garden.

"She isn't even from Kair Toren. She's from a backwater village, and yet she holds herself apart as if she were better than us. Everyone looks down on her. They are just too afraid to voice it."

More words, deeper hole.

"She thinks she has the second prince, but everyone knows that man grows bored with women after a week. She doesn't even practice the Three Arts. She doesn't sing, she doesn't dance. All she has is her body, wrecked by childbirth. Her breasts droop, her stomach has scars, the color of her flower is no longer a fresh pink."

You evil harpy.

"Inhan will be done with her in a fortnight, and then the wrath of Hreban will come full force. He does not forgive. The Garden cannot stand against him."

Hade's face betrayed no emotion.

"When that time comes, we will have only two choices. We can send her to Hreban and hope he still wants her, or we can deliver her corpse. If she stays here, she will doom us. Would it not be better to let her go? I can take her place. I am younger and more skilled. I've kept my body pristine. Highborn lords fight each other for the privilege of spending half an hour in my company. I can do so much better than she can. You must see it. If the survival of the Garden matters to you, you must make the right choice."

"Gag her," Hade said.

A pulse of red tore from the mage. It burst against Arale and jerked her up on her toes, snapping her into a rigid, tortured pose. She must've tried to move and been unable to, because nobody could stand on their toes like that without pointe shoes.

"The Garden thanks you for your gracious assistance," Galiene told me and glanced at the guards. "Show our guests to the East Room. Ciste will be with you shortly."

It was time for my exit. I turned and followed the guards out, Solentine and Everard in tow.

"May I have her?" the mage asked behind me. "They are hungry."

"You may," Galiene said.

As we stepped out of the room, the guards shut the door behind us, but before it closed, I caught a flash of bright gold spiraling out of the mage's hands. It looked like a swarm of glowing butterflies. As they streamed toward Arale, the look in her eyes was pure terror.

The East Room was lovely. The three of us sat at a large table, enjoying the view of the hill from a large window. Arale's panicked eyes kept popping up out of my memory, and my mouth tasted like ash. I really wanted to get out of here.

The door swung open and Ciste came inside and sat at our table. He looked about as happy to be here as I was.

"Thank you for agreeing to meet us," I said.

No response.

I pushed the contract toward him. "Can you tell us if there is a spell on this contract?"

He passed his hand over it and stared at the paper like it was a snake about to bite him. "Burn it."

What?

"What is it?" Everard asked.

"It is *lugur campur*," he said.

"A life chain?" I asked.

Ciste narrowed his eyes. "You speak Sareso."

Apparently I did. Sareso was the language of magic. That opened all sorts of possibilities, but right now I needed to concentrate on the contract.

"What does 'life chain' mean?" I asked.

"When you sign this contract and seal it with your blood, you will be bound to it. If the contract is destroyed, it will kill you."

Oh my god.

"This a vile thing born of the Crimson Usurper and his death mages," Ciste said. "It is made with blood and suffering, and it's been outlawed for three hundred years."

Three hundred forty years ago, a usurper mage claimed the throne of the Crimson Empire and unleashed a cult of his death mages on the continent. He reigned for almost three decades, bringing war, slavery, and mass sacrifices everywhere he went until he invaded Rellas, and his legions fell before the meat grinder of Rellasian knights. In the final battle, Romel Savaric sang his way through the Usurper's sorcery and personally cut off the dictator's head. The

Crimson Empire recoiled, Rellas gained a new ruling dynasty, and owning human beings was outlawed in both countries, which made it illegal on the majority of the continent.

The mage stared at us, his dark eyes unreadable. "Should you be found with it, you will be stripped of your name, your lands will be forfeit, and you will be exiled."

The fractured pieces of an idea that had been floating in my head snapped together.

"What if someone has more than one?" I asked.

"Death."

Perfect.

This could work. It was a reckless plan that hinged on me being able to read Sareso correctly, and that was a massive, huge *if*. If I failed . . . It didn't matter. I had to succeed because we were out of options.

"Last question," I said. "Why does it push me away when I try to touch it?"

"You have too much magic. It seeks to protect you from harm, so it warns you not to hurt yourself."

"Thank you," I said.

The mage rose and walked away without another word.

Everard and Solentine got up at the same time.

"We're leaving," Everard said under his breath.

"The sooner, the better," Solentine muttered.

Three minutes later we were in the carriage, rolling away from the Garden plaza.

Solentine pulled the coif off his face. "Is there no low Hreban won't sink to?"

"Apparently not," Everard said.

"I have to go to the harbor," I said.

The two of them turned to me.

"Hreban's grandfather was an evil, hard son of a bitch, and he had high hopes for his grandson. Ulmar grew up by his desk, and from the time he was a toddler, Ulmar saw people fawn, bow, and scrape before his grandfather, while their hearts brimmed with contempt and hate. Ulmar doesn't trust people. He trusts signatures. He is compulsive about putting things in writing, because his grandfather taught him that people lie, but once you have their signature, you have them in your grasp."

I pointed at the contract. "This is irresistible to him. A foolproof way to ensure that he isn't betrayed. These contracts can't be easy to get, and they don't come cheap. The mercenaries on Otrade's crew wouldn't have lived long anyway and if they were caught, even if they implicated Hreban, their word doesn't matter without proof."

"And yet he wasted a contract on Tillmar," Everard said.

"He can't help himself," I said. "Knowing that he holds the power over their lives in his hand and he can snuff them out at will keeps him warm at night. This is what he lives for. Silveren would never sign one of these, but . . ."

"The Butcher might have," Solentine said. "His magical talent was minor. Even if he felt the pressure of the spell, he wouldn't know what he was signing."

"So there's a contract out there that has Hreban's name, the Butcher's, and the Sun Margrave's," I said.

"If this is exposed, nothing will save Hreban," Everard said. "Sauven is desperate to reinforce the support for his bloodline. His dynasty was founded on killing an enslaver. Sauven will not miss the opportunity to do the same."

"And he will make it as public as possible," Solentine agreed. "Especially since Colart Jenicor is the target. It will be the loudest trial since they convicted Ralinbor's wife."

I faced Everard. "This is it. This is how we stop him. We expose this, and the whole of Rellas will rise to bring him down."

"But to do that, we need the contracts," Everard said.

"Hreban would never keep these contracts at his house. Too much risk," Solentine said.

"We don't have to look for them. I know where they are. But getting to them will be difficult, which is why I need to go to the harbor."

"Where in the harbor?" Everard asked.

"The Ribs Bazaar."

"I will take you," Solentine promised. "We are dropping you off at the house, Ramond. And this time, for the love of all that is holy, stay put. If you are discovered and she is caught with you, there will be Void to pay."

The largest aquatic animal species on Earth was the blue whale, one hundred feet long and roughly four hundred thousand pounds. I remembered those useless facts because when I was seven years old, our teacher told us that a blue whale was as long as three school buses put together. The idea that any animal could be that large had exploded my baby brain.

The largest aquatic animal in the West Ocean, on the coast of which Kair Toren was located, hadn't been determined because the ocean was deep and liked to keep its secrets. However, this was a world of monsters, and one day, decades ago, one of those monsters had died and washed ashore at the poor section of the Kair Toren wharf during a terrible storm.

The monstrous creature was too large and too heavy to move, so the city took it apart where it fell. The fishmongers had carved off its flesh and harvested everything they could use: the scales, the protective spines, and some of the innards. The Chamber of Works claimed the head and carted it off to be displayed at Eagle Roost. The Mage Tower sent its mages for the monster's tail and the rest of its insides, which were delivered to the Tower for research and use in protective talismans. When Kair Toren was done, only the creature's ribs and spine remained.

Over the years, sun, wind, and rain stripped and bleached the skeleton. Eventually, a market sprouted inside of the rib cage. Sail canvas was strung on top of the bones, rugs were brought in for the vendors to sell their wares, little stalls sprang up all around it, and the Ribs Bazaar was born.

The bazaar quickly became Kair Toren's version of a tourist trap and for good reason. I was looking at it now, and it was at least two hundred thirty feet long and thirty feet tall. The biggest blue whale in our world would be this monster's newborn.

I walked into the front entrance of the bazaar, where the giant vertebrae sticking out above my head hinted at the remnants of a neck. Rows of vendors sat on rugs along the walls, offering baubles, cheap jewelry, talismans, phony remedies, shells, scrimshaw, weird sea creatures encased in glass and resin, and other useless oddities. In other words, tourist junk.

Next to me Solentine was doing a fine impression of a bodyguard, complete with a cloak and covered face. This wasn't his turf. He wouldn't be welcome.

I strolled between the rows. The air smelled of pungent incense, a poor attempt to cover up the stench from the nearby fishing dock. The vendors eyed me, trying to gauge my suitability as a potential mark, saw Solentine following me, and lost interest. His hood was up, and he walked with purpose, seemingly knitted from menace. People glanced at him once and then decided they had pressing business elsewhere.

There she was, midway on the left, a stout older woman wrapped in a shawl, with harsh features and graying blond hair. Unlike most of the vendors, who sat on rugs, she had a display table and a chair. I stopped before the table filled with sea glass jewelry.

"Greetings, Darotha."

She squinted at me. "You look better than the last time I saw you."

I made a show of examining the jewelry. Most of it was leather cord bracelets and necklaces with wooden beads and a chunk of sea glass in the center. The sea glass ranged from bright red to pale turquoise. There was a certain etiquette when it came to this kind of transaction.

"You told the Garden where to find me."

"Our business was concluded, and discretion costs extra."

I picked up a bracelet with a chunk of green glass, draped it on my wrist, and tilted my arm, letting it catch the light.

Darotha watched me, amused.

"How much?"

"Five dens."

I could buy four bottles of wine for that price. Outrageous. Apparently, Darotha *was* the Thieves of the North. All of them.

I nodded to Solentine, and he put a silver noma on the table. Before you talked to someone like Darotha, you paid an entrance fee. This was the proper way to do it, and I was very generous.

Darotha reached out, almost lazily, and took the coin off the table. A minor vendor would have snatched it so fast, I wouldn't have even seen it. It would have just vanished. This was Darotha demonstrating her clout. She didn't have to grab the money. Nobody would try to take it from her.

"What can I do for you?" she asked.

"I'm looking for a beggar woman," I said quietly.

"There are lots of beggar women in the city."

"This one is worth fifteen nomas," I said.

Darotha's eyes shone. She looked like a shark coming for you through shadowy water. "That narrows it down a bit."

Even for Darotha, who had her crooked fingers in many underworld pies, fifteen nomas was significant money.

"She is about my age, average height, bright red hair. She keeps to herself, doesn't really beg, but mutters under her breath. Other beggars leave her alone, because her mumbling is disturbing, and if they try to touch her, painful magic stings them. There is no need to apprehend her. I just need to know where she is. She must be alive and uninjured, and I need to find her fast."

"The city is large, and the beggars are many," Darotha said. "It may take some time. I will send one of my kids to your new place when we know something."

We smiled at each other.

"One more thing. If you keep telling people about me, we cannot do business."

"I will keep that in mind."

I turned around and walked out without another word.

Outside the air stank of salt and fish, and after that choking incense, it tasted like the pristine atmosphere of a flower-filled alpine meadow. We took a street running east, away from the wharf and back toward the city.

"How do you know Darotha?" Solentine asked.

"The same way I know everything else."

"Are you going to explain why we need that woman?"

"No, because you won't like it."

If he and Everard realized what I was planning, they would lock me up inside the house and throw the key into this damn harbor.

He laughed softly. "Refreshing honesty. Will this work?"

"I don't know," I said. "A month ago I would've thought this was a brilliant idea, but I've been burned too many times. I hope to the Aspects it works, because I don't have anything else, and I don't know what else I can do to turn things around."

I sounded so tired and bitter. Everything was riding on finding Isadau in time, and then I had to jump the hurdle of bringing her around. Even if I managed that somehow, there was no guarantee she would help me. And if I screwed this up, the Sun Margrave would die, and the future would resume its grim march toward a cliff. I didn't have the energy to pretend to not worry about it.

"My people are looking for Cai," Solentine said. "I can't promise we'll find him, but I will do everything I can."

"Taking out Cai alone won't be enough. We must remove Hreban at the same time, in one blow. We have to make such a huge hole in the timeline that it can't reassemble itself."

"You speak of it as if the future were a living thing."

"Sometimes it feels that way. I've become . . . disturbed by it. It's this kingdom, Solentine. This city. It messes with my mind. It has changed me, and there's no going back."

"Perhaps it simply showed you who you truly were."

"That is a terrifying thought."

We kept walking. I needed to get back home and go to work. Here was hoping my perfect recall of the books held, because if I made a mistake with this, it could kill me. Possibly permanently.

"Speaking of things I know, Krasta had younger brothers."

"I'm aware," he said.

"He'd left the city and traveled back home shortly before you and he had that fight. He let his brothers in on his plans. You did kill him, right?"

"I did."

"That means his three brothers will be back in Kair Toren by the second of Redberry looking for you."

"I will make sure they'll find me."

"Is that wise?"

"They are an annoyance I don't need. The sooner I deal with it, the better."

"You could've avoided it altogether. I told you not to get into that carriage. You have an infuriating habit of listening to the warning and then doing whatever you want anyway and then you get mad at Ev—*Ramond* for doing the same."

"I have a reputation to consider," he said. "Sometimes long-term strategy demands short-term risks."

"I don't want anything bad to happen to you, Solentine." I gave him a big smile. "After all, you're my favorite cousin."

"Thank the Aspects for that," he muttered.

Chapter 33

"Your first defense is always to scream and run away," Everard said.

After our trip to the Ribs, Solentine had delivered me back to the house. My plan was to go back to my room and work. There was a passage from the book written in Sareso I wanted to reproduce. But Everard had decided it was a good time to teach me how to use a dagger, and now I was in the courtyard.

The day was lovely. Ragged clouds floated in the sky, and sunshine dappled the yard. The sunlight played on Everard's dark hair, sliding over his harsh, handsome face. The wind was blowing east, and the air smelled of salt and ocean.

"Don't go toe-to-toe with your attacker, especially if they are larger than you," Everard said. "Make noise, draw attention to yourself, and try to gain some distance."

I nodded.

"We're going to assume that you tried to run away and failed." Everard nodded at the three knives waiting on the table to the side. "Pick the one that seems the most comfortable."

I studied my options. The first knife was single edged, with a six-and-a-half-inch, slightly curved blade and a short wooden handle. The second knife looked like a classic, straight-edged Ka-Bar. My dad had one that looked just like it, except his was larger. This one was a smaller version, lighter, with a six-inch blade. The third was a traditional, double-edged dagger, the same blade I had stabbed into the Butcher's corpse.

I took the dagger and pulled it out of its leather sheath. It was slender, light, and very sharp.

"Good choice," Everard said. "Put it back in its sheath."

I sheathed the dagger and faced him.

His eyes turned cold. He advanced. Menace rolled off him in waves. He moved like someone who hunted and killed people, and some animal instinct inside me recognized him as a predator and screeched in fear.

I took a step back.

He kept coming.

I took another step.

Another.

My legs hit the wine tree table. Nowhere left to go.

Everard loomed in front of me. His hand snapped out and clamped my neck.

The breath caught in my throat.

He didn't squeeze. He just held me, but the urge to frantically flail and kick myself free gripped me. My heart thudded in my chest. In some books I'd read this would've been a sexy moment when the hero used this opportunity to demonstrate his hot, possessive ways and gently caress the heroine's neck, but nothing about this was sexy. It was scary as hell, and the panic inside me convulsed like a feral cat caught in the loop of a dog catcher's pole.

Everard held still. "Deep slow breaths."

I was shaking. Not with fear but with suppressed fight response. I needed to hit him and claw my way free. I knew he wouldn't hurt me. I knew it, but my instincts were screaming in blind terror. This had to be some kind of reaction to trauma. Kair Toren had done this to me.

"Breathe, Maggie."

I forced myself to take a slow shuddering breath.

"Good," Everard said. "Again. Deep breath."

His voice was reassuring and steady, but he still looked terrifying, as if one man were talking and a different man had his hand on my neck.

"Good. You're looking for calm. Calm and cold."

I breathed. The electric prickling on my skin faded slowly.

"Got it?" he asked.

I swallowed and felt my throat tense against his hold. I nodded. Talking was beyond me right this second.

"Don't raise your arm. Don't look at the knife. Keep looking at me."

I stared into his green eyes.

He pulled me toward him. "Stab."

I jammed the dagger in its sheath at his body.

"Lower."

I jabbed again.

"That's the spot. Most men will be taller than you. Jab here and you will hit the femoral artery. If you do it right, they will bleed out before they can do any real damage. I'm still holding you. Keep stabbing."

I jammed the sheath into him again.

"Where is the woman who smashed the Butcher to a pulp?"

That mix of rage and panic that had driven me into a frenzy inside the Butcher's lair bubbled up. I stabbed him four times in a single breath, fast and hard.

"Just like that." He released his hold on my neck and took a few steps back.

The air rushed out of me. I tasted metal in my mouth.

"If you can't get away, look them straight in the eye as they're coming. Men who hunt women want to see the fear in their eyes. A professional paid to grab you off the street will also look at your face to make sure they have the right target."

The handle of my knife was sweaty. I wiped it on my skirt.

"You're going to look straight at them, so they hold your gaze, and when they put their hands on you, you're going to stab. Clover will add padded pockets to your dresses so you can carry your blade without a sheath. Don't bother taking the dagger out. Stab right through the dress."

I nodded.

"Here I come," he warned.

He started toward me again. I forced myself to stand still.

Everard grabbed me by my shoulder and yanked me to him. I stabbed his thigh three times, and he let go.

"Good," he said.

It felt like I had run a sprint.

"Let's do it again. This time, thrust, and drag the knife to the left, giving it a twist as you pull it out. Just a slight turn will do."

Will came out the door carrying a ham.

"That's for you," Everard said. "To practice."

Will winked at me.

It would be okay. This was just practice, and I was safe. No matter how uncomfortable Everard made me, I could end it at any moment by stabbing him.

"The hardest part of fighting with a knife is commitment," Everard said. "You must make the decision to hurt someone, and you must commit completely. You get one chance at a good thrust. If you fail, your attacker will kill you."

I had learned that lesson already from Lecke on the Estret Bridge.

My mouth felt dry, so I had to force the words out. "Commitment isn't a problem for me."

Everard smiled. The grin lit up his face, and the menacing predator melted away in an instant.

"No, I imagine not. It's getting you to stop that's the problem."

I had never thought of myself as a violent person. I had gotten into a couple of school fights, once in elementary school and once when I was thirteen, but neither time was I the aggressor. Nothing in my twenty-six years had indicated that when pushed into a corner, I was capable of beating a human being to a bloody pulp.

Maybe Solentine was right, and this was inside of me all along. It just never had a chance to come out because my life used to be blissfully peaceful. I had never appreciated how safe I was until I came here. If I somehow found a way back, could I even return to my life? Would I be able to slide right back in where I left off or would it be like trying to hammer a square peg into a round hole?

"We're going to do this again, and this time, you're going to run away," Everard said. "Remember, thrust until you get free, then turn and flee. Don't try to finish me off. Don't kick at me while screaming obscenities. Stab and run."

I gripped my knife. "No promises."

Osor dor mi Damaes. Re braste ca . . .

Or was it *re braste cä*? It could be read either way and something was telling me that there should've been a squiggle above the *a* to indicate that, but there wasn't one in the books. Maybe they didn't bother with it . . .

"Yes, Kaiden?"

He blinked in the doorway with my study door half-open. "How did you know I was there?"

I pointed at the candle on the table. The evening was really dark tonight, so I'd added it to my two lanterns.

"The flame moved when you swung the door open. You'll have to do better if you want to be sneaky. Do you need something?"

"Lute says someone named Digi is here with her bodyguard."

"Here? At our front door?"

He nodded.

Crap. Everard was in the basement, having another private meeting with one of his retainers. I had no idea how he would react to finding the stepdaughter of the man who had killed his mother on our doorstep.

Damn it.

"Lute says he has a rag Clover used to mop the floor, so If we need for Digi to wait, he's got the rug handled."

Oh for the love of . . . Apparently, Lute didn't just hold grudges, he cuddled them and tucked them in at night.

"Tell him to show them to the meeting room. And ask Clover to brew some of that fancy tea; it would be lovely."

"Yes, my lady." He gave me a mock bow.

"And don't tell Everard. I mean it this time."

"Yes, my lady."

"And be less of a smartass."

He grinned and took off.

I blew my candle out and headed down the stairs.

The meeting room was a new addition to the house. Gathering in the kitchen for private meetings worked well, but we couldn't exactly bring strangers there. Meeting them outside by the wine tree was fine during the day, but not in the evening or during bad weather. I didn't want random people in my office either, so we had cleared out one of the larger rooms, put a simple table in there with some chairs, and designated it as the meeting room.

Digi waited for me in one of the chairs. The large woman who had almost stabbed me with a spear stood behind her chair watching Gort, who leaned against the wall. Apparently, he was my designated protector for this meeting.

I nodded to everyone. "Calm winds and tranquil sky."

"Warm sun and safe harbor," Digi responded.

I sat in a chair.

Digi wore a hooded robe that hid her from top to bottom. Her hood was down now, revealing her hair, which was pulled back into a simple ponytail. Her clothes under that tattered robe were probably plain. She hadn't wanted to be recognized. Her bodyguard was wearing one of those generic Rellasian cloaks, the kind you could buy for a couple of dens at any market.

How did they find me? I'd expected Digi would make contact eventually, but not that soon. Did they track the mordok somehow? Or was it Darotha again? No, they wouldn't know to look for her. It must've been the mordok.

"Have you come to retrieve your creature?"

"Tzeri was a gift," Digi said. "She is yours."

"I'm relieved. Lute is trying to tame her. He says he is doing well, and she has only bitten him once today. He would be so disappointed if you came to take her back."

Digi smiled. "A mordok chooses its tamer, not the other way around."

Clover came in, carrying a platter with a teapot and two cups. She nodded to me. "My lady."

"Thank you," I said.

Clover set the tray down, poured the tea, and departed.

I sipped my tea. Mmmm, the client special occasion tea. So delicious.

Everard walked through the door, dressed in all black, his eyes green and cold.

I almost choked on my tea.

Digi and her bodyguard froze.

Gort bowed his head and left the room. Everard pulled out a chair and sat on my left.

Nobody said anything. Damn it, Kaiden. Little traitor.

Digi stared straight at me, as if willing Everard to disappear from her peripheral vision. Behind her, her bodyguard clenched her spear. Digi was practiced at hiding her emotions, but the woman behind her was teetering on the edge of panic. It wasn't for her own sake. She realized that if Everard attacked Digi, she was powerless to stop him.

I cleared my throat. "What can I do for the honorable *orsi*?"

"I have three questions," Digi said.

"What have you brought in trade?"

Digi flicked her fingers. The bodyguard set a small wooden box on the table.

Digi opened the box. A small amulet lay inside, a clawed silver paw with long talons holding a black pearl.

"A stone of remembrance," Digi said. "If you squeeze it, the talons will crush the stone, and the person in front of you will see and hear the one they love most in your place. They will tell you their darkest secrets. You are someone who deals in knowledge. It will be of great value to you."

Nice. "How long will the magic last?"

"Forty breaths. Enough for a clever woman to save a life or ruin it."

About two minutes or so. That was a really valuable trade. "Ask your questions."

Digi leaned forward slightly. "Which of my siblings share a father with me?"

"Your third brother, your sister, and your fourth brother are children of your parents."

"Does the husband of my mother know of their parentage?"

Word choice was very important in the Okulan language. Not the *tair*, not my stepfather, the husband of my mother. She would've owed allegiance to the *tair* and familial respect and care to her stepfather. The *husband of my mother*, however, didn't rate any consideration.

"The *tair* knows. He found out when you took the first of the Heir Rights. The Grand Priest is not your ally. He also knows, and he has since tested the blood of all your siblings."

Digi fell silent, pondering the implications.

"We have cleaned our house," she said. "The *tair* was having my father poisoned. Small doses slipped into his food. My father had already noticed himself growing weaker. In another six months he would have wasted away. The traitor has been found and dealt with."

"As expected." Digi was meticulous. She and Clover would get along.

"My father is the First Sword. The defender of our clan. His death would be a huge loss to our people. It is a crime."

Aha. Now I knew where she was going. She did this in the books, too, but it took her a lot longer to arrive at this course of action, and Mrest had died of unknown causes by then. I'd changed the future and maybe this time it would stick. Although was this change for the better or worse? How much bloodier would their quiet war get now that Digi was forewarned?

"You seek to accuse the *tair* of Blood-burning. The *tair* who betrays the clan in the name of self-interest burns the blood of their people and isn't worthy to rule."

Digi nodded. "You know our ways."

"You need three crimes to prove his guilt. The poisoning of your father is one."

"The corruption of trade is the other. The *tair* has put his sister, Tarak's mother, in charge of the silk trade. She has embezzled funds and distributed them through the family with the *tair*'s knowledge. She has been clever about it, but she shared her scheme with my cousin. Tarak is a soft man, unaccustomed to any discomfort."

Oh, there had been a hell of a lot of discomfort, I was sure. The Harzi were not known for their gentleness when it came to interrogating prisoners.

"You need a third crime. Is that your final question?"

"Yes," Digi said. "Give me a third crime that the *tair* committed. Something I can take back to my people to prove the Blood-burning."

Her stepfather had done a lot of shady shit. Let's see, what would qualify and have the right emotional weight to enrage the clan?

Ah. That.

"There is a man named Amur among your retainers. Do you trust him?"

"Yes."

"Amur's grandfather travels to the Mountain Temple every year at midsummer, during the longest day. This year Amur should accompany his grandfather to the temple. You must secretly meet them there. Don't tell Amur's grandfather of this plan. Let it be a surprise."

Digi nodded.

"Make sure the abbot of the temple is present for this meeting."

She nodded again.

The Blood-burning required specific conditions. To prove a case in the clan's court, one would need the injured party, a blood relative, or a sworn sibling who could speak to the impact of the crime, and an impartial witness to confirm the testimony.

"The abbot must be your witness," I warned. "The Grand Priest will support the husband of your mother, and the abbot is the only one with enough sway to counter the Grand Priest's influence."

"Understood."

"When you meet Amur's grandfather, ask him if he still mourns his dogs on the longest day of the year. You must appear as if you already know the answer. Then let him speak. All you need to do is listen."

Digi opened her mouth and closed it. She had asked three questions. Anything else would cost her extra.

"If his grandfather hesitates, tell him that you never cared for the number seven."

"Thank you."

A moment passed. Another.

"And what of Selva's wishes?" Digi asked.

Behind her, her bodyguard clenched her spear.

Everard's posture was relaxed and his voice calm and measured. "As long as all of the blood stays on your side of the border, Selva will not cross it."

Oh, how clever. The way he put it could mean that he expected all of the fighting to stay on their side of the border or all of their people, because the Okula referred to their clanspeople as *the blood*.

"For how long?" Digi asked.

The Harzi clan territory directly bordered Selva. She wanted to make sure he wouldn't stab her in the back while she secured her position.

"My quarrel is with the husband of your mother," Everard said. "Should the Harzi find themselves a new *tair*, that *tair* can count on lasting peace and a calm border."

"May such a *tair* have that in writing?" Digi asked.

And she had just questioned his integrity.

A thin curl of black smoke slipped out from Everard, circled around his forearm, and melted into nothing. The bodyguard looked like she might faint at any minute.

"Treaties and accords are made between rulers," he said. "Become your people's ruler. Until then, my word must suffice."

"The Sleepless Duke has never broken a promise to me," I said. "His word is carved in stone." *Take the hint. You're pushing too far.*

"And if I did go back on my word, she would never let it pass," he said.

What?

Digi looked at me.

"It's getting late." *Go while you can.*

"So it is. Should you wish to have tea without any trade, Lady Maggie, you know where to find me."

"I would like that."

Digi pulled the hood over her head. The poor bodyguard woman almost collapsed in relief.

"Kaiden!" I called.

He popped out of thin air in the doorway.

"Please escort our honored guests to the door."

The two Harzi women departed.

Everard turned to me.

"So the smoke. Do you control it or does it happen on its own . . ."

The dark swirled around him like tongues of some cosmic flame and vanished again. "It's the start of the Fatefire. The same as Arvel's radiance just before he shapes his barrier. I find letting it loose at the right time makes an effective statement."

No shit.

"You made it seem as if I have much more influence over you than I do."

"I believe I'm the ultimate authority on the amount of influence you have over me."

It was best to just leave that alone.

"Tell me about this," he said.

"What do you want to know?"

"Digi's parentage."

"When Rogh Dareel won the war of succession with his siblings, his reserves were exhausted. He needed money in the worst way, so he approached a rich merchant family, seeking to marry their heir, Asali. Asali turned him down in public. He pulled some strings and made sure her brother's trade convoy was captured and then offered to negotiate for his release."

"If Asali married him."

"He told her that she could either lose a brother or gain a husband. The choice was hers. She married him. They had a grand wedding with contests of strength and skill, as is the Okula's tradition. While Rogh was getting drunk and basking in congratulations, Asali evaluated the contestants and settled on Mrest Eser. He had won everything except the singing. He can't carry a tune in a bucket. Have you ever met her?"

"No."

"She is stunningly beautiful and twice as smart. She realized that what Rogh treasures the most is his legacy. She has six children. Two of them are Rogh's and the rest were sired by Mrest Eser."

Digi's mother didn't do revenge halfway.

Everard frowned, thinking. "In the Okulan tradition, every child is legitimate no matter the circumstances of their birth. They anticipate wars of succession, so the children start to build their alliances early."

I nodded. "By now all of Mrest's children are very well established, with strong allies. If their parentage comes to light, Mrest Eser will claim them as his own, and the balance of power within the clan will drastically shift to the Eser family. It's even better because he never married or had other children, so they'll have no competition."

"If this comes to pass, the Esers will pull Rogh Dareel off the Oak Chair."

"Exactly. Rogh found this out just over a year ago. He has two choices for an heir of his blood: his oldest son, who is nowhere as capable as Digi, or his youngest son, who is barely eight. He sent Digi off and scrambled to build up his older son's support. Now that she knows, she will fight them both until she carves them into bloody ribbons."

"And Amur's grandfather?" Everard asked.

"He breeds the best hounds in Okula. Years ago, when Rogh was fifteen and named the heir, he came to Amur's grandfather looking for a puppy. The grandfather gifted the pick of the litter to him. But the dog required a lot of work. One day he bit Rogh, and Rogh snapped the puppy's neck."

Damn dog killer. Every time I read that scene, I wanted to murder him.

"Hardly a surprise." Everard's tone was ice-cold.

"After Rogh Dareel became the *tair*, he came to get another dog. He wanted one of those hounds to sit by him while he ruled from the Oak Chair. It would show everyone that he had the support and approval of the whole clan. Amur's grandfather refused. The next morning his entire kennel was dead. Poisoned. Decades of careful breeding, a life's work, wiped out in a single night."

"What happened?"

"The entire household wept over the dead puppies. Rogh Dareel had bribed a servant to do it, and she was so broken up about it that she confessed and surrendered the gold coin he'd given her as payment. The High Clans of the Okula are called High Clans because they have the right to mint their own gold and silver. When a new *tair* ascends, a new run of coins is struck, and these coins are numbered. The first ten coins are given to the new *tair* and are meant to be kept for a lifetime."

I probably wasn't telling him anything he didn't already know.

"What was the number on the coin the servant gave up?" Everard asked.

"Seven."

Everard smiled. I fought off a shiver. In moments like this, I didn't know if he just had an occasional spike of bloodlust or if his mask slipped, revealing a glimpse of his true nature underneath. The second possibility was much more alarming.

"How capable is Digi?" he asked.

"She's her mother's daughter. You should've seen her. If you told me that my father didn't sire me, I would need to take some time to deal with it. She took one moment and then announced a celebration in her real father's honor."

In all fairness, Rogh was a lousy father, mostly absent from his children's lives. When he did take an interest, it was because they had achieved something that benefited him and even then, he was moody and quick to snap. His offspring had to walk a fine line between accomplishing enough to stand out and be a credit to the family, but not so much that they outshone him.

"Will it bother you that you won't be the one to kill him?" I asked.

"Watching a child he raised as his own burn everything he built and then dance on the ashes of his kingdom will be much more satisfying."

Okay then. Glad we'd cleared that up.

"Why did you go to the Ribs?"

"Don't worry about it, Your Grace."

A thin streak of darkness snaked toward me. I waved my hand, dispersing it. "You don't scare me. You promised you would keep me safe, and your word is cut in stone."

"It was worth a try," he said.

Chapter 34

Planter 31

"Turn your wrist a bit more," Gort suggested, raising his head from the map he was drawing.

I stabbed the straw dummy, twisting my wrist, straightened, and exhaled.

Gort nodded at me from his seat at the laundry table. "Better."

"It's really difficult to cut through packed straw," I said.

"A human leg is thick. Lots of muscle," Gort said.

Kaiden, who sat cross-legged on the table next to him, mimicked my stabbing with his hand.

I stretched my shoulders.

In the past seventy-two hours, I had stabbed such a wide variety of humans and objects, I had dulled my dagger and had to learn how to resharpen it. Sharpening knives wasn't my strong suit. I had ended up dulling it more and had to have Shana help me.

My arm hurt, but cutting things was helping with my stress. There had been no word from Darotha. She hadn't found Isadau, Solentine hadn't found Cai, and I could feel time slipping away. Stabbing random crap was better than pulling my hair out.

The straw dummy was the latest target for my self-defense adventures. It had been made with packed straw, tightly wrapped with cords, set on a wooden base, and dressed in old rusty chainmail. I had no idea where the brothers had gotten it, but they had presented me with it yesterday and were so proud of themselves, I told them that it was the best gift ever.

Soon I would have to switch back to producing soap. The Garden had sent a messenger. They had loved it so much, they wanted to buy some. I sent Clover to negotiate. The Garden found our prices agreeable—Clover was sure that they thought we were suckers who were selling our soap to them dirt cheap. They ordered so much that we made a whole gold grest on the sale. Clover had presented the gold coin to me in the courtyard in front of everyone and then did a little dance. But now our inventory was running low.

Also, Solentine had sent two large chests with various items selected to convince anyone that I was a Demarr, including two paintings, several lacquered crests, and other silliness. I had to sort through it at some point.

A bell rang inside. Will exited the house and went to the front door.

Now who could that be?

"Where is he?"

That sounded suspiciously like Solentine.

A moment later my cousin emerged, with Will right behind him rolling his eyes. Solentine wore his incognito outfit, a plain brown jerkin and dark pants with a worn cloak, and he still looked elegant. And pissed off.

Solentine marched across the yard, holding a large wooden scroll case like a club.

"I told him. I said—" He saw me and stopped. "What are you doing?"

"Learning to stab straw people with a dagger." I showed him my knife.

"Why in the world would you learn that from them when you have me?"

Um.

Solentine motioned me away from the dummy. I joined Gort and Kaiden at the table.

Solentine set the scroll case on the table and extracted two small, slender knives from somewhere in his jerkin. They had short blades, maybe four and a half inches long, curved like claws, with the inside edge sharpened. Their handles were bone, carved to provide a textured grip, with a ring large enough to slide a finger through at their ends.

"Ooh, ooh, he's going to do the two-dagger thing!"

Yessss. His signature fighting style from the books. Yes, yes, yes!

"His Grace doesn't need two daggers," Kaiden said.

"Hush and watch," I told him.

Solentine spun the two blades in his hands and struck at the dummy, lightning fast and yet smooth, flowing like water. His left blade slashed the dummy's face, while his right hooked an imaginary arm and sliced through the inside of the elbow. He spun around the dummy, sinking his knife into the kidneys, stabbing into the armpit, slashing across the spine, and finished with a wide, beautiful cut to the throat.

I reached over and pushed Kaiden's chin up to close his mouth.

"Straw doesn't fight back," Will said.

Solentine grinned at him. "Do you?"

Will pulled his knife.

The door opened, and Everard stepped out.

"Will, don't you have blades to oil? Solentine, do not debone my soldier."

Will sheathed his knife, bowed his head to Everard, and went inside.

"You ruin all my fun," Solentine said. He flicked the knives, and they vanished back into his jerkin.

"Do you have news?" I asked. If he had figured out the missing link, I needed to know it right now.

"Yes, but not the kind we wanted."

Solentine picked up the scroll case from the table and lobbed it at Everard. Everard snatched it out of the air, pulled the scroll out of the case, glanced at it, and swore.

"I told you. I fucking told you there would be consequences," Solentine said.

"What is it?" I asked.

"We need privacy," Solentine said.

"Let's go to my office."

We went up the stairs into my office, and I shut the door.

"Um," Solentine said.

A small green fish lay on my desk. I sighed, picked it up by the tail, and carried it to the plate I'd stolen from the kitchen. I put the fish on the plate and slid it under my bed.

"I'm not even going to ask," Solentine said.

"It's Sushi," I told him. "You insulted her by calling her the guard vermin last time you were here. She keeps trying to feed me because I'm garbage at catching fish."

Sushi decided to poke her nose out from under the bed, gave Solentine a warning hiss, and vanished back into the gloom.

I wiped my hands on a towel, threw the ruined paper into the wastebasket, and sat in the chair behind my desk. "So, what's going on?"

"Sauven is throwing a joedurar," Everard ground out. "My attendance is requested."

Joedurar, pronounced jaw-doo-ruhr, translated to *meeting of the brows* in the Old Tongue, and by brow they meant forehead or mind. Long ago, when Rellas was barely a kingdom and its monarchs were only slightly more powerful than their vassals, a joedurar was called to plan strategies in response to invasions and critical issues that threatened the stability of the region. Since the lords trusted each other about as far as they could spit, each noble would arrive with a detachment of their forces.

While the lords met behind closed doors to sort out their problems, their troops would feast, drink, and dance. The hope was that having a good time would cut down on inevitable friction between different factions.

The modern joedurar wasn't much different. There would be a strategy meeting behind closed doors, followed by a combination of a formal dinner and a ball. Attendance wasn't optional. To defy the king's invitation was to risk being accused of treason.

"This is what happens when you start throwing the Fatefire to and fro," Solentine growled. "Sauven got tired of waiting for the Conquerors to find you, so he's trying to flush you out."

"What in the blazes does he want to talk about?" Everard growled.

Solentine shrugged. "The revolt in the north. The stirrings of the Empire. Who knows? He'll find something."

"When did the rider leave?" Everard asked.

"Two days ago, in secret. You must leave tonight." Solentine shook his head.

If Sauven's messenger arrived in the Selva Dukedom, and the Sleepless Duke wasn't there, it would confirm Sauven's suspicions that Everard had snuck into the city. There was no telling how he would react.

The only way to sidestep this would be to have Everard receive the messenger on arrival, as if he'd been in Selva the entire time. Sauven wouldn't believe it, but he could hardly accuse Everard of breaking the Accords based on a weird scar in some random plaza without any other evidence.

At least ten days to Selva by horse.

"Can you make it?" I asked Everard.

"Oh yes."

"How? I know Villain is a great warhorse, but the messenger is likely riding the Rellasian yarras."

Rellasian yarras were a magical breed. The best horses back home could clear forty miles per day, if they were used to running. Villain could easily cover fifty miles, possibly more. But the yarra horses, big chestnut mounts with blond manes, would leave him in the dust. They were bred specifically for cross-country marathons, and they were fast and tireless. You wouldn't want to take one on a mountain path or into battle, but as long as they had a road, they would get you from point A to point B in record time.

"I'm not going to ride Villain. I'm going to ride a drezmur."

Zmur was any large predatory bird, *dre* was probably from the Old Tongue *dreog* . . .

"Fear bird?" What the hell was a fear bird?

Everard focused on me. "Maggie, do you know what a drezmur is?"

There was zero chance he would believe me if I lied. "No."

"So you've never seen one?" He looked like a cat luring a mouse to play with his claws. "Would you like to meet a drezmur?"

Solentine shook his head at me.

Are you kidding me? "Yes, I would."

My cousin rolled his eyes.

"Does Sauven know about you riding drezmurs?" I asked.

"No," Everard said. "If all goes well, I will be in Selva tomorrow, but it will take me at least twenty days to return."

The messenger had left two days ago, so eight days to reach Selva, then about ten days to get back by normal means. And Everard would have to arrive in

Kair Toren in a very public manner, with his knights. That meant they would travel as fast as their slowest horse. He could take a ship, but that would take even longer.

"You will be alone for almost three weeks," he said. "I don't like it."

"She will be well protected," Solentine said.

"Right now Hreban doesn't know that his crew reached the house," Everard said. "For all he knows, they were intercepted by Velpor, had some sort of disagreement, and then killed each other. However, that doesn't mean he has forgotten that Maggie exists. He wants to silence her at the very least. He will try again."

"If he does, my people will take care of it. Besides, with the Conquerors breathing down his neck, he will be highly unlikely to send more killers. Too risky." Solentine picked up a box from my shelf, looked into it, and pulled a bar of soap out. "Is this the soap you gave to the Garden?"

"Yes."

"I'll need a big box. At least twenty-five bars."

"What in the void are you going to do with that much soap?" Everard demanded. He sounded irritated. His Grace really didn't want to leave me unsupervised.

"I'm going to send it to her mother."

"Why?"

"Because when a woman makes soap, perfume, embroidery, or any other home-related craft, she will gift it to her mother first. If someone comes to Demarr to confirm her identity, the soap will seal the deal."

"You can have that box," I told him. "It's our sampler."

Solentine picked up the box. "I will pick you up tonight, Ramond."

Everard waved him off.

Solentine gave me a long look.

Right. "Let me see you off," I said.

I got up and we walked together down the stairs and across the yard.

We were almost to the front door when he said, "Under no circumstances must you allow him to get you onto a drezmur. No matter what he says, do not go near it, or you will wake up tomorrow in Selva."

"Understood."

"Good. Ramond isn't the only one who has to leave the capital. I've received orders to escort my father to the joedurar in person."

"Why?"

"I have no idea."

"Did you do something to alarm Sauven?"

"I've done absolutely nothing. I don't know what he is scheming, but I will have to make a public exit tomorrow. That means that neither Ramond nor I will be here for almost three weeks. You will have the protection of my people, but without my presence, you will be vulnerable. Do you want to make the trip with me?"

"I can't. I have to stay here and finish what I started."

He nodded. "I thought as much. I will respect your wishes. We will talk more tonight, after he leaves."

He knew I'd seen him shaking his head when Everard asked me about a drezmur. I'd ignored him, but he didn't chide me. He didn't criticize, he just moved on to mitigate the damage. That's how he handled his siblings' messes. He'd explained it in the books once. He saw no point in berating his brother and sister for their mistakes. He trusted that they were smart enough to realize when they blundered. Only fixing it mattered.

In this moment Solentine was treating me the way he did family. It was . . . touching.

"I promise not to get onto the drezmur."

"If you do, I won't be able to get you off it."

"I understand."

I opened the door for him. "One last thing, before you go. Who did Sauven send as the messenger to the Selva Dukedom?"

Solentine grimaced. "Joris. His new favorite dog."

Oh no.

I locked the door behind him and hurried across the yard. I ran up the stairs, crossed the hallway, and rushed into the room.

Everard had remained in his chair. I caught a glimpse of his expression as I came through the doorway. His face was harsh and cold, as if carved from ice with a razor-sharp sword.

"The messenger is Joris."

"What about it?"

"He will poison you. He will use omaran, the same poison that killed your father, and blame the Crimson Empire for it."

A spark of brilliant green flashed in Everard's eyes. "Will he, now?"

That's what happened in the books. The joedurar was called after the assassination of the Sun Margrave, which should've happened months from now, but I'd sent the timeline to hell in a handbasket. In the old timeline Sauven dispatched Joris to fetch Everard with orders to poison him. Joris had done exactly that, and Everard barely survived that attempt. It took him months to recover. He couldn't even attend the joedurar, which was why Sauven demanded his presence at the Winter Hunt. He was still sick at the Hunt. And then Kiel was murdered, and Kair Toren went off the rails.

"Joris will do it on the way to Kair Toren. The poisoning will be severe enough that you will return to Selva instead of pushing on."

Everard didn't seem concerned.

"Listen to me."

I strode to his chair, leaned my arms on the armrests, and stared straight into his eyes.

"When you meet Joris, don't touch anything he offers you. If he brings you a gift of wine, don't taste it. If he offers you a beautiful dagger, don't hold it. If he gives you a dog as a gift, don't pet it. If you smell strong perfume, find a way to exit the room. Don't eat with him, don't drink with him, don't share any items. Touch nothing his hands have touched."

His eyes widened.

"Joris is very good at what he does, and omaran has no antidote. If you feel sick, don't take the extract of wodon flower. It will make things worse. Drink a glass of water and make yourself vomit, and then do it again, and again. Your only hope is to dilute and purge the poison before your body digests it. Promise me."

He stared.

"Ramond, promise me!"

"I promise."

"You swear?"

"I do." He nodded. "I'll be careful. Trust me, Maggie."

I realized I was still clutching his chair and let go.

"Thank you for warning me," he said.

"Don't thank me." I dropped into my chair. "Just don't die."

We fell silent. Everard stood up and looked at the window, thinking about something. He looked very regal right now, elegant and focused, his face severe and unforgiving.

I didn't want him to die.

He was leaving the house, which played right into my hands. I needed to do things, and his presence would make them impossible. He would never let me rescue Isadau. More, this was my chance to escape his grasp. When he came back, he would arrive in public. The Accords he'd signed limited his movement in the capital and he would be closely watched. This was our last chance to spend time together.

It felt like someone had stabbed me in the heart and twisted the knife.

I would miss him. No, that was nowhere near adequate. Not having him hear would feel like a hole had been torn in my life. He was at once a threat and my safety net, and he took up so much room. As long as he was in this house, no intruder would make it past him, but that's not what I would miss the most. I would miss his wit, his sharp mind, his rare smiles, the way he looked at me, his body, his voice . . . *Him*, I would miss him.

Oh, I'd fallen really hard. If there was any doubt before, it was all gone now, because when I thought about Joris, panic punched me right in the heart. I was terrified Ramond would die.

Damn it.

"How did he do it in your future?" he asked.

"He gifted you a dagger."

"Was the blade poisoned?"

"The sheath. He soaked the leather in a solution of powdered omaran, and the sheath felt slightly sticky. Once you handled it, you washed your hands, and the water activated the poison. Then you rubbed your face, getting it into your eyes and mouth." I took a deep breath. "You bled from your eyes for three days, Ramond."

"Killing me puts the entire northern border at risk," Everard said. "I don't have an heir, so the Dukedom would pass to my cousin. Her Fatefire is only a shadow of mine, and she is barely fourteen. That daft prick would risk his kingdom and his throne to kill me."

"Sauven is afraid for his crown prince," I said. "Every time he builds a coalition around his son, Kiel does something to fracture it. Sauven sees you as a threat that can end his line. He fears you more than he fears the Crimson Empire. And he hates you."

"Because I look like my father? Because I refuse to tolerate his inane nonsense?"

"Because you are everything Kiel Savaric is not. You inspire people. They devote themselves to you. Kiel has his magic, his sword, and his glib charm, but his arrogance and rage keep him from truly understanding human emotions. He doesn't form bonds of loyalty; he manipulates, intimidates, and uses people, and they recognize it. He hasn't built a foundation for his throne, and he never will. Sauven knows it. It keeps him up at night."

He walked around the desk and leaned his back against it, leaving me no room to get up off my chair. There was barely any space between us.

"Come with me to Selva."

It was almost a plea.

"You know I can't."

"I don't want to leave you here without my protection."

"I have the Magnars and the Shears."

"Come with me. I swear on the memory of my father I will bring you back to Kair Toren in twenty days."

"I can't. There are things I must do here. The future—"

"Fuck the future. If I come back here and find you gone, I will level this damn city. If you care for Kair Toren, come with me."

I had to put some distance between us. I stood up. He wrapped his arms around me, pulling me close, and rested his forehead against mine. "Maggie . . ."

Oh, no. My whole body sang when he touched me.

"Don't leave me alone. Let me take you to Selva."

I had to break free of him, and not just because I couldn't trust him or because he would use me. I needed to know if I could survive in Kair Toren without him. I'd been leaning on him like a crutch, first when he was Reynald and then again when he was the Sleepless Duke sleeping under the same roof. I had to find out if I could make it on my own.

"Let me go, Your Grace." Against all odds, my voice sounded calm.

He raised his arms and took a step back. It almost hurt to be let go.

I was on the right track. It was time to stand on my own two feet.

"I can't leave any more than you can stay. Let's not talk about it anymore."

Everard wasn't used to hearing no. He had to be frustrated, but none of it reflected on his face. His control was ridiculous. It would've been so much easier if he was an open book.

"Promise me you will be careful," he said. "Twenty days. Stay in the house, make soap, don't do anything reckless."

"I promise," I lied.

The boat slipped along the dark sea, fast and nimble. I sat at the bow and watched the sky spreading above us, the stars glittering so bright, Prata waning, Drao in first quarter, and Broe a sliver of a crescent, almost an afterthought.

Solentine's people came to get us, as promised. Everard and I boarded the small vessel, the sails went up, and a few minutes later we slipped out of the city and headed into the open sea. That was always the trouble with Kair Toren. You could lock the city gates, but blockading the harbor was a lot harder.

We reached a couple of islands, dark jagged tops of submerged hills thrusting through the water. At first, I thought we'd stop at one of them, but instead we passed them on our right and kept going.

Half an hour later, the boat made a turn toward the shore. The hills rose high here, a dark wall sloping sharply to the water. Dense vegetation covered the nearly vertical surface, shrubs, strange-looking grasses, and dense, thorny thickets of rudberry. The boat slid to a small dock, and we disembarked.

A soft high-pitched whir came from the cliff above us. If humpback whales could purr, they would have sounded just like this, haunting, beautiful, and uncanny.

Everard steered me to a path clinging to the side of the hill, leading upward the apex. We began to climb. Halfway up I began puffing and huffing, while Everard didn't even break a sweat. He must've been part mountain goat.

Finally, we reached the top. I followed him through the narrow gap between two bushes and walked into a clearing facing the ocean.

A huge white beast stood by the cliff, fully eighteen feet tall at the shoulder. It had a body like a greyhound, with a long ermine-like tail and four long legs, powerful but slender, with paws armed with crescent talons. Its deep chest narrowed to a ridiculously small waist. Its neck was long and flexible, almost swan-like, except much thicker, topped with a sleek head that ended in an eagle's beak. The feathers on its body were so fine, they looked almost like fur, but on the back of its head, they grew into a long secretary bird crest, darkening toward the ends to a shimmering golden brown.

The creature saw us. Its turquoise eyes shone. It spread its enormous wings, blocking the sky. They were golden near the leading edge and white at the contour feathers. Two giant curved claws tipped the wing bends.

Nothing in my life had prepared me for this. There was no equivalent in our world. This was magical. This creature shouldn't have existed but here it was, in front of me, and it took my breath away.

The beast leaned forward, stretching its neck. Its head lowered and came toward me, lower and closer, and closer . . .

"Easy." Everard stepped forward.

The beast nudged him out of the way with its head, its eyes fixed on me. It bumped me with its beak and blew air out with a soft huff.

"Oh, she likes you." Solentine walked out of the shadows.

I reached out. Some part of me realized that the drezmur could cut me in half with one crunch of that beak, but I couldn't help myself. My fingers slipped through the pale feathers on the bridge of her nose. Oh wow. Soft and silky, like a kitten.

"The drezmurs live in the northern mountains." Everard stroked the feathers next to my hand. "They require both flesh and magic to survive, so they hunt creatures rich in magic, like peibasas, kugats, or dorseem. They are always hungry. And they will allow you to ride and steer them, as long as you feed your magic to them."

Ride them?

He laughed softly. "You should see your eyes, Maggie. They are so big."

Who was the first person to even think of riding one of these? How?

"It takes a great deal of magic to make them carry you," Solentine said. "Very few people can do it. Especially outside of the Selvan Mountains. You must be brimming with it because she is dying for a taste."

"What happens if you run out of magic before you get where you're going?" I asked.

"If you lose consciousness before you land, the drezmur will fling you off their back and devour you," Solentine said.

I turned to Everard.

He nodded. "Luckily for us, I have a lot of magic."

Now the exhausted Solentine from a few days ago made sense. He'd said he had to go around a thunderstorm, which added three hours to the flight. It must've drained his magic reserves to nothing.

Everard's face had a speculative look, as if he had just thought of something. "Would you like to ride her?"

Oh wow.

"We can go for a short test flight above the sea."

Under no circumstances must you allow him to get you onto a drezmur.

Saying yes was out of the question, and if I took a step back, he would grab me and pull me onto this creature. I had no idea how I knew it; I just sensed it. I held perfectly still.

"You're not taking my cousin onto a drezmur," Solentine said. "It's one thing for you and me to risk our lives, but there is no need for her to flirt with death. Come on. You're wasting the moonlight."

Everard's eyes said *Come with me.*

I opened my mouth. "Safe journey, Your Grace."

He sighed and raised his hand. A barely perceptible curl of dark smoke shimmering with green slipped from his fingers and sank into the pale feathers.

The drezmur raised her head and crouched.

The sound of hoofbeats came from the shadows. A man walked out of them, leading a big stallion. The horse was the color of smoke, and its face was pure white.

Hello, Villain. We meet again.

The drezmur let out that high-pitched purr again.

Villain stopped and blew air out of his nose. The man pulled on the lead. The stallion snapped at him.

"Foul temper," Solentine told me. "Like his master."

Everard walked over to his horse, took the reins from the man, petted the stallion's face, and walked him to the side, where a narrow wooden crate waited. I hadn't even noticed it until now.

Everard pulled the blinders over Villain's eyes. The stallion stopped again.

"Come on. We've done this before," Everard told him.

Villain huffed, stepped from foot to foot, and then walked into the crate. Everard secured the ropes leading from the harness, tying them down inside the crate, and shut the door, locking the big horse inside. There was a chain attached to the crate, looping under it, and another on top . . .

"Are you going to fly him to Selva?"

Everard looked at me and grinned. "How else would he get there in time?"

"But he's so heavy, and the crate and the chain must weigh so much . . ."

"I once saw a drezmur pick up a trader boat fully loaded with cargo," Everard said. "Trust me, this is nothing."

He strode to the drezmur, then turned.

"Will you give me a kiss for luck, my lady?"

"Absolutely not," Solentine said.

"I didn't ask you," Everard told him.

He was pulling out all the stops, huh.

"Come back safe, without getting poisoned, and you will get one."

Ramond turned and stepped on the drezmur's forepaw. The beast raised it, and he climbed onto her back.

"Wait for me," he called out.

"Maybe," I told him.

The drezmur reared. Her wings snapped open, blocking half of the sky. She thrust her beak into the loop of the chain on top of Villain's crate. It slid over her head onto her neck, the crate dangling from it like a locket. The giant beast spun toward the cliff, sprinted, leaped, and soared into the night.

"Thank you, Divine." Solentine exhaled. "Finally."

Chapter 35

Redberry 5

"I can't smell it." Shana sniffed the small block of soap and put it back on the kitchen table, next to the other six bars.

"We can't put any more in there," Clover said. "The soap won't hold."

"That settles it. No honey." I crossed honey off the soap additives list. It had been a long shot anyway. In our world, I would have used honey fragrance oil, but there was none to be had here.

Everard had been gone for five days. The house felt strangely empty. I wouldn't know if he had survived for another fifteen days, possibly longer.

I had done everything I could to warn him.

"Yes, you did," Shana said.

I hadn't realized that I had spoken that last part out loud.

"His Grace is very intelligent," Clover said. "He won't let himself be poisoned."

"Clover is right," Shana told me. "People have been trying to kill him since he was a boy and he's still here."

Kaiden dashed into the kitchen. "There are guards outside."

"What guards?" I asked.

"City guards."

"Teal tabards?"

Kaiden nodded.

"What do they want?"

"To talk to you."

Why would the guards want to talk to me? Were they looking for Everard? I couldn't think of any other reason, unless the Filderon thing had come back to us, but so much time had passed . . .

I got up and marched to the front door.

Will and Lute had parked themselves in the tunnel in front of the outer door, blocking access. Gort stood directly behind them, brandishing his axe.

"What is going on?" I asked.

Gort bowed. "My lady, these guards are requesting to speak to you."

It was time to channel a noble. I made a *step aside* motion with my hand. I'd seen Everard do it often enough. The Magnars parted and I saw three men in chainmail and City Guard tabards.

The leader held out a scroll. "Knight Captain Jehan invites you to join him for a conversation."

I stared at him.

He held my gaze for a long moment, then added, "My lady."

I nodded at Will. He took the scroll and presented it to me.

"A conversation where?" Gort growled.

"At the Southern Guard Station," I said. "No reason given."

The Magnars squared their shoulders in unison. The lead guard took a small step back. His two colleagues put their hands on their weapons.

As far as I knew, the guards had no authority to remove me from the house without a written order. Rellas took the concept of "my home, my castle" very seriously. We could shut the door in their faces. However, that would only postpone this confrontation. There was a decent chance that they would come back with more guards or try to snatch me up when I was out in the city.

No, it was better to do this now, on my terms.

"I will require at least an hour to get ready. You may wait here, or you may return at that time."

"We'll wait." The lead guard took what my father would call the "at ease" position. They wouldn't be moving from their spot.

"You have a carriage, I assume? Or were you going to march me through the streets?"

The lead guard blinked.

I sighed. "Willem, procure a carriage for me while they're waiting. Let us not advertise the Guard's lack of courtesy."

The lead guard turned slightly red.

I gave Will a pointed look. *Go to the Shears and get a carriage.*

Will bowed his head, stepped out into the street, and shut the door behind him. I headed into the courtyard.

"This is ill-advised," Gort said.

I kept my voice low. "There is absolutely no reason for city guards to be here. Someone is behind this, and we need to know who."

"What if they detain you?"

"On what charge?"

"On whatever charge they come up with while they have you there."

"Then we'll wait for the Shears to get me out. I'm sure my cousin left detailed instructions. Don't do anything. Wait for me. I will be back."

Knight Captain Jehan had a dilemma on his hands. I wasn't sure what he had expected, but I clearly wasn't it. I wore a gown in a beautiful green—Clover had made it for me to replace the one the Butcher had ruined. My hair was braided and styled to the latest fashion with silver cord and appropriate ornaments. My makeup was flawless, and I was looking at him as if he were a mosquito buzzing around me. Clover stood behind my chair, her hands demurely folded, her eyes downcast.

Knight Captains acted in the same capacity as police lieutenants in most large cities back home. Kair Toren had four main City Guard stations, each headed by a station commander, who had anywhere from four to six Knight Captains under his authority. The Knight Captains supervised the sergeants, who in turn supervised the guards. In terms of position, Jehan was upper middle management, and he hadn't gotten that far by being dense. Intimidating a commoner was one thing, although under Rellasian law, even a commoner could appeal. Detaining a noblewoman without a solid cause was an entirely different matter, and if handled incorrectly, could cost him his career.

I had been ushered into his office three minutes ago, and he had yet to say a single word.

The Knight Captain gave me a heavy look. He was in his mid- to late thirties, maybe even early forties, a tall man with a severe expression and some silver in his hair. He wore a black and teal tabard over dark chainmail. A teal half cloak hugged his throat and draped down his back with a metal pauldron on one shoulder. A complicated belt of dark leather wrapped his waist, offering a variety of pockets filled with various things a City Guard Knight Captain might find handy.

His office was a large square space in the middle of the Southern Guard Station. He sat behind a heavy wooden desk, with stacks of paper and scrolls on both sides. Behind him the Kair Toren flag stretched across the wall, teal, edged with black, with a stylized Skyline of Eagle Roost in gold. The Justice Chamber was attired in royal colors, mostly purple, but as municipal police force, the City Guard had its own color scheme.

One of us had to start this conversation or I would be here all day.

"Knight Captain Jehan, I presume?" I asked.

"Correct. Whom do I have the privilege of addressing?"

"You sent your people to my house. Surely you know who I am?"

"That is what we are here to determine."

I had brought the full set of my papers and the metal crest of the Demarr family complete with my name on it. Solentine had helpfully left all of it for me. If I showed it, Jehan would have a hard time keeping me here. There was always a chance that he might detain me under some pretext of verifying my identity, but it would be a huge gamble for him.

Somebody was using him to figure out who I was. My money was on either Hreban or Silveren, and I wanted to know who was pulling Jehan's strings.

Knight Captain Jehan was treating me to the medieval version of the "you're in big trouble" cop stare.

"So you do not know who I am." I crossed my arms. "Is this how you find out? When you're not sure who lives in a house, you just have them dragged down here? It seems like an odd use of the Guard's time and resources."

He didn't say anything.

"Or perhaps I am a special case? I can't help but note that the Guard station closest to my residence is in the north. Instead, I had to travel for the better part of an hour and cross two bridges to be brought here. Why?"

He glowered at me. "Here, I ask the questions."

"Please start then. Whatever we can do to speed this thing along."

He opened his mouth.

Something thudded outside the office, followed by the sound of raised voices.

"Just one question before we begin," I said. "Am I charged with a crime?"

He unhinged his jaws. "Not yet."

The commotion got louder and closer.

"Am I being detained?"

"Not exactly."

"If not, am I free to leave?"

Welcome to twenty-first-century police-encounter protocol.

"Just a moment." He turned toward the door.

"If I am being detained, I request the services of a law scribe."

"Hold that thought." Jehan rose, stepped outside, and shut the door behind him.

Behind me Clover snickered.

A deep male voice roared something in the distance. I couldn't quite make it out, but it might have been "Where?" Whoever he was, he sounded pissed. Rhythmic thuds drew closer. Somebody was coming down the hallway in heavy boots.

The door flew open, and Lord Bellen marched into the room, enormous in full Defender armor, with a huge sword on his hip and a white Defender cloak billowing behind him. His helmet was off, and his blond hair looked slightly tousled.

Bellen saw me. His blue eyes lit up.

"Lady Maggie! There you are."

"Lord Bellen! Did they drag you in here, too?"

"Not at all."

Behind Bellen, two more Defender Knights in full armor shouldered their way into Jehan's office, one dark haired with olive skin, and the other with ash-blond hair and the kind of complexion that guaranteed a sunburn in thirty seconds. The Knight Captain was the last one through the door.

"What is the meaning of this?" Bellen roared at him.

Jehan raised his chin, clearly not willing to be intimidated in his own office. "We received a report that this woman—"

Bellen glared at him.

"—this noblewoman is conducting business without a permit."

Bellen glanced at me.

"Is this about the soap?" I did my best to sound shocked.

"What soap, my lady?" Bellen asked.

"I make perfumed soap for my family, and an acquaintance asked me to sell her some."

Bellen flicked his fingers. The dark-haired knight took a step forward. "I am Sir Owyn, Baron Ragvart, Senior Law Scribe of the Defender Order. Am I to understand, Knight Captain, that you sent guards to a noblewoman's home, removed her from her abode, brought her, under guard, here, to your office, detained her, and questioned her without cause because she didn't file for a trader permit? Is that correct?"

Oh wow. Bellen had brought lawyer support.

"Knight Captain, is this correct?" Owyn demanded.

"In part." Jehan looked directly at Bellen, judging him to be the biggest threat.

"Since when does the City Guard oversee compliance with trade permit laws? Is that matter not under the purview of the Treasury?"

Jehan said nothing.

"Answer the question!" Bellen thundered.

"I *invited* the lady—"

"Do you have a warrant?" Owyn demanded. "Who signed it?"

"We were simply conversing." Jehan glanced at me.

I actually felt sorry for him. "The Knight Captain extended his invitation to me, and I voluntarily accepted. I was not arrested, although he did neglect to provide a carriage."

Bellen somehow got even larger. "Did she walk, or did she have to pay for her own carriage to be interrogated?"

Jehan took a step back, almost out of his own office. "Lord . . ."

"Be silent!" Bellen stepped over to me and offered his arm. "My lady, would you do me the honor of allowing me to accompany you out of this place?"

The entire point of coming here had been to figure out who had arranged this mess. That ship had sailed. All I could do was let Bellen complete his rescue in a blaze of glory.

"I would be delighted, my lord."

"Splendid." Bellen gave me a brilliant smile.

I put my hand on his arm and stood up.

"We are leaving," Bellen announced.

As he led me out of the office, Bellen pointed at the Knight Captain. Before the door swung closed behind us, I saw the other two knights close on Jehan like two hounds cornering a raccoon.

Outside, sunshine flooded the streets. Lord Bellen gave me another brilliant smile. The man looked overjoyed.

"Lord Bellen, that was amazing. Thank you for my rescue."

"Don't mention it."

He was leading to the right, where a massive white horse waited.

"My carriage . . ." Where the hell was the Shears' carriage?

"Won't be necessary," he assured me. "With your permission."

He didn't wait for my permission. He picked me up and lifted me onto the horse. Oh crap. The saddle was neither Western nor Eastern. It had a weird-padded bar. It was probably a war saddle, designed to keep you on the horse no matter what.

What was I supposed to do with my dress?

Screw it. I swung my leg over and sat in the saddle properly. Clover stepped forward and tugged my dress into place with a perfectly neutral expression and subtly nodded. Oh phew. I had done the right thing and dodged a social bullet.

Bellen took the horse's reins.

"My lord, is this your warhorse?"

"Indeed."

He started down the street. A couple of guards turned the corner, heading toward the Guard station, saw us, and gaped.

"I cannot possibly ride your warhorse."

Rellasian knight warhorses were highly trained and prized, and they tended to be loyal only to their rider. Touching a knight's horse without permission was taking your life in your hands.

"Of course you can. You are doing it right now. You're so light, he barely noticed."

"I can walk."

"Please, my lady, I couldn't possibly tolerate you overexerting yourself in my presence."

You've got to be kidding me. "My lord . . ."

Bellen gave me another grin. "Lady Maggie, this is a proper rescue. Having bested a corrupt Knight Captain, we must now make our exit in style."

What? "What if we made a quiet getaway instead?"

"Impossible. The Holy Order of the Defender must maintain its reputation. You have done us a great service by warning us about the danger to Dame

Eliarde. It is only fair that we demonstrate to everyone that you are under our protection. Anything else would displease Lord Arvel."

I glanced at Clover. She made big eyes at me. Right. No help there either. I just had to sit here on top of this colossal horse and try to maintain some dignity. The last time I went riding was two years ago and it was on the beach, in Galveston. My mount had been an old mare, and I rode her at a gentle walk.

The Shears' carriage was supposed to wait for me. Instead, it was nowhere to be found. In Solentine's absence, Avaria was in charge, and I had a feeling she did not care for me.

We reached an intersection. We should've turned right, north, toward our house. Instead, we turned left, south.

"My lord, I think we're going the wrong way."

He frowned. "No, I'm quite certain this is the shortest route."

"Where are we going?"

"To the Citadel, of course."

Of course. What was I thinking?

"Why are we going there?"

"To celebrate your glorious rescue."

"My people will be very anxious about my safety."

"No worries," he assured me. "Once we reach the Citadel, I will send your maid to inform them of your whereabouts in a carriage. Clover, is it?"

"Yes, my lord," Clover answered.

"Have no fear. Your lady will be perfectly safe. I'm reasonably certain the Defender Knights can withstand an assault from the City Guard."

Bellen winked at me.

I sighed. "When I was younger, my mother said, 'If a man is charming and smooth-tongued, you must ask yourself how he got that way.'"

"Your mother sounds like a very wise woman," Bellen said.

"My lord, I think you are the man my mother warned me about."

He laughed.

I shut up and concentrated on staying in the saddle. At least I had gotten out of the Guard station without revealing my identity. Hreban was still in the dark. Even Bellen only knew my first name, and I needed to keep it that way.

Twenty minutes later we rode into the Citadel's courtyard. Bellen lifted me off the horse. A female squire came running out and took the reins.

"Get a carriage for Tress Clover," Bellen ordered.

Clover gave me a look. I nodded. He seemed very intent on separating me from my maid. Might as well find out why.

"This way." Bellen offered me his arm again.

I put my hand on his forearm, and we ascended the massive staircase, going up to the keep. Midway up, Bellen stopped and frowned. I looked in the direction of his stare. The entire city lay below us, miles of roofs and walls, interrupted by the flat ribbons of the rivers, and in the distance the thin spire of the Mage Tower thrust to the sky. Above it a huge fireball churned, a sphere of brilliant red flames, spinning and turning. Dear god, it had to be bigger than a city block.

"What in the void is he doing now?" Bellen growled.

Another knight descended a staircase, a lean, dark-haired man. Bellen pointed toward the Mage Tower.

"Apparently, we are expecting a rock from the heavens," the other knight said.

"Again?"

"It's a larger one than last year's. He sent the dispatch to the Eagle Roost this morning. At least he warned us this time."

"Thank the Aspects for small favors," Bellen said.

The fireball blazed with pure white. A laser beam of light shot out of it toward the sky, sucking the fire into itself. A sonic boom pulsed through the city and smashed into my ears. The Citadel shuddered.

Bellen wrapped his arm around me. It was like being steadied by a mountain.

A wind gust fanned us and died.

"My apologies." Bellen let go of me.

The space above the Mage Tower was perfectly clear.

A shower of sparks lit up the sky above the city. They flared and melted into the blue.

Holy fuck. Damaes had just blasted a meteor out of the sky. Probably before it even hit the atmosphere.

This was a man I was picking a fight with. Damaes was a power unto himself. He recognized Sauven's authority, because Sauven was the king, but not anyone else's. If he decided to take issue with what I was doing, nobody could stop him. There would be no discussion, no negotiations. He would just do whatever he did and then our house would turn into a smoking crater.

Maybe I should rethink the whole Isadau thing.

No, I was committed now. I had no choice. Besides, now that I knew I could read Sareso, leaving Isadau where she was wasn't an option. I couldn't bring myself to do it.

"I swear, one day that man will destroy the city." Bellen pointed toward the entrance to the keep. "This way, my lady."

He led me into the keep. I had expected a dungeon-like fortress, but it was a bright, beautiful space with soaring ceilings and tall arches. We crossed the floor to a patio, where two squires were setting up a table.

"A light lunch?" Bellen asked.

To decline would be rude.

"I would love to."

He held the chair out for me. I took my seat. The view from the patio was stunning. I looked at the array of finger foods in front of me.

"You have rescued me and fed me, Lord Bellen. I'm afraid I have no way to repay you."

"The pleasure of your company would more than suffice."

He looked so pleased with himself, it was hard not to smile back.

"Wine?"

"I would prefer tea."

"As you wish."

One of the squires reached for the teapot. Bellen waved him off and poured the tea for me. The squires withdrew.

"This is too much, really. I can pour my own tea."

"You are so easy to overwhelm, Lady Maggie. You must endeavor to be more demanding."

I sipped the tea. Delicious. "How did you know I was at the Guard station?"

"Interesting, that. A child brought a note to the Citadel. It said that you had been arrested and were held at the Southern Guard Station."

Another note. Who the hell was sending these?

"Was it from one of your people, perhaps?" Bellen asked.

"No. I gave them strict instructions to do nothing and wait for me. Did you question the child?"

"He said a priest paid him a quarter to deliver it."

Interesting. "Did he say which Aspect?"

Bellen shook his head. "No. The child was too young and didn't pay attention."

"I'm at a loss then. I do not have close ties to any of the temples."

Bellen studied me. "Why leave the safety of your house?"

"Because city guards do not usually come to the door of law-abiding citizens and *invite* them to meet with a Knight Captain. Especially not over something so trivial as a trade permit. I wanted to know who was behind Jehan."

Bellen nodded. The charm and humor were gone now. The man sitting across from me was sharp and focused. "A sound strategy. Might as well flush the culprit out into the open. You must've been quite frustrated when I pulled you out of that office."

"Never." I smiled at him. "You were so gallant it was worth it."

One of the squires returned with a note and withdrew. Bellen glanced at it.

"Ah. Just in time. Owyn's chat with the Knight Captain was most productive. Is there a reason Ulmar Hreban might want to intimidate you?"

That's what I thought. Jehan had mentioned the soap. Silveren wouldn't have paid attention to that, but Hreban was a businessman. If he somehow figured out that I had sold soap to the Garden and he wanted to know my identity, he would check for a trade permit. Since one wasn't filed, he'd used its absence as a pretext to get my name.

I wished I could tell how much to freak out over this.

"I can't imagine what that would be," I lied. "We've never been introduced. Our families have no conflicts or mutual trade interests. It is puzzling."

Bellen frowned. "Hreban is a difficult enemy with many resources at his disposal."

The question was, what was Hreban really after? I doubted the Butcher had shared the fact that he had gotten his ass kicked with his employer. Hreban had the warehouse watched, and his people saw my rescue. For all he knew, I was a random woman the Butcher had grabbed off the street for fun, and my family had found and saved me. That would be far preferable to him knowing the truth.

"Do you have family in the city?" Bellen asked.

"Yes, but my cousin is away at the moment."

"Do you wish to prolong your visit to the Citadel, my lady? We could arrange a short stay. As you can see, we have plenty of room." He leaned forward slightly, his blue eyes warm and inviting. "I personally would find a chance to share time with you most agreeable."

Bellen had just hit on me. What the hell?

"Wouldn't that put you in conflict with Hreban?"

"He sought to harm you. He is already my enemy."

What?

He reached over and covered my hand with his.

"Won't you stay, my lady? I would be truly delighted."

If Everard knew that a handsome Defender knight had rescued me, brought me to his castle, fed me snacks, and was now trying to persuade me to temporarily move in, he would lose his mind.

So far Bellen had been perfectly courteous, but he'd basically kidnapped me. He didn't seem in a hurry to let me go either. Quite the opposite. I needed to lay some boundaries and fast.

"It wouldn't be proper, my lord. Besides, the Lord Commander will likely take a dim view of some random woman staying in his Citadel."

"I'm sure I can smooth things over," he said.

"I can't. My family would not approve."

"Then perhaps you'll give me a chance to change their mind."

"If I didn't know better, my lord, I'd think you're trying sweep me off my feet."

"I am," he said. "Is it working?"

Good question. If Hreban and Silveren weren't an imminent threat and if I were free of the tangled ball of feelings Everard evoked, it would absolutely work. Bellen was stunning, and funny, and he treated me with flawless courtesy, but I sensed a core of steel underneath all of that. There was more to Lord Bellen than he was willing to show. I was on thin ice, and I had to tread carefully.

"I'm flattered, my lord. Any woman in my place would be overjoyed."

"But you're not just any woman." He said it as if he meant something deeper by it.

"I'm not. Also, we barely know each other."

He smiled at me. "Well, that's something we will have to remedy, isn't it?"

Chapter 36

Redberry 6

The light of the early morning played on my desk and the pages of a genealogy book. Escaping the Citadel yesterday had taken some doing. Clover had returned with Gort and the brothers, and nobody had told me. Who knew how long Bellen would've kept them waiting, except that he got a message via another squire. Something had happened that required his attention, so he regretfully released me.

Bellen's interest in me was a new development. He wasn't in the books, so I was flying in the dark. If this had been the first week of me being here, that fact would've sent me into a spiral of anxiety, but I had adjusted now. This world was so much bigger, and I'd already seen too much of it.

I had other ways of getting information now. He had to be fairly high in the Defender Order. I needed to figure out which noble family he was affiliated with. Trouble was, Derog's genealogy books were way out-of-date.

Someone rapped their knuckles on the doorframe. I looked up. Will leaned in the doorway of the office. His color was off, his face looked like he had slept on it, and a spectacular shiner clutched at his left eye. Blue and purple, it had swollen to a glossy puffiness like some sort of awful jewel.

"Rough night?" I asked.

"You might say that."

I pointed at one of the chairs. Usually he dropped into them, but this time he sat kind of carefully, like he was sore.

"What happened to you?" I waved my finger around my left eye, indicating his shiner.

He grinned. "I picked a fight with some mercs from the South. We threw some punches and then got drunk together."

"Did you get anything good?" He wouldn't have done that unless he had an agenda.

"A busted eye, a hangover, and the Butcher's name."

The reed pen fell out of my fingers. Finally.

"Tell me."

"His name was Serem Vor. Born to a family of weavers out of Kwinspir. He was from the Lower Middle Fields."

"Hreban's domain."

"Yes. He enlisted in the King's Army at seventeen and was assigned to the Blir."

The southern border of Rellas ran along the Copper Mountains, an older, drier mountain range. On the other side of it lay the Jastoro Tribe Horde, a nation of a thousand tribes united by faith in Kamagant-God, the Great Serpent. The Jastoro was a tribal theocracy, where chiefs ruled their tribes with the blessing of the tribe high priests, and every high priest fancied himself a prophet.

Serving at the southern border meant repelling a constant tide of raids as the roving tribes took turns testing Rellasian defenses. It was a small never-ending war. And if you were captured, you would be tortured and murdered. Kamagant-God liked his sacrifices well tenderized.

"Serem Vor was knighted at twenty-three for talent and wartime achievements," Will continued. "Most of his fighting happened on the Jastoro border. The clansmen raid constantly. It's a shit post. The way people tell it, the stuff that happens at that border will turn your hair white."

"The Jastorons don't see other people as people," I told him. "To them, only those who worship the Kamagant-God are human. Everyone else is just a living corpse without a soul. One doesn't have to feel bad about atrocities committed against a corpse."

Religious extremists rarely had room for compassion. They were too busy making their religion into everyone else's problem.

"That's what I heard," Will said. "Most people only last a few years at the border, then they get transferred. Serem Vor did twenty-two."

"Did he upset someone important?" I guessed.

"Several people, but that wasn't what kept him there. He was offered a transfer several times. He declined. Word is, he liked it. Fit right in and gave as good as he got. The Jastorons had a name for him. I can't pronounce it, but they called him the blood reaper."

Ah. So that's how he'd honed his human-cutting skills.

"He wasn't well liked, but it was known that if he went out to repel a raid, that clan wouldn't come raiding for a while. The man was uncanny at tracking. He could find some tiny scrape on a rock and tell you how many of the clansmen passed and which way they went."

"Makes sense." That's how he had noticed me.

"A year ago, the Blir got a new commander. He arrived with a fresh detachment of knights and two of his kardars. Serem Vor was told to take one of the kardars and her knights to the mountain border passes and give them the tour. Show them the lay of the land."

"How did that go?"

"On the way, they ran across a Jastoron party gathering herbs, no warriors, only civilians. Serem Vor charged them, running down the women and children without provocation. The kardar ordered him to stop. Serem ignored the command and killed two kids before the kardar knocked him off his horse. Serem Vor lost his shit. The knights surrounded Serem, and he told them that they had all better fucking learn how things were done around there and decide which side they were on before they ended up on Jastoron sacrificial poles wrapped in their own guts. He was detained, brought back to the fort, and tried for failure to heed command. They stripped him of his knighthood and released him from the king's service. He got to keep his head in light of his many years of meritorious tenure, but not much else."

And now the Butcher's hatred of knights made perfect sense. He had climbed the ladder from a weaver's son to a soldier and then to a knight, who was respected and trusted. His ascent to the knighthood must've meant a great deal to him. It had given his life meaning. Then the King's Army stripped him of his identity and spat him out with nothing.

"When did they throw him out?" I asked.

"Just under a year ago."

A long time to stew in his anger.

"Here is the best part." Will smiled. "Serem Vor had one friend during his years of service. Likatine of Praul Grast."

"Aha."

"He runs security for Castle Hreban in Lower Berem."

"The Butcher's best friend is the head of Hreban's hometown guards?"

Will nodded.

Perfect. If we managed to get the contracts, they would be damning. But If we failed, this link would come in handy, and Will had just brought it to me on a silver platter.

"Will, this is amazing. Thank you."

"You're welcome." Will squared his shoulders. "I've been meaning to talk to you about something else for a while. First, the old man lied to you and never apologized for that."

"I've had this conversation with Lute. Your father did what he thought was best for your future. He didn't know me, and he owed me nothing."

"I know. As I said, first the old man lied to you. Then we failed to kill the Butcher. Then Lute allowed you to be taken. We keep fucking up and I'm tired of it. That's not the way we usually do things."

"I don't see it that way but go on."

"The old man has his ideas about the Sleepless Duke and what serving him means. But that's his plans. Lute and I talked it over. The Sleepless Duke is a force, but you were the one who kept the old man from dying. You have my axe and Lute's sword."

"Didn't you swear fealty to Everard?"

He shook his head. "No."

For some reason, I had assumed they had.

"The Sleepless Duke can do so much more for you than I can," I told him.

"We know. We are our own men. We've made our decision."

"Are you sure? Because I'm about to pick a fight with Damaes of the Mage Tower."

Will raised his eyebrows and winced when the skin above his black eye stretched. "Well, I've never gone up against an Archmage before. Might be fun."

I felt so touched.

"I appreciate it more than I can express, Will. I will not treat your loyalty lightly."

"Maggie!" Clover called from downstairs. There was a slight note of alarm in her voice.

I sighed. Something else had happened.

Will smiled at me and we headed downstairs to put out another fire.

The scroll case lay on the kitchen table. It was about a foot long, a wooden tube treated with resin. Decorative vines, carved with precision and care, wrapped around it. It looked expensive.

"Where did you find it?" I asked.

"On the side by the northern wall. It was attached to an arrow," Lute reported.

The six of us pondered the tube.

"You don't suppose there is a snake inside?" I asked.

Clover gave me an odd look. "Why would there be a snake?"

"No reason." Digi's aunt had once sent a poisonous viper in a scroll tube to someone she hated.

Kaiden pulled out his knife. "If there's a snake, I'll kill it."

"Where did you get that?" Shana demanded.

Kaiden looked at Gort.

"You gave him a knife?" Shana asked.

"He's old enough."

"He'll cut himself."

"That's what he said," Kaiden said. "He also said cutting myself would teach me to be careful with it."

Gort, a fan of consequence parenting.

"Get your knife ready," I told Kaiden.

He raised his dagger.

I pulled the top off the scroll case and tapped it on the table. The edge of a scroll came out. No snakes.

I pinched the edge of the scroll and pulled it out. Slowly.

Nothing, except the scroll itself. It was thin and light with a trace of golden flecks embedded in the paper.

"Gilded vellum," Clover whispered.

"Expensive?" I guessed.

"Very." She nodded.

I unrolled the scroll and read out loud, "His Royal Majesty, King Sauven Savaric, the Sword and Shield of Rellas, father of the nation, long may he reign . . . blah blah blah, it's good to be the king, very impressive . . . invites the bearer of this scroll to bask in the presence of His Majesty at the Joedurar on the twentieth of Redberry . . ."

Clover gasped.

"A snake would've been better," Shana said.

I read the scroll again. It didn't say anything different.

"You can't go," Gort said. "It's too dangerous."

"I absolutely have to go," I said.

"Gort is right. Nothing good can come from being near Sauven," Shana said. "He's not right in the head."

"This didn't come from Sauven. If the king wanted to see me, he would wave his hand, and people in armor with scary weapons would drag me out of this house and deliver me to him." I tapped the vellum. "These invitations are sent in batches. Meaning if Sauven wants to see Everard at the joedurar, he will send him not just one, but several invitations, which Everard will then distribute among his people. Every Great Family gets a few. This is probably one of those extras."

"Could it have come from His Grace?" Clover wondered.

"Not a chance. It isn't from Solentine either. If it was, the Shears would've hand-delivered it with explanations."

Neither Everard nor Solentine would want me anywhere near the joedurar. To borrow Everard's metaphor, Rellas was an ocean of monsters and going to the joedurar would be like jumping into the deepest part of it.

"If it isn't from the king directly, then all the better," Shana said. "Sauven doesn't know you exist. If you skip, nobody will know."

"It doesn't matter if it didn't come from Sauven directly. Ignoring it is still treason against the Throne. And it's not just me. I'm now a lady of a noble family, and everything I do in public reflects on my parents and relatives. If I don't go, the entire Demarr family could be in hot water."

Shana swore. Clover stared into space, her eyes distant.

"But does anyone even know you're a Demarr?" Will asked.

"There is no way to tell. Solentine could've updated some official records somewhere. Sauven sent him home to fetch his father in person. That tells me that he is paying close attention to the Demarrs right now. I can't afford to give him any excuse to find fault with them. Whether anyone knows or not doesn't matter. The fact is, I'm now Lady Marigold Demarr. I have to conduct myself as my name dictates."

"Everard said not to let you out of the house," Kaiden said. "Before he left, he talked to Gort, Will, and Lute, and he said that if something happened to you, he would not forgive."

Thank you, Your Grace. So lovely of you to terrorize the Magnars. "And where were you when that talk took place?"

"Hiding on the wall above them."

"I'm unlikely to get murdered at the joedurar, Kaiden. This is the king's special gathering. If anyone embarrasses him in any way during it, he will have their head. I should be safe. I will go there, show my face, turn right around, and come home."

"We will need a dress," Clover said.

"I'm sorry?"

"We'll need a dress in the Demarrs' colors." She broke her trance and looked at me. "We'll need jewelry, footwear, and accessories. In fourteen days."

"How long does that usually take?"

"For a gown fit for the king's court? Six weeks. Two months would be better."

"Can you do it?" Shana asked.

Clover raised her chin. "Absolutely."

Shana and I looked at her.

"We have fourteen days to brush up on dinner etiquette and dancing. You will be fine."

"Dancing?" That's right. The joedurars ended in a combination dance and banquet.

"Yes," Clover confirmed. "What dances do you know?"

"None."

Clover blinked. "None at all?"

"None that wouldn't get me instantly killed."

Throwing my hands in the air and seductively wiggling my hips would probably get me decapitated.

"I could go and just not dance," I said.

"That may not be an option," Clover said. "Some invitations shouldn't be declined."

She was right. The entire upper echelon of Rellasian society would be there, not to mention the foreign dignitaries. In those circumstances, dancing went beyond simple social entertainment. If I refused the wrong person, I could make an enemy, and once again the Demarrs would be dragged into it.

Having a family was turning out to be a lot more complicated than anticipated. I could picture Everard leaning against the wall across from me like a tall dark wraith. *I warned you.*

Yeah, well you can just shut the hell up.

Clover wrenched a smile back on her face. "Don't worry. We have fourteen days. We can do a lot in fourteen days."

Shana put her hand over her face.

"Fourteen days," Clover repeated like a prayer. "Stay right here. I need to get you measured."

Chapter 37

Redberry 7

"Raise your arms, my lady," Clover said. It sounded like an order, and the "my lady" was clearly tacked on.

I obeyed.

The gown I wore flowed over me in delicate folds. It was breathtakingly beautiful, with a luxuriously full skirt, long sleeves, and delicate embroidery. It floated as I walked, fit me well, and was perfect in every way except one: It was a ghastly greenish yellow. It was probably some sort of fancy shade of chartreuse, but the color was less French liqueur and more diarrhea slime.

A shop assistant held up a large mirror so I could see myself. Yep, I was the prettiest digestive-upset princess ever.

Clover pursed her lips. "Ereglin family?"

The shop owner, a woman in her early forties in an impeccably fitting blue gown, nodded. "A wedding fell apart. I was told to burn it, but I couldn't bring myself to do it."

Clover pondered the dress. If she concentrated any harder, the gown would catch on fire.

Making the kind of dress I needed for the joedurar in fourteen days was impossible. Our only option was to purchase one and alter it. We'd spent the whole day taking the carriage from one dressmaking shop to the next, with both Will and Lute watching over us and Kaiden on scouting duty.

The unfortunately colored gown wasn't just our best option. It was our only option. Attending the dance in one of my regular gowns was out of the question. I might as well show up in a bean sack.

"Do you think it will take the dye?" Clover asked.

The owner frowned. "It should. Although I cannot guarantee it. We had to soak it for three days in a vat of goseweed to get this shade. The dye is very saturated."

"I was thinking cantolin powder," Clover said.

"Hot or cold?"

"Hot, then cold-set with vinegar and a dash of burgundy dust."

"To counteract the undertone from the yellow?"

"Yes. I need rust, not orange."

The two women peered at me.

"The embroidery is gold thread," the shop owner said. "It should hold."

I cleared my throat. "Tresses?"

They looked at me.

"Can I put my arms down?"

Clover turned red. "Of course, my lady."

Oh good. Actually, I could've held out longer. My arms weren't that tired. All of that daily stabbing I'd been doing was paying off.

"I will let it go for half a grest," the shop owner said.

Clover gasped. "Fifty nomas? For a dress that should be burned?"

"This is Olvian silk!"

"In a hideous color! For all we know, the dye will eat holes in it. And since they told you to burn it, you were already paid for it."

"Forty-five. The embroidery alone took a month."

"Fifteen. The embroidery is gold which doesn't even fit our family colors."

"Thirty-five."

"Twenty."

"Meet me at thirty or leave," the shop owner ground out.

Clover raised her chin. "Thirty it is."

"We'll take it," I told the dress shop owner. "Thank you for your help. It will not be forgotten."

The owner smiled at me. "Yes, my lady."

Ten minutes later, we exited the shop with the dress securely wrapped in a fat roll of canvas. Clover had counted out the coins and taken it with a sour face.

Outside, Will and Lute flanked us. We'd walked for about half a block when Clover broke into a brilliant smile.

"It's a two-grest dress and we got it for thirty nomas. Let's go fast before someone arrests me for this robbery."

She hugged the bundle to her.

"That was amazing, and I'm the luckiest 'lady' in Kair Toren," I told her.

Clover gave me a brilliant smile. I didn't have the heart to ask her what we'd do if the dress failed to take the dye.

A small dirty child darted toward us. Will caught her by the shoulder before she could reach me.

The little girl grinned at me. One of her teeth on the top was missing. "Buy a bracelet, my lady? Only two dens!"

She held out a bracelet of shells and sea glass. The excitement dashed down my spine. Darotha had found Isadau.

I held up three fingers. Lute pulled three dens out of his pocket and put them into the little girl's grimy palm.

"Two for her, one for you."

She handed the bracelet over to him, and Will released her.

"Do you have news about my special order?" I asked.

She nodded. "Come to the knight statue tonight when the bells strike ten. Bring a carriage. It is far."

She giggled and dashed off into the crowd.

The carriage from Broad Street was the Kair Toren equivalent of the Texas white pickup truck. Perfectly nondescript and anonymous, but solid. It was also spacious enough for four people to ride comfortably, but Gort was a bit oversized. Shana sat on my right, Darotha sat across from me, and next to her Gort had barely enough room to stretch his legs.

Darotha rode in nonchalant silence, pretending that Shana wasn't there. She hadn't reacted to Will or Lute, gave Gort an appraising once-over, and snorted at the driver that came with the Shears' carriage. But Shana had gotten a wary look. Something about her set Darotha's teeth on edge. She watched her out of the corner of her eye, and Shana, in her chainmail and armed with a mace, did the same.

The carriage rocked slightly. In the past hour, we had crossed two bridges, steadily making our way north, to the maze of crooked narrow streets that made up the Tangle, a warren of the city's slums. That was why both Will and Lute rode next to the driver, a burly, broad-shouldered man who looked like he wrestled bears on his days off.

"How much farther?" Gort asked.

Darotha edged the curtain on the window aside and glanced out. "Four streets."

And once we got there, it was up to me to make things work. I had no idea if I could. I had never done magic before.

In theory, anyone with enough power and the ability to read Sareso should have been able to manage it, but Kair Toren had a habit of shoving my theories to the ground and stomping on their faces.

I had the power covered. Both the contract's resistance and the drezmur's reaction to me confirmed that thanks to whatever had brought me here, I had plenty of it. That made sense: Bringing dead me back to life had to require a wallop of magic. The problem was with Sareso. It was a weird language, and the entire sound of a vowel could be changed depending on tiny marks next to the word. Mispronouncing things could turn me into atomic dust.

I was so full of nervous tension my skin felt too tight. It was taking all of my will to not fidget.

If I failed, I had no idea how we would get Isadau into the carriage. And leaving her there wasn't an option. I trusted Darotha about as far as I could throw her. If we left here without Isadau, she would disappear, and I would have to pay Darotha more money to "find" her again. She could string me along for weeks. I had to get this right the first time.

If Damaes had some kind of warning system set up and decided to respond in person... Well, there was no point in worrying about that because if he showed up, we would all instantly die. Even I might not come back from being hit with that much magic.

The carriage turned right. Darotha checked the window.

"Stop here."

Gort knocked on the wall behind him.

The carriage came to a stop. Gort got out. Shana nodded to Darotha. She got up and climbed into the street.

Shana leaned toward me. "Last chance to turn around and go home."

"We must do this."

"If I say run, you run. No heroics."

"I promise."

I wore my clothes from the time we had confronted the Butcher by the Knight Vanquisher statue. I had also brought my dagger with me, but I had no illusions. My best bet to keep my escorts safe was to run away from danger as fast as I could, so they could run away with me. I hadn't even bothered with the cloak.

Shana got out, and I followed her.

We formed a diamond on the street, Gort in the lead, Will and Lute on my sides, and Shana behind us. The Magnars had their weapons out. The driver stayed with the carriage.

The brothers eyed the night streets like they expected a pack of wolves to charge us. Even Darotha's face turned grim. She hunched her shoulders, glancing at the dark three-story buildings boxing the street in. If I hadn't been nervous before, this would have done it.

The carriage driver eyed us. I had a flashback to coming out of the Guard station with my carriage nowhere to be seen. Fighting our way back out of the Tangle would be very difficult. And it would be just like Avaria to leave me stranded.

"Quickly," Darotha said.

"I need a private moment." I faced the driver.

Shana and Gort herded Darotha down the street, while Will and Lute flanked me. When the others were half a block away, I turned to the driver.

"I don't know what Avaria told you, but I'm telling you that Solentine is my cousin. If I come back here and the carriage is gone, I will make it out of the Tangle alive and then I will tell Solentine that you left me here. Do we have an understanding?"

The driver gave me a dark look. "We do."

"Good."

I turned and chased Darotha.

The street opened into an oblong plaza. An ancient building rose on our left, a dark five-story ruin peppered with alcoves. Elaborate carvings, smudged by time and the elements, decorated its façade: grotesque monsters twisting, people with contorted faces, strange symbols . . . In the center, colossal stone gates stood slightly cracked, the six-foot gap between them lightless like a bottomless pit.

It felt incredibly dark, ancient, and malignant. A place meant to be timeless that hadn't endured. It had fallen to ruin, but the power inhabiting it was still there.

Dread settled over me. The tiny hairs on the back of my neck rose.

Evil.

I couldn't explain how I knew. I felt it all the way in my bones.

"What is this?" I asked, keeping my voice low.

"A temple," Darotha said.

"To whom?"

"Nobody knows. Many dead are buried here. Walled in."

This wasn't in the books either. I was flying blind.

Why was nothing ever simple in this damn city? Was the threat of Damaes and reading this incantation not challenging enough?

"There she is." Darotha pointed to the bundle of old rags, thrown carelessly on the temple's steps.

I walked toward it. Will and Lute came with me. Gort moved to the side, watching the temple. Shana hung back, watching Darotha and the street behind us.

My steps sounded too loud, each fall of my feet like the strike of a blasphemous bell, an insult to the temple's forgotten god. The darkness within the temple watched me through the gap between its gates, waiting, deciding if it should crush the trespasser or allow me to approach.

My teeth chattered.

Remember why you're here. You're trying to keep Kair Toren from burning and Rellas from eating itself. You're doing it so Ramond doesn't have to fight a bloody war and Clover, Kaiden, and Matheo survive . . .

My pep talk wasn't working. I wanted to run away screaming and keep running into the night, all the way home.

I reached the stairway and stepped on the first step.

A cold wind tore from inside the temple and fanned my face, flinging the stench of decay and wood rot at me. Cold sweat broke out at my hairline.

One step. Two. Three.

The bundle of rags was right there.

A flicker of blue light pulsed in front of me. I stopped. Another step and magic would electrocute me.

This was it. Do or die.

I cared way too much about these people to let their lives turn into a nightmare.

I pulled a piece of paper from my pocket and checked it again. I had written the incantation down from memory. Every other time I tried to reproduce something from the books, I was able to do it exactly, but the incantation in the books wasn't in English. It was in Sareso, spelled phonetically in English letters. So it was basically two paragraphs of mystical-sounding nonsense. I had tried my best, but I was only ninety-five percent sure I had recalled it correctly.

Right now five percent seemed like an enormous margin of error.

The paper in my fingers trembled. The longer I stood here, the more danger I invited. I just had to read it and get out.

"*Osor dor mi Damaes!*"

Magic clamped me. Each syllable was an effort, as if I were hitting a wall made of rubber as hard as I could, and the impact of it reverberated through my body.

Something stirred in the temple, deep in the primordial darkness.

"*Re braste ca!*"

The rags flew aside. A woman jerked upright, her body rigid, her mouth open, a filthy mass of red hair swirling around her head as if she were underwater. Her eyes rolled back into her head, the stark whites glaring at me, unseeing.

"*Sonta mih perss, cro su geñi . . .*"

A blue glow gripped her, pulling her off the steps up into the air. The knot of power inside the temple slithered toward me. Every word hurt.

"*Mimpro bo ullu taprin . . .*"

My jaw locked open. I strained, trying to make my mouth move.

An enormous hand, each finger as tall as me, reached out through the gap and grasped the side of the stone door. It was translucent and black glyphs slid over it, like ghostly tattoos. My mind refused to process it.

A second hand stretched out of the darkness, then two more, another pair, another . . . They grasped the doors, sliding over each other.

My jaws still wouldn't move. My heart hammered against my ribs, my blood pounding through my head and throbbing in my ears. An invisible cord of magic connected me and the woman in the air. I felt her through it, like a fish on the end of a line.

The phantom hands pushed. The stone slabs of the door slid a couple of inches. Something in me knew that if those doors opened all the way, an unimaginable horror would seize all of us and pull us into the darkness. I had to finish it. I had to do it now.

Something crunched in my mouth. The salty taste of blood washed over my tongue, wetting the words as they tore out.

"Galbir os re cuar!"

A column of bright neon blue light burst out of the woman, turning her mouth and eyes a pure, brilliant white. A ring of light pulsed out of her and smashed into me in an explosion of heat and radiance, as if a star had burst into life in front of me. Magic sizzled on my skin. The light hit the temple doors and slammed them shut.

The woman collapsed onto the steps, fell on her side, and rolled down to the street.

The night turned completely silent. Nothing moved.

I swallowed a mouthful of blood and ran down the stairs to her. She was on her back, her face to the sky. I dropped to my knees and checked the pulse in her neck. Alive. Oh good. Good, good, good.

"Grab her, and let's get the fuck out of here," Gort growled.

Will scooped her off the ground, slung her over his shoulder, and we ran for the carriage.

Washing an unconscious person was surprisingly difficult, especially since Shana and I were on our own. Clover was in the kitchen, watching the vat containing my dress and the dye boiling slowly on the stove. Her face looked haunted, and when I asked her if she was fine, she gave me a look that was pure zombie.

Will had brought the unconscious woman into the bathroom for us and departed. We heated up water, filled the tub, stripped her, and lowered her in. Shana shoved a rolled-up towel under her head to keep it above water and we started scrubbing. She wasn't just dirty. The grime was layered and thick. Her *dirt* had dirt.

Normally I would've waited to bathe someone until they came to, but in her case, there was no telling when that would be. She could wake up in a minute, in a week, or not at all. She'd been on that street for months, without any awareness of her own hygiene or injuries. Her legs and arms had several cuts and scrapes, some of which were clearly infected, and her hair was full of lice. Getting her clean was a medical necessity and spot cleaning wouldn't do it. We had to let her soak.

Shana had mixed some sort of botanical powder with oil and rubbed it into the woman's scalp and mane of red hair, and now we waited for it to work. Shana said it would take about half an hour, and it would kill both lice and their eggs.

I heated more water and carefully added it to the tub. In winter, we'd build a fire directly under it, but considering her condition, gentle and lukewarm was best.

Shana checked the hair and got a fine-toothed wooden comb out. I picked up a small brush and started carefully washing her left hand, working the dirt from the cracked skin of her knuckles and from under her fingernails. Between the soaking and the scrubbing, the filth was coming off. Our soap kicked ass.

"Who is she?" Shana asked.

"The best mage of her generation," I said. It was kind of hard to tell with all the dirt, but she was only twenty-eight, barely three years older than me.

"I thought Archmage Damaes was the best mage of the current generation."

"So did he."

Shana made a face.

I'd worked my way up to her elbow. The stink was epic.

"Does Damaes know her?"

"Yes. He's the reason she's like this."

Shana dropped the soap. "Maggie!"

"Yes?"

"Tell me we didn't just cross the Archmage? Tell me you didn't drag my kids into it?"

"It will be fine," I told her.

"Nothing about this is fine. That man is not in his right mind, and he can blast rocks from the sky with a flick of his fingers."

That fire beam took way more than a flick but now seemed like the wrong time to quibble about the details.

"He cares about her," I said. "Her mind is too fragmented for her to have realized she needed to panhandle. She is dirty, but she isn't thin. He sends someone to feed her every day and she isn't in bad health."

"Does that mean he's going to come looking for her? Did we just kidnap someone who belongs to him?"

"The word you're looking for is rescued."

"Aspects preserve us!"

"If he decides to get upset about it, I will take the blame and let him kill me."

"Maggie!"

"I'll come back to life, and it will be fine. Besides, if she wakes up, she will handle Damaes herself."

"Is she going to murder all of us when she comes to?"

"I hope not."

Shana swore. "Just tell me that my children aren't going to be turned into torches."

"Again, if anyone is going to be set on fire, it's me."

Shana resumed scrubbing.

"I wonder about you."

"Which part?"

"All the parts!" She sighed. "You need her for something. I understand. But even so, here you are washing a filthy stray you picked up in the Tangle and plucking lice out of her hair knowing that she might murder you when she wakes up."

"We can't leave her in this state. Clover is dying my dress, and I wouldn't expect you to do it for me. This is not a one-woman job."

"What if she refuses to help you?"

We would be screwed. "Then we did a good deed and saved her."

Shana pointed her soapy comb at me. "That's exactly what I mean. Ours isn't a time for kindness. Too much compassion will get you killed. Sooner or later, you're going to get yourself into trouble."

"Shana, look at her. Would you leave her on the street?"

"In an instant."

"I don't believe you."

"Believe it." Shana set the comb aside. "Pour the water for me."

I scooped some water out of the bucket with a large ladle and gently poured it over the woman's hair.

"What's her name?"

"I don't know the one she was born with. Her mage name is Isadau. It means Flame-bloom."

Isadau jerked upright like a corpse popping out of a coffin in a cheesy horror flick. Shana shied back. I froze.

Isadau looked at me with eyes that were a deep, golden amber.

"Put down the ladle," she said.

I dropped the ladle. It clattered as it fell to the floor.

"What date is it?"

It was after midnight. "Redberry 8 of the year 3044."

"Two years," she whispered. Her hands clenched the side of the tub, the freshly cleaned knuckles turning white. The water in the tub steamed.

"Easy," I told her.

Her gaze fastened on me. "Do I know you?"

"No."

"Do you belong to Damaes?"

"No."

"Who are you?"

"I'm Maggie."

She blinked. "Never heard of you."

"I'm not important."

"Are you a mage?"

"No."

"Then how did you break the spell?"

I shook the water off my fingers, reached into the pocket of my dress, pulled out my incantation, and showed the paper to her.

"*In the name of Damaes, be whole. Let that which was shattered be healed.* That fucking bastard." Isadau held up the paper. "There are three misspellings in this. It should've killed you. How are you alive?"

"I'm Maggie the Undying."

Isadau stared at me and shook the paper. "Where did you get this?"

"I wrote it down from memory."

"How?"

"She knows things. That's what she does," Shana told her. "You'll get used to it. Look, I understand you've been through a lot, but it's past midnight and we have a full day tomorrow, so how about you shut up and let me finish washing the dead lice out of your hair? You have lovely hair. It'd be a shame if the powder ate through it and turned you bald."

Isadau clamped her mouth shut. I got up, picked up a bucket, and emptied it over her head.

Chapter 38

Redberry 8

My dancing teacher was tall, with striking ash-blond hair cut to flatter his handsome face. He wore a tailored black doublet, black pants, and black boots, and as he entered our courtyard, he moved with easy, smooth elegance. A young woman in a yellow gown followed him, carrying a wens, a stringed instrument similar to a zither.

Lute trailed them, with Tzeri perched on the pauldron on his shoulder. He'd discovered that she really liked seedrocks, a hard candy made from honey and sunflower-like seeds. Lute had been giving her little bits of it as training aids and over the past week she had finally stopped screaming every time someone came near. The way to a mordok's heart was clearly through her bottomless stomach.

The dancing teacher was Clover's idea. She'd informed me that he was highly sought after and expensive, but worth every den. I was getting worried about Clover. After we cleaned up Isadau and situated her in a spare room, I had gone to check on Clover before heading off to bed. She was still in the kitchen, and when I woke up, she was back in the kitchen again. I wasn't sure she had even slept. Fingers crossed that the dress took the dye, because I really didn't want her to have a breakdown.

The dancing teacher approached me and executed a beautiful bow. "My lady, my name is Erodel. I'm dapchel and a ranowen. You may address me as he and him. It is my privilege to serve you today."

Ah. In Rellas, like in every society, some people didn't fit the stricter definitions of gender roles. Dapchel were designated female at birth but lived their life as men, while darchel were designated male at birth but lived as women. Both identities embraced the feminine and masculine parts of themselves as one harmonious whole, not one gender but rather both. It was a complex philosophy centering on acceptance.

Dapchel often worked as ranowen. The word meant *battle brothers* in the Old Tongue, but their actual duties were much more complicated. They served as escorts in a strictly nonsexual sense. They were well educated, had impeccable manners, and were highly skilled in combat arts. If you had to attend a social event where bringing a bodyguard wasn't appropriate or just needed a sympathetic ear without any judgment, you would schedule a date with a ranowen.

"It is my privilege to benefit from your instruction."

"We will begin with simple stretching," Erodel announced. "Listen to the music Ruana plays, my lady, and try to find the rhythm."

The stretching took a full fifteen minutes. Apparently, I had a good sense of rhythm and was flexible, but my footwork would need major improvement. We progressed into making small circles around each other, with strategic turns and arm raising.

"Our time is limited, so we can only concentrate on a single dance," Erodel said. "Luckily, we only need one. Although joedurars include dances, the main point has always been conversation."

He reversed the direction, and I followed, trying to mirror his movements.

"I will teach you how to dance the polhe. It's not a particularly fast dance, with only five main parts, and it's danced in pairs and designed to keep you moving at just the right pace to easily converse with your partner. It's a way to have a private talk in a very public setting."

"So it's an excuse for flirting?"

"Single people such as yourself have limited opportunities to interact with other single people their age unless they are chaperoned. This is a way to sidestep that limitation. And that is our next move. We sidestep to the left . . . and to the right. And again, to the left . . . and to the right. Very good. You will not be chaperoned at the joedurar. The invitation is for you alone. You cannot bring a companion."

I was painfully aware of that.

"During a polhe, the entire gathering acts as your chaperone. If anything untoward were to take place, the perpetrator would be instantly condemned by everyone. There is nothing society loves more than tearing down one of their own when they stumble in a public way. You will be perfectly safe during this dance."

"What happens if they don't play a polhe?"

"They will. They will likely play it more than once as well. The first dance at the joedurar will be an exhibition dance, something fast like a sarett. It will be danced by a single pair handpicked by the Chamber of Ceremonies, usually someone young, of good birth, and excellent at dancing. The sarett will be followed by a polhe, then a fast dance since the dancers will have warmed up, then a polhe again. Raise your hand like this, my lady."

He raised his hand as if for a high five. I mimicked him and we touched our fingers.

"So far this doesn't seem too complicated."

"The polhe is an old dance. It's relatively simple. The challenge isn't in learning all of the steps, my lady. The challenge is in training your body until the dance is so familiar, you can do it without thinking and with casual ease, so you won't stand out."

"So I don't look like I'm trying too hard?"

"Exactly. The focus should be on the conversation. The dance is simply an excuse to have it. Please don't look at your feet. Look at me instead."

My foot hit his. "Sorry."

"No worries."

"I'm guessing developing 'casual ease' will require a lot of practice."

Erodel gave me a small smile. It was the same kind of smile Everard had given me when I asked him how much time it would take for me to get good with my dagger.

I surrendered to my fate and concentrated on not stepping on my teacher's feet.

Dancing for three hours straight was harder than stabbing the straw dummy. At some point, Isadau exited the house and sat on the stone wall around the wine tree watching me struggle. She wore one of Clover's gowns—mine were too short for her—and her hair, a wavy mass of deep red, fell all the way down to her waist. In the books she was known as the beauty of the Mage Tower, and I could see why.

Erodel finally relented and let me and Ruana have a long break. I stumbled to the wine tree and landed in the chair by the little table. Ow, my legs. Ow, my feet. Ow. Ow. Ow.

Isadau leaned over and stared at my shoes.

"Yes?"

"You don't have two left feet. Surprising."

"Ha. Ha."

I closed my eyes.

"I can kill all of you, you know," she said. "I can burn this place to the ground."

"You won't."

"What makes you so sure?"

"You're not that kind of person."

"You speak as if you know me."

"You have your magic, and I have mine." My legs hummed like I had attached two phones to my thighs, and they were vibrating.

"Do you know what happened between me and Damaes?"

"Yes."

"Tell me."

This was a test, and one I had to pass. I opened my eyes.

"There are twelve circles of magic, each requiring progressively greater understanding. The top two ranks are theoretical. Nobody has ever ascended past the tenth circle."

But every mage in existence spent way too much time speculating about what that might be like. Mages were the ultimate power hounds. No matter how great their achievements were, they always wanted more.

"Two years ago, you were in the seventh circle, while Damaes was in the eighth and on the way to the ninth. The eighth circle is the art of unlocking the mystery of existence through which the mage gains complete control over their body and achieves the Fade, a state of existing without the physical form."

The Fade wasn't an astral projection but rather an ability to turn your physical body incorporeal, which rendered you immune to most physical attacks. It could only be maintained for a few moments, and many eighth-circle mages couldn't hold it for longer than an instant.

"You had been in the seventh circle since you turned twenty-two. Up to that point, your rise was meteoric, and then you got stuck."

Isadau grimaced.

"For years, you'd refined your magic and discovered new ways to employ it, but no matter how hard you tried, you couldn't achieve the Fade. You were frustrated, especially because the mage society is filled with jealous, pissy academics who snipe at each other and squabble over petty things. You were exceptional and that chafed at some of them, so once you couldn't break through to the eighth circle, even the mages who couldn't dream of ever reaching it started making comments about you hitting your limit."

She opened her mouth to say something but changed her mind.

"Meanwhile Damaes was relentlessly pursuing the ninth circle. He always paid special attention to you, which you found flattering, and over time, you became his right-hand person. You practically ran the Tower, and he was consulted only on the most important decisions. The Mage Tower possesses the Eye, which is a source of great power. You wanted Damaes to allow you access to the Eye so you could boost your power and ascend. He refused and told you that you needed to think less."

She clenched her teeth.

"You told him that you had ambitions, that you wanted your own Tower one day, and he said that he didn't see you as the head of a Tower. Your place was at his side as his subordinate and his woman. Although he had never communicated that kind of interest, in his head the two of you were in a relationship. You simply hadn't had the opportunity to consummate it, it was glaringly obvious to anyone with half a brain, and he was annoyed that you were being deliberately dense about it."

She barked a short laugh. "He didn't even ask me. The thought that I might reject him never crossed his arrogant brain. His woman. Not *the one I love*, not a partner, not a wife. His woman."

"Damaes was born in the Highlands of Grador. His father is a hunter, and his mother is a bow maker. If you took away his magic and dropped him into the mountain wilderness with nothing but a knife, he would find his way back and come out of the woods carrying a delicious mountain goat he had hunted on his shoulders."

Isadau gave me an odd look.

"While his actions are deeply problematic and criminal in multiple ways, calling you his woman wasn't an insult," I told her. "That is how Grador bandmen speak. They refer to their loved ones as *my man* and *my woman*. It is their term of endearment."

"I don't care."

"That's fair. Do you want me to finish the story?"

"Yes."

"You had an argument, and then you attacked him. He defended himself. You had a duel. You lost and he shattered your mind and used his own name as the key. He placed a spell that prevented anyone from touching you and turned you loose in Kair Toren. He made sure someone came by to feed you every day and heal your injuries, and he watched you. By now he knows you're gone. Did I leave anything out?"

"No."

I shifted my weight in my chair and rubbed my thighs. Ow. Maybe sitting had been a mistake.

"I suppose you want something from me," Isadau said.

"I could use your help."

"I can't teach you to dance. That would take a miracle. I'm a mage, not a saint."

"It was my first polhe ever. Leave me alone."

"I don't like debts." Her voice had an edge. "Tell me what you want."

"I want a door opened."

"Who does it belong to?"

"Ulmar Hreban."

"Are you trying to rob the richest man in Rellas?"

"Do you know what *lugur campur* is?"

She made a hissing noise. "How did you come by that?"

"Someone has been making those contracts for Ulmar Hreban. They are hidden in his secret vault, which is sealed with a spell."

Isadau raised her left eyebrow. "And you want that spell cracked?"

"Yes. There is a catch. Ten years ago, when Damaes had just come to power, he needed a lot of money fast. Hreban offered him an outrageous fortune to seal his vault, and Damaes did it."

"Fool."

Damaes understood magic and little else. He spent his time contemplating incredibly complex spells, but he never quite got the complexity of human relationships. To Damaes, doing something for Hreban in exchange for gold was a simple barter. Political or moral implications hadn't crossed his mind. It was a weakness Isadau had compensated for when they were working together.

"If you break the seal, Damaes will come to see who dared."

A glint of golden fire sparked in her eyes. "That's not a catch. That's a bonus."

"You will fight again."

"I'm counting on it."

"Don't you need time to meditate and recover?"

Isadau raised her hand. A beautiful red glow coated her fingers and trailed as she moved them.

"Mages meditate to build up their reserves. We set the world ablaze with our spells, so we must stack wood within our soul to fuel them. For two years, I sat by that temple like a mindless beast, while my body absorbed and cycled magic, storing it within me. Had I been in my right mind, I would've been spending it casting spells and training. But I wasn't. My tower of wood is so high, it scratches at the heavens. I'm so full of magic, I'm about to burst. I must burn some of it."

And it would be one hell of a bonfire.

Isadau cracked her knuckles.

"Take me to this door."

"Let's make sure you're fine first."

"Tonight," she said.

"Let's do it in three days."

Getting the contracts was crucial. Everything was riding on it. But I wanted her to rest, and eat, and get her bearings.

Erodel motioned me over.

I got up.

"Maggie!"

"Three days. I want you to remember what it's like to live before you decide you want to fight Damaes again. He might kill you this time."

Her eyes shone with red. "Not in his wildest dreams."

Chapter 39

Redberry II

The boat glided across the midnight-black water, propelled by the oars in Will's and Lute's hands. The river was silent except for the gentle whisper of the oar blades sliding under the surface. No wind troubled the night, and our sail drooped from the mast, secured by a line.

Above us, an endless sky glittered with alien, unfamiliar constellations. The world seemed huge, the river and the sky blending into one, and our boat with the lone lantern on the bow was just a speck of cosmic dust within it.

I stood at the stern, working the rudder. Steering the boat was a lot less complicated than I had expected. We'd been going upstream for a couple of hours now and I wasn't even tired.

Sushi crouched by me. She had crawled into the boat before we cast off and perched by my feet. There had been a brief commotion, until I picked her up to assure everyone that we were on a petting basis, and she wouldn't be biting any ankles.

Isadau sat on the nearest bench, wrapped in a cloak, her amber eyes swirling with starlight. She was cycling magic, drawing it into her body and pushing it out, and it tugged on me with every shift. Next to her, Clover looked over the water, deep in thought. I'd pulled her away from my dress. I needed every pair of hands I could get, and Gort and Shana had to stay home. Someone had to protect the house and Gort wouldn't be able to move fast enough to help us anyway.

Gort really didn't want to let me go. He told me it was ill-advised, then that it was stupid, and then he brought up Everard's instructions, and I told him that Everard wasn't here, and he owed me for Falcon Point. This was me collecting.

It wasn't fair, but I had called in that favor, and now we were on the boat sailing to an almost certain death. I would survive it, but my death wasn't the one that mattered. I'd dragged five people into this boat with me and I had to bring them home.

Sushi made a short trilling sound. Isadau smiled.

"Of course, you would have a pet stelka."

"Why 'of course'?"

"They are attracted to magic. That's why they make their burrows in the cities. We, humans, burn with magic, and these little guys bask in our afterglow."

"What about gold butterflies?" I asked.

"Ah. You've met Ciste. Is he still hanging out at the Garden?"

I nodded.

"His mother sold her body," she said. "He grew up in a place a lot like the Garden."

"What happened to it?"

"Nothing good," she said. "Damaes tolerates his moonlighting, because Ciste is a gifted summoner. Did you see a swarm of glowing butterflies?"

"Yes. He summoned a sea monster and stelkas, too."

She smiled. "Was it beautiful?"

"Very."

"Ciste doesn't summon illusions, only weapons. Everything he conjures is created for violence."

Oh.

"Those beautiful golden butterflies feed on your blood. The more magic you have, the richer their feast. A larger swarm can turn a living being into a husk in moments."

When they had swarmed me, I thought they were beautiful. They thought they'd spotted a Thanksgiving dinner.

"Do other mages know about the butterflies?"

"Some," Isadau said. "Depending on how informed they are."

Was that how Silveren had zeroed in on me? Was he a mage? I'd been thinking about Lute stopping in the middle of the street. Magic would be a logical explanation for that.

"Is that the island?" Kaiden stood up at the bow.

Ahead, the river widened. A small island, no more than a couple of acres in size, jutted from the water. It was free of trees and brush, just a wedge of grassy land rising about fifty feet at its highest point. One side ended in a drop, the other sloped to the water. A narrow shore ringed it.

"That's it," I confirmed.

The boat shot out into the open. The water in front of us was like polished volcanic glass with the entire universe reflected in it, and we sliced through it at top speed.

The island grew larger and larger.

Breathe. Breathe. This will be simple. Get in, grab what we need, get out before all hell breaks loose.

If we lingered even a second too long, it would cost us all our lives.

Isadau squinted at the hill. "A palisade cluster with a triple spiral. Simple and boring, but effective."

"Can you crack it?"

"Yes."

The island loomed in front of us. The brothers lifted the oars, and the boat softly bumped against the shore.

"Clover, the sacks," I murmured.

She held out big canvas bags. I grabbed one, Lute and Will took one each, and Clover held on to two, one for herself and the other for Kaiden.

"We are not here for gold or jewels. We're here for his contracts. Take scroll cases, loose scrolls, and papers. Don't waste time reading them, just grab every document you see."

We disembarked. The hill lay in front of us, the fat side of the wedge to our left, the sloping end to our right.

Isadau stepped onto the shore, took three measured steps forward, and raised her hand. A faint blue light pulsed from her fingers, dashed to the side and up, and melted into nothing, as a perfect transparent half sphere covering the hill flashed in response to her touch.

"Once I break it, you will have one hundred breaths," she said.

Five minutes. That little?

"Damaes will never serve as someone's guard dog," Isadau said. "He won't go after you, but he won't spare you if you get in the way. I won't spare you either. Don't look to me for protection. Once I break this, we are even, and all debts are paid in full."

I glanced at Kaiden. He pulled a small leather pouch out of his shirt and opened it. The moonlight glinted from an array of weird tools.

Isadau braided the fingers of her hands, her thumbs pointing straight up, and opened her mouth.

"*Osor dor mi Damaes, da der englofrosos iti . . .*"

She was right, I shouldn't have been alive. When I'd cast the incantation, I'd struggled with every word. She was firing them out with barely any effort.

Power stirred around her. Green sparks flashed in the air.

"*. . . da der englocreptesus si . . .*"

The sparks flared into a bright beryl-green glow. It spun around Isadau in a tight spiral, dense and potent, her own personal cyclone of magic.

"*. . . der odod sen grejos tro . . .*"

The hill in front of us shuddered. The ground under my feet shook.

"*. . . da yu or grolcin doafe mi . . .*"

Pressure gripped me, squeezing my body.

"*IRCES!*"

A wall of fire and light sprang into existence in front of Isadau, constructed with translucent spiked columns. The two columns directly in front of her slid into the ground, revealing the second wall, then the columns on their sides, and on and on. The first wall sank into nothing, then the second, and finally the third. The soil on the side of the hill melted, revealing a big double door, carved from gray stone and secured by a bar with a complex metal padlock.

"We are even." Isadau walked away.

Kaiden sprinted to the door, pulling tools out of his leather satchel. Will followed, carrying the lantern with him. Kaiden looked into the keyhole, thrust a small tool into it, and wiggled it around.

"Good lock," he murmured.

"Can you open it?"

"It's a good lock, not great." He stuck his tools into his mouth.

I paced along the shore. Every second counted.

Lute was looking up. I glanced in the direction of his gaze. Isadau had climbed the hill and stopped at the highest point, just before the drop.

"What is she doing?" Lute muttered.

"Waiting."

A spark shot upward in the distance like a golden flare, fired ridiculously high.

Damn it.

The spark burst into a star.

"Kaiden!"

"Almost there."

The star streaked across the sky toward us.

"Hurry!"

Kaiden twisted the tool inside the lock. The padlock popped open with an audible *click*. Kaiden pulled it free, and the double door swung open with a screech.

Will ducked inside, carrying the lantern, and I ran in behind him.

On the walls, lanterns ignited on their own, illuminating a small vault, a square cavern cut in the rock. Shelves lined the stone walls, filled with chests. Fuck. I was hoping for the papers to be in plain view.

I glanced at the doorway. The star was heading toward us, a painfully bright pinpoint of light.

I sprinted to the nearest chest and yanked it open. Gold. I slammed the lid and threw the next lid open. Scrolls in wooden cases. I tried to heave it up, but it was too heavy. Will grabbed the chest out of my hands and took off with it. Kaiden darted back and forth.

A dull roar rolled through the night, growing louder and louder. Damaes was coming.

I dug in the next chest. Spiky chestnut-looking nuts. No clue.

Next chest, gold.

Next, jewels.

Scrolls. I grabbed the chest—it had to weigh fifty pounds at least—and ran outside. At the boat, Will slid his own chest in place and took mine.

The star was almost on us. It twisted, growing longer, slimmer, twisting into a giant . . . lance. Oh shit.

"Leave it!" I screamed. "We have to go! Now! Now, now!"

Clover ran out, hauling a big sack. Kaiden was right behind her. I grabbed Clover's sack and dropped it in. She climbed into the boat. Kaiden took a running start and vaulted over the edge.

Will grabbed me by the waist and lifted me into the boat.

Lute was still missing.

High above us, the lance streaked upward like a fighter jet at an air show. It was enormous, radiant with gold and white.

"Lute!" I howled.

Lute came running, dragging a huge chest. Behind him, the stone doors clanged shut and melted into the hill.

The lance turned, pointing down at Isadau standing on the apex.

Lute dropped the chest in and threw himself against the boat's bow. The small vessel slid off the shore. He chased it, and Will grabbed him by the hand and pulled his brother in. They hit the oars.

The lance plunged down, roaring like a tornado. Flames burst from its point, and I didn't know if it was air friction because it was solid, or magic spilling out.

Isadau watched it come.

I grabbed Sushi and wrapped my arms around her.

The lance smashed into Isadau. Flames and light exploded, turning the tiny island into a giant fireball. Water and steam geysered in the air. Heat slammed into us, and I turned my back to it. The blast wave rocked the boat.

Clover gasped.

I turned back and raised my head. The flames washed over the water and drained down, revealing Isadau unharmed at the top of the hill above the steaming river. She hadn't even moved.

The magic lance hovered a foot from her head, stopped by some invisible force. Isadau raised her hands to the side and thrust them straight down. The steam swirled around the island, thickening, twisting, sliding, and spiraled up, solidifying into a pure white serpent with Isadau's amber eyes.

Holy shit.

The enormous snake lunged at the lance, coiling about the shaft. The scaled body flexed.

The lance shattered. Thunder pealed. Magic slashed at me, and every hair on the back of my neck stood straight up.

A glowing sphere swirling with purple flames appeared above where the butt of the lance would have been. The flames melted, revealing a man's silhouette inside a vertical ring of magic. Its rim sizzled with black and electric purple, like some twisted antithesis of a sun's corona against a spray of distant stars.

The snake struck.

Damaes flicked his hand. Black orbs tore from the rim of the ring and sliced through the steam serpent. For a millisecond, its body hung in the air, severed in three pieces, and then it crashed into the river, breaking into liquid.

I wished Everard could see this. It was amazing.

Isadau was doing something complicated and pretty with her hands.

Sushi squirmed out of my arms. The Magnar brothers rowed like a well-oiled machine, putting more and more distance between us.

The ring tilted with Damaes inside it. More orbs tore from the rim, like gobs of black ink, and sped toward Isadau.

She raised her head. A circle of ruby blades flared in front of her, like a windmill made of swords. The windmill whirled, shredding the incoming projectiles.

The ring around Damaes spun, spitting a barrage of dark orbs.

Behind me Will swore.

The ruby fan of blades collapsed on itself bowing inward, toward Isadau, catching the orbs in the funnel of its blades, sparked with bright white, and sprang taut, firing a torrent of brilliant red at Damaes. The current of magic hammered the ring, breaking against an invisible wall. The impact careened the spell, shaking the Archmage inside.

"Kick his ass!" Lute yelled.

The red current died, exhausted. The ring around Damaes flared with purple and shed a copy of itself. The second ring expanded around the first and copied itself. Again, again . . . Three, four . . . eight.

"The Scream of Undensos. That fucker is actually trying to kill her." I clenched the side of the boat with my free hand.

The rings rotated, some faster, some slower, each glowing with furious purple.

Isadau stared at the spell above her.

The rings snapped still. Purple lightning streaked forward from their rims, merging into a single ball of magic in front of Damaes. The Archmage raised his hand.

Isadau waited, defiant.

Damaes paused. The spell crackled in front of him. He was giving her time to escape.

Move, Isadau. Move, damn you.

She stood still.

The lightning popped, expanded into a circle, and tore a hole in the fabric of existence. Darkness churned inside the ring, primordial, terrifying, alien, so terrible that I didn't want to look straight at it.

Isadau tilted her head.

The darkness tore out of the spell in a horrifying beam, searing the air with a deafening hiss and smashed into Isadau. The top of the hill disintegrated. It didn't catch fire. It didn't break. It just became nothing.

She was dead. That was an eighth-circle spell. It didn't just kill, it undid the very matter we were made of. She couldn't possibly—

The beam vanished. Isadau floated above the ground, her form translucent and glowing slightly.

The Fade! She had achieved the Fade!

I screamed and clapped my hands.

Isadau solidified. A fountain of bright red sparks burst from her, twisting into a glowing red flower. The flame-bloom—her signature spell.

The flower expanded. Fire and magic surged toward Damaes, wrapping him in a curtain of red. He fired back with an icy-blue meteor shower.

The river dragged us downstream, farther and farther. Soon we could no longer see the two mages, only the glowing explosions of light from their magic.

"Will she win?" Kaiden asked me.

"I don't know," I told him.

"You know everything."

"I wish."

"You're asking the wrong question," Clover told him. "Can she win?"

"Possibly." Both Damaes and Isadau were monsters. He was more skilled, but she was beyond furious. It was anyone's guess who would win.

"Let's hope she does," Lute said.

We glided into the night, our boat filled with our loot.

When Gort opened the secret door to us, the relief on his face was so obvious, it wasn't even funny.

"See," I told him. "Back in one piece."

"You missed it, old man," Lute said. "It was a show to remember."

"Once in a lifetime," Will said.

"Shut up and get inside, before someone sees you."

"Empty everything on the floor in the basement, please," I asked.

"And one of you tell your mother you've survived!" Gort growled.

The Magnar brothers, Clover, and Kaiden dragged our stolen loot past me. Sushi had ditched us as soon as we pulled up. She was probably back in my room now, in her nest under the bed.

"Where is the mage girl?" Gort shut the door and slid the heavy bar in place.

"She was still fighting when we left." I hefted my sack.

Gort took it from me and carried it into the basement.

"Think she'll survive?"

"I don't know."

Fighting this duel was Isadau's choice. The thing between Damaes and her was so complicated and screwed up, even the two of them couldn't make sense of it.

It took us only a couple of minutes to dump everything on the floor, and we began sorting through it. I had already shown Tillmar's contract to everyone so they would know what to look for.

I picked up the first scroll. Some sort of bill of sale . . .

An IOU . . .

Another IOU . . .

The letters crawled across the scroll. I blinked, trying to focus. There were other scrolls left in the vault. Other papers. We hadn't gotten everything. There had been no time. What if the Butcher's contract was left behind? What if . . .

It hit me all at once. The floor tried to slide sideways. I landed on the bench. It was that or I would pass out.

Gort's heavy hand settled on my shoulder. "Breathe."

I was trying.

"My lady!" Clover jerked upright.

I tried to say something and couldn't.

"She's fine," Gort said. "If you want to help, find those damned papers."

Clover bit her lip, crouched, and went back to digging. She and Will almost bumped heads.

"Even if the contracts aren't here, we will find a way," Gort said quietly.

"There is no other way. Not in time."

"You will think of something. You always do."

In my head, the city was burning.

Moments dragged on, slow and viscous, like cold syrup.

"Got Otrade," Lute reported.

He leaned over a pile of papers and thrust a scroll at Gort. Gort took it and held it in front of me. Exactly the same as Tillmar's contract, except for the names. I ran my hand over it.

"It's inert. The spell is gone, and there is no magic in it."

"Otrade is dead," Gort said.

That made sense. There was no life bound to this paper because that life had already ended.

I raised the contract to the light. The contours of the spell were still there, woven into the paper. We could still use this. A qualified mage would be able to tell what the spell did even if it wasn't active. We had Tillmar's blank contract, too . . .

"Another mercenary," Will reported.

A second scroll made its way to me. Exact same contract. Also dead.

Another. Another.

Kaiden scrambled to his feet, leaped over the papers, and stuck a scroll under my nose.

> Let it be known to all who read or hear these words that on this day, a covenant of duty is forged between the undersigned:
> Lord Ulmar Hreban, Baron of the Realm, Lord of Lower Berem, Vaterna... (hereinafter referred to as The Liege)
> and
> Serem Vor, a knight of sound mind and unwavering resolve (hereinafter referred to as The Contractor).
>
> Article I: The Task
> The Liege, acting under the authority of his station, does hereby commission the Contractor to deliver the death of Lord Colart Jenicor, the Sun Margrave, now deemed a threat to the prosperity and interests of the Liege and the stability of the realm.
> The Contractor shall employ whatever means deemed fit, provided the act is carried out with due discretion...

I scanned the last line. Here it was, the Butcher's signature. I yanked the scroll up. The contours of the spell were distinct and clear.

It was here, right here, in my hands. The key to eliminating Ulmar Hreban. There would be no reign of terror.

Something wet my cheeks.

Kaiden's eyes went wide. "Maggie, don't cry. Don't cry!"

I passed the scroll over to Gort before my tears fell on it. I'd held it together all this time and now the tension was leaking out. There was no stopping it.

"Give me a scroll case!" Gort ordered.

A cocoon of red light popped into existence right by the basement stairs.

Gort yanked me off the chair and shoved me behind him.

The light exploded into nothing, leaving Isadau. She stared at us. Her hair stood out from her head, smoking slightly. Strange glowing dust peppered her face.

We stared at each other.

"Did you win?" I asked.

She raised her chin. "No. But he didn't win either." She wiped the shiny dirt off her cheek. "I'm going to my room to take a nap."

Mage naps and normal-people naps were two different things.

"For how long?" I asked.

"Two weeks. Maybe more. Don't bother me. Don't try to feed me, and don't call a physician. I'm not dead."

"Okay," I said.

"I don't know what that means. Remember: not dead."

Isadau turned and strode up the stairs.

She had almost given me a heart attack.

A panicky thought flared in me. "The Butcher's scroll?!"

"I have it right here." Lute held up the scroll case. "Safe!"

I landed back in the chair and grabbed my head with both hands, trying to get a grip. My heart hammered in my chest.

"Maggie," Clover said quietly.

"Yes?"

Will and Clover stood together, looking like they had just seen a whole army of ghosts.

"You said those contracts were inert," Will said.

"Yes."

"These are not." Clover raised a scroll. "It stings my fingers."

Kaiden brought it to me. I slid my hand over it. The spell was alive and active. There was a name and a thumbprint on the signature line.

"I know that name," Gort said. "She is one of Sauven's royal guards. I served with her father."

Oh crap.

"This one is not inert either." Will showed me another one.

"How many of those are there?"

Will pointed down at the big black chest by his feet. It was filled with scrolls.

Redberry 12

Avaria stared at me across the desk of my study. The sky was overcast today and in the diffuse light she looked like a stylized fantasy painting: lean, mean, dressed in gray jerkin and pants, wearing a complicated leather belt with way too many knives hanging from it. The kind of woman that would kick you in the throat, stab you twice, and then knee you in your face as you fell down. The hostility rolled from her in waves.

Unfortunately for her, I'd had a very long night and was suffering a pounding headache, and I was too tired to be intimidated.

"You have a problem with me," I told her.

She gave me a derisive look and cocked one artfully shaped eyebrow. "Whatever do you mean, my lady?"

"I mean that I'm a woman who showed up out of nowhere. You don't trust me farther than you can throw me. You're strong, but that still wouldn't be very far."

"Oh I don't know. If I was properly motivated . . ."

"When I first contacted Solentine, he likely expressed doubts about me. You're a cautious woman, who is suspicious by nature. That paranoia has kept you alive so far."

"Don't talk like you know me."

"You try to solve Solentine's problems. I was a problem, and because of Everard he couldn't remove me directly. He might have shared that frustration. You're not fond of Everard either. You think that the Sleepless Duke is too dangerous to have as an ally so if Solentine and Everard went their separate ways, you'd likely open a bottle of wine to celebrate."

She didn't say anything.

"Bearing all of that in mind, you decided that it would be very convenient if something untoward happened to me through no fault of Solentine's. You know, like the Butcher grabbing me off the street and then cutting off my fingers, shattering my kneecaps, carving up my liver, and so on."

"You seem whole to me," she said.

"Magic can do wonderful things." I wiggled my fingers back at her. "They work like new. No stumps."

Her eyes widened slightly.

"Then I became Solentine's cousin. He told you to keep me safe, but he likely did not explain why. He probably said something like, 'Assist her in all things. She is family, so if she tells you to do something, treat it as if it came from me.'"

Avaria's mouth tightened. Yep. That was exactly what he'd said.

"Except that you don't think I'm family. For no obvious reason, Solentine is giving me access to secret matters I have no right to be a part of and he is putting the Shears at my disposal. You view me as a threat. You can't disobey Solentine directly, so instead you chose the path of quiet sabotage. You allowed a team of killers to enter the house. You took me to the Guard station and then recalled the carriage. You've dragged your feet uncovering the identity of the Butcher. You instructed the driver to leave us stranded in the Tangle."

She smiled at me. "You do like the sound of your own voice."

"Vasilianus would be proud, Despina. That's a page right out of his book. He always preferred subtlety over direct violence."

The dagger was in her hand so fast, it practically leaped into her fingers. One moment she was standing, the next she crouched on my desk, the dagger against my neck.

"Dramatic, but unnecessary," I told her.

"How do you know?" she snarled.

"The same way I know a lot of things. Your name is Despina Lustina Rasteros.

You were sold by your family to the Obsidian Veil at the age of seven and trained as a whisper. Your three masters were Kronia, Vasilianus, and Lakeros, and you preferred Kronia over the other two, because direct combat comes naturally to you. Also, your alchemy work is sloppy, and you kept poisoning yourself in Lakeros's laboratory, so you fantasized about stabbing . . ."

She held her left hand up. "Stop."

I gently nudged the dagger away from my throat with my index finger.

"Does Solentine know?" she asked.

"That you were sent here as a Crimson Empire spy and then defected? Yes. He figured it out years ago."

"How?"

"You put milk in your tea. You're supposed to be the daughter of a shoemaker from the Middle Fields. The Rellasians from that region drink their tea with honey and jam. You have to go all the way east, toward the border, before you start seeing milk served with tea."

She sat cross-legged on my desk. "That's all?"

I nodded. "He is sharp. He doesn't need much. You trust him, and eventually you gave yourself away with little things. Too much nuance in understanding politics. Too much knowledge about the weakness of legionnaire armor. He accepts you as you are. He knows you will not betray him."

"It was a horrible life," she said.

"I know. I mean, I really do know, Avaria. The Hole, the killing of Sominia, and so on."

The Obsidian Veil served as the Crimson Empire's CIA. They obtained their trainees young and put them through a crucible of physical and mental conditioning so extreme it would make seasoned Marine Corps drill instructors weep. Avaria had been sent to Rellas to infiltrate Eagle Roost. Instead, she went AWOL. The Veil tried to kill her a few times, but she murdered them instead and eventually found a home with the Shears.

"Would you like to know how you die?" I asked.

Avaria pondered me.

"Within two years, the Crimson Empire pours over the border like a tide. Solentine's father dies in battle trying to stop them. Solentine loses his grip on reality and refuses to leave Izarn's body. As you try to drag him away, Theodoros of Gavalia, who rides with that legion, recognizes you and shoots you with his bow. The arrow takes you in the back, and when you fall, his horse stomps over you and crushes your skull. You knew he was a vindictive little shit when you ratted him out for stealing that knife from Vasilianus. He's been waiting years for his revenge."

She stared at me.

"I'd like to keep all of that from happening." I picked up a stack of papers.

"I have a list of names here. I need to know everything about these people. Who they are, what they do, what weaknesses do they have that someone with Ulmar Hreban's resources could exploit. The High Court Session begins on the twenty-fifth this month. We must give this to them with some time to spare so we can all survive and live happily ever after. Do you think you could help me with that?"

"Yes," she said.

"Thank you. Before we begin, I know he isn't your favorite person, but have you heard from Everard lately?"

She shook her head.

I still had no idea if he was dead or alive. Worry gnawed at me like a hungry snake and there was absolutely nothing I could do about it.

I sighed and went to work.

Chapter 40

Redberry 20

"No peeking," Kaiden warned, leading me forward.

"No peeking," I promised, keeping my eyes firmly shut.

"You look amazing, my lady," Clover said.

"Stunning," Erodel said. "You have nothing to worry about."

Kaiden let go of my hand. There was some thudding.

"Ready," Will said.

"You can look now," Kaiden announced.

I opened my eyes. Everyone was in the courtyard. The sky above us was golden with afternoon sunshine.

"Good job!" Shana told Clover.

"This way," Lute called. I turned and saw myself in a full-length mirror he had dragged into the courtyard.

Oh.

After the dress had come out of the dye vat, Clover had taken off the sleeves and gone to work. I wasn't allowed to look at it, and when I asked her how it was going, she made growling noises and shooed me away.

The dress was amazing. The color turned out to be a breathtaking rust, almost as deep as Isadau's hair. The neckline was a variation of a Queen Anne, but instead of the triangular shoulder pieces, the embroidered straps were rectangular, flowing into complex bell sleeves, layered with rust and cream and bordered by wide bands of gold thread embroidery. The chain of Digi's amulet was hidden under my neckline.

The fitted bodice transitioned into a light-as-a-feather outer skirt, slit on the sides to expose an even thinner cream skirt underneath when I moved. A two-inch-wide embroidered cloth belt caught my waist and from it, on a cord of a deep beautiful blue, hung the wooden puck of the Demarr crest. Clover had matched the color scheme with uncanny precision.

The hair from my temples was gathered up and plaited into an elaborate braid, leaving the rest of it free to drip down my back in wavy locks. I'd had to sleep in wooden curlers, and it was hell, but my hair looked spectacular—shiny and wavy. Clover had woven a matching blue cord into it and secured the whole thing with a cascade of tiny gold chains. I had done my own makeup and adjusted it with her feedback to match the Rellasian formal occasion standards. My shoes were tiny blue slippers with little heels.

It was as if all of my fantasy princess fantasies had somehow come to life. I looked . . . I looked . . .

"You can't cry, my lady!" Clover snapped. "You'll ruin your face!"

"I won't cry," I promised.

Kaiden rolled his eyes.

"What do you think?" I asked him.

"You're pretty," he said.

"I'll take that."

Erodel offered me his arm. He was the picture of elegance in a silver doublet edged with light blue. A slender sword hung on his hip. Companions weren't allowed at the joedurar, but as a ranowen, he could escort me all the way to the doors.

"It's time," he said.

I took a deep breath and put my hand on his elbow. We started toward the door, with Lute and Will following us. Both wore the Demarr shade-down of darker brown.

Behind me Lute said, "Hey, Maggie?"

"Yes?"

"Survive, get paid."

Surviving was a good goal. An excellent goal, actually.

"No risk, no gold," I told him.

Erodel led me to the carriage and loaded me into it. I painstakingly followed Clover's directions to smooth the fabric over my butt before I sat down to keep from crushing my dress. Erodel climbed in, the brothers got onto the driver's bench, and we were off.

If Everard hadn't been poisoned, he would be at the joedurar. I'd thought he would let me know when he arrived in the capital, but there had been nothing. No sign at all. I'd asked Avaria to let me know if he rode in, and she didn't send any word either. The joedurar was my last chance. If he wasn't there . . . I had no idea what I would do but I would do something.

We would've heard something if Joris had poisoned him. Surely, we would've heard something.

"Anxious?" Erodel asked.

"Very."

"It is fitting that you are anxious. If you were not, I would be worried that you've become overconfident. You are going into a den of predators. The apprehension you are feeling is natural. I taught you well, and you worked very hard to prepare. You should be confident but wary."

I nodded. Confident but wary.

"You know every step of the polhe by heart."

"I had a nightmare about it last night. I fumbled the transition to the second partner and fell off a cliff into molten lava."

Erodel smiled.

In the middle of the polhe, the pairs of dancers broke up and switched partners for a brief period and then kept switching until they had made their way around the room to their original partner. It required a turn to the left. For some obnoxious reason, I could turn to the right all day long but turning to the left threw me a little off-balance. Not much, just enough to disastrously stumble at exactly the wrong moment.

"That damn dance now haunts me."

"You will execute if flawlessly. I have no doubt."

I smoothed my skirt.

"It will be fine, my lady. You know the dance, you know the etiquette, and you look just right. Beautiful, but not ostentatious. You will fit in perfectly."

I nodded. This was helping.

"Let's go over what happens again," he said.

We had practiced it all, the entrance, the proper manners, what the guards might say, what the nobles might say . . . I took a deep breath.

"The joedurar will be held in the left wing. Will and Lute must stay with the carriage. You will escort me up the stairs. We will be greeted at the door and my invitation will be checked."

Sudden fear stabbed me.

"Do you—"

He lifted the scroll case. "No worries, my lady. Continue."

"Right. My invitation will be checked. You will stay behind and return to the carriage once I go in. A guard will escort me to the ballroom. Since I am arriving slightly late, I will be asked if I want to be announced. I will decline."

"Correct," Erodel said.

"The nobles will form a ring around the open dance floor. Once I am in the ballroom, I will move to the front, directly facing the dance floor. I will stay there for exactly ten breaths to let myself be seen, and then I will step back, out of sight."

"Correct. The etiquette dictates that only those of high standing remain in the front row, but it is proper and polite to let yourself be seen on arrival, so your allies know you have entered."

"After I have been seen, I will find an out-of-the-way spot. Somewhere I can have a quiet conversation. I will not eat or drink."

"Correct again. You're doing so well, my lady."

"Should I wish to use the washroom, I will tell the guard at the doorway, and he will escort me back and forth."

"And if you are asked to dance?"

"If it's a polhe, I accept the invitation. It is safer to accept than to offend someone powerful by refusing."

"And if you are asked to dance a fast dance?"

"I demur and suggest a polhe instead." Declining fast dances was somewhat socially acceptable.

Erodel leaned closer. "You have done everything possible to go through tonight with grace. It will be fine, my lady. I have complete confidence in you."

I was as prepared as I was going to be. Get in, be seen, get out, and get home. I could do this.

The castle was ancient. I was met by guards at the entrance, and one of them politely offered me his arm to escort me to the ballroom. As we strolled through the hallway, the age of the walls was almost palpable. The very stone radiated centuries of power and conquest. The Eagle Roost had changed hands countless times. Thousands of people had died between these walls, some with a sword in their hands, others with a dagger in their back. Their blood had soaked into the stone floor tiles. I couldn't see it, but it was there.

"Thank you, Lady Maggie," my escort murmured.

When the older knight had asked me for my name as he reviewed my invitation, I had introduced myself as Marigold.

The guard raised his head. The light from the ballroom illuminated his features. His skin was rich brown, his dark hair was cut short, and his eyes were light gray. *Matheo.*

How was he here? Why?

"Are you all right?" I squeezed his arm.

"I'm well," he told me. "I've been watching you. I've met Tillmar."

He's been farseeing to keep an eye on me. How did he know who I was? Never mind, that wasn't important right now. "The warning notes! That was you."

"Yes."

He'd been trying to help this entire time.

"Hreban doesn't know who you are or what you look like," Matheo murmured. "He thinks the Butcher took a noblewoman off the street to satisfy his urges and her family rescued her, killing him. Lord and Lady Bors visited him and threatened him over Velpor's death. He knows the Conquerors are watching him, and he's wary. He still wants to silence you, but he will bide his time."

"You mustn't escort the Sun Margrave on the day of the High Court. There will be a killer . . ."

"I know," he said. "That's why I have to do it. It's my duty to keep the Sun Margrave safe."

"Matheo—"

"My father would not want me to run. I will do what I must. It is my responsibility."

Ahead, the ballroom glittered, framed by the arched doorway. We had run out of hallway.

"Matheo..."

"Thank you, from the bottom of my heart," he whispered. "I will be forever grateful."

He stepped aside, bowed, turned, and walked back the way he came.

Damn it.

Another person appeared at the far end of the hallway, escorted by a different guard. I had to go into the room, or I would cause a traffic jam.

I took a deep breath and strode forward, quiet, unassuming, slipping into the ballroom in anonymous silence, just another noble in a lovely dress. In front of me, bright light spilled onto the crowd from enchanted chandeliers: men in their best doublets, women in gowns of every color, hair ornaments glinting, jewels shining, voices murmuring to the echoes of the fading music. Some people wore their crests in plain view, like me. Others didn't bother because they were well known.

The last notes of a fast melody faded out. The opening dance had just ended. Perfect.

The who's who of Rellas mingled around me. *The ocean of monsters*, Everard murmured in my memory. Truer words had never been spoken. In these stormy waters, I was prey. I needed to get my thirty seconds of spotlight out of the way and then I would fade into the background.

The music had died. The next dance would begin in ten minutes.

I took a deep breath and stepped forward to the front of the gathering loosely ringing the dance floor. The floor didn't crack under my feet and swallow me up. So far so good.

I scanned people's faces. *Where is he?*

A clump of red and silver—Wynand Bors holding court directly across from me. He was easy to spot. He stood five foot five, but he weighed about two hundred pounds, all of it bone, sinew, and muscle. He was enormously strong, and he'd been known to pick up taller opponents in full armor and throw them if they pissed him off enough. His doublet mimicked armor, as if his tailor had tried to reproduce a cuirass with cloth and leather. A bright red cloak dripped from his left pauldron in artful pleats.

To the right of Bors, a group of people in copper, cobalt, and gray watched the crowd with flat expressions. The Yolentas' faction. Dreantia Yolenta stood with her two sons and her daughter, who sat in a wheelchair. The resemblance between them was unmistakable. All four had the same squarish faces, the same arrogant bend to their eyebrows, and the same rare shade of ash-brown hair. No DNA test needed.

No sign of her niece, though. She was the only blond of the lot.

I looked to the left of the Yolentas. Scarlet, gold, and black. Ulmar Hreban. I didn't jerk. I stayed calm.

He had the same look he had worn on his face in the Garden. The pale woman next to him was his wife. Her black and red gown was beautifully tailored, and her dark hair was studded with jewels. She was about ten years younger than Hreban, which put her in her early thirties, but there was something petulant about her expression. She was like the most popular girl at school who was forced to attend someone else's party, and not being the star was eating at her.

Everybody under the sun was in the damn ballroom except for Everard. Had he been poisoned?

I took a tiny step forward, trying to move past a large man next to me to take a look at the rest of the dance floor to my right.

Rust and cream. Solentine.

Even among all this finery, he stood out, cutting an elegant figure in a tailored doublet that also resembled armor. That must've been the formal fashion, and it was perfect for Solentine. Everything my new cousin did, from the tilt of his head to the casual gesture of his hand as he spoke to an older man next to him, was refined and graceful. Solentine dripped sophistication.

Our gazes met. Solentine Dagarra did a double take. And then he looked to the side.

I turned slightly to follow his gaze.

Everard. Alive.

Thank God he was alive.

He wore black from head to toe, leather and cloth with a green inlay on the chest. Black leather pauldrons broadened his shoulders, his green cloak dripping from them in structured folds. He looked like some infernal prince in armor forged of cosmic darkness. Behind him, the retainers of Selva stood shoulder to shoulder, in black and green.

His face was glacial. Cold and unyielding, as if cut from stone.

I never should've come. Seeing him like this, in those clothes, was not good for me. I had won my freedom from him, and I had to keep it.

Wait. He was fine. So was Solentine. Both of them were here, in perfect health, and neither of these assholes had thought it was worth their time to let me know that they had arrived safely or that Everard wasn't dead. I had driven myself up the wall worrying, I had lain awake at night thinking he might have gotten poisoned, and they didn't even bother to send a note. One word: Alive. That's all I needed.

It was crystal clear to me now. I was a weapon. A tool, like a dagger. Ramond vi Everard was content to use me when it suited him and to ignore me when it didn't. That Solentine did it bothered me less, but Everard had lived in my head rent free almost since the moment I came to this wretched city. He'd lied to me, he'd saved me, and then he'd lied again by pretending he cared for me, and I kept deluding myself and buying into his lies.

You know what, screw this.

Shock slapped Everard's face. He had finally seen me. His eyes flared with green.

Yes, yes, here I am. Didn't expect that, did you?

The entire Selvan delegation was focused on me now. Somebody would notice this. They were painfully obvious about it.

I glanced at Solentine. He started moving to his right, the shortest path around the room and to me.

Okay then, time to impersonate Homer and the hedge and fade into the background. I took a careful step back.

A taller woman walked into me. She stopped at the last moment, so she didn't quite knock me over, but we did bump into each other.

Blond hair, piercing blue eyes, rose, teal, and white crest. Eliarde. Arvel's second cousin and the Butcher's would-be victim #3. Crap.

She glared at me. And she was pissed off. Awesome.

"Who are you?"

"Excuse me, my lady." I took a small step back toward the wall, clearing her path. She preferred to be addressed as dame, but in the formal setting the noble title took precedence.

"I asked you a question," she ground out.

The two women following her stared at me. The one on the left, in a blue dress, sighed. "Let her be, Elie."

"No, I want to know what makes her think she can stand in the front row."

I saved your life, you ungrateful cow.

"I don't recognize these colors." Eliarde took a step toward me.

No surprise there. Izarn Demarr was a border commander, who visited Kair Toren once in a blue moon, while Eliarde was a Silver Eagle, part of the royal garrison. The only way she would ever see the Trihorn would be if Sauven personally went there. But recognizing the colors or no, I was a woman with a crest in an expensive dress who was allowed to enter the joedurar. Most people would've taken that into account.

Eliarde was not most people. I could tell by the set of her jaw that common sense had left the station. Something had irritated her, and she was looking for a lightning rod to scorch. She'd done it multiple times in the books. When something annoyed her, any target was a good target.

"Why are you here?" she demanded.

"Because I was invited," I told her.

"By whom?"

"By His Majesty, Sauven Savaric." Chew on that.

"Isn't it blindingly obvious?" another female voice said.

I glanced to my left. A stunning woman with light brown skin and a wealth of curly hair braided into a gorgeous arrangement bore down on us. The bodice of her dress, a beautiful gray, resembled armor, and her skirt was like a gush of arterial blood. Two women accompanied her, waiting a step behind.

Lady Ilandra Bors.

Great. Just great. The two candidates for the deadliest female knight in the kingdom who hated each other with the passion of a thousand suns and me, the gnat stuck between them.

"She is here because she was invited," Lady Bors repeated.

"By the king," a taller woman on her left added. "Imagine that."

"Isn't that why all of us are here?" the shorter woman asked. "Unless Lady Eliarde somehow snuck in? Could it be that you didn't receive an invitation?"

"This doesn't concern you, Magrefondretta," Eliarde snarled.

Hurry up, Solentine.

"Why can't we take an interest? It is so amusing to watch," Lady Bors said. "I can't wait to see how you will embarrass yourself further. Perhaps you should throw her to the ground to vent your ire."

The two women behind her chuckled softly.

This was not helping. Eliarde couldn't attack Ilandra Bors directly, not without issuing a formal challenge and disrupting the joedurar, which would bring Sauven's wrath down on her head, but she sure as hell could attack me. As far as she was concerned, I was a nobody.

Eliarde pivoted to me.

Yep, just as I thought.

"You still haven't answered my question." Every word dripped with menace. "Who—"

"Lady Maggie," a deep rumbling voice said behind her.

Eliarde spun out of the way. Lord Bellen looked at me. His colors were blue and white, and his clothes were cut like Everard's, armor replicated in cloth and leather with exquisite detail. His white doublet clasped his frame, widening already huge shoulders. A stunning inlay of pale blue curved across his chest, accented with gold. His sky-blue cloak dripped from his left shoulder. He looked enormous, his blond hair nearly glowing in the light of the enchanted chandeliers.

Everyone stared at us. Suddenly we were the focal point of the room.

"Lord Arvel," Eliarde gasped.

Please no. No, no, no . . .

He was looking at me. "My lady, you've made me the happiest man in Rellas by accepting my invitation."

Some woman behind Eliarde made a choking noise.

You have got to be kidding me. What the actual fuck?

Arvel leveled a stare at Eliarde. It was flat, heavy, and cold. She took two steps back. He turned to me.

"I have been so looking forward to our reunion."

I needed morr beads. Or a drezmur. I needed to not be here.

He bowed. Bellen—*Arvel*—was *bowing* to me.

Eliarde's eyes were as big as saucers. Lady Bors would need a crane to lift her jaw off the floor.

"Will you grant me the honor of a dance?"

Oh fuck me.

He held out his hand.

All around us people went quiet. I had no choice. None at all.

"The honor is mine, my lord."

I rested my fingers on his. His hand swallowed mine, and he led me onto the dance floor.

The first notes of a polhe floated in the air. I took up the position, moving on autopilot. Thank you, Erodel.

Arvel was looking at me like I was a delicious snack.

Twice. Kair Toren had done this to me twice. First, Everard, then him.

We stepped forward in unison, beginning the first set of movements.

"You sent me the invitation."

"Guilty as charged."

"Over the wall. Attached to an arrow."

"I thought of that myself. That was my idea. Added a bit of excitement and mystery."

"Anxiety, my lord. It added a great deal of anxiety. I had no idea who it came from."

He beamed at me. The man looked ridiculously pleased with himself.

"Wouldn't it be simpler to deliver the invitation by courier?"

"You deserve the extra effort."

That was neither here nor there. "You lied to me about who you were."

"I did not. I am Earl Bellen on my mother's side."

"Your knight lied to me, also."

"Oh?"

"When I visited the Citadel, I saw a knight in beautiful armor at the top of the stairs. I asked my escort if he was you and he said he was."

"Felidor is an accomplished liar. A rather useful talent."

"You are completely unrepentant."

"It was a bit of harmless deception," he said. "Should I beg forgiveness?"

Arvel and *beg* in the same sentence. Let me off this train . . . "Not at all, my lord. Although putting you and *harmless* in the same sentence is a crime."

"Have no fear, my lady. No harm will come to you in my presence. From me or anyone else."

We started the second set of movements.

"You look exquisite tonight," he said.

"My lord, I have to ask, what is it about me that ignited your interest? Was it because I warned you about harm to your cousin?"

"It was the way you spoke of the war," he said. "Of what happens to those mangled by what their duty requires them to do."

"I do not recall . . ." Berengur's bodyguard. The giant man in the full helmet. "You were Lord Berengur's escort?"

He nodded. "He has returned to the Citadel. You will be relieved to know that he did not disturb his brother's quest for inner peace. His conversation with the abbot was fruitful and his hope for an eventual reunion is renewed."

Yes. Excellent. I smiled without realizing it. He tilted his head, looking at me. I remembered where I was and killed the smile.

"Thank you for letting me know, my lord. I wish them only the best."

"As I knew you would. I remember our first encounter with startling clarity, my lady. Things you said during that meeting touched my soul."

"I only stated the obvious."

We made a circle around each other. The move gave me a glimpse of the ballroom. Eliarde stood frozen like a statue. She didn't seem angry. She seemed shellshocked and confused, like her brain couldn't process what she was seeing.

"Surely there are many women who choose to serve as knights and who understand everything I said in much greater depth. I can only imagine the horrors of war, while they live through them."

"You are right. Knights share many things. We are bound by our purpose and duty. But when I walk off a battlefield, I want . . . Something else. Someone else. Someone who understands yet isn't stained by the same blood. A ray of sunshine after the storm."

His blue eyes were so warm and there was just a hint of vulnerability in their depths. The shadow of longing.

"I think you could be that to me," he said.

Was this real? Was Doran Arvel pouring his heart out to me? Couldn't be.

"What about your second cousin?" I asked.

He glanced in her direction, then back at me. "Ah, Eliarde. My apologies for her rudeness. She and I will speak."

He didn't raise his voice. He just loaded so much cold disdain into the words, I almost shivered. It sobered me right up.

"She is under the impression that your match is assured."

"There are two wars fought in this kingdom," Arvel said. "One that requires blades and armor and the other that demands subtlety and understanding the currents of power. My cousin has chosen her battlefield, and on it she is spectacular. Relentless, courageous, and formidable. However, I require more."

"Oh? But her military achievements are second to none."

He nodded. "So she tells me. In great detail. Repeatedly."

Oh, Eliarde.

"A few weeks ago, she brought up the curious notion of 'enhancing' my bloodline through a union."

What? "But you're already an Arvel."

He sighed. "Indeed, I am. Once again, you understand me perfectly."

In Rellasian terms, Doran Arvel was the pinnacle of what a man could achieve. He had gotten a great head start with an ancient pedigree, wealth, and hereditary magic, but he also worked very hard at surpassing expectations. His martial skills were unmatched. He wasn't just admired, he was renowned for his competency, valor, and general awesomeness, and he wielded that reputation like a weapon. And to top it off, he was so handsome and charming he probably needed to carry a shield wherever he went to keep an entire generation of women from pouncing on him in the street.

"It isn't arrogance on my part," he said. "I bring this up only to show you that Eliarde doesn't understand my needs. Because of who I am and my achievements, my bride's background doesn't matter. No matter who she was before, when I slide a ring on her finger, she will become Lady Arvel, and our children will be the heirs of Arvel."

You couldn't climb higher unless you sat on the throne. By telling him that she could enhance his bloodline, Eliarde showed a complete lack of awareness of where he stood. She hadn't just crossed her name off the potential bride list, she had taken a big black permanent marker and obliterated it.

"My wife doesn't need to be a skilled knight," Arvel said. "I'm happy to bear that burden. Her battlefield will be here, in Kair Toren. She will be a woman who can carry a conversation, a woman who is sharp, who understands the power landscape and knows when to stab and when to withdraw. A woman to whom I will entrust my soul and the future of my Family."

And that was *Family* with a capital *F*. Right.

"You have an entire room of astute, smart women to choose from." I nodded at the crowd around us. "Perhaps the future Lady Arvel is watching us right now."

"She isn't."

We took a step apart from each other and closed the distance again. The third movement. That stupid left turn was coming up.

"How do you know?"

He leaned a little closer to me. His blue eyes were dark and tinted with humor. "When I was younger, I thoroughly explored my options."

"You worked your way through the eligible ladies of Kair Toren?"

"Yes." His smile was sinful. That was the only word for it.

We backed away and came together again.

"It was great fun in the beginning. Eventually, though, I grew bored. I kept looking for someone special and not finding her. Until now."

I needed to nip this in the bud.

"I'm no one special, my lord."

I raised my hand.

"I beg to differ."

He touched his fingers to mine. Perfectly acceptable, and yet it felt like a caress somehow.

"I've made inquiries," he said. "Nobody knows who you are or where you come from. You returned my friend's brother to him, then you saved Eliarde, and both times you've asked for nothing in return."

If only he knew.

"Eliarde attends court events every year. This is your first time, and yet you made her look like a fool with two sentences."

"I did nothing of the sort. She dug that hole herself."

His eyes told me he was stripping the dress off me in his head. "I don't know how or where they've been hiding you, but there is something about you, Maggie. I have a feeling there is no one else like you. Look around you. This is the only battlefield worthy of you, and you are radiant."

And we were on a first-name basis. Oh no, you don't.

"*Lord Arvel*, I believe you are mistaken. There is nothing special about me. Your life is filled with powers and magic, and I'm but a dim spark. I'm happy being a spark. It suits me."

He stepped to the side, and behind me, keeping my right hand in his, placed his other hand on my lower back, and guided me in a small circle. Erodel did not teach me this. I had to just go with it. Arvel's touch was featherlight, but I knew with absolute certainty that I couldn't get away. For a moment, my back was to his chest, our heads close.

His voice murmured in my ear. "What do you want, my lady? What do you really want? Tell me and I will make it yours."

He returned me back to the right position, across from him, the backs of our hands touching.

I stared right into his eyes. "No."

"No what?"

"No anything. And no more creative dance moves. In case you've forgotten, my lord, we are in public. We're going to finish dancing and go our separate ways."

I should've said that in a different way and a different tone. Too late now.

He looked thrilled. "Irresistible."

Damn it.

The tempo changed, signaling a partner switch. Here we go. I spun to my left, praying I didn't trip, and a man glided in place across from me. Face like an angel, eyes like a wolf—Silveren.

"And we meet again, my lady," he purred.

Bite me. "Indeed, we do, my lord."

"Truly, I encounter you in the strangest places. I told you I would see you again."

That magic voice washed over me like warm honey. He wore the Redeemer sage, gray, and dark brown, and against those colors his dark blond hair and those golden eyes almost glowed. He was sinfully beautiful.

"Imagine seeing you on Arvel's arm."

We touched our hands and made a circle around each other.

"However did you manage that?"

"I have no idea what you're talking about."

We stepped away from each other and came together. His face was entirely too close. His voice was an intimate caress.

"Does he know you led me around on a leash?"

Aha. "That was coincidental, my lord. I'm not into bondage, and if I were, you're not the partner I would choose."

The music changed again. I executed another left turn without tripping, and Solentine caught me.

"Get me out of here," I snarled under my breath.

"Why are you here in the first place?" he hissed through his smile.

"Why do you think? I got an invitation, and I didn't want to endanger the family by not coming."

We circled each other, and I caught sight of Arvel. He was completely ignoring his partner. His body was making all the right moves, but his gaze was on me.

"How do you even know Arvel?"

"Not important right now. He's watching me."

"Yes. I know. Everybody here is watching him watch you."

"It's not my fault," I squeezed out.

"How did you even manage this? Arvel views women as amusements or irritations. I've never seen him get territorial."

Ugh. "Silveren just asked me the same thing."

"We have a bigger problem."

Solentine spun me the same way Arvel had, giving me a glimpse of the northern side of the room. Black smoke coiled around Everard. It was barely visible, but it was there, snaking around his chest and arms. His eyes were a bright piercing green.

"He's smoking," I ground out.

"I've noticed. No man wants Arvel as a rival."

"They're not rivals."

"Does he know that?"

"Stop being clever and help me."

"We're almost there. After the next turn, walk with me. Don't stop. Don't say anything."

We turned. Solentine locked my hand on his forearm. We slipped out of our spot among the dancing couples, and he steered me toward the crowd. People edged out of the way to let us pass. A moment and we were through the clump of nobles, right in front of a small arch leading to a narrow hallway guarded by a knight.

Solentine pulled me into the hallway, which was barely wide enough for the two of us to pass side by side. We speed-walked through it, turned left, and exited into a much wider hallway, with tall arched windows lining its opposite side.

"We need to run now." Solentine made another left.

I grabbed my skirt, and we broke into a jog.

"A joedurar scroll comes out of nowhere, and you accept it?" Solentine growled.

"It was shot into our courtyard with an arrow, right after a City Guard Knight Captain invited me into his office trying to figure out my identity. I couldn't refuse it."

Ahead of us, Arvel stepped out of a side hallway, blocking our path.

"Shit." Solentine stopped and I stopped with him.

"How?" I whispered.

"The castle is a maze. There is more than one way to get anywhere. He had to race to catch us. Congratulations, my sweet cousin. You're the only woman in Rellas who can make Arvel run after her."

Arvel started toward us, his steps measured and steady. Solentine watched him approach, his face unbothered.

"Remember: You're a Demarr," he said quietly.

Arvel was almost upon us, doing an excellent impression of an unstoppable force.

Solentine frowned, as if puzzled.

"Step away from her," Arvel ordered.

"Or what?" Solentine asked.

Arvel's eyes narrowed. Getting into a brawl during Sauven's special party would create difficulties even for him.

"My lady, this man is a notorious cad. You are not safe in his company. His very proximity may tarnish your reputation."

"Trust me, I'm well aware of his reputation." I glanced at Solentine. "It is a frequent topic of discussion at our dinner table."

"His intentions are base," Arvel said.

"My intentions are pure as fresh snow," Solentine said. "Since we are on the subject of intentions, Lord Arvel, what are your intentions toward my cousin?"

"Your cousin?"

"Are you saying that you invited her here, claimed the first dance, and then chased her through the castle without knowing her family name?"

Arvel narrowed his eyes, sighting Solentine as if he had a sword in his hand and was about to swing it. All of that charm and smoothness had vanished, replaced by pure menace. The one-hundred-eighty-degree turn was shocking.

Solentine didn't even blink. "May I present Lady Marigold Demarr, daughter of Brune and Griele Demarr. She is the only daughter of my aunt and uncle, which makes her my treasured cousin. Are you getting all of this?"

Arvel shook his head. "We both know this is bullshit. Whatever you're scheming, she is to be left out of it. Walk away."

A tall, auburn-haired man came out of the side passage. He was in his late twenties, handsome, and wearing rust and cream.

"Sol, there you are—" He saw me. His eyes went wide. "Maggie! What are you doing here?"

My new brother, Rumian. Awesome timing.

"I'm sorry." I didn't even have to pretend to sound dejected.

"What happened to living quietly? By the Aspects, Mother is going to kill us."

"She won't kill us if she doesn't know," Solentine said.

"Sol is right." Rumian dragged his hand through his hair. "I don't know what's going on, but we must get you out of here before Uncle Izarn sees you, because he *will* tell Mother. Excuse me, Lord Arvel. I must rescue my sister from a fate worse than death."

He cut in front of Arvel and took me by the arm. Solentine grasped my other arm, and we walked down the hallway, right past Arvel.

"When you embarked on this little adventure, you swore to me that you would mind your safety. One year. Is it so much to expect?" Rumian asked. His tone said he wasn't mad, just very disappointed.

We kept walking.

". . . We all agreed you wouldn't draw attention to yourself . . ."

We kept moving down the hallway.

Rumian droned on. ". . . Mom nearly sent a team of knights to retrieve you.

I stuck up for you. I promised that you wouldn't do anything rash. I said that you were smart and sensible . . ."

I glanced over my shoulder. Arvel was now a good hundred feet behind us. He wasn't chasing us. He was looking at me like a tiger who had wounded a gazelle and was watching it run away. His prey had escaped for the moment, but his face told me that the chase wasn't over yet. I was in so much trouble.

"I promised Father . . . Is he still watching us?"

"Yes, he is," I murmured.

"Do you think he will chase us?" Rumian raised an eyebrow at me. "That would be fun."

"He's welcome to try," Solentine said. The darkness in his eyes was deep enough to drown in.

Solentine Dagarra didn't take kindly to orders, not even from his own father. If Arvel tried to chase us, Solentine would fight him. I had zero doubt of it. The sooner we got the hell out of here, the better. At least Everard hadn't come after us. Dodged a bullet there.

We turned the corner. I exhaled.

"Thank you for rescuing me."

"Did I do well?" Rumian gave me a charming smile. "Was I too stern?"

"You were wonderful."

"Splendid," he said. "I always wanted to be an older brother."

Chapter 41

As soon as we cleared the castle doors, a boy ran up to us. "Which carriage?"

"The Magnars'," I told him.

The boy took off down the wide staircase. My cousin and my brother tore down the stairs after him at top speed, pulling me with them.

"Stop or I'll break my neck!"

The two of them let go of me. I picked up my skirt, gripped Rumian's arm, and continued down the stairs. We conquered the stairs. Our carriage pulled up, Will and Lute looking like they were ready to fight.

Solentine jerked the door of the carriage open and saw Erodel. And then there was a dagger at Erodel's neck.

"No!" I grabbed Solentine's forearm. "He's with me."

Solentine slid the dagger back into his doublet and half shoved, half helped me into the carriage.

"I'll go with her!" Rumian announced. "In case something happens."

"Thank you, but no." I blocked the door. "Arvel won't do anything to me. He knows where I live, so he doesn't have to rush. But he might pick a fight with Solentine."

"Why do I never get to do anything exciting?" Rumian demanded.

"Now isn't the time," Solentine snapped.

Rumian sighed. "I suppose I will stay and help defend the family name."

And he would defend it well. Rumian was the fastest blade in Rellas. Faster than his father or Solentine.

"If you could manage," Solentine squeezed out. "If it wouldn't be too much trouble."

They should take their show on the road and charge admission.

Solentine slapped the carriage door shut. "Ride like dursans are chasing you! Don't stop for anything. If you see Defender colors, ride harder."

Will barked a harsh command, the carriage jerked, and we sped down the King's Way.

"What's going on, my lady?" Erodel asked.

The carriage clattered down the cobblestones at full speed, jerking us to and fro. I needed to invent some seatbelts.

"Why are we riding so fast?"

"Lord Arvel has taken a liking to me," I said. "My brother and my cousin are afraid he might chase us down with the Defender Knights and try to retrieve me."

"Lord Doran Arvel? Commander of the Defender Knights?"

"Yeah. Huge, blond, blue eyes. That one."

Erodel opened his mouth, closed it, then opened his mouth again. "Should it come to that, I will do my duty as your escort, my lady."

"It absolutely won't come to that."

We took a turn at hair-raising speed. If I were an egg, by the time we arrived home, I would be an omelet.

"This is ridiculous. I'm allowed to leave the dance. Arvel isn't going to ride after us. He knows where I live, so he'll come to see me at his convenience and probably expect tea and snacks. Nobody will be chasing us."

The sound of hoofbeats thundered all around us. Erodel jerked the curtain on the window aside.

"We're being chased."

Oh for the love of . . . "Is it the Defenders?"

Erodel turned a shade paler. "It's worse. It's the Sleepless Duke."

I pulled the curtain aside. Selvan knights in black and green surrounded the carriage. Directly in front of me, Everard rode atop Villain, black smoke pouring off him like a royal mantle.

That colossal jerk. Of all the ridiculous things he could've done . . . Argh.

"What do you think you're doing?!" I yelled at him.

No answer. Just smoke and green eyes.

"Get back into the carriage, my lady!" Erodel pulled me away from the window.

I sat back down. Erodel unsheathed his sword, put it across his lap, and adjusted the glove on his right hand.

"No need to worry. It's just Everard." I pounded on the carriage wall. "Will! Slow down!"

The carriage slowed. Erodel looked like he was ready to storm a castle.

"It will be fine," I assured him. "I promise."

<hr />

The carriage rolled to a stop. The door swung open, and Everard loomed in my view, his eyes green and bright. His gaze slid over Erodel. "Out!"

Erodel gripped his sword and put himself between me and Everard. "What is the meaning of this?"

"Don't hurt him," I told Everard. "He's my ranowen. There is no need for violence. Erodel, His Grace is my childhood friend. I will be perfectly safe in his presence."

"Are you sure, my lady?"

"Yes. Thank you for your services and the pleasure of your company. Your courage and expertise are unmatched. I couldn't have wished for a better companion."

Everard took a step aside.

Erodel gave him a wary look.

"Thank you again for everything," I told him. "I'm safe. I promise."

"It was a pleasure, my lady."

He exited the carriage. Everard climbed in and slammed the door shut.

"Have you lost your mind?" I demanded. "This isn't Wilkair! You can't just leave the joedurar and ride like a wild man across the city. Not only that but you've endangered—"

He wrapped his arms around me and crushed me to him.

"Ramond . . ."

He kissed me.

My heart fluttered in my chest. I was suddenly flying, exhilarated and terrified at the same time, and I didn't know how to stop.

It was possessive and intense and unbelievably, searingly hot. He kissed me like I belonged to him, and he couldn't get enough. Like he would kill anyone who dared to interrupt.

His tongue slid between my lips and touched mine, stroking, tasting . . . This wasn't a kiss, this was sex. He was making love to my mouth, and I took him in like I needed him to live. The heat of him, the scent of him, the heady taste, the feel of those powerful arms embracing me, it was too much. He destroyed me. I forgot where I was. There was no thinking anymore, no fear, no doubt, only the irresistible need in my body and the fireworks in my soul.

He broke the kiss. I was breathless. My head spun.

He looked at me with those wicked green eyes. If he kissed me again, I would strip him naked in this damn carriage.

He pushed the door open, took my hand, and pulled me out onto the street. We were in front of our house. He led me through the tunnel. Some part of my brain registered the familiar faces—Clover, the Magnars . . . Behind us, Everard's knights loomed.

"She does not leave this house," Everard ordered in his Sleepless Duke voice. "Nobody comes in, nobody goes out."

Reality slammed into me. My brain restarted in a cold rush.

"I don't think so," I said.

He turned to me.

"Last I checked, I was a free woman. I will go out whenever I want."

Everard looked at Clover. "Take your lady to her rooms."

She bit her lip but didn't move.

"Did you not hear me, Clover?" Everard asked.

"Do not take a step," I told her.

Will and Lute moved to flank Clover.

"What the fuck are you two doing?" Gort growled.

Will ignored him. "My lady made her wishes known, Your Grace."

Lute put his hand on his sword.

"You seem to think that you can order my people around," I said. "You've forgotten where you are. This is not Selva."

Behind us two of Everard's knights walked through the tunnel.

"Maggie," he started, a warning in his voice.

"Lady Demarr. This is not your house, Your Grace. We are not your people. Do not presume that you have any power here."

Black smoke slithered from him across the courtyard, writhing like a living thing.

"I guess Solentine was right," I said. "No man wants Arvel as a rival."

His voice was cold enough to freeze blood in your veins. "I'm at the very limit of my patience."

"You saw me dance with Arvel, realized that your pet secret weapon might be slipping through your fingers, and dramatically rushed over here to make sure I was secure under house arrest and pull me back in line. The kiss was pretty good, I will give you that. Omelyana is a lucky woman."

"Maggie!"

"Lady Demarr!" I bit back. "Did you think that if you kissed me, I would be so overcome that my brain would turn off and I would meekly obey you without question on the off chance you might condescend to climb into my bed?"

Behind Everard, one of his knights winced. The other just stared, motionless like a statue.

"I don't care that you danced with him!" Black smoke boiled out of Everard. "You were hidden and safe. Arvel dragged you out into that nest of vipers and made sure that every single one of them noticed you! If any of them find out what you're capable of, they will crush every bone in your body for a crumb of the knowledge hidden in your head."

"But they don't know what I'm capable of, and instead of helping me fade into obscurity, you added to the spectacle by dropping everything and thundering through the streets to escort my carriage! You know Sauven watches you like a hawk. Everyone you interact with becomes suspect in his eyes. What were you thinking?"

"I kept you safe!" he snarled. "Arvel thinks laws don't apply to him. He's trained in defensive warfare, he plans and lays traps, and when they fail, he takes what he wants by force."

"And yet neither he nor his knights are here, are they? The only one here trying to force me is you."

His eyes were two green points of light. "I don't have to force you. You're already mine."

Okay, that was it. That was the last fucking straw.

"I wish you would stop with this shit. For two and a half weeks I lived on pins and needles, wondering if you were poisoned and dying. Ramond, you didn't even bother to let me know you were alive. If I hadn't gone to the joedurar, I still wouldn't know if you'd survived. It didn't cross your mind, because to you I'm a tool, and tools do not warrant that kind of consideration. They are supposed to stay at home, nice and neat, waiting quietly until you need to use them. So please, for the love of the Aspects, stop and be honest."

You broke my heart. Own up to it.

The whole courtyard was filled with his smoke now. We were ankle deep in it. It churned and roiled, sparking with green when it collided with itself. Magic saturated the air, so thick and potent, it sizzled on my skin. At this rate, he would wake up Isadau and adding her to this mix would only make things worse.

A third Selvan knight ran into the courtyard. "My lord, our absence was noticed. Crown Prince Kiel is on his way to Razmur. He's accompanied by Silveren and the Redeemers—"

I faced Everard. "Answer me one thing: If I hadn't danced with Arvel at the joedurar, would you be here right now?"

"My lord," the knight called, his voice tight with urgency. "We must—"

Everard raised his hand and the knight fell silent.

Everard looked at me. "I want to be with you and just you. If you never told me another secret again, I would still want you. Nobody can take you away from me. Not Arvel, not Sauven, not the Archmage, not the entirety of the Crimson Empire. The only person who can come between us is you. And I promise you, from this point on, I will bring the full power of everything I am to win you over. You will put your hand in mine, Maggie, and you will do it gladly."

When hell froze over. "Leave my house."

He turned around and marched out, his knights in tow. Will followed him and barred the door.

The remnants of Everard's power faded into the night air.

"You fucking fools," Gort said, his voice bitter.

"Not your call," Will told him.

Lute grinned. "They're our lives, old man."

"I told you," Shana said.

I cleared my throat.

"The joedurar went very well," I said. "I danced with Arvel and, Clover, he said I looked exquisite."

She blinked. "He did?"

"Yes. He also said I was radiant. I do believe you are the most skilled lady's maid in the entire city."

She raised her chin. "Damn right."

I looked at Shana. "Do we have any wine?"

"I have two jugs of Favonian red mead," she said.

"That will do." I took off my shoes and headed into the house.

Chapter 42

Redberry 21

"Maggie!"

Someone was shaking my shoulder, and I was absolutely sure it wasn't Mom. Because I didn't live at home anymore. I had moved out to my own apartment ages ago.

"Maggie!"

My eyes snapped open. Clover leaned over me. My head pounded like someone was beating my skull with a hammer.

"What time is it?"

"The bells have struck eight."

I'd gone to bed drunk just after midnight.

"My lady, Lord Arvel is here."

"What do you mean here? *Here* here?"

"Here, downstairs, by our front door. He is waiting in the street."

I sat up and winced. My poor head.

"Your hair is a mess," Clover said.

I hadn't bothered unbraiding it last night. I'd just taken all the metal out.

"How many people does he have with him?"

"Just one knight."

"Please let them into the courtyard and put them at the table by the wine tree. Do we have any snacks?"

"I already have tea brewing. Let me help you with your hair."

Clover held up one of my house gowns.

Twenty minutes later, I was in the courtyard, sitting across the table from Arvel and his guard. The Golden Knight wore a plain hooded cloak and his face looked like he was about to lead an army into battle.

Gort and the brothers formed a triangle behind Arvel, maintaining a respectable distance. If he decided to make himself into a problem, there wouldn't be much they could do to stop him. His magic made him invulnerable, so I had to win this fight on my own.

I wouldn't be running from that confrontation. No, I welcomed it. That was one good thing about having your heart broken—you stopped giving a crap, and he'd just presented me with a target for all of my frustration.

"What an unexpected visit, my lord. The last time I visited the Citadel, you served such wonderful tea. I'm afraid mine can't compare. But our pastries are second to none."

"They are indeed superb."

"To what do I owe the pleasure of your company?"

"I know you're not a Demarr."

Straight to the point.

I sighed. "Lute, bring the painting from my office."

"The large or the small one, my lady?"

"Both."

"Yes, my lady."

I turned back to Arvel. "I'm exactly who I say I am. But I fail to see why it matters to you, my lord."

He leaned back in his chair. "I would like to know everything there is to know about you, my lady. And I will. Right now, I want to know why you are lying."

I sighed. "I see you intend to make your interest in me into my problem."

Lute returned, placed the small painting on the table, and held the larger one up.

I looked at the small painting. On it Griele Demarr hugged a ten-year-old girl who resembled me. Griele's smile was soft and warm. She didn't look anything like my mother. My eyes grew hot.

Arvel watched me like a hawk.

Don't cry, don't cry, don't cry. "This is my mother and I."

He looked at the painting. It was a beautiful work of art. I had no idea where Solentine had found the artist on such short notice.

I nodded at the bigger painting. "These are my parents and my brother."

Arvel stared at the painting. In it Brune and Griele Demarr sat in chairs, while Rumian and I, both adults, stood behind them in our family colors.

"This proves nothing."

"Would you like to see the official papers? Perhaps my Demarr family crest?"

"Papers can be forged, and I doubt the Demarrs have a shortage of crests."

"This is bordering on rude, my lord. I had a long and eventful night. I'm tired. You show up first thing in the morning and demand the proof of my lineage without any justification for it."

"I've never heard of Brune and Griele Demarr having a daughter."

"I can't help that you are poorly informed."

He leaned forward. "You don't look like your parents."

Clover gasped behind me.

He glanced at her.

"It's all right, Clover. He didn't hurt my feelings." I glanced at Arvel. "I was adopted at the age of nine."

Arvel drew back slightly. *Yes, you were inexcusably rude.*

"Do you have any other pointed insights to offer, my lord, or can we conclude this meeting?"

"I don't know what Solentine has on you, but I will find out and I will free you of it."

"Solentine is the best cousin I could ever wish for. He is caring and protective, and he respects my freedom and independence."

"He is slippery, conniving, and dangerous. He appears to be a cad, and he cultivates his unsavory reputation . . ."

"Are you worried that my cousin's reputation will somehow stain yours? Please have no fear. I do not intend to pursue you, my lord. I'd promise you that I have no desire to end your chastity, but as you've assured me, that dursan flew long ago."

He blinked again. This conversation wasn't going the way he had expected. *Leave. Go away.*

Arvel leaned forward and fixed me with his gaze. Wow.

"You told Berengur that your father was touched by the horrors of war. I've met Brune Demarr. He's a simple man who likes war because he is good at it. He has the depth and insight of a wooden spoon. In his wildest dreams, Brune could never raise a daughter like you."

I had always wanted to say this. "How dare you?"

I stood up.

Arvel jumped to his feet. The pressure in his stare faltered. He'd realized he'd gone too far.

"Do you think, Lord Arvel, that only men like you have the monopoly on being scarred by the violence you unleash? Has it ever crossed your deep and insightful mind that I might have seen a side of my father he had not shown others? Or that I saw something in him even he himself didn't acknowledge?"

I took a step toward him. Arvel took a step back.

"I have sat here and listened to you smear my cousin and question my parentage, but I will not tolerate an insult to my father. Get out. I may not be a Demarr by blood, but I had their training, and by the Aspects, I will draw blood. Leave my house."

A golden glow flared in his eyes. For a moment they blazed with lethal radiance, and I felt a stirring of a power. It was like a distant hurricane waking up.

The glow died. He smiled and bowed. It was a graceful, deep bow, the kind a man of his position would offer to a woman he appreciated.

"Apologies, my lady."

"You can apologize by leaving. Your welcome is withdrawn."

He spun around and marched to the front door. Kaiden chased after to close it behind him.

Clover slapped her hand over her mouth and snickered into it.

Will leaned forward. His voice had a touch of awe. "You chased Doran Arvel out of the house."

"He'll be back."

The look Arvel had given me wasn't the look of a man who had given up. It was the kind of look you saw in the movies, when a skilled martial artist was trying to cool things down, and someone decided to sucker punch him in the mouth. It said *Good punch. Brace yourself.*

I had to figure out some way to redirect him away from me and fast. I had too much to do and no time to waste.

I took an envelope out of my sleeve and handed it to Kaiden.

"Three Moons?" he asked.

I nodded.

There was a single piece of paper inside with a short note in the Shears' cypher on it. It said, *I have the contracts. Get me an audience with the Sun Margrave.*

The last of the Shears background on the contracted people had been delivered yesterday, just before I left for that infernal dance. I would use today to finish organizing it.

With or without Everard, I would change the future of this kingdom.

The carriage rocked slightly, rolling through the streets soaked in afternoon light. Solentine sat on the bench across from me, wrapped in a nondescript cloak.

"I didn't tell you that Ramond survived because I didn't think about it," he said. "I should have realized how worried you would be, but it didn't occur to me."

"It's for the best," I told him. "Now he and I both know where we stand."

"I doubt that." Solentine frowned. "I should've taken your feelings into consideration."

"We've only been relatives for less than a month."

"And we were doing so well, but now there is a coldness between us."

I gave him a look.

"Maggie, I would rather have honesty than politeness."

"Of course there is a coldness, you ass. You have a hundred people at your disposal, and you couldn't send one to notify me. If only I had repeatedly asked your agents if there was any news about Everard—oh wait, I did."

He blinked. "I'll make it up to you."

"No need. I no longer care. Besides, you arranged this audience on very short notice. That's enough. I'm surprised you pulled it off."

The frown got deeper. "I'm equally surprised. I don't have influence over the Sun Margrave. Even my father would have to wait at least a few days for a meeting."

"Maybe the stars aligned."

I looked down at the floor of the carriage, where a large chest waited, filled with scrolls and papers. I didn't care how we'd gotten the audience, as long as we got it.

The carriage stopped. Lute knocked on the front wall. We'd reached our destination.

Solentine picked up the wooden chest with all of our papers and stepped out. I climbed out after him without waiting for Will to help me out of the carriage. I didn't have time for all the proprieties.

A large square building rose in front of us, a small fortress in the middle of the city, complete with two knights protecting the door. A woman stood between them, dressed in the black and purple colors of the Justice Chamber.

We approached the guards.

"Lord Dagarra and Lady Demarr," Solentine said.

"You are expected. The lady only."

"That's fine."

I took the chest from Solentine before he could open his mouth.

"Follow me," the woman said.

We walked through a long, well-lit hallway into a large, three-story tower. Shelves ringed the walls, filled to the brim with books, odd objects, and scrolls and interrupted by arched windows letting in the afternoon light. A wide balcony with a blocky wooden rail traced the walls about fifteen feet up, offering access to the higher shelves.

In the middle of the tower stood a massive wooden desk, heavy and ornate. The man behind it was in his early sixties. He wore a black tabard with a stylized gold sun embroidered upon it. The symbol of his rank for, like the sun, he was meant to see all and purge the darkness. His hair, very curly and cropped short, had gone almost completely white. His face was long, made longer by a short graying beard in stark contrast to his deep brown skin. His cheekbones were prominent, his nose broad and flared. His eyes under sparse eyebrows were smart and watchful.

Colart Jenicor, the Sun Margrave.

"Here she is," he said. "You can stop haunting me now."

Someone moved on the balcony. A man in black and green stood up from a chair.

Everard.

Damn it.

"Lady Demarr, I presume," the Sun Margrave said. "The Lord of Selva tells me you have something vital for me. Something so important that he showed up at my office with the first rays of the sun and refused to leave. I'm eager to hear what it is."

What was it he had said to me when we were trying to figure out what to do with the Yolentas' salt? *I have a friend who works for the Justice Chamber...*

I set my chest on the floor, took out the first scroll case, and offered it to him. Colart Jenicor pried the case open, extracted the scroll, and unrolled it.

His face changed. He looked at me, his expression unreadable. The magic pulsing over the signature line was obvious even from this distance.

I plucked out the second scroll and handed it over. He put the first one down as if it were a snake, took the second scroll, glanced at it, and put that one atop the first.

I reached into the chest and began stacking the scroll cases on his desk. He watched me without a word. I placed the sixteen remaining scroll cases into a neat little pile and passed him a piece of paper with a list on it. Eighteen names, everyone who was bound to Hreban by a life chain and still alive. Two clerks in the Chamber of Ceremonies, a woman very high up in the Treasury, a knight of the Silver Eagles, one Defender, two Redeemers, a royal cook, two royal guards, a City Guard Knight Captain, a sprinkling of officials, and a prosecutor from the Justice Chamber. That last one had to hurt. He worked directly under the Sun Margrave.

I plucked a stack of papers from the chest and put it in front of him. Detailed background on the eighteen with as much information as the Shears could find: their origins, their careers, their sins. Most of them had sold themselves for basic, human reasons. Some had nowhere to turn, others were just greedy.

The Sun Margrave flipped through the papers, scanning them with surprising speed, and looked back at me.

I handed the Butcher's scroll to him. He stared at it, shocked.

If there was anything a liberal arts education taught you how to do, it was to read a bunch of different sources and vomit all the information in an organized and structured manner. I had wrapped this case in shiny paper and slapped a beautiful bow on top of it.

The Sun Margrave met my gaze.

"I know the kind of man you are. I know you will do the right thing. But if something stops you from saving the kingdom, I've kept enough evidence, and I will use what I have."

I turned and walked out.

Redberry 24

I walked on the Sun Margrave's left, through a long hallway. Ahead, a knight with a torch led the way. Behind us, two more knights brought up the rear.

In my head the word *dungeon* always conjured up either a dimly lit maze or something that came out of a LitRPG, but the dungeon of the Eagle Roost was nothing like that.

It looked like the rest of the Eagle Roost, ancient, foreboding, impenetrable, a wide hallway lit by lanterns, its floor swept clean and its thick stone walls free of grime. On our left, rows of cells ran the length of the hallway, guarded by solid iron bars, cages to contain human evil. On our right, narrow windows let the inmates glimpse a bit of the sky. A little hope was a terrible thing.

"Remember his power. Do not allow yourself to be hurt," Jenicor said.

"I will not."

The day of the audience with the Sun Margrave, I had made it all the way home, and fifteen minutes after I walked through the door, a carriage bearing the Sun Margrave's standard arrived with the Sun Margrave's second-in-command. Colart Jenicor had formally asked for my help. I'd climbed into the carriage and had yet to get home.

Ulmar Hreban was arrested the following day on an emergency warrant signed by Sauven himself.

The opening of the High Court's session had to go forward. It was a massive public event, a celebration that had happened for twenty-five years, ever since Jenicor announced the case against Ralinbor's widow and the High Court unanimously sentenced her to death. Tomorrow the Sun Margrave had to ascend the steps of the Eagle Roost escorted by three squires. Surrounding him with an escort of armored knights would send all sorts of wrong signals about the stability of Sauven's reign.

Worse, I didn't find a contract with Cai's name on it. That meant that Hreban had hired his replacement assassin via ordinary means. If Cai failed tomorrow, he would face no magical repercussions. He would survive that failure.

Cai of Sunder always made his kill. If tomorrow didn't work out, he would bide his time and kill Jenicor later. We couldn't take that chance.

The Justice Chamber had interrogated Hreban for two days, trying to squeeze the location of the assassin out of him, but he revealed nothing. I was their last chance. It was a very long shot.

Ahead the knight stopped and raised her torch.

"Take care with your heart," the Sun Margrave said.

"I will."

I walked to the cell. The Sun Margrave and his escort retreated to one end of the hallway, out of earshot. The knight who escorted me thrust the torch into a holder on the wall, between the lanterns, and walked to the other end of the hallway. There was twenty yards of open space on both sides of me.

In the cell, Ulmar Hreban sat on the stone floor, stripped of his finery, wearing a plain tunic and pants with simple sandals on his feet. But the expression on his face was still the same. Pouty, arrogant, the man who expected his due.

I sat on the floor by the bars well out of his reach. We looked at each other.

"You're wondering how you ended up here," I told him. "It was me."

"I do not know you." His voice was deep and even.

"But I know you. I was there when your grandfather let you hide under his desk as he destroyed the merchant guild of Barder. I saw your father kill your uncle. I witnessed you assaulting a maid because you wanted her and your lust turned to violence, and then I watched as your parents had you whipped because you had dishonored your house. I know your thoughts. I was in your head. Look into my heart and see if I am lying."

He stared at me, and for the first time ever I saw his expression change slightly. A new emotion shivered in his eyes. Fear.

"Who are you?"

"Someone who came into this world to stop you."

He frowned. "Why would you want to stop me? The world needs order. It needs a strong hand. My hand."

"You're right. The world needs order, but that's not what you offer. You offer tyranny."

"What is the difference?"

"Order is imposed to allow the majority of people in a society to survive and prosper. It curbs violence and provides protection by enforcing laws and limitations. Tyranny concentrates power in the hands of the few and benefits only them. The rest suffer."

"The rest aren't fit to govern. I see into your heart now and it's filled with contempt for me, but I am what people made me. You don't know the nature of human hearts. They are woven of false promises and full of deceit and hatred. The world is filled with the weak, the stupid, the easily deceived and easily led."

"You cherry-pick your truth. You saw other things in people's hearts, like love and kindness. Compassion. Valor. Empathy. But you chose to discard them."

"They are illusions," he said. "Lies people tell themselves to aggrandize their petty ambitions. In the end, only the self-interest matters, and they will sacrifice everything they profess to love just to survive. I am the only one who isn't blind to it."

I shook my head. "You think your life is the most valuable life out there, but it's just one of many. We are all unique, yet in the eyes of the law we must be equal. Only then can we survive and thrive. You're just like everyone else, Ulmar. You bleed like any other human, and soon the kingdom will take your head."

"No. I'm Ulmar Hreban," he told me. "They will not kill me."

"Oh, they will. You've planned to murder the Sun Margrave, a cornerstone of Sauven's reign. The king will never let it pass. However, the Sun Margrave is prepared to spare your life if you tell me how to find Cai of Sunder."

"So, this is why you're here."

"Does it not bother you that you will be dead while Silveren is free?"

This was a gamble. In all of his papers, I had found no mention of Silveren. No hint, not even a whisper.

Hreban gave me a smug smile. "You do not know."

"Why don't you enlighten me?"

"When all is said and done, I will walk out of here and you will be brought to me in chains."

"Are you imagining me in *contemplation* right now? Perhaps with a proper sign suspended from my neck?"

He drew back.

"You're counting on Silveren to free you, but if human hearts are as treacherous as you claim, why would he? Does he truly need you? What do you offer besides money? If Cai succeeds, your head will be the first to roll, and nobody can implicate Silveren in the killing. How neat and tidy that would be."

A hint of doubt appeared in his eyes.

"Follow your self-interest, Ulmar. Make this deal. At the very least, it will preserve your life long enough for you to find out if Silveren will come to your rescue. Tell me how to call off your pet assassin."

He laughed a quiet bitter laugh. "I can't."

"Why not?"

"I will not allow you to beat me."

I reached into my bodice and touched Digi's amulet hanging around my neck. If I broke it, Hreban would see the person he loved must. It would likely be his grandfather. Of course, knowing him, it could be himself. The question was, would he tell that person what I wanted to know?

I looked into his eyes and let go of the amulet.

"I don't believe you." I leaned forward. "You are too selfish to gamble with your life. You can't call him off even if you want to, can you? You have no idea where he is or how he will strike."

"You fear failure," he said. "It gnaws at you and keeps you up at night. You will fail tomorrow, and I will savor it. Come and see me again, so I can drink in your despair."

I got up.

"You have some time left before they kill you. Look into your own heart, Ulmar, if you're brave enough. Come to terms with all that darkness so you can go in peace. We will never meet again. The next person to speak to you will be your executioner."

I walked back the way I came, to where the Sun Margrave waited.

"Nothing?" Jenicor guessed.

"No. He set this in motion, but he can't stop it."

"Then I will have to put my faith into my armor and my blade tomorrow," he said.

He was never the best with a blade. Jenicor was a competent fighter back in the day, but he'd been fighting a paper war for the last two decades.

"If I might make a suggestion?" I asked.

"Of course."

"Cai of Sunder is very fast. He relies on that speed to deliver the killing blow."

"But?" the Sun Margrave said.

"But I know someone who is faster."

"Would they be willing to put their life on the line?"

Why do I never get to do anything exciting?

I smiled. "In a heartbeat."

Chapter 43

Redberry 25

The Eagle Roost crowned the apex of Castle Hill like a battle helm, its ancient walls and towers growing from bedrock. Just to the side of the castle, a small stone spire jutted, barely wide enough to support a single slender tower connected to the main hill by an eighty-yard stone bridge. Seven stories tall, the tower was the highest building in the city, and I stood on the observation deck at its very top.

The weather had decided to comply with the celebration, and the day was glorious, all blue sky, golden sunshine, and plump white clouds hanging low above us. From my vantage point, the Eagle Roost's vast courtyard was a square bordered by a wall, with the main castle rising on the right and the gatehouse offering entrance on the left. On the other side of the gatehouse, the King's Way, a wide, paved street guarded by a two-story wall, rolled down the hill into the city.

Today, crowds lined the sides of the King's Way, held back by ropes decorated with narrow black and purple ribbons. The royal guards, wearing purple cloaks and armed with spears, protected the ropes. The sun reflected from their pale gray breastplates, and their full-face helmets made them look like menacing living armor.

The Sun Margrave would arrive by carriage at the bottom of the King's Way, then walk about a third of a mile up to the castle with his escort. He would pass through the Eagle Roost gates, cross the four hundred yards of the courtyard, and finally reach the royal perron, a long outdoor staircase, flanked by two spectator galleries filled with nobles, government officials, merchants, heads of craft guilds, and other prominent citizens.

The perron led to the top landing in front of the Eagle Keep, where King Sauven and the three judges of the High Court waited. The grand staircase had four landings besides the top one, and each landing offered two smaller galleries, eight in total, reserved for the Great Families. The closer you were to Sauven, the higher your Family was regarded. The right top platform was all blue and white, with a splash of pale yellow—Arvel's squad. The top left platform, red and gray, clearly belonged to Bors. Everard's black and green was all the way down, the lowest platform on the left, just above the spectator galleries.

My original plan was to be in one of the spectator galleries down below, possibly next to Solentine and therefore perfectly safe. Both my cousin and my brother had nixed that plan as too dangerous, and the Sun Margrave had offered me the tower instead. Solentine had a spyglass delivered to the house, so I wouldn't be tempted to sneak into the courtyard, and I was putting it to good use scanning the crowd. I'd scrutinized the galleries three times now, and Silveren was nowhere in sight.

Everard was there, though. The last time I'd leveled my spyglass at him, he'd turned and looked directly at me as if he'd sensed me looking.

I did not have a good feeling about this.

I missed my run-around-at-night outfit. Today I was dressed like a lady again. At least my dress had a knife pocket in it. Solentine had offered me one of his daggers, but I'd brought the knife Everard had given me. It was familiar and comfortable, and its weight was reassuring. I still had Digi's amulet as well. Just in case.

War horns sounded, sending a low, menacing note into the sky. I pivoted left with my spyglass.

A carriage rolled through the square, pulled by a pair of beautiful black horses. The crowd cheered.

The Sun Margrave exited the carriage, stern and foreboding in his armor and formal black tabard. A herald in matching black armor stepped forward, carrying the banner of the High Court, the sun in golden splendor on a black background, waving from the top of a very sharp spear.

The Sun Margrave raised his arm to greet the crowd, then took his place behind the herald. Three squires in the armor of their respective Orders stepped up as his honor guard. The Defender squire in blue and white took the position on the Marshal's right, the Conqueror squire in red and gray on his left, and the Redeemer squire in sage and brown behind him.

I focused on the Redeemer squire. Matheo. As expected.

The horn sounded again.

The herald started up the slope, and the Sun Margrave and his escort followed. Very slowly. Very stately. If a turtle was ascending the King's Way next to them, it would have won this race. They had a third of a mile to go, and the Sun Margrave was an older man wearing about thirty pounds of armor. He couldn't be too out of breath by the end of it either. That would have been unseemly.

According to Solentine and my brother, if they were Cai, they would dress up as one of the royal guards, stab Jenicor, and use a morr bead to bug out. Logic said the assassination would happen closer to the top. The whole point of a public killing was to let everyone on the platforms see it in gory detail.

The procession crawled up the slope. The crowds cheered.

Of course, Cai could also hit the Sun Margrave now and use the resulting chaos to teleport away.

"Maggie," Lute said behind me.

I almost jumped. The Magnar brothers insisted on sticking to me like glue until the ceremony was over, but somehow, I had forgotten they were there. Tzeri on Lute's shoulder gave me the evil eye.

"If you don't relax, you'll fall off the tower," Lute said.

"It will be fine," Will told me.

We were about to watch an assassination unfold, and if it succeeded, the entire kingdom would collapse. I had given everything I could to prevent this moment. Nothing about this was fine.

A third of the way up.

A half.

Two-thirds of the way up. This was going to take all fucking day. If I got any tenser, I would explode.

The Sun Margrave's face was serene. Here I was, safe and stressing the hell out, while he was down there, walking toward his possible death, cool as a cucumber. Not a hint of worry showing.

They reached the gates. The two guards blocked their way. The herald spun his spear in an expertly executed flourish and bellowed, "The Sun Margrave seeks entry."

By the keep, Sauven nodded. The war horn roared again, and the guards stepped aside.

This would be the perfect moment to kill him. I held my breath.

The herald, the Sun Margrave, and the three squires passed through the gates and started across the courtyard, walking between two rows of sparsely placed royal guards.

The first pair of sentries. The second. The third . . .

The tension was killing me.

The fourth pair. The fifth . . .

I rocked back and forth.

Will took me by my shoulders and very deliberately pulled me back from the rail.

The sixth. The seventh. The eighth . . .

The guard on the right dropped his spear and lunged forward, blindingly quick. Before his discarded spear had a chance to fall, he darted past the Defender squire, a slender black blade in his hand. The poor kid had no chance to react. He just gaped as Cai flew past, arm raised for the kill.

The herald *moved*. I didn't see him do it, but he must have, because his spear slid into Cai's chest.

The assassin froze, arrested in mid-step. The herald had skewered him right through his armor.

Blood drenched Cai's armor, leaking from under his breastplate.

The Sun Margrave stopped, looking straight ahead, as if the whole thing weren't worthy of his attention.

The herald took a step forward and thrust, putting all of his strength into it. The spear emerged from Cai's back. The assassin dropped his blade and fell to his knees.

The herald freed the spear with a sharp tug. Blood dripped from the black standard.

Cai fell forward, face down.

The herald raised his spear, bloody standard dripping in the wind, and started forward as if nothing had happened.

I exhaled.

Rumian was truly the fastest swordsman in Rellas. If there was any doubt, this cinched it.

The platforms were deadly silent. Rellas held its collective breath, unsure what it had just witnessed.

Slowly it sank in.

Cai was dead. The Sun Margrave was alive. Matheo was alive. My brother hadn't died.

It was over. Finally, it was all over.

An eerie roar rolled through the sky, a bloodcurdling sound of something huge and enraged.

Tzeri screamed. It was a screech of sheer panic. The small beast shoved herself at Lute, trying to crawl into his jacket.

A shadow blotted out the sun, a dark shape, growing larger, its roar getting louder until it was deafening. It plummeted down and landed in front of the Sun Margrave, between him and the perron.

A dursan.

It was huge, larger than any elephant, larger than the statue, so big my brain refused to deal with it. Nothing that big should have been able to fly. Nothing that big should have had those enormous wings studded with spikes.

The dursan roared.

I had heard a version of this roar before. That sounded like the baby beast in the Harzi kennels, the one who was crying for its mother.

The hair on the back of my neck rose. The fractured facts snapped together into a crystal-clear picture.

The boy in the cellar who fell and broke both legs.

Silveren broke his legs somehow during his service and they bother him when it rains.

The crying baby dursan in the Harzi stables.

They have something that doesn't belong to them. I came to retrieve it.

The magic voice, the one that wrapped around you like a caress.

Ralinbor of the Wilds inherited the power of Exultant Call from his father and the affinity for the dursans from his mother.

"Ah, but I wouldn't be the counselor."

"Who would you be?"

"The king, of course."

Silveren was Mirabor Savaric, son of Ralinbor and Aelis, and twenty-five years ago, in this courtyard, Colart Jenicor had brought charges of high treason against his mother. She had died right there, in that courtyard, wrapped in chains, and he had used Hreban to collect on that bloody debt.

It was right there, in front of me, the whole time. I had all the clues. He all but told me who he was, and I did not see it.

Somewhere, a cold, logical part of my brain informed me that Silveren had seen his revenge impaled on a spear and couldn't handle it. He must not have fully trusted Hreban to pull it off. This was his plan B. He had waited so long for this moment, he wanted it so much, he had imagined it for decades, and now he would not let it slip from his grasp. He would kill the Sun Margrave one way or the other.

The dursan hunched its shoulders. The bladelike scales on its chest and back stood erect. Its triple tail lashed the air, slicing through it like a bladed whip.

How is this real?

The beast raised its wings, aiming the spikes at the Sun Margrave. It clawed the stone, its black talons scraping across it, dipped its huge horned head, and roared. The blast of sound was like a tornado, and Rumian, the Sun Margrave, and the three teenage squires were right in its path.

Run!

The Sun Margrave gaped at the dursan, shocked.

Run! Run away!

My brother spun his spear. Next to the beast, it looked like a toothpick. I was about to see him die.

The dursan swung one massive paw, ready to swat Rumian like a fly.

A searing wall of green light sliced through the courtyard. Somehow the dursan sensed it coming and shied to the side, but the green flames caught it as it turned, slashing through its front paw and stopping three feet short of Rumian.

The dursan screeched. The giant paw fell, cut free from the beast.

Everard stood on the staircase. Black smoke boiled from him, and his sword burned with green fire.

The dursan spun around and charged, going straight for Everard, mouth gaping, sword-sized fangs bared.

Everard spun his sword. His magic shot out of him like a demonic blade. The green streak of the Fatefire slashed toward the dursan, angling to the right and leaving a wall of flames in its wake. The dursan leaped over it, but Everard had already struck again. The second slice singed the dursan's remaining forepaw.

The beast reared, trying to avoid the lethal inferno.

Everard sliced in a vicious horizontal arc. The flat wave of green flames cut straight across the dursan's exposed belly. The top half of the beast slid aside, smoking, its guts instantly cauterized.

Nothing moved. The courtyard had turned silent as a tomb.

A dull, layered roar came from above. I looked up.

The sky above us darkened. Dursans rained down, slicing through the clouds. Five, ten, no, more, landing all over the courtyard.

One of them, a giant beast, hung above the cascade. I turned my spyglass up. There was a rider on its back, dressed in black, his face hidden by a hood.

Silveren. It had to be.

On the platforms, people screamed. By the gates, the crowds on the King's Way echoed the screams and ran, stampeding down the street toward the safety of the city.

Everard started down the stairs, a mass of churning magic, his eyes blazing. His knights streamed from his platform, a wave of black and green, running ahead of him, fanning out toward the dursans.

A deep male roar came from the right. Bors was on his feet, his arms raised, gripping a war axe in his right hand. His body shook, rigid, the motion nearly jerking him off his feet. His eyes turned scarlet. A wave of blood-red glow pulsed out of him, washing over Lady Bors by his side. It jerked her upright, holding her still, and splayed out past her, to their knights. Lady Bors landed back on her feet, glowing with translucent red, and screamed, her voice pure fury, a chorus to her husband's roar. Behind them the knights howled as one.

Bors leaped over the low platform, landed on the stairs, and charged down. His wife was only a step behind, her sword in her hand, her face deranged. The Conquerors spilled out onto the stairs and tore down, roaring.

Arvel vaulted over the rail of his platform, jogged up the stairs, as if he had all the time in the world, and stopped by Sauven. A bright golden glow flared from him, wrapping around his body like a cocoon of light. For a moment, Arvel levitated, weightless, his face serene. The golden radiance of the Enduring Flame pulsed from him, expanding past the first landing. A wall of translucent gold rose just below the top platforms, sealing them and the top of the perron in a translucent dome.

Sauven sat in his chair, impassive, looking slightly bored. How was he bored?

Was he so out of it, he didn't realize what was happening? Did he not understand that his nephew had come back from the dead?

The Defender Knights spread out across the top two platforms, moving with military precision into a perfect line. A knight with a golden pauldron on his shoulder made a chopping motion with his hand. The Defenders pulled their bows off their backs, nocked arrows, and fired as one. The arrows pierced the golden wall and bit into the nearest dursan, turning it into a hedgehog.

In the courtyard, Everard was cutting and slicing, the Fatefire shooting from him in every direction, impossibly fast. He cleaved one dursan in half. A second leaped at him from the side. Everard threw himself to the left. The dursan chased him, trying to pin him down. Everard stabbed his sword into the giant beast's paw, impaling it. The Fatefire-coated blade cut through flesh like it was warm butter. The creature screamed, and three Everard knights skewered it with spears, taking it to the ground.

Don't die, Ramond. Please, please, don't die.

People poured from the lower platforms, some running up, others charging down into the fight. I caught a glimpse of Solentine, his face lit up by joy, as he dove into the slaughter next to an older man who had to be his father.

A body flew out of the melee, one of the Conquerors, mangled and torn like a stuffed toy caught by the blades of a lawn mower. He skidded across the stones and lay still, a ruin of flesh and metal. The Rageglow shimmering over his body died.

A big pale dursan roared, its mouth bloody. Lady Bors lunged into the opening, swinging her crimson-coated sword. Bors dropped to one knee. She stepped on his back and leaped. Her blade caught the dursan just behind the neck, and she slid down, carving a path through its flesh.

To the left, a dursan bit a woman in half. She screamed as it flung the top half of her aside. Blood wet the stone. The dursans snarled, clawed, and roared, their tails lashing. The humans charged them and died.

It was hell. A violent terrible hell of magic, blood, and beasts, and Silveren was still above it all, hanging in the air and watching it.

A voice rose from the castle, a beautiful voice that floated in the air, fueled by magic. On the top of the stairs, Sauven had risen from his chair. He was a horrible human, paranoid, vicious, petty, but he sang like an angel.

The magic of his voice rolled through the battlefield and splashed against me. I felt stronger, faster, steadier somehow. The fear was still there but it didn't seem important. I wasn't alone. I belonged with the others. I was a part of an unstoppable whole, valiant and powerful, and we would win this fight. The victory was ours. We just had to reach out and take it.

My mind cleared. I saw Everard rampage across the battlefield, I saw Bors, and Solentine. Where was the Sun Margrave?

I scanned the courtyard, desperately trying to find him. Not in the middle of the melee, not by the galleries, where the hell . . . There! A short figure in Redeemer colors shielding the Sun Margrave in black as they ran along the wall toward the gates. They had no choice. The only safe place was by Arvel, and there was no way they could make it there with the battle raging. But going to the King's Way wasn't better. It was deserted, and Silveren was still hanging in the sky on his giant beast. Once they made it out of the gates, they would be out in the open, between the walls bordering the street. He would see them.

There was only one break in those walls before the bottom of the hill—the arched entrance to the bridge that connected our tower to the main hill. They had to be going for this bridge. I had to hide them in the tower. It was their only hope.

"We have to hide the Sun Margrave." My voice came out clipped. "Get the door!"

The Magnars turned and dashed down the stairs. I followed, skipping over two steps at a time.

The stone stairs flew by. I reached the bottom. Lute unbarred the gate, and the three of us burst onto the bridge.

The air stank of charred flesh. Out of sight behind the wall, one of the dursans roared again and I almost clamped my hands over my ears. Sauven sang louder, the magic of the Savarics' battle hymn holding back the terror.

I ran forward. The arch that led through was ahead of me and still empty.

Come on, come on . . .

Two figures appeared in the opening. Matheo, pulling the Sun Margrave by the arm. Blood wet the margrave's face. He stumbled.

"Take the margrave into the tower and stay with him!" I snarled.

Will and Lute sprinted forward, grabbed the margrave, and hauled him back, past me. I backed away toward the tower, waiting to see if anyone would follow. Matheo ran up to me, his sword bare, and stopped.

"Go with them!" I told him.

"I will protect you."

I opened my mouth.

A dursan landed on the bridge. The stones quaked. The rider slid off the beast's back and dropped lightly to the ground. His hood fell back.

Silveren.

Shit.

The bridge was long, and Will and Lute were less than halfway across it.

"Go to the tower and bar the door, Matheo. Do it now."

He took a few hesitant steps back and stopped.

"Do it now!"

The sound of his retreating steps told me he'd finally listened.

Silveren started across the bridge, his gaze fixed on the retreating Sun Margrave. Wind stirred his hair. He carried a sword in his hand, long, sharp, and white as if it were cut from an iceberg. The beast behind him followed, paw over paw, like a cat walking along the top of a fence.

I blocked his way.

"You don't have to do this."

His face was feral. He didn't even register me. He would walk right past me, and his dursan would brush me off the bridge. Matheo would die next, and then the brothers, and the Sun Margrave. Even if they reached the tower, that door wouldn't hold for long. If all else failed, he could bring the tower down on their heads.

The Sun Margrave would die. Reynald's line would end with Matheo. Silveren would rampage unchecked, and Kair Toren would burn.

I reached for the chain around my neck. My fingers found Digi's amulet. I ripped it free and squeezed the claw. The gem broke in my fist. A burst of magic pierced me, the pain so intense I almost blacked out. She hadn't mentioned that part.

For forty breaths, Mirabor Savaric would see the person he loved most in my place. And I knew exactly who that was.

"Little bird?" I said.

Silveren froze. "Mother?"

I walked toward him.

"Mother..." he said. His face was slack with shock. Tears wet his golden eyes.

"You've done so well."

I reached him and stroked his face with my left hand, brushing his cheek. He raised his hand and put it over mine.

"You were so brave. You worked so hard. But it is enough now. You have to stop."

His voice was a tortured snarl. "I can't!"

"Of course you can. Just let go. You are stronger than this. Live for me, my little bird. Live and be happy. That's the best revenge."

A tear slid from his eyes. The sadness in them was enough to make you cry with him. He shut his eyes for a long moment, swallowed, and when he opened them again, they were frozen over with hard fury.

Oh no.

Silveren shook his head. "I can't. I can't, because Father is dead, Mother."

His voice was cold.

"They killed him. And they killed you, too."

He pointed over my shoulder. "That man killed you. I don't want to live. I don't need to be happy. I want him to die. I want them all to die."

I was running out of time.

"Please, Mirabor. Please, for me. No more death. No more killing. Just run away and live."

He shook his head harder. "I will kill them all. And when they're dead, I will build a pyre of their bodies, so the rest of this cursed city can choke on the smoke rising from their corpses."

A hint of awareness crept into his eyes. He stiffened under my touch.

I stabbed him through my dress, exactly like Ramond had taught me. My dagger bit into his thigh, and I stabbed him again and again. Fast and hard.

He snarled. His left hand clamped my throat, cutting off my air. There was no panic. There was only icy cold. I knew what to do and I did it. I lifted my dagger and stabbed him in the kidney. He let go, his face contorted.

"I'm sorry," I told him. Tears wet my face. "You've suffered, and I'm so sorry. I wish they hadn't died. I wish you'd had a long and happy life, loved by your mother and father. I do not have the power to make it right. I would if I could, but I don't."

Silveren crumpled in front of me.

Behind him, the dursan stared at me with its terrifying eyes, suddenly aware I existed. Silveren's control was gone. It was free to choose its prey, and I was right there.

There was nowhere to go.

The dursan took a step forward, stretching its neck toward me. Its mouth opened, baring a forest of knife-long fangs. Drool slipped between its teeth and dripped to the ground.

Even if I tried to run, it would catch me. I was about to be eaten alive. It would hurt. Oh my god, it would hurt so much. Could I even come back if it digested me? What if I had no body left to resurrect?

The dursan raised its head.

This was it. This was how it would all end.

The beast flexed its wings. I watched it strike in slow motion. It raised its shoulders, it leaned forward, its mouth gaped . . .

A wall of green flames severed it in half, stopping just a foot from me. I froze on instinct, unable to even breathe.

The dursan split in two, bisected. The two halves of it fell apart, toppled over the low rails, and fell into the gap below.

Ramond stood on the bridge, sheathed in black smoke, his sword spilling green flames. Blood spattered his face and armor.

His Fatefire died.

He started toward me.

I ran to him.

We collided halfway, and he hugged me to him, gripping me tight, as if afraid I would break apart in his hands if he couldn't hold on to me. The black smoke coiled around me like armor.

Ramond kissed me, his lips searing hot, and hugged me to him again, breathless, his eyes shining. "Made it this time."

I hugged him and didn't want to let go.

Epilogue

I stood on the wall of our house, wrapped in a shawl against the night chill. I'd never appreciated shawls until I came to Rellas. They were soft, warm, and comfy. A hoodie would've been better, but shawls held their own.

All three moons were out, and the river surface glowed slightly, reflecting their light, like polished black glass. The sound of celebration came floating up from our kitchen. Matheo and the Sun Margrave had survived. We had stopped a disaster from coming. Hreban was behind bars and Silveren was hopefully dead. The future had to change this time. It had to.

I had told Shana that we should celebrate while we could.

Kair Toren was celebrating as well. Sauven had opened the royal cellars to commemorate the new victory. Tonight would be a night of free ale and mead, courtesy of the Eagle Roost. The population was disturbed, and this would go a long way to calming things down. The Savarics had sat on the throne for over three hundred years. They knew how to keep it.

I had tried to enjoy our little feast, but at some point, it became too much, so I excused myself, grabbed my lantern, and came out on the wall for a few minutes of quiet.

I missed Ramond.

It was the worst feeling. I knew better than to trust him, but I wanted him here with me. I'd had to let go of him on that bridge because the fight was still raging. He had gone back into the slaughter, and I had run to the tower and stayed there, until the last of the battle died down and the people of the Justice Chamber came to fetch us. They took me, the Magnars, and Matheo to our house.

Later in the day, Avaria delivered a message from the Shears. Solentine and Rumian were fine. The dursans were dead, order was restored, and Silveren's body had disappeared.

That last one sent a shiver down my spine every time I thought about it. I had stabbed him at least four times. Surely he was dead.

Someone ran up the steps. I turned and saw Matheo. He was tall for fifteen, but still slender rather than lean. His face had traces of Reynald's hard features, but his expression was completely different. His light eyes were bright and hopeful.

He grinned at me. It was a beautiful contagious smile, and I grinned back.

"I found you," he said.

"You did."

He came to lean on the wall next to me.

"When did you first start keeping an eye on me?" I asked.

"About five weeks ago. Up until then, I mostly saw Ulmar Hreban. I didn't know why. I can't always control my visions. Sometimes they come unbidden."

"Like sparks from a fire." That's how he had described it in the books.

"Yes, like that. The spark glows, and I catch a glimpse. Sometimes I see what I am seeking. Sometimes I see something different. I saw my father die."

Oh.

"I saw Hreban cutting off someone's hands. I think he was a thief. I saw Lord Everard riding. And then I started seeing you. At first only hints, then more and more."

"I did my best," I told him. "I am sorry I wasn't in time to help your father."

"It's not your fault. You weren't here. You saved me instead. He would be grateful."

Matheo unsheathed his sword and showed it to me. He carried Reynald's blade.

"When did you get this?"

"His Grace left it with the Sun Margrave. There was a note with it. It said that my father carried this sword with honor, and I had to strive to be worthy of it. I carried it with me into that battle. It tasted dursan blood."

He smiled at me.

Fifteen-year-olds. They thought they were immortal.

"I think my father would be proud."

"He would be. You didn't run. You performed your duty with honor. What will you do now, Matheo?"

"I will become a knight of Selva."

"Is that what you truly want?"

He nodded. His face turned somber. In that moment he was a mirror of Reynald, hard and slightly mournful. He looked like a boy with two dead parents who had been abducted by slavers, sold to a knight order, and then had to pretend to be content and dutiful to survive.

"My father trusted His Grace," Matheo said quietly. "When he was backed into a corner, he went to ask him for help because of a promise made over a decade ago, and Everard honored it. I want to know what kind of person he is for my father to have trusted him that much. I will learn from him and if his cause stops being just, I will find someone else to follow. But right now, he has my loyalty."

He reached into his jerkin and handed me a small velvet pouch. "He left this with the sword for you."

I took the pouch. "Thank you."

"I'm going downstairs to get some pastries."

And that was the perfect teenager for you. *I will devote my life to the Sleepless Duke, but first I will get some pastries.*

"I'll be right behind you."

He nodded and ran down the stairs.

I opened the pouch. There was a note inside and something else. Something metal. I held the note to the lantern and unfolded it. On it, in Everard's strong hand, was a single sentence:

I'll see you tonight.

Right. With Sauven's guards watching his house like they thought it would catch on fire any second. I seriously doubted it.

I put the paper down, reached into the pouch, and pulled the metal thing out. A beautiful hair ornament with three simple white flowers. They looked like little forget-me-nots, with five petals and a tiny spark of a golden gem in the center. Around the flowers, slender silver branches held small triangular leaves. Each leaf was a bright breathtaking green crossed by bands and swirls of darker and lighter shades . . .

I almost dropped it. This was the hair clip Ramond's father gave his mother on the day of their engagement. The flowers were cut from the white opal that was a sister to the one in Selva's crown and the leaves were malachite from the throne in Wilkair. It looked simple, but it was anything but. I was holding a priceless treasure passed down through the Everard Family. A crown meant to go into the hair of Selva's duchess.

That fool. That epic fool.

He couldn't possibly mean it. It would be ridiculous. And he was coming here tonight. What the hell was I going to do?

I would have to give it back to him. That was the only . . .

A soft melody made me pause. It floated around me, suffused with magic, enchanting, seducing, captivating, like a soft mirage that faded in and out of existence. The male voice that sang it curled around me, caressing my skin.

Ice drenched me.

I turned. Clover stood at the edge of the wall. She held very still, and her eyes were oddly blank.

Silveren stepped out from behind her. He was walking on his own. He didn't seem pale or injured. His eyes were cold and vicious.

How?

"Hello, Mother," he said.

Fuck me.

I took a step back.

He hummed, and Clover stepped onto the stone rail bordering the wall.

I froze.

"Good call," he said. "What's in your hand?"

I made my mouth move. "A hair ornament."

"Show me."

I raised my hand.

"I like it," he said. "Put it in your hair."

I slipped the flowers into my hair, locking them in place.

"Lovely."

"How are you alive?"

"No thanks to you, clearly."

He flicked his fingers. A big dursan plunged down and landed on the wall, straddling it.

"Get on the dursan, or I will sing her off the wall," he said.

All the advice I'd ever heard about being assaulted started with "Do not let yourself be transported to another location."

"I can just jump off the wall instead and save you the trouble," I offered. "It's a long fall, and I'll break my neck." I would survive it.

"Where would be the fun in that?" He hummed a note.

Clover tilted forward, one foot over the edge.

"If you jump, she will join you. If you break my hold on her, like you've done with your guard, she will lose her balance and plummet."

I jerked my hands up. "I'll come with you. I won't fight or try to escape. Please make her step back to safety."

If I told him to let her go, he could drop her over the wall for laughs.

Silveren hummed again. Clover stepped back off the wall like a living doll. His Exultant Call was way more powerful than his father's ever was.

He nodded at the dursan.

I took a step toward it. The huge beast held still. I took two more steps and hesitated. "I don't know how . . ."

Somehow, he was behind me. His arms gripped me. The dursan ducked. Silveren stepped onto its forepaw and lifted me onto its back, into a long saddle. He pulled himself up and slid into the saddle behind me.

"Hold here." He reached around me and gripped a wooden handle thrusting from the front of the saddle. "We wouldn't want you to fall. It's a long way down, and we still have things to discuss."

I took the handle. He locked his arm around my waist and sang a soft note. The dursan shot into the night. The cold air rushed at me. I caught a glimpse of Clover staring at us open-mouthed, and then we were flying up and over the river toward the ocean.

The future always had the last laugh.

Acknowledgments

This Kingdom was a labor of love for us, but it was still a labor. A lot of labor. Luckily for us, we had help along the way. We would like to thank the following people:

Stephanie Stein, for shaping a hopeless mess into an actual story—this Kingdom would not be possible without you, and we are deeply grateful for your expert guidance;

Sanaa Ali-Virani and Julianna Kim for their dedication and editorial suggestions;

Bailey Harrington for copy editing and going above and beyond, and Terry McGarry and Carol Rutan for proofreading;

production editor Megan Kiddoo, for incredible attention to detail;

production manager Jim Kapp and managing editor Rafal Gibek for keeping everyone on track;

Peter Lutjen for the beautiful cover design and Andrew Davis for the gorgeous cover art;

Tyrinne Lewis and Eileen Lawrence for helping our book land in stores;

Jocelyn Bright, Caro Perny, and Sarah Reidy for helping the audience find our work;

and the TPG leadership: Claire Eddy, Will Hinton, Lucille Rettino, and Devi Pillai for taking a chance on us and our imagination. Thank you.

In addition, we are very grateful to Nancy Yost and the team at NYLA for helping this project find a home and always taking our phone calls; Jeaniene Frost for her infinite patience and reading the manuscript three times; Jessie Mihalik and Jill Smith for their friendship; Rossana Sasso for so many things, but most of all for the attention to detail, patience, kindness, and friendship; Mary Zambreno, PhD, for linguistic help; the original beta team who read the first iteration of the book and somehow survived: Veronika "Lyra" Kovaničová, Karen Wood, Harriet Chow, Laura Martinez, Dianne Blust, Michele Schenck, Francesca Virgili, and Edie Lang; and the moderators of the fan group, who read the later draft and also survived: Kerris Humphreys, Katherine Heasley, Wendi Adams, Loredana Carini, and Louise McCoy Vickers.

But most of all, we are grateful to you, our readers. We hope you will love Maggie.

About the Author

Ilona Andrews is the pseudonym for a husband-and-wife writing team. Ilona is a native-born Russian, and Gordon is a former communications sergeant in the US Army. Contrary to popular belief, Gordon was never an intelligence officer with a license to kill, and Ilona was never the mysterious Russian spy who seduced him. They met in college, in English Composition 101, where Ilona got a better grade. (Gordon is still sore about that.) Gordon and Ilona currently reside in Texas with their two children and many dogs and cats. They have co-authored several bestselling series, including the No. 1 *New York Times* bestselling Kate Daniels urban fantasy series, The Edge rustic fantasy novels, the Hidden Legacy paranormal romances and the weekly serial Innkeeper Chronicles. For a complete list of their books, fun extras and Innkeeper instalments, please visit their website at: ilona-andrews.com.